THE OXFORD BOOK OF

Latin American Essays

THE OXFORD BOOK OF

Latin American Essays

EDITED BY
ILAN STAVANS

NEW YORK   OXFORD
OXFORD UNIVERSITY PRESS
1997

Oxford University Press

Oxford   New York
Athens   Auckland   Bangkok   Bogotá   Bombay   Buenos Aires   Calcutta
Cape Town   Dar es Salaam   Delhi   Florence   Hong Kong   Istanbul
Karachi   Kuala Lumpur   Madras   Madrid   Melbourne   Mexico City
Nairobi   Paris   Singapore   Taipei   Tokyo   Toronto   Warsaw

and associated companies in
Berlin   Ibadan

Published by Oxford University Press, Inc.
198 Madison Avenue, New York, New York 10016-4314

Oxford is a registered trademark of Oxford University Press

Library of Congress Cataloging-in-Publication Data

The Oxford book of Latin American essays / edited by Ilan Stavans.
      p. cm.
   Includes bibliographical references and index.
   ISBN 0-19-509234-1
      1. Latin American essays—20th century—Translations into English.
   2. Latin American essays—19th century—Translations into English.
   I. Stavans, Ilan.
   PQ7087.E5089   1997
   864.008'098—dc21   97-10976

Because this page cannot legibly accommodate all of the acknowledgments, pages
505–511 constitute an extension of the copyright page.

9   8   7   6   5   4   3   2   1

Printed in the United States of America
on acid-free paper

Contents

Preface

Choices, choices. . . . Every anthology creates its own double. Its contents must be measured not only by what was included but also by what was left out. Compromises are obviously made along the way, and the compiler's freedom of choice is subject to a variety of factors, not excluding the permissibility of copyright material. Space limitations forced me to eliminate estimable essayists whose impact is considerable, such as Esteban Echeverría, Rubén Darío, Ricardo Palma, William Henry Hudson, Macedonio Fernández, Alberto Gerchunoff, Silvio Romero, José Luis González, Alberto Zum Felde, Sergio Buarque de Holanda, João Guimarães Rosa, Mariano Picón Salas, Mario Benedetti, René Marqués, Edmundo O'Gorman, and Marta Traba. It may therefore be advisable to explain the scope and ambition of the book I ended up shaping.

This is an anthology of modern Latin American literary essays written in Spanish and Portuguese and translated into English. The period covered spans a century and a half, from 1849 to 1994. Within this time frame I searched for the type of entry that would appeal to a broad English-speaking readership, one interested not only in literary affairs per se but in a broader, all-encompassing view of culture. This meant looking for works of high artistic caliber and lasting intellectual insight and stamina, windows through which to begin contemplating the central dilemmas of an entire civilization. In selecting the material I not only reacted to my own tastes and predispositions, but I also struggled to give adequate representation to each historical period. These two factors explain why in the table of contents several decades are more heavily populated than others. My goal was to offer as engaging and provocative a selection as possible. I hope this collection can serve as a compass to more than one explorer.

The almost eighty essays are ordered chronologically by the author's date of birth. The wide orbit of themes ranges from the bloody crossroads where literature and politics meet to journalistic accounts of natural disasters like the 1886 earthquake that devastated Charleston, South Carolina; from intellectual explorations of the Hispanic collective psyche to personal letters and manifestos; from autobiographical evocations of a particular Brazilian landscape to summations of a memorable friendship and anxious meditations on the loss of one's own mother tongue. Each entry is accompanied by a brief headnote presenting information pertinent to understanding the writer's biographical background, as well as a sample of book titles with the original Spanish publication dates. These titles are listed in English only when the book has been translated. The headnotes usually conclude by placing the entry itself in context.

All of the essays are self-sufficient and can be read as independent units. My criteria for selection were based on the significance of the writer in this literary tradition and the relevance of the essay itself. Not all the entries began as such. Many were designed as reportage, lectures, diaries, poetic studies, magazine portraits, introductions, afterwords, and book reviews, a fact that speaks to the amorphous spirit of this literary form. A very small number are part of book-length works. To be able to present a wider selection, I limited myself to finding essays between five and ten pages long. This often meant replacing a classic text with a lesser-known but equally representative one. On very few occasions I disregarded this limitation; in some cases I went beyond, and in a few others—as in the distinct case of Augusto Monterroso—the number of pages ended up being far smaller.

Both in choosing the essays and in writing my introduction I consulted and drew from a number of anthologies and critical studies. I should mention particularly those of José Miguel Oviedo, Emir Rodríguez Monegal, Octavio Paz, Raquel Chang-Rodríguez and Melva E. Filer, Peter G. Earle and Robert G. Mead, Ernesto Mejía Sánchez, José Luis Martínez, Alfonso Reyes, Enrique Anderson Imbert, Norma Klahn and Wilfrido H. Corral, Doris Meyer, and John Skirius. Earlier discussions of mine on the Latin American literary essay appear in my books *La pluma y la máscara* (Fondo de Cultura Económica, 1993) and *The Hispanic Condition* (HarperPerennial, 1996).

Finally, I wish to thank Linda Halvorson Morse at Oxford University Press for her original invitation to edit this anthology, as well as for her inexhaustible enthusiasm, support, friendship, and meticulous editorial eye; Mary Jacobi and Karen Murphy for their kindness and expeditious energy; Margaret Gorenstein for her willingness to penetrate the treacherous universe of copyrights and permissions in Latin America; and Jesse H. Lytle, José Matosantos, and Laura Santiago for their help in preparing the manuscript. And my wholehearted gratitude to the extraordinarily talented cast of translators I depended on to bring these Spanish-speaking essayists to English. This book is theirs.

Introduction

Intellectuel = celui que se dédouble.
—Albert Camus

Of what use is the essay in Latin America? Odd as it may seem, this is a question worth asking. Bookstores around the world are filled with novels and short story collections from south of the Rio Grande about mysterious universes invaded by storms of butterflies and epidemics of insomnia, with lavishly baroque narratives about forgotten soldiers and flamboyant prostitutes. What is almost completely absent from their shelves, in contrast, are volumes of essays displaying the intellect of Latin America's inhabitants. This absence is all the more evident to anyone who has browsed through bookstores in the Southern Hemisphere, where original essay collections are displayed prominently on every wall. Selective reading? No doubt—which leads to the question of why. Stereotyping, perhaps? Surely the region has come to be known for its magic and exoticism, for intermingling the primitive and folkloric with the ultramodern. But the issue runs far deeper, I am afraid. Dreaming and critical thinking are two very different mental activities. Both are essential to our capacity to function as rational entities; without either one we are only half complete. It is symptomatic, then, that the former seems to be among the most valuable export items in the region, whereas the latter is all but eclipsed, as if European and North American readers consider Latin Americans incapable of holding opposing ideas in mind and still retaining the ability to function.

Dreaming, needless to say, does figure prominently in the mental life of Hispanics, but so does critical thinking, although the latter has its own unique metabolism. To understand, one needs to tackle the role of critical thinking in the development of Hispanic civilization. Unlike the United States and most European countries, Latin America was born to modernity without passing through a Reformation period, which allowed for critical reflection and political debate on schisms within both clerical and governmental spheres. Martin Luther and the Protestant movement ignited, first in Germany and then throughout the Old Continent, a reform that scrutinized codes of morality and reevaluated the role of the individual vis-à-vis the community. But the Iberian Peninsula was alien to this change. Spain and Portugal were still relatively awkward, xenophobic, feudal societies in the late fifteenth and the sixteenth centuries. These nations ventured across the Atlantic at a time when religious and racial tensions prevailed and already ineffectual governments were further hindered by

3

corruption and abysmal economies. The riches of gold, silver, and other natural elements found in the New World made Spain and Portugal overwhelmingly powerful. They had a florid cultural, artistic, and intellectual life, but what they did not have was the will to initiate self-reflection conducive to the type of antiecclesiastical, bourgeois individualism sweeping the rest of Europe.

The result is obvious. The prototypical Iberian knight who traveled to the Americas was a macho bachelor who left wife and children behind, a daydreamer of chimeras, unconcerned with notions of tolerance or antidogmatism—therein the proclivity to dream, south of the Rio Grande. His goal was to amass power and fortune and to enchant the king. He never contemplated beginning anew by building a rejuvenated society purged of handicaps. This, in part, explains why Latin America is often perceived as a gathering of banana republics. Many politicians in the Southern Hemisphere are considered *políticos* for their dictatorial styles. Some have been derivative and mediocre in their critical approach to government. And perhaps their greatest failing has been an inability to value ideas espoused by their political opponents. Indeed, for them *opponent* seems to be synonymous with *enemy*—and the best way to deal with an enemy is by annihilation. For all this, Latin America has been rich in fantasy but poor in political thought.

Let me invoke the word *democracy* at this point, for democracy and critical thinking go hand in hand. One cannot live without the other; one depends on the other not only to survive but to thrive. Democracy, as Winston Churchill would have it, is the worst form of government—excluding all the other forms that have been tried from time to time. To endorse democracy one needs to trust its foundations. One needs to believe both that there is wisdom in majority rule and that all politicians chosen by and for the people are accountable for their acts. Furthermore, there is the belief in democracy as an art—the art of governing by discussion. But discussion, the sharpening of useful ideas by means of argument, can only prevail when people understand that destroying your enemy may make you temporarily stronger, but not wiser or better.

The knighthood, the machismo, that brought Latin America to its modernity is not democratic at heart. Webster's *English Dictionary* describes the macho as one "aggressively virile," with "an exaggerated or exhilarating sense of power and strength." No wonder, then, that the most memorable fictional characters from the region are spitfires or virginal beauties, torturers or gigolos, and that critical thinking is not their forte. What are they if not reflections of their milieu? Paraphrasing William Butler Yeats, in dreams begin responsibilities . . . and end. For thinking to be done critically, a space must be opened by the appropriate democratic institutions.

Such an opening is the result of certain historical circumstances, absent in Latin America. This does not mean, of course, that Latin America is devoid of thinking—far from it. What it does mean is that critical thinking is forced to the fringes, to a marginal stance, unendorsed by the state and often done against the prevailing intellectual atmosphere. Latin America is filled with critical thinkers, but they are by definition outcasts, advocates for social change forced to articulate their vision without the support of the powers that be. This is what defines the lack of democracy: the impossibility to effect change from within the system.

Both the novel and the short story are artistic expressions of a democratic spirit. They are modern products of the Enlightenment, and their design is malleable enough to accommodate a symphony of voices and moral values. Their availability in mass-market books makes them subversive articles, conduits of collective introspection and change. But fiction can never pass for *truth*: In its drive to enthrall and absorb the reader's imagination, it embellishes or diminishes its subject matter to the point of complete reconfiguration. To confront, to dispute, to contradict, to *think* through vital issues from inside out and top to bottom is the job of the essay, which is also a residue of the Enlightenment, designed simultaneously to inform and persuade, to educate and unsettle. The essay values itself as a platform to discuss personal and social experience with dignity and seriousness of purpose, and, thus, it also has an implicitly democratic bent. "We must remove the mask," said Montaigne, for "every man has within himself the entire human condition," and we do this by "interrogating our ignorance" and "thinking ourselves through." To think is to generalize, to abstract, to integrate and disintegrate patterns of thought, to summarize and forget differences; and that is what the essay does best, particularly in a hemisphere so profoundly injured by vast differences and yet so hesitant to recognize and discuss these injuries openly.

In my eyes no other literary genre seems more suitable to map the Latin American psyche, its labyrinthine patterns, its unspeakable secrets. No other literary form is more akin to educating while generalizing. Indeed, the word *essay* comes from the French *essayer*, "to try, to experiment," and ultimately from the Latin *exagium*, the act of meditating, weighing, and thinking. Like the novel and the short story, the essay is free-minded, ambitious, and seems to satisfy many needs at once: it entertains, it enlightens, it obfuscates, it confesses, it laments. It uses the personal "I" or it takes an idiosyncratic angle—what Elizabeth Hardwick once called "the soloist's personal signature"—and regards all sorts of issues, large and small, relevant and futile, as though they were matters of unequivocal importance. What the essay cannot do, however, not even when it desperately tries to, is hide the truth: Its texture is too crystalline, too genuine to hide the unhideable, and because essayists are lonely voices crying in the wilderness, their argument generates discomfort, and they are often censored by the powers that be.

But Latin America has never been about silence. Essayists invariably find alternative venues of expression, astute side routes to make their message heard. All of this, in turn, transforms the genre into the perfect mirror, an essential and obligatory instrument to examine life, to reflect on society's strengths and weaknesses. This mirror also forces the region to confront its intolerance and dogmatism. To what extent that confrontation generates change is, of course, another matter. Add to this accessibility, and you have a formula for debate: Whereas novels and short stories ask for the intimacy of solitude and an investment of time and attention, essays are by nature extroverted; they make use of the most public of forums—newspapers, monthlies, book reviews, lectures, and addresses—to create a feeling of community, of solidarity. Therein lies their rebelliousness. Therein, too, their Jeffersonian value.

Once again, the fact that bookstores elsewhere across the globe display few, if any, volumes of essays by writers from south of the Rio Grande does not mean that such volumes do not exist. It means only that, in the process of translating Hispanic culture to the world, they have been left forgotten, replaced by colorful genealogical narratives about love, violence, and corruption. True, for the unusually patient and curious reader, essayistic volumes by Eduardo Galeano and Carlos Fuentes, with a strong political overtone, and others, more philosophically minded, by Borges and Octavio Paz, can be found on the shelf. But these volumes are only a minuscule fraction of what is available in their place of origin, and hardly representative of the genre's wide range of offerings from Latin American authors. Actually, essays are as ubiquitous in Latin America as is any other literary form—and perhaps even more so. In a land obsessed with mirrors and masks, essays hold a prominent place in daily life, reflecting on a certain behavior, commenting on an aspect of life, reevaluating a legend, or analyzing a collective dream. Everywhere one turns, an essay stands as an *aleph* reflecting the entire continent for us: Essays encompass the transcribed recollections of Rigoberta Menchú, a Guatemalan Indian awarded the Nobel Peace Prize in 1992 for her Mayan activism; the Marxist manifestos of José Carlos Mariátegui, an early-twentieth-century Peruvian intellectual who became the spiritual leader of the Peruvian Maoist group Shining Path; the longings for independence by the Puerto Rican educator and activist Eugenio María de Hostos during the Spanish-American War; and the invectives against Fidel Castro by Guillermo Cabrera Infante, a Cuban émigré living in London.

The essay is certainly much more than merely a pliable ideological barometer. Resistant to superficiality, it parades itself as an instrument through which Latin America meditates on its history and comes to terms with its behavior. It is ambitious and all-encompassing, the equivalent of the lens of a ubiquitious camera that knows magically when, how, and why to freeze a crucial slice of reality. This is not to say, obviously, that all Latin American essays are sophisticated, complex, and nondoctrinaire. What is unquestionable is that, whatever form the essays come in, the genre is unparalleled in deciphering the troubled status of critical thinking among Hispanics and in navigating the bumpy road toward democracy.

Inevitably, in any attempt it makes to communicate and reach outward, the intelligentsia in Latin America is forced to subscribe to the European code. First of all, it must use Spanish and Portuguese, both "foreign" vehicles, to convey its messages. Its problem is not only one of vehicle, however, but also one of form: Any literary genre employed—such as the novel, the short story, or the essay—is also a foreign artifact, imported from across the Atlantic, where that genre originated and took shape, and where the written word acquired an elevated status, placed at the heart of Western civilization. The essay tradition has a long list of early European practitioners: Plato, Plutarch, Seneca, St. Augustine, Machiavelli, and Erasmus of Rotterdam, to name a few. The birthplace of the modern essay is France, where Montaigne published his first series of *Essais* in 1580, and where Voltaire, Rousseau, Diderot, and Montesquieu raised it to dazzling heights. Its development continued in Britain, and it was there, in the pens first of Francis Bacon and then of Charles Lamb, William Hazlitt, Thomas De Quincey, and Thomas Carlyle, that it reached its most impressive early plateau. One notes that, with the exception of Seneca, this list of European predecessors is entirely devoid of Spanish and Portuguese names. This, I must say, is not altogether surprising. The Iberian Peninsula did not catch up with others employing the essayistic genre until late in the nineteenth century, when it was approached with some timidity, primarily in Spain, until the *Generación del 98*, and especially philosophers José Ortega y Gasset and Miguel de Unamuno, brought the essay to the fore. This late awakening—which came despite the fact that Golden Age luminaries such as Fray Luis de León, Santa Teresa de Ávila, and Francisco de Quevedo could be considered early essay practitioners—can be explained as the result of the unsophisticated climate in which the entire peninsula lived both after the Spanish invasion of Portugal in 1580 and after the fall of the Spanish Armada, which, eight years later, left the Iberian imperial dream of world domination in ruins.

Indeed, not until very recently has the Spanish word for essay, *ensayo*, established itself in the Iberian Peninsula in Montaigne's sense of the word as "an instrument to explore our natural faculties." In comparison, the first modern Latin American essayist, Venezuelan Andrés Bello, began printing his opinion pieces in exile in London around 1810, approximately six years before the first Latin American novel, *The Itching Parrot*, by José Joaquín Fernández de Lizardi, appeared in serialized form in Mexico City.

This fact is also not surprising. While the Iberian Peninsula in the early nineteenth century was deep in its postimperial depression, Latin America spent its energy seeking independence and searching for refreshing ideological and intellectual models in its countries' various journeys toward nationalism. Indeed, the passage of the essay into modernity south of the Rio Grande can be traced, with astonishing precision, to the edict of the Cádiz Court in 1812, when freedom of expression and of the press was allowed for a brief period of time and when the ban on imported European books was lifted. The strict ruling of the Church against fiction and secular literature, for fear they would pervert the minds of parishioners, had prevailed throughout colonial times. This brief period of liberty was to inaugurate a fiesta of possibilities.

Of course, one can go further back, as literary historians such as John Skirius and José Miguel Oviedo have done, to trace the genealogy of the Latin American essay—as far back as 1493, when Columbus drafted his personal diaries and letters to the Catholic monarchs, Isabella and Ferdinand. In chronicling what he witnessed, Columbus, a native Italian-speaking Genoan, in poor and misspelled Spanish, intertwined fiction and reality; thus he could be considered either the first magical realist novelist in the region or its first enchanting essayist. Either way, he started the tradition of appropriations which, when used with talent, can create astonishing novels, short stories, and essays. This debut is quite intriguing. That the first so-called essays in the region were written by a nonnative Spanish speaker is, of course, a metaphor, a foreshadowing, and clearly in tune with the strategy used by Rigoberta Menchú, whose autobiography was transcribed by anthropologist Elisabeth Burgos-Debray from Menchú's Mayan viewpoint to a language and narrative structure accessible to Western readers. Obviously, this degree of "inherent translation," of linguistic revamping and appropriation, is evidence of the wondrous adaptability of the Latin American essay.

All in all, the offspring of Columbus could not but be multilingual and multiracial, with issues of conflicting identity and the never-ending quest for legitimate roots—historical, psychological, theological, and linguistic—permeating their work. The annals of colonization and conquest by such witnesses as Bernal Díaz del Castillo, Gaspar de Carvajal, Gonzalo Fernández de Oviedo, and "El Inca" Garcilaso de la Vega, and the denunciations of Iberian atrocities by Fray Bartolomé de las Casas and Antônio Vieira, are summoned by literary historians as cornerstones of the essayistic tradition as well; some even include the Mexicans Carlos de Singüenza y Góngora and Sor Juana Inés de la Cruz (a magisterial nun responsible for some of the finest baroque lyrical poetry to come from the Hispanic world, forced to silence by the Church in 1691) as literary forerunners. With some imagination, Sor Juana's "Response to Sor Filotea de la Cruz" and "Spiritual Self-Defense" could be treated as epistolary essays with clear feminist overtones, which would make them the only early examples produced by a woman in a genre that up until very recently was dominated by men. But none of these chroniclers, none of these colonial writers, wrote essays in the modern sense of the word—brief argumentative pieces, engaging and self-sufficient, with humor, graceful style, easy structure, freshness of form, and freedom from affectation—on a subject pertaining to Latin America as an autonomous entity.

The job was left to the intellectual generation of Andrés Bello and others, who devoted themselves to establishing and carrying on the legacy of the so-called Age of Independence, which fell, loosely, between 1810 and 1855. This generation included Bello, Domingo Faustino Sarmiento, Juan Montalvo, Eugenio María de Hostos, Manuel González Prada, José Martí, and Euclides da Cunha, all writers from different countries (Venezuela, Argentina, Ecuador, Puerto Rico, Peru, Cuba, and Brazil, respectively) and with different upbringings. Bello was born in 1781 and da Cunha died in 1909, so their collective oeuvre spans the entire nineteenth century. But while, for the most part, these essayists read each other, many of them never met face-to-face; their styles were essentially different, and in an age of intense utopianism and patriotic redefinition, so were their political objectives. Hence, it is inappropriate to describe these authors as members of an aesthetic movement. Instead, their work formed a foundation that allowed the essay to find its place among Latin American readers.

Because all of these writers were voracious readers, the names of Montaigne and Bacon were quite fresh in their minds, as were those of Michelet, Carlyle, and de Tocqueville, and later on Emerson and Whitman. In fact, many of them were polyglot readers capable of consuming an enormous amount of literature in various languages. They were the conduits through which romanticism, positivism, and Modernismo gained disciples south of the Rio Grande, and they benefited from the availability of printing presses, which although often targeted by repressive regimes, did not stop disseminating democratic values.

As the Age of Independence unfolded, an emerging class of enlightened *criollos*, close in spirit to the fighters of the American and French Revolutions of 1776 and 1789, consolidated itself all across Latin America. This class's democratic vision, its passion for the printed word, found its most perfect mode of expression in the newly formed periodicals and high-minded dispatches produced by an ambitious intelligentsia enamored with freedom and self-determination. Bello, for instance, edited the influential newspapers *Biblioteca Americana* and *Repertorio Americano*, in which he refined his views on education; da Cunha was a correspondent for the mainstream Brazilian daily *O Estado de São Paulo*, for which he wrote the first version of his classic *Os sertões*, known in English as *Rebellion in the Backlands*, a multilayered chronicle devoted to the struggle against anarchy and religious fanaticism; Sarmiento was editor of the short-lived journal *El Zonda*, in which he fought against the Juan Manuel de Rosas tyranny; Montalvo founded and ran the magazines *El Regenerador* and *El Espectador*, in which he constantly attacked corruption and abuse of power; and Martí was a foreign correspondent for periodicals in various Latin American capitals, including for the prestigious Buenos Aires daily *La Nación*, to which he sent dispatches describing, in vivid prose, natural and social disasters, and denouncing all forms of human exploitation.

It is often said that no Latin American writer can come to terms with his craft until he lives in exile, be it voluntary or forced: Distance, more than anything else, will grant him maturity and perspective. It is no surprise, therefore, that almost all of these essayists, from Bello to Martí, produced their best work in England, France, Spain, the United States, or elsewhere in the Southern Hemisphere: Bello lived in London from 1810 to 1829; Sarmiento traveled extensively through the United States; Montalvo wrote his classic *Capítulos que se le olvidaron a Cervantes* during his European exile; Hostos spent many of his adult years in Spain, Peru, Chile, the Dominican Republic, Venezuela, and the United States; and before his premature death at forty-two, Martí lived in New York and Florida.

This generation of essayists is also responsible for solidifying a trademark in Latin American letters: that of the link between the sword and the pen, between politics and the written word. No matter how they each individually envisioned the essay—as journalistic chronicle, pedagogical treatise, combative attack against governmental corruption, or meditation on the crossroads where geography and psychology meet—politics was always their main ingredient. So much so that with perhaps the exception of Bello, it is almost impossible to distinguish where the activist ends and the writer begins: Montalvo is best remembered as the intellectual nemesis of Ecuadorian tyrant Gabriel García Moreno; the young Sarmiento was an opponent of the Juan Manuel de Rosas dictatorship, and the mature Sarmiento became president of Argentina (1868–74); Hostos was active during the Spanish-American War, advocating independence for Cuba and for his native Puerto Rico; Martí, a quintessential freedom fighter and the spirit behind Fidel Castro's revolution in Cuba in 1959, spent his life in the struggle against imperialism in Latin America and died on the battlefield; and González Prada, an aristocrat by birth, is known as an antiestablishment essayist whose *Indigenista* viewpoint was decisive for later-day Marxists in Peru.

The inclusion of the Brazilian Euclides da Cunha in this list of modern masters merits a comment on the boundaries of Latin America as a civilization. Brazil is the largest nation in the Southern Hemisphere and also the most populous. Independent since 1822, its history follows a pattern similar to that of other countries in the region. And yet its Portuguese lineage and its language have forced it to inhabit an oddly isolated place as an integral yet discrete unit on the Latin American map. This dual standard is, however, more generous than the standard applied to French- and English-speaking Caribbean nations such as Jamaica and Haiti, islands completely denied a Latin American identity. Brazil's essayists have to some extent followed similar patterns as their Spanish-speaking counterparts, but they have also generated distinct aesthetic and intellectual movements to which the outside world grants little attention. Many Brazilians keep themselves informed on intellectual matters in their neighboring Spanish-speaking countries; however, often the reverse is not true. Thus, a figure such as Euclides da Cunha, much like Oswald de Andrade, Mário de Andrade, Gilberto Freyre, and Clarice Lispector, responds to such far-reaching influences as Bello and Sarmiento, but because da Cunha wrote in Portuguese, some of his Spanish-speaking counterparts would either exclude him or simply ignore his contribution to the continental camaraderie. This ambivalence is often at the heart of Brazilian essays dealing with collective and particular identities. They ask questions such as "Where do we fit in?" with considerably more vehemence that do other Latin Americans.

Whatever the object of their attention, modern essayists sought to develop their genre, whether in Spanish or Portuguese, as an intellectual tool. The goal was to use the essay critically to explore behavioral patterns, to discuss cultural forms (music, dance, cuisine, and pictorial art), and to consider the divided ties of Latin America to both the Old Continent and its own aboriginal past. Writers commented on natural disasters, on the role of education in society, on the impact of technology, always searching for clues to unravel the nature of their collective identity. But, to reiterate an earlier point, they were using a strictly European genre in their quest for self-discovery. At what point did the essay cease to be a foreign import and acquire a distinctively native quality? While some might argue such a transformation can never fully take place, there is no question that the Latin American essay reached high levels of sophistication. And certainly some sense of uniqueness, of singularity, would be a gift of the twentieth-century successors of Bello and his compatriots, beginning with José Enrique Rodó, whose groundbreaking *Ariel*, a slim volume published in 1900 in Montevideo, summarizes all of the great themes in the Latin American essayistic tradition.

Rodó was a member of the Modernista aesthetic movement, framed roughly between 1885 and 1915, and of which Martí, together with Nicaraguan poet Rubén Darío, was a prominent leader. Their achievement was to renew the Spanish language on this side of the Atlantic and to establish a sense of camaraderie and shared feeling of belonging among writers from the different nations in that region. Before Martí and Darío, that sense of community was all but absent—writers like Bello and Montalvo were contemporaries isolated from one another. But the *modernistas*, most of whom were poets whose style was strongly influenced by French symbolism and Parnassianism, came to be seen as a homogeneous group, although from diverse national backgrounds. In this context, *Ariel* is a singular gem. Designed as an open letter to Latin American youth, it borrows the characters Ariel and Caliban from Shakespeare's *The Tempest* to explain, from Rodó's perspective, what makes the entire region function: the dialectical opposition between materialism and idealism, between looking inward and looking outward, between loyalty to the native pre-Columbian roots and the Westernized influence that forces betrayal of these roots. *Ariel* is the first book-length essay to embark on such an ambitious undertaking. Before it, essayists engaged in lively discussions without offering an understanding of the larger picture; that is, their essays were *textos de ocasión*, random, disconnected pieces responding to single events but never offering a systematic theory of Latin America as a civilization. Rodó was the first to do so. True, in 1845, Sarmiento, in *Facundo: Civilization and Barbarism*— a hybrid piece of writing, part biography, part novel, and part philosophical inquiry—had embarked on an equally ambitious undertaking: the exploration of the Argentine's unique identity. Likewise, Euclides da Cunha, in *Os sertões*, had investigated the tension between rural and urban Brazil, between fanaticism and cosmopolitanism. But their subject matter was limited to Argentina and Brazil only, whereas Rodó, a *modernista*, looked at the entire continent.

Rodó is indeed a figure of such breadth and vision that one can divide the history of the Latin American essay in half—before and after Rodó. His progeny would return to Rodó's favorite themes time and again from multiple perspectives, but from Mário de Andrade and Fernando Ortiz to Borges and Alfonso Reyes, from Ezequiel Martínez Estrada to Alejo Carpentier and Octavio Paz and Angel Rama, the central theme of culture as a struggle between complementary opposites would survive. Yet much has happened since that was new and unforeseen in the essay, particularly after World War I. It is said—and not lightly—that while the second half of the nineteenth century belongs to Russian masters like Chekhov, Turgenev, Gogol, Tolstoy, and Dostoyevsky, the second half of the twentieth century belongs to Latin American luminaries—Jorge Luis Borges, Alejo Carpentier, Octavio Paz, Miguel Angel Asturias, José Lezama Lima, Guillermo Cabrera Infante, Severo Sarduy, Jorge Amado, Augusto Roa Bastos, José Donoso, Carlos Fuentes, Mario Vargas Llosa, Julio Cortázar, and Gabriel García Márquez, among the most representative, all of whom are not only outstanding poets or novelists but also, in various degrees, unforgettable essayists. The generations of essayists that succeeded Rodó retained his continental breadth and continued to link politics to literature. Its members devoted their energy to understanding the speed with which modernity was forcing the continent to sacrifice its past to accommodate itself to a global future. A serious analysis of what Alfonso Reyes and Leopoldo Zea called "the American mind" was under way, and the arrival of psychoanalysis as a tool to examine individual and national behavior left its mark on essayists like Samuel Ramos, whose influential volume *Profile of Man and Culture in Mexico* discussed the Mexican inferiority complex. But after World War II, primarily as a result of an explosion of literary creativity known as *El Boom*, essayists ceased to be interested solely in content and began exploring form in all its potential.

This transformation is perhaps the most dramatic the essayistic genre has experienced in the region. Once again, political repression forced many writers into exile, but rather than nurturing a kind of nostalgia, exile became an end in itself. Even more than with Bello and Martí, the perception of Hispanic civilization as a diaspora, an ever-expanding map of immigrants in constant movement from one latitude to another, gained momentum during this post–World War II era. Most Boom writers came of age in the 1960s in Barcelona, Paris, and even New Delhi, where they served as cultural attachés or newspaper correspondents. Many returned home after extended absences but eventually made their residence in the United States, England, France, or Spain, and they did so only by subscribing to a kind of globe-trotting lifestyle, delivering lectures before congresses and at prestigious universities, serving as judges at film festivals, and advising European and American presidents on Hispanic matters. This lifestyle, together with the precipitous drive toward industrialism and consumerism that overwhelmed most Latin American countries, injected Latin American literature with the cosmopolitan. If the readership of Bello's generation clearly lived in what the writer called "home," the one courted by the Boom writers was more globally minded: They wrote not only for their compatriots but for the world at large, which meant infusing their material with a higher dose of the exotic, making it at once more deeply rooted in its native soil and more universal. Essayists like Vargas Llosa delivered beautiful books and serialized pieces on subjects of international interest, such as *Madame Bovary*'s impact on his adolescent writing and thought, or his reflections on Jean-Paul Sartre and Albert Camus's intellectual debate on the scope and nature of a writer's political and artistic commitment.

Similarly, Octavio Paz seemed perfectly comfortable writing monographs about French intellectuals such as Claude Lévi-Strauss and Marcel Duchamp, about Western concepts of love and eroticism, about Spanish Golden Age poetry, about Buddhism and Greek mythology. And the bookishness of Borges, a writer at ease discussing G. K. Chesterton and

Oscar Wilde, *A Thousand and One Nights,* Kafka and Paul Valèry, made readers feel he was a European by choice and an Argentine by sheer accident. What's more, in a bold move that made Latin America's multilingual reveries more overt, a handful of these writers temporarily abandoned the Spanish and Portuguese languages to write essays in other tongues: Borges, for instance, in collaboration with one of his many translators, Norman Thomas di Giovanni, wrote "An Autobiographical Essay" in English for the *New Yorker;* Cortázar wrote introductions in French for Gallimard and Biblioteque La Pléyade, as did Sarduy; likewise, *Myself and Others* by Fuentes was crafted in English, as were *A Personal History of the Boom* by Donoso and *Holy Smoke* by Cabrera Infante. In short, the achievements of these luminaries are enormous: By proving that the essayistic tradition could be enriched by contributions written in Miami, Prague, Munich, or Tel Aviv, and that Spanish and Portuguese had ceased to be the sole vehicles of communication, they forced the world to realize that Latin America, more than a mere geographical presence, is a state of mind. These writers' critical thinking allowed people in the Southern Hemisphere and the world at large to understand how receptive the Latin American collective mind is and how willing it remains to find strategies to fit into the maze of modernity.

As did Bello and Martí, the Boom writers fortified the irrevocable marriage of pen and sword. They defended the right to "go out on the street," to become speakers for the silent segment of the population. Many were self-appointed "political ambassadors," using their craft to call attention to the abysmal inequalities in their societies. Consequently, their essays can be approached as a barometer of the historical and intellectual events that shook the twentieth century, from the atomic bombing of Hiroshima to the Soviet gulag and the 1968 student massacre in Mexico City's Tlatelolco Square, from Fidel Castro's revolution to the fall of the Berlin Wall. Some, like Fuentes and Paz, were members of the diplomatic service; others, like Vargas Llosa, ran for public office. A few, such as Cabrera Infante, continued the tradition inaugurated by Juan Montalvo, using verbal combat to oppose a tyrant.

Because a rapidly changing society needs a type of literature that is flexible and versatile, the main legacy of the Boom years, in terms of the essay, was the essay's increasing "promiscuity," its ability to mix with other literary forms, thereby appropriating a handful of their qualities. Its became chameleon-like: It disguised itself as a novel, as in the case of *Hopscotch* by Julio Cortázar; at other times the essay appeared in the form of a pop-culture questionnaire, as in the case of the work of Carlos Monsiváis, a member of Latin America's New Journalism school; it also paraded as a collage, as in Elena Poniatowska's *Massacre in Mexico,* a chronicle of the Tlatelolco massacre that includes newspaper clippings, interviews, reminiscences, photographs, poems, and graffiti; or as a letter to the international press by Subcomandante Marcos of the Ejército Zapatista de Liberación Nacional, a *guerrillero* in the tradition of Ernesto "Ché" Guevara, leading an armed struggle in Chiapas, southern Mexico, in 1994; or as a meditation on cheap Hollywood movies or on kitsch and gay themes by Manuel Puig, the Argentine author of *Kiss of the Spider Woman*; or as a kitchen recipe, a grocery list, a satirical poem, or a political communiqué. More often, though, the essay intermingled with the short story—that is, a short story could pass as an essay and vice versa—all but erasing the thin line between fiction and nonfiction, a comment on the fluidity between dreams and reality in Latin American thought. This practice calls to mind the heading of George Orwell's London *Tribune* column: "I Write as I Please."

Of all of the essayists who gained notoriety after World War II, two stand highest in the firmament: Jorge Luis Borges and Octavio Paz. Whereas for most of the others the genre was another facet of their intellectual endeavors, for these writers it came second to none. They cultivated the form endlessly and passionately, with rigor and commitment, pushing it to new frontiers. Borges and Paz understood the role of the writer in society in different ways. Borges saw himself primarily as a librarian: For him, reading was a substitute for life, and his essays are filled with bibliographical references—often in Latin, French, German, and English—a handful of which are fictional. His apolitical stance not only made him unpopular among left-wing intellectuals, but it is also the reason why his essays, even when they deal exclusively with Argentine idiosyncracy, are almost invariably abstract. And while Borges's writing evolved from an obtusely baroque to a dense yet readable style, his essays in *A Universal History of Infamy* and *Other Inquisitions*—because of the sophistication of their ideas and universal subject matter—seem suspended in time. They read as short stories and, in turn, his short stories read like essays.

Octavio Paz, on the other hand, was a man concerned with the ideological and social upheavals of his time. From *The Labyrinth of Solitude* to his essays on language and technology in *Convergences* to his 1982 biography of Sor Juana Inés de la Cruz, entitled *The Traps of Faith*, he used his poetic style to deliver difficult truths to the modern world. Awarded the Nobel Prize for literature in 1990, Paz is a writer whose intellectual odyssey functions as both a map and a compass. Politically, he began as a Socialist but became disillusioned with the Left after Fidel Castro's revolution and embraced a right-of-center ideological stance; artistically, he first fell under the spell of French surrealism, switched to structuralism, and soon endorsed an eclectic, free-for-all system of thought based on the principle of dialectical binaries; intellectually, he was initially concerned with Mexican culture and then expanded his vision to Western civilization and the Far East.

Whereas Borges's essays are essentially palimpsests, Paz's are the shifting mirrors of the events that shook his life and those of his contemporaries: In the spirit of Rodó, they reflect what is particular and universal, what is parochial and cosmopolitan in Latin America.

But despite the exciting contributions of Paz and Borges, and despite the versatility and stamina the essay acquired in the pens of the media-courting Boom generation, the Latin American essay remains, beyond its regional borders, an eclipsed literary genre. Can it ever compete for the spotlight granted to Latin American fiction? What will it take for bookstores worldwide to clear space on their shelves for essays from the region in English translation?

A technological twist suddenly makes the answers to these questions fascinating. True, the Latin American essay seems doomed when it comes to international exposure, but that is because book publishing is such a self-censoring industry. However, our fin de siécle culture seems to be less about the printed word and more about the written word. That is, while hard-copy newspapers and magazines are slowly becoming obsolete, their relevance put in question by the slow speed with which they deliver their message, an explosion of electronic channels of communication—what has come to be known as the information superhighway—is connecting people the world over in a matter of seconds . . . and by means of the written word. I am talking, of course, of E-mail and the Internet. These channels, instead of diminishing the value of the essay as a literary form, instead of turning it into an inefficient and outmoded genre, are actually increasing its value and applicability. The Internet alone is an infinite medium with a most voracious appetite: Its users are obsessively hooked to the written word in ways previously unseen, and the essay is malleable enough to reflect upon and digest at great speed. Obviously, these electronic channels generate special concerns in Latin America. If at this late stage in history, illiteracy is still one of Latin America's most urgent and unsolved problems, the introduction of the information superhighway is likely to widen the divisions of haves and have-nots: Those who possess the technology will be "hooked," becoming contemporaries of the rest of the world, while the dispossessed will be pushed even further to the margins, alienated from the huge volume of information that unifies people around the globe.

The generation of Andrés Bello, Euclides da Cunha, and Manuel González Prada was able to make its reputation by disseminating democratic values by means of the printed word; so did the Boom writers, who, thanks to mass-marketing techniques, could reach a much larger audience by similar means. But future generations of essayists south of the Rio Grande, in tune with contemporary global practices, will depend less on printed and highly publicized periodicals and more on the electronic venues. This means that their readership will be the residents of Tokyo and Bangladesh,

Rio de Janeiro and Johannesburg—everywhere and nowhere. In their search for an audience of their own, the message these essayists will deliver, sent through the Internet, will be fashioned to readers far beyond their immediate milieu: In their thirst to achieve the universal, they might accentuate the local—Latin America as a small integral neighborhood in the global village.

But this model of the future bears its own opposite. Technology is in essence subversive and centrifugal; rather than acquiesce, it functions to diversify and unsettle. Let me invoke, by way of example, the 1994 uprising of the southern Mexican Zapatista insurgents, mostly poor Indians, led by Subcomandante Marcos. Firearms were of secondary importance to the rebels' most effective weapon: fax machines and the Internet, through which Subcomandante Marcos sent instantaneous essays-qua-news releases to a world hungry for information less one-sided and offering more complexities than that provided by the censoring Mexican government. A freedom fighter in the tradition of Enriquillo and "Ché" Guevara, Subcomandante Marcos is also the first postmodern multimedia *guerrillero* and an original Internet essayist ready to put technology at the service of ideology, with on-line readers able to reply instantly to his messages. In his hands, the essay had gravity and punch, but it also announced the unavoidable: Its life span was reduced to a matter of hours. And that, in truth, is the most crucial challenge future generations of essayists are apt to face. Writing for posterity will be a contradiction in terms. For them, the contemporary reader may well become the one and only target, because of the gratification of immediate rewards.

So what does all of this mean? Of what use will the essay be in the Latin America of the twenty-first century and beyond? Bookstores in Europe and the United States may continue to ignore the essay, making fiction the sole trademark of the region, but the information superhighway has without a doubt already embraced the essay; and it will continue to do so wholeheartedly, opening up fresh and unexplored possibilities of development in which thinking and dreaming are closely linked, in which immediate feedback from the reader is crucial. The essay will unquestionably prevail, its democratic vibrations finding echoes in other manifestations. It cannot cease to be what it has always been—a mirror, a map to the labyrinth.

Andrés Bello

Venezuela
(1781–1865)

Diplomat, educator, and poet, Andrés Bello is considered by many to be the first South American humanist and the region's first modern essayist. Bello was a well-rounded intellectual, versed in a vast array of complex subjects, including grammar, the sciences, literature, and international law. He edited numerous journals of Latin American thought in London, where he served as secretary to the Chilean legation in England. A native of Caracas, he returned to live in Chile from 1829 to 1865. His major works include the unfinished poetic collection, *América*, and *Gramática de la lengua castellana destinada al uso de los americanos* (1847), which is still in use and which many have praised. His most famous and often anthologized poem is "Ode to the Agriculture of the Torrid Zone," written in London and meant to be part of a descriptive poem on the New World. In it he recommends peace and working constructively to the survivors of the wars of independence that shook Latin America in the early part of the nineteenth century. In the following small newspaper note, first published in 1849 under the title "Prophecy," Bello dwells on a central theme in the Latin American identity: ambivalent origins. In his astonishing bibliothecal wisdom, he elucidates a handful of references in chivalry novels preceding Columbus's 1492 voyage to the so-called New World and announces—as would many of his successors in the next couple of centuries (such as Alfonso Reyes, Germán Arciniegas, and Edmundo O'Gorman)—that the Americas were already in the European imagination before Columbus first set foot in the Bahamas.

Curious Occurrences

In a chivalric poem of the mid-fifteenth century, the *Morgante Maggiore* by Pulci, there is a passage that in the clearest possible way announces the discovery of America. The passage is found in stanzas 229, 230, and 231 of Canto XXV. What follows is a description of the passage included by M. Ginguené in his *Historia literaria de Italia*.

The demon Astarot goes to Italy in search of two paladins, Reinaldo and Ricardeto, and charges them with a mission; he then enters the body of Bayardo, Reinaldo's steed, and his comrade Farfadete enters that of Ri-

19

cardo's mount Rabicán; forthwith both horses and both riders are made to soar through the air. On the second day of their aerial voyage, they pass over the Strait of Gibraltar, and Ricardo, recognizing the place, asks his guide what the ancients meant by the phrase *the columns of Hercules*. "That expression," replied Astarot, "had its origin in a venerable error that has persisted in the world for many centuries. Those who believe that one cannot sail beyond that point hold a vain and false opinion. The waters are flat as far as they extend, even though together with the land they form a sphere. In the time of the ancients, the human species was rude and ignorant. If Hercules were to return today, he would be ashamed for having planted those two columns that prevented ships from passing beyond them. It is possible to enter the other hemisphere, because all things gravitate to their center, and by a divine mystery the earth is suspended among the stars. Beneath us there are cities, castles, empires; but antiquity was unaware of them. Those places are called the antipodes; the people there worship false gods; they have domestic animals and plants, as you do, and like you they live in a state of constant war with one another."

To properly appreciate this passage (continues M. Ginguené), it is necessary to remember that when it was written, Copernicus and Galileo did not as yet exist, and that Christopher Columbus made his first discovery in 1492, some years after the death of Pulci.

Another significant prophecy is the one mentioned in the *Diario de los Debates* on January 8th and 9th of this year. Mr. Idler, of Berlin, asked by Baron von Humboldt to estimate how many years of our era have corresponded to the great conjunctions of Saturn, which, according to the Cardinal of Ailly in his work *Tractatus de concordia astronomicae veritatis cum narratione historica* (published in Louvain in 1490) usher in extraordinary events, found that one of the planet's periods of greatness should transpire in 1789. With reference to that year the Cardinal wrote: "If the world lasts until then, something only God could know, there will be important and numerous vicissitudes and astonishing revolutions, especially in the field of law": *si mundus usque ad illa tempora duraverit, quod solus Deus novit, multae tunc et magnae et mirabiles alterationes mundi et mutationes futurae sunt, et maxime circe leges*. Baron von Humboldt, citing this marvelous coincidence, asks whether the devotees of mystery and darkness have taken note of this prediction of a revolution that occupies such an honored place in the annals of human history. "Since we believe," says the *Diario de los Debates*, "that his erudite work (*The History of the Geography of the New Continent*) is the first to call attention to it, we recognize it here as a truly curious occurrence."

TRANSLATED BY JO ANNE ENGELBERT

Domingo Faustino Sarmiento

Argentina

(1811–1888)

———•◦••◦•———

Domingo Faustino Sarmiento, a career politician, served as president of his native Argentina from 1868 to 1874. During this time he attempted to eradicate the gaucho culture he had derided in his *Life in the Argentine Republic in the Days of the Tyrants* (1845), a volume also known as *Facundo: Civilization and Barbarism*, translated into English by Mrs. Horace (Mary) Mann and published in New York in 1868. The book is an extraordinary hybrid, intertwining biography, sociological and anthropological analysis, and political thinking. Before his rise to power, Sarmiento was a member of the Asociación de Mayo, a movement opposed to the dictator Juan Manuel de Rosas and his Federalist Party. Sarmiento and his political allies, who supported the creation of a unified Argentine republic, spent long tenures exiled in Chile and Uruguay. His views on the *gaucho* as primitive were probably developed during an early childhood and adolescence spent in a violent and rustic environment in Argentina's pampas. A devoted reader of the Bible and of Benjamin Franklin's *Autobiography*, Sarmiento was one of the early chroniclers of North American culture, and as an educator with a scholarly interest in de Tocqueville, he recorded his forays to foreign schools in the travelogue *Viajes por Europa, Africa y América*, known in English as *Travels* (1845–47, 1847–51), from which the following "Niagara" is part. The value of the essay is found not only in Sarmiento's fascination with nature, an aspect also present in the writing of Ezequiel Martínez Estrada and many other Argentine intellectuals, but in his passion for the North American landscape. Sarmiento was also a devotee of James Fenimore Cooper and an admirer of other North American 'frontier' writers. In his later years, Sarmiento published a memoir on his hometown called *Memories of Provincial Life* (1850), as well as *Life of Dominguito* (1886), a biography of his son, who was killed in the war against Paraguay.

Niagara

The sight of Buffalo, a city rather small for the number of its inhabitants, had a peculiar effect on me. A cluster of steamboats gave off thick columns of smoke from their still lit furnaces. The unloading of buffalo hides and other products of trade with the Indians went against the stream of passengers headed for the port. Turning back to look at the city you

21

could see hundreds of workers on the tops of buildings erecting more buildings, expanding the city to accommodate a growth rate of twenty thousand people a year. Like all centers marked for future commerce in the Union, Buffalo has a coal deposit not far away, on the peninsula formed by Lakes Michigan and Huron.

From Buffalo on, the works of man—railroads, nascent cities, and new farms—contrast with the sublime works of nature. To the north begins the earth's most beautiful region. The Niagara River emerges from Lake Erie tame and transparent, reflecting in its ripples a jumble of rhododendrons and evergreens. In the distance, blue vistas of primeval forests; within those fastnesses one can still see the mysterious moccasin tracks of the untamed Indian. The river splits in two to pass around Grand Island and then gathers its waters to prepare for the sublime play of waters that begins in the rapids and ends in the falls. The distant rumble of this portentous jump, the mist that forms in the air, the excitement caused by the approach of sensations long awaited, make the traveler anxious and impatient with the slowness of the train that carries him. Finally you come to Niagara Falls, a town that feeds the gathering of the curious, and there the fearsome din of the falls pounds in your ears, the tornado of water is more visible, standing out whitely over the treetops; and, as you approach, through the clearings made by the tree trunks, a slice of the rapids contrasts with the darkness of the gloomy branches, like a fragment of burnished silver. These rapids are underwater cascades in which the immense mass of the Niagara River moves over an invisible bed of sharp rocks which give the water its marmoreal whiteness. A thousand tragic accidents have taken place here: the Indian hunter, who let himself be distracted for a moment by the chase, felt himself carried along by the current in his fragile canoe, and after superhuman efforts to resist, he drained the whisky in his gourd and standing with his arms crossed, let himself be carried over the falls, which do not return the corpses of their victims; the prisoners who had taken control of a ship but did not know how to steer it, watched it head straight for the falls, and were buried forever in the bottomless abyss that the falls have carved away. There was talk about the recent death of a child who had slipped into the rapids; they had caught him by the hand from Goat Island but he got away from them.

To try to describe such an extraordinary scene would be futile. The colossal size mitigates one's impression of fear, just as distance causes the stars to look small. Let me quote these lovely verses which the spectacle inspired in a young lady:

> Flow on for ever, in thy glorious robe
> Of terror and beauty. God hath set
> His rainbow on thy forehead; and the cloud

Mantled around thy feet. Awe he doth give
Thy voice of thunder, power to speak to Him
Eternally—bidding the lip of man
Keep silence; and upon thine altar pour
Incense of awe-struck praise.

I thought of myself as a reasonably erudite tourist as far as waterfalls go.
I had seen the ones at Tivoli, so beautiful, so artistic, and so poetically
accompanied by historical memories; the ones in the Rhine, the largest in
Europe; and the hundred that enliven the Swiss landscape. But Niagara
Falls defies all comparison. It alone is the earth's most terrifying spectacle.
Its colossal dimensions, the enormous masses of water and the straight lines
of its shape, divest it of all beauty, inspire only sensations of terror, admiration and that sublime delight caused by the spectacle of great conflicts.
Imagine a crystalline river like the Bío-Bío dropping sharply from an upper
plane to a lower one. Cutting over the edge perpendicularly, the water
will describe a right angle as it moves from the horizontal plane to the
vertical, and from there, after turning over itself in silvery vortexes, it follows the new, lower plane as meekly as it had the upper one before falling.
The beauty of the falls is created by the points of rocks jutting out, which
force the water to fall back on itself, leap into the air, and shatter into atoms
or become impregnated with light.

The sight of other waterfalls has made me smile with pleasure. But
looking at Niagara I felt my legs trembling and that feverish sensation when
the blood drains from your face. Approaching from Goat Island which cuts
it in half, you arrived cheerfully prepared by the less violent landscape of
the rapids, where the Niagara drops fifty feet in a mile. The primeval forest
that covers the island and hides the nearby town behind its branches, the
view upstream in which the river approaches undulating—this is one of
those smiling, virginal landscapes so frequently encountered in the United
States. The Canadian side of the falls has the shape of a horseshoe, and four
stages of evolution without irregularities or interruptions. On the American
side the falls are two hundred yards wide and for that reason they are called
the little falls. In both the water drops 165 feet and the channel scooped
out of the rock below is 100 yards deep and 130 yards wide. Seeing these
measurements written down, one becomes aware of the human eye's inability to encompass vast surfaces. Saint Peter's in Rome seems a structure
of natural dimensions, and Niagara Falls shrinks to the eye, reducing itself
to our small size.

The thickness of the mass of water is 21 feet. Since light cannot penetrate
it, it retains its green color at the center of the falls. This detail, which
reveals to the eye the magnitude of the scene, increases the fear that it
inspires. Look at it from the roof of a watch station on Goat Island; or,

even better, look at it from the Canadian shore, from which the eye can follow the vertical line of the drop and gauge the depth of the abyss that growls like a thunderstorm or a rain of cannon fire. You can see it in all its magnificence and splendor from on board a steamboat that comes up every day from Lake Ontario. Loaded with passengers, it floats to within a hundred yards of the falls and halts there with its motor ready to counteract the suction of the whirlpools, the hull shivers on that stormy water, and foaming as if in delirium, retreats with its passengers, who have had their fill of terrifying emotions. But the falls cannot be felt or touched except by descending into the abyss at their base, wrapping yourself in a rubber cape and letting yourself be led by the hand by a guide right under the cascade itself, where a path has been carved into the rock and provided with an iron railing to save one from slipping on the hundreds of viscous eels that get caught in the cracks in the stone. At the end of this singular corridor, you are amazed, bewildered by the noise, and on your body you take the brunt of thick streams of water. You see in front of you a glass wall that would look solid and stable were it not for the leaks and droplets betraying the presence of the liquid element. When you emerge from that watery hell and look again upon the sun and sky, it might be said that your heart has experienced the sensation of the sublime. A battle between two hundred thousand soldiers could not provoke deeper emotions.

On the Canadian side there is a magnificent hotel and a museum where live buffaloes are exhibited, and sea sponges and fossilized corals broken off from the floor of the falls are sold. This was the bottom of the sea in another era!

These falls differ from others in the world, in that they are situated in the center of a plain, and at first glance you cannot guess the reason for their existence. However, going downstream toward Lake Ontario, the explanation of the phenomenon becomes obvious. Lake Erie is in the middle of an immense platform without any irregularities at all. This plain is the upper surface of a plateau whose border is near Lake Ontario, which is situated on another, lower plateau. The difference in altitude between the two lakes is 300 feet, and the falls in the Niagara River which unites them should really be at the edge of the higher plateau, not far from the shores of Lake Ontario. Instead, the falls are seven miles farther up and the rock breaks off into a large trench of the same depth as the drop. In other words, the falls have been shifting, actually moving slowly toward Lake Erie where one day they will be. The distance the falls advance every year is visible to the observer, as the water tears down and eats away at the bedrock, and from it a part of the earth's age may be guessed. According to the geologist Lyell, supposing that the falls only receded one foot per year, it has taken 39,000 years to reach the present position from the edge of the cliff near the city of Queenstown. But this estimate is modified by differences in the height of the falls at each location and the diverse resistances of the types of stone in the water's path. The falls were first described in 1678 by French missionaries, who also made a drawing. Another description dates from 1751, but geological observations do not begin until very recently. From 1815 on the shape of the two falls has been changing due to slides of enormous chunks of rock, and since 1840 Goat Island has lost several acres of land. As far away as four miles downstream, Lyell discovered the ancient bed of the river at an even higher altitude than the Niagara River's present one. The fragments of fresh-water shells found in heaps on Goat Island are similar in kind and epoch to those found on a line running toward Lake Ontario: this line reveals the river's former course. According to the geologist, the precipices left by the Niagara provide us with a chronometer that roughly measures the immense magnitude of the interval of years separating the present from the time in which the Niagara River ran many miles further north, on the top of the plateau. This chronometer shows us how the two events which were thought to have been simultaneous, namely the extinction of the mastodons and the period in which the earth first came to be inhabited by man, might in fact be infinitely far apart in time. Lyell adds that a geologist may ruminate on these events until, full of terror and admiration, he forgets the presence of the falls themselves, stops perceiving the movement of the waters, and no longer hears their stampede as they plunge into the deep abyss. But when his thoughts return to the present moment, his state of mind and the sensations awakened in his heart will be in perfect harmony with the grandeur and beauty of the glorious scene that surrounds him.

TRANSLATED BY ANDRÉE CONRAD

Juan Montalvo

Ecuador
(1832–1889)

An uncompromising opponent of Ecuadorian dictatorships, Juan Montalvo attacked two tyrants, the theocratic Gabriel García Moreno and, later on, General Ignacio de Veintimilla, in his scathing essays. His opposition condemned him to a life of exile in Ipiales, Colombia, and in Paris, where he founded *El Espectador* (1886–88), a very individualist magazine inspired by Joseph Addison's *The Spectator*. This was just one of three major periodicals he established; the others were *El Cosmopolitano* (1866–69) and *El Regenerador* (1876–78). Montalvo's expulsion from Ecuador by Veintimilla in 1869 set a pattern for similar political rejections in his life, as he was also refused membership to the Spanish Academy of Language. However, his personal frustration never seemed to demoralize Montalvo, who is considered by many, alongside Andrés Bello, to be Latin America's finest nineteenth-century essayist. Montalvo was praised and admired by Victor Hugo and Miguel de Unamuno, among other. Among his most important work is his denunciation of General Veintimilla, entitled *Catilinarias* (1880). He published *Siete tratados* (1882–83), a collection of essays considered a masterpiece reminiscent of Montaigne both in the variety of the essays' subjects and in the abundance of metaphors, and they are considered a precursor of the Modernista movement that swept Latin America from 1885 to 1915. Montalvo also authored a novel, *Los capítulos que se le olvidaron a Cervantes* (1895), but *Siete tratados*, which includes "Washington and Bolívar," the essay reproduced here, remains his most enduring legacy. In it his anticlerical ideas and his views on politics and education are unmistakable. By examining the personalities of George Washington and Simón Bolívar, he compares the idiosyncrasies of the United States and Latin America and attempts to explain their essential differences.

Washington and Bolívar

Washington's fame isn't based on his military feats as much as it is on the very success of the work he went ahead with and completed with joy and sound judgment. Bolívar's fame brings with it the noise of weapons, and in the brilliance discharged by that radiant figure, we see the specters of tyranny fall, flee, and disappear; the clarions sound, the horses neigh, and everything is a warlike clamor around the Spanish American hero. Washington is presented to one's memory and imagination as being a great citizen before being a great warrior, as a philosopher before being a general. Washington would feel very much at home in the Roman Senate next to the old Roman general of the fourth century A.D., Papirio Cursor, and in being an old monarch, he would be Augustus, that serene and poised man who likes to sit between Horatio and Virgil, while the nations reverently revolve around his throne. Washington and Bolívar share the same end purpose, such that their yearning is summarized in the liberty of a people and the establishment of a democracy. The difference between those two very illustrious men and the superiority of one over the other lies in the unmeasurable difficulties one of them had to overcome, and the enjoyment with which the other saw his work coronated. Bolívar, during various periods of the war, didn't count on the slightest recourse, nor did he know where to go looking for it; his unyielding love for the fatherland, that strong sense of honor which existed in his chest, that fertile imagination, that sovereign will, that prodigious activity which constituted his character, would inspire the knowledge of making the impossible feasible; and would endow him with the power to return from nothing to the center of the real world. A military leader inspired by providence, he strikes the rock with his magic wand and a torrent of murmuring crystalline water gushes forth; he walks with a purpose, and the land becomes populated with numerous combatants, those who the patroness of the oppressed people sends without our knowing from where. The Americans from the north were naturally rich, civilized, and powerful even before their emancipation from the mother England; and in the absence of their military leader, one hundred Washingtons would have appeared instantly to fill that void, and not at a disadvantage. Washington was surrounded by men as remarkable as he was, not to mention more worthy: Jefferson, Madison, men of lofty and profound counsel; Franklin, genius of the land and sky, who when he snatches the scepter away from the tyrants, snatches the ray from the clouds, *Eripuit celo fulmen sceptrumque tyrannis*. These and all the rest, as eminent and as numerous as they were, were all united in the cause, rivals in obedience, each of them placing their contingent in the immense rapid stream that flowed over the armies and the enemy fleet and destroyed the British Command. Bolívar had to curb his lieutenants, combat and defeat his own fellow countrymen, and struggle with a thousand plots against him and the independence, while at the same time battling against the Spanish army to either defeat them or be defeated. Bolívar's work is more arduous and, for the same reason, more meritorious.

Washington is presented as more respectable and stately when contemplating the world; Bolívar as more intense and radiant. Washington founded a republic, which after a short time has become one of the greatest nations in the world; Bolívar also founded a great nation, but, less fortunate than his firstborn brother, he saw it crumble away, and even though his work wasn't destroyed, it was defaced and lessened. Washington's successors, great citizens, philosophers, and politicians, never thought of shredding their mothers' sacred cloak in order for each of them to adorn her scars with a piece of purple cloth; all of Bolívar's friends attempted to destroy the "real" Colombia, namely, the Great Republic of Colombia, which afterward was divided into four countries: Colombia, Venezuela, Ecuador, and later Panama, seizing as much as possible for themselves, crazy with ambition and tyranny. In the era of the gods, Saturn would devour his children; we have seen and are seeing certain children devour their mother. If José Antonio Páez, a general during the wars of independence and three-time president of Venezuela to whose memory we owe the most profound respect, had not taken part in this crime, I was already prepared to make a terrible comparison to those associates of parricide who destroyed our great fatherland; and moreover, since I had to mention a worm and remember the sad demise of the hero of the battle of Ayacucho in 1824, the hero of the war and virtues, I return to the business of suppressing this painful indignation of mine in my chest. Washington, less ambitious, but less magnanimous, more modest, but less exalted than Bolívar; Washington, his work concluded, accepts the almost humble presence of his countrymen, while Bolívar rejects the millions offered to him by Peru. Washington turns down the third U.S. presidential term, and like a patriarch retires to live quietly in the comfort of private life, enjoying the consideration of his fellow man without any tinge of hatred, venerated by the community, loved by his friends; he had no enemies, a happy and uncommon man! Bolívar accepts the enticing command which for the third time, and this time from an impure source, comes to vex his spirit, and dies reprimanded, persecuted, and ridiculed by a good portion of his contemporaries. Time has erased this light stain, and we only see the brilliance that surrounds the majority of South Americans. Washington and Bolívar, august personages, the glory of the New World, the honor of humankind, join the most illustrious men of all classes and all time.

TRANSLATED BY HARRY MORALES

Eugenio María de Hostos

Puerto Rico
(1839–1903)

—◆•◆◆•◆—

An advocate of Cuban and Puerto Rican independence and of the abolition of slavery, Hostos, nicknamed "America's citizen," was a lawyer and a moralist. A positivist thinker with rather strict definitions of morality, he traveled widely throughout Spanish America (mainly Peru, Brazil, Argentina, and Chile) in defense of independence. His approach to writing was multidisciplinary, as his works addressed politics, sociology, philosophy, morality, international law, economics, biography, and literary forms such as theater, epistles, novels, and the short story. In an essay titled "Moral Social" (1888), written after his arrival in New York City, he repudiated literature and from then on refused to acknowledge his early forays into fiction. One of his works, *La peregrinación de Bayoán* (1863), reflects Hostos's lifelong campaign for the independence of Puerto Rico and Cuba. However, Hostos's political activism never did bring him much gratification. After resuming his struggle against colonial rule in Puerto Rico against the American regime that followed the Spanish-American War, Hostos's efforts were largely ignored as he was unable to garner support on both the island and in the United States. His frustration would eventually persuade him to spend the remainder of his days in the Dominican Republic, where he was named director of El Colegio Central, created several schools and progressive institutions, and finally died of a sudden illness—although the Dominican Pedro Henríquez Ureña claimed Hostos died of "moral asphyxia." The essay presented here, "At the Tomb of Segundo Ruiz Belvis," is one of the most moving epistolary works ever written in Spanish. Segundo Ruiz Belvis (1829–67) was a Puerto Rican abolitionist who fought against the colonial government and chose exile, first in New York and later in Chile. In 1873, when Hostos reached Valparaíso, Chile, he wrote this homage invoking his patriotic idol and finding parallels to his own condition.

At the Tomb of Segundo Ruiz Belvis

Thousands of miles away from the homeland.
    I'm in Valparaíso, the commercial center of this beautiful, quiet, free, and civilized Republic of Chile. I'm here alone with my prevailing idea. She's the one that supports me when I'm exhausted, the one that pushes me onward, the one that extinguishes my secret tears in her inextinguishable fire, the one that makes me superior to solitude, sadness,

29

poverty, slander, mimicry, the disdain and neglect of my people, and the resentment and insults of our enemies. She is my homeland, my family, my newlywed, my only friend, my only assistant, my only protector, my faith, my hope, my love, my strength. She is the one determining my duty in Puerto Rico, symbolizing my stimulus in Cuba, showing me Latin America's great future homeland, creating a doctrine out of my own neglect, abnegation and sacrifice; the one who has replaced my memorized beliefs with this religion of duty and the American homeland, who has replaced the easy glory of words and the vicious triumphs of political individualism with this indifference for the glory of talent and this vehement hostility toward the triumphs of miserable feelings; she is the one who loves me as I am, which is also why men don't love me.

They say you get to the cemetery by climbing this hill. A bit more effort and I'll be at the top. Oh, but I'm always making an effort, and I never reach the top!

All hills are tiring, and the one I'm climbing is tiring me. I climb two at a time. Which of the two is the more tiring: my prevailing idea or this hill? Over there is the top of the hill. Where is the apex of the idea? Oh, blessed are those who climb and reach the top! How spectacular! Near the ravines and on the slopes of all the hills that surround the city are ranches, shacks, country houses, and luxurious mansions; below, the ordinary streets of this unusually picturesque city; on the lower plane, the movement of labor, the thousand local trade embarkations, and the thousand ships of universal commerce; at the bottom, the chiaroscuro band of the boundless Pacific horizon; to the right, the harmonious chain of mountains that dominate the giant Andes, felicitous Aconcagua, in front of which no other light shines but the first, nor is the pure air ever harmful. Behind me the bastion of the hills rises, which, rising higher with each step, continues to do so until it becomes erect in the impregnable fortress of the Andes. There, in the fissure of two hills, appears an enclosed wall inside of which there is a city turning white. It's the city of the dead. And it's where Segundo Ruiz Belvis is having the first quiet sleep of his life. I'm going to visit the forgotten one.

Luxurious tombs and grand mausoleums are everywhere. The community of the rich is not one the poor man can live in, nor is the community of the aristocracy one that that representative of democracy would tolerate. Ruiz isn't here.

If there were a community of blacks in the city, he who first asked for the liberation of blacks in Puerto Rico would happily be living in it. If there were a community of slaves . . . I'm not in Puerto Rico, I'm in Chile, and here everyone is free; I'm not in the world of the living, I'm in the world of the dead, and this is where the emancipation of the misconceptions, interests, feelings, and vices that enslave you begins.

Where could Segundo Ruiz be? Like all of us who conceal the country's shame, he must have gone into the darkest corner to hide!

Don't the inhabitants of these tombs know where an atoning victim of the Caribbean homeland lives? An arrogant Puerto Rican who didn't want to suffer the enslavement of his homeland? A vagabond of the liberation who came to Chile looking for help for a recalcitrant revolution? A patriot, not the first nor the last, who went around begging for charity to reconquer the homeland? A man who, like many others, committed the unforgivable error of being ahead of his time and his country? Here I've been told that he lives and came here, around 1868. . . .

But what do the eternally oppressed know about the times; whether or not those who are engaged in the evolution of the universal life of substance concern themselves with the revolutions of the society; or what these pathetic rich people, whose homeland was money, or those poor miserable people whose homeland was pain, know about their country? If the tombs of Carrera, Camilo Henríquez, Freire, Infante, and Francisco Bilbao were here, I'm sure that Segundo Ruiz would be living among them; the good ones live together.

How impetuous of me! I should have had the patience to ask any Puerto Rican for the location of Ruiz's last house. . . . Puerto Ricans! They forget about the living and should not forget about the dead; they forget about themselves and should not forget about others; they forget about a commitment, and should not forget about a right! It's 1873, and the republic of charlatans has begun in Spain. How could Puerto Rico not have devoted itself to the pleasure of blessing that great day? How does one urge them to turn away from a childish game that will soon end?

I'm not looking for a dead town: I'm looking for a man who is asleep.

Ruiz! Segundo Ruiz! . . . He doesn't respond. The sleep of death is deep.

As is a dark death, secretly suffered in the corner of a hotel, casually witnessed by one or two brothers . . . Oh, now I remember! His brother the doctor who saw him die, who arrived too late for the resources of his science to do any good, who could convince himself only that this dying man was dying because he had persisted in reaching the country of his hopes despite having a fever that was devouring him; it was his brother the doctor who, because of the details of that quick death during which he barely had time to sign a roll of documents, gently squeeze a hand, and smile with his last smile, gave me the location of the tomb.

But all the tombs of the forgotten ones look alike! It wouldn't be so hard for me to find my colleague's final home if Puerto Rico would remember him. Puerto Rico? . . . Puerto Rico will be celebrating the joy of its new illusoriness, signing the sentence of disgrace with a happy face.

Ruiz, Segundo Ruiz! The homeland is in danger of perpetual enslavement! The homeland is forming a pact with Spain!

Even the dead respond to that shouting: only the colonists are deaf. The tomb has responded to me. Here is Ruiz.

Friend of my ideas! Companion of arduous work! You did well in resting from existence. You rested just in time. You didn't see Cuba persecuted, Puerto Rico ridiculed, the heroes vainly clamoring for help, or the slaves dancing to the sound of their chains. You didn't see the Spanish republicans sanctioning the torture of the regenerated island in the name of the republic, or the degenerated island begging for the leftover crumbs from its master's banquet. You didn't see the biggest republic, the most solid democracy, the strongest town, disputing its living right to the nascent republic, refusing to recognize the new democracy, agreeing upon the price of spilled blood with the executioner. You didn't see the brother towns forgetting about their unfortunate brother in the midst of their own good luck. You didn't see an entire town lift its thin arms to the sky, while another town, eager for the same form of government and the same enjoyment of liberty and justice, unloaded the most treacherous and cruel blows upon it, nor did you see the town we were preparing out of our love for justice between both arms, impassive toward the brother's scream and overlooking the atrocities of the executioner. You didn't see the most civilized nations in the land deliberately becoming silent in the midst of the wanton barbarism against Cuba, nor did you see our own country ridiculed by serving as a witness against Cuba before the world that looks at her contentedly. You didn't see the nations of this continent in which you rest in peace take a stand in a moment of futile enthusiasm in favor of Cuba, in order to surrender to a designation of these governments that can do everything to harm itself, and know nothing about the power to do a good deed. You didn't see logic get trampled on. You didn't see the repudiation of justice. You didn't see the ridicule of all that is good. You didn't see the denial of all that is true. You didn't see the betrayal of universal rights, the death of the most conscientious hopes, the purest aspirations of the human soul in ashes, the dearest truths reduced to muddy realities. You didn't see the orgy of injustice, of all the misconceptions, the carnival of indignity, the infernal quickness of all the illnesses, the golden age of all the repugnant egos, the iron age of all the abnegations, the universal omnipotence of gold, the absolute impotence of rights, the canonization of the most abject feelings, the haughtiness of all the barbarism, and the final judgment of common sense in our species.

You did well to rest, Segundo Ruiz. Rest in peace.

TRANSLATED BY HARRY MORALES

Manuel González Prada

Peru
(1844–1918)

Born in Lima, Manuel González Prada presided over the Peruvian Literary Circle, which eventually became the National Union Party. He joined the Literary Circle in order to oppose the government he viewed as responsible for Peru's defeat at the hands of Chile and the humiliating Treaty of Ancón. González Prada's persuasive, economical writings analyze the failings of his country's political structure, reveal his anarchist convictions, and often point out the mistreatment of Peruvian indigenous populations. He believed that a writer's style should be accessible to a large audience. In his eyes, the writer's task was to write clearly and convincingly rather than obscurely. Although the ruling classes often offered him positions of power, he refused to compromise his ideals for a bureaucratic post. He published numerous volumes of romantic poetry. His work includes *Horas de lucha* (1908) and a defiant early essay, "Páginas libres" (1894), in which he argued against the spelling standards of the Royal Academy of the Spanish Language and wrote about his idols Ernest Renan, Virgil, and Victor Hugo. "Our Bedouins," written in 1889, is González Prada at his sharpest: The essay is an indictment of Peruvian politicos, corrupt exploiters who constitute the nation's most dangerous class. He also describes his amazement at the docility of the Peruvian people and questions whether there is hope for change. The piece was composed exactly a decade after the disastrous Pacific War with Chile, which slowed Peru's progress dramatically and angered many intellectuals, who considered the war an ill-conceived political affair.

Our Bedouins

We consider men who have ruined a country to be bad politicians, even if they speak like Cicero and write like Tacitus.

Where have our Guizots and our Bismarcks led us? Let them respond to whether the nation's reputation is superior to that of Turkey, if the Peruvian name signifies honor or castigation, if Peru causes envy or pity.

For our public figures, that is to say, for the Bedouins (things should be called by their names), Peru was a tent pitched in the desert of a second Arabia: they overtook and and robbed the owners, but they don't leave because they still exploit a few remnants of grandeur and don't see a tent to attack and rob.

33

If, as Letourneau assures, half of England belongs to one hundred and fifty individuals and half of Scotland to ten or twelve people, Peru suffers under the rule of a few privileged beings. It's always the same men, their children or their parents!

Like the alchemists of the Middle Ages who would bequeath the task of finding the philosopher's stone from fathers to sons, the Bedouins of Peru pass on the job of turning the blood and sweat of the nation into gold from ascendants to descendants. Entire families, like gigantic octopuses, unravel a thousand and one byways to the treasury. Those men would laminate us between the cylinders of a sugar mill, filter us over the sink of a distillery, and burn us in an oven used to melt down metals, if they could extract a single milligram of gold from the remains of our bodies.

The struggle with the Bedouins has to be long, difficult, and bloody, not because they might be prepared to spill their own blood, but because they would find a way to let others allow themselves to be killed for them. They lack courage, but they are very astute. In the war against Chile, they proved their cowardice by not even being angry enough to defend against the seizure of dung and saltpeter; this very day, their ability is manifested in the seesaw of our politics, doing it all when they don't enjoy popularity and are generally bored. They're born like fungi in the dung heap, adhere to rock like the oyster, propagate in the intestines like the tapeworm, and slip through the narrowest gratings like the air. They possess the subtlety of hydrogen and the ductility of gold. Where one of them fails, a thousand fail, everyone fails, because they form a hypocrisy of tailcoats and a free-masonry of stew. They change their name and disguise, remaining the same. In the same way that clerks continue as clerks, even though they call themselves archivists, actuaries, secretaries, notaries, or ministers of legal authority, the Bedouins don't stop being Bedouins by calling themselves what they call themselves, by following the flag they follow, or by practicing the profession they practice. Who rules in the Congress? The Bedouins. Who rules in the government? The Bedouins. Who rules in the judiciary? The Bedouins. Who rules in the customhouses, charities, municipalities, embassies, consulates, banks, and newspapers? The Bedouins.

They live their life hypnotizing governments or performing the fox circle dance at the base of the presidential tree; they are the first to enjoy the benefits and the last to confront the dangers; they, like worthless soil, receive the seed and drink the water without ever producing fruit; they, like the snake of popular stories, weld their lips to the nipple of the nation, suck until they extract blood, and give us the tip of their nauseating tail.

What harm did they not cause? About them, one can affirm something similar to what Attila said about his horse: "Where it stamps its hooves, grass will never grow again."

And the harm comes from up above; the schemes for all the iniquities are consummated at the highest elevation. Here the contagious putrid matter hides underneath the frock and tailcoat, not underneath the shirt or the poncho. In Peru, the meaning of corruption is the opposite of what one is accustomed to: in the more civilized nations there exists a primitive nature from where the elements of barbarism rise to the surface; but within ourselves there exists a superior class, and in that class, a *crust*, from where the germs of all misery, debasement, and all vices descend to the bottom. Our thousand revolutions failed or were counterproductive because that crust, after momentary immersions, always floated. Presidents were overthrown, the blood of the wretched was spilled, but that which was at the bottom never turned upwards, nor was any real social liquidation put into practice.

What occurred yesterday occurs today, and who knows if it won't occur for many years. The nation (and not only the nation, but many men who have pretensions to being thinkers and cultured) imagines that it accomplishes quite a bit by applauding and whistling, forgetting that in the saturnalias of Rome the slaves had a right to get drunk and speak shamelessly to their masters.

We were offended, trampled on, and bloodied like no other nation, but the war against Chile has not shown us anything nor has it cured us of any of our defects: like intercurrent illness, the Araucanian infection disappeared, leaving all of us chronically ill.

Today, the next presidential election feigns signs of life in this paralyzed and nearly dead organism: the candidates struggle—the struggle of crows to peck at the bloodied head of a dying soldier; the politicians become agitated—the agitation of vibrio bacteria in the entrails of a cadaver; the newspapers quarrel—the quarrel of prostitutes in the puddle of a small plaza.

We attend a useful and necessary spectacle, although cynical and nauseating: all the men in public office, protecting themselves with authentic documents, smear on their face the mud they amassed along their route. It looks like the revelation of all the accumulated filth in a hospital of syphilitics and lepers. The only thing left is for the nation to release a good dose of carbolic acid.

The people, the nation's masses, remain stupidly indifferent. Regardless of who will govern, nothing matters; come what may, little attention is paid; they endure everything, accept everything. Peru, like an unhappy woman chained to a highway post, can endure the insults of an outlaw, an imbecile, a lunatic, and even an orangutan.

Some people still think about enlivening the everlasting vendors of ham sandwiches, when the only scream of all the honest men should amount to: Bedouins get out!

TRANSLATED BY HARRY MORALES

José Martí

Cuba
(1853–1895)

José Martí first joined the cause of Cuban independence in 1868, immediately after Cuba's first battle for independence against Spain. He was sentenced to hard labor, and his imprisonment resulted in an exposé on prison life, *The Political Prison in Cuba* (1871). He was then exiled to Spain and subsequently landed in the United States, where he wrote for the *New York Sun* under the pseudonym M. de S., politicked to garner support for the 1895 U.S. invasion of Cuba, and involved himself in the careful planning of the Cuban Revolution. He worked with exiled generals and raised money for the island's cause. As one of the precursors of Latin America's Modernismo, Martí was one of the leaders of this literary movement, which sought to renovate the Spanish language. He admired the French romantics and symbolists, but remained deeply rooted in Spanish literature. An incredibly prolific writer whose complete oeuvre in Spanish fills more than two dozen volumes, Martí's major works include three books of poetry, *Ismaelillo* (1882), *Versos sencillos* (1891), and *Versos libres* (1913), a number of prose pieces about contemporary life in the United States, and a novel penned under the name Adelaida Ral. A return to Cuba in 1895 was rapidly followed by his death in combat, but his tragic end only served to elevate him to the stature of martyr. Innumerable guerrilla fighters in Latin America have made Martí their inspiration, and Fidel Castro's revolution in Cuba turned Martí's face into an icon to be equated with Karl Marx, Friederich Engels, and Ernesto "Ché" Guevara. The following essay is an extraordinary display of Martí's talent as a journalist. Written in New York City on 10 September 1886, for the newspaper *La Nación*, in reaction to the tragic earthquake in the city of Charleston, South Carolina, its reportorial style incorporates vivid images of natural destruction with astonishing doses of human compassion. Martí wrote scores of similar articles on a wide range of American topics (the Statue of Liberty, the Brooklyn Bridge, Black Harlem, for instance), which, when read together, offer a *sine qua non* understanding of the United States as perceived by a Latin American outsider of the times.

The Earthquake at Charleston

To the Editor of *La Nación*:

An earthquake has destroyed the city of Charleston. Only ruins remain of what yesterday had been a flower; on one side the lovely city had contemplated her reflection in the sandy waters of her two rivers, poised elegantly beside them like a basket of fruit; looking inland, her gaze had extended along a garland of beautiful villages ringed with magnolia and orange groves and gardens in full bloom.

Defeated whites and prosperous blacks have lived here since the war in languid harmony; the trees here do not shed their leaves, and the sea can be glimpsed through tremulous gowns of Spanish moss. Over there, at the edge of the Atlantic, almost hidden by sand, rises Fort Sumter, whose walls were struck by the bullet that finally called the South and the North to war. And this is the place where the unfortunate passengers of the good ship *Puig* were received by the city with generous compassion.

The streets of Charleston lead directly to her two rivers. The city is bordered by a promenade that runs along the water's edge; a bevy of ships lie at bay loaded with cotton for England and India. King Street is for commerce; Meeting Street boasts fine hotels; but the blacks are crammed into a crowded, noisy neighborhood. The rest of the city consists of beautiful residences, not built cheek by jowl like the mean, immodest houses of the cold cities of the North, but with a noble space around them that favors the poetry and decorum of life. Each house has its rosebushes and its lawn with sunflowers and orange trees to grace the entranceway.

In the morning light, bright colors stand out against the white walls of the houses: rugs and ornaments, spread along the veranda railings by smiling black women, their heads covered by blue and red scarves. In other opulent dwellings, the raw hue of bricks is muted by the dust of defeat. Living in that tranquil, dark-eyed city, people develop strength of spirit and radiance of mind.

But today, the railroad that wends its way to Charleston's gates has halted mid-path on twisted, severed rails, heaved up from their beds. Towers have toppled; residents have spent the week kneeling in prayer; blacks and their former masters have slept under the same tarpaulins and eaten the same loaf of grief before their ruined homes: crumbled walls, fallen pillars; here and there lie pieces of iron grillwork, wrenched from the stone and thrown far from their bases.

Startled in the small hours of the night by a tremor that shook their houses as if they were bird's nests, the fifty thousand inhabitants of Charleston now live in its streets and plazas in tents and wagons, in makeshift huts draped with their clothing.

Eight million dollars ground into dust in twenty-five seconds. Sixty persons have died, some crushed by falling walls, others by fear. And at the same tremendous hour, a number of children were born into the world.

Misfortunes launched from the bowels of the earth must be contemplated from the heights of heaven.

From that vantage, earthquakes with their terrible legacy of human suffering are nothing more than the adjustment of the earth's visible surface to the compression of its vitals, a movement indispensable for the equilibrium of creation: for all the majesty of his suffering, for all the ocean-power of his judgement and that vast universe of wings that beat within his cranium, man is no more than a gleaming bubble bobbing blindly in a sunbeam! A poor warrior of the air, clad in gold, hurled back to earth by an enemy invisible to him, he always staggers to his feet, reeling from the blow, and readies himself for the next fight, even though his hands never succeed in wiping away the torrents of blood that blind his eyes.

But he feels that he is rising, like the bubble in the sunbeam! He feels in his breast all the pleasure and light of nature, all her storms and strife, helping to lift him!

All this majesty crashed to earth at the hour of horror of the earthquake in Charleston.

• • •

It was about ten o'clock at night. Like golden bees, the good brethren who make newspapers were toiling over their type cases; the devout, who in Charleston, a place of scant science and ardent imagination, are numerous, were concluding their prayers; doors were being locked, and those who next day must defend the hearth were seeking strength from love or from repose; the slow, suffocating air could scarcely bear the heavy fragrance of the roses; half of Charleston lay asleep: the velocity of light is not faster than the speed with which disaster struck.

The earth had never trembled here, in this soft point of land that leans forward toward the sea: the city is built on spongy soil, that of the coastal plain; the region had never known volcanoes nor vents, nor columns of smoke, nor geysers, nor solfataras: the only columns here have been fountains of fragrance, the perfume of orange trees perpetually covered with white blossoms. Nor had the ocean, whose shallow coastal waters gild the inlet's rim with yellow sand, ever hurled up those mighty waves, dark as a maw, that can suddenly heave up when its floor becomes unbalanced, splits, or is propelled upward—ruinous waves that swell in force and curl at the crest to slam against the shore like ravenous mountains.

In the patrician peace known to Southern cities, night was beginning to fall when a noise was heard that sounded vaguely like a heavy body being pushed very fast.

To mention it is to hear it again. The sound grew louder: lamps and windows trembled . . . a fearsome artillery had begun to rumble under the earth: the typesetters dropped their letters in the cases; the clergy fled, still wearing their vestments; women, forgetting their children, rushed unclad into the street; men ran headlong between teetering walls: Who had grabbed the city by the belt and begun to shake it in the air, with a terrible hand, dislocating all its joints?

The ground undulated, walls split apart, houses swayed from side to side, half-naked people kissed the earth, crying out, "Oh Lord! Oh, beautiful Lord," their voices choked. Look! A whole portico has crashed to the ground! Valor has fled, thought is confounded; now it is growing quiet, the shaking is subsiding, now it ceases; dust from the fallen houses has risen above the roofs and treetops.

Desperate parents take advantage of the truce to get back to their babies; a young mother of great beauty begins clearing away the wreckage of her own door with her hands; brothers and husbands are gently dragging or carrying in their arms women who have fainted; a poor wretch who jumped from a window is crawling on his belly, uttering horrendous cries, his arms and legs broken; an old woman is seized by a fit of violent trembling and dies; another woman, who is dying of fear, agonizes in an uncontrollable spasm; the faint gas lights, barely perceptible in the murky air, provide scant light for hapless people running back and forth, waving their arms in the air and crying out for Jesus.

Without warning tall fires flare up in the darkness; their broad flames, waving slowly, bathe the scene in a red splendor.

In the sudden light all faces reveal that they have seen death: around many visages, reason floats in shreds; around others it seems to grope, blinded and stunned, as if looking for its seat. Now the flames form a canopy; the fire is rising; but who can express in words what happens next? The muffled noise is heard again: people mill about as if looking for the best exit; they begin to run in all directions; the wave down under is magnified, undulates; every single person feels that a great tiger has pounced on him.

Some fall to their knees; others fall face down; old people are carried in the arms of their faithful servants; great cracks open in the earth; solid walls flutter like a handkerchief in the wind; the cornices of facing buildings graze each other on high. Human dread is augmented by that of animals: horses unable to shake loose from their wagons heave them over, first on one side, then on the other, with violent movements of their flanks; one beast kneels on his front legs; others sniff the ground; the eyes of another glow red in the light of the flames; his body trembles like a reed in a storm: What fearsome drum is rousing the bowels of the earth, calling them to battle?

• • •

Then, when the second wave subsided, when all souls were already pregnant with fear, and when from beneath the rubble, like long arms reaching upward, the faint moans of the moribund began to rise; when the shuddering horses had to be tethered to the ground like wild elephants; when toppling walls pulled telegraph wires and posts down with them; when the injured struggled to free themselves from the broken bricks and timbers that blocked their escape; when poor women, with the marvelous perception of love, discerned their ruined homes; when fear kindled the tempestuous imagination of the blacks; then above that carpet of prostrate bodies a clamor began to arise that seemed to emerge from previously unsuspected depths and soared, quivering in the air on wings that pierced it like arrows. That great cry hovered above our heads and seemed to rain down tears.

The few brave souls who were still standing—and they were very few!—tried in vain to stifle that growing clamor that made their flesh crawl: fifty thousand creatures praising God with the most outlandish blandishments of fear!

The bravest put out the fire, picked up the fallen, leaving behind those who no longer had any reason to get up, carried on their backs elderly persons paralyzed by horror. No one knew what time it was; all clocks had stopped at the moment of the first tremor.

• • •

Dawn revealed the disaster.

With the light of day, one could begin to perceive the cadavers strewn on every street and the mountains of rubble, the walls reduced to dust, the porticos sliced completely in half, the bent and twisted wrought iron grills and metal posts, the houses collapsed in crumpled folds upon their foundations, the crumbled towers, the tallest spire dangling from the church by a slender wire.

The sun began to warm hearts: the dead were taken to the cemetery where that Calhoun who spoke so well lies forever mute, along with Gaddens, and Rutledge and Pinckney; doctors attended to the sick; a priest heard the confessions of the frightened; on louvered shutters and door panels the wounded were transported.

Rubble was piled on sidewalks. Houses were ransacked for sheets and quilts for making tents; blacks hustled to get some of the ice distributed by wagon. Certain houses were still smoldering; through deep fissures recently opened in the earth, a fine sand had emerged, reeking of sulfur.

Everyone is carrying or transporting something. Some are making straw pallets. Others are lulling a child to sleep on a pillow, shading him with a parasol. Still others flee from a wall about to collapse; crack! a wall crushes two elderly people who could not manage to get out of the way! A bearded son, tears streaming down his face, repeatedly kisses the cheeks of the dead man he is carrying in his arms.

A blue tent shields the many babies who were born during the night; one young woman has given birth to twins.

St. Michael's of the sonorous bells, St. Phillip's of the proud tower, the Hiberian Salon, where speeches were said to gleam like bayonets, the guard house, in short, the best of the city has fallen and reclines upon the earth.

A crippled man with a thin face and a huge black mustache approaches a group sitting sadly on a broken pediment, his eyes ablaze with joy. "It hasn't fallen, boys, it hasn't fallen." What hadn't fallen was the courthouse where on hearing the Confederate army fire on Fort Sumter, the ardent patriot McGrath had thrown off his judge's robe: he swore to give the South his blood, and give it he did!

What desolation in people's homes! In the entire city there is not a steady wall nor an intact roof. The roofs of many verandas hang suspended without the support of their columns, like faces lacking a lower jaw; wall lamps and chandeliers have shattered on the pavement; statues have descended from their pedestals: the water stored in roof tanks has leaked through cracks, flooding houses: at the entrances of homes, even the flowers seem to have understood the damage: the jasmine has withered on the stem and the roses are wilted and forlorn.

• • •

For the first two days there was great anguish throughout the city. No one could go home. Nothing was bought or sold in the market. One tremor followed another, although they gradually became less violent. The city was in a state of exalted religious excitement, and whenever the tremors grew more alarming, haughty whites humbly added their voices to the hymns improvised by the blacks. Innumerable poor black girls tugged at the skirts of white women and begged them with tears in their eyes to take them home with them—such is the power of habit to transform abuse into virtue and lend it poetry: these children—conceived in misery by parents whose spirit had been frozen by slavery—still attribute supernatural powers to the caste that subjugated theirs; such is the goodness and humility of that race which the wicked disparage and disdain! Whatever its shortcomings, our obligation to pardon it is very great indeed.

Caravans of blacks hurried into farm country in search of better conditions; they hastened back, appalled by what they saw. For twenty miles inland the earth was pitted and laid open: cracks two feet wide seemed to be bottomless. A multitude of new wells had opened up: some spewing up a fine white sand mixed with water, or sand alone that piled up around the rims as around the mouths of anthills; others spouted water or bluish mud, or little mounds of mud piled atop others of sand, as if beneath the surface the top layer of earth were pure mud with a layer of sand just below. The new water tasted like sulfur and iron.

A hundred-acre reservoir had gone dry at the first tremor and lay full of dead fish. A dam had broken and its waters had swept away everything in their path.

Trains could no longer enter Charleston, because rails had been lifted from the roadbed and hurled into the air or had writhed like serpents and buckled on their supports.

At the time of the first tremor a locomotive, approaching at a triumphant clip, suddenly leaped into the air, shaking behind it as if it were a rosary, a long string of cars lifted from the tracks; it then plunged head downward into a crevass opening before it, and the engineer was killed on impact. Another whistling merrily a little distance away was lifted bodily by the earthquake and tossed into a nearby reservoir, where it now reposes under forty feet of water.

· · ·

Trees are the new homes of all frightened townspeople of the surrounding area; farm folk have taken refuge in their churches where they listen in terror to messages of wrath that visit the heads of foolish pastors; the singing and praying of rural congregations can be heard for miles around. The entire town of Summerville has crumbled and seems now to lie at the bottom of a huge pit in the earth.

In Columbia people lean against walls as if they were seasick. In Abbeville the tremor set the church bells aringing, now jangling wildly, now tolling plaintively. In Savannah, fear reached such a pitch that women plunged out of windows with nursing infants still at their breasts, and at this very moment one can see a column of smoke rising straight from the sea a few meters offshore.

The night of the quake, the forests began to fill with city folk who ran from shaking roofs to take refuge under trees, kneeling in the woodland darkness to sing praises to the Lord in chorus, entreating Him to be merciful. In Illinois, Kentucky, Missouri, and Ohio the earth also trembled and fell open. A terrified Mason, who was being initiated into a lodge, fled into the street, a cord still tied around his waist.

A Cherokee Indian who had just laid a brutal hand on his poor wife fell to his knees when he felt the earth move beneath his feet, swearing to the Lord that he would never punish her again.

· · ·

What a strange scene greeted those who, jumping across crevasses and huge holes in the earth, finally succeeded in reaching Charleston with donations of money and camp tents! They arrived at night. The roads were lines of wagons, like the wagontrains of the West. In the plazas, which are small, families slept in tents improvised out of blankets, towels, even linen suits. Purple, scarlet and yellow tents; blue and white tents with red stripes.

The walls that seemed most in danger of toppling had already been razed. Canopies erected around the ice wagons and fire pumps gave the impression of a fair. From far away, as if in distant villages, one could hear a tremendous outcry. Women were falling into each other's arms and weeping on finding one another still alive; their sobbing was the language of gratitude to heaven; falling silent, they knelt and prayed, then went their separate ways, consoled.

Like pilgrims, people with tents on their backs stop to sit down, then walk about aimlessly, or join a chorus without seeming to find a safe place for their rags or for their fear. They are blacks whose primal fear of natural phenomena has been rekindled in their passionate race by doleful hymns and terrible dances.

Dreadful birds unseen by other eyes seem to have seized them by the head, picking at their flesh and beating them with their wings in mad fury.

Since the horror of that night it has been apparent to anyone who had eyes to see with that out of the distant memories of the poor blacks a strange nature was emerging: the compressed spirit of the race, the Africa of parents and grandparents, the characteristic sign that every nature imprints upon the individual so that despite any accident or human violation, he lives out his unique life and makes his way on earth.

Every race brings it mandate into the world, and if the harmony of the universe is not to be disturbed, the way must be kept free for each to make use of its strength to fulfill its mission, enjoying all the fruits and the full dignity of natural independence. Who believes that the spiritual harmony of the universe can be interrupted with impunity, that advancement can be blocked under the pretext of a supposed superiority of one of the races based on nothing more than a degree of historical time?

It almost seems that the people of Africa are illumined by a black sun! Their blood is fire; their passion, a flash of teeth; their eyes, flames; everything in their nature has the energy of their poisons and the potency of their balms.

Black people have immense inherent goodness, which neither suffering nor slavery can pervert and which cannot be obscured by displays of bravura.

But more than other races, the black race has such close communion with nature that it seems better able to perceive its changes, be moved by them and respond to them.

There is something supernatural and marvelous in their fears and joys that does not exist in other primitive races, something in their movements and their gaze that is reminiscent of the majesty of the lion: in their emotions there is a loyalty so gentle that it reminds one not of dogs but of doves, and there is such clarity, steadiness and intensity in their passions that they seem like rays of sunlight.

A miserable parody of that sovereign constitution are those creatures deformed by fear and the whip and so exhausted they can only transmit to their descendants, engendered in fearsome and tormented nights of servitude, the bestial emotions of instinct, sad vestige of their free and uninhibited nature.

But even slavery, capable of extinguishing the very sun, cannot destroy completely the spirit of a race: and this was what was seen to well up in these silent souls when the greatest fear of their lives stirred in the legacy of their blood what it retains of jungle airs, swaying reeds, the rustle of cane. Thus was reborn, in all its melancholy barbarousness, in the breast of those blacks, born for the most part in America and educated in its customs, the most violent and ingenuous fear, common to their whole passionate race, of those incandescent changes in nature that nurture the poisonous *manzanillo* in the realm of plants, and the lion in the kingdom of the animals!

They have been taught the Bible and voiced their fear in its prophetic language. Within an instant of the first tremor, the blacks were experiencing extreme horror.

Jesus belongs to them, and in their prayers they call Him "My Lord Jesus," "My Sweet Jesus," "My Blessed Christ." They prayed to Him on their knees, slapping their heads and thighs as they watched spires and columns fall to the ground. "This is Sodom and Gomorrah," they told each other, trembling. "It will open up, Mount Horeb is going to open up!" they exclaimed, trembling, and threw up their arms, bodies rocking back and forth. A keen awareness of their exile, the terrible exile of their race, came over them, perhaps for the first time in their lives, and since we love that which we can see and that which makes us suffer, in their terror they clung to the whites and begged them to let them stay with them "until the judgment was over."

They were coming and going, dragging their children to and fro in frantic dashes; and when the poor elders of their caste appeared, elders sacred to all human beings except the white man, they prostrated themselves around them, in large groups, listening to them on their knees with their foreheads pressed against the earth, and repeated in convulsive chorus their mysterious exhortation, which projected such priestly strength from the vigor and ingenuousness of their nature and the divine attribute of age that the whites themselves, even the educated whites, in deep veneration, added the music of their troubled souls to that tender and ridiculous dialect.

In the saddest hour of the night, about six black youths began to drag themselves along the ground in a group, prisoners of the frenzy inherent to the race for which religion provides forms of expression. They were literally crawling on hands and knees. Inexpressible anguish quivered in their chant. Their faces were bathed in tears. "It's the angels, it's the angels knocking at the door." They sobbed, softly, the same song they had sung in full voice. Then came the refrain, full of supplication, "Oh tell Noah to make the ark soon, make the ark soon, make the ark soon." The prayers of the elders are not lengthy utterances, but the short phrases of genuine emotion and of primitive races.

Their spirituals have the contortions, the monotony, the force and the fatigue of their dances. The people who are listening contrive a rhythm at the end of the phrase that seems musical to them, in tune with their spiritual mood, and without previous consultation they all join in the same refrain. "Oh my Lord, don't touch, oh my Lord don't touch, oh my Lord, don't touch my city again!"

"The birds have their nests. Lord, leave us our nests!" and the whole group, faces to the ground, repeats with the agony that is taking possession of their souls, "Leave us our nests!"

At the entrance of a tent there is a black woman to whom great age has given a fantastic appearance. Her lips are moving, but you cannot hear her speak. She rocks her body back and forth; she rocks it incessantly, backward and forward. Many blacks and whites surround her with visible eagerness until she breaks into this hymn: "Oh let me go, Jacob, let me go!"

The crowd surrounds her; all are singing, all are swaying from one side to another, raising their hands toward heaven, clapping their ecstasy. One man falls to the ground, begging for mercy. He is the first convert. The women bring a lamp and crouch down around him, and take him by the hand. He trembles, stammering a prayer; his muscles flex, he clenches his fists; his features relax beneath a veil of ecstatic death; he remains there, in a swoon, alongside the tent, where he is soon joined by others. And at every tent, a scene exactly like this one is repeated. By sunrise neither the song nor the old woman's rocking has ceased. In these benighted neighborhoods, the beasts who abound in all races fall, under the pretext of religion, into abominable orgies.

· · ·

Now, after seven days of fear and prayers, people are beginning to return to their houses. The women, being both easily alarmed and quick to adjust, were the first to return, lending courage to the men: the mayor dwells once more with his family in what is left of their sumptuous residence. Railroad cars roll along the repaired tracks, loaded with cotton; the city, already famous for valor in war and now for valor in catastrophe, once again fills up with strangers; the municipality negotiates a federal loan of ten thousand dollars to repair damaged buildings and replace those that have toppled to the ground. From stock markets, theaters, newspapers and banks arrive generous contributions of funds: many of the tents the government improvised in gardens and parade grounds are being folded for lack of occupants. The ground is still trembling as if it had not yet firmly established itself upon it new base: what could have been the cause of this violent trembling of the earth?

Can it be that the earth's outer crust, its interior shrunken as a result of heat loss through hot springs and lava flows, has contracted to adjust to its changed and reduced inner core, which is calling the surface to itself?

The earth, then, when it cannot resist the tension, contracts and buckles in waves; then cracks and the openings of the cracks mount one atop the other with a terrible clash—and successive tremors of adjacent rocks, always flexible, push the earth upward and outward until the echo of the crash subsides.

But there are no volcanoes in the extensive area where the earthquake was felt; and the sulfurous vapors expelled through holes in the surface and cracks are those that naturally abound because of the geological formation of the low, sandy plain of the Atlantic coast.

Perhaps in the deep declivities of the sea, as a consequence of the same gradual cooling of the fiery center, the seabed, too large for the reduced dome it ought to cover, has buckled and cracked like any body under violent contraction, and upon closing with enormous force upon the broken edge, has shuddered violently, the tremor rising with a roar to the surface of the waves. But in that case the surface of the sea would have curled in a monstrous wave, and from its mouths the wounded earth would have poured out its pain upon the handsome city that nurtures flowers and dark-eyed women upon the unstable sand of the shore.

Or can it be that the shelf of fragmentary rock that leans toward the sea, its rivers laden with ancient rocky residue, has cracked off violently, yielding at last to the weight of the mass of gneiss descended from the Alleghenies, and slid upon the granite base which three thousand feet below the surface sustains it at the edge of the sea, the weight of the fallen mass compressing the lower levels of the plain, causing the ground to swell and shaking the cities lifted on the fold of earth created by the shock?

That is indeed what is believed to be the case: the warm, crumbling Atlantic coastal plain, yielding to the weight of the residue deposited upon it in the course of centuries by the rivers, slid upon its granite bed in the direction of the sea.

Thus, very simply—swallowing men and women and carrying off their houses as the wind carries away leaves—did the earth comply with its law of formation, with all the majesty appropriate to acts of creation, the travail of nature!

Man, wounded, stanches the blood that streams into his eyes, gropes for his sword to combat the eternal enemy and goes on dancing in the wind, striving to follow his path, that of an atom, climbing always, like a warrior scaling a sunbeam!

Charleston is already reviving, although its agony is not yet over, although the ground beneath its swaying houses is not yet still.

Friends and relatives of the dead have found that work replaces in the soul the roots that death has snatched away. Humble blacks, the fire that flickered in their eyes now extinguished, return to their gentle tasks and their numerous progeny. Brave young women sprinkle rose dust on the rebuilt porticoes.

And in the town square, the twins born in a blue tent at the very hour of desolation are laughing merrily, one on either side of their smiling mother.

TRANSLATED BY JO ANNE ENGELBERT

Baldomero Sanín Cano

Colombia

(1861–1957)

———◆•※•◆———

Baldomero Sanín Cano was born in Rionegro, Colombia, and was contributing to periodicals in the city of Medellín by the age of twenty. A perspicacious reader with a legendary intellectual curiosity, he taught himself English, Italian, French, German, Latin, and Danish. After a brief tenure as a teacher in Medellín, he took an active role in liberal politics in his country. This interest took him to Europe, where he worked for the government of General Rafael Reyes. Sanín Cano lived in Madrid, Geneva, and later in Buenos Aires, where he directed the international politics section of *La Nación*. Many of his essays were devoted to politics, and these works reveal Sanín Cano's deep aversion to absolutist conclusions. He hated words like *always, never, everything,* which imposed a defined and indisputable character on ideas. This perspective led to him to explore hidden meanings and to engage the complexity of the issues he was addressing instead of settling for simple answers. Sanín Cano's perception of Colombia's general isolation from the international community reflects such a pattern of thought. Although Sanín Cano acknowledged Colombia's relative obscurity internationally, he argued that Colombia's isolation from its national character was at the root of this problem, rather than blaming it only it on a racist international climate. *La civilización manual y otros ensayos* (1925) and *Indagaciones e imágenes* (1926) are among his most notable works. In the spirit of Montalvo's "Washington and Bolívar," Sanín Cano's "Theodore Roosevelt," published in the magazine *Hispania* on 1 July 1914, is a depiction of the adventurous leader of the Rough Riders in the Spanish-American War and the twenty-sixth president of the United States. Roosevelt was disliked by many Latin American intellectuals; Rubén Darío, for instance, profiled him in an ode, included in *Cantos de vida y esperanza,* where Roosevelt is at once primitive and modern, simple and complicated, a bit like George Washington. Sanín Cano portrays Roosevelt—already a Nobel Prize winner and the loser of a presidential election in which he was the Progressive Party candidate—as a nearsighted, unintelligent army man, celebrated by his fellow nationals but ignorant of other people's views.

Theodore Roosevelt

Colonel Theodore Roosevelt is an exponent of his time. He was born in the twentieth century to live the restless, superficial, and noxious life of a journalist dedicated to politics. He was born to bring havoc to that place where civilization has not penetrated with its egalitarian tools. The world is his setting. One day, he fights the war in Cuba. At dawn on another day, he organizes a South American revolution in Washington. He governs a state, a nation, and by virtue of this is depicted as an arbiter of a continent. With his colonel's epaulets and the less ostentatious spoils of war of a Central American revolutionary, he displays the Nobel Peace Prize. When Yankee politics became exasperated with his irritating chatter, the colonel went to Africa in search of big game. He was followed to dark Africa by reporters, cinematographers, and his imperturbable nerve. A few elephants or hippopotamuses would have preferred he not visit them; they would have changed their lives for the momentary fame he, Colonel Roosevelt, bestowed upon them, already dead.

And it appears that the god of the century, a kind of sandwich, an avid man of formidable dimensions, would follow him everywhere. The horns of announcement, conquerors of fame, proclaim his arrival in Egypt, his Sorbonne nonsense, his marvelous lack of tact during his receptions in London, his serene and portentous ignorance, and his inimitable boldness.

When he arrived home, public sentiment showed signs that it wanted to forget about the boisterous Colonel Roosevelt, whose good fortune afforded him the opportunity to file a lawsuit for slander against an indiscreet man who had called him a drunk. The process lasted long enough for the colonel to remain in the spotlight for a few weeks. It appeared as if he had planned the exciting incident himself. And the stormy sea of journalism, whose waves take away and bring back the name of this vigorous champion of the biggest headlines, had barely started to calm down when a treacherous hand fired a bullet into his chest. Fortunately, it just so happened that the colonel was wearing a very thick overcoat, and in one of the pockets of that overcoat, he had many sheets of paper, as if to form a breastplate. Colonel Roosevelt received a slight wound because the bullet seemed to have orders to pause in his overcoat, travel through the padding, and perforate the pages of an impromptu lecture that the apostles of the new gentiles usually carry. Not even the most somber suspicions can assume that this painful turn of events would have been planned in advance; it was nothing more than further proof of how carefully fate guides the colonel's path.

Everything happens in this world, and the American press was starting to get tired of upholding the importance of this world figure. His name would disappear from the biggest headlines. It was important to look for a new form of gratification to satisfy the public's curiosity. South America remained. Colonel Roosevelt imagined, and his vision of the near future proved to be true, that in the intricate Amazonian jungle there were wild beasts in whose ears this sonorous Dutch name had not sounded; in addition, he imagined that there are still commercial marketplaces in South America where one can find an assembly of unconditional praise for the right price. His foresight about the future went as far as considering that his descriptions of the Amazonian jungle, portrayed as zoological dissertations, could possibly find space in English newspapers. Amazingly, here too he discovered his feelings for the issues. The *Daily Telegraph* has been publishing the description of the events Colonel Roosevelt has taken part in and witnessed in the Amazon. And this account isn't published in a carefree manner, but by reinforcing it with all kinds of privileges. At the end of every article there is a series of comments detailing the risks taken by the unwary regarding that material published without a large number of precautions. One day the Ark of the Covenant would fall. One of the faithful who was present put up his hand to avoid the collapse. Jehovah gave the owner of that sacrilegious hand a sudden death. Reading the very earnest comments of the *Daily Telegraph* opposing the possible violators of the literary property Theodore Roosevelt has granted it, one thinks about the Ark of the Covenant. If the wind could carry off into the air something as heavy as the *Daily Telegraph*, in which the colonel of the light cavalry demonstrates his knowledge as a naturalist, then no one would dare to stop that plaything in the air. He could be punished for his audacity in the same manner as the person who put his hand on the Ark of the Covenant. "Strict ownership rights," reads the headline. The following words are located at the end of each article: "All rights reserved, including translation into other languages, even Scandinavian." To which is added: "These articles are fully protected by copyright, which imposes [it was necessary to add] severe penalties for their infraction." Not having anything to do with Colonel Roosevelt, anyone might say that there is a certain lack of manners in threatening one with the law, after having endured reading three imaginative columns by this gentleman.

And let's see what he writes. The colonel went there with the affectation, look, and all the tools of a naturalist. He was going to look for big game for the museums and for his own consumption. One of his victims was the anteater. He needed two or three specimens for the museums and to observe their stomachs. It's one of the internal organs that attracts the ex-president the most. In the stomach of the *Myrmecophaga* he found a certain amount of dirt and discreetly observed: "There is no doubt that the dirt has been swallowed accidentally." The colonel cannot assume that a person would eat dirt without a motive. In the swamp, he found a deer stuck in the mud up to its knees, and his sense of logic, which is firm and acute, compelled him to enlighten us about the habits of this animal in a clear and rapid manner: "It is a marshy animal, because we found it stuck in the mud of the papyrus swamp." So that the deer that comes to drink in the afternoon and steps into the river, the deer that fords the small currents or swims across the biggest currents fleeing from its enemies, is a marshy animal, like the frog. In matters of Darwinian science the colonel is a portent of wisdom. While talking about his dogs, he incidentally says: "There is no doubt that the household dog descends [what prudence!] from at least a dozen different species of wild dogs, wolves, and jackals." In which case, it would no longer be necessary to launch a paternity investigation into this matter. Darwin required many years of experimentation and observation to reach this conclusion. Roosevelt, traversing the jungle on horseback and quickly observing the languid bodies of the tropical hunting dogs under the imperious sun, was surprised suddenly by this amazing discovery.

Colonel Roosevelt doesn't spend much time organizing his report of his observations. He jumps from the anteater to the ruminants, from the ruminants to the dog, and with a certain lack of tact, when he has finished describing the representatives of the canine species, he begins to describe Colonel Rondón, whom he then quickly disregards in order to talk about the deer again. It's taking the mania of zoological classification a little too far. Without a doubt, Colonel Rondón is two-handed, but his comrade has been able to place him in better company. The worst thing of all is that the description of Colonel Rondón is as depressing as that of the other zoological species. Roosevelt says: "Colonel Rondón is not only an official and a gentleman. He is a fine naturalist in the outdoors, a competent explorer experienced in the work, a man of science, a researcher, and a philosopher." Roosevelt could talk to Colonel Rondón about everything: never was there more consummate praise for an individual's knowledge, because the former president, as evident from the proceedings, especially likes to talk about what he doesn't know, and his *not-knowing* extends for a few millimeters. Among Colonel Rondón's distinctive characteristics, Roosevelt identifies the positivism of his philosophical criterion. It's as if to describe the girls of New Jersey he were to say that they have flat feet. All of Rondón's countrymen, or almost all of them, are positivists. With this indication we understand very little though.

Mr. Roosevelt immediately describes one of his banquets in the jungle. He ate jaguar, which is like saying he ate cat. It was one of the principal objectives of this journey initiated for the benefit of humanity, zoological science, and the barbers from the East End of London, who read the *Daily Telegraph* free of charge. This is how Roosevelt describes his first gluttonous experience in the presence of the cooked flesh of an incautious jaguar: "Its meat, incidentally, proved to be good to eat when we devoured it at dinner time; even though it hadn't been cooked enough nor prepared in an appropriate fashion. I wanted to taste it because the puma had looked like a good dish; I've always regretted that I didn't eat lion meat in Africa, which I'm sure must be excellent." And then he adds a line followed by an indifference that makes the readers' hair stand on its end: "The next day it was my son Kermit's turn." Doesn't the reader feel goose bumps? Read the *Daily Telegraph* from April 28, 1914, page 9.

The seriousness of the sentence coincides with the following opinion of Mr. Roosevelt, expressed later on: "In this particular vicinity the average jaguar almost doesn't disturb the livestock, if not because from time to time it eats one of its offspring." The eating of one's descendants is a very bearable nuisance for Colonel Roosevelt.

It's important to leave evidence of one of his methods of reasoning. Mr. Roosevelt, who probably visited the zoological gardens of his country and a few in Europe, deserved to be interested in what an armadillo is. Nevertheless, Mr. Roosevelt was greatly surprised to see an armadillo fleeing from man in a brisk run through the Amazonian jungle. And Colonel Roosevelt would say: "How is it possible that an animal with a shell like a turtle can run so fast?" In other words, this is the colonel's reasoning: the turtle has a shell; the turtle moves slowly; hence the shell and the slowness are inseparable qualities.

This reasoning shows us the degree of his intelligence. Being intelligent doesn't definitely mean anything other than being capable of separating the ideas that the infantile brain of an unintelligent man maintains united, among other reasons, because such appears to be the general trend of thinking and because language, created by infantile brains, was formed by arbitrary associations, sometimes monstrous. Separating ideas is, then, the sign of real intelligence. The work isn't simple: quite the opposite; it requires exceptional patience and insight. If all solid bodies were necessarily transparent and all transparent bodies were solid, humanity would not have been able, until centuries later, to separate the two concepts of solidity and transparency that language, naturally, had confused as being one word. Being capable of separating concepts of this kind implies, in psychology, an insight, a capacity to eliminate the useless detail, similar to the qualities displayed by the man who discovered argon in the air's atmosphere. Not everyone has them in the same degree as William Ramsay; but not to have them at all or use them in an adverse manner to associate the edentates with the chelonians and Colonel Rondón with the ruminants is an unmistakable sign of a lack of intelligence, which was what one wanted to demonstrate.

TRANSLATED BY HARRY MORALES

Euclides da Cunha

Brazil
(1866–1909)

----•◦•◦•----

Following the death of his mother when he was three, Euclides da Cunha was raised by his relatives until he was old enough to attend boarding school. A witness of both the abolition of slavery and the collapse of the Brazilian Empire in 1889, da Cunha lived in a turbulent age. Far from being isolated from all of this turmoil, he was an active participant in the movement to make his native country a republic. In 1888, as a student in the military school of Praia Vemelha, he led a political protest that led to his expulsion from the school and imprisonment in the Fortress of Santa Cruz. However, the young idealistic republican would eventually develop a broader view of Brazilian politics. This evolution led to his increased interest in the complexity of the War of Canudos and thus to the writing of *Os sertões* (1902), known in English as *Rebellion in the Backlands* in a 1944 translation by Samuel Putnam. This is da Cunha's most remarkable work, which Mario Vargas Llosa reworked in his ambitious novel *The War of the End of the World*. In this analysis of the War of Canudos, which he composed progressively while on assignment as a reporter for the daily *O Estado de São Paulo* from 1897 on, da Cunha, like Sarmiento in his *Facundo: Civilization and Barbarism*, combined the tenets of a sociopolitical treatise and the creative facility of an epic novel. Though da Cunha worked for the Brazilian government as a military engineer from 1892 to his death, he is better known for the aforementioned text, his posthumously published essays called *A margem da história* (1909), and articles collected in *Contrastes e confrontos* (1907). Da Cunha was inducted into the Brazilian Academy of Letters in 1903. He died in 1909, shot while trying to kill his wife's lover. "The Rubber Men" is a little-known, firsthand chronicle of Brazilian working men, written in 1904. It is part of da Cunha's book of assembled reportage, *Um paraíso perdido* (1976).

The Rubber Men

On this side of the right bank of the Ucayali River and the rolling terrain where the Javari, the Juruá, and the Purus Rivers have their source, a new society appeared about fifty years ago. It was formed in obscurity. Lost for a long time in the stifling jungle, it was only known to some few merchants in Pará, where from 1862 on, coming from those remote points, the dark gray slabs of another elastic gum in competition with rubber latex began to arrive for the demands of industry. It was gum rubber. And *caucheros*, rubber men, was the name given to these adventurers in the interior who were boldly vanquishing those unknown corners.

They came from the west, crossing the Andes and enduring every climate in the land, from the bleak Pacific shores to the icy high plains of the mountain range. Between them and their native soil were two walls twenty thousand feet high and a long trench gaping with chasms. Before them lay the Amazon lowlands, a stretch of thousands of miles to the northeast, that disappeared without a trace into the broad Atlantic, with no hint of a hill to delimit the immensity. Never had such an imposing stage been set for such tiny actors.

It was natural for the explorers to roam for long years, scattered, diminutive, invisible, feeling their way along in the perpetual twilight of those distant forests where, even more serious than the immense distances and wild underbrush, other difficulties hounded or perturbed their careful steps. In the region where the border between Brazil and Peru is still drawn in dotted lines, irradiating in four directions are the headwaters of the Purus and the Juruá, the northernmost tributaries of the Urubamba, and the last branches of the Madre-de-Dios. It is one of the least known regions of the Americas, not so much because of its exceptional physical features that were overcome by F. Castelnau in 1844 as because of the fearsome reputation of the tribes that inhabited it and who became, under the generic name of Chunches, the major fear of the bravest pioneers.

It won't be necessary to name them all. A person going up the Purus to the approaches of Cahoeira and contemplating from time to time the rare Pamarys is scarcely reminded that these were once masters of those floodplains, and on upstream from there the inoffensive Ipurinans, or starting at the Yaco the Tucurinas, who are now born old as the decrepitude of the race is reflected so much in their palsied makeup. He will have the greatest surprise as at the headwaters of the river he comes upon the singular forest dwellers who inhabit them. Of differing customs and origins, there they have been squeezed together in forced assembly: the docile Amauacas, who gather at the posts of the rubber gatherers; the indomitable Coronauas, lords of the headwaters of the Curanja; the copper-skinned Piros, with shining teeth dyed with dark *rena*, which, when they smile, gives their faces an indefinable trace of somber threat; the bearded Cashillos, close to extermination after two hundred years of inroads suffered by remnants of the missions on the Pachiteá; the Conibos with deformed skulls and breasts frightfully striped in red and blue; the Setebos, the Sipibos, and the Yurimauas; the corpulent Mashcos on the Mano, bringing to mind with their misshapen figures the giants of the fables of the early map-makers of the

Amazon region; and, above all, ahead of them in fame and valor, the warlike Campas of the Urubamba. . . .

The variety of tribes in such a limited area is responsible for the strange pressure that constrains them. Adjustment is perforce necessary. They are obviously in the last redoubts into which they have poured as the result of an age-old campaign that went from the apostolate of the Maynas to modern expeditions and whose culminating episodes have been lost to history. The narrator of these days is coming to the end of a drama, and he views it with surprise as its last act makes ready to close. Civilization, barbarously armed with ruthless rifles, has laid complete siege to the natives found there. Peruvians to the west and south, Brazilians in the whole northeastern sector, and in the southeast, cutting across the Madre-de-Dios River valley, Bolivians.

And the rubber gatherers appear as the leading jungle beaters of the sinister indoctrination with fire and steel that goes along in those remote backlands exterminating the most interesting of South American aborigines. This historic mission was visited upon them through the fragility of a tree. The rubber gatherer is by circumstance a nomad sworn to battle, to destruction, and to a wandering or tumultuous life because the *castilloa elastica* that furnished him with the rubber he covets does not allow like the Brazilian *heveas* for a stable exploitation through the periodical renewal of the vital juice extracted from it. It is exceptionally sensitive. As soon as it is cut it dies or is debilitated for a long time, useless. So the extractor cuts it down completely in order to take full advantage. He saws it up, foot by foot, from the roots to the last twigs of the crown, and with it open on the ground, from shallow rectangular cavities along the felled trunk, at the end of a week he takes out the valuable slabs, while the remains that adhere to the bark, to the edges of the cuts, or scattered at random on the ground are gathered up to make the *sernambi*, of inferior quality.

The process, as can be seen, is rudimentary and rapid. The most flourishing rubber grove is exhausted in a short time, and since the *castilloas* are not distributed regularly through the forest but scattered in clumps that are often quite far apart, the exploiters move on to other places, repeating almost without variation all the actions in that random life of tree hunters. In that way nomadism takes over. For them it is an absolutely necessary condition for success. They plunge boldly into the wilderness, isolate themselves in successive sites, and never retrace the paths taken. Condemned to the unknown, they become accustomed to trackless and completely new locales. They reach them, abandon them, continue on their way, and do not settle down in locations conquered with great difficulty.

Having come upon a stretch where rubber trees are discovered, on the edge of a clearing they erect the first *tambo*, or shed, of rasp palm, and plunge into their most active task. Their main tools for work are a Winchester carbine—the short rifle purposely designed for encounters in the underbrush, the sharp machete that untangles vines for them, and the pocket compass that shows them the way through that maze of openings. They take them and set out in a cautious inspection of the area. They go in search of savages whom they must fight and exterminate or enslave, so that in the same operation they will get complete security in the new working site and hands to do the work.

Very few are the times that they venture out on this obligatory and bold preliminary: half a dozen men scattering and plunging into the thickets. And there they go, investigating and sounding out every pocket, inspecting inch by inch every suspicious corner, making mental notes in an exhaustive topographical survey, memorizing a great variety of landmarks. At the same time with their eyes and ears alert to the most fleeting aspects and the vaguest sounds in the murmuring air of the forest, they go along on the qui vive with the prudence and wiles required in that fearsome Sevillian duel with the wilderness.

Some do not come back. Others return unharmed to their camp after a useless search. One of them, however, at the end of a fatiguing search, catches sight in the distance, half indistinct through the foliage, of the first huts of savages. He has trouble repressing a shout and returning immediately to tell his comrades of his find. He sharpens his extraordinary astuteness. He hugs the ground and, crawling, sniffing out danger, he gets as close as he can to the unaware enemy. There is really a moving touch of heroism in this action. The man, lost in that absolute solitude, goes looking for the barbarian, accompanied only by the eighteen rounds in his loaded rifle.

It's a long, tortuous, and slow crawl in which he takes advantage of all natural features, hiding behind tree trunks or making an opening through large roots, slipping noiselessly over the piles of rotting branches, or sneaking in among the joined stems of the broad-leafed heliconias for cover until, at the end of a silent and anxious incursion, he's able to observe and listen from close by, almost on the rim of the clearing, to the unskilled enemy, unaware of the sinister civilized man who is spying on them and counting them and observing their ways and evaluating their defenses— and then he returns from his minute examination, bringing to his waiting comrades all the necessary information for the "conquest."

Conquest is the favorite term used as a kind of atavistic reminder of the ancient marauding teams of Pizarro's expeditionaries. But they won't bring it off with weapons before they exhaust the effects of a rudimentary diplomacy of the gifts most hungered after by the savages. I once heard one of them explain the process as follows: "You bring them to the *tambo* by means of gifts: clothing, rifles, machetes, etc., and without making them work. You let them go back to their village and tell their comrades how they've been treated by the rubber men, who didn't make them work but only asked them to do a little of their own free will in order to pay for what they were given. . . ."

These peaceful means usually do not work, however. The general rule is a pitiless hunt with bullets. It's the heroic side of the enterprise: an insignificantly small group going on the hunt after a multitude. There's no need to go into detail with episodes. They follow an invariable tactic: maximum speed in shooting and maximum boldness. These are sure guarantees of victory. The number of small battles fought in those backlands is incalculable. In them small well-armed groups take over whole tribes, sacrificed all at once by their crude weapons and by the fearlessness with which they charge the running fire of the carbines.

Let us cite a single example. When Carlos Fitz-Carral arrived at the headwaters of the Madre-de-Dios in 1892, coming from the Ucayali along the channel opened in the isthmus that bears his name, he tried to find the best way to win over the indomitable Mashcos who ruled there. He brought along from the Piros, whom he had conquered, an intelligent and loyal interpreter. He succeeded without any difficulties in seeing and talking to the *curaca*, or chief, of the savages. The parley was swift and quite curious.

The famous explorer, after introducing the "infidel" to the equipment he had brought and his small army, in which the disparate faces of the tribes he had subjugated were mingled, attempted to demonstrate to him the advantages of the alliance he was offering him as against the inconveniences of a disastrous battle. As his sole reply the Mashco asked him about the arrows he was carrying. And Fitz-Carral, smiling, handed him a Winchester cartridge. The savage examined it at length, taken with the small size of the projectile. He tried, in vain, to wound himself, pushing the bullet hard against his chest. Unable to do so, he took out one of his arrows, plunged it into his other arm, penetrating it. He smiled then, indifferent to the pain, and he watched proudly as his own blood spurted out . . . , and without saying a word he turned his back on the startled explorer and returned to his village with an illusion of superiority, which would shortly be completely undone. A half hour later, in fact, nearly a hundred Mashcos, including the recalcitrant and ingenuous chief, lay riddled with bullets on the riverbank whose name, Playamashcos, even today is a reminder of that bloody episode. . . .

That's how the wild region is being tamed. With the surrounding area scouted out, the natives within a radius of a few leagues dead or enslaved, the rubber seekers work feverishly with frantic haste. In a few months other *tambos* have sprung up alongside the original one. The solitary hut has been transformed into a large shed or a noisy pier, and sometimes the living quarters grow into settlements, like Cocama and Curanja on the bank of the Purus, suddenly gleaming in the wilderness with the mirage of a progress that rises up, develops, and comes to an end within the space of ten years. The rubber men settle there until the last rubber tree has fallen. They arrive, destroy, and leave. Generally they ask nothing of the land except some small plantings of cassava and bananas, cared for by the domesticated Indians. The only regular agriculture, on a very small scale, that can be seen along the Upper Purus beyond the last shacks of our rubber prospectors is the cotton of the settled Campas, who even here reveal their native independence: picking, carding, spinning, weaving, and dyeing the *cushmas* they wear, which reach from their shoulders to their feet with the design of long, crude togas. So, among the civilized strangers who arrive there suddenly, wounding and killing men and trees, settling only for the time needed for both to be extinguished, then continuing on to other parts where they repeat the same damage, passing through like a devastating wave and leaving savagery that is even more savage—those singular barbarians display the only peaceful aspect of the cultures. The contrast is striking. Going from the Campa settlement of Tingoleales to the Peruvian site of Shamboyaco near the mouth of the Manuel Urbano River, the traveler isn't passing, as he might believe at first, from the most primitive to the most elevated stages of human evolution. He has a great surprise. He goes from frank barbarism to a kind of crippled civilization in which all the stigmas of the former stand out more incisively in the midst of the very conquests of progress.

He approaches a Peruvian settlement, and for the first few hours he is enchanted by the picture of bustling and noisy existence. The main residence and those around it, arranged along streets as in a small town, are always built on well-chosen spots overlooking the river. And even though they are built exclusively with the leaves and stalks of the rasp palm—which is the providential palm tree of the Amazon region—they generally have two stories and, in the elegance of their lines and in the open verandas that encircle them, have an appearance that is completely the opposite of the sad look of the low huts of our rubber gatherers.

On the broad terrace ending on the crest of the ravine, falling in a living avalanche down to the river with an animated and rapid movement, powerful stevedores pass in long successive files, bending under the slabs of rubber. Active administrators burst out of the doors on the ground floor and run all about to the warehouse filled with supplies or to the blazing tents where hammers and anvils clang in the repair of axes and machetes.

Below on the dock crammed with swift dugouts, where loincloths are waving in the breeze, the gabble of pilots and oarsmen can be heard; spreading out on the water are rafts made exclusively of rubber, forming the "moving road" of the "merchandise that leads the leaders." And in all of that movement winding from there up to the top of the embankment, the red skirts and white blouses of the graceful half-breed women from Iquitios pass and mingle like festive bunting. . . .

The traveler passes through these active groups and the surprises never cease. He mounts the steps that take him to the front veranda, onto which the main divisions of the house open. At the top, the rubber baron—a jovial and robust man, triumphant on the stout heels of his jungle boots—greets him noisily, opening the doors wide for him in spectacular and frank hospitality. And the enchantment is complete. Having lost the notion of time or the long distance of the thousands of miles spent going along solitary rivers to reach that distant plantation, the outsider unconsciously imagines that he is in some commercial establishment in some city on the coast. There's nothing to hinder the deception: on the long pine counter bordering the main room and closing off the area stand shelves loaded with merchandise; solicitous servants obey the orders of a most proper book-keeper, who greeted him as he entered and immediately returned to his writing, curved over a slanting desk. The glass of beer they give him instead of the traditional *chicha*, the artistic calendar on the side wall marking the proper day of the year, the newspapers from Manaus and Lima, and even— which is unusual—the elegant and cultured torture of a phonograph that insistently stutters in the depths of that wilderness a favorite aria of a famous tenor. . . .

But all that surprising exterior disappears before an observation that permits the visitor to see what his distinguished host doesn't show him. Disillusionment then strikes him quickly, and impressively. That reflection of a finer life doesn't extend beyond the small strip of land covering less than a few acres and restricted between the close-by and threatening forest to the rear and the steep ravine down to the river. Outside that false setting the real drama that takes place is almost inconceivable for our time.

Beneath the wealthy rubber dealer in a deplorable scale from the half-breed from Loreto who goes there in search of a fortune to the dispirited Quechua brought from the Andes, there is an undefined series of the ex-ploited. In order to see them one must get through the dark recesses of the pathless forest and look for them in the solitary campsites where they work completely alone, accompanied only by their inseparable rifles, which guarantee their existence with the fortuitous product of the hunt. There they slave unprofitably for long years, fall ill, devoured by vermin, and fade away in absolute abandonment. Four hundred men, whom sometimes no-body sees, are scattered through those gullies and appear only from time to time at the straw castle of the hardened baron who enslaves them. The "conqueror" doesn't keep watch over them. He knows they won't run away. All around in a radius of six leagues, which is his whole domain, the region swarming with other infidels is impassable. The wilderness is a perpetually watchful overseer. It keeps them in slavery for him. Even the arrogant Campas that he captured, manipulating masterful perfidy against the ingenuous wildness of the barbarians, do not leave him anymore, afraid of their own wild brothers, who have never forgiven them their temporary submission.

In this way the happy adventurer, who ten years before in Lima or Arequipa was most genteel in his dealings with people, feels himself entirely free of the pressure of the infinite correctives of social life and, acquiring the feeling of unlimited command at the same time as he is taken by a feeling of impunity for all whims and crimes, falls all at once into the most primitive savagery, which he enters without having had time to lose the superior attributes of the milieu into which he was born.

In reality, the rubber baron is a type previously unknown to history. He is above all antinomian and paradoxical. There is no place for him in the most detailed ethnographic chart. At first he looks like an ordinary case of a civilized man who has become barbarized in a fearsome retreat where his superior characteristics are transformed into primitive forms of activity. That is an illusion. He doesn't combine those opposite stages, creating a hybrid activity that is defined and stable. He only joins them together without blending them. It is a case of psychic mimicry in a man who pretends to be a barbarian in order to defeat the barbarian. He is a gentleman and a savage, depending upon the circumstances. The curious dualism of a person trying to maintain intact the best moral upbringing alongside a morality established especially for the wilderness reappears in every act of his mingled existence. The same man who with enviable rectitude makes an effort to pay his debts, which are sometimes more than a thousand *contos* to exporters in Iquitos or Manaus, does not hesitate to cheat the miserable peon who works for him out of a few pounds of common *sernambi*. Cases of this nature are common, as told by Peruvians themselves. A canoe leaves Iquitos loaded with merchandise of the kind most sought after by inhabitants along the river bank. It comes to a *tambo* of infidels or half-breeds on the Ucayali. The dealer leaps ashore and immediately starts this invariable dialogue with the owner of the place:

"Have you got any rubber?"

"Yes, I have, but it belongs to merchant F——. I owe him for the supplies he sent me four months ago. From what I know his launch is coming to pick it up in a few days. . . ."

"Don't be a fool, man!" the rubber dealer answers and adds, lying imperturbably, "F—— can't send for the rubber because his launch has broken down. . . ."

"It doesn't matter," the savage replies. "I'll keep my word and wait for the orders he sends."

And the civilized man, insistent:

"So in the meantime you'll be hurting yourself, because F—— will never pay you more than 12 *soles* an *arroba* and I'll give you 16 *soles* right now. . . ."

The peon, avid for unexpected profit, gives in. The rubber dealer skillfully takes advantage of his hesitation.

"Let's go to my launch. I invite you to a good drink. . . ."

There they go. In a short time the drunken peon will turn over to the rubber dealer the best part of his holding at the lowest price.

Sometimes the dealer moves from the most refined gentility to the greatest brutality, stopping in the midst of a captivating smile and implacable calm to leap with a roar, knife flashing in his fist, onto the disobedient half-breed who has challenged him. Savagery is a mask that he puts on and takes off at will.

He cannot be compared to the incomparable mold of our *bandeirante* pioneers. Antônio Raposo, for example, stands out admirably among all South American conquerors. His heroism is brutal, sturdy, without cracks, without folds, without disguises. He advances unintelligently, mechanically, inflexibly, with a natural unleashed force. The diagonal line of fifteen hundred leagues that he drew from São Paulo to the Pacific, cutting across South America, over rivers, clearings, swamps, stagnant marshes, deserts, mountains, snow-covered uplands, and harsh shores, along with the fright and the ruin of a hundred supplanted tribes, is a fearsome deed worthy of an epic. But well-contained in that individual act of daring is the marvelous concentration of all acts of an epoch. The *bandeirante* was brutal and inexorable but logical. He was the superman of the wilderness.

The rubber baron is irritatingly absurd in his elegant brutality, in his bloody gallantry, and in his ragged heroism. He is the homunculus of civilization. But this antilogy is understandable. The adventurer goes there with the single preoccupation of getting rich and returning, returning as soon as possible, fleeing that melancholy and swampy land that doesn't seem solid enough to bear even the material weight of a society. Accompanying him at all points in his nervous and hasty activity is the spectacle of vast cities where he will shine one day, transforming the black gold of rubber into sterling. Dominated completely by an incurable nostalgia for the native parts he left precisely to see once again in possession of resources that will provide him with greater levels of happiness, he plunges into the forests, eliminates and subjugates the savages, resists malaria and fatigue, is madly active for four, five, six years, accumulates a few hundred *soles*, and suddenly disappears. . . .

He turns up in Paris. He experiences the noisy splendor of theaters and salons, six months of a delirious life without a single sign showing through the impeccable correctness of his clothes and manners or the slightest hint of his professional nomadism. He goes into ruin elegantly and he returns. . . . He picks up his former task again: another four or six years of hard work, a new fortune quickly acquired, a new leap across the ocean, and, almost always, a new and anxious return in search of an easily lost fortune in a stupendous oscillation between the gleaming avenues and the solitary forests. The most curious versions in this regard can be heard in which famous rubber barons of Manaus stand out.

In this oscillating life everything he does to the land that he devastates and hates gives it a provisional character—from the house he builds in ten days to last five years to the most intimate relationships that sometimes go on for years and which he destroys in a day. In this point especially his unrivaled inconstancy stands out. One of them, when we asked him in Curunja where he had married the most charming Amahuaca woman who attended him for ten years with the care of a model wife, retorted a bit sarcastically: "She was given to me as a gift in Pachitea." A gift, a present, a rag he would abandon at the first eventuality without caring.

An established dealer in that rundown village, who would have been a fine model of a peaceful and abstemious bourgeois in Lima or Iquitos, there, hungry for women, introduces his friends and the casual stranger to his scandalous harem that includes Mercedes of the doe eyes who cost him a battle with the Coronauas and the enchanting Facunda with her great savage and pensive eyes who cost him a hundred *soles*. And he talks about that criminal traffic with laughter, in absolute impunity, without fear.

There are no laws. Each one carries his penal code in the rifle under his arm, administers justice as he sees fit without anyone's calling him to account. One day in July 1905, when it reached the last rubber outpost on the Purus, a mixed investigation commission made up of Brazilians and Peruvians saw a naked and horribly mutilated body that had been thrown onto the left bank of the river by a clearing. It was the corpse of an Amahuaca. He had been killed out of revenge, it was vaguely explained later. And nothing more was done about the incident—a trifling and trivial thing in that region which had been turned upside down by people who pass through, do not settle, and leave it sadder still with the ruins of abandoned ranch houses. . . .

Such things are found at every bend along the Upper Purus in a sad display of different types, from the humble huts of the peons to the once lordly quarters of the rubber men. A short way up the Shamboyaco there was one that especially impressed us as we were coming down. It had been a first-class post. We leaped out to examine it and, climbing the almost stepless embankment with difficulty, we discovered at the top the old pathway invaded by wild sorrel. We reached the terrace where the inextricable underbrush was penetrating and covering piles of old jars, a repugnant mélange, the remains of tools and rubbish left in piles by the inhabitants who had gone away. The main house, with the front half fallen in, roofs collapsed, walls crumbling, breaking away from the perpendicular stakes as they fell, seemed to be held up only by the vines that penetrated it at all points, piercing the cover, wrapping around the shaky beams, tying them and stretching out like cables to the nearest trees where they twined about and prevented a complete collapse. The lesser buildings alongside were covered with climbers that were exuberant in their smiling flowers, disappearing little by little into the irresistible constriction of the forest that was reconquering its original terrain.

We did not have much time, however, for the magnificent regenerative work of the plants as they covered those deplorable ruins with crowns and festive wreaths. The abandoned seat wasn't entirely uninhabited. In one of the better-preserved shacks the last inhabitant was awaiting us. Piro, Amahuaca, or Campa, his origins were impossible to distinguish. The very traces of the human species were transformed by his repulsive appearance: his misshapen trunk, inflated by the effects of malaria, made his whole figure a complete contrast to his thin arms and lean and crippled legs that looked like those of a monstrous fetus. Squatting in a corner, he was watching us impassively. He had the sum of his possessions on one side: a bunch of green bananas. That indefinable thing, which by cruel analogy suggested by the circumstances looked to us less like a man than a ball of rubber tossed there at random, forgotten by the tappers, answered our questions in an almost inaudible yawp and in a completely incomprehensible language. Finally, with great effort, he raised an arm, stretched it out slowly to the front, as if pointing at something he'd followed for a long way beyond all those forests and rivers, and he babbled, letting his arm drop heavily, as if he'd lifted a great weight:

"Friends."

We understood: friends, comrades, partners in those busy harvest days who'd left for other parts out there, abandoning him to absolute solitude. Of the Spanish words he'd learned, that was the only one he had left, and the poor wretch, by murmuring it with a touching gesture of longing, was cursing, without knowing it—with ever so bitter irony—the lawless adventurers who at that time were continuing on with their devastating chores, opening with bullets from their carbines and blows from their machetes new paths for their twisting itineraries and revealing other unknown places, where they would leave, as they had left there, in the collapse of the buildings or in the lamentable figure of the sacrificed native, the only fruits of their tumultuous struggles as builders of ruins.

TRANSLATED BY GREGORY RABASSA

José Enrique Rodó

Uruguay
(1871–1917)

———◆•❉•◆———

Uruguay's José Enrique Rodó is most renowned for his booklong essay *Ariel* (1900), a work that added critical depth to Latin America's Modernismo and gave rise to the term *arielismo*, the equivalent of spiritualism. He uses the famous characters of Caliban and Ariel, from Shakespeare's *The Tempest*, to personify a forking road to the future: Caliban represents the United States, a country he admires but feels is too materialistic, too utilitarian, and Ariel represents Latin America. The book has been reprinted hundreds of times and has inspired scores of intellectuals and diplomats. Its charm lies in Rodó's approach: He shapes it as a letter to young Latin Americans coming to terms with their continental identity. After the Spanish-American War, Rodó perceived the United States as Spain's imperialist successor and as a dangerous materialist influence on Latin America. Born in Montevideo, Rodó was the seventh and youngest child of a wealthy Uruguayan family. However, the family's financial troubles later forced Rodó to work as a clerk at the age of fourteen. His performance in school was unremarkable in every subject with the exception of history and literature. He founded the important *Revista Nacional de Literatura y Ciencias Sociales*, taught literature at the University of Montevideo, and later contributed to Uruguayan politics by serving in the House of Representatives. He was the first to write a serious critical study of Rubén Darío. His other important literary achievements include *The Motives of Proteus* (1909), translated into English by Angel Flores, and a collection of his pieces from *La Nación*, called *El mirador de Próspero* (1913). While on tour in Europe, Rodó died nearly penniless in Sicily. Published in the newspaper *El Telégrafo* on 24 September 1914, the following account is an extraordinary testimonial to the importance of the press in Latin America. Rodó establishes a series of principles to guide the function of the press and portrays it as the most important instrument to achieve democracy in society. As such, it is an anthem to freedom of speech, which, in a land of revolutions, counterrevolutions, and tyranny, is not an ever-present factor in daily life.

How a Newspaper Should Be

R ather than as an isolated activity within the range of social activities, the function of journalism should be conceived as a collection of all functions that, materially or morally, interest the social organism. Nobody can forgo this complement without forfeiting his strength and productivity. There has never been an institution in the world so entirely identified with society's complex development as, in our era, the institution of the journalistic Press.

One does not work, nor fight, nor study, nor spend life in leisure and relaxation, without having some critical point of contact with the Press. This universality of relations, of course, produces an infinite complexity of character and structure in the modern newspaper. But were we to attempt a classification of the journalist's proper role, we could begin with two fundamental orders: information and commentary.

Of these two applications, only the first is truly essential to and inseparable from the modern newspaper's nature. Commentary is, without a doubt, something higher and of a superior hierarchical dignity than the news, but in no way does it represent a more positive or important social interest than the former. For as much as we overcome the concept of utility, reality will always remain that the daily Press's superior utility is based on being a medium of information, because it is thus that the newspaper performs a role in communication and social sympathy for those with no possible equivalent. The book, the pamphlet, the tribune can also deliver, with comparable opportunity and effectiveness, the Press's commentary and propaganda. But no other form of publicity can deliver the rapid and extensive diffusion of facts that may attract a large or small portion of general interest.

The Press's importance, then, is not reduced, nor is there a propensity to adapt it to a bastardized utilitarianism, when its informative function is indicated as its principal character. As the social medium that fosters its development grows in magnitude and diversity, the interest in that function grows, because there are more types of events with repercussions on collective and individual life, and it is easier to spread them through the Press's written transmission than by other means. It goes without saying, on the other hand, that within the limits of journalistic information fit all the forms of exposition that, based on the naked reference of fact, give the chronicle its amenity and interest and earn the relative value of art that fits in this small, daily history stamped upon the pages of the newspaper.

• • •

But if information must necessarily be more alluring and complex every day, it seems equally certain that we should exclude or limit some of the manifestations that predominate in the actual uses of the Press. There does exist, of course, an informative complacency that I do not hesitate to label as pernicious and brutal, which correspondingly satisfies the lowly preferences of popular taste. I refer to the "delinquent delight" with which nearly all of our era's journalism quests for details, photographic exactitude, the realistic minutiae in the description of scenes of ferocious criminality; of the events where the human beast appears in all its repugnant nakedness. Here the utility of protracted detail is null, and instead the vulgar reader, whose propensity for ignorance praises itself, welcomes the suggestion of cruelty and stupidity. It has been a long time, even in the genre of literary fiction—where art enters as a purifying element—since the morbid predisposition toward the false realism of the repulsive and hateful aspects of our nature has fallen into disfavor. Crime, vice, degeneration should only interest as far as they can be motivation to teach, by negative example: never as incentives for unhealthy curiosity.

There is one exceptional moral aberration, an object of psychic contagion, which by virtue of its existence has prompted a unanimous response in the human interest of eliminating it from Press reports. I am referring to suicide. There is generally support for a legal sanction mandating such silence. In my opinion I would prefer an unstated journalistic convention pointing to the same ends, which would perhaps better ensure this outcome, if one considers that anything forced and imposed seems to inherently invite furtive contravention in the form of allusion and reticence, which are beyond the law's reach.

Another aspect of publication that merits certain restriction, if not absolute elimination, is that of personal attacks, realized or avoided. Such tactics of personal retribution will probably subsist in society until we reach a social conscience that is more just and effective in its moral sanctions, so that it is free from the need for reparation.

The only thing worthy of exploration at this time is to limit such duels to cases of true seriousness, unresolvable through any other means. And in the meantime, although the law should lift or modify the penal code for a crime that is no longer considered one by today's prevalent customs and feelings, the Press should, in turn, abstain from helping to foment it and encouraging its diffusion by setting an example or stimulating vanity.

• • •

But although the newspaper is, above all, an organ of information, it is also a commentator, a censor, a propagandist. As those two characters are not mutually exclusive, but complementary and somewhat dependent upon each other, it is difficult to exclusively limit information without producing an incomplete and ineffective sort of newspaper in which the public draws conclusions by sensing the absence of a yearning, needing force. I am a supporter, then, of the newspaper that states its opinion on every important issue of human, national, or professional interest, or anything within the collective scope over which current events may spark debate. I understand the "impartiality" of the Press as its tribute, based on respect and culture, to all sincere opinions and to all legitimate interests; but I do not admit that such a condition will inhibit the frank and definite personality of the newspaper in the slightest. I still recognize that, by dealing with a militant concept through politics—not as a movement of ideas developed around the administrative and legislative life of the country, but as a struggle of permanent or accidental passions and associations—there may exist newspapers that, by their trade-specificity and their own tradition, disregard politics strictly speaking, or reserve themselves only for intervention based on the notion of an exception that can be justified by the solemnity of the proceedings and by the authority inherent to their own impartiality.

Given that the newspaper, in general, should opine, should aspire to be a force in public debate, how shall it interpret that participation incumbent upon it? Should it be a guide? Should it be a reflection? Should it rise above popular currents like a beacon dominating them, or will it be content as a register for one who comes to know a trend of collective feeling? There cannot be different answers to this question, if one considers it from the perspective of the Press's social responsibility and dignity. The newspaper ought to strive to direct and not be directed, to be a mentor and not a spokesman; and even when its opinion is fundamentally identified with that of a popular collective, it should always try to be, in relation to the group's feelings, like the filter that removes the dregs of error, passion, and injustice.

It would be a mistake to deduce an absolute consensus of what the majority thinks and feels at a given instance. Not only is the majority's impression of an event always interesting, but it is also impossible to deny it its just worth, based sometimes upon intuitions and guesses that may be superior to even the most authorized reports within one's personal criteria. Therefore, without infringing on its independence or its personal and definite thought, the newspaper should foster an ample spirit of hospitality and embrace all the opinions it promotes by virtue of their presentation, if not the authors behind them, even when such opinions dissent from those the newspaper states as its own.

A moment ago I was discussing newspapers whose character stems from serving as organs of certain trades; for example: commerce, or rural industries. There is nothing more justifiable than this fundamental and preferential dedication to a specific category of social interests; but on the condition that, despite their specialization, they maintain the complexity of content and interest that satisfies the harmonic and upright notion of how a "newspaper" should be. I feel relatively the same about this as I do about educational specialization. I was never partial to the mutilations of secondary teaching, which tend to keep the preparatory studies of the lawyer, the engineer, or the doctor separate from the materials that have no direct relationship with the studies they should emphasize in their professional consecration. Since the lawyer will have scarce opportunity to return to an interest in natural sciences, or the doctor to literary studies, it is important that his preparatory teaching communicate the general initiation necessary for all men of higher culture to maintain the solidarity between his spirit and the other directing elements of society. The trade newspaper should conform to similar criteria. It should emphasize ideas, feelings, and interests that are not immediately connected to the style of life and work that a particular species of reader has as a profession. Together with the sections that contain specialized information and commentary relative to professional interests, newspapers should include items that transmit a general notion of activities and concerns from other spheres of society, from which nobody could remain absolutely isolated without the deterioration of his culture and professional effectuality.

On the other hand, a newspaper should not consider its jurisdiction limited to themes of strict reality or utilitarian interest. These are, without a doubt, the principal objectives by the nature of the daily Press; but the portion containing selfless material, in which concessions are made to letters, science, art, popular interest, or instruction, represents an extremely precious element in modern newspapers, because it contributes to an end, which is also their own, by "democratizing culture," delivering reflections where books rarely penetrate, and attracting attention toward questions of purely spiritual interest in such a continuous and insinuating way that they would otherwise be stuck in the library or the cathedral, were it not for that vehicle allowing them to resonate in open air, along with the various echoes of everyday movement.

•   •   •

"The evil that plagues the Argentine Republic is that of extension," Sarmiento said in his admirable introduction to *Facundo*.

The evil that plagues modern journalism is that of extension.

The material produced by the development of the great urban centers, increasingly active and complex; international communication, more intimate and assiduous every day, plus the consequent growth of interest in news from around the world; the progressive demands of the reading public, as the average level of culture rises and the majority's intellectual needs increase; everything seems to conspire to indefinitely expand the newspapers' extension and capacity.

But as this material development has already become excessive and the growing impositions from which it stems are impossible to avoid, the formula for the future of journalistic evolution can be no other than "concentration": to maintain the substance of facts and commentary, with superior density, eliminating everything protracted, vain, superfluous. That Spencerian theory of style that we learned in school reduces the secret of good literary form to the economy of attention, is totally ineffective and false when it tries to penetrate the character of true artistic expression, but it does well to define the ideal of journalism's peculiar form, where the economy of attention and time is a direction naturally imposed by a style of reading done among the urgencies of everyday work and with clear awareness of the ephemeral condition of what is being read.

Increasingly identified with the complex life of a society, but in a necessarily shallow and malleable form, the daily Press should be the shadow of the social body: true and faithful like the shadow, and like the shadow ethereal and fleeting.

TRANSLATED BY JESSE H. LYTLE

Fernando Ortiz

Cuba
(1881–1969)

————◆◆◆◆●————

Renowned for his multifaceted work on Afro-Cuban culture, Fernando Ortiz was called "Our Third Discoverer" in his native Cuba. Elected as a representative to the House of Representatives for the Liberal Party in 1917, he was forced to flee his homeland in 1930 because of his opposition to the Cuban dictator Gerardo Machado. Ortiz directed the *Revista Bimestre Cubana*, which he used as a catalyst and forum for Cuban national studies, and later founded the International Institute of Afro-American Studies in Mexico. His published work spans the history, linguistics, sociology, archaeology, and arts of Afro-Cuban culture. His magnum opus is *Contrapunteo cubano del tabaco y el azúcar* (1940), translated into English as *Cuban Counterpoint: Tobacco and Sugar* by Harriet de Onís in 1947. Ortiz, whose house was the setting of many late-night discussions, was both a mentor and inspiration for several generations of Cuban artists and intellectuals. Integrating positivist elements with his profound interest in history, biography, archaeology, lexicology, and music, he delivered a multifaceted reading of Cuban culture. His oeuvre includes titles such as *La rebelión de los afro-cubanos* (1910), *Un catauro de cubanismos* (1923), *Las cuatro culturas indias de Cuba* (1943), *El engaño de las razas* (1945), and *La africanía de la música folklórica de Cuba* (1950). The following segment of *Cuban Counterpoint* is a showcase of Ortiz's talents as a hypnotic essayist. It illustrates the dichotomies of the Caribbean self: darkness and whiteness, bitterness and sweetness. In essence, Ortiz's thesis is that the Cuban character is a result of the ongoing tension between these sides.

Tobacco and Sugar

Tobacco is born, sugar is made. Tobacco is born pure, is processed pure and smoked pure. To secure saccharose, which is pure sugar, a long series of complicated physiochemical operations are required merely to eliminate impurities—bagasse, scum, sediment, and obstacles in the way of crystallization.

Tobacco is dark, ranging from black to mulatto; sugar is light, ranging from mulatto to white. Tobacco does not change its color; it is born dark and dies the color of its race. Sugar changes its coloring; it is born brown

70

and whitens itself, at first it is a syrupy mulatto and in this state pleases the common taste; then it is bleached and refined until it can pass for white, travel all over the world, reach all mouths, and bring a better price, climbing to the top of the social ladder.

"In the same box there are no two cigars alike; each one has a different taste," is a phrase frequent among discerning smokers, whereas all refined sugar tastes the same.

Sugar has no odor; the merit of tobacco lies in its smell and it offers a gamut of perfumes, from the exquisite aroma of the pure Havana cigar, which is intoxicating to the smell, to the reeking stogies of European manufacture, which prove to what levels human taste can sink.

One might even say that tobacco affords satisfaction to the touch and the sight. What smoker has not passed his hand caressingly over the rich *brevas* or *regalías* of a freshly opened box of Havanas? Do not cigar and cigarette act as a catharsis for nervous tension to the smoker who handles them and holds them delicately between lips and fingers? And what about chewing tobacco or snuff? Do they not titillate their users' tactile sense? And, for the sight, is not a cigar in the hands of a youth a symbol, a foretaste of manhood? And is not tobacco at times a mark of class in the ostentation of brand and shape? At times nothing less than a *corona corona*, a crowned crown. Poets who have been smokers have sung of the rapt ecstasy that comes over them as they follow with eyes and imagination the bluish smoke rising upward, as though from the ashes of the cigar, dying in the fire like a victim of the Inquisition, its spirit, purified and free, were ascending to heaven, leaving in the air hieroglyphic signs like ineffable promises of redemption.

Whereas sugar appeals to only one of the senses, that of taste, tobacco appeals not only to the palate, but to the smell, touch, and sight. Except for hearing, there is not one of the five senses that tobacco does not stimulate and please.

Sugar is assimilated in its entirety; much of tobacco is lost in smoke. Sugar goes gluttonously down the gullet into the intestines, where it is converted into muscle-strengthening vigor. Tobacco, like the rascal it is, goes from the mouth up the turnings and twistings of the cranium, following the trail of thought. *Ex fumo dare lucem.* Not for nothing was tobacco condemned as a snare of the devil, sinful and dangerous.

Tobacco is unnecessary for man and sugar is a requisite of his organism. And yet this superfluous tobacco gives rise to a vice that becomes a torment if it is denied; it is far easier to become resigned to doing without the necessary sugar.

Tobacco contains a poison: nicotine; sugar affords nourishment: carbohydrates. Tobacco poisons, sugar nourishes. Nicotine stimulates the mind, giving it diabolical inspiration; the excess of glucose in the blood benumbs the brain and even causes stupidity. For this reason alone tobacco would be of the liberal reform group and sugar of the reactionary conservatives; fittingly enough, a century ago in England the Whigs were regarded as little less than devils and the Tories as little less than fools.

Tobacco is a medicinal plant; it was so considered by both Indians and Europeans. Tobacco is a narcotic, an emetic, and an antiparasitic. Its active ingredient, nicotine, is used as an antitetanic, in cases of paralysis of the bladder, and as an insecticide. In olden times it was used for the most farfetched cures; according to Father Cobo, "to cure innumerable ailments, in green or dried leaf form, in powder, in smoke, in infusion, and in other ways." Cuban folklore has preserved some of these practices in home remedies. Snuff was used as a dentifrice. At the beginning of the nineteenth century a very bitter-tasting variety, known as Peñalvar, was manufactured in Havana and exported to England for this purpose; it contained a mixture of powdered tobacco and a kind of red clay. Tobacco has always been highly prized for its sedative qualities, and was regarded as a medicine for the spirit. For this reason, if long ago the savages censed their idols in caves with tobacco to placate their fury with adulation, today one burns the incense of tobacco in the hollows of one's own skull to calm one's worries and breathe new life into one's illusions.

Sugar, too, has its medicinal side and is even a basic element of our physiological make-up, producing psychological disturbances by its deficiency as by its excess. For this reason, and because of their scarcity, sugar and tobacco were sold centuries ago at the apothecary's shop. But in spite of their old association on the druggist's shelves, tobacco and sugar have always been far removed. In the opinion of moralists tobacco was vicious in origin, and was abominated by them and condemned by kings as much as it was exalted by the doctors.

Tobacco is, beyond doubt, malignant; it belongs to that dangerous and widespread family of the Solanaceæ. In the old European world the Solanaceæ were known to inspire terror, torment, visions, and delirium. Mandragora produced madness and dreams and acted as an aphrodisiac. Atropa gave its name to one of the Fates. Belladonna gave the sinful blackness of hell to the pupils of beautiful women's eyes. Henbane was the narcotic poison of classic literature. The various daturas were the source of alkaloids that the Indians of Asia as well as those of America employed in their rites, spells, and crimes. In our New World this family of cursed plants was regenerated. Even though the Datura, of which the lowly Jimson weed is a species, still works its diabolical will here, inspiring the mystic frenzy of Aztecs, Quechuas, Zuñis, Algonquins, and other native tribes, America has paid its debt of sin with interest, bestowing on mankind other plants of the solanaceous family, but upright, edible members, such as the potato, which today is cultivated more extensively throughout the world than wheat; the tomato, the "love apple" of the French, whose juice is considered a stimulating wine today; and the pepper, that king of spices, which carries to all the globe the burning and vitamin-rich stimulus of the tropical sun of America.

But in addition to these exemplary plants with their nutritious, homely, respectable fruits, the Solanaceæ of America set afoot in the world that scamp of the family, tobacco, neither fruit nor food, sly and conceited, lazy and having no other object than to tempt the spirit. The moralists of Europe were fully aware of the mischief-making properties of that irresistible Indian tempter. Quevedo said in Spain that "more harm had been done by bringing in that powder and smoke than the Catholic King had committed through Columbus and Cortés." But those were rogues' days and nothing could be devised to halt this Indian tobacco which, like the Limping Devil, went roving all over the world because everywhere it found a longing for dreams and indulgence for rascalities.

In Europe tobacco became utterly degraded, the instrument of crime, the accomplice of criminals. In the eighteenth century there was a general fear of being poisoned by deadly poison mixed with snuff. "Perfumed snuff was at times the vehicle of poison," says the historian of tobacco, Fairholt. "In 1712 the Duke of Noailles presented the Dauphine of France with a box of Spanish snuff, a gift which pleased her mightily. The snuff was saturated with poison, and after inhaling it for five days the Dauphine died, complaining of a severe pain in her temples. This caused great excitement, and there was great fear of accepting a pinch of snuff, and likewise of offering it. It was generally believed that this poisoned snuff was used in Spain and by Spanish emissaries to get rid of political opponents, and also that it was employed by the Jesuits to poison their enemies. For this reason it was given the name of 'Jesuit snuff.' This fear persisted for a long time." In 1851 tobacco was guilty of murder. The Count of Bocarme was put to death in Mons for poisoning his brother-in-law with nicotine that was extracted from tobacco for this purpose.

As though to heighten the malignity of tobacco, there is that special virus, or ultra-virus, which attacks it, and produces the dread disease known as mosaic. Sugar cane, too, suffers from a mosaic; but that which preys upon tobacco is produced by the first of the filtrable viruses, which was not only the first to be discovered, in 1857, but is the most infectious of all. It is stubbornly immune to ether, chloroform, acetone, and other similar countermeasures. There is something diabolical about this virus of tobacco mosaic. Its behavior is almost supernatural. It has not yet been ascertained whether it is a living molecule at the bottom of the life scale, or merely a macromolecule of crystallized protein. As though it had a double personality, the virus is as inert as distilled water, as inoffensive as a cherub, until it comes into contact with tobacco. But as soon as it penetrates the plant it becomes as active and malignant as the worst poison, like a mischievous devil in a vestry room. It almost seems as though it were in the essence of the tobacco that the virus finds the evil power by which it mottles the plant, dressing it up like a devil or a harlequin. The instant the tiniest particle of the infernal virus establishes contact with the protoplasm of tobacco, all its evil powers come to life, it infects every healthy plant, reproduces by the million, and in a few days a whole crop is stricken and destroyed by the virosis. As though the virulence of tobacco were the most deadly, when the Indians had to sleep in places infested by poisonous animals they were in the habit of spreading tobacco around themselves as a defense, for, as Father Cobo says, "it has a great malevolence against poisonous animals and insects" and drives them away as by magic.

Now to the traditional malignity of tobacco another and more cruel power is being attributed: the power to cause cancer by means of the tars extracted from it. An Argentine doctor (Dr. Angel H. Roffo) smeared these tars on the skin of rabbits, and cancer resulted "in every case." This did not occur with the tars distilled from Havana tobacco, but even with these half of the cases experimented with developed cancer.

At the same time scientists are still studying the possibility that cancer may be produced by an ultra-virus, that is to say, one of those protein viruses which, although chemical compounds, behave with lifelike activity, multiplying when in contact with certain living organisms, growing and dying like living cells. A scientist (Dr. W. W. Stanley), who achieved fame by isolating certain viruses in the form of crystals, holds the belief that whether those viruses that are invisible even with the microscope are the cause of cancer or not, they hold the secret of those irritations of the tissues, and in them are to be found the governing factors of the vital process in all cells, whether normal or cancerous. The puzzling feature of this horrible disease, which seems to consist in a wild reproduction of living cells out of harmony with hereditary structural rhythms, and the no less puzzling phenomenon of this ultra-virus of tobacco mosaic, which also manifests itself as the unforeseen coming to life of certain molecules that suddenly lose their inertia on coming into contact with tobacco, and reproduce and proliferate madly, carrying the germs of life, add a new mystery to the nature of tobacco. Can it be that there is something in tobacco that is a powerful stimulant of life, that can make cells proliferate in this wild manner and give to inert molecules the vital power of reproductivity, just as its smoke stimulates the weary, guttering spirit so it may flame up anew and live with renewed vigor?

TRANSLATED BY HARRIET DE ONÍS

José Vasconcelos

Mexico

(1882–1959)

An educator, writer, journalist, lawyer, and historian considered by some to be the Rousseau and the Saint Augustine of the Hispanic world, Vasconcelos first gained prominence through his philosophical pursuits, along with the likes of Alfonso Reyes, Antonio Caso, Martín Luis Guzmán, and Pedro Henríquez Ureña. He studied law in his native Mexico at the National School of Jurisprudence and had a private practice for several years. Before the outset of the Mexican Revolution he organized political clubs, wrote articles against the Díaz regime, and worked for the anti-Díaz Progressive Constitutional Party. He served Francisco Madero and other revolutionary leaders in the Mexican Revolution in 1910 as a representative in Washington, D.C., during which time he also published a number of philosophical and literary essays while in exile, such as *Pitágoras: Una teoría de ritmo* (1916) and *Divagaciones literarias* (1919). Vasconcelos left Mexico after he was arrested by the government of Victoriano Huerta following Madero's downfall. Upon his return, he was named president of the National University, where he established the Ministry of Public Education and began a cultural and educational renaissance as Mexico's secretary of public education. Under Vasconcelos, the ministry developed policies that sought to reform both elementary and adult education. He ran for president in 1929, losing due to an electoral fraud. The 1930s saw a political realignment for Vasconcelos, as he shifted to the right and published a number of Iberian-American nationalistic essays such as *Bolivarismo y Monroísmo* (1934). During this period he taught at the University of Chicago, the University of Puerto Rico, Stanford University, and the University of California at Berkeley, and he wrote his autobiography, published in four volumes: *Ulises criollo* (1935), *La tormenta* (1936), *El desastre* (1938), and *El proconsulado* (1939). But his most famous titles are *La raza cósmica* (1925) and its sequel, *Indología* (1926), in which he offers visionary social and racial theories—at times with anti-Semitic undertones—of the future of the Hispanic people. "Books I Read Sitting and Books I Read Standing," engaging and free-spirited, is part of *Divagaciones literarias*.

Books I Read Sitting and Books I Read Standing

To distinguish books, I have followed the practice for some time of using a classification which corresponds to the emotions they arouse in me. I divide them into books I read sitting and books I read standing. The former may be pleasant, instructive, beautiful, splendid, or simply stupid and boring, but all are incapable of arousing us from our normal posture. On the other hand there are some books which, the moment we begin reading, make us get up, as though they derive from the earth a force that pushes against our heels and obliges us to make an effort to rise. In these we do not just read: we declaim, we assume a lofty pose, and undergo a genuine transfiguration. Examples of this kind are: Greek tragedy, Plato, Hindu philosophy, the Gospels, Dante, Spinoza, Kant, Schopenhauer, the music of Beethoven, and others, if more modest, not less exceptional in their qualities.

To the quiet type of book, which one reads without being stirred up, belong all the rest, of infinite number, in which we find instruction, delight, charm, but not the palpitation of our consciousness which lifts us up as if we were witnessing a revelation of a new aspect of creation, a new aspect which incites us to move in order to be able to contemplate it in its entirety.

Moreover, writing books is a poor consolation for being unadaptable to life. Thinking is the most intense and fruitful function of life, but descending from thought to the hazardous task of writing it down weakens pride and reveals a spiritual inadequacy, indicating a fear that the idea will not live if it is not put in writing. This is an author's vanity and a little fraternal solicitude on the part of a traveller who, for the benefit of future travellers, marks along the arid way the points where there has been found the ideal water, indispensable for the continuance of the journey. A book, like a journey, is begun in anxiety and finished in melancholy.

If it were possible to be profound and optimistic, books would never be written. Men filled with energy, free and fecund, would not devote themselves to imitating with dead letters the ineffable worth, the perennial self-renewing of a life which absorbs and fulfils its impulses and all its longings. A noble book is always the fruit of disillusionment and a sign of protest. The poet does not barter his visions for his verses, and the hero prefers to live his passions and heroisms rather than sing them, however capable he might be of doing so in full and sumptuous pages. The people who write are those who cannot do things or are not satisfied with what they do. Every book says, expressly or between the lines: nothing is as it ought to be.

Woe to the man who takes up his pen and begins to write, while outside there is every potential which attracts human endeavour, when all the unfinished work calls forth emotion to consummate it in a pure and perfect reality!

But woe also to the man who, devoted to the world outside, neither reflects, nor becomes revolted, nor has ambitions ever more exalted! This man lives complacently only for the external and does not give up and die only because he is not yet born or reborn. For to be born is not merely to come into the world, in which life and death persist together and succeed each other; to be born is to proclaim oneself a non-conformist; to be born is to tear oneself away from the sombre mass of the species, to rebel against every human convention, to wish to strike out and rise up under the stimulus of the books that are read standing, books radically unsubmissive.

I do not know to what we are born when, like Buddha or Jesus, we renounce the world, but there is certainly no doubt about the nobility of a renunciation which anticipates the fatal dictum of death and defies death. Yes, unquestionably it is necessary, after knowing life, to be able to say to it: "That's enough!" Without that renunciation and without that demanding of something better, it appears that life has no value for us. It appears that new incarnations will be necessary in order that we may again attempt to surpass in our hearts all that is human, in order to rise to the state of the demigod, the angel, or the blessed.

Good books reprove life, without for that reason giving in to discouragement and doubt. To understand this, it is sufficient to read them, and to observe how strong, healthy temperaments judge them; because the sick man desires health, as the weak man reveres strength and as the mediocre man seeks happiness, and all three are optimistic. But the man who is healthy and glad of heart, the valiant and the bold, become demanding and clamour for what is not found here. Before the sybarite who offers me pleasure and the prophet who points out to me the vale of tears, I may waver, but I understand and respect the one who says to me: "It is necessary," and I laugh with scorn when I come upon the one who exclaims: "How beautiful!" or "How splendid!"

This is because truth is expressed only in a prophetic tone, and is perceived only in the tremulous atmosphere of catastrophe. So it speaks in the word of Aeschylus, so it is woven gloriously into the dialogue of Plato, so it bursts forth in the opulent modern symphony.

Euripides too, one of the free and great who have passed by, had such a clear understanding of the human that, moved by compassion, he began to write his visions, taking care to repeat at every moment the wise and sincere counsel, to which we are so deaf: "Be distrustful, be not puffed up in your joy. Call not yourself happy till the hour of your death; before then you know not what fate has in store for you. Why do you wish glory, beauty, and power. . . . Look at the house of Priam; listen to the lamentations of Hecuba. The faithful Andromache shares the bed of the victor! The little son of Hector has just perished, and of all the illustrious race there remains only the procession of Trojan slaves, imploring in vain as they march towards exile. Why have children!"

But as the truth inspires terror and many are alarmed by the corollaries which any thoroughly sincere spirit might deduce from these immortal gospels, the representatives of those who refuse to die, and who still, furthermore, indulge the instinct to engender offspring—the representatives of such beings, the intelligent men, with Aristotle at the head, invent for us attenuated interpretations, as they do in telling us that tragedy gives relief because the portrayal of pain causes joy, and that in this way the principle of life triumphs over its negations. They seem to fear that some day men will understand, and therefore they write books which restore our calm and good sense, books which deceive us: books which we read sitting because they attach us to life!

TRANSLATED BY H. W. HILBORN

Pedro Henríquez Ureña

Dominican Republic
(1884–1946)

———◆•∗•◆———

Born in Santo Domingo, the child of one of his country's presidents and poet Salomé Ureña, and sibling of critic Max Henríquez Ureña, Pedro Henríquez Ureña traveled broadly, living and working in Cuba, the United States, Argentina, and Mexico. His stay in Mexico is of particular importance, as he became an integral component of that country's intellectual renewal. An early positivist and a deep admirer of Eugenio María de Hostos, Henríquez Ureña later turned toward skepticism; however, his work shows that he never completely abandoned positivism. Although he did not allow for the existence of any universal ideals in terms of philosophy, Henríquez Ureña believed in a universal meaning of life. He was a prominent essayist and editor of anthologies. His first book, written in Havana, was *Ensayos críticos* (1905), and more than three decades later he coedited, with Jorge Luis Borges, *Antología clásica argentina* (1937). However, he is perhaps better known as an educator. During his tenure as a professor in Argentina, he contributed to several student publications and encouraged students to militate in favor of a liberal, parliamentary, secular, anti-imperialistic, and socialist democracy. He was particularly concerned with the Spanish language and its historical tradition. Included in his vast collection of published works are his posthumously published *Estudios de la versificación española* (1961) and *En la orilla: Mi España* (1922), although *Seis ensayos en busca de nuestra expresión* (1928), about the role of the intelligentsia in the Americas, is his most frequently cited and reprinted work. In 1940–41 he delivered the Charles Eliot Norton Lectures at Harvard University, subsequently published as *Literary Currents in Hispanic America* (1945). (The Spanish version was produced by the distinguished publisher Joaquín Díez-Canedo.) Published in the Buenos Aires daily *La Nación* on 4 February 1940, "Indian Things" is an ethnographic piece from a linguistic perspective. The author's concern is the European linguistic appropriation of the New World that has taken place since 1492. A man of inexhaustible knowledge, Henríquez Ureña makes a catalog of objects in the Americas and of the peculiar labels Europeans have chosen for them.

Indian Things

The traveler who leaves his home for foreign lands is amused to find faces similar to those he left behind. And he hopes to define the flavor

79

of unfamiliar fruits. In America, explorers searched for European similarities in everything. Columbus thought he heard nightingales singing in the Antilles; I do not know what bird had him fooled. Now nightingales are called one of the indigenous birds (the *Mimus polyglotus?*). Later the conquistadors named the *ananá*, pineapple; the *zapotillo*, loquat; the *puma*, lion; the cockerel, *gallipavo*; and, finally, they named turkey to the Cuban *guanajo* or the Mexican *guajolote*; the Argentine weasel is a marsupial, but it is inaccurate to refer to it as *mustélido*, as is done in the Iberian Peninsula. The South American thrush and calandra lark are not their European counterparts. Europeans invent fantastic names for New World things, like *manzana de tierra*.

The literature from the century of explorations and conquests comprises two currents: one that tries to paint new things in all their novelty; the other that translates the unknown to the familiar. That century had its Stevensons and its Lotis, its Lawrences and its Morands. *The Great Kingdom of China* by Fray Juan González de Mendoza saw more than forty editions in seven distinct languages. The chroniclers of the Indians describe everything from the new stars to the surprising insects. Father Bartolomé de las Casas, Oviedo, and Father Acosta write comprehensive treatises on American zoology and botany, in which the reader can enjoy novelistic fruition. They know—I do not recall if they say—that there is hardly any animal or plant like those in Europe. Among the poets, Juan de Castellanos, essentially a journalist in verse, packs his *Elegies* with fauna and flora bearing Taino and Caribbean names. Nothing picturesque eluded Madrid native Eugenio de Salazar, a poet of daily life, in his odes to Doña Catalina Carrillos, letters to his friends, and sonnets for the nearby nuns in the Church's heyday:

Allí el bermejo "chile" colorea	See the red "chile" come alive,
y el naranjado "ají" no muy maduro;	and the unripe orange "*ají*";
allí el frío "tomate" verdeguea . . .	see the cold "*tomate*" revive . . .

Another poet of rancid stock, the Sevillian Juan de la Cueva, praises the *mamey*, the avocado, the guava, the sapodillas. . . .

Ercilla, perhaps because he believed that the epic style could not convey the excess of local color, keeps prudently silent about the scenery, save the fine description of the Chiloé Archipelago and the brief images of "the great mountains and the high sierra" covered by inaccessible snow. When he ventures precisions—rare instances—he mentions the Italian gondola and the indigenous piragua together, as well as the vicuña and the "longhaired sheep" (would it be the alpaca, or the llama?), the corn and "the tiny crowned fruit which produces the virtuous *murta*"; what is this myrtle of edible fruits?

But some poets close their eyes to what they see. They bring their Mediterranean scenery, that of Virgil and Ovid and Horace, their natural history by Pliny, even their mythological zoology with its fauns and newts.

And those most addicted to their artificial scenery are the poets who were born on this side of the ocean. The Mexican Francisco de Terrazas makes Huitzel the Indian talk about deer—the classical "wounded deer," to whom María Rosa Lida has consecrated precious study—and about the plaintive turtledove, the no less classical "tender fowl."

Chilean Pedro de Oña populates the Araucanian meadows and forests with plants and animals that neither they nor he himself knew, for the most part, beyond books:

Aquí veréis la rosa de encarnado,	The crimson rose here you see,
allí el clavel de púrpura teñido,	there the purple stained
los turquesados lirios, las violas,	carnation,
jazmines, azucenas, amapolas . . .	irises turquoise, and violas,
	poppies, Madonna lilies,
	jasmines . . .

Vense por ambas márgenes poblados	Thickly settled on every side
el mirto, el salce, el álamo, el aliso,	poplar, willow, alder, myrtle,
el sauce, el fresno, el nardo, el	weeping willow, ash, spikenards,
cipariso,	cypress
los pinos y los cedros encumbrados	the towering pine and cedar . . .
. . . *	

Entre el verde juncia, en la ribera,	Among the reeds, along the
veréis al blanco cisne paseando . . .	riverbank,
Pues por el bosque espeso y enredado,	you see the white swan
ya sale el jabalí cerdoso y fiero,	promenading . . .
ya pasa el gamo tímido y ligero,	While in the thick and tangled
ya corren la corcilla y el venado,	forest green
ya se atraviesa el tigre variado,	comes the warthog, porcine and
ya penden sobre algún despeñadero	wild,
las saltadoras cabras montesinas	goes the fallow deer, slight and
con otras agradables salvajinas . . .	mild,
	the roe deer and the stag run by,
	prowls the tiger in its vibrant
	stripes,
	the leaping mountain goats
	suspended high above some
	precipice
	among other pleasant savages . . .

---

*Since Oña did not have a clear notion of these trees, he does not know that *salce* and *sauce* are two forms of the same word.

As one would expect, the mythological entities that covered these Chilean meadows and forests are not Indian deities, but:

Las Dríadas, Oréades, Napeas	Dryads, Oreads, Napes
y otras ignotas mil silvestres deas,	wild spirits yet unknown,
de sátiros y faunos perseguidas . . .	satyrs and fauns in pursuit . . .

All poets of the colonial era are surpassed in profusion by the great and luminary Bernardo de Balbuena, who brought a new and original American note to Baroque art, for although it was not born here, it came to reside here while it was young, around the age of two or three. In his opulent poem "Grandeur of Mexico" (1604) he adorns the land where he was educated with all the vegetal richness of classical literature. Many of the plants he mentions had already arrived from Europe by then, but surely not all:

La verde pera, la cermeña enjuta,	The luscious pear, the lean cermeña,
las uvas dulces, de color de grana,	sweet grapes, cochineal colored,
y su licor, que es néctar y cicuta.	and its liqueur, at once nectar and venom.
El membrillo oloroso, la manzana	The aromatic quince, the apple succulent
arrebolada, y el durazno tierno,	turned ruby, the tender peach,
la incierta nuez, la frágil avellana.	the unexpected nut, the fragile hazelnut.
La granada, vecina del invierno,	The pomegranate, winter's denizen
coronada por reina del verano,	crowned the summer's queen,
símbolo del amor y su gobierno. . . .	symbol of love in all its reign. . . .
Florece aquí el laurel, sombra y reparos	Here flourishes the laurel, shade and heaven
del celestial rigor, grave corona	from celestial rigor, earnest crown
de doctas sienes y poetas raros.	of seasoned knowledge and poets rare.
Y el presuroso almendro, que pregona	And the hurried almond that proclaims
las nuevas del verano, y por traerlas	the news of summer and, to make them known,
sus flores pone a riesgo y su persona;	its blossoms jeopardizes and its being;

el pino altivo, reventando perlas	and the aerial pine vivacious
de transparente goma, y de las perras	with pearls of lucent gum, and
frescas uvas, y el gusto de cogerlas.	the lusty
	grapes, tasty and a pleasure to the
	touch;
Al olor de jazmín ninfas bizarras,	Fancy water lilies, scenting of
y a la haya y al olmo entretejida	jasmine,
la amable yedra con vistosas garras	and the affectionate ivy
. . .	intermingled
	its defiant tendril claws in beech
	and elm . . .

And he continues: the bloody mulberry tree, the shady willow, the oriental palm, the sad cypress, the straight fir, the plain box, the *taray*, the rugged oak, the perfect poplar, the gnarled holm oak, the tree strawberry, the cedar, the walnut; and then the flowers: the snowdrop, the red poppy, the rose, the carnation, the basil, the sandalwood, the verbena, the sunflower, the jasmine, the wallflower, the iris, the violet, the rosemary, the thyme, the Madonna lily, the hyacinth, the narcissus. . . .

There is, moreover, a luxurious enumeration of fine horses; everything within has semblances of truth, for even in its early stages the conquest of Mexico was famous for its stables and horsemen. Valbuena offers many interesting names: the choleric brown, the crazy sorrel, "made of fire in its color and spirit," the dappled *hovero*, the gray *rucio*, the dew-covered *rosillo*, the white dotted with black flies; the chestnut, the ashen *gateado*, the sloe, the *zabruno*, the *picazo*, the cream horse.

· · ·

The transplant of European scenery to American literature was credited to the rhetoric of the Renaissance: in poetry as in painting, the scenery served to adorn and obeyed traditional formulas.

But America flowed back into Europe in a thousand ways. First and foremost, if the Europeans brought wheat and rice, the cow and the sheep, the horse and the dog, America sent back corn and potato, cacao and tobacco, cinchona and cocoa, the turkey and the turtle. The "marvelous Indian things," as they penetrate European life, also penetrate literature. Shakespeare mentions yams—tidbits then appreciated like marrons glacés are now—but still does not mention tobacco. Spaniards, imitating the Indians of the Antilles, learned to smoke before the English: Tirso, at least, mentions the cigar, the "tube of tobacco" which "gives benediction" after the meal. It is true that his character—in *The Village Girl from Vallecas*—is an Indian, on his way back to Spain.

After a short while the American origins of many things were forgotten.

Spaniards said "Málaga yams" in the sixteenth century. In England they called them "Spanish potatoes." And the potato, then, the "Irish potato": a name that circulates, paradoxically, in American English. Eastern origins have been attributed to corn, and Italians call it *granturco*, "Turkish grain." Victor Hugo has his *Cautiva*; in the Orient they speak of "fields of corn."

There are unexpected confusions: cactus, which is exclusively autochthonous to America, was bred and transplanted to the Mediterranean with such speed that it appears in seventeenth-century paintings as characteristic vegetation of arid lands—for example, when Palestine is represented in religious paintings.* And Flaubert, despite his fabulous studies and voyages, which provided the research to write *Salammbó*, makes the same mistake and speaks of chameleons that climb through the cactus stalks in the vicinity of Carthage.

Recently, Jean Giraudoux, in his admirable *Electra*, put tomatoes, Mexican in name and origin, in ancient Greece. Because his work is never for want of irony, we will attribute it as such, as a deliberate anachronism, the tomatoes in the long-haired Argives' gardens.

TRANSLATED BY JESSE H. LYTLE AND ILAN STAVANS

---

*I owe this information to the eminent Argentine botanist D. Lorenzo R. Parodi.

Gabriela Mistral

Chile
(1889–1957)

The first Spanish-American recipient of the Nobel Prize for literature, awarded in 1945, Gabriela Mistral was born Lucila Godoy Alcayaga. She began her career penning newspaper columns, and then, after adopting her pseudonym, she released four volumes of poetry: *Desolación* (1922), *Ternura* (1924), *Tala* (1938), and *Lagar* (1954). Invited to Mexico in 1922 by José Vasconcelos, she became a teacher in the rural Mexican countryside and wrote children's songs for her pupils. In addition to her poetry, Mistral also produced a great quantity of letters and articles printed in Hispanic-American newspapers. These works focus primarily on Americanist, Christian, pedagogical, and biographical themes. Although Mistral avoided involvement in politics, she was deeply concerned about the living conditions of women, children, and Indians in Latin America. Mistral's early guidance was crucial in the development of other Chilean writers such as Pablo Neruda. Four collections of her essays were published posthumously in 1978: *Cartas de amor de Gabriela Mistral, Gabriela piensa en . . . , Garbiela anda por el mundo,* and *Prosa religiosa de Gabriela Mistral.* Known chiefly as a poet, Mistral nevertheless wrote a solid number of highly allegorical newspaper essays, such as "My Homeland," reproduced here, first published in 1923 and part of her essay collection *Lecturas para mujeres* (1924), which resulted from her days in Mexico.

My Homeland

Chile: a land so small that it comes to look on the map like a beach between a mountain chain and the sea; a parenthesis between two dominant centurions and to the south the tragic caprice of the antarctic archipelago, torn into pieces, creating an immense laceration in the ocean's velvet.

And the natural zones, clear, defined, reflecting the character of the race. To the north, the desert, the salt bank, whitened by the sun, where man proves himself through effort and pain. Immediately thereafter, the transition zone, devoted to mining and agriculture, the provider of the race's most vigorous fellows: a landscape of austere sobriety, akin to an ardent spirituality. Then comes the agrarian zone, with its affable landscape, joyous spots from its fields and dense spots populated by factories; the placid

85

shadow of a peasant rupturing itself through the valleys, and the working masses walking like agile ants into the cities. At the southern end the cold tropic, with a jungle that exhales in the same manner as the one in Brazil, but one that is black, dispossessed of the color's lechery; islands rich in fishing, wrapped in a livid mist, and the *Patagonian* plateau, horizontal and desolate, our only land blessed with a broad sky, a pastoral land for the innumerable cattle herding below the mountain snow.

Small land, not small nation. Reduced soil, inferior to the ambitions and the heroic nature of its people. It does not matter: we have the sea . . . the sea . . . the sea!

A new race without Lady Luck as its fairy godmother, still in need of an exacting spartan mother. In the Indian period it doesn't reach the rank of kingdom; savage tribes walk with leisure through its lands, blind to their destiny in such a way that in divine blindness they lay unconsciously the foundations of a people that would be born strangely, in a stupendously vigorous manner. Later the Conquest, cruel like in other regions, the rifle fired until it succumbs upon the rigid back of the Arauac, like a crocodile's loins. The Colony, not developed like in the rest of America with permissiveness and refinement due to the silence of defeated Indians, but illuminated by that tremendous flash of lightning, which stops the night in Mexico, as a result of the struggle against the Indian, which does not allow the conquistadors to put their weapons down to sketch a *pavana* over the ballrooms. . . . Finally, the Republic, the serene and slow creation of the institutions. Some colorless presidencies, only vouching for the work of heroic and ardent presidencies. From time to time, passionate creators distinguish themselves: O'Higgins, Portales, Bilbao, Balmaceda.

Our America convulses in a minimum of revolutions, two wars in which the race resembles David the shepherd who makes himself a warrior by saving his people.

Today, in the basin of mountains considered too closed to universal life; and yet the world's thundering hour reverberates. People have the fiery panting on a resting lion. On their path through the republican life, they will always be inspired by it: Their severity of strength is well known and not exaggerated.

The nation's race possesses a virile differentiation, an originality that is a form of nobility. Indians will shortly become exotic because of their scarcity and, thus, a mixed race covers the territory and doesn't have the weakness some might detect in impure races.

We don't feel the coldness or even the distrust of the European people, the white race acting as the civilizer, ordering energies and building the collective organisms. Germans have made and continued to make their southern cities, arm in arm, with the Chileans, to whom they have been communicating their confident organizing sense. Yugoslavians and English men and women build their settlements in Magallanes and Antofagasta. Let us praise the national spirit allowing them to cooperate with our sacred task of thickening the eternal vertebrae of a homeland, without hate, with a noble understanding of what Europe has given us through them!

Yes, we aren't a defined race unlike the old and rich. No, we have something of a primitive Switzerland, whose austerity is a result of its stubborn mountains. As that resounds in our ear, it begins to inflame us. Poverty should make us sober. It should never make us surrender to the powerful countries who corrupt through insinuated generosity. Caupolicán's gesture, relentless over the log that opens the soul, is tattooed in our soul.

TRANSLATED BY JOSÉ MATOSANTOS

Alfonso Reyes

Mexico
(1889–1959)

Known as a diplomat for his native Mexico as well as for his writing, Alfonso Reyes's prose and poetry clearly display his strong work ethic and profound understanding of Western culture. He joined Justo Sierra in 1912 and founded the School of Higher Studies, the first humanities division of the National University. His diplomatic career, which began in 1913 when he became the second secretary of the Mexican legation in France, lasted for twenty-five years. Reyes also lived in Argentina and Madrid, where he directed the cultural section of José Ortega y Gasset's *El Sol* and established strong bonds with the celebrated Spanish writers Miguel de Unamuno and Juan Ramón Jiménez, among others. Upon his return to Mexico in 1938, Reyes and President Lázaro Cardenas established El Colegio Nacional de México, a cultural research center that opened its doors to exiled Spaniards. He also cofounded El Colegio Nacional in 1945, which every year brings together twenty of the most distinguished Mexican scholars to offer public lectures. The great height of Reyes's literary and artistic achievements has prompted many to place him on a pedestal among Latin American figures. His early works such as *Cuestiones estéticas* (1911), *Visión de Anáhuac* (1917), and *Simpatías y diferencias* (1921–26) reflect insight into a wide array of subjects, including theater, film, literature, and travel. He later moved on to other subjects, writing serious literary critiques and sociocultural analyses of Greek and Roman civilizations. By the end of Reyes's career, his complete works in classical studies filled five tomes. "Notes on the American Mind" is an influential essay addressing emotional, intellectual, and psychological issues. It was published in *Sur* in September 1936 and was included in *Ultima Tule* (1941), a volume of essays about Europe's "invention" of America. Eventually, it was published in volume 19 of Reyes's complete works.

Notes on the American Mind

1. My observations are confined to what is called Latin America. The need to abridge forces me to be inaccurate and unclear, and to exaggerate to the point of caricature. All I propose to do is to provoke or set moving a conversation, without trying to exhaust the groundwork of the problems

I raise, much less to offer solutions. I have the feeling that, while using America as a pretext, I am doing nothing more than touching a few universal themes in passing.

2.   To speak of American civilization* would be, in the present instance, inopportune: it would lead us into archaeological regions which lie outside our theme. To speak of American culture would be somewhat equivocal: it would suggest to us only one branch of the European tree which has been transplanted to American soil. On the other hand, we can speak of the American mind, and the American view of life and action in life. This will permit us to define, though only provisionally, the American colouring.

3.   Our drama has a stage, a chorus, and a character. By a stage I do not now mean a space, but rather a time, a time in almost the musical sense of the word: a beat, a rhythm. Having arrived late at the banquet of European civilization, America goes leaping over steps along the way, hurrying and racing from one form to another, without having given the preceding form time to mature completely. At times, the leap is bold and the new form looks like food taken away from the fire before it is fully cooked. Tradition has had less weight, and this explains the boldness. But we do not yet know whether the European rhythm—which we try to overtake with long strides, not being able to match it at its measured pace— is the only historical tempo possible; and no one has yet demonstrated that a certain acceleration of the process is contrary to nature. This is the secret of our history, our politics, our life, dominated by a call to improvise. The chorus: American populations are formed, principally, from the old autochthonous elements, the Iberian throngs of conquerors, missionaries, and colonists, and the later contributions of European immigrants in general. There are conflicts of blood, problems of cross-breeding, efforts at adap-

---

*The seventh meeting of the International Institute for Intellectual Co-operation was held in Buenos Aires, from the 11th to the 16th of September, 1936, on the theme: "Present relations between the cultures of Europe and Latin America." In it the following took part: G. Duhamel, P. Henríquez Ureña, J. B. Terán, L. Piérard, F. de Figueiredo, J. Maritain, B. Sanín Cano, A. Arguedas, E. Ludwig, [H. A.] Keyserling (by letter), F. Romero, R. H. Mottram, C. Ibarguren, W. Entwistle, A. Peixoto, J. Estelrich, A. Reyes, C. Reyles, E. Díez-Canedo, G. Ungaretti, J. Romains, and S. Zweig. Duhamel opened the discussion in the name of Europe, and the notes published here represent the introduction of the subject in the name of America, which was entrusted to us. The impossibility of exhausting such a vast and enticing theme in such short sessions occasioned our being called later to meet with Pedro Henríquez Ureña and Francisco Romero to continue the discussion on our own account. In several meetings, from October 23 to November 19 in 1936, we took some notes from which perhaps some day a work in collaboration will be produced.

tation and absorption. In different regions, there is a predominance of the Indian or Iberian hue, the grey of the half-caste, the white of the general European immigrant, and even the huge marks of the African brought in past centuries to our soil by the old colonial administrators. The gamut allows every kind of tone. The laborious womb of America is little by little intermingling this heterogeneous substance, and day by day there is now coming into existence a characteristic American humanity, an American spirit. The actor or character in this case is the intelligence.

4. The American intelligence is operating upon a series of conflicts. Fifty years after the Spanish conquest, that is, in one generation, we already find in Mexico an American manner: under the influences of the new atmosphere, the new economic set-up, with the coming together of the sensibility of the Indian and the property instinct which arises out of having occupied the land, there appears among the Mexican Spaniards themselves a sense of a New World aristocracy, which already clashes with the aggressive ambitions of Spanish newcomers. On this point there are abundant literary testimonies: both in the satirical and popular poetry of the period, and in the subtle observations of the peninsular sages, like Juan de Cárdenas. Literary criticism has centred this phenomenon, as in a luminous focus, in the figure of the Mexican dramatist don Juan Ruiz de Alarcón, who, through Corneille—who passed it on to Molière—had the good fortune to bring influence to bear upon the modern French theatre of customs. And what I say of Mexico, because it is more familiar and better known to me, might be said to a greater or lesser degree of the rest of our America. In this incipient prickling, there was already throbbing the long yearning for the independence of the American states.

A second conflict: as soon as independence is won, the inevitable dispute between Americanists and Hispanists appears, between those who lay stress on the new reality, and those who lay it upon old tradition. Sarmiento is above all an Americanist. Bello is above all a Hispanist. In Mexico one recalls a certain polemic between the Indian Ignacio Ramírez and the Spaniard Emilio Castelar which revolves around the same themes. This polemic was often turned into a conflict between liberals and conservatives. The emancipation was so recent that neither father nor son had learned how to live with it in an attitude of mutual tolerance.

Third conflict: one pole is in Europe and the other in the United States. We receive inspiration from them both. Our constitutional utopias combine the political philosophy of France with the presidential federalism of the United States. The sirens of Europe and those of North America both sing to us at once. In a general way, the mind of our America (without for that reason denying affinities with the most select individuals of the other America) seems to find in Europe a vision of what is most universally and most basically human, and in closest conformity to its own way of feeling.

Apart from historical suspicions, fortunately less and less justified and which must not be touched upon here, we dislike any tendency towards ethnic segregations. To keep to the Anglo-Saxon world, we like the naturalness with which a Chesterton or a Bernard Shaw contemplates the peoples of all climes, conceding to them equal human authenticity. Gide does the same thing in the Congo. We do not like to consider any human type as a mere curiosity or an amusing exotic specimen, because this is not the basis for true moral sympathy. The very first mentors of our America, the missionaries, lambs with hearts of lions, people of fierce independence, lovingly embrace the Indians, promising them the same heaven that was promised to them. The very first conquerors founded equality in their impulses towards cross-breeding: so, in the West Indies, we have Miguel Díaz and his Cacica, whom we find in the pages of Juan de Castellanos; we also have that soldier, a certain Guerrero—who without this story about him would be unknown to us—refusing to follow the Spaniards with Cortez because he was getting along fine among Indians and, as in the old Spanish ballad, "had a beautiful wife and children most lovely." Likewise, in Brazil, we have the famous Jão Romalho and el Caramurú, who fascinated the Indian women of San Vicente de Bahía. The conqueror Cortez himself enters into the secrets of his conquest when he rests upon the bosom of Doña Marina; perhaps there he learns to fall in love with his prize in a way that other captains with colder hearts could not (like Caesar of the Gauls), and begins to harbour in his mind certain ambitions for autonomy which, behind closed doors and within the family, he was to communicate to his children, later tortured for conspiracy against the Spanish motherland. Imperial Iberia, much more than she administered our affairs, simply kept bleeding herself over America. Here, in our countries, we continue to think of life in that way—as open and generous bleeding.

5. Such are the stage, the chorus, and the character. I have mentioned the principal alternatives in conduct. I spoke of a certain call to improvise, and I must now explain myself. The American mind is necessarily less specialized than the European. Our social structure requires it so. The writer here has closer links with society, and generally practises several professions. He rarely succeeds in being merely a writer, and is almost always a writer "plus" one or more other things. Such a situation offers advantages and disadvantages. The disadvantages: a call to action—the mind discovers that the order of action is the order of transaction, and this brings suffering. Frustrated by continual necessary duties, intellectual production is sporadic, and the mind is distracted. The advantages arise from the actual state of the contemporary world. In crisis, in the turmoil which keeps us all astir nowadays and requires the effort of all, and especially mental effort (unless we resign ourselves to allowing only ignorance and desperation to contrive to frame the new human patterns), the American

mind is more accustomed to the air of the street; among us there are not, there cannot be, ivory towers. This new alternative of advantages and disadvantages also allows a synthesis, an equilibrium which resolves itself into a peculiar way of viewing intellectual work as a public service and a civilizing duty. Naturally this does not rule out, fortunately, possibilities of a withdrawal, of the luxury of pure literary leisure, a fount to which we must return to bathe with a salutary frequency. But in Europe, the withdrawal could be normal. The European writer is born, as it were, on the top level of the Eiffel Tower. With an effort of a few metres, he is right up on the mental heights. The American writer is born, as it were, in the region of central fire. After a colossal effort, in which often he is aided by a stimulated vitality which almost resembles genius, he just barely succeeds in getting up to the surface of the earth. Oh, my European colleagues, under many a mediocre American is frequently concealed a storehouse of qualities which certainly merits your sympathy and study. Evaluate him, if you please, from the standpoint of that profession superior to all the others, mentioned by Guyau and by José Enrique Rodó: the general profession of being a man. Under this light, there is no danger that learning would become detached from its main body, bottled up in its isolated conquests a millimetre long by another millimetre wide, a danger the consequences of which Jules Romains described to us so lucidly in his inaugural address to the Pen Club. In this peculiar American situation there is no danger either of a cutting-off of links with Europe. Quite on the contrary, I have a feeling that the American mind is called to fulfil the most noble complementary function: that of establishing syntheses, even though necessarily provisional; that of applying the results promptly, verifying the value of the theory in the living flesh of action. Along these lines, if the economy of Europe has need of us already, the very mind of Europe will in the end have need of us.

6. For this beautiful harmony which I foresee, the American mind offers a peculiar faculty, because our mentality, even though so strongly rooted in our own countries, as I have stated, is naturally internationalistic. This is explained not only by the fact that our America offers conditions for making it the melting-pot for that future "cosmic race" of which Vasconcelos has dreamed, but also by the fact that we have had to go looking for our cultural machinery in the great European centres, thus accustoming ourselves to handling foreign ideas as if they were our own. While the European has not had to go to America to construct his world-system, the American studies, knows, and lives Europe from the primary school. From this arises a most interesting consequence which I point out without vanity or rancour: in the balance of errors in detail or partial misunderstandings found in European books that deal with America, and those found in

American books that deal with Europe, the count is in our favour. Among American writers it is actually a professional secret that European literature makes frequent errors in quotations in our language, the spelling of our names, our geography, etc. Our innate internationalism, happily supported by the historic brotherhood which unites so many republics, implants in the American mind an undeniable pacifistic inclination. It passes through armed conflicts, winning each time by dexterous manipulation, and makes itself felt in the international order even in groups most contaminated by a certain fashionable bellicosity. It will facilitate the delicate grafting of the pacifistic idealism which inspires the greatest minds of North America. Our America must live as if it were always prepared to realize the dream which its discovery inspired among the thinkers of Europe: the dream of utopia, the happy republic, which lent singular warmth to the pages of Montaigne, when he came to contemplate the surprises and marvels of the new world.*

7. In the new American literatures there is quite perceptible an insistence upon autochthonism which merits all our respect, especially when one does not cling to the easy note of local colour, but tries to extend the sounding right down to the heart of psychological realities. This pubescent ardour corrects that hereditary sadness, that bad conscience with which our

---

*I thought these explanations would suffice to clarify the sense I gave to the concept of the synthesis of culture, a synthesis for which our America seems singularly fitted. In the volumes published in 1937 by the International Institute for Intellectual Co-operation, in Spanish and in French in Buenos Aires and Paris, respectively, in which appears the review of the talks to which these notes on America served as an introduction, it may be seen that Francisco Romero agreed with me in appreciating a certain synthesizing ability in the American mentality, a coincidence which was not the result of a previous interchange of ideas, and this makes it the more weighty. But, on speaking of "synthesis," neither he nor I was correctly interpreted by our European colleagues, who thought we referred to an elemental summary or compendium of European achievements. According to this superficial interpretation, the synthesis would be a terminal point. But no: synthesis here is a new point of departure, a structure made of previous scattered elements which, like any structure, is transcendent and contains new things within itself. H_2O is not only a combination of hydrogen and oxygen, but it is also water. The quantity 3 is not only the sum of 1 plus 2, but it is also something which neither 1 nor 2 is. This capacity to look at the incoherent panorama of the world and at the same time to establish objective structures, which signify a step further, finds in the American mind a fertile and prepared soil. As compared to the American setting, the European setting appears to be shut up behind a Chinese wall, and irremediably so, like a cultural provincial. So long as they do not perceive this and do not modestly accept it, the Europeans will not have understood the Americans. It is not a matter of vulgar judgments regarding what may be superior or inferior in itself, but of different points of view with respect to reality.

elders contemplated the world, feeling themselves children of the great original sin, of diminution in stature on account of being American. I permit myself here to utilize some pages I wrote six years ago.*

The generation immediately preceding us still believed itself born within the prison of several concentric misfortunes. The most pessimistic felt this way: in the first place, the first great misfortune, which of course consisted of being human, according to the saying of the ancient Silenus picked up by Calderón:

> Because the greatest crime of man
> is to have been born.

Within this circle came the second, which consisted of having come very late to an old world. Still unsilenced were the echoes of that Romanticism which the Cuban Juan Clemente Zenea epitomized in two lines:

> My verses are those of ancient Rome
> And my brothers died with Greece.

In the world of our letters, a sentimental anachronism dominated the average person. The third circle, besides the misfortunes of being human and being modern, was the very specific circle of being American, that is to say, born and rooted in a soil which was not the present focus of civilization, but a branch-office of the world. To use a saying of our Victoria Ocampo, our ancestors felt themselves "proprietors of a soul without a passport." Once one was American, another handicap in life's career was to be Latin, or, in short, of a Latin cultural heritage. It was the period of "Wherein lies the superiority of the Anglo-Saxon?" It was the period of submission to the present state of things, without hope of a definitive change or faith in redemption. One heard only the harangues of Rodó, noble and ingenuous. Once belonging to the Latin sphere, another misfortune within it was to belong to the Hispanic sphere. The old lion had been in decline for some time. Spain seemed to have gone back home from its earlier greatness, and was now sceptical and weak. The sun had set over her dominions. And, to cap it all, the Spanish American was on bad terms with Spain, which was true until a short time ago, until before the present sorrow of Spain, which pains us all. Within the Hispanic world, we were still reduced to being a dialect, a derivation, something secondary, a branch-office once more: Spanish-American, a name bound together by a hyphen as with a chain. Within the Spanish-American, those near me still lamented having been born in the region where the Indian strain was

---

*Monterrey, *Correo Literario* of A. Reyes, Rio de Janeiro, October 1930. No. 3, pp. 1–3, and *Sur*, Buenos Aires, 1931, No. 1, pp. 149–58: *A Bit of America.*

strong: the Indian, then, was a burden, and not yet a proud duty and a strong hope. Within this region, those still nearer to me had reasons for distress at having been born in the fearful neighbourhood of an aggressive and plethoric nation, a feeling now transformed into the inappreciable sense of pride in representing the forefront of a race. Of all these phantoms which the wind has been blowing away or the light of day reforming into different shapes to the point of converting them, at least, into acceptable realities, something still remains in the corners of America, and it must be chased out, opening the windows to full width and calling superstition by its name, which is the way to put it to flight. But, basically, all that is now corrected.

8.   Having established the foregoing premises and after this examination in court, I venture to assume the style of a juridical summing-up. For some time there has existed between Spain and us the sense of a levelling process and of equality. And now I say before the tribunal of international thinkers which is listening to me: acknowledge that we have the right to the universal citizenship which we now have won. We have attained our majority. Very soon you will get accustomed to having us with you.

TRANSLATED BY H. W. HILBORN

Oswald de Andrade

Brazil
(1890–1954)

———◆◆◆◆◆———

A writer of prose, poetry, manifestos, and plays, Oswald de Andrade was a vanguard writer with strong Marxist tendencies who tried to create a modern understanding of Brazilian culture through sarcasm and parody. In fact, if anything defines
his writing style, it is his witty sense of humor and his strong criticism of Brazil's upper
class. Strongly influenced by cubism and futurism, Andrade's works reconstruct
Brazilian society in a fragmented style. His plays are imbued with a strong dose of
satire. His most memorable works are *Sentimental Memoirs of John Seaborne* (1923),
Brazilwood (1925), and *Seraphim Grosse Pointe* (1926). "Anthropophagite Manifesto," from the first issue of São Paulo's *Revista de Antropofagia*, a journal in which
his companion, Tarsila do Amaral, Brazil's most famous modern painter, was associated as well, is a decisive essay in the tradition of Latin American letters. Published
in May 1928, Andrade's thesis states that for Brazilian art to achieve authenticity and
originality, it first must "devour" all things European. The idea is revolutionary in that
intellectuals south of the Rio Grande have always looked at the European legacy in
an ambivalent fashion—either as an invasive force to be denied or as an admirable
constellation of symbols and meanings to be emulated. Oswald de Andrade takes
neither perspective—or perhaps he takes both. His solution in the search for a collective Latin American identity is to assimilate as much as possible from the Old
Continent, and then turn it upside down.

Anthropophagite Manifesto

Only anthropophagy unites us. Socially. Economically. Philosophi-
cally.
The world's only law. The disguised expression of all individualisms, of
all collectivisms. Of all religions. Of all peace treaties.
Tupy or not tupy, that is the question.
Down with all catechisms. And down with the mother of the Gracchi.
The only things that interest me are those that are not mine. The laws
of men. The laws of the anthropophagites.
We are tired of all the dramatic suspicious Catholic husbands. Freud put
an end to the enigma of woman and to other frights of printed psychology.
Truth was reviled by clothing, that waterproofing separating the interior

from the exterior world. The reaction against the dressed man. The American cinema will inform you.

Children of the sun, the mother of mortals. Found and loved ferociously, with all the hypocrisy of nostalgia, by the immigrants, slaves and tourists. In the country of the giant snake.

It was because we never had grammar books, nor collections of old vegetables. And we never knew what urban, suburban, frontiers and continents were. We were a lazy spot on the map of Brazil.

A participating consciousness, a religious rhythm.

Down with all the importers of the canned conscience. The palpable existence of life. The pre-logical mentality for M. Lévy-Bruhl to study.

We want the Carahiba revolution. Bigger than the French Revolution. The unification of all successful rebellions led by man. Without us, Europe would not even have its meagre Declaration of the Rights of Man. The golden age proclaimed by America. The golden age and all the girls.

Descent. Contact with Carahiban Brazil. Où Villeganhon print terre [sic]. Montaigne. Natural man. Rousseau. From the French Revolution to Romanticism, to the Bolshevik Revolution, to the Surrealist revolution and the technical barbarity of Keyserling. We continue on our path.

We were never catechized. We sustained ourselves by way of sleepy laws. We made Christ be born in Bahia. Or in Belém, in Pará.

But we never let the concept of logic invade our midst.

Down with Father Vieira. He contracted our first debt, so as to get his commission. The illiterate king told him: write it down on paper but without too many fine words. And so the loan was made. An assessment on Brazilian sugar. Vieira left the money in Portugal and left us with the fine words.

The spirit refused to conceive of the idea of spirit without body. Anthropomorphism. The need for an anthropophagical vaccine. We are for balance. Down with the religions of the meridian. And foreign inquisitions.

We can only pay heed to an oracular world.

Justice became a code of vengeance and Science was transformed into magic. Anthropophagy. The permanent transformation of taboo into totem.

Down with the reversible world and objective ideas. Transformed into corpses. The curtailment of dynamic thought. The individual as victim of the system. The source of classic injustices. Of romantic injustices. And the forgetting of interior conquests.

Routes. Routes. Routes. Routes. Routes. Routes. Routes.

The Carahiban instinct.

The life and death of hypotheses. From the equation—me as part of the Cosmos—to the axiom—the Cosmos as part of me. Subsistence. Knowledge. Anthropophagy.

Down with the vegetable élites. In communication with the earth.

We were never catechized. Instead we invented the Carnival. The Indian dressed as a Senator of the Empire. Pretending to be Pitt. Or appearing in Alencar's operas, full of good Portuguese feelings.

We already had communism. We already had surrealist language. The golden age. Catiti Catiti Imara Natiá Notiá Imara Ipejú.

Magic and life. We had the relation and the distribution of physical goods, moral goods and the goods of dignity. And we knew how to transpose mystery and death with the help of grammatical forms.

I asked a man what Law was. He told me it was the guarantee to exercise the possible. That man was called Gibberish. I swallowed him.

Determinism does not exist only where there is mystery. But what has this got to do with us?

Down with the stories of men, that begin at Cape Finistère. The undated uncountersigned world. No Napoleon. No Caesar.

The determining of progress by catalogues and television sets. They are only machines. And the blood transfusors.

Down with the antagonical sublimations. Brought in caravels.

Down with the truth of missionary peoples, defined by the sagacity of a cannibal, the Viscount of Cairú:—A lie repeated many times.

But they who came were not crusaders. They were fugitives from a civilization that we are devouring, because we are strong and vengeful just like Jaboty.

If God is the conscience of the Universe Uncreated, Guaracy is the mother of living beings. Jacy is the mother of all plants.

We did not speculate. But we had the power to guess. We had Politics which is the science of distribution. And a planetary social system.

The migrations. The flight from tedious states. Down with urban sclerosis. Down with the Conservatoires and tedious speculation.

From William James to Voronoff. The transfiguration of taboo in totem. Anthropophagy.

The *pater familias* and the creation of the Moral of the Stork: real ignorance of things + lack of imagination + sentiment of authority towards the curious progeny.

It is necessary to start with a profound atheism in order to arrive at the idea of God. But the Carahiba did not need one. Because they had Guaracy.

The created object reacts like the Fallen Angel. After, Moses wanders. What has this got to do with us?

Before the Portuguese discovered Brazil, Brazil had discovered happiness.

Down with the Indian candleholder. The Indian son of Mary, godson of Catherine de Medici and son-in-law of Sir Antonio de Mariz.

Happiness is the proof of the pudding.

In the matriarchy of Pindorama.

Down with the Memory, source of custom. Personal experience renewed.

We are concretists. Ideas take hold, react, burn people in public squares. We must suppress ideas and other paralyses. Along the routes. Believe in signs, believe in the instruments and the stars.

Down with Goethe, the mother of the Gracchi, and the court of João VI.

Happiness is the proof of the pudding.

The *lucta* between what one would call the Uncreated and the Creature illustrated by the permanent contradiction between man and his taboo. The daily love and the capitalist *modus vivendi*. Anthropophagy. Absorption of the sacred enemy. In order to transform him into totem. The human adventure. The mundane finality. However, only the purest of élites managed to become anthropophagous in the flesh and thus ascended to the highest sense of life, avoiding all the evils identified by Freud, catechist evils. What happens is not a sublimation of sexual instincts. It's the thermometric scale of the anthropophagous instinct. Moving from carnal to wilful and creating friendship. Affective, love. Speculative, science. Deviation and transference. And then vilification. The low anthropophagousness in the sins of the catechism—envy, usury, calumny, murder. Plague of the so-called cultured Christianized peoples, it is against it that we are acting. Anthropophagi.

Down with Anchieta singing the eleven thousand virgins of the sky in the land of Iracema—the patriarch João Ramalho, founder of São Paulo.

Our independence has not yet been proclaimed. A typical phrase of João VI:—My son, put this crown on your head before some adventurer puts it on his! We expelled the dynasty. We must expel the spirit of Bragança, the laws and the snuff of Maria da Fonte.

Down with social reality, dressed and oppressive, registered by Freud—reality without complexes, without madness, without prostitution and without the prisons of the matriarchy of Pindorama.

—Piratininga, the year 374 after the swallowing of the Bishop of Sardinia

TRANSLATED BY CHRIS WHITEHOUSE

Victoria Ocampo

Argentina
(1890–1979)

In typical Argentine style, Victoria Ocampo was classically educated and heavily influenced by European thought and culture. She learned French, English, and Italian at an early age and did much of her writing in French during the early part of her career. Although Ocampo faced a male-dominated literary world resistant to accepting women, she quickly earned the praise of the Spanish philosopher José Ortega y Gasset. In 1931 she founded the magazine *Sur*, which became one of Latin America's most important literary forums. *Sur* achieved international renown and promoted some of the region's greatest writers, including Borges and Adolfo Bioy Casares. Ocampo later became director of the National Foundation of the Arts, and by the 1950s she had attained worldwide recognition. When Juan Perón's government arrested her in 1955, both Gabriela Mistral and Jawarhal Nehru interceded on her behalf and arranged her release. A strong activist for women's rights in Argentina, Ocampo cofounded the Argentine Union of Women. Her own translations, essays, and creative pieces reflect her interest in literature that has arisen from beyond traditional Western sources, and these works have spanned two generations of Latin American literature and thought. She masterfully links seemingly unrelated anecdotes and references in a smooth and fluid narrative, free of pedantry and artificiality. The tone and outlook of most of her work is optimistic. She published twenty-six volumes of essays, of which nine are entitled *Testimonios*. "Women in the Academy" was Ocampo's speech on 23 June 1977, upon being inducted into the Argentine Academy of Letters. It was later included in *Testimonios*, volume 10: 1975–77. She was invited to occupy the chair named for Juan Bautista Alberdi, a statesman and writer who was a contemporary of Domingo Faustino Sarmiento. Her message is clear-cut: By discussing two personal friends, Virginia Woolf and Gabriela Mistral, she talks, in a poised yet spirited fashion, about the role of women in the pantheon of national letters.

Women in the Academy

I congratulate us—first you members of the Argentine Academy of Letters, then us women—for the decision you have taken to include a woman among your members. I congratulate you first because *motu propio*

us rather imperfectly about them. In the back of our heads, you say, there is a spot the size of a shilling that we cannot see with our own eyes. Each sex must assume the responsibility of describing that spot for the benefit of the other. We women, therefore, should not show ourselves ungrateful. We should repay men in kind."

Not to hesitate at any subject, however trivial or vast it may seem, was exactly my thought. In 1924, Ortega y Gasset published my first endeavor, my commentary on the *Commedia*. I shall never forget the way he extended his hand to me.

To return to Virginia—she and I agreed perfectly about the place that women should occupy in literature. She achieved that place. And today, when her work is so often studied, no one questions her feat. Her triumph comforts me, as does that of Emily Brontë, lost in the moors of Yorkshire, who never knew the fate that awaited her books. She was not one of those who enjoyed public recognition during her lifetime. But it was not essential. When human beings are truly individual, recognition or lack thereof doesn't change them.

The Nobel Prize didn't change Gabriela Mistral, who was half Indian and was born in the Valley of Elqui. This Chilean woman, a school teacher in her youth, was one of the most mysterious, attractive, stubborn, and noble figures I have ever known. I mention her today because she represented America in a very special way that few have been able to match. In 1937, she spent her entire visit to Argentina in my home in Mar del Plata. After a few days, she wrote me (we would write from room to room): "You have done me a great deal of good. I needed to know, *to know*, that an entirely white person could be genuinely American. You cannot fully understand what this means to me." And later she added: "I was enormously surprised to find you as criolla as I." I took Gabriela to several estancias near Mar del Plata during that autumn, and together we looked at plants, stones, and pastures. In Balcarce I showed her some *curros*, spiney bushes covered, in March, with little white flowers that smell of vanilla. The curro is considered a national plague. Nonetheless I like it so much that when it blooms, I always pay it a visit. After her departure, Gabriela wrote me: "I still see you with the stones, pastures and little animals of our America. Even if you weren't so noble or superior, I would see you that way; . . . Do you remember that magnificent bush that was at the estancia you took me to and from which you had some branches cut? I see that geometry of thorns, that look-at-me-but-don't-touch, that machine-gun of silence. . . . That could be *you* (and *I* was that way too at times), at least that's the way I think of you. Because that plant, also disconcerting, is truthful, and what ties me to you most is your truthfulness. Your culture and so on, I can get from others in Europe. Your truth and your vital violence, only *you* can give me. It's the most open-air American style there is." I know Gabriela believed that. It's the only letter of recommendation I want to offer you.

After Gabriela died, I found out something that would have given her even more of a surprise. I used to accuse her, half-jokingly, half-seriously, of being a racist. She had a passion for the *inditos* (dear little Indians, as she called them), and she felt herself a part of them. What I discovered was that, on my mother's side, I am descended from Domingo Martínez de Irala, a companion of don Pedro de Mendoza, and a Guaraní Indian woman, Agueda. This Spanish man and this American woman had a daughter whom her father legally recognized as his. Given my feminist "prejudices," I sympathize more with Agueda than with the one who spoke to the founder of Buenos Aires on equal terms. This is not a demagogic stance. I am as incapable of demagogy as I am of pedantry. But in my capacity as a woman, it is both an act of justice and an honor to invite my Guaraní ancestor to this reception at the Academy and to seat her between the English woman and the Chilean. Not because she deserves, as the others do, to enter an Academy of Letters, but because I, for my part, *recognize* Agueda.

This has nothing to do with literature, you will probably say. No. Though perhaps it has something to do with inherent justice and with poetry. Or so Virginia's fantasy would have imagined. And so would Gabriela's passion, as when she wrote in her "Saudades":

> On earth we shall be queens
> and of a truthful kingdom . . .

For this "truthful kingdom" to exist, we need some ideas and attitudes that Agueda was not aware of, nor, most certainly, was the Spanish conquistador. The "truthful kingdom" will be born out of great patience. And my most fervent wish is that a woman never accept a position for which she is not qualified or one which does not coincide with her authentic personal aptitudes. That's why I insist on pointing out that my presence here is the result of my eagerness to remove barriers, nothing more. That is also why I repeat these explanations. If one is to be queen, one must reign truthfully.

And so I have made my confession to you. It's the only thing that I think appropriate under the circumstances. I bring with me today three women because I owe to them something that has mattered in my life. To one, a portion of my existence. To the others, in part, my not having been content just to exist. The one who would be most astonished if he could see us here today would be Domingo Martínez de Irala.

In a letter of petition sent to the conquistador in 1556 by a navigator, a certain Bartolomé García, from Asunción, García said: "Worthy sir: this is to bring to your attention how much I have worked and served in these lands." I, too, have worked and served as a navigator of other voyages in these not always peaceful lands. Four and a half centuries had to go by after Irala lived before I was allowed—before we women were allowed—to tread the lawns of universities.

You, my dear colleagues, know this. And you know that changes are taking place everywhere. The world is adapting to a new reality, one that can no longer be denied, one that will benefit you as much as it will us women.

TRANSLATED BY DORIS MEYER

Graciliano Ramos

Brazil
(1892–1953)

Despite his relative obscurity, few scholars would deny that Graciliano Ramos belongs among the elite of Brazilian letters. A self-educated man, Ramos learned English, French, Latin, and Italian; he also organized and taught at a school for children. He made a reluctant entry into politics as the mayor of Palmera dos Indios in 1928 and later became the director of the state printing office. In 1936 he was incarcerated without explanation by the regime of Getúlio Vargas, but was later given a government post by the same regime that had imprisoned him. He was first shipped from Maceio, where he was director of public instruction, via Recife and prison-ship to Rio de Janeiro, and was passed from prison to prison for a year until his release. His writing centered around the poor northeastern region of Brazil and focused on tensions between the authorities, the people, progress, and nature. Ramos wrote only four novels, but two, *São Bernardo* (1934) and *Barren Lives* (1976), have gained popularity since film versions were released. His prison diaries, published a few months after his death, are as fascinating for their Kafkaesque tone as for the way they shed light on the Brazilian collective character. They are a chronicle of inhuman oppression and a laud to human kindness. Ramos turns the essay into an autobiographical artifact and uses his own experiences to understand his national heritage and the role of the individual in a labyrinthine society.

Jail: Prison Memoirs

Outside of reading I spend hours making a mess of my finger with the nail clippers. I change it from nicotine-yellow to iodine-red and then bandage it with adhesive tape. The dryness in my throat and numbness of my stomach seem to be letting up. The sickening sight of food no longer brings nausea with it. I try eating a little, to overcome this madness, and as my memory comes back to me the mental fog lifts and more distant shapes fall into focus. But the inner emptiness persists through despondency, indecisiveness and the certainty that these papers I've scribbled so laboriously will be worthless anyway. Not only that, but Captain Mata seems to multiply himself. I don't have a minute's rest, —it's impossible to concentrate on anything in his presence. He laughs, he sings, he even has a project for some literary exercise of his own. Once I criticized the excessive number of *so*'s in one of his cacophonies. He completely suppressed the word from his vocabulary. Later he even managed to successfully compose a letter to his wife in which not a single *so* was to be found. He tells stories, recites sonnets, explains the meaning of every bugle-call. He tells me that in order to remember them the recruits make up all kinds of crude songs. This one's for *about-face*:

> *Who's that walking down the street,*
> *Your MO-ther?*

And this one too:

> *Never saw a woman screw,*
> *Like YOURS does!*

Some were fouler. Sometimes he'd pause in the middle of such facetiousness and become a little sad. Finally I realized that the bugle was really upsetting him. He trembled as he listened to it, translating its language to me, and only calmed down a long time after it was over. Then he would drift slowly back into some conversation or into the one song he never finishes, —or starts, —but keeps repeating.

"The words are stupid," he once confessed, "but I like the music. It's a good tune."

Then later on with a suddenly serious look, his face all screwed up apprehensively, at the sound:

"The Major just arrived. The Commandant is back."

I couldn't imagine why the hell he was worrying about what the Major or the Company Commander were doing. Turned out he *wasn't*, about *them*. And by catching a word here, a word there, I finally discovered what it was all about: Mata was scared some General might come to visit the camp. Simple as that. It surprised me to see such a talkative, happy guy fretting about nothing at all. I couldn't see any reason for it. Later I changed my mind. Anyway, for a Police Captain a visit from a flesh-and-blood General has to be a pretty serious thing. Reveille, inspection, orders of the day, all of that must really come down on some petty officer who's already completely deformed from discipline. And if this particular officer happens to be losing his mind in a cellblock, trying to interpret the noises outside or to decipher the grimaces of some condescending guard, the notion of their enormous General gets to be an extremely painful obsession. This invisibly remote authority can simply wipe out, in the most casual sort of way, with an order, our whole social existence. Can put us in solitary, —us or Sebastião Hora, who's maybe just horsing around with a bunch of guys a few steps away in the Sergeant Barracks. I began to understand how exclusively we depended on the good will of this type of *Cavalier*. No

interrogations, no witnesses for the prosecution, none of the normal procedures for trial seemed to be about to materialize in our case. Not even
the simple words of an accusation. And maybe we'd have to go on just
like this. Probably there's a reason for segregating us like this, but silence
is always frightening. Why aren't we part of some official *auto-da-fé?* Why
are there no witnesses? Even false witnesses to simulate some kind of ju-
dicial procedure? Of course it'd be a farce, but even in a mock-trial we'd
have a vague possibility of defending ourselves. Or at least of giving the
prosecutor a hard time. Even a dehumanized tribunal has some value. Even
a rotten judge hesitates before passing a totally contemptible sentence: fear
of public opinion. Or, the last resort: a reasonable jury. This kind of fear
occasionally does compromise persecution. But here there's no sign of even
wanting to bring us to trial. Possibly we've already been tried and sentenced, without knowing it. Our rights, already completely suppressed
down to the last shred. No idea who might be involved. Possibly one
single individual was enough to pass sentence: the General? And Captain
Mata, listening to the bugle, has a right to be scared.

I tried to convince him, —to convince myself, —there's no need to be
frightened. The simple appearance of the man couldn't do us any harm:
he might clarify things for us. We'd be looking at a well-educated human
being, I was sure of it. When we first came here, a subordinate officer
presented himself,—and hadn't I mistaken him for a superior officer because he acted so courteously? Every morning the Commandant visits us,
and we hear what he always has to say with some slight variation in his
cool amiability. Captain Lobo continues to differ only with respect to my
ideas, which I've yet to mention. Moreover, I still haven't managed to
grasp his own. It still pleases me, however, to be able to see him. To enjoy
his almost rude frankness, clear voice and quick, incisive gestures. And in
his dark look, the spark of a tendency toward sidestepping intentionally
into madness. Out in the hallway, rigid and automatic figures pass by. But
those with whom we come into contact seem comprehensible and hu-
mane. Even the guard, our clownish little hairbrained kid with his prison
grids of crisscrossed fingers, jeering: "Not even rats escape." Even the duty
officer. While unwrapping the things I'd requested from him, I offered
him a small token. The boy refused. Without making any fuss about it.
Without taking offense. If the inhabitants of the place are so well disposed
towards us, why should we be frightened by some outside General who
visits? Well, my cellmate was just daydreaming. At times he'd sing:

> *Where are you going my* (something-something) *young son,*
> *With your rifle slung on your shoulder?*

But the strident tones of the bugle still affected him. And always, for a few
minutes, with his face apprehensively screwed up in anger, he'd give up

the song, his lunch, nail-clipping, those literary exercises and his efforts not to use cacophonous conjunctions. I tried to distract him:

>—*Who's that walking down the street,*
>   *your MO-ther . . .*

The truth is, I was getting nervous myself. For the most part I practice a form of auditory indifference, but his uneasiness began to infect me.

"*Who* just arrived?"

No one. Just a group of soldiers. Just the silence. Just reveille. The differing sounds possess no meaning for me. And all of them enter the room with news of the invisible enemy.

•   •   •

One morning as we crossed the hall on the way back from the shower, we met the Commandant. He was accompanied by a tall, thin, serious-looking man. We nodded hello to the Commandant and he stopped us.

"General," he introduced us, "these gentlemen . . ."

End of introduction, but the tall man continued to look at me, rather irritated:

"A Communist, eh?"

I was confused, but answered: "No."

"No? Why, you're a confessed Communist!"

"No I'm not. I never confessed to anything at all."

He stared at me for a minute of stern silence, then said out loud:

"If only the Government'd give me the chance I'd have you shot!"

I barely managed to whisper, "Why, General? You've got me here in prison, don't you?"

But I quickly decided it's better to keep still: hell, he might take what I had to say as some kind of challenge, and I couldn't exactly back it up. Luckily, the man didn't pay any more attention to me, turned his back on me to deal with my cellmate, whom he now interrogated fiercely. Captain Mata, the same as always, straightened himself up and swore he was the victim of some slanderously false persecution. But the way he was standing, in his pajamas with a towel around his neck, made the whole thing ridiculously comic.

"I'll prove to Your Excellency *yet* how devoted a patriot I can *truly* be!"

Now there's a suitable turn of phrase, fit for mouthing in any military outpost. I could never manage to come out with such a declaration. How could I call myself a devoted patriot? I've never really considered myself a patriot. It'd be dishonest to start now, but certain words have power over some people whether or not they contain any truths. Captain Mata never referred to proofs to demonstrate the real substance of his hypothetical virtue: he simply promised additional proofs sometime in the future. And that was enough. The General, without compromising his rather serious countenance, duly appreciated the manner and speech of the accused. Then he expended just a bit more energy in our direction but soon left us, — with dignity, —followed by the Commandant. That's more or less how it was, or I think so. We retreated, tired and abashed, returning to our cell. I walked along with my ears burning up.

"Fuck!"

Captain Mata was completely exhausted. He swore I'd behaved dangerously. How? What the hell! Wasn't that the proper way to talk to a General? Matter of fact I never understood that sort of thing, but I was convinced I'd done nothing disrespectful. To swear I wasn't a Communist, —that was the truth: I didn't belong to the *Party*. Of course, had I been a member, I still wouldn't have confessed to illegal activities, but I wasn't a member. The only thing left to consider was that improbable business of my execution. But no one was going to shoot me, because there was nothing to be gained from it. I was too insignificant. No one would notice. I'm useless as an example. And they certainly don't want to make anything out of my death: it might just backfire. It might turn me into a martyr or create the illusion of qualities I've never possessed. Which could provide useful propaganda for the opposition, —clandestine newspapers and such. Change me into a celebrity. No, no point in shooting me. Besides when you plan to murder someone, you don't advertise: you do it. If you can. An ingenious method, his: to threaten people indiscriminately, without really caring if it frightens them or not. Here in Brazil, we still haven't gotten to the stage of public executions. Even in the most fascistic of countries some semblance of legality is still requisite, and public opinion is still not the least important factor. Here, bloodshed in the open is still frowned upon: governmental cowardice tends to restrict itself to beating and torturing prisoners and to news from time to time of some mysterious suicide. That's more or less the case with those implicated in the events of 1935. But what the hell've I got to do with that? They're really not about to shove needles behind my fingernails or push me out of a high window. So I must be ok, I thought. And I certainly didn't see how anything I might've said was going to upset the authorities.

My cellmate still felt I'd reacted carelessly in response to the mention of my execution. His imagination was overwrought. He was adding words I'd never come out with and putting a different emphasis on things until they sounded more and more reckless even to me. He was certainly exaggerating: that I could expect only the most serious consequences. Bullshit. It's true, I fail to behave properly toward any men in uniform: I can't be expected to salute with a stiff hand, tight spine and straight legged. Even if the last thing I'd said to the guy was out of place, it didn't count for so much: he hadn't paid attention anyway: he'd just moved on, turned his back on me and his mind off me. In his infantile way, —looking tough and hard-nosed, raising his voice, —he probably considered me dead already. Most likely pretty happy with himself. More important things to deal with. Probably. At the moment we were the last thing he'd want to think about. So I figured there was really nothing to worry about. And there wasn't. Nothing new happened in the next couple of days.

We got back into the routine of things: eating our grubby rations from a tray; visits from the Commandant; long talks with Captain Lobo; attempts to fill out the empty, frustrating hours with vain efforts at amusing one another. Out there close to the two cannons a group of soldiers in light fatigues were marching back and forth: a smiley lieutenant carrying a whistle, devising elaborate exercises. On the opposite side of the courtyard some guys were now struggling to get a basketball through a hoop attached to the wall. The bugle plays, sounding its question: *who's-that-walking-down-the-street-your-MO-ther.* And my friend Captain Mata is no longer upset by the question. The scares seemed to be over now: no reason to be afraid that among various announcements would come the arrival of a General. The guard keeps an eye on us, making his funny faces and, when no one's around, he chats in a whisper. The duty officer comes to ask us about supplies. Captain Mata's suitcase opens and out comes needle and thread, a moment's devotion to the task of sewing loose buttons back on trousers. The index finger of my left hand has begun to leak pus. I still coat it with iodine but the nail is separating from my finger. My poor paperbacks, three of them, are disintegrating from rough usage. I listen to the sounds of orders, strident about-faces, parades, silence.

I've written a letter to my wife in pencil, asking her again if she's mailed the short story to Buenos Aires. Does the post office, with all this censorship, allow such works to be exported? It's an ordinary story with endless twists around the same basic idea, a real potboiler. It has no value as a work of art or as a political tract, but there's always the chance they'll see dynamite in it. The police-censors, so stupidly, can only judge a work of art by the name of the author. Almost never by the content. I'm still a reasonably shadowy figure, virtually unknown: two works, rather short ones, have awakened only mild interest and mostly disdainful consideration. I'm a provincial hack-writer, hated in the provinces, unknown to the metropolis. Why waste time criticizing my works; condemning them only draws the attention of the masses. I suppose the authorities could quietly find me guilty, toss me in with criminals: precisely the people I've wanted a closer look at. The most likely thing is to lock me up with the rebels from the Natal uprising, the 3rd Regiment or the Air Force Academy. Whatever they decide to do, I was thinking, I'd be running into different kinds of people and maybe I'd get some materials together for something a little less useless than the two rather insipid novels which were busy gathering dust on the publisher's shelf. This presumptuousness of mine, however, failed to take into account the enormous difficulties I always encountered whenever I would pick up one of the pads the duty officer'd brought for me. I always write very slowly: I end up sitting in front of a page for hours on end without managing to dispel my mental blocks for a moment. Trying vainly to stick a few ideas together. Clean them up a little, polish them. And now everything's so much worse that even the idea of torturing myself in order to eke out of my existence a half-dozen lines of prose ceases to interest me: I feel indifferent, dried out, incapable of overcoming the enormous lethargy which at each hour suddenly appears out of nowhere. And all efforts, to my mind, have become useless.

My decision to keep a diary is weakening, faltering from the lack of any stimulus within me or without. The facts, once they occur, no longer seem to hold any interest. Only four or five incidents stand out, but, as soon as they begin to take shape, they wither into seeming insignificance. It's getting more and more difficult to find any circumstances to lend them color or brilliance: they all come out almost naturally faded, dull sounding, — irremediably so. The prose of some vagrant reporter. Terrible obstacles even for sketching out the simplest commentary. *Ora*, commentary! If even the exterior narration and the dialogues falter continually, how's there ever going to be a chance of reaching any depth? I've a stone in my head. And to think I imagined once upon a time I could create a novel in prison, slowly and methodically, page today, page tomorrow. It reminds me of an article I read years ago on the creativity of the criminal: "a contradiction in terms." And doubts continue to assail me. Are we creatures, just naturally insensitive? Boorish animals? Or does prison rob us of our energies? Warp the mind and the senses?

• • •

I was ordered one day to present myself in the room to the left of ours, situated opposite the cell where Sebastião Hora and Nunes Leite were being held. I dressed quickly and in less than a minute was in the courtyard, knotting my tie, headed for a place which, for lack of something better to call it, I christened the administrative office. I entered the office in a state of commotion and presented myself to a young soldier in uniform. He was leaning on a table covered with papers. I've been getting used to the different ranks lately: in spite of my anxiety, I was able to count his stripes to see he was a Captain. He offered me a chair and handed over an envelope to me. Why should I take a seat if he just wanted to give me a letter? I wanted to oblige and at the same time stay on my feet, but a week of confinement in this environment has taught me that refusals signify a lack of discipline. I acquiesced to his demand. Then I took the letter from him and was about to put it into my pocket, get up and leave, when he stopped me with a motion of his hand.

"I'm obliged to ask you to open the letter in my presence."

"Sorry, sorry." I mumbled embarrassingly, taking the letter opener he handed me. "Of course."

Obediently, I handed the sheet of paper to him. He took it from me, and quickly turned it over to the blank side so as to cover whatever might be written on it. He also turned some photographs over the same way and spread them out face-down on the table, discreetly, to avoid looking at them:

"I'm satisfied. Pardon. Just a formality."

I got up, left the room in a grateful state of confusion, hardly believing my eyes and ears. Strange. That's really stretching the routine a bit far to make some poor bastard do something or other and then tell him it doesn't really matter because it's just some needless requirement. An extravagant waste of time. With such procedures we'd soon be thinking there's no such thing as responsibilities and everything's really aimlessly permitted. Maybe they just want me to understand how easily they can make me behave this way or that. Sit me down or stand me up. Burn my letters or leave them intact. No, that'd just be stupid, a cat and mouse game. A mild gesture from a flaccid paw shows me to a chair. Then suddenly a pink claw emerges out of the amiable flaccidity: "I'm obliged to ask you. . . . Pardon. Just a formality." It never entered my head. Did they actually suppose that inside of a flat three-by-five quadrilateral of no thickness whatsoever, there might be weapons, dynamite, poison disguised by a letter and photographs? If the writing paper and the pictures aroused no curiosity, it seemed unnecessary to have to show them. With such unreasonable, bureaucratic exigencies censorship must tend to degenerate. In the end I'm left with a feeling that the official in charge seems to be a very amiable sort of person. That and nothing more.

"Please sit down. Fine. I'm satisfied. Pardon. A formality."

Well educated, that's understood, but it'd be even more understandable if it had to do with something a little more productive. In this kind of situation I begin to suspect that their function in life is a purely parasitical one. Although my opinion's of no importance whatsoever as far as they're concerned, the facts remain the same, and whoever observes the same situation would have to agree with me. I felt almost angry the guy hadn't looked at the packet from my wife, hadn't seen the distant faces she was sending me in the mail. It couldn't cause me any trouble for him to be aware that a few of my pages were destined for some journal or magazine in Buenos Aires. I probably had some fucking inadmissible pride going on in all this, maybe some cowardly wish to prove I had nothing to hide. I wasn't aware of it though, and I mention such a degrading notion just because it's always possible. What the hell do I know about what was going on inside of me? It's hard to be objective under such circumstances; naturally we all share a tendency to justify ourselves, and it's looking at someone else's behavior that sometimes reveals us to ourselves as the miserable creatures we are. Makes us want to escape from ourselves, disgusting as we are, and encourages us to make some superficial corrections. To be honest, by watching myself every second I seemed to be able to keep clear of low sentiments. But who's to say if such sentiments really cease to exist deep down? Inside of us, everything tends to be ambiguous, contradictory, confusing, and only our acts are truly revelatory. We tend to surprise ourselves when we least expect it, by saying things and doing things which are horrifying. The fact is I still haven't experienced any fear in this place. There hasn't been any reason to. At times, however, I'm filled with apprehensiveness about the possibility of experiencing it one day. An absurdly anguished sensation: fear of fear. Nothing the matter, apparently, we're calm. Then suddenly we're touched by a troubling sensation that spreads over us until we're in a cold sweat: "—If danger comes my way, how will I behave? Will I react like a decent human being or will I succumb to god knows what? Trembling until I'm completely debased?" We all resist these painful uncertainties by pretending to feel secure. Until, in the end, we accomplish just that, by talking freely and giving vent to strong emotions. Bullshit. What about the fact that they judge us to be harmful and so they lock us up in complete isolation? But our thoughts skirt such issues with minds on more important things: "—Did I show any weakness, am I too malleable? Do they think I'm willing to sell myself?" The idea of prostituting oneself terrifies us, —and the terror itself makes one behave reasonably somehow. Captain Lobo seems to be decent enough. So what? We'd be on his side if his ideas didn't conflict with our own. But what exactly are Captain Lobo's ideas? We ourselves have a certain number of fixed ideas, that's true, but refuse to believe in discarded formulas. Good a century ago, maybe, but worthless today. Seeing him and hearing him, we have to understand that he's still on the other side and that makes him an enemy. Realizing his integrity, we watch him just as carefully.

Obviously, I didn't figure all this out on the way back from the administrative office, while looking at family photos and briefing myself on the latest news of them. The short story, meandering and poorly worded, had been mailed to Benjamin Garay, who, frankly, well I didn't know who the hell he was. Someone offering to start some Brazilian thing in Argentina. Who the hell's Benjamin de Garay? He'd gotten to me with his amiable letters, but suppose he saw me now, staring at the guard outside and the two pieces of artillery decorating the entranceway? He'd give up writing me quickly enough, prudently enough, timidly enough. He keeps mentioning his *qualified* translators, *calificados*, supposing me to be a reasonable bastard with a penchant for notoriety and for the Academy. At least my imprisonment would rid me of Garay and his *calificados*. All of this passed unnoticed by the Captain who'd just finished dismissing me with an agreeable wave of the hand, "—Just a formality." Why act that way? Does he figure I'm completely malleable, manageable by any politician or general? That must be it. Most likely it wasn't just the tiresome repetition of conventional signs and bureaucratic phrases at work here. He'd perceived in me someone from his own class, someone confused and easily brought around, so he'd decided to be civil. The promise of execution was inapplicable in my case: he couldn't even pretend to such exaggerated powers. So while I'd been fumbling around with the letter opener, he'd had time to observe me, to judge I was completely inoffensive, probably involved through some misunderstanding, not worth the inspection. If he had observed any suspicious sign, he'd have dropped the feigned disinterest quickly enough: he'd have read the letter attentively, carefully searching for any clue hidden away in the simplest news. Nothing though. He'd looked away with an almost humiliating condescension. I was obviously not one for tossing hand grenades, for barracks' mutinies. After all, I was just here to provide the middle class with some evidence of the many unsavory elements in a society. Threatening the country.

TRANSLATED BY THOMAS COLCHIE

Mário de Andrade

Brazil

(1893–1945)

————◆◆◆◆————

Often considered one of Brazil's most cultivated men, Mário de Andrade was a poet, essayist, sociologist, musicologist, novelist, and educator. He was leader of an avant-garde group that promoted São Paulo's Modern Art Week in 1922 and pushed for a rejuvenation of Brazilian art, and he actively promoted the concepts of Brazilian modernism. Not only was he central to the development of nationalist Brazilian art, but he also remained very interested in preserving the native folk art and music of his country. While cooperating with the Ministry of Education and Culture, Andrade organized the Department of Culture of São Paulo in 1937 and was named director of the Institute of Arts of the University of the Federal District in Rio de Janeiro. His literary style underwent some changes after 1930, as his writings reflect an increased interest in politics. Among his best-known works are *There Is a Drop of Blood in Every Poem* (1917), *Hallucinated City* (1922), and *The Modernist Movement* (1942); but his greatest literary triumph was his "rhapsody" *Macunaíma* (1926), an exploration of myth and folklore with segments in an invented language with Tupí words and modern Brazilian slang. The book won international recognition, becoming a film and a play. By the end of his life Andrade came to be recognized as the greatest representative of Brazil's early modernism. His complete works, published in twenty volumes in 1944, include the following newspaper note, first printed on 23 August 1939, well into Getúlio Vargas's first presidential period.

Of Hypocrisy

Sometimes, in the middle of the path of humanity's great technical accomplishments, it is not at all unfortunate to recover ideals and notions that new scientific discoveries persuaded us to abandon. Could those aged budgets and doctrines be entirely useless? . . . Medicine's renewed interest in the study of the human character provides a healthy example. Fecund observations and renovated possibilities of analytical certainty are presently extracted from a field of study that had been abandoned for centuries.

Contemporary psychology also began to scrutinize the mechanism of artistic individuality with its keen eye, exploring the reasons why an individual becomes an artist and the anaesthetic causes and effects of art; as a result, new truths emerged. Today we speak of enlargement, of transference, and employ several other important and undoubtedly valuable words. The modern belief in the certitude of scientific inquiry strangles the romantic adornments through which the artist was evaluated in an earlier age: an age in which the artist was considered the chosen of the gods, an intimate friend of the Muse, and the adventurous rider of several Pegasuses. The artist is presently a poor devil; he was vitally incapacitated and devoured by insomniac phobias. Anyone who is incapable of earning money through courage complains about life through free verse. Those who lack the courage to declare their love paint a Venus or sculpt several complacent Amazons. In summation, psychology and sociology are creating a historical age that could very well be called that of the dismantled artist: an age that is incapable of ridding itself of its desolating relativism and its absurd insufficiency despite its concern with the truth. I deem it necessary to remount the artist on his Pegasus, to introduce him to the Muses, and submit him to the vote of the gods. Man is not only flesh and bones. That is why the psychological causes currently employed to explain the existence of artistic works and the artist (i.e., financial, sexual, intertwined with phobias, incapacities and internal ambition) advance less in the aesthetic knowledge of art than an analysis of the tale of the birds pecking grapes in the region of Apeles. I say more: They are profoundly immoral. Artists are becoming conscious of the hypocrisy that adorns true art. Nowadays it is very easy for any artist to "invent" an attractive complex and sweeten his works, offering generous material for future psychoanalysts. And despite his lyrical sensitivity, the artist will end up forgetting his true human destiny and allow himself to be devoured by hypocrisy.

The writer who, in my judgment, studied and confessed his artistic hypocrisy and that of his colleagues in the most shameless manner was Arnold Bennett in *The Truth about an Author*. In his book, Arnold Bennett unmasks with impressive sincerity the reasons that induced him to become a journalist, novelist, critic, and playwright. None of the illusions, the virtues, the fervor for art, or the yearnings for glory that stalk the artist and that are usually believed to be the cause of the existence of artists are described there. None of what turns man into humanity, the visible being, or the moral being concerns him. He is only concerned with the secret reasons . . . the small, lowly acts, all that exists inside us and that we hide from others and from ourselves with the utmost care.

Arnold Bennett had a precursor of similar impertinence in Edgar A. Poe (without mentioning the psychologists of art . . .) when he studied the making of "The Raven" in a celebrated and irritating essay.

But even if those essays might represent a particular truth, these Anglo-Saxons are not absolutely right. Yes, every artist undoubtedly demonstrates a good dose of hypocrisy when he says that he is also driven to create by harmful or pernicious causes that are impossible to confess and which he tries to hide from himself. In fact, that matter about the artist sacrificing a great deal of his spontaneity, of commotion itself, and of his own ideas in favor of the ideas and agitations of others is also hypocrisy. The true artist will never lose sight of his audience, and the dosage of arrogance inherent in that should escape no one. The complete artist will never lose sight of the ambition of recovering or continuing his status as a celebrity and that is hypocritical. And because it is the public which forges the greatness of an artist (I say "public" even in the sense of a small elite, which some artists possibly prefer), these two ambitions regarding the public—one which will judge and another which will be responsible for the artist's celebrity status—direct the creative behavior of the artist to a great extent although they are alien to the specific concept of art.

There are, as well, other ideas that denaturalize the ideal beauty of the artist and encourage the creation of works of art such as rivalries, struggles for subsistence, jealousy, and sexual vanities. Only for the perfect artist, for the complete artist, for the legitimate artist, shall these agents always remain subconscious forces, repressed feelings, secret notions and secret causes. It is commonplace to say nowadays that they are the ones that direct us and that the ends we openly and consciously confess to pursue are not more than the mask that hides those inferior wretched aspirations.

Well then, I think that the contrary occurs, and I will provide my reasons. Secret ideas are not the only motives that direct us. I would argue that we are directed by the mask we give these secret ideas. I know and recognize that the secret agents, the contemptuous ambitions, and hypocrisies in general are the origin of all our social gestures and our social behavior. Thus, they are also the origin of the infinite majority of works of art. But the fact that it is the original agent does not mean that it is necessarily the directive agent. Although these secret motives are only defeated momentarily, they are constantly being repressed and defeated inside us. They are defeated because the life of man among men creates that "fictitious" entity we all are socially, and that we need to become so that social organization remains plausible and flows, consolidating its moral normative intention.

And in fact, secret motives are not only repressed as a sacrifice to the social life; there are other individual reasons. We spend the greater part of our existence hiding from our earthly being. Our intelligence, after listening to the so-called "voice of our conscience," comes to acknowledge that our true self is in many ways an abject and horrifying thing. It is only after our intelligence faces up to that reality that we are able to defeat with patience and untiring attention all the vile, wretched, and repugnant things that our life and our behavior can produce.

The apparent agents then surge, the ailing ideas of presentation, not the original ideas anymore but rather ideas concerned with the final project whose destiny is really charitable and ennobling. Pure hypocrisy, the pure falsification of values, a noble and necessary hypocrisy composes and saves our works. It adds a tone to our artistic creations and channels them. Sincerity survives this hypocrisy regardless of whether or not Edgar A. Poe and Arnold Bennett desire its survival. These apparently insincere agents, masks of an original reality, form part of our total sincerity.

The secret ideas, the contemptuous agents, were seized. The intention of writing a novel, sculpting a statue, celebrating the feats of a captain were born from these secret ideas. But we will still come out screaming into the public plaza proclaiming that we question the suitability of the customs, creating beauty with capital words, and celebrating the hero. And we will repeat that same insincere hypocrisy when our conscience appears with its mirror during the darkest nights. But what work of art emerges then? *War and Peace* emerges, the *Venus* of the Medicis and *Camoes's Lusiads* emerge. And the sublime in all of this is that these works of art are really punishing traditions, creating Beauty, and celebrating heroes. The second idea, the mandate that excuses us, is the mask; she is the one that truly created them. And the mask itself was created.

And that is why Edgar A. Poe and Arnold Bennett were mistaken. Edgar A. Poe simply lied when he claimed that the unique and astute intention of creating praiseworthy art served as the origin for "The Raven" (". . . I mean that Beauty is the sole illegitimate province of the poem . . .); and he lied when he disclosed the more or less sagacious means from which he served himself to create the coldness and the inhumanity with which he invented the theme and the technical features of his marvelous poem. He forgot or, rather, he hid the analysis of the composition, all of which he placed into his experiences, his suffering, and his ideas; in sum, he hid everything that, in addition to the causes of the flesh, enters in a more determinate fashion into the amazingly complex phenomenon of creation. Edgar A. Poe provided the possible origin of his poem, but he took particular care to hide the associative and lyrical forces that guided him later, and which were, exclusively, the ones that made "The Raven" a generous source of beauty instead of a hypocritical and beautiful work of art.

When Arnold Bennett affirmed that only the desire to earn money and the vanity of seeing himself celebrated encouraged him to explore every literary form, he hid the fact that although these abject reasons might have been the origin of his works, the commotion, his creative imagination, experience, culture, and his vast intelligence immediately took over the construction of the books in the same way that the hypocrisy of the presented ideas fortified and enlarged them; and it ennobled them.

Neither Poe nor Bennett remembered to publish such confessions before letting their works become known. "The Raven" was already a triumph when Edgar A. Poe wrote *The Philosophy of Composition*. Arnold Bennett was universally recognized when he remembered to "scandalize" the British *pruderie* by telling them *The Truth about an Author*. Only the previous triumphs justify these outbursts of false sincerity.

And for all that, one proves that the hypocrites were not the Poe of the poems or the Bennett of the novels. But in their confessions, be it out of masochism, because of a sentimentalism inspired by the need for self-punishment, in the desire for scandal, or in the concealment of the total truth that they brought about, they were extremely hypocritical.

TRANSLATED BY JOSÉ MATOSANTOS

José Carlos Mariátegui

Peru

(1894–1930)

———◆◆◆◆———

Self-educated, and abandoned by his father at an early age, José Carlos Mariátegui began supporting his family at the age of fifteen. The first influential Marxist thinker in Latin America, he got his start in literary journalism in Lima. Although his original post at *La Prensa* was that of copyboy, he quickly became a respected journalist. At the age of twenty, Mariátegui shifted his focus to radical left-wing thought, and after cofounding *La Razón* he became an important figure in Peruvian labor politics. Following a stint in Europe, Mariátegui returned to Peru as an ardent socialist, published his first book, *Historia de la crisis mundial* (1925), and became the editor of *Claridad*. He was Peru's most famous leftist at the time and openly discussed his ideology in both his lectures and writings. Throughout the late 1920s, Mariátegui published *Amauta*, another Marxist magazine. (The name *Amauta*, that of the ancient Inca philosopher, would eventually be used by his disciples as Mariátegui's nickname.) Later he became integrally involved in proletarian solidarity movements and in the 1928 founding of the Peruvian Socialist Party. That year also saw the release of his most famous work, *Siete ensayos de interpretación de la realidad peruana*. Despite his ardent Marxism, because of his strong Catholic beliefs Mariátegui was considerably more flexible in his approach than were orthodox Communists. Since he was one of the first thinkers in Latin America to propose that religion should transcend the private spiritual life and enter the material world, he is sometimes considered a precursor of liberation theology. His political thought was also endorsed by the terrorist group Shining Path in the 1980s. In fact, its leader, Abimael Guzmán, known as Presidente Gonzalo, named Mao Tzedong and Mariátegui as his two undisputed inspirations. Written in Lima on 3 November 1926, the following manifesto illuminates Mariátegui's views on art and politics. The link between these two subjects is at the heart of the Latin American literary tradition, and few others have been able to articulate so successfully the challenge of bringing them together.

Art, Revolution, and Decadence

It is important to dispel with the utmost speed a misleading idea which is confusing some young artists. We must correct certain hasty definitions, and establish that not all new art is revolutionary, nor is it really new. Two spirits co-exist in the world at present, that of revolution and that of decadence. Only the former confers on a poem or painting the title new art.

We cannot accept as new, art which merely contributes a new technique. That would be flirting with the most fallacious of current illusions. No aesthetic can reduce art to a question of technique. New technique must also correspond to a new spirit. If not, the only things to change are the trappings, the setting. And a revolution in art is not satisfied with formal achievements.

Distinguishing between the two contemporary categories of artists is not easy. Decadence and revolution; just as the two co-exist in the same world, so they co-exist within the same individual. The artist's conscience is the arena for the struggle between the two spirits. This struggle is sometimes, almost always, beyond the comprehension of the artist himself. But one of the two spirits ultimately prevails. The other remains strangled in the arena.

The decadence of capitalist civilization is reflected in the atomization and dissolute nature of its art. In this crisis, art has above all lost its essential unity. Each of its principles, each of its elements, has asserted its autonomy. Secession is the most natural conclusion. Schools proliferate *ad infinitum* because no centrifugal forces exist.

But this anarchy, in which the spirit of bourgeois art dies, irreparably fragmented and broken, heralds a new order. It is the transition from dusk to dawn. In this crisis, the elements of a future art emerge separately. Cubism, Dadaism, Expressionism, etc., signal a crisis and herald a reconstruction at the same time. No single movement provides a formula, but all contribute (an element, a value, a principle) to its development.

The revolutionary nature of contemporary schools or trends does not lie in the creation of a new technique. Nor does it lie in the destruction of the old. It lies in the rejection, dismissal and ridicule of the bourgeois absolute. Art is always nourished, consciously or unconsciously—it's not important—by the absolute of its age. The contemporary artist's soul is, in the majority of cases, empty. The literature of decadence is literature with no absolute. But man can take no more than a few steps like that. He cannot march forward without a faith, because having no faith means having no goal. And marching without a goal is standing still. The artist who declares himself most exasperatedly skeptical and nihilistic is, generally, the one who most desperately needs a myth.

The Russian Futurists have embraced Communism, the Italian Futurists have embraced Fascism. Is there any better historical proof that artists cannot avoid political polarization? Massimo Bontempelli says that in 1920 he felt almost Communist and in 1923, the year of the march to Rome, he felt almost Fascist. Now he feels totally Fascist. Many people have made fun of Bontempelli for that confession. I defend him; I think he is sincere. The empty soul of poor Bontempelli has to accept the Myth which Mussolini lays on his altar. (The Italian avant-garde is convinced that Fascism is the Revolution.)

César Vallejo writes that, while Haya de La Torre thinks the *Divine Comedy* and *Don Quixote* have political undercurrents, Vicente Huidobro maintains that art is independent of politics. The causes and motives behind this assertion are so old-fashioned and invalid that I wouldn't ascribe it to an Ultraist poet, assuming Ultraist poets are capable of discussing politics, economics and religion. If, for Huidobro, politics is exclusively what goes on in the Palais Bourbon, we can clearly endow his art with all the autonomy he wishes. But the fact is that politics, for those of us who, as Unamuno says, see it as a religion, is the very fabric of history. In classical periods, or periods of supreme order, politics may merely be administration and trappings; in romantic periods and regimes in crisis, however, politics occupies the foreground.

This is evident in the conduct of Louis Aragon, André Breton and their fellow artists of the Surrealist Revolution—the best minds of the French avant-garde—as they march towards Communism. Drieu La Rochelle, so close to this state of mind when he wrote "Mesure de la France," and "Plainte contre l' Inconnu," could not follow them. But since he could not escape politics either, he declared himself vaguely Fascist and clearly reactionary.

In the Hispanic world, Ortega y Gasset is responsible for part of this misleading idea about new art. Since he could not distinguish between schools or trends, he could not distinguish, at least in modern art, between revolutionary elements and decadent elements. The author of *The Dehumanization of Art* did not define new art. Instead, he took as features of a revolution those which are typical of decadence. This led him to state, among other things, that "new inspiration is always, unfailingly, cosmic." His symptomological framework is, in general, correct; but his diagnosis is incomplete and mistaken.

Method is not enough. Technique is not enough. Despite his images and his modernity, Paul Morand is a product of decadence. A sense of dissoluteness pervades his literature. After flirting with Dadaism for a while, Jean Cocteau now gives us "Rappel à l'ordre."

It is important to clarify this matter, to dispel the very last misconceptions. The task is not easy. Many points are difficult to reconcile. Glimpses of decadence are frequently seen in the avant-garde even when, overcoming the subjectivism which sometimes infects it, they want to achieve truly revolutionary goals. Hidalgo, thinking of Lenin, says in a multidimensional poem, that the "Salome breasts" and "tomboy hairstyle" are the first steps towards the socialization of women. This should not surprise us. There are poets who think that the jazz band is a herald of the revolution.

Fortunately there are artists in the world, like Bernard Shaw, who are capable of understanding that "art cannot be great unless it provides an iconography for a living religion, but it cannot be completely objectionable either except when it imitates the iconography of a religion which has become superstition." This path seems to be the one taken by various new artists in French and other literature. The future will mock the naïve stupidity with which some critics of their time called them "new" and even "revolutionary."

TRANSLATED BY ANN WRIGHT

Ezequiel Martínez Estrada

Argentina
(1895–1964)

———◆◆◆◆◆———

Although he was born in rural Argentina, Ezequiel Martínez Estrada moved to Buenos Aires as a young child, which may help explain his fascination with the many facets of Argentine life. Eternally frustrated with the pattern of corruption and misfortunes in his beloved homeland, he grew especially bitter during the dictatorship of Juan Perón and remained a pessimistic observer until his death. A frequent contributor to *La Nación, Sur, Nosotros*, and other Argentine periodicals, in which his essayistic style was shaped, Martínez Estrada lived in Mexico and in Cuba, where he worked for the Casa de las Américas publishing house. Although his early efforts were in poetry, by 1929 he had shifted his energy toward analytical essays on Argentine culture. Despite his solitary nature, he was a good friend of fellow writers Horacio Quiroga, Leopoldo Lugones, and Victoria Ocampo. In *X-Rays of the Pampa* (1933), Martínez Estrada had already begun to explore the unhealthy historical, social, and psychological aspects of his homeland. Other books of his are *La cabeza de Goliath* (1940) and *Muerte y transfiguración de Martín Fierro* (1948). His writings were strongly influenced by Freud, Nietzsche, and other thinkers who shared an interest in the subconscious and the dark forces that drive mankind. A determinist, he viewed Argentina as a polarized society that could not rid itself of its barbarism or restrain its desire to establish a "higher culture." Martínez Estrada continued to teach and publish in Buenos Aires, and by his death he had produced twenty-eight essay collections and over three hundred journalistic pieces. "Thoreau," included in *En torno a Kafka* (1966), allows Martínez Estrada to underscore the relevance of the New England philosopher in the context of the Southern Hemisphere.

Thoreau

In general, sensible people (I mean good people who easily become alarmed at the remote threat of imaginary dangers) have considered it a kindness to humanity to caution against true benefactors. Until the balance sheet is drawn up, quite a long time from now, no one will know with certainty who has worked for God and who for the Devil. A man of lucid intelligence and a free spirit, Henry David Thoreau quickly perceived in his youth "that there is no uglier odor than that which is given off by

127

corrupted goodness." From that moment he took sides, if not for evil, then for wild nature and for the wild life that he preserved in his heart.

I do not pretend to be able to condense his thought, which he condensed in a few pages, into a few words. But I think that I can assert that one of his axioms was that if progress in the moral and social order is so slow and difficult, compared to what has been realized in the material world, it must be due, among other things, to the intervention of those agents of good will who serve in the enemy ranks.

That is very often the case: the case of someone, like Orlando, who in the blindness of battle, attacks his companions which is the same as fighting for the other side. Thoreau resolved to take sides for himself, for his conscience, at the risk of being denounced as a disturber of an order which is thought to be divine in the worldly order. Since he had more than enough ability to take care of his own defense, he left judgment up to Time, like Aeschylus. Time is proving him right, even though his case is lost. Mechanical civilization is a matter of money and not of conscience.

His adventure of living among friends who adhered to the strictest rules of philosophical and social orthodoxy proves to us, thank God, that foolish or paradoxical people, heretics or whatever one wants to call them, are the indispensable counterbalance. They fight, almost always risking their well-being and life, in order to clear away the primary world in which the inhabitant of large cosmopolitan centers lives contentedly. With only the precepts of the very ancient philosophers of the forest, without any political sociology, Thoreau not only thought paradoxes of this sort but also put them into practice, living according to them. Expressed in another way, he was one of those men who become rarer every day, one who decided to take upon himself the guilt of the inhabitants of the comfortable western world, persisting in enriching and embellishing the plot of land which he had the luck to inhabit.

He built his house, lived from what he produced and—in plain language—on departing, he left his land a little cleaner, more ordered and more prosperous than he had found it. He belonged to the most closed and exclusive environment of the United States: to the State of Massachusetts, to the area of Concord, to the municipality of Boston, to Harvard University and to the *petit bourgeoisie*, a stronghold of prejudices and conventionalism. He studied at and graduated from Harvard and was a private teacher by vocation as well as a pencil-maker by necessity. At a certain peak in his life while still quite young—he lived for forty-five years, from 1817 to 1862—he abandoned his family and scholarly attire and retired to the shores of Walden Pond. There he built a long and narrow cabin, with two windows and a door; he furnished it with a table, two chairs and a cot, all constructed by his own hands, using an adze which was loaned him and some rustic tool of his own. For two years he lived on what he produced in his garden: vegetables, a few fruits and many beans from whose abundance he carried on a business well accounted for in cents and fractions of a cent. After that experience and the surprise that man can live on a tenth of what he produces from almost any unspecialized labor, Thoreau formulated his own economic theory, which is still ignored by the specialists; namely, that man should only work a couple of weeks each year and dedicate the rest of his time to contemplation, meditation and study which—even though there is no exercise more noble or more necessary than manual labor—is what best suits humanity.

On some Sundays, friends and admirers, people who were curious and inclined toward extravagance, would come to visit him, and he received them with no other ceremony than to have them enter his cabin. In this he was more courteous than Diogenes. These were the years of his most valuable literary production, when he collected the most diverse knowledge: agronomy, zoology and botany, oriental philosophy, poetry and all those useless disciplines which defied the authentic Yankee spirit that abounded everywhere. In a way that no one had up until then, he observed nature in order to understand it and not in order to know it—with wisdom and passion. He loved nature with the heart of a satyr, of a forest animal, and he left behind some valuable suggestions for travelers who want to save their souls in this world without competing for the haunts of other creatures. To save his soul in life and also after death: "I become wilder every day," he wrote, "as if I ate raw meat. My domesticity is no more than the relaxation of my indomitability. I dream of contemplating summer and winter with a free gaze from somewhere else, from the side of some other mountain."

He was, I mean to say, a moralist and a philosopher who preached the conformity of man with nature, of the known with the unknown and the respect for conscience and its imperatives. A catechism as simple as Antigone's and at the same time as astute as Lao Tse's. In this passion for nature and what is natural he was a disciple of Rousseau and a teacher of Tolstoy, although we should look for Thoreau's teachers in China and in India, above all in the holy books—the *Bhagavad Gita*, most of all. To explain what his originality consists of and what his value is as a naturalist and a philosopher of the wild without any direct connections would take a lot of time. But it may be enough for me to say that something happened to Thoreau which is similar to what happened to our William Henry Hudson, who was a naturalist and a writer like many and like no one else. Would it make any sense if I said that he thought and felt—let's suppose—as a squirrel or a marmot might if it possessed human wisdom? His philosophy is that of a child of nature, much more profound, wilder and finer than Jean Jacques; that of a pantheist, if you want, that of a person who worships what is divine more than the divinity. Certainly not a rustic man; but, rather, an exquisite one in the manner of untouched nature: "In the wildest nature there exists not only the material of the most cultivated life and a type of anticipation of the final outcome, but also a refinement greater than man can ever reach."

Because he belonged to an exotic species he has been pinned down on many taxonomists' boards: anarchist, transcendentalist, theosophist, moralist, misogynist, atheist, mystic, panpsychist. Actually, there was a little of all of these in him and of the many other definitions from the botanical or zoological nomenclature of free thought—all of whose species are unclassifiable—definitions which would fit him well with some adjustment. What no one can accuse him of is trying to win by cheating in life, as many other forest-philosophers and sociologists of slavery did: of bending his head before the despot or preaching a creed in which he did not believe or of which he believed that one should not believe. It has never occurred to me to ask about his relatives, his ancestors or his offspring. We should content ourselves with him alone.

Thoreau is one of those men of whom we should not ask whether he was right or wrong, whether or not his doctrine is valuable for progress and civilization. There are questions that ought not to be asked, not even of bus drivers who more or less know which way they are going and where they are taking us. In this journey, which we are taking and whose itinerary Thoreau knew very well, things other than the route and the destination are important. We have no yardstick to measure it, no scales to weigh it nor abacus to count it. My feeling is that only in a world that has sealed off the vigorous bright fountains of life, in a society that has put a price on all that man does and dreams, can Thoreau be prosecuted and brought before a court of appeals. And so he has been, by many segments of public opinion—but who will be the prosecutor?

His most dangerous thesis, which has caused a true revolution in the souls and in the tentacular empires—perhaps even the French Revolution has not had such consequence—is that of *On Civil Disobedience*, a pamphlet of thirty-five pages. There is nothing more placid and silent, more powerful and effective than persisting in the truth. Tolstoy received this apocalypse as a chrism and transmitted it to Gandhi, who dispersed it over the face of the earth, as an insurmountable, infinite power of gentleness and peace. It is the same path but dramatically opposed to that of violence to the point of death: docility to the death. Simply, one of the paradoxes of Lao Tse.

This simple and extraordinary idea or revelation was born in a jail—this is the danger of jails—Thoreau being a prisoner for having refused to pay the treasury a tax of one dollar for the war in Mexico. He established the legally and morally irrefutable principle that the State can collect taxes for public services, including free education, but not for the mass extermination of human beings. In such a case the citizen can resist the levy, and, if he is forced, can remain quiet, neither resisting nor paying. It is the "satyagraha," the song of the distaff of liberty, of Mahatma Gandhi. But this is the figure of Thoreau brought down to the political level of his philosophy of the sacred duties of man to himself and to his society, the principal article of the transcendentalist credo whose two eminent apostles were Thoreau and his close friend Emerson.

His love of the Creation at its height—of animals and plants—bordered on devotion and ecstasy. And because that devotion was pure and free from any religious intentions or imperative obligation of the creature to the Creator, it approached reverential wisdom. I do not know if I should excuse myself for presenting him as an example worthy of being understood and loved. My deep and sincere conviction is to do so; and since our younger generation already knows enough about politics and economics, what better advice is there than that of a purifying vacation at Walden Pond? A rest in that sanctuary where the daylight is so radiant that it illuminates even the most hidden recesses of the soul.

TRANSLATED BY GREGORY KOLOVAKOS

Concha Meléndez

Puerto Rico

(1895–1984)

———•◦•◦•———

Recognized as one of the preeminent figures in Puerto Rican literature, Concha Meléndez devoted her life to scholarship, teaching, and literature. Educated at the University of Puerto Rico, Columbia University, and the Universidad Nacional Autónoma de México, Meléndez's diverse studies and poetry earned her the Puerto Rican Woman of the Year Award in 1971. She received numerous literary prizes from the Institute of Puerto Rican Culture, as well as the Orden Andrés Bello from the Venezuelan government and an honorary doctorate from Dowling College in Long Island, New York. Some of her most important critical work can be found in *La novela indianista en hispanoamérica: 1882–1889* (1934), *Pablo Neruda: Vida y obra* (1936), *Figuración de Puerto Rico y otros ensayos* (1958), *Personas y libros* (1970), *La literatura de ficción en Puerto Rico* (1971), and *Poetas hispanoamericanos diversos* (1971), which includes an excellent piece on Pablo Neruda. "A Visit to the Alphonsine Chapel," sparked by the reading of an essay collection by Carlos Fuentes, is a tribute to the vision and wisdom of Alfonso Reyes and to Mexican culture as a whole. Written in Santurce, Puerto Rico, on 8 December 1970, the essay was published a year later in *Revista de ficción de Puerto Rico*.

A Visit to the Alphonsine Chapel

I

I've just finished reading a book of essays by Carlos Fuentes: *Casa con dos puertas*.* The reading, upon my return from Mexico after having fulfilled my loyal obligation to the memory of Amado Nervo on the centennial of his birth, was the result of serendipity, a word that surely pleases the author of *Casa con dos puertas*, who will approve of the observant wisdom of the Princes of Serendip.

One September morning, I went to the Alphonsine Chapel at 122 Benjamin Hill Street. I had dreamed about that visit for more than twenty years, ever since my teacher and friend wrote to me saying that he had a

———

*Joaquín Mortiz, Mexico, 1970.

house built so that he could live among his books. I prepared to return to Mexico, the city of my exhausting studies at the Universidad Nacional Autónoma de México and experiences in archaeology, art, and Americanism that affected and enriched me forever.

I prepared and promised. . . . I could not keep my promise when Alfonso Reyes was alive in life. That morning I would keep my promise by feeling he was alive in death. But what does all of this have to do with the Princes of Serendip? The three young Persians would orient their lives according to the unexpected that presented itself to them. And the unexpected was "sure chance," which would open the path for something significant and beneficent in the development of their adventures.

I was talking to Alicia Reyes, the Tikis who loved the old man very much and now protects the reason for that love by taking care of his books, keeping alive the quiet dialogue their owner maintained with them through persistent visits. I was accompanied by Ernesto Mejía Sánchez, who revises and prologizes his teacher's unpublished works—the same Mejía Sánchez who, besides having followed his lead in El Colegio de México, learned from him the art of friendship in its finest and noblest gestures.

I had looked at his collection of books and had seen part of his unpublished work in the drawers near his writing desk. I was saying good-bye when an expressive elderly, pleasant, man arrived. Alicia made the introductions, and when I told him that I had seen Alfonso Reyes only once, in Rio de Janeiro, when he was Mexico's ambassador to Brazil, he told me: "I was Alfonso Reyes's secretary. I was a diplomat for many years." And with obvious satisfaction, he added: "I'm the father of Carlos Fuentes, who just published a book of essays: *Casa con dos puertas*. I think this book surpasses all his essay work up till now." The serendipity of this encounter sent me to the university bookstore the next day. I brought the book with me.

In it I found an essay on Alfonso Reyes that illustrates how his work "is a response to the social and political fatalism of Mexico." The last paragraph gives the great Mexican the endurance necessary in the future of his town. Alfonso Reyes did not stop stoking the fire of the intelligence with which he lived, wrote, and created his world; he was an educator for his town and all towns, deeply rooted "in projects of will and intelligence."

But in addition, *Casa con dos puertas* opens wide one of them in order to present, for our reflection, three excellent essays on the novel, not the present-day novel, which is renowned in Hispanic America among our critics and readers, but novels from an earlier time: "The Novel as Appreciation: Jane Austen," "The Novel as Symbol: Herman Melville," and "The Novel as Tragedy: William Faulkner."

This examination of the novel "using three methods of narration" ends with an appendix that confirms "the death and resurrection of the novel," placing the resurrection in a discovery: "During the sixties, the novelists and their readers discovered that, above all, the novel is a verbal structure."

II

If the novelists and their Hispanic American readers discovered the novel as a verbal structure in the sixties, the discovery had been gaining momentum in the areas that I'm most familiar with, English and North American criticism of 1948. I refer to the year because that was when I became aware of the work of a new literary foundation, the School of Letters, which met during the summers, first at Kenyon College, Ohio, and later at Indiana University. I was fortunate to study at the School of Letters during the summer of 1949, where I had been preceded by Nilita Vientós Gastón in 1948. The organization was composed of a president, three honorary members—F. O. Matthiessen, John Crowe Ransom, and Lionel Trilling—and twenty-two members, almost all of them valuable critics of the novel, poetry, and theater. Among them were Richard Blackmur, Robert Penn Warren, Eric Bentley, William Empson, Herbert Read, Mark Schorer, Allen Tate, and René Wellek.

No one did any research while studying at the School of Letters; the classes were critical discussions of works that had been read, literary criticism writing exercises, weekly forums, and conferences conducted by the professors in the school's auditorium. At the bookstore, one could buy literary criticism from every time period, among them anthologies of criticism like *The Importance of Scrutiny*, by Eric Bentley, and *Criticism: The Foundations of Modern Literary Judgment*, by Mark Schorer.

I selected the following study courses: "The Techniques of the Novel," by Mark Schorer; "Tolstoy and Dostoyevsky," by Philip Rahv; and "The English Lyric," by Yvor Winters. The course I followed with the most interest, the one that opened up for me new perspectives in the interpretation of the novel, was the course taught by Mark Schorer. His anthology, *The Story: A Critical Anthology*, containing critical analyses of stories, was very useful to me in the preparation of my own book of criticism, *El arte del cuento en Puerto Rico*. The course, "The Techniques of the Novel," included a critical analysis of *Emma*, by Jane Austen; *The Portrait of a Lady*, by Henry James; *Middlemarch: A Study of Provincial Life*, by George Eliot; *Hard Times*, by Dickens; and *Sons and Lovers*, by D. H. Lawrence.

I used the experience I gained at the School of Letters when I returned to the University of Puerto Rico, where in 1950 I taught a new course called "Techniques of the Hispanic American Novel." The class became filled with students and teachers, among them Ciro Alegría, who was teaching Hispanic American literature as a visiting professor. One day as he was leaving class he told me: "In Hispanic America, novelists write their novels any way they desire." It was a comment that reminded me of Count Keyserling, and I told him so. But the "desire" in him led him to study Balzac, Thomas Mann, and Faulkner. According to Carlos Fuentes, "desire" is now a verbal exploration, "visual, aesthetic, and sonorous, opening itself to the universality of linguistic structures."

My course began with the study of the technique used in *María: A South American Romance* by Jorge Isaacs, which in no way should be cast aside, because "all the scholars in Latin America have been walking along Isaac's idyllic paths with tears in their eyes," as one very intelligent critic, Luis Harss, wrote in his book *Into the Mainstream*.

The result of our study of Jorge Isaacs's novel at that time was my essay "El arte de Jorge Isaacs en 'María,' " which reveals interesting impressionistic scenes, effects of light which lend themselves to cinematography, the literary sentiment of the voice, the use of time in the old recourse of settings, and the psychological effect of an absence of three days on the protagonists.

III

Although it does not appear so, the two preceding parts of this essay are the introduction to a review of the novel *El fuego y su aire* by Enrique A. Laguerre.* In it, Laguerre presents the Puerto Rican situation, which is dragging along the vicissitudes of its history, the confusion of its circumstances, its increasingly complex problems—including immigration to New York—viewed with bitterness, irony, despair, and implacable social criticism.

The kindled fire in the novelist, whose air caused it to suddenly blaze into a first novel, has continued to burn in a vocation sustained by an eagerness for perfection. For years he explores his subject matter and, upon applying the technical methods needed to create the novel, discovers the theme those methods will reveal to the reader: spiritual and egoistical deterioration and the fatal distraction of that which is false with its sequence of vice and death.

The integration of the materials supporting the subject matter occurs by inventing the characters and placing them in a plot that develops by way of symbols, the repetition of memories of determinant events in the characters' destiny, and alternating points of view between the narrator in third person and the character who explains his circumstances in a stream of consciousness. This occurs without any transition in the progress of the entire novel.

---

*Losada, Buenos Aires, 1970.

El fuego y su aire departs from the fluctuating rhythm of the historic moment in which we live that disturbs "a juvenile conscience in crisis." These are words from *La llamarada*, Laguerre's first novel, written in 1935. They seem to be modern-day words. The fluctuating rhythm of the historic moment has not changed in 1970 in *El fuego y su aire* but has grown in urgency and seriousness of death. Now, the social problems of the sugar cane plantation seem to be substituted with real political problems, moral deterioration in the opulent urban life, the lives of the immigrants in New York, the agony of ancient class prejudices, the invasion of artificial paradises, and, above all, the danger of the loss of Puerto Rican identity intensified in the protagonist, Pedro José. The symbolism of Pedro José as a seeker of his identity allows the other characters also to reveal themselves as symbols of different sentiments and attitudes, but is unsuccessful in those who reject general alienation. In it move lifeless beings, already without fire or air, victims of the remoteness from what they should have been.

IV

To arrive at the presentation of such a complex world, Laguerre used his style of delving deeply behind appearances, characterization, symbolism, and the use of words as an instrument without the old limitations that the distinction between literary language and everyday language would raise with walls of artifice.

These methods start to become accentuated in the novel *La ceiba en el tiesto* and begin to approach the atmosphere of *El fuego y su aire* in *El laberinto* and *Cauce sin río*. Here the integration of the diverse elements is realized all at once with an obvious sense of structure. With intense resonance, this is first achieved with the title that we have identified as a symbol and two others, which appear spaced throughout the course of the novel: the octopus, which eats its own tentacles, and the carrier pigeon, which is eaten by its owner in the middle of the jungle.

Laguerre has used this recourse in the structure of meaning of his previous novels: *La ceiba en el tiesto, La resaca,* and *El laberinto*. In none of his other novels does the recurrent symbolic title weave the structure of meaning with more intentional depth than in *El fuego y su aire*. This is insinuated with the quotation in the first chapter: "Candles without wicks." The adolescent Pedro José's own formulated thoughts are inserted in the narration, which begins in the third person, without any transition, a technique that persists in those two movements, narrator–character, throughout the entire novel.

A short paragraph explains the circumstances: Pedro José is going to be twenty years old; he has lived in a hospice for the mentally retarded since he was eight years old; feels fine in this world, but is removed from there by the musical talent Father Fabiano discovers he has, and since the priest wants to develop the music school, he offers to help him.

He couldn't explain how he found himself cold and hungry at the entrance of the hospice's chapel in this unfamiliar city. His first words had been "Puerto Rico." He was two years old before he started talking and couldn't describe the first years of his childhood, "an abstract picture painted with a few figurative strokes." The candles without wicks of this first chapter allude to Pedro José's fire in the symbol "fire and its air." The child would play by lighting the candle stubs that his little Dominican friend, Ulises Pichardo, who was in school near the hospice, would find for him.

The title of the novel joins the entire narration in a structural continuity. The process of the search for identity begins when Antoñón, the hospice servant, tells Pedro José that he is as quiet as an oyster. It was then that the jigsaw puzzle Pedro José composed in the end sprang forth in him in an imaginary vision: sails on the tropical sea, landscape of palms, to which he later added a window open to the sun. That picture lights up and shuts off repeatedly throughout the novel, and together with other similar recurrences, sustains the structural thread of events.

V

The barracuda as a symbol in the problem of liberty in *El ceiba en el tiesto* is intentionally related to the neurotic octopus that eats its own tentacles in *El fuego y su aire*. But here the meaning expands to "the living image of man's actual insanity," who, when his ambitions fail him, turns on himself in a dangerous, suicidal manner.

The most repeated symbol in social criticism is the carrier pigeon that is eaten by its own master in the middle of the jungle, burying himself in the quagmire of that which is ignoble, of materialistic and inhuman alienation. It appears in the mouth of Lori, the young and rich heiress who notices the poor surroundings that suffocate her, that make her feel lonely and unsatisfied in her artificial home, filled with luxurious objects lacking any spiritual meaning. She happens to think about Oscar Martín, the "enterprising" young man her mother wants her to marry. Lori rejects him because she sees in him "the kind of man who when he gets lost in the jungle and becomes hungry doesn't object to eating the carrier pigeon." At this moment, the author, according to his consistent point-of-view technique, inserts Lori's stream of consciousness: "In Puerto Rico, all— businessmen, professionals, and politicians, all of them—eat the carrier pigeon when they become hungry. We only want to satisfy physical hunger."

Therefore, the carrier pigeon is the flapping of spiritual hunger stifled by the zealousness to satisfy physical hunger. Not exempt from that fatal disablement in Lori's stream of consciousness are the priests who would also commit the unforgivable sin. From this point on, the symbol appears in other passages of the novel. It is Lori herself, deathly ill, who repeats it. The narrator remembers it when friends of Lori, Elda Astol and Adalberto Linares, visit Lori's parents, who distressingly comment about the end of their world. It's a dismal memory: they all committed the unforgivable sin and "perished trapped in the labyrinth of the jungle."

Between the priesthood, "with the purpose of working next to the needy in front of the baronage in any part of the world," or joining "any group in any part of the world who would also be actively opposing the abuses of the powerful cartels," Pedro José decides to follow the second path. In La Parguera, he disappears after the inquiry into his secret identity, joining an invasion against the Dominican dictatorship. In some way, that is how he thought he would also avenge the death of his most faithful friend from his years at the hospice until his return to his island, Ulises Pichardo.

The novel ends with the following words, which destroy the symbolic structure in a final exclamation: "It wasn't known, no, if he fell on the sandbar or if he managed to reach the mountain. After all, what did it matter? He had decided to defy suffocation; he was looking for air with which to stoke his fire."

VI

Do all fires go out because there isn't any air? Are the dogs of Actaeon on the loose? Is there no longer anyone who will take care of and protect their carrier pigeon? Is it afternoon everywhere, as Adalberto Linares, the sociology professor, said to Lori, aware of his surroundings and declaring himself defenseless at this hour of the world? Is it the convulsions of today's Christianity, as Pedro José says, that enlarge the edge of apocalyptic shadows?

As a teacher of a different concept of the Christianity that Pedro José was taught at the hospice, I know "a resurrection will follow" the agony that commentary alludes to. There are prominent extremes of pessimism in *El fuego y su aire*: in the presentation of the situations and a few insistences in those situations which could be eliminated without losing the efficacy of the necessary statement of caution against what we shouldn't ignore.

A much older part of humanity knows that it is much more than a physical body. With the astronauts, we've seen our planet from the moon's perspective. From there we've seen a world, a humanity, a society. That perspective foretells the passage of revolution to a renovated concept of evolution. Above all, from within, it is trying to express the love and understanding that attracts love and understanding.

There is a peremptory calling within us to experience a transformation that will place us in nobility and piousness. It is like that for everyone. We know that weapons are symbols that attract and justify their use. And that the discussions about disarmament among the most powerful armed towns in the land are winds of peace that announce the growth of the fire of universal love.

The world in Laguerre's novel contains the dogs of Actaeon, the destructive activity of its own faults. That activity allows itself to be felt anywhere that world exists in the land. In order for man to live in the four-dimensional universe that science glimpses today, he would have to express abilities equivalent to the expansion of his conscience.

Teilhard de Chardin warns that to place our hopes in a social order achieved by external violence is to give up all hope of leading the spirit of the land to its destiny. But he adds that the energy of humans and the universe are expressions of an infallible and irresistible movement that will finally arrive at the natural completion of evolution. A new age is approaching "in which the world will break its chains and surrender to the power of its internal affinities."

TRANSLATED BY HARRY MORALES

Samuel Ramos

Mexico

(1897–1959)

———◆◆◆◆———

Known as the first modern student of the Mexican identity, Ramos pursued the study of medicine, psychology, and philosophy during the early stages of his career. After moving to Mexico City, he abandoned medicine and became heavily involved in the city's intellectual community. In Mexico City, Ramos came into contact with established figures such as Antonio Caso, José Vasconcelos, and Pedro Henríquez Ureña. By 1925 he had inherited the editorship of *La Antorcha* from Vasconcelos and had taught at the National Preparatory School. He also contributed to *Exámen* and *Contemporáneos*. Ramos entered Mexico's intellectual arena at a crucial juncture, when scholars were losing interest in both positivist philosophy and the study of intuitive action. As a result, he and other Mexican intellectuals became interested in the cultural existentialism of European philosophers such as the Spanish philosopher José Ortega y Gasset. Ramos stressed the importance of reason in human acts. His books include *Diego Rivera* (1935), *Más allá de la moral de Kant* (1938), and *Hacia un nuevo humanismo* (1940). But his crowning achievement, which includes "The Use of Thought," is *Profile of Man and Culture in Mexico* (1934), a study of the Mexican identity from a psychoanalytic perspective. His main subject of discussion is *el pelado*, a lower-class street person in Mexico whose language and manners were, in the essayist's eyes, "symptomatic of the nation's inferiority complex." Often Ramos falls into easy stereotyping; nevertheless, his book was highly influential. In fact, there is no doubt that without it Octavio Paz's slim volume *The Labyrinth of Solitude* (1950), the most probing analysis of the Mexican mind, would not have been possible.

The Use of Thought

Thinking is not a luxury, but rather a vital necessity of man. Thought is born of life and turns to life qualities that broaden its horizons and give it depth. By virtue of thought, life is not only present but past and future as well. Thought is the possibility of making the present benefit by recollecting past experience; at the same time it is the instrument for anticipating the future. But, as far as intelligence and comprehension are concerned, thought is above all a window to the world through which we communicate with men and things. It is therefore our means to spiritual relationship with society and the world, and it allows us to determine our place in life. Thanks to knowledge, we are not lost on our march through existence; only thus can we discover which road to travel. But the use of intelligence is, unfortunately, neither an easy nor a secure task; it is fraught with difficulties and constantly exposed to error.

If in the beginning, as Descartes thought, all men are equally endowed with intelligence, it does not follow that all know equally well how to apply it, and many are deprived of its benefits. One might add that some men are reluctant to use intelligence, possibly because they have not been taught its potentialities, or because their temperament restrains them. We should remember that intelligence does not have equal preponderance over other psychic forces (such as will and sentiment) in every race. In some races will is the guiding force in life; in others, sentiment; in still others, intelligence or reason. All have heard the well-known opinion that the Hispanic race to which we belong has not distinguished itself in history by the products of its thought; by implication, then, it is an unintelligent race. But the truth is that a quite different spiritual force has assumed the direction of life: sentiment, or more precisely, passion. Intelligence is there, but subordinated, enslaved by other more potent drives which infringe upon it and impede its movements. This, at least, seems to be the case with Mexicans. The contact I have had with a large number of young people at the University convinces me that our race is well endowed with intelligence. The young Mexican who has not yet suffered the mental deformations that life produces can make intelligence work freely, and just as well, I believe, as that of any of the "superior" races.

The work of some thinkers and scientists shows, moreover, that our intelligence is not inferior to that of the Europeans. But if this fact is to constitute the rule rather than the exception, there will have to be a change in circumstances, which today are scarcely conducive to intellectual activity. Young countries must first organize and develop their material existence in order to attend later to less pressing needs. Deep meditation and abstract thought are fruits of a liberation which is possible only when the elementary problems of life have been solved.

This does not mean that one can actually live without thinking. Only at the cost of lowering life to the most abject level would such an existence be possible. Without thought, man would vegetate in the obscurity of instinct and scarcely surpass the level of animal existence. In justice to our race we should recognize that ideas have played a role of considerable importance in our history, to the extent that if criticism is deserved it is due to the frequent preference of ideas to everything else. Utopianism is no more than an exaggerated rationalism, or the innocent assumption that reality submits to the dictates of reason.

If in Mexico, then, there exists some capacity for thought, it has yet to be effectively developed and disciplined. The primary cause of the exercise and development of intelligence is the urge to know the truth about all that is problematical in life. It is not easy to submit oneself continuously to truth, because truth is not always pleasant, nor does it answer to the most intimate demands of the will. There are accordingly many individuals who deceive themselves, declaring to be true that which they would like to be true. Dignified exercise of the intelligence requires effort, sometimes painful, and intellectual and moral discipline. The thinking person must protect not only his learning process, but also his entire spirit, against the many subjective influences that will result from his inquiries. No one ignores the fact that this self-criticism is extremely difficult to practice. That is why veracity is considered a virtue of great worth. Are there many truthful people in Mexico? I should like the reader to answer this question for himself, relying on his own experience and discretion.

I limit myself to pointing out how readily ideas and theories imported from Europe are accepted in Mexico without any criticism whatsoever; this betrays a minimal effort and idleness of spirit. I wonder if our tendency to imitate, especially in philosophy, is not really idleness in disguise. Aside from all these circumstances that weaken thought, one cannot ignore the fact that truth has not, by any means, been indispensable to our social and political existence. Our national life is ensnared in a thick web of deceptive appearances and conventional lies which are deemed essential to its sustenance. Truth is relegated to the category of an undesirable object.

In spite of all this I still believe that the cultivation of thought and reflection in every activity is an urgent necessity in Mexico. It seems to me that many abortive projects, many errors and deviations, are due not to evil intent but to a lack of reflection, to an insufficient and inadequate use of intelligence. I do not mean to say that talent is lacking; there is simply an erroneous application of it. If in using our talent we fail to be objective and to direct it toward precise objectives, its efficiency will be nullified.

For some time I have wanted to show that the only legitimate course in Mexico is to think as Mexicans. This must seem like a trivial and platitudinous affirmation; but in our country it is a necessary one, because we often talk as if we were foreigners, far removed from our spiritual and physical surroundings. All thought must be based on the assumption that we are Mexicans and have to see the world in our own perspective, as the logical consequence of our geographic destiny. It naturally follows that the object or objects of our thought should be those right around us. Seeking knowledge in the world at large, we shall have to see it through the particular circumstance of our little Mexican world. It would be a mistake to interpret these ideas as the mere result of narrow-minded nationalism. It is rather a question of ideas which have a philosophical motivation. Only the man who can see the world about him in his own perspective has vital thought. Leibnitz said that every individual reflects the world in his own way. This, however, does not mean that there are many truths, but one only. It is logical to suppose that concerning any one object no more than one truth can exist, for if there are many, none is *truth*. A spherical segment seen from one side is concave, from the other, convex. Therefore, two individuals who see this object from opposite points will have two different views of it; each will be partial, but within this limitation they will each see the truth.

By disciplined action, Mexico needs to cultivate an authentic style of national thought, and its truth or context of truths, just as other countries have done. As long as this is missing we will be vulnerable to strange ideas which, having nothing to do with our needs, will eventually deform our national character and create problems still more serious than those now at hand. I believe that all men in our country who can think must take the responsibility for withdrawing—though it be only momentarily—from the whirlwind of life, so as to explore objectively the various realms of Mexican reality. Great regions of this reality are entirely unknown; they have not yet been formulated in concepts. It seems to me that the tasks awaiting our consideration are essentially two: 1) What is each aspect of Mexican existence really like? 2) What should it be like, within the limits of possibility? The most concrete and detailed definition of problems to be solved, that is, the statement of Mexican problems, is a preliminary theme, and perhaps the most difficult one to study. We'll postpone for a while our attempt to define in precise formulas any of the basic problems of Mexico.

TRANSLATED BY PETER G. EARLE

Jorge Mañach Robato

Cuba

(1898–1961)

———•◦•◦•———

Born in the province of Las Villas, Cuba, Jorge Mañach Robato engaged in both politics and literature with a remarkable passion. During the 1940s he served as Cuba's secretary of state and as a senator in the Cuban congress, but he was also considered by many to be the best Cuban essayist, he was the central theoretician of Cuba's vanguard movement. In 1923, Mañach Robato joined a group of young Cuban intellectuals, *Grupo Minorista*, and began to address Cuba's cultural and political problems through his writings. By 1927 he and four other intellectuals had founded *Revista de Avance*, for which notable Spanish and Latin American writers such as Miguel de Unamuno, Américo Castro, Eugenio D'Ors, Jaime Torres Bodet, César Vallejo, and Miguel Angel Asturias wrote numerous articles. His most famous work is *Martí, Apostle of Freedom* (1933), which is still considered the best biography of José Martí. He is also well known for his *Indagación del choteo* (1928), a study of Cuban humor. Mañach Robato received numerous honors outside Cuba and was elected to the Royal Academy of the Spanish Language. The following essay, "America's Quixotic Character," is part of his book *Examen del Quijotismo* (1950).

America's Quixotic Character

Life is for living. . . . We can't wait until the mysteries have been resolved, until every pathway of the ideal we carry within us has been illuminated. If we are surrounded by gloom, we must show the way with some provisional light. And there they are, our new nations, longing for their destiny, that double set of values that seem to issue from Don Quixote and Sancho. Toward whom should we lean?

We Latin Americans inherit through our blood all that is naturally present in the quixotic character, and no small amount of its history. Strip from this man the offspring of that progeny, which in our lands other races and a partially new one had to add, and we shall see with far greater clarity our true psychological and moral face where the Spanish features have lost much of their prominence and integrity only to gain a greater flexibility. The early American-born Spaniard retained his rugged individualism but already lacked that combative willpower; he was quick-witted and imaginative but already somewhat skeptical, sensitive when it came to honor but now with an obliging and decorative quality. His conscience adjusted itself to sensuality and his religion to ritual. Moreover, America's open space, the exclusion of dramatic compromise at the level of the flow of ideas, permitted him to go about forging an unfettered and even frivolous soul, a mentality receptive to experience and a range of ideas. Nevertheless, at heart, he was still the grandson of Don Alonso Quijano, able to produce a small quixote at the slightest provocation. . . .

With the Conquest and the colonial period, we also acquired impulses and social conditions that to a certain extent conspired to preserve our quixotic qualities. One writer recently filled an entire book to demonstrate that the conquest of America was a "chivalric enterprise." The exploits and exploitation of the conquistadors weave together a kind of quixotic temperament that is both barbaric and magnificent. It is born of a geographical faith nourished by millenarian utopias and insistent greed; it is encouraged by an arrogant confidence in its own abilities when faced with obstacles that to any sensible disposition would seem invincible in the light of such meager resources. That limited force, potentially effective to fabulous degrees of audacity and resistance, merges with the cross and the sword, the spirit of the Middle Ages and the vigorous humanism of the Renaissance. But it collapses in a violent struggle of peculiarities, and the imposition of the will works—in the name of a higher redemption (that of the soul)—against the weak Indian, taken to be the victim of evil sorcerers. The quixotic nature reversed. Its efforts do not turn out to be ineffectual, for it is attended by the entire weight of its historic era, and rather than opposing reality, the quixotic character works in reality's favor. The greatest civilization invariably triumphs over the elementary and sluggish one. That compound of quixotic and Sanchoesque qualities, turned barbarous by their own irresponsible remoteness, attempts to govern the great promised isle. It does not give birth to the all-for-sale rule as prescribed by Don Quixote, but rather an empire of the instincts in hypocritical forms— the greed and suspicion of a Sancho who would only have undergone a superficial quixotry.

Thus we Latin Americans inherit all of this, the natural provocation and the historical stamp. And we have taken pleasure in it and suffered from it to the extent permitted by a new physical environment. When the momentum of the Conquest was spent, the challenge of our external nature was less an invitation to heroism as it was to submission; the weakening of imported traditions left more room for sensuality than for moral consciousness. For these same reasons, given that the quixotic vice flowed in our blood, that social tenuousness had to at last awaken the will to redemption and dominion. Isn't that double dimension of moral idealism (though already somewhat theoretical and aesthetic) and imperious authoritarianism (though already more prudent in its adventures) manifested in the spirit of independence, represented in the archetype of Bolívar? Wasn't this spirit also able to dream of premature worlds of freedom, confront fearful obstacles, constantly rise again from the ashes of its own misfortunes and hold its ground until it suspected, already on its death bed, that it had been "plowing the ocean"? And did it not wish, in effect, to do too much or to do it too soon?

Romantic constitutionalism, with its fundamental confusion between what is and what one desires, paved the way for the barbarous rule by caudillo, which identified the political right with personal choice. As long as Don Quixote's furrow remained, our land was sown with high ideals and heroic urgency, but also with futile gestures, tragic glorification of trifles, arrogant particularism under the pretext of race, caste, or national border, or simply that our small Quixotes could not admit that anyone might lay claim through doctrine to a more beautiful lady than one's own. Underlying all of this was the intractable conflict between the more or less ideal norm (learned from the books of political chivalry) and the third primary reality of America, of which Sancho constantly reminded us. The infiltration of positivism was an initial solvent for that petty quixotic character and a theoretical call to common sense—it was even perhaps a bit Sanchoesque. Thus did the image of a European world make its appearance among us, and as we found it so foreign, it looked anti-Spanish to us. People like Sarmiento, Lastarria, Bilbao, and Altamirano sought to speak an anti-quixotic tongue with no awareness of the Quixote they carried within themselves. They did not know, as did Martí, that they were still Spaniards, although not "of the vine" but "of the husk." Montalvo called for freedom in the name of the chapters forgotten by Cervantes, Romanticism reproached a weary Spain for having abandoned its particular genius, and Comte and Spencer were constantly confronted by a thoroughbred nostalgia.

Lacking its own philosophy, our twentieth century was a product of this oscillation between the temptations of convenience and the bad habits of conscience, between tradition as it was crudely understood and a naïvely simplified modernity. It was an attempt to make the norm viable, to technologize life and the environment, to pave the way for a workable discretion, muting the presumptions of creed, race, and caste, diluting the inclination toward individualism with collective considerations, in short, disciplining the Quixote we carried within since we were no longer able to uproot him. But from time to time we would feel a sudden nostalgia for that voice of the blood and wanting in a way for a more profound dignity. And then we would take up the rallying cry of returning once more to stand beneath the deity Ariel, repenting of Saxon practices and of French aestheticism, reclaiming mystical values and lifeless ethics vaguely attributed to the patrimony of "The Race."

So then: neither the one nor the other. Neither Sanchos nor Quixotes. America is a continuation, but it is a vocation as well. It cannot renounce its roots but neither should it bury itself among them. Its own environment calls for blossoming flowers, choice fruit, fertile seeds. The quixotic character is, on the one hand, a psychological and historical excretion; on the other, an indication of absolute moral idealism. As psychology and history, it goes a way toward explaining us and in more than one sense reveals who we are, but in no way does it present us with an obligation. As the sum total of our highest values and aspirations, it represents a tradition of which we should be proud, for its essential nobility and because, as the ethical base of our culture, we are indebted to it for much of the best of who we are. But this duality I have endeavored to lay bare must be understood properly. The quixotic character as psychology produces nothing but futile gesticulation, an illusory inundation that very rarely fills the surrounding hollowness with any lasting substance: it scorns experience too much to be able to build upon it. The quixotic character in moral culture is like an allegory of the forces of the spirit: of the perfection to which man aspires for himself and his world and of the generous and constant effort to which his greatest destiny beckons him.

But the work of humans is never definitive; it is always progressive. It consists in obtaining at every moment and at every place the highest level of perfection that is naturally accessible, which is always—although we may not like the word because of the complacency to which it submits—a transaction between ideal speed and sluggish reality. We are obliged, by the very limitless vocation of our spirit, by something like the dignity of the species, to maintain the most elevated ideals and apply to things the full demands they imply. But we must not forget, at the risk of frustrating every improvement, that each objective situation has its own degree to which it may be permeated by the ideal. Reality itself takes care to indicate to us that very assimilation: when reality resists, it is an indication that we are demanding of it more than it can offer, and, on the other hand, the success of an undertaking, if we truly invested it with our most noble industry, is an indication of its justness, of its justice.

(That this sounds pragmatic should not disturb us. The Greeks had already defined the good as the capacity to achieve the end in itself. What is important is that it actually be a matter of the end *itself*. In this regard, nature is thoroughly impregnated by pragmatism: favored as much by omens as frustrated when it comes to vice.)

Our American styles of conscience and behavior—let us say this without mincing words—fluctuate between crass utilitarianism and an idealistic hypocrisy. A perverse pleasure in the instinctual dominates the general tone of life, a laughter arising from material advantage, a cynical indifference toward all transcendence, though it be purely historical. This "Sanchoesque nature" is corrupting not only our moral education and our civilization but our destiny as well. A melting pot of social resentment, certain kinds of dogmatic "idealism," are seen taking advantage of it in order to decry the political and economic structures that permit it and—more serious still—to discredit democracy in favor of military or theocratic solutions or supposed radical advancements, no less totalitarian. And contributing as well to this exploitation in the regions of most discreet calculation has been a false, traditionalist "idealism," gesticulating and rhetorical, whose swindles are not for that reason any less beneficial to the denunciation of bourgeois hypocrisy.

The truth is that genuine democracy—the only set of values I have an interest in defending—still constitutes the purest of idealisms and the one most in line with the deeply rooted vocation of our race. It is based on the capacity to transcend the human spirit: the notion that man, though he may not be fundamentally good, is at least able to ascend to goodness on the roads of a free and responsible existence in which success might mean the achievement of his reward and mistakes lead to his punishment without the whip of exterior authority. It responds to a valuation of the person whose rights from childhood are not contingent in the end upon any form of entelechy or dogma and seek to provide discipline through a deliberation in which he himself participates, through education and the coercion permitted by the law rather than through terror or the improvisations of violence. It consecrates, in short, that sense of individual dignity; it praises that conscience imbued with courage and its particular strength, deeply rooted features of our character whose suppression or smothering has happened in America without its societies feeling impoverished and the plunderers revealing their sinister sterility.

America is a vocation of freedom and without it no true dignity shall prosper. What does prosper is the deformation or the negation of dignity: the providentialist quixotic character that humiliates society by imposing its redemption and assuming its every form of justice and ruthless dogmatism that, in the name of a supposed salvation of the human race, dries up the spring of critical consciousness that is the very condition of the spirit, the will's goading force, and the glory of intelligence.

America is in need of an idealism more moderate in its language and more effectual in its deeds. The quixotic character has lent itself to an excessive extent to throwing a cloak—the threadbare cloak of a nobleman from Toledo—over our squalor, to deluding us with the idea that, because we are a people of literary traditions and with ardent and sentimental characteristics, we are more idealistic than the blonde pragmatists with whom material greed and ideological hypocrisy (of which we have no lack) are at least frequently offset by around-the-clock vigilance, noble private institutions, a genuine zeal for greater spiritual dignity.

In fact, we must settle in our own roots and defend our personality, yet not with bitter disdain or sublime rhetoric. Our true essence can be found in that illustrious Spanish realism that, as I have already said, illuminated the crux of the matter without its thus becoming mercurial, that realism to which Cervantes aspired when he wished for Don Quixote and Sancho to live together and not to part except to disappear into their respective destinies of the darkness of death and the oblivion of the village. And our America wishes neither to molder in tradition nor to be reduced to a province. It still has its whole future ahead of it, large as the world itself.

TRANSLATED BY MARK SCHAFER

Miguel Angel Asturias

Guatemala

(1899–1974)

————————

Following the footsteps of his politically oppressed father, Miguel Angel Asturias studied law in his native Guatemala, during which period he produced *El problema social del Indio* (1923), a book indicative of his interest in the native population of his country. He believed that Guatemala's problems were the direct result of the marginalization of the nation's indigenous people coupled with the tremendous power of the literate minority. Asturias lived his early childhood among rural peasants in the remote town of Salamá, where his family settled. To complete his education, he spent his adolescence in Guatemala City amid the oppressive climate of Manuel Estrada Cabrera's dictatorship. Asturias helped found the People's University of Guatemala after Estrada Cabrera's downfall. A subsequent trip to Europe resulted in his involvement in the surrealist movement, his establishing contact with James Joyce and Paul Eluard, the abandonment of his positivist leanings, and the publication of his first book. His return to Guatemala saw him move through journalistic circles until he undertook a diplomatic role in Guatemala's progressive governments from 1946 to 1954. Exiled in 1954, Asturias returned to journalism in various Latin American countries, and he was awarded the Nobel Prize for literature in 1967, the second ever given to a Latin American writer. His many books include *Legends of Guatemala* (1930), *El Señor Presidente* (1946), the masterpiece *Men of Maize* (1949), and *The Green Pope* (1954). Asturias served as ambassador to France and as a cultural attaché in Mexico. His later works are *Latinoamérica y otros ensayos* (1968) and *América, fábula de fábulas* (1972); the latter includes the following essay, "Lake Titicaca," originally published in 1958.

Lake Titicaca

The wind blows, making calls. We listen to it pass. Gusts. And we are still distant. Two, three condor flights. We know we must keep our eyes. Not let our eyes be stolen by the altiplano that emerges and submerges in every direction. They grow. They grow. The hills, the highlands, the mountains grow. Waves. Waves of a gigantic, seamless mass from the Cretaceous that become, at the height of the American world, the fairest crown of water: Titicaca.

Mineral water. Other American lakes have vegetable waters. The sun knows it. And it is not a heavenly body, but a foundry in the west. Water with the cold and shimmer of precious stone. Its sweetness surprises. Water in which the armor of the Incan empire's conquistadors has not rusted. And it has been entombed already for centuries in its profound vase.

Now close your history books. I saw, as the sun was setting, the conquistadors' steel shadows sink in search of the city of gold, hidden by the waters of this Andean sweet-lake sea. They accompanied me from the high solitudes, and we discerned, not burning, but set ablaze by the sun, boats that looked more like the braided tresses of women, basaltic reflections of pick-cut rocks; the reflection here is palpable, bulrushes shaking with every sight of the advancing night, solemn, with all its stars lying in wait, through the Puerta del Tiahuanaco, and the island on which man and woman, the first ones, created by the dying star, went crazy and broke their golden canes.

You're not going to cut my hand off . . . ! I heard the voice of the Indian whose wrist I had just taken unexpectedly, in a no-man's-land of waters and silences, to raise the hollow of that fingered conch to my ear, like an aquatic snail, with curdled lines of cabalistic marks, tiny fingernails of yellowish mother-of-pearl, gnawed by an avian beak, and the skin of labor.

I heard, I discovered the origin of man, in the hollowed hand of that Indian, who belonged to the oldest race on the planet, the lone example who spoke a language like water falling from his lips, and then I wrote these verses:

> The Indian knows full well what this means,
> it is to be from here, whence America comes.

When I released his hand, he told me of his riches, and I understood that he spoke of the great lake of ears of corn that all of us Indians have in our heart and from which we get tiny drops of moonlight to adorn the liquid, nocturnal gods, whose faces mimic the dark sky with eyes.

Other tributaries of the great lake join us as we walk. They travel with their llamas. They see me, knitting their cheeks to contemplate me with tiny eyes. Do I not deserve to be seen by their big eyes? They play with bulrush roots with their magnificent teeth. The path narrows, weaves through the hills; it will elude us if we do not follow it closely. Another grove of craggy heights and deep, sleeping waters. We approach the shore. Dizzily, we descend. The wind. The waves unfolding upon the sand. Someone. The stranger's feet are not dragging, but they seem to drag, the blistered skirt is so low. From the hat, one would say a man. But it is a woman, by her tresses and her clothing. Her hands do not rest. She weaves with black thread. From what old hegemony does that sorrow come? Other Indians accompany her. But far behind. And others farther. The space does not separate them, but unites them.

The great emptiness and the immense silence. The scarce vegetation. Perspectives persist in angles that open and close, and the innocence of the transparent air, through which some bird of prey crosses, while the clouds quilt the sky, and we have time to turn around to see Lake Titicaca from an even higher footing.

TRANSLATED BY JESSE H. LYTLE

Jorge Luis Borges

Argentina
(1899–1986)

One of the greatest icons of all Latin American culture, Jorge Luis Borges was a bookish poet, essayist, and short story writer, with little interest in politics. Both English and Spanish were spoken in his household, and most of his earliest readings were in English. He translated Oscar Wilde's *The Happy Prince* at the age of nine and published his first story at thirteen. The early part of his career was devoted to poetry, but he wrote mostly short stories and essays in the late 1930s and early 1940s, many of them while working as a librarian. His fame remained local until he shared in 1961, with Samuel Beckett, the Formentor International Publishers' Prize; as a result, the entire Western world became fascinated by him, and he was given honorary degrees at Harvard, Oxford, and other institutions. A most original essayist, given to producing hybrid forms in which fiction and nonfiction intermingle, he subverts our conventional views by creating labyrinthine connections between obscure bibliographical references and direct quotes from previously written works. The result, always tantalizing, forces us to reconsider the boundaries between life and dreams, between the finite and infinite. His language is complex and precise; his themes, cerebral and abstract. Borges's classic books are *A Universal History of Infamy* (1935), *Ficciones* (1944), *The Aleph* (1949), *Other Inquisitions* (1952), *Doctor Brodie's Report* (1970), and *The Book of Sand* (1975). He also coedited many anthologies with friends and students, among them the groundbreaking *Antología de literatura fantástica* (1940). The selection chosen here, "Pierre Menard, Author of the Quixote," is probably the most influential essay ever written in Latin America. It was originally published in Victoria Ocampo's prestigious magazine *Sur* (May 1939), and was collected a year later in *Ficciones*. In an autobiographical essay Borges wrote for the *New Yorker*, he tells of a life-threatening accident he had on Christmas Eve 1938. Before that he had written fiction only timidly, but the possibility of losing control of his mind stimulated him to write short stories with fervor. The result was his quasi-essay on Pierre Menard, a French symbolist who decided to rewrite—not copy, but rewrite—Cervantes's *Don Quixote*. The story is, of course, a parody and a commentary on reading as rewriting, but its implications are many, not the least of which is his questioning of our modern concept of originality; he thus obliquely insinuates that culture in Latin America is, by definition, derivative.

Pierre Menard, Author of the *Quixote*

The *visible* works left by this novelist are easily and briefly enumerated. It is therefore impossible to forgive the omissions and additions perpetrated by Madame Henri Bachelier in a fallacious catalog that a certain newspaper, whose Protestant tendencies are no secret, was inconsiderate enough to inflict on its wretched readers—even though they are few and Calvinist, if not Masonic and circumcised. Menard's true friends regarded this catalog with alarm, and even with a certain sadness. It is as if yesterday we were gathered together before the final marble and the fateful cypresses, and already error is trying to tarnish his memory. . . . Decidedly, a brief rectification is inevitable.

I am certain that it would be very easy to challenge my meager authority. I hope, nevertheless, that I will not be prevented from mentioning two important testimonials. The Baroness de Bacourt (at whose unforgettable *vendredis* I had the honor of becoming acquainted with the late lamented poet) has seen fit to approve these lines. The Countess de Bagnoregio, one of the most refined minds in the principality of Monaco (and now of Pittsburgh, Pennsylvania, since her recent marriage to the international philanthropist Simon Kautsch who, alas, has been so slandered by the victims of his disinterested handiwork), has sacrificed to "truth and death" (those are her words) that majestic reserve which distinguishes her, and in an open letter published in the magazine *Luxe* also grants me her consent. These authorizations, I believe, are not insufficient.

I have said that Menard's *visible* lifework is easily enumerated. Having carefully examined his private archives, I have been able to verify that it consists of the following:

a. A Symbolist sonnet which appeared twice (with variations) in the magazine *La conque* (the March and October issues of 1899).

b. A monograph on the possibility of constructing a poetic vocabulary of concepts that would not be synonyms or periphrases of those which make up ordinary language, "but ideal objects created by means of common agreement and destined essentially to fill poetic needs" (Nîmes, 1901).

c. A monograph on "certain connections or affinities" among the ideas of Descartes, Leibniz, and John Wilkins (Nîmes, 1903).

d. A monograph on the *Characteristica universalis* of Leibniz (Nîmes, 1904).

e. A technical article on the possibility of enriching the game of chess by means of eliminating one of the rooks' pawns. Menard proposes, recommends, disputes, and ends by rejecting this innovation.

f. A monograph on the *Ars magna generalis* of Ramón Lull (Nîmes, 1906).

g. A translation with prologue and notes of the *Libro de la invención y arte del juego del ajedrez* by Ruy López de Segura (Paris, 1907).

h. The rough draft of a monograph on the symbolic logic of George Boole.

i. An examination of the metric laws essential to French prose, illustrated with examples from Saint-Simon (*Revue des langues romanes*, Montpellier, October 1909).

j. An answer to Luc Durtain (who had denied the existence of such laws) illustrated with examples from Luc Durtain (*Revue des langues romanes*, Montpellier, December 1909).

k. A manuscript translation of the *Aguja de navegar cultos* of Quevedo, entitled *La boussole des précieux*.

l. A preface to the catalog of the exposition of lithographs by Carolus Hourcade (Nîmes, 1914).

m. His work, *Les problèmes d'un problème* (Paris, 1917), which takes up in chronological order the various solutions of the famous problem of Achilles and the tortoise. Two editions of this book have appeared so far; the second has as an epigraph Leibniz's advice *"Ne craignez point, monsieur, la tortue,"* and contains revisions of the chapters dedicated to Russell and Descartes.

n. An obstinate analysis of the "syntactic habits" of Toulet (*N.R.F.*, March 1921). I remember that Menard used to declare that censuring and praising were sentimental operations which had nothing to do with criticism.

o. A transposition into Alexandrines of *Le cimetière marin* of Paul Valéry (*N.R.F.*, January 1928).

p. An invective against Paul Valéry in the *Journal for the Suppression of Reality* of Jacques Reboul. (This invective, it should be stated parenthetically, is the exact reverse of his true opinion of Valéry. The latter understood it as such, and the old friendship between the two was never endangered.)

q. A "definition" of the Countess of Bagnoregio in the "victorious volume"—the phrase is that of another collaborator, Gabriele d'Annunzio—which this lady publishes yearly to rectify the inevitable falsifications of journalism and to present "to the world and to Italy" an authentic effigy of her person, which is so exposed (by reason of her beauty and her activities) to erroneous or hasty interpretations.

r. A cycle of admirable sonnets for the Baroness de Bacourt (1934).

s. A manuscript list of verses which owe their effectiveness to punctuation.*

Up to this point (with no other omission than that of some vague, circumstantial sonnets for the hospitable, or greedy, album of Madame Henri Bachelier) we have the *visible* part of Menard's works in chronological order. Now I will pass over to that other part, which is subterranean, interminably heroic, and unequaled, and which is also—oh, the possibilities inherent in the man!—inconclusive. This work, possibly the most significant of our time, consists of the ninth and thirty-eighth chapters of Part One of *Don Quixote* and a fragment of the twenty-second chapter. I realize that such an affirmation seems absurd; but the justification of this "absurdity" is the primary object of this note.†

Two texts of unequal value inspired the undertaking. One was that philological fragment of Novalis—No. 2005 of the Dresden edition—which outlines the theme of *total* identification with a specific author. The other was one of those parasitic books which places Christ on a boulevard, Hamlet on the Cannebière, and Don Quixote on Wall Street. Like any man of good taste, Menard detested these useless carnivals, only suitable—he used to say—for evoking plebeian delight in anachronism, or (what is worse) charming us with the primary idea that all epochs are the same, or that they are different. He considered more interesting, even though it had been carried out in a contradictory and superficial way, Daudet's famous plan: to unite in *one* figure, Tartarin, the Ingenious Gentleman and his squire. . . . Any insinuation that Menard dedicated his life to the writing of a contemporary *Don Quixote* is a calumny of his illustrious memory.

He did not want to compose another *Don Quixote*—which would be easy—but *the Don Quixote*. It is unnecessary to add that his aim was never to produce a mechanical transcription of the original; he did not propose to copy it. His admirable ambition was to produce pages which would coincide—word for word and line for line—with those of Miguel de Cervantes.

"My intent is merely astonishing," he wrote me from Bayonne on

---

*Madame Henri Bachelier also lists a literal translation of a literal translation done by Quevedo of the *Introduction à la vie dévote* of Saint Francis of Sales. In Pierre Menard's library there are no traces of such a work. She must have misunderstood a remark of his which he had intended as a joke.

†I also had another, secondary intent—that of sketching a portrait of Pierre Menard. But how would I dare to compete with the golden pages the Baroness de Bacourt tells me she is preparing, or with the delicate and precise pencil of Carolus Hourcade?

December 30, 1934. "The ultimate goal of a theological or metaphysical demonstration—the external world, God, chance, universal forms—is no less anterior or common than this novel which I am now developing. The only difference is that philosophers publish in pleasant volumes the intermediary stages of their work and that I have decided to lose them." And, in fact, not one page of a rough draft remains to bear witness to this work of years.

The initial method he conceived was relatively simple: to know Spanish well, to reembrace the Catholic faith, to fight against Moors and Turks, to forget European history between 1602 and 1918, and to *be* Miguel de Cervantes. Pierre Menard studied this procedure (I know that he arrived at a rather faithful handling of seventeenth-century Spanish) but rejected it as too easy. Rather because it was impossible, the reader will say! I agree, but the undertaking was impossible from the start, and of all the possible means of carrying it out, this one was the least interesting. To be, in the twentieth century, a popular novelist of the seventeenth century seemed to him a diminution. To be, in some way, Cervantes and to arrive at *Don Quixote* seemed to him less arduous—and consequently less interesting—than to continue being Pierre Menard and to arrive at *Don Quixote* through the experiences of Pierre Menard. (This conviction, let it be said in passing, forced him to exclude the autobiographical prologue of the second part of *Don Quixote*. To include this prologue would have meant creating another personage—Cervantes—but it would also have meant presenting *Don Quixote* as the work of this personage and not of Menard. He naturally denied himself such an easy problem.) "My undertaking is not essentially different," he said in another part of the same letter. "I would only have to be immortal in order to carry it out." Shall I confess that I often imagine that he finished it and that I am reading *Don Quixote*—the entire work—as if Menard had conceived it? Several nights ago, while leafing through Chapter 26—which he had never attempted—I recognized our friend's style and, as it were, his voice in this exceptional phrase: the nymphs of the rivers, mournful and humid Echo. This effective combination of two adjectives, one moral and the other physical, reminded me of a line from Shakespeare which we discussed one afternoon:

Where a malignant and turbaned Turk . . .

Why precisely *Don Quixote*, our reader will ask. Such a preference would not have been inexplicable in a Spaniard; but it undoubtedly was in a Symbolist from Nîmes, essentially devoted to Poe, who engendered Baudelaire, who engendered Mallarmé, who engendered Valéry, who engendered Edmond Teste. The letter quoted above clarifies this point. "*Don

Quixote," Menard explains, "interests me profoundly, but it does not seem to me to have been—how shall I say it—inevitable. I cannot imagine the universe without the interjection of Edgar Allan Poe:

Ah, bear in mind this garden was enchanted!

Or without the *Bateau Ivre* or the *Ancient Mariner*, but I know that I am capable of imagining it without *Don Quixote*. (I speak, naturally, of my personal capacity not of the historical repercussions of these works.) *Don Quixote* is an accidental book. *Don Quixote* is unnecessary. I can premeditate writing. I can write it without incurring a tautology. When I was twelve or thirteen years old I read it perhaps in its entirety. Since then I have reread several chapters attentively, but not the ones I am going to undertake. I have likewise studied the *entremeses*, the comedies, the *Galatea*, the exemplary novels, and the undoubtedly laborious efforts of *Pérsiles y Sigismunda* and the *Viaje al Parnaso*. . . . My general memory of *Don Quixote*, simplified by forgetfulness and indifference, is much the same as the imprecise, anterior image of a book not yet written. Once this image (which no one can deny me in good faith) has been postulated, my problems are undeniably considerably more difficult than those which Cervantes faced. My affable precursor did not refuse the collaboration of fate; he went along composing his immortal work a little *à la diable*, swept along by inertias of language and invention. I have contracted the mysterious duty of reconstructing literally his spontaneous work. My solitary game is governed by two polar laws. The first permits me to attempt variants of a formal and psychological nature; the second obliges me to sacrifice them to the 'original' text and irrefutably to rationalize this annihilation. . . . To these artificial obstacles one must add another congenital one. To compose *Don Quixote* at the beginning of the seventeenth century was a reasonable, necessary and perhaps inevitable undertaking; at the beginning of the twentieth century it is almost impossible. It is not in vain that three hundred years have passed, charged with the most complex happenings—among them, to mention only one, that same *Don Quixote*."

In spite of these three obstacles, the fragmentary *Don Quixote* of Menard is more subtle than that of Cervantes. The latter indulges in a rather coarse opposition between tales of knighthood and the meager, provincial reality of his country; Menard chooses as "reality" the land of Carmen during the century of Lepanto and Lope. What Hispanophile would not have advised Maurice Bariès or Dr. Rodríguez Larreta to make such a choice! Menard, as if it were the most natural thing in the world, eludes them. In his work there are neither bands of gypsies, conquistadors, mystics, Philip the Seconds, nor autos-da-fé. He disregards or proscribes local color. This disdain indicates a new approach to the historical novel. This disdain condemns *Salammbô* without appeal.

It is no less astonishing to consider isolated chapters. Let us examine, for instance, Chapter 38 of Part One "which treats of the curious discourse that Don Quixote delivered on the subject of arms and letters." As is known, Don Quixote (like Quevedo in a later, analogous passage of *La hora de todos*) passes judgment against letters and in favor of arms. Cervantes was an old soldier, which explains such a judgment. But that the *Don Quixote* of Pierre Menard—a contemporary of *La trahison des clercs* and Bertrand Russell—should relapse into these nebulous sophistries! Madame Bachelier has seen in them an admirable and typical subordination of the author to the psychology of the hero; others (by no means perspicaciously) a *transcription of Don Quixote*; the Baroness de Bacourt, the influence of Nietzsche. To this third interpretation (which seems to me irrefutable) I do not know if I would dare to add a fourth; which coincides very well with the divine modesty of Pierre Menard: his resigned or ironic habit of propounding ideas which were the strict reverse of those he preferred. (One will remember his diatribe against Paul Valéry in the ephemeral journal of the superrealist Jacques Reboul.) The text of Cervantes and that of Menard are verbally identical, but the second is almost infinitely richer. (More ambiguous, his detractors will say; but ambiguity is a richness.) It is a revelation to compare the *Don Quixote* of Menard with that of Cervantes. The latter, for instance, wrote (*Don Quixote*, Part One, Chapter 9):

> . . . la verdad, cuya madre es la historia, émula del tiempo, depósito de las acciones, testigo de lo pasado, ejemplo y aviso de lo presente, advertencia de lo por venir.
>
> [. . . truth, whose mother is history, who is the rival of time, depository of deeds, witness of the past, example and lesson to the present, and warning to the future.]

Written in the seventeenth century, written by the "ingenious layman" Cervantes, this enumeration is a mere rhetorical eulogy of history. Menard, on the other hand, writes:

> . . . la verdad, cuya madre es la historia, émula del tiempo, depósito de las acciones, testigo de lo pasado, ejemplo y aviso de lo presente, advertencia de lo por venir.
>
> [. . . truth, whose mother is history, who is the rival of time, depository of deeds, witness of the past, example and lesson to the present, and warning to the future.]

History, *mother* of truth; the idea is astounding. Menard, a contemporary of William James, does not define history as an investigation of reality, but as its origin. Historical truth, for him, is not what took place; it is what we think took place. The final clauses—*example and lesson to the present, and warning to the future*—are shamelessly pragmatic.

Equally vivid is the contrast in styles. The archaic style of Menard—in the last analysis, a foreigner—suffers from a certain affectation. Not so that of his precursor, who handles easily the ordinary Spanish of his time.

There is no intellectual exercise which is not ultimately useless. A philosophical doctrine is in the beginning a seemingly true description of the universe; as the years pass it becomes a mere chapter—if not a paragraph or a noun—in the history of philosophy. In literature, this ultimate decay is even more notorious. *"Don Quixote,"* Menard once told me, "was above all an agreeable book; now it is an occasion for patriotic toasts, grammatical arrogance and obscene deluxe editions. Glory is an incomprehension, and perhaps the worst."

These nihilist arguments contain nothing new; what is unusual is the decision Pierre Menard derived from them. He resolved to outstrip that vanity which awaits all the woes of mankind; he undertook a task that was complex in the extreme and futile from the outset. He dedicated his conscience and nightly studies to the repetition of a preexisting book in a foreign tongue. The number of rough drafts kept on increasing; he tenaciously made corrections and tore up thousands of manuscript pages.* He did not permit them to be examined, and he took great care that they would not survive him. It is in vain that I have tried to reconstruct them.

I have thought that it is legitimate to consider the "final" *Don Quixote* as a kind of palimpsest, in which should appear traces—tenuous but not undecipherable—of the "previous" handwriting of our friend. Unfortunately, only a second Pierre Menard, inverting the work of the former, could exhume and resuscitate these Troys. . . .

"To think, analyze and invent," he also wrote me, "are not anomalous acts, but the normal respiration of the intelligence. To glorify the occasional fulfillment of this function, to treasure ancient thoughts of others, to remember with incredulous amazement that the *doctor universalis* thought, is to confess our languor or barbarism. Every man should be capable of all ideas, and I believe that in the future he will be."

Menard (perhaps without wishing to) has enriched, by means of a new technique, the hesitant and rudimentary art of reading: the technique is one of deliberate anachronism and erroneous attributions. This technique, with its infinite applications, urges us to run through the *Odyssey* as if it

---

*I remember his square-ruled notebooks, the black streaks where he had crossed out words, his peculiar typographical symbols, and his insectlike handwriting. In the late afternoon he liked to go for walks on the outskirts of Nîmes; he would take a notebook with him and make a gay bonfire.

were written after the *Aeneid*, and to read *Le jardin du Centaure* by Madame Henri Bachelier as if it were by Madame Henri Bachelier. This technique would fill the dullest books with adventure. Would not the attributing of *The Imitation of Christ* to Louis Ferdinand Céline or James Joyce be a sufficient renovation of its tenuous spiritual counsels?

TRANSLATED BY ANTHONY BONNER

Lydia Cabrera

Cuba

(1900–1991)

———◆•◆•◆———

Although the Negrista movement in Cuba—devoted, from the 1920s to the 1940s, to exploring the African cultural legacy of the island—was best known for its influence on poetry, one would not know that from Lydia Cabrera's corpus of narratives. Known as a short story writer and anthropologist, she was born in New York City, the daughter of a well-known historian and lawyer. Her journalistic debut took place in 1913, when she began to write, under a pseudonym, on social events of Cuban high society for the magazine *Cuba y América*. In 1922 she moved to Paris to study painting, art, and Asian culture. She remained in the French capital until 1939, and it was there her interest in primitive cultures was awakened. Upon her return to Cuba, her passion for the nation's African population deepened, particularly for its folklore and mythology. In 1959, after the triumph of Fidel Castro's revolution, she moved to the United States, where she settled until her death in Miami, Florida. *Cuentos negros de Cuba* (1940) was her first major work, published by Gallimard in France before it appeared in Spanish. It is one of the finest examples of Afro-Cuban literature. The book was followed by *¿Por qué?* (1948) and *El monte: Notas sobre las religiones, la magia, las supersticiones y el folklore de los negros criollos y del pueblo de Cuba* (1954), the latter an adventurous portrayal of African languages and customs in Cuba. Her later works include *Refranes de negros viejos* (1955), *La sociedad secreta Abakuá, narrada por viejos adeptos* (1959), *Otan Iyebiyé: Las piedras preciosas* (1970), *Ayapá, cuentos de jicotea* (1971), *La laguna secreta de San Joaquín* (1973), from which the selection "El Socorro Lake" is taken, and *Yemayá and Ochún* (1974).

El Socorro Lake

Many years ago, Ma Francisquilla Ibáñez, a centenarian still strong enough to be aroused by the drums and to sing and dance to her gods for three solid days, brought us to Lake El Socorro. The lake, as the woman explained, took its name from the old sugar plantation on which it was located. She had known the long-deceased owner, Doña Socorro de Armas, an authoritarian woman of exceptional energy who had been initiated into the secrets of Palo Monte. That is, the same lady who could travel to Europe and revel in luxury and refinement could also—not as a curious spectator but as a believer—take part in the "games" or rites of the Congo slaves who invoked the Ngangas (the dead and the spirits of trees, or *palos*). This, incidentally, is the source of the name Regla de Palo or Palo Monte, used in Cuba to refer to the religion or magic of the blacks of Bantu origin, the Congos. It wasn't unheard of in the past for mistresses and masters of plantations—as we've found out from their descendants— to be seduced, like Doña Socorro, by the beliefs of their slaves. Other ladies preferred the Orishas of the Lucumís to the Nkisi, Wangas, Nkitas, and Mumbomas of the Congos.

As Roger Bastide says, "African mysticism is a passionate, complex, and beautiful form of mysticism. A spring in which thirsty souls can slake their thirst and drink in heaven." Lake El Socorro has a special charm. Ma Francisquilla implied that, and no sooner had we gazed upon it at a distance, from which it seemed almost to inscribe a perfect circle, than we felt ourselves touched by its charm, its *aché*.

The lake: a pure horizon composed of sky and a few solemn ceiba trees, majestically self-absorbed. Along with a few scattered and distant carobs that spread their wide green umbrellas, the ceibas are the only trees growing there. This is not—plain, sky, and the sky-blue lake—what is usually understood to be a picturesque place. But in the very nakedness of the scene there is a mystery, a soul one can feel. The old black woman, always talkative, never stopped chatting during the trip, laughing, pretending to fall with every lurch of the jeep. But she fell silent when we stopped about 90 feet from the lake. Serious now, she took me by the hand, plunged into the thick vegetation with its humid fragrance, saturated with holiness, and led me to the shore. The day was overcast, gray, and as the local people told us they would, the milky, tranquil, seemingly bottomless waters trembled when we approached. The lake seemed to have awakened and blinked in surprise when it discovered our presence.

It was inhabited by thousands of small turtles about a foot long that from time to time bite and break the glassy surface. Mysterious creatures, half spirit, with indecipherable markings on their stony, spherical bodies, they are not daughters of the water but of fire: They only live in rivers and ponds so they won't burn up.

Now Ma Francisquilla carries some modest offerings wrapped in paper. She lies down and intones, "Mó yuba, mó yuba olodó Awoyó mi ré." Then, on her knees, she falls silent, as if awaiting a response. "Mó yuba mó yuba," she repeats, as if someone had heard her, pouring honey from a little bottle she had in her packet.

Leaning over the edge of the lake, she calls me over to her, introduces me to the water with a beautiful gesture and forces me to humble myself by imperiously placing her rough, dry hand on the back of my neck. She speaks in Lucumí to the goddess who lives at the bottom. She explains—

I could understand her—that the "eleyo, la obiní oibó," the white, foreign woman, was there to greet her. And she goes on with persuasive compassion, in the tone we use to speak to children in order to convince them of something: "Obiní eleyibó omó etié. Omó etié Iyami olodomí." That is, the white woman is also your daughter, your daughter, mother of mine, Lady of the Water.

A long prayer followed, of which I could catch only a few words. This phrase: "ma oto kokán kokán." (I beg you with all my heart.) She was praying in a low voice for herself and for me with intense fervor, abstracted, still with that old, tree bark hand of hers forcing me to remain in an attitude of adoration before the goddess who listened to her, perhaps even materializing before her believing eyes. And for an instant the ingenuous and humble mysticism of the old woman, its roots deep in nature, the sensation of being in a virgin world, in the presence of a mystery, made a fear flower in the most ancient part of my "obiní oibó" soul, in what remained there of my childhood.

Francisquilla finished her prayers—"greetings"—washed her face, drank, ordered me to moisten my forehead, and walked away from me taking extraordinarily agile, rhythmic steps, as if an invincible joy, the invincible joy of her race, obliged her to dance the ancestral burden she bore with such lightness on her century-old but almost youthful shoulders. We watched her dance her way around the lake, gathering the herbs she needed to purify and cure her patients and pausing from time to time to talk to a spirit.

Perhaps the absence of the aggressive sun of the tropical afternoon was indispensable for such a subtle, celestial, and crystalline magic. Without the pure, ineffable nature of that pale setting, that absolute silence, the light that scattered shades of an infinite delicacy on these waters, calm again like the sleep of the maternal and beneficent goddess who had gone back to sleep, I would have been limited to watching Ma Francisquilla coldly, to interrogating her and filling my notebook with jottings. I wouldn't have felt the holiness of the water.

The old woman returned holding in her arms the fresh bundles of herbs. Now her impatient voice evaporated the magic suspension, the mysterious poetry of enchantment. It was time, because at the plantation they'd gone back to making everyone stick to a schedule, to return to the mill, occupied day and night in satisfying the voracity of another divinity. A modern, steel divinity, the mechanical, precise god of a huge sugar mill in whose teeth miles and miles of sugarcane groan and bleed.

A little later and it would not be prudent to rely on the apparently unchanging, good-natured serenity of the water. Lake El Socorro never gave back the corpses of those who drowned in it.

Later I visited other sacred lakes. But none as beautiful and unfathomable as this memorable Socorro lake, in which, thanks to the abiding faith of the old slave who led me to it, transporting me to the beginnings of time or to my childhood, when I feared unknown powers in the solitude of a river or the sea, I had such a genuine and poetic demonstration of the durability of a millennial and universal belief in the divinity of the water.

TRANSLATED BY ALFRED MACADAM

Gilberto Freyre

Brazil

(1900–1987)

————•◦•◦•————

Born and educated in Recife, Freyre was taught in Latin, Greek, and English at an early age. He earned a bachelor's degree from Baylor and a master's from Columbia. At Columbia, Freyre studied under the anthropologist Franz Boas and the philosopher John Dewey, both of whom influenced him significantly. After studying anthropology and ethnology in Europe, Freyre returned to Brazil and entered the political arena as secretary to the governor of the state of Pernambuco. He founded *Region Tradition*, a movement critical of Brazilian modernism and its adoption of European literary trends. Freyre and other writers sought to develop a distinctly Brazilian national literature. His prose often combines creative writing with historical inquiry. As a result, his novels often seem to be written by a historian, whereas his scholarly works read like creative texts. Freyre's first publications include *Sobrados e Mucambos* (1936), *Nordeste* (1937), and *O mundo que o portugues criou* (1940). His most famous work, however, is *The Masters and the Slaves* (1933). Although his fiction is not as well-known as his essays, his "semi-novel" *Mother and Son: A Brazilian Tale* (1964) earned him much praise. Freyre was a visiting lecturer at schools all over the world—from Stanford to Columbia to King's College to the Sorbonne. In 1946, he helped draw up the Brazilian Constitution, and he was a delegate to the United Nations in 1949. The following article, "Slaves in Newspaper Ads," was included in *O escravo nos anúncios de jornais brasileiros do século XIX* (1963). It exemplifies, in Freyre's persuasive yet idiosyncratic style, his anthropological and ethnographic interests.

Slaves in Newspaper Ads

When it comes to dealing with demographic history or the anthropological past—a past which constantly casts a shadow before it onto the present and the future—advertisements are the best fresh material available for the study and interpretation of certain aspects of the nineteenth century in Brazil. Not only can they help us to interpret the period; they throw light on many little-known facets of our collective psychology. For example, they are helpful to a study of the development of the Brazilian language. Not until well along in the twentieth century does the literary language of our fiction and poetry reveal anything like the spontaneity and independence found in newspaper advertisements throughout the nineteenth century. These were then already full of African and Tupí-Guaraní words and pungent Brazilianisms: *sapiranga* [blepharitis (inflammation of the eyelids)], *cassaco* [mill or railroad worker], *cambiteiro* [splindleshanks], *aça* or *assa* [very light mulatto], *xexeu* [stink], *troncho* [stump], *perequeté* [dapper], *mulambo* [rag or weakling], *munganga* [grimace or sweet talk], *cambado* [bandy-legged], *zambo* [sambo], *cangulo* [bucktoothed], *tacheiro* [millhand], *engurujado* [dried up], *banguê* [sugar mill or litter for dead slaves], *banzeiro* [unruly or homesick for Africa], *batuque* [Afro-Brazilian dance or gathering], *munheca* [strong, vigorous man], *batucar* [pound, beat, or hammer].

The notices in the gazettes which our great-grandfathers used to read so tranquilly by the light of a candle or an oil lamp were written the way people talked: Portuguese was already being written in a Brazilian way. Just compare the language of advertisements in 1825 with the stale purity of speeches by the members of the Imperial Government: they are diametrically opposed, two languages at sword's point. Compare the phrasing of political articles or literary features with that of an advertisement in the same newspaper: the superiority of forceful expressiveness and, I will go so far as to say, the beauty of the advertisements is enormous. If George Borrow had visited Brazil he would have said, as he did of Spain, that the language of this people is greater, far greater, than its literature. The language of the paid announcements in Brazilian newspapers in the last days of Portuguese rule and of the Empire often seem to me to be superior as an expression of the Brazilian nation to the whole of our literature of the same period, including the novels about *moreninhas* and *iaiás* who were beginning to be a little less Portuguese than their predecessors. If I had the authority to do so, this is what I would advise young people to read to counteract the influence, no doubt indispensable up to a point, of the Portuguese classics: newspaper announcements from the days of the Empire. They constitute our first classic literature, above all the announcements about slaves, which are the frankest, the liveliest, and the richest in Brazilian flavor.

Whoever has the leisure to leaf through a collection of any of our newspapers from the beginning or the middle of the nineteenth century—leisure and caution, because the paper often crumbles from rottenness or old age in the fingers of the careless researcher—whoever is patient enough and careful enough to do this is bound to reach the same conclusion: far more clearly than in history books or novels, the internal history of Brazil in the nineteenth century is preserved in the commercial pages of its newspapers. A great part of that history during most of the century is the history of the exploitation of slaves—though this was done with a measure of indulgence, for Brazil has never been a country of extremes, all things tending to melt into temporization and soften into compromise: by the plantation owner, usually stout and rather flabby, with occasional outbursts of cruelty; by his wife, also stout, sometimes obese, at times terribly jealous of the slave girls; by the sons and daughters of the house, the chaplain, the overseer, and the man in charge of catching runaway slaves. And since the economic history of Brazil before abolition is to a great extent the history of Negro workers, the significance of notices concerning slaves is of capital importance. There was a time when these notices took up a third or even half of the pages not devoted to news. They were incomparably the most vivid, humanly interesting part of the paper: the one most closely linked to the patriarchal, agrarian economy of the age and to life as it was lived by Brazilians, whether in the towns or, more commonly, on the plantations and the farms large and small, and in farm or plantation houses big enough to need slaves, if not slave cabins. . . . Many of the slaves described in the newspapers were men or women on whom excessive hard work had left deep scars or deformities. This is so true that among the identifying marks of runaway slaves were color: black, high yellow, whitish, or mulatto (generally mulatto); character: smart, sly, or ignorant; hair: woolly, frizzy, straight, curly, Indian, light, reddish, even blond; size and shape of hands and feet: usually large, with widespread toes; shape of nose: not always flat, but sometimes sharp like those of the half-castes in the now classic study of Eugen Fischer;* teeth: almost invariably white and whole; tribe or "nation": distinguished by self-inflicted gashes, cuts, and scars. The stigmata of hard labor are often emphasized: the professional deformities, one might say, of the slaves' hands, feet, gait, and form.

Notices such as these frequently appeared: "Caetano, runaway, age 12 more or less, Angola nation, last seen wearing tow pantaloons and cotton shirt, has a cross branded on his left arm and hair worn off the middle of his head from carrying weight . . ." (*Diário de Pernambuco*, 1/23/1830). This little twelve-year-old slave boy who already had a tonsure which had not been shaved off with pomp and ritual like those of the white boys who went off to the seminary to study for the priesthood, but had been worn bald by the weight of heavy loads, ran away from a dress goods store at No. 13, Rua do Queimado, in Recife. Here is another notice of the same kind: "Runaway slave in the Province of Alagoas . . . with the following marks: name Joaquim, toes missing through kneading lime with the same; lime-opened sores and rotted toes. . . ."

The notice of Joaquim's escape goes on to say that he was a man "black in color, with whitish hair, broad face, big eyes . . . Cacanje nation, easy to understand when he talks because he came over as a pickaninny, has whip marks and hobbles a little when he walks" (*Diário de Pernambuco*,

---

Rasse und Rassenentstehung bein Menschen (Berlin, 1927).

3/31/45). In addition there are the fugitive slaves from workshops and dockyards in the towns, like Manoel Congo, eighteen years old, sinewy arms, long broad feet, and "callused hand" (*Diário de Pernambuco*, 6/2/34), and Antônio Cacanje, with "very crooked callused hands, he being a carpenter" (*Diário de Pernambuco*, 6/16/34), or again a high yellow, "Manoel by name, calls himself Moraes"—so runs a notice in the *Jornal do Commércio* on the third of January, 1833—"tailor's journeyman, you can tell by his fingers." The cases of professional deformities, more pronounced in slaves than in other men, are too numerous to mention. Many of the notices describe young millhands whose hands had been cut off at the wrist by the grinder, and innumerable men with bald spots rubbed by the heavy weights they had to carry on their heads—boards, bricks, sand, "shitbarrels," water butts. One slave in Recife who ran away on June 14, 1836, was a black man named João, nicknamed Smarty, Cabinda nation, thirty-six years old, average height, sparse beard, big eyes, right leg a little bowed, hurried in gait and speech, with stammering speech and trembling hips—a canoemaker, he too had his martyr's crown: "a round bald spot from carrying weight on his head" (*Diário de Pernambuco*, 11/23/36). In the September 24, 1830, edition of the same newspaper is a notice of two runaway boys, both with "bald spots on their pates from carrying sand." The Negro Luis, announces an ad in the *Diário do Rio de Janeiro* of January 2, 1833, had "his fingers pricked all over by the needle because his job is to trim wooden clogs." Francisco, a boy of the Angolan nation, above average height, mulatto, low brow, new scars from a bullwhip on his back, no beard, is described by his master as having "calluses on the joints of his fingers from kneading bread" (*Diário de Pernambuco*, 8/8/33). The same was true of Pedro, also Angolan: calluses on his fingers from kneading bread, besides the marks of a chain to keep him from running away. Pedro had escaped from a bakery in the Rua de Cinco Pontas in Recife. There are also examples of runaway tailor's apprentices with "scars on their fingers from sewing with a needle" (*Diário de Pernambuco*, 8/9/30). Maria, a Benguela slave, age forty, short stature, head flattened from carrying heavy weights, already trembled and walked with a limp (*Diário de Pernambuco*, 9/10/31). Apolinária—Brazilian-born Negress, tall, stout, mulatto, with an ugly face, fleshy lower lip, no teeth missing in front, large breasts—had "such fat arms, feet, and hands they look swollen" (*Diário de Pernambuco*, 1/30/30). Actually, such big, swollen, deformed hands and feet were so common that fugitive slaves could hardly ever be identified by those marks alone. Truly rare were slaves with "little hands" or "long, muscular feet." Occasionally some favorite female house slave with a "pretty figure," who had been brought up almost like a daughter, would run away, with her mulatto swain perhaps, and leave her white master lonely and missing her fingers in his hair, her pretty ways and endearments. Little black Luisa was such a one, with her thin lips, big eyes, small feet, tall slender figure, and pert pointed breasts. She ran away from the Rua das Violas, right here in São Cristóvão, in 1833 (*Jornal do Commércio*, 1/8/33).

TRANSLATED BY BARBARA SHELBY

Germán Arciniegas

Colombia
(b. 1900)

—•:•:•—

Despite being born in Colombia, Germán Arciniegas was faithful to his mother's Cuban heritage throughout his career, especially in works such as *Biografía del Caribe* (1947) and *Nueva imagen del Caribe* (1970). His academic career was centered in Bogotá, where he was extremely active in student organizations and published a series of essays and studies on university life in Spain and America. Arciniegas played a large role in the unionization of Colombia's university students and directed two magazines while he was a student, *La voz de la juventud* (1919–20) and *Universidad* (1925–29). A spokesman for Latin American unity, Arciniegas often focuses his analyses on the history of the common people. An example of what some have referred to as "populist history" can be seen in his treatment of Spain. Although Arciniegas was always a strong critic of the Spanish Conquest, he claims to admire the ordinary Spaniards who launched themselves into the project, risking their lives in the hope of leaving their poverty behind. This tendency can also be seen in his writing style, as he tries to write in an accessible manner without resorting to esoteric references. He published a wealth of material on Latin American culture, much of which has been translated into English, such as *América, tierra firme* (1937), *Este pueblo de América* (1945), *The Green Continent* (1945), and *America in Europe* (1975). He also focused on his own Colombia in books such as *Los comuneros* (1938), *El Dorado* (1942), and *Fernando Botero* (1977). Arciniegas served as Colombia's ambassador to Italy, as a congressman, and as a member of the Colombian Academy of Letters. He has taught at the University of California, the University of Chicago, Mills College, and at Columbia University, where he was a full professor from 1947 to 1959. The following essay is part of Arciniegas's *El país del rascacielos y las zanahorias* (1945), pertaining to the knowledge the so-called civilized world has of Latin America.

Do They Know Us? Do We Know Them? Do We Know Each Other?

An excellent writer who visited us a few years ago and wrote a lovely book about his travels through Nueva Granada found himself in London when planning his trip, and, explaining his projects to a distinguished lady of the city, received this comment: "If you're going to Colombia, you must send me a souvenir from Buenos Aires."

The writer tried to explain that Buenos Aires was farther from Bogotá than London was from Cairo. But the lady left him speechless, dismissing any possibility of discussion with these words: "Such confusion is reasonable, because we see all those countries where bank robbers and such take refuge as one single thing. . . ."

Even at risk of acknowledging a land of fugitives from the law, the writer bade a shaken farewell to the enchanting lady, came to Colombia, and wrote, as I mentioned, a very lovely book.

He does come across angrily in his book, because we adopted the expression "Colombia"—a word he did not understand, because in Spanish one says Colón rather than Columbus—to replace the old and beautiful appellation of Nueva Granada, and thus he baptized his work in an archaic manner. Even in this minor detail one can see the affection he holds for us.

When I read the incident of the traveler and the lady in London, which appears in the same book's prologue, I remembered the first chapter of *Green Mansions*, W. H. Hudson's precious novel, which today is part of any respectable collection of English classics and was set in the lands bathed by the Orinoco.

In this novel, written not too long ago, Hudson says:

> Every nation, someone remarks, has the government it deserves, and Venezuela certainly has the one it deserves and suits it best. We call it a republic, not only because it is not one, but also because a thing must have a name; and to have a good name, or a fine name, is very convenient, especially when you want to borrow money. . . .

With this background, the reader can already imagine a South American traveler's anticipation when he ventures into the other world. The other world is, in turn, for him, a jungle: one of peoples we call "civilized," perhaps obeying the same conventions exposed by Mr. Hudson: because everything must have a name, and so much the better if it is a fine name. . . . Naturally, to the South American there remains no other way to defend himself but to make the most of the current ideas about his country.

I had unprecedented success in London, as I have mentioned many times, when the woman who owned the pension where I was living begged me not to damage the chairs by sitting on their arms, and I replied: "Pardon me, ma'am, I'll never do it again. Forgive me, but understand me, for we, in my country, receive our visitors on tree branches. . . ."

From that day on I was the favorite pet in the pension, the South American who presented himself to visitors.

Eliseo Arango had a similar experience in Paris. He was courting some girls, or a girl, to whose house he was frequently invited. Once, out of either mere disinterested curiosity or the strong sense of dowry that adorns the French people, the conversation drifted toward the business of the Eliseo family. And Eliseo, to give himself a touch of class, invented a little story:

"I am," he told them, "from a land which produces the most beautiful snakes in all of America: it is called Chocó, in Colombia, South America. The people live off the platinum, which comes in stones in the sand or river mud. But my fathers, for generations, have remained faithful to the family tradition, and have never done anything but charm serpents. I have come to Paris to study, as you know, literature and law at the university; this will be nothing but decoration for my career, for when I return to Chocó, I will spend my time with a flute between my lips, like papá, watching snakes shake their tails to ring bells or stick out their quivering tongues."

Eliseo's case was a tragic one. The girls became interested in the ophidians' life, about whose customs Eliseo had scarce knowledge, and then the poor man, to escape his predicament, had to miss a number of afternoon conferences at the Sorbonne so he could work through volumes in the library to get some substance to punctuate his lies.

As one can see, we ourselves contribute to the complexity of the problem of awareness toward our countries. And thus there is no need to be confused if suddenly the South American sees books or hears conversations that leave him stupefied.

I don't want to proceed on this theme without saying, in passing, that traveling usually involves the South American encountering two extremes: those who know nothing of us and those who know too much. When Dr. Olaya Herrera arrived in New York, already president-elect, there were a few days in which our name was frequently seen in columns. And not just columns but shop windows too. One day I saw, in one of the most elegant jewelry shops on Fifth Avenue, a little exhibition of Colombian items: it was reduced to a small pile of gold powder on a saucer and a few fish hooks of the same metal. Beneath were two inscriptions: "Powdered gold used for trading by natives in Colombia, South America," "Fishing instruments used by Colombian natives . . . , etcetera."

In those times I was an ingenuous young fellow, and it hurt me a bit to see this new representation of El Dorado. I tried, furthermore, to find out if such things occurred in all of New York's spheres, and I had the nerve to seek out certain directors of large financial institutions to solicit their opinions of our country and the president-elect, who, as I understood, should have been a well-known figure to them. Dr. Olaya himself had the courtesy to give me a few names, and with clean shoes and white handkerchief I approached them, brimming with curiosity.

I will never forget the experience I had with one, who had never visited

Colombia but had tried to become informed based on the memories of his correspondents. He graciously asked me to sit in that chair that executives have beside their desks to hear their clients' confessions and give them spiritual counseling, and without further ado, instead of waiting for my questions, began his interrogation:

"Ah! From Bogotá, Colombia? What a pleasure! Tell me something, has Chucho Marulanda finished the house he was building on Carrera Quinta? . . . And tell me, how's Chato Jaramillo Isaza, playing a lot?"

And so on and so forth. Few are the Colombians, not to mention South Americans, who have read a little book by Julio Posada, entitled *El machete*. Of course, I think *El machete* is the best book ever written in Colombia. I know no other in which such a dramatic plot is executed with such grace, cunning, malice, delight, without the author ever transcending the vocabulary of the muleteers and blacks on the plantations.

El machete was released in a limited edition that never sold. It was originally published in the magazine *Alfa*, from Medellín. The curious part is that one day, in conversation with Professor Kany, the author of a beautiful and well-documented book about the customs and popular life in eighteenth-century Spain, he said: "Follow me and I'll show you something good from Colombia."

And from his library shelf, in his office at the University of California, in Berkeley, he produced a copy of *El machete*, bearing meticulous notation. Then he told me: "I've learned a lot from this book: look how many times I've cited it in my studies on Colombian popular speech."

And, in fact, among the mass of citations Kany usually has supporting his language studies, published in U.S. science magazines, I stumbled onto Julio Posada's name and citations from *El machete* numerous times.

Kany, of course, is a hopeless observer. The first time I ran into him was in Bogotá. He passed through here, like many other American cities, with the sole agenda of collecting the hand gestures of our people. One night he had me for over five hours, in an interrogation of mimicry, asking questions in this tenor: "How do you indicate that someone is stingy? When you have your fingers like this, what do you mean?"

In this manner Kany gleans a cornucopia of points for his notebooks, in which there is nothing but the concern that keeps the author's very spirit awake: exactitude. Something that is, by the way, very common among northern college professors. If the reader, for example, wants to know in its intimacies and minutiae the history of our loans to North American bankers, up to the exact detail of who received the commission, he has only to read Professor Rippy's book, *The Capitalists and Colombia*.

Or if one wishes to know the history of the Panama Canal, even its Colombian intricacies, one must read Mack's book, *The Land Divided*. And if one is interested in the third of November, in *Cadiz to Cathay*, Mr.

Duval's book, one will find the most meticulous analysis of the correspondence of Tomás Herrán, the best Colombian source on the episode, which one can only find otherwise at the U.S. university to which Herrán willed his papers.

Naturally, not the whole world is as rigorous in its annotations as Kany, Mack, or Duval. Once, Virginia Paxton came here, lived a couple of years in Bogotá, met Jorge Cárdenas, the daughters of Dr. Olaya Herrera, and two or three other people. Later she returned to the United States and wrote a book, *Penthouse in Bogotá*, which on just the second page already says things like this:

> Go into the homes where solid gold service is used at formal dinners . . . roll down Calle Réal in a *coche*, and watch the girls in black shawls bearing trays of orchids on their heads . . . you will see lepers occasionally on the street . . . in Bogotá you will find the bones of Indians laid in hallway mosaics. . . .

It is very possible that Ms. Paxton, to write her book, had gone over the proceedings of another North American journalist who came to South America on a goodwill trip, arrived in Buenos Aires where she was offered a tour by my friend Spec, one of the most helpful and generous men I have ever known, and whom many Bogotanos will remember because this was the origin of his affectionate nickname "Spec," by which he is known as far away as Argentina. Spec said to the journalist: "If you are planning to write a book about South America which discusses Buenos Aires, I think you should visit El Tigre, which is typical of this area. . . ."

"Thank you, no," she replied. "I really think this place is interesting, but I wrote the respective chapter before I left New York."

That writer, naturally, was more clever than Gunther, because Gunther hoped at the very least to fly over each country before writing its respective chapter. Another phenomenon occurred to him: he was flying with such speed that he put items from one country in the text of the next, and we were lucky that he had already edited his volume on Asia before coming to Latin America, because otherwise our history would be intertwined with parts of the Far East's.

Furthermore, Gunther's book, which, according to the engineer Uribe Uribe "is not so bad," at least paints a picturesque and not too unfavorable idea of Colombia for the North American reader, for it was from him that our good neighbors learned that in Bogotá the shoe shiners use oranges to polish leather, and that the first question the Bogotano asks of a foreigner is this: "What do you think of Marcel Proust?"

We can never do enough justice to Ms. Romoli for writing her magnificent book about our homeland, after living in it with great consciousness, walking through fields and cities, reading books about the nation and producing a more judicious, discreet, and cordial book than any Colombian had ever done.

In Colombia, when we read absurdities from northern travelers, or when we have some experiences with outsiders' ignorance, a surge of indignation rises to our heads. This indignation, however, is not well-founded. Because how well do we know the United States? Clearly an American off the street in New York may not know if Bogotá is the capital of Bolivia or Ecuador, but does the reader know the capital of Texas?

Without trying to offend whoever has read thus far—offensiveness under these circumstances would be too much—I want to ask you: Do you know the capital of California?

I include these two examples simply because each of these two states, both with very Spanish histories, is so big that it has more land area than many of the republics of our America, and both managed to have periods of independent rule.

Through mature and thoughtful reflection, I have come to believe that to initiate the so-called era of mutual understanding between the United States and the republics labeled as Latin American, we already have a common, perhaps favorable, base in our mutual ignorance. The differences, if any, are of degree.

This ignorance is explainable. The panorama of things to know in the world grows in such a way that no formula exists to determine what to learn, through reading or academia, to provide that degree of middle culture to which we aspire. Discoveries and inventions multiply. When I studied in secondary school, there were no radios, the airplane seemed problematic, nobody had figured out that one could get penicillin from the scum on rotten cheese, nor that the bread rolls we ate, like black bread, which were offered to nobody, would come to be that bundle of vitamins which today are recognized by any gentleman; I mean, rather not a gentleman: a self-respecting woman.

Today, one must know a little of all these things, and a little bit more history, because any servant's child, like Mr. Hitler, may fill a thousand new volumes. Bachelors can no longer devote the time we once dedicated to the catalog of Asian rivers, which used to give us such mastery over the world that lies between the Obi and the Yang Tse Kiang. But, despite all of these difficulties, we will still need to augment the quantity of our understandings in all spheres, and even more in the Americas, so that North Americans will know more about Bolívar, and we more about Lincoln.

TRANSLATED BY JESSE H. LYTLE

Nicolás Guillén

Cuba

(1902–1989)

———◆•◈•◆———

Widely acclaimed as one of the great recent Cuban poets, Nicolás Guillén left a body of work that spans *Modernismo*, folklorism, social protest, and, most notably, *poesía negrista*. In what was a radical departure from the previous treatment of blacks in Cuban literature—his predecessors and contemporaries often treated blacks as exotic—he portrayed blacks or blackness as an integral element of Cuban culture and a necessary component of the search for a national identity. As a result, his works immediately caught the attention of those unwilling to accept the realities of racial conditions in Cuba. He was the editor of the newspaper *Información* and the weekly humor journal *El loco*. Then, after being dismissed from his job as a typist in the Department of Culture, Guillén increased his involvement in politics. He joined the Cuban Communist Party, which led him to be named Ambassador-at-large and Plenipotentiary Minister of the country's foreign service under Fidel Castro's regime, and, also, president of the Cuban Writer's Union. He published *Cantos para soldados y sones para turistas* in 1937, the same year he joined the party, but his most famous works came later: *El gran zoo* (1967), *El diario que a diario* (1972), and *Poesías completas* (1973). His poetry has been widely translated. In 1972, for example, both *Patria o muerte: The Great Zoo and Other Poems* and *Man-Making Words: Selected Poems* were published in the United States. The following essay, which appeared in December 1950 in the Venezuelan daily *El Nacional* and was incorporated into the second of the three-volume *Prosa de prisa: 1929–1972* (1972), is a lucid reminiscence of the appearance of the black American jazz singer Josephine Baker in Havana, with Guillén's racial and rhythmic motifs beautifully mapped.

Josephine Baker in Cuba

Smoothly rubbing his hands together in a polished display of attentiveness, the employee confessed his impotence with a hypocritical, almost sad smile: "You must understand how embarrassed we feel. You have no idea how sorry we are. However, there isn't a single room available. . . ."

And then he added mysteriously: "Imagine! At the height of the tourist season!"

An embarrassing silence followed. A silence soft and thick as a heavy rug. The presumed guest stood there for a few moments, unsure, drumming his fingers on the thick glass of the counter top. By his side, a slim black woman, still young, her small head topped by a gray beret, questioned him in French. She was none other than Josephine Baker—"the world-famous *vedette*" according to the boisterous announcements promoting her performance in Havana. The man was her husband, Jo Bouillon, white, an orchestra conductor. Nearby, several Cuban friends who had met them at the airport understood the situation all too well but were helpless in their indignation.

What had happened? Nothing but a now familiar occurrence in the sociology of Americans of pure European blood. The splendid Hotel Nacional was refusing lodging to the great artist because of the color of her skin. Of course they had rooms available. But what excuse could the management have offered the blonde North Americans—who cannot stand to be close to "colored people" in their own land—when they found themselves obliged to eat in the same hall as that filthy creature here in Havana? Of course, the teeming tribe of Smiths that overruns this exclusive mansion now and then produces a sudden gentleman, an improvised lord who blows his nose in a napkin or who sticks a fork piled high with rice into his mouth like a domestic fakir. But the whiteness of his skin is beyond all doubt: a slightly pinkish white resembling that of certain tumors just before they are sliced open by a surgeon; their eyes swim in a bluish water; their hair, plastered against their skulls, runs the full gamut of yellows, from ripe wheat to dysentery.

So Mrs. Baker and her husband left the hotel and went to take a room in another, more modest, hotel where the Cuban Constitution offered them greater guarantees. What more could you ask for? As occurs with the fiction of international law by which embassies are extensions of the country to which they belong, so are there many places here where our laws are not worth the paper they're written on. The Hotel Nacional, for example, is Yankee territory. In Havana it stands for a piece of Virginia or Georgia, places where to be black is barely a humanized form of being a dog. Having said that, let us be fair: it must be noted that at no time did Mrs. Baker run the risk of being lynched as she would have in Richmond or Atlanta. Is this not a clear sign of progress, for which we Cubans should pride ourselves?

• • •

The next day, the star of the Folies-Bergères, Parisian to the bone although she was born in the United States, speaking English with a slight inflection from the Boulevard Saint-Michel and placing the stress—in the French manner—on the last syllable of her surname, made her debut in the America Theater before a packed and convulsed hall. The audience received her with a truly torrential standing ovation. Despite her years—now numbering fifty-four—Josephine Baker is still Josephine Baker. Lithe, lively, fiery, and bursting with spirit. Only now, she dances fully clothed.

"Where are the bananas?" a spectator shouted from the balcony.

"I ate them all during the war!" Josephine responded.

And she continued dancing, her marvelous body wrapped tightly in a practically polar, almost Antarctic white suit, a suit like snow slashed by the sun and filled with shining stones. Diamonds? Apparently so. . . . Flowing from her shoulders was a black and white cape that the *vedette* moved like the wings of an enormous butterfly. The ensemble—she herself said so—cost thirty thousand dollars. No wonder, for her complete wardrobe is worth eighteen million francs.

Thus every appearance Josephine makes is like the rising of the sun. No sooner does she emerge than a murmur of amazement rises from the audience like a cloud of words. Hundreds of eyes ambitiously examine her body from head to toe. Immediately, she fills the set with her sensual presence, her broad smile, her mischievous eyes overflowing with fresh, crowd-pleasing charm, her warm, mellow voice like a hand knowingly caressing the most sensitive regions of the skin. Then the murmur turns to a charged, phosphoric anguish that finally explodes in a tempest of thunder and lightning. This takes place every single afternoon, the theater packed to the rafters, the box office sold out by an endless line of men and women, and Josephine, in the admiring embrace of all Havana, squeezed to the point of suffocation.

• • •

It goes without saying that the presence of Josephine Baker among us has already enriched our repertoire of popular anecdotes. They say that on the day of her first performance, people were waiting for her for more than thirty minutes in the Radiocentro building where she was to rehearse. Her eminence notwithstanding—and perhaps because of it, for this happens at times—someone there was one not to mince his words and reprimanded her as was her due for being late. Immediately, Josephine—buoyant, smiling, sophisticated—apologized in Spanish with such grace, such elegance, that the tension dissolved right away. The artists from this radio station immediately surrounded her in an atmosphere of warm sympathy. Present as well was the producer of a certain sponsored program for which the *vedette* had been hired: Señor José Antonio Alonso.

"Señora Baker," he said. "We thought you might sing three numbers for us. Is that all right with you?"

"Just two, Señor Alonso," responded the artist.

"However," the producer insisted, "in these types of performances it is customary to do three numbers."

"I'm sure it is," Josephine responded, "but two, that's it."

Señor Alonso agreed—what could he do!—and then they went on to settle certain technical details of the transmission.

"You will sing the first number, Señora Baker, then there will be a commercial message and afterward, you—"

The producer, distressed, could not finish his sentence. With a firm smile, Josephine had interrupted him.

"No, Señor Alonso. Only two numbers, one right after the other. Between my first and my second number not a word shall be spoken. . . ."

And so it was.

The very modern America Theater has the most luxurious dressing rooms in Havana. When the great black *vedette* was shown to hers, she protested: "Oh no! I can't go in there. I need mirrors on all the walls, a rug on the floor—but a big rug, one that covers the entire floor—and flowers, lots of flowers. I can't live without flowers."

Only a few minutes later, she was satisfied.

• • •

Josephine Baker was great friends with Eliseo Grenet, the acclaimed composer of popular music who had died a month earlier. "He wouldn't wait for me," she said with moist eyes while still in the airport. The next day she visited the cemetery to place a bouquet of roses on the grave of the author of "Mamá Inés." She has said that she will bring the "sucu-sucu" with her to Paris and debut it there, "as he would have wanted, as he would have done."

"Do you like Havana?" a reporter asked her the other day. One of those reporters present in every aerodrome and seaport throughout the world whose function it is to ask equivalent stupidities of illustrious travelers.

"Quite," Mrs. Baker answered courteously. "I have always been obsessed with this country, so warm, so full of fire, with such a dazzling sun. Only . . ."

"Only what?"

"Only . . . it's so cold!"

So it was. The thermometer had been registering—already in November—fifty-seven degrees. . . .

TRANSLATED BY MARK SCHAFER

Eduardo Mallea

Argentina
(1903–1982)

Considered a member of Argentina's intellectual aristocracy, Eduardo Mallea, not unlike Borges, was heavily influenced by European thought. He is often criticized for his elitist tendencies and his perceived apathy toward social injustice. A lawyer by training, Mallea always devoted himself to literature. He cofounded the *Review of America*, had a fifty-year association with *Sur*, and was the editor of *La Nación*'s literary section for over twenty years. Mallea's writing, both in essays and novels, was intensely focused on Argentina's national identity. His writings explore two Argentinas: the visible one, whose character can be seen in the country's institutions and in the life of its citizens; and an invisible one, which represents the nation's essence. Mallea's exploration of the national character is significantly different from that of his predecessors. While, for instance, Domingo Faustino Sarmiento tried to capture the spirit of the country's physical landscape and its psychological impact on the population, Mallea wrote about inner struggles often independent of the physical world. His characters struggle against their own fears and emotions. His essay *History of an Argentine Passion* (1937) and novel *The Bay of Silence* (1937) earned his ideas national and worldwide recognition. Later, more modern novels such as *La red* (1968) and *La penúltima puerta* (1969) were equally thoughtful but did not achieve the recognition of his initial works. Mallea was awarded the First National Prize of Letters (1945), the Grand Prize of Honor of the Argentine Association of Writers (1946), and the Grand National Prize for the Arts (1970). He was Argentina's representative to UNESCO in both Paris and New Delhi. "To Be Argentine," the essay presented here, is the preface to Mallea's *History of an Argentine Passion*.

To Be Argentine

After trying fruitlessly for years to palliate my affliction, I feel the need to shout the anguish caused by my country—our country.

From that anguish is born this reflection, this almost indescribable fever, by which I am incurably consumed. This hopelessness, this love—hungry, impatient, fastidious, intolerant—this cruel vigil.

Behold that suddenly this country exasperates me, discourages me. Against this discouragement I rise up, I touch the skin of my country, her temperature, I am on the watch for the slightest movements of her conscience, I examine her gestures, her reflexes, her predispositions, and I revolt against her, I reproach her, I violently call to her very being, her profound being, when she is on the brink of succumbing to the temptation of so many indiscretions.

I feel the presence of this country like something corporeal. Like a woman of incredible, secret beauty, whose eyes are the color, the majesty, the awesome height of her northern skies, her waterfalls in the jungle; whose body is long, slender at the waist, broad at the shoulders, smooth. Her femininity is the province; her living embryonic child, the active heart of the territories, the governments, the metropolises. Her head lies unflinching near the tropics, at once nearby and distant, a separate thing. Her womb is in the estuary, the incredibly strong womb of humanity, which extends to her heart through two powerful fluvial channels; her svelteness, her nervous system, seem to rest, erect, eternal, in the vertebral system of the Andes. Smooth, effeminate bust around her beautiful, turgid pectorals, the deserts, the sheets, the mountains of the indomitable north; the belly, the pampa, extensive and unwavering like those of normative sculpture. Her members harmonic and long, shaped by the long, stone hills of the Patagonia, not without the regular hair of the valleys. Her feet point to the south; they rest upon the glacial strait; they touch the sterile cliffs and deserts of Cape Horn; and they let the English—once enraged—entertain themselves with the loose slipper of the Falkland Islands.

I want to see her this way, as a woman, because a woman attracts love, as does the motherland.

What can the people born from this motherland be? The embodiment of virility, serenity, courage, intelligence, and virile beauty. Before birth, none can be presumed to betray such a magnificent womb.

The truth: the people born from that womb have been all that. And something more, still something more; in them, intelligence has always been a form of kindness. To love in spirit is to pity, Unamuno said, and he who pities more, loves more.

Of these virtues I have wanted to know which exist and which are on the verge of dying.

I do not want a soliloquy, but rather a dialogue with you, with the Argentines whom I prefer. What fruit would this confession bear, if not the responses it elicits? What effect but the inquietude it awakens, the care, the scruple it provokes, the state of conscience that it can create with its own state? I cannot teach, I cannot—nor do I want to—oblige any thought, I cannot instruct; I would like only to move you, or rather to bring you along with me.

Toward our Argentina, sleepless Argentines; toward a difficult Argentina, toward an easy Argentina. Toward a state of intelligence, not toward a state of panic. I want to say with intelligence: the inception of a distrust in ourselves together with the trust; only this is fruitful. While we live sleeping in certain vague states of well-being, we will be forgetting a destiny. Something else: the responsibility of a destiny. I want to say with intelligence: the total comprehension of our obligation as men, the inclusion of this living comprehension in the life of our nation, the inclusion of a morality, of a defined spirituality, in a natural activity.

You must go toward it, do not be detained, Argentines, taciturn Argentines, Argentines who suffer Argentina like a physical pain.

It is to you that I speak. Not to others. It is not to the Argentine who gets up, calculates the dawn, according to commercial terms, vegetates, speculates, and procreates. It is not to our so-called Patriotic Man, so often sold to ignominiously material gods (and with these appears the extra burden that, over a certain breed of men, exerts the dark blindness of ignorance, the clouded destiny of noncomprehension, and the sad rhythm of emphasis). It is not to those who "make" and "live off" Argentina. No. But to you, who form a segment, perhaps, of that deeply submerged Argentina to whose worthy and noble glory this book is dedicated. To you who are as young as the dawn.

Those others are irrational, the irrational part (to be precise: animal) of our people. And only to the extent that the rationality of a man is lofty, intrinsic nationality, immanent nationality, all which is national grows toward its root. There is nothing more dismal and terrible than the nationalism of men of short reason. It is not by chance that beasts do not recognize a country, but rather wherever they may find safety and sustenance. The rationality of a human being is so much higher; the tree that his nation plants is larger, and it spreads within him. I fear one thing, and it is love without intelligence in the heart, because this is the kind of love that kills but does not protect.

We are verging on so many evils in this land of so much sun, so much land, and so much sky, that I see no way to change course, other than through a categorical, radical, complete mobilization of consciences. Mobilization is maturation: when all the particles of a living organism begin an agitated, dynamic movement is when that organism's fruit will ripen, when the entire organism moves in the sense of its secret prescience, and all of its cells have gained the fortune of organic lucidity. And if we are still a green people, an unripened people, it is not because we are "a young people"—a candid, innocent lie, now that there is no longer youth or age in the world, and in any case it is even older because of certain youthful frustrations—but because our conscience is lagging behind, she has not arisen from her wellspring, from her lowland, but remains on the verge of herself, as if she were closed. What we lack is real fruit, and only our Creole tree branches have spread in the false space of an apparent supercivilization.

The children of the children of Argentines, what are they like? This is a question one must anxiously feel. I know what they are like in their vital form, but I do not know what they are like in their moral form. I know they will be rich, I know they will be physically strong; technically able; what I do not know is whether they will be Argentines. I do not know if they will be Argentines because I know their parents have already lost their sense of Argentineness.

The sense of Argentineness. Even in enunciating it, it sounds strange, because it hardly carries any credit with us; it does not have the necessary credulous, responsible history. It is a white prayer, like those white voices they use in America to speak of spiritual and cultural things, that is to say, in purely locutory, insubstantial terms. And if this fundamental prayer is a white prayer, one need not shout to the heavens, but to the soul; one must shout to the soul. One must shout to the soul, because we face the proof of a certainty, and it is that our conscience stays immature and we run the risk not just of remaining but of becoming increasingly premature men.

Those who were born as a people were not so. We are increasingly so through an involution, a process of involution before which one must stop and say no. Not by remaining in our affliction, sunken in the arid reflection of our lair, but rather by precipitously, passionately, leaving our chamber to carry to our neighbor's home the declaration of our critical decision and our hunger, our "no" to this sluggish advance whose progress is like a stupor, which displaces itself on men, masses, and cities.

No, the Argentina we want is another. Different. With a conscience in motion, a conscience like it should be, in other words, natural wisdom. If, according to the Socratic theory recorded by Plato in his *Phaedon*, science is reminiscence, what we need at all times is reminiscence, or call it previous understanding of the origin of our destiny; and in the origin of our destiny is the origin of our feeling, conduct, and nature. Our natural origin potentially contains our evolution; if we lose our memory, or call it the science, of our interior origin—what more can we be than a roving optimism? To have originated is to constantly originate, to be born is to keep being born—and if we do not know how and why we possess this constant birth, our ignorance will acquire, under the guise of self-perpetuating life, the value of repeating death. Notice that these reflections, carried to their extreme consequence, do not leave me calm. Every day I see the real Argentina pervert herself through some act or other. One moment she is there, present; the next she is gone. Futile to try to get her to look at herself; her voice is muffled by the circumstantial sum of ignorances. Which prompts her to strike an attitude not unlike that of certain youths, who will just as soon please as discourage. What to do with this country which plays out the parable of the Prodigal Son? She has gone off in search of happiness and wealth; it is impossible not to notice that she has also distanced herself too far from something she should never leave: her sense of interior progress.

And peoples, like men—once more, mister, like men!—were not masters of their ends, but of their paths. No species living on this planet knows its end; everything lies in the path. Men are living paths, path the winged bug who dies in oil. Path is life and path is death. Everything is path. Path is the body and path is the soul headed toward a remote consumption. Path the love, path the charity, path the hatred that divides and the hope that rises in the east with every dawn. Path the apparent immobility of the mobile constellations; the doubt, the joy, and the agony. Path the man who lurks in the shadows to strike with treachery and the woman who—flesh and blood—kills in the name of love; path the dream of the taciturn, the courage of the brave, the activity of the active, the laziness of the lazy, woman's periodic evil, and the height of her poetic anguish and her twilight delirium, the gait of a child, the cruel reservation of the atheist, the lie of the bad Christian, the pride of the prosperous, and the bitterness of the poor. These are all paths.

We are poor masters of our paths when we begin to neglect them. Because then, according to the parable in the Scriptures, he who goes in search of opulent days and nights returns on the path of sorrow as a hog farmer. Machiavelli understood this all too well, with his prescient discretion and his face of dark, suspicious imbecility (as can be seen in the corner of the Florentine ducal chamber), when he was counseling Lorenzo the Magnificent: "Some have believed and others keep on believing that God controls all things in this world, and fate, without man's prudence influencing changes or knowing how to remedy them . . . , but I dare venture that if half of our acts depend upon fate, then man controls, at least, the other half."

Nothing is controlled, to be honest, for we live on the plain, a point from which one does not command; but it is or is not so, depending on whether or not we wield the courage of our conscience. This, which could seem almost nothing, is such a critical thing that, because of it alone, a Man was imprisoned in the Olive Garden and was dead by nightfall, on a Saturday eve, and dead, by the same token, the good and evil thieves, and an evil judge lost, and some centurions saddened without apparent motive, and many people buried alive in the catacombs of the Roman countryside and, epoch upon epoch, men thrust against men, with no more to give than themselves, and at the end of their lives, in the cruelest of their wars, a weak moan and a belated nostalgia for peace and survival.

Our people have only recently become lost; it has been but in this century: now barely more than thirty-something. I have seen immigrants before and immigrants after; in them one can study one's self, like the deep disturbances in a countenance, the history of our decadence as a country, more than as a nation or a state. (And they are hardly upset, those whom these truths affect; the greater their sense of outrage, the worse will be their guilt on the day when enough decide to better themselves.) I have seen foreigners who arrived in our country when the voices of our greatest intelligences were still alive, and, for these men, that which was Argentine was a state of religiosity; land and tree, house or man, everything from here inspired highly original devotion in men who came from peoples where human power had lost efficiency; they were here to see the almost heroic rise of a nationality where anything could be created, from the metropolitan parks, the urban line of dwellings, the martial songs, the political foresight, the organic reality of the extrinsic and intrinsic sides of the country, to the invisible articulation of her intelligence. It was the moral exploit and the material of a territory fabulously oriented to the future. But this was not an illusory and deserted future, rather an active and inhabited future, a present future, like the futures of all that which is created by a volitive act, in which the future is no more than the progress, or subsequent form, of an actual act. And before the spectacle of that authentic potential grandeur, men gathered from other lands, consubstantiated, kept silent. I have seen in their antiquity, in the antiquity of such men, the traces of this fervent suffering, so simple, so emotional, and so pure. And before them I have been touched with an emotion from my land, because in those faces full of black wrinkles, like those of old peasants, friends of the eternal, free of earthly avarice, that expression endured; none other than the look of a new man, the spectacle of a dawn which lasts until midnight and then begins again. They had felt all around them, around these foreigners, the buzz of a wisdom: the buzz of ideas, feelings, hopes, faces, wills in motion, the buzz of a world of recent men which gives birth to itself, but not in darkness, but rather as a child who makes his way through the darkness of the maternity ward. They spoke of Argentine things, of the old guardian men (like the discourse of [Nicolás] Avellaneda upon the repatriation of San Martín's remains), of this or that sensible virtue in this or that new man in his new land, with the same tender, slightly solemn voice with which, in their birthplace, beyond the ocean, they had learned to decipher Ecclesiastes.

And I have seen the subsequent immigrant. And in vain I have wanted to sense in those youthful, ambitious faces the brilliance with which they may understand something more than the letters of the metropolitan advertisements, hear something more than the songs in the cafe, see something more than the physical image of a comfortable country, perceive, all in all, something more defined and profound than the mere feeling of a pretentious national orchestration. I have seen them: happy on the outside, deaf on the inside. Tied to our destiny, without really knowing us: without having any anticipation of us, without seeing beyond our skin.

Is it their fault? No; it is ours, Argentines. Because their deafness is a mode we must attribute to our silence. In our silence we prefer not to think. We believe that we have had enough of proclaiming our innermost thought: onward! And God will provide.

What a hoax! What a hoax! Because God will not provide. It is written: "He who seeks to save his soul, shall lose it." He who wants to save his soul; it is thus that our free will is lost when it is not ordained to a transcendental principle, when we let it go the way of our virtue, of our heart, and our knowledge—these being not only the fertile hands of man, but the branches of the fundamental tree, the principal principle, because there are no principles that do not flourish on those three branches.

Now it is inevitable that I begin to talk about me. So inevitable, so essential! These pages are dictated, I have already said it, by an anxiety, by an aspiration, by a need for dialogue. I would like to have some Argentine faces turned for an instant to my own discomfort, to my own struggle, to my own hopes, to my agonies and renaissances before a people whose destiny keeps me at the outer limits of my anxiety. My word is almost only fervor; I almost want no more than to share this fervor with others, that is, to confess, to make my faith common with others. There is no absolute friendship that is not based on an uninterrupted confession, in an understanding, watching, feeling of everything, by confession. Confession means unity, without which there can be nothing between you and me, the reader who must judge, love, abominate, or suffer through me.

With which, the pretension of these pages is not unsubstantial, and too grand is its purpose; because its pretension and purpose are to find some men in their paths and stop them so they may share the causes of their contrition, of their faith, and say, "That is why we live, that is why we suffer, that is why we struggle, that is why we love, that is why we bleed, and that is why we die."

I do not know that there is on earth, with the exception of faith itself, any other possibility of consolation.

TRANSLATED BY JESSE H. LYTLE

Luis Cardoza y Aragón

Guatemala

(1904–1992)

———◆•✦•◆———

Born in Antigua, Guatemala, Luis Cardoza y Aragón was forced to a life of exile by the highly unstable political situation in his homeland. He moved first to New York and then to Paris, where he befriended Peruvian *Vanguardista* poet César Vallejo and Mexican critic Alfonso Reyes. From 1932 to 1944 he lived in Mexico, where he would return and settle down permanently in 1952, after spending less than a decade in Guatemala. His initial work was a volume of poetry, *Cuando termine mi segundo engendro* (1926). But his most prolific period was in Mexico, where he established himself as a perceptive art critic. His critical works include *La nube y el reloj* (1940), *José Clemente Orozco* (1964), and *México: Pintura de hoy* (1964). Upon his return to Guatemala in 1944, Cardoza y Aragón became a player in the political sphere, publishing the important journal *Revista de Guatemala* for a number of years. Back in Mexico, he published *La revolución guatemalteca* (1955) and his most acclaimed work, combining fiction, history, and political commentary, *Guatemala: Las líneas de su mano* (1955), which includes the evocative essay "A Macaw at the Pole." His vast oeuvre includes other volumes of poetry, stories, and collections of essays. Cardoza y Aragón's fractured, experimental autobiography, *El río: Novelas de caballería* (1986), discusses his relationship with César Vallejo, Alfonso Reyes, Diego Rivera, Pablo Neruda, and Gabriel García Márquez, among many other prominent Latin American intellectuals.

A Macaw at the Pole

Guatemalans, an inhibited people, neither sing nor speak. Introverted; on guard; ignored and ignorant. Dialogue is accomplished by subtraction, through inference, questions, feints, ellipses, parentheses: amphibological communication—slippery, semi-encoded, reticent. Smiles, gestures, formulas of courtesy and elusion, diminutives, and diminutives of diminutives complete this veiled language of circumlocution that either shouts or hides behind the discreet conditional tense. It is a language that resists reduction to a simple yes or no. Rather, it simulates, invents, eludes, lies to itself so it can lie to others, dons a disguise and mimes itself so the disguise ceases to be one and becomes a skin, passes from mere appearance to become a new reality, a created, reserved, invented nature that never conceals itself as fully as it would prefer.

This deformation is a consequence both of our social structure and of the brutal rigidity of our despotisms. What taskmasters we have had! How many years have we enjoyed without oppression, let's not even say with genuine liberty, between 1524 and 1821, the year of our independence, and between that date and the October Revolution of 1944? Perhaps—perhaps!—fifteen years, and this only for a minimal part of the population: the indigenous people have never known anything but suffering. "They have the custom of never affirming the things they know and see," observed Fuentes y Guzmán, a Creole historian of the seventeenth century. "They always answer, 'Perhaps this may be so, perhaps that may exist,' even though they have full knowledge of the matter they are being queried about because they have seen it with their own eyes. . . ." In the time of Justo Rufino Barrios, the Nicaraguan Enrique Guzmán wrote in his *Diario íntimo*: "Discretion is obligatory in the Republic of Guatemala. It is impossible to find people more reserved than the *chapines* or Guatemalans. Even the drunkards here are circumspect."

Guatemalans speak in a low voice, insinuating, evading, expressing demands and affirmations through questions. Thus they seem gentle and somewhat evasive, even when they are imperious and arbitrary. Always contained, timid and self-absorbed, they grow hard from having to bury alive so many of their thoughts and wishes. Whenever they try to speak out, the results backfire. Their teeth have been broken. They shield themselves with a pretended indifference or reserve, as if half asleep; they have been on guard for centuries, waiting for the smallest opportunity to shout their misery for all to hear, to fight for and perhaps win their liberty. Their stubborn will persists, and when it has exploded at certain moments, it has destroyed dikes with the natural violence of centuries of retention. It can remain dormant through long seasons of terror like those trees that seem dead during winter, their branches dramatically bare, but which, as soon as they sense the approach of the sun, long before we do, poke new sprouts through their bark, and in a matter of days grace the countryside with the brilliance of spring green. This is how I perceive the people of Guatemala: down deep, their sap is alive; their lush abundance of blossoms and fruit is hidden from view. Not the land of eternal spring, but the land of eternal tyranny. An abused, silent, truthful people who do not sing.

Their silence, always fresh, seeming always to have just begun, is truly tragic. For centuries the Indians have braced themselves for coercion—anticipating the muzzle, the red hot branding iron, the gunpowder, even when they are being questioned about their wants. Their infinite muteness is almost mineral; they are mere earth, earth that plows the earth. Their music, spare, scarce, all but forgotten, is an endless monotonous wail. Their dance, the *son*, is a sad tapping of soles in the livelier cadences of a primitive melody that is repeated endlessly. The imagination we see in temples, stelae, frescoes, magic books, and folk art lies hidden, an ember that does not flame. Its inner warmth still comforts bones, eases torments, but the people will not know the light through their own eyes nor through their own songs until, naked, they lie down at last to rest in the earth, faces toward the sun. The eclipse is total, and if they do not explode in their muteness, it is because something is relieved through religious rites in jungle and mountain; in these festivals, communing with nature far away from Creoles and mestizos, they may get drunk in desperation; having been desperate for so many centuries they no longer know they are desperate.

Despite the beauty and color of their cultures, silence confers upon the indigenous people an Edenic, melancholy character. I think that through the gorgeous color of their clothing, the marvelous objects they create, their pottery, they seek escape, just as they seek it through alcohol and prayer. Without those costumes, without the beauty of the land, they would already have exploded as if from dynamite. With the gayest clothing in the world, total color, and in a landscape opulent as a ripe fruit, total color, the Indian is total melancholy. Because for Guatemalans, the sadness of the Indian is not a cliché; this sadness is exuded through the country's every pore. There is no literature in its very real extremes of misery and abandonment. What human being anywhere in the world is more vulnerable? Taciturn country, sun-baked and austere. An atmosphere in which everyone seems to have fled the scene of a crime; the silence that follows a catastrophe. One might entertain any thought except that a happy song was about to be heard. An obstructive silence, because one can never determine why and how a word about to be spoken can be so dangerous. Our silence is made of songs we have not been able to sing. The tension of the social climate has not allowed for song; it shrivels it even as it is born; to flourish, song must have a nursery. Perhaps song might be possible for the Indian in the depth of the forest where laughter, like orchids, is born fresh and acclimated. In the village, in the city, laughter seems alien; it makes no echo. One realizes, accurately, that joy would splinter the quiet glass air. A rousing song would be like a shot.

Suddenly at a party a little marimba of *tecomates* [gourd resonators] takes off like a frisky pony that begins to buck and tries to throw its rider, then just as suddenly reverts to its lament. The Guatemalan *son*, rhythmic and monotonous, intones its cadences over the fragrance of pine in the air. The *aguardiente* [a potent local liquor] flows in a melancholy stream. The party may go on for several days. Pigs, chickens, turkeys, and calves may be killed for the revel. Tamales are cooked. Guns are fired. But the atmosphere remains tense and sad, like a funeral drum. The sound of the marimba, which is part of a Guatemalan childhood, like the scent of pine and camomile of the manger scenes, the aroma of coffee, of chocolate, of tamales and *chipilines*, is nasal, guttural, with a persistent undertone of rain and whippings. When it is struck with mallets covered with crude rubber, the vibrations merge because there are no pedals to damp them, and the sound produced is a wooden rain shower. If the marimba is a bad one, resonance is poor, and the wooden bars produce a dead sound like a thump on a table.

The marimba of *tecomates* sings sweetly, sadly. Its sound is pleasant and controlled. The Guatemalan *son* performed on it gives an idea of native music of the sixteenth century. It is curious that traces of black heritage cannot be identified here, because it must have exerted an influence on rhythm and dance. Perhaps this has not occurred because of the relatively small number of slaves imported from Africa. It was they who brought us the marimba, which many believe to be autochthonous. Cherished and nurtured here, it had a new birth. One would have thought that other testimonies of African presence might have survived. Music and dance constitute a beautiful language of theirs known in the United States, Cuba, Venezuela, Colombia, Brazil, Puerto Rico, Santo Domingo and, of course, Haiti. In both popular and high culture, black music and dance are pre-eminent. Jazz, spirituals, rhumbas, *danzones*, and other variants are admirable for their rhythm and expressive power. Black and indigenous peoples have provided the basis of some of our contemporary achievements in art. As we develop greater awareness, we advance toward the expression of the genuine. Sometimes, not knowing how to react, we force ourselves to be what we are not and in our resentment rage against everything European. Resentment grows strong and next we spurn everything indigenous and end up despising everything we possess, however solid or admirable, then swing to the opposite extreme: a totally false obsession with everything European. There is a childish confusion in all of this, often political in origin, a harmful and primitive politics, created for self-defense, to give ourselves an alibi.

We get drunk in order to be more alone. We get drunk in the company of others in order to augment our loneliness. There is no conversation, only monologues. Even in conversation there is really no dialogue; each speaker is obsessed with his or her private concerns. We do not openly break our cover, our suspicious, reserved, introverted character. It is hard for us to venture out of our shells; if we do, it is precisely in order to burst into a monologue. We shout, empty our revolvers into the air, lean back in our chairs to hear ourselves better: we are really talking to ourselves. Our insecurity cannot abide contradiction or difference of opinion. We are intolerant, passionate—fanatics whose fetish has been profaned. What a lack of imagination!

Guatemalans prefer not to put their identity to the test in conversing.

They prefer to sink slowly into a river of alcohol. If a Guatemalan is calm, we discover his presence from time to time, like that of whales, by the spout he shoots up in the air: a joke, an off-color remark, an ancient howl. In the meantime, a marimba hammers out a Viennese waltz. We speak and act for ourselves. Company may provoke a monologue, expand it, turn it angry; but its development remains in the mode of a monologue. Our is not a sociable drunkenness. We don't sing together in chorus. Violence, born of resentment, is perhaps the consequence of believing that anybody who has been kicked ought to kick somebody else. . . .

Drunkenness is gloomy and seldom leads to joy, laughter, singing. The marimba of *tecomates* siphons its lethargy into the Indian conviviality: a soft, submissive sound, born of the plant kingdom. The marimba bemoans the slavery of blacks and Indians. Their exhausted voices are blended in its sound. Without alcohol the fiesta won't come to life; everyone would retreat into silence, impassive and absent. People drink to the point of tears, to the point of killing, even dying.

The country drinks brandy and the people's enthusiasm for it is evident, because when people drink, they drink to excess. The Conquest, colonial subjection, the tyrannies and economic discrimination all play a part in this excess and in the kind of parties we have. In the year of Justo Rufino Barrios, liquor provided the second highest revenue for the State. If people sang, they would not drink this way. If they danced, if they could laugh. If only they could. The climate doesn't permit the budding of such a bloom. Laughter still does not germinate here except in a very attenuated way. How rare it is—like glimpsing a quetzal in flight—to hear an Indian really cut loose and guffaw.

Our drunkenness is a solitary drunkenness; we take our egos' hour of hiding, terrified that somebody will look at them. Oppressed, pinched egos, unaccustomed to the light—scorned, insulted, slandered, denied, deformed, mutilated, and distrustful. In drunkenness the ego does not succeed in opening itself, in revealing itself in its ideal form. The mestizos of all social classes get drunk in the same way. The latest statistics prove that if we calculate, fairly accurately, that a half million people drink alcoholic beverages on an average of 16 liters apiece annually, this comes to nearly one and a half liters per month per person. As a way of debasing the Indians, people have tried to spread the idea that they drink to excess: their consumption, however, does not even begin to approach that of the upper classes. Marimba music is also the music of the non-Indian or *ladino*, and is heard at clubs and society parties. Guatemala has transformed the marimba into a nearly perfect instrument, with a keyboard similar to that of the piano. In the best bands there is never just one marimba, but two that play at the same time: the small one has a higher tone whose vegetable timbre is enhanced by the sound of jazz trumpets. We are so marimbatized, it is practically blasphemous to even suggest this.

The roads are traveled by devotees of the *cofradías* or religious brotherhoods who go from town to town, and with them come the marimbas, like great alligators, carried on someone's shoulders. Marimbas, along with trumpets, saxophones, cymbals, and drums, play "classical music" (generally overtures of Italian operas) as well as popular tunes—the latest Afro-American dances; in both cases the effect is rather unfortunate.

How could our people be expected to sing? It is a fact of history that only yesterday the people were on the ground, face downward, beaten to a pulp. Today they are right back there. They had begun to lift their heads cautiously, open their eyes fearfully, to wonder whether things had actually changed. It was difficult for them to stand, to walk, to speak. They had forgotten how to smile. Today, nevertheless, life still stirs in their bodies, like spring sap rising in an old tree. They smile once more, sometimes, with a bristly tenderness. A belly laugh is completely improbable—the flash of a macaw at the North Pole.

The fundamental causes of underdevelopment are the imbalance in land distribution and the system of exploitation; this is the origin of the poverty of the immense majority of the dispossessed population, the campesinos. Another factor is the machinations of foreign companies that dominate our economy, creaming off the super-earnings of a colonial power. Dictators are an effect, not a cause, the result of the lack of property division, which has also impeded the development of a domestic market and the growth of the working class and the middle class and of national capital that could create industries. All our strongmen have served the large landowners; they have been the puppets of imperialism. Their identification with the dominant class is the only thing necessary to explain their existence. Individual variants—liberal or conservative—have sometimes been quite important, but they have not had an impact on our basic problems, because all the dictators, without exception, have concentrated solely on perpetuating the power of the same class.

For our people, a revolution that does not solve the fundamental problem of land does not deserve to be called a revolution.

These are some aspects of life in Guatemala. A great deal more could be added if I had not proposed to make this a brief synthesis. In my remarks on the dynamics of the economy, I would not want anyone to forget that my simplified treatment could not do justice to the complexities responsible for the magnitude of our problem.

TRANSLATED BY JO ANNE ENGELBERT

Alejo Carpentier

Cuba
(1904–1980)

Born in Havana to an immigrant family, Alejo Carpentier sought to integrate and even harmonize the Spanish and African traditions of his native Cuba with his French background. He studied music theory and wrote theatrical and musical critiques for Cuban newspapers and magazines in Paris, where he lived with his paternal grand-parents. His popular *La música en Cuba* (1946) attests to the writer's deep interest in music. He also studied architecture in Havana but abandoned his studies in 1922 for economic reasons. From then on, Carpentier devoted himself to writing. In his homeland he helped inspire the *Vanguardista* movement before moving to Paris as a political refugee and then settling in Venezuela. In 1959, after Fidel Castro's revo-lution, he returned home and was later sent to France as a diplomat. His novels include *Ecué-Yamba-O!* (1933), *The Lost Steps* (1953), *The Chase* (1956), *Explosion in the Cathedral* (1962), *Baroque Concert* (1974), and *The Harp and the Shadow* (1978), and he received the prestigious Cervantes Prize in 1978 for his contribution to Hispanic letters. Carpentier's prologue to *The Kingdom of This World* (1949) is a turning point in the intellectual and artistic history of Latin America. Written after a trip to Haiti in 1943, it is at once a voyage of identity and a manifesto of Carpentier's aesthetic ideas. In it he discusses for the first time the concept of *lo real maravilloso*, which eventually was turned into magical realism. In his eyes the people in the New World did not need the artificial stimuli of surrealism, an important artistic movement in Europe in the forties, because Latin America itself as a whole has a magical reality. With time Carpentier grew uncomfortable with the prologue because in essence it opposed the socialist realism of Fidel Castro's revolution. He eliminated it from future editions of *The Kingdom of This World*, but made it part of his collection *Tientos y diferencias* (1964). Very few essays have had a similar impact on the Latin American consciousness.

Prologue: The Kingdom of This World

What we are to understand in this matter of metamorphosis into wolves is that there is an illness doctors call lupine mania.
—The Toils of Persiles and Segismunda

Toward the end of 1943, I had the good fortune to be able to visit the kingdom of Henri Christophe—the poetic ruins of Sans-Souci, the massive citadel of La Ferrière, impressively intact despite lightning bolts and earthquakes—and to acquaint myself with the still Norman-style Cap-Haitien (the Cap Français of the former colony) where a street lined with long balconies leads to the cut-stone palace inhabited once upon a time by Pauline Bonaparte.

After feeling the in no way false enchantment of this Haitian earth, after discovering magic presences on the red roads of the Central Plateau, after hearing the drums of Petro and Rada, I was moved to compare this marvelous reality I'd just been living with the exhaustingly vain attempts to arouse the marvelous that characterize certain European literatures of these last thirty years. The marvelous, sought for by means of the old clichés of the Forest of Broceliande, the Knights of the Round Table, Merlin the Magician, and Arthurian cycle. The marvelous, poorly suggested by the acts and deformities of sideshow characters—will the young poets of France ever get tired of the freaks and clowns of the fête foraine, to which Rimbaud bade farewell in his Alchemy of the Word?

The marvelous, obtained through sleight-of-hand, through bringing together objects ordinarily never found in the same place: the old, lying tale of the fortuitous encounter of the umbrella and the sewing machine on an operating table, which engendered ermine spoons, the snails in the rainy taxi, the head of a lion on the pelvis of a widow in surrealist exhibitions. Or, even more to the point, the literary marvelous: the king in Sade's *Juliette*, Jarry's supermacho, Lewis's monk, the hair-raising theatrical props of the English gothic novel: ghosts, walled-up priests, lycanthropy, hands nailed to the castle door.

But, by attempting to arouse the marvelous at all costs, the thaumaturges become bureaucrats. Invoked by means of all-too-well-known formulas that make certain paintings into a monotonous mess of molasses-covered clocks, of seamstress' dummies, of vague phallic monuments, the marvelous is left behind in the umbrella, the lobster, the sewing machine, wherever, on an operating table, within a sad room, a stony desert. Miguel de Unamuno said that having to memorize rule books meant a poverty of imagination. And today there exist rule books of the fantastic based on the principle of the burro devoured by the fig, posited in the *Chants de Maldoror* as the supreme inversion of reality, to which we owe many of André Masson's *Children Menaced by Nightingales* or *Horses Devouring Birds*.

But we should note that when André Masson tried to draw the forest on the island of Martinique, with the incredible entangling of its plants and the obscene promiscuity of certain fruits, the marvelous truth of the subject devoured the painter, leaving him virtually impotent before the empty page. And it had to be a painter from America, the Cuban Wifredo Lam, who showed us the magic of tropical vegetation, the uncontrolled Creation of Forms in our nature—with all its metamorphosis and symbiosis—in monumental paintings whose expression is unique in contemporary art. In the face of the disconcerting poverty of imagination of a Tanguy, for example, who for twenty-five years now has been painting the same petrified larvae under the same gray sky, I feel the urge to recite a phrase that was the pride of the Surrealists of the first generation: *Vous qui ne voyez pas, pensez à ceux qui voient.*

There are still too many "adolescents who take pleasure in raping the cadavers of beautiful, freshly murdered women" (Lautréamont), without realizing how marvelous it would be to rape them alive. It's that so many people forget, because it costs them so little to dress up as magicians, that the marvelous begins to be marvelous in an unequivocal way when it arises from an unexpected alteration of reality (a miracle), from a privileged revelation of reality, from an illumination that is either unusual or singularly favorable to the unnoticed riches of reality, from an amplification of the scale and categories of reality perceived with particular intensity by means of an exaltation of the spirit that leads it to a kind of "limit-state."

In the first place, the sensation of the marvelous presupposes a faith. Those who do not believe in saints cannot be cured by the miracles of saints, in the same way that those who are not Quixotes cannot enter, body and soul, the world of Amadis of Gaul or Tirant lo Blanc. Certain remarks about men being transformed into wolves made by the character Rutilio in Cervantes's *Toils of Persiles and Segismunda* are prodigiously believable because in Cervantes's day it was believed there were people afflicted with lupine mania. The same applies to the character's journey from Tuscany to Norway on a witch's cape. Marco Polo allowed that certain birds flew carrying elephants in their talons; Martin Luther saw the Devil right before his eyes and threw an inkwell at his head. Victor Hugo, so exploited by the book-keepers of the marvelous, believed in ghosts, because he was sure of having spoken, while in Guernsey, with the ghost of Leopoldina.

All Van Gogh needed was to have faith in the Sunflower to capture its revelation on a canvas. Thus the idea of the marvelous invoked in the context of disbelief—which is what the surrealists did for so many years—was never anything but a literary trick, and a boring one at that after being prolonged, as was a certain "arranged" oneiric literature, as were certain praises of folly, which we left behind long, long ago. But by the same token, we are not, for all that, going to yield to those who advocate a *return to the real*—an expression that takes on, in this context, the value of a political slogan—because they are merely replacing the magician's tricks with the commonplaces of "committed" literary hacks or the scatological delights of some existentialists.

But it is unquestionably true that it is hard to make a case for poets and artists who praise sadism without practicing it, who admire the supermacho because of their own impotence, who invoke spirits without believing they answer their chants, and who found secret societies, literary sects, vaguely philosophic groups, with passwords and arcane goals—never achieved—without being able to conceive a valid mysticism or to abandon their pettiest habits and risk their souls on the play of a frightening card of faith.

All of that became particularly evident to me during my stay in Haiti, where I found myself in daily contact with something we could call the *real marvelous*. I was treading earth where thousands of men eager for liberty believed in Mackandal's lycanthropic powers, to the point that their collective faith produced a miracle the day of his execution. I already knew the prodigious story of Bouckman, the Jamaican initiate. I entered the La Ferrière citadel, a structure without architectonic antecedents, portended only in Piranesi's *Imaginary Prisons*. I breathed the atmosphere created by Henri Christophe, monarch of incredible undertakings, much more surprising than all the cruel kings invented by the surrealists, who are very fond of imaginary, though never suffered, tyrannies.

With each step I found *the real marvelous*. But I also realized that the presence and authority of the real marvelous was not a privilege unique to Haiti but the patrimony of all the Americas, where, for example, a census of cosmogonies is still to be established. The real marvelous is found at each step in the lives of the men who inscribed dates on the history of the Continent and who left behind names still borne by the living: from the seekers after the Fountain of Youth or the golden city of Manoa to certain rebels of the early times or certain modern heroes of our wars of independence, those of such mythological stature as Colonel Juana Azurduy.

It's always seemed significant to me that in 1780 some perfectly sane Spaniards from Angostura, set out even then in search of El Dorado, and that, during the French Revolution—long live Reason and the Supreme Being!—Francisco Menéndez, from Compostela, traversed Patagonia hunting for the Enchanted City of the Caesars. Looking at the matter in another way, we see that while in western Europe dance-related folklore has lost all its magic, spirit-invoking character, it is rare that a collective dance in the Americas does not contain a profound ritual meaning that creates around it an entire initiatory process: the *santería* dances in Cuba or the prodigious Black version of the feast of Corpus, which may still be seen in the town of San Francisco de Yare in Venezuela.

There is a moment in the sixth song of Maldoror when the hero, chased by all the police in the world, escapes from "an army of agents and spies" by taking on the shape of diverse animals and making use of his ability to transport himself instantly to Peking, Madrid, or Saint Petersburg. This is "marvelous literature" at its peak. But in the Americas, where nothing like that has been written, there existed a Mackandal who possessed the same powers because of the faith of his contemporaries and who used that magic to inspire one of the most dramatic and strange uprisings in History.

Maldoror—Isidor Ducasse himself confesses it—was nothing more than a "poetic Rocambole." All he left behind was a short-lived literary school. The American Mackandal, on the other hand, has left behind an entire mythology, accompanied by magical hymns, preserved by an entire people, who still sing them at Vaudou ceremonies. (There is, on the other hand, a strange coincidence in the fact that Isidore Ducasse, a man who had an exceptional instinct for the fantastic-poetic, was born in the Americas and bragged so emphatically at the end of one of his chapters of being "Le Montevidéen.") Because of the virginity of its landscape, because of its formation, because of its ontology, because of the Faustian presence of the Indian and of the Black, because of the Revelation its recent discovery constituted, because of the fertile racial mixtures it favored, the Americas are far from having used up their wealth of mythologies.

The text that follows, even though I didn't propose it to myself in a systematic fashion, responds to this order of concerns. It tells a sequence of extraordinary events that occurred on the island of Saint Domingue over the course of a period which does not exceed an entire human life. It allows the *marvelous* to flow freely from a reality followed strictly in all its details. The reader must be warned that the story he is going to read is based on an extremely rigorous documentation which not only respects the historical truth of the events, the names of the characters (even the minor ones), of the places, and even the streets but which hides under its apparently non-chronological façade, a minute collation of dates and chronologies.

And yet, because of the dramatic singularity of the events, because of the fantastic bearing of the characters who met, at a given moment, in the magical crossroads of Cap-Haitien, everything seems marvelous in a story it would have been impossible to set in Europe and which is as real, in any case, as any exemplary event yet set down for the edification of students in school manuals. But what is the history of all the Americas but a chronicle of the real marvelous?

TRANSLATED BY ALFRED MACADAM

Pablo Neruda

Chile
(1904–1973)

———◦•••◦———

Chilean Pablo Neruda, one of the great poets of the twentieth century, spent the early portion of his career publishing his poetry in magazines and newspapers. Later he released *Twenty Love Poems and a Song of Despair* (1924) and coauthored a book of essays, *Anillos* (1926). Born Ricardo Eliecer Neftalí Reyes, he took the name Pablo from his idol Paul Verlaine and the surname from a Czech gothic novelist. His poetic style was popular in its appeal as he became not only a national poet but the poet of a continent. Although he sometimes uses complex structures, the language and metaphors of Neruda's works remain relatively accessible. For two decades, Neruda traveled the world in a diplomatic capacity, during which time he produced *Residence on Earth* (1925–35) and *España in Our Hearts* (1937), followed by his masterpiece, *Canto General* (1950). Throughout the 1940s Neruda became increasingly politically active as a communist (he was a close friend of Mexican muralists Diego Rivera and José Clemente Orozco), writing *Carta íntima para millones de hombres*, *Yo acuso*, and *Viajes*. Other works include *Elementary Odes* (1954–59), *Extravagaria* (1958), and *Memorial of Isla Negra* (1964). Two posthumous autobiographical volumes are also noteworthy: *Confieso que he vivido: Memorias* (1974), known in English simply as *Memoirs*, and *Para nacer he nacido* (1978). Neruda was awarded the Nobel Prize for literature, and the following essay is his Stockholm acceptance speech, delivered on 13 December 1971. Its echoes are fascinating: Around that time Neruda ran for president of Chile but, in the final quest, decided to endorse the campaign of his friend Salvador Allende. The bloody coup d'état that brought General Augusto Pinochet into power in 1973 and forced Allende to suicide pushed Neruda to a terrible depression. He died that same year of a heart attack.

The Nobel Address

My remarks will trace a long voyage, a personal journey through far regions in the antipodes whose remoteness does not lessen their resemblance to the landscape and solitudes of the North. I am speaking of the extreme south of my country. We Chileans retreat farther and farther until we come to the boundaries of the South Pole that is the source of our similarity to the geography of Sweden, whose head brushes the snowy northern pole of the planet.

There in the remote wilderness of my native land, where I found myself because of a series of events now forgotten, if one must—and I had to—reach the Argentine frontier, one must first cross the Andes. In those inaccessible regions one travels through great forests as if through tunnels, and along that dark and forbidden route there were very few recognizable landmarks. And yet, in this land where there were no tracks, no trails, I and my four companions, in a snaking cavalcade—overcoming the obstacles of imposing trees, impassable rivers, enormous outcroppings of rock, desolate snows—had to seek—more accurately, to reckon—the route to my freedom. The men accompanying me knew the direction we must travel, the potential routes through the heavy undergrowth. But to be more certain on their return—after they had abandoned me to my fate—from their horses they slashed at the bark with their machetes, blazing a trail on towering trees.

Each of us rode forward awed by that limitless solitude, that green and white silence, the trees, the huge climbing vines, the humus deposited over the centuries, the half-toppled trees that suddenly confronted us, one further barrier to our progress. Nature was bedazzling and secret, and at the same time an ever-increasing threat of cold, snow, persecution. Everything coalesced: solitude, danger, silence, and the urgency of our mission.

Occasionally we followed a faint trail left perhaps by smugglers, or possibly by outlaws, and we had no way of knowing how many of them might have perished, suddenly surprised by the icy hands of winter, by the raging snowstorms of the Andes that can smother an unwary traveler, burying him beneath seven stories of whiteness.

On either side of the trail, in the midst of that savage desolation, I saw something resembling human handiwork, lengths of piled-up branches that had suffered many winters, the offerings of hundreds of travelers, tall mounds of wood to commemorate the fallen, to remind us of those who had been unable to continue and who lay forever beneath the snows. With their machetes my companions lopped off the branches brushing against our faces, boughs sweeping down from the heights of the enormous evergreens, from the oaks whose last leaves were trembling before the onslaught of winter storms. And I, as well, left on each mound a memento, a calling card of wood, a branch cut from the forest to adorn the tombs of those many unknown travelers.

We had to cross a river. Those small streams born in the peaks of the Andes rush down precipitously, discharging their violent, vertiginous force, become cascades, crush earth and rock with the energy and momentum carried from those noble heights; but we were able to find a pool, a broad mirror of water, a ford. The horses waded in till they lost their footing, then struck out toward the opposite shore. Soon my horse was almost completely swamped by water, and I began to sway, nearly unseated; my feet churned as the beast labored to keep his head above water. And so we crossed.

We had no sooner reached the far shore than my guides, the countrymen who were accompanying me, asked with the trace of a smile: "Were you afraid?"

"Very. I thought my hour had come," I said.

"We were right behind you with our ropes ready," they said.

"My father went down at this very spot," one added, "and the current carried him away. We weren't going to let that happen to you."

We rode on until we came to a natural tunnel that might have been carved in the imposing rock by a roaring, long-since-disappeared river, or possibly an earth tremor had created in those heights the rocky channel of hewn-out granite into which we now penetrated. After a few yards, our mounts were slipping and sliding, struggling to find a foothold on the rough stone; their legs buckled beneath them, their hoofs struck sparks; more than once I found myself lying on the rocks, thrown from my horse. My mount was bleeding from the nostrils, his legs were bloody, but doggedly we continued along the unending, the splendid, the arduous road.

Something awaited us in the middle of that wild forest. Suddenly, as in an extraordinary vision, we came to a small, gleaming meadow nestled in the lap of the mountains: clear water, a green field, wild flowers, the sound of rivers, the blue sky overhead, munificent light uninterrupted by foliage.

There we paused, as if within a magic circle, like visitors at a holy shrine; and the ceremony in which I participated had even greater overtones of holiness. The cowboys dismounted. In the center of the enclosure was set—as if for some ritual—the skull of an ox. One by one, my companions silently walked forward and placed a few coins and scraps of food in the openings of the skull. I joined them in that offering destined for rough, wandering Ulysseses, for fugitives of every ilk, who would find bread and assistance in the eye sockets of a dead bull.

But that unforgettable ceremony did not stop there. My rustic friends took off their hats and began a strange dance, hopping on one foot around the abandoned skull, retracing the circle left by the countless dances of others who had come this way. I had some vague comprehension then, standing beside my taciturn companions, that there could be communication between strangers—solicitude, pleas, even a response—in the farthest, most isolated solitudes of the world.

Farther along, very close now to crossing the border that was to separate me for many years from my country, we were navigating by night the last ravines of the mountains. Suddenly we saw a light, a sure sign of human habitation, but as we rode nearer, we saw only a few ramshackle structures, a few rickety sheds, all seemingly vacant. We entered one, and in the light of a great fire saw tree trunks blazing in the center of the room, the cadavers of giant trees burning there day and night, whose smoke escaped through the chinks in the roof to drift through the shadows like a thick blue veil. We could see great wheels of cheeses piled there by those who made them in this high country. Near the fire, clumped together like burlap bags, lay several men. From the silence we heard the chords of a guitar and the words of a song which, born of the glowing coals and the darkness, carried to us the first human voice we had heard in our long trek. It was a song of love and far horizons, a lament of love and of longing for the distant spring, for the cities from which we had come, for the boundless infinity of life. They had no idea who we were; they knew nothing of a fugitive; they did not know my poetry or my name. Or did they know it, know us? What mattered was that we sang and ate beside their fire, and then we walked through the darkness to some very primitive rooms. Through them ran a thermal stream, volcanic water in which we bathed, warmth released from the cordillera, which gathered us to its bosom.

We splashed like happy children, sinking into the water, cleansing ourselves of the burden of that long ride. When at dawn we set out on the last kilometers of the journey that would separate me from the eclipse fallen over my beloved land, we were refreshed, reborn, baptized. We rode away singing, filled with a new spirit, with a new hope that propelled us toward the great highway of the world awaiting me. When (I remember vividly) we tried to give those mountain men a few coins in payment for the songs, the food, the thermal bath, for the roof and bed, that is, for the shelter we had so unexpectedly stumbled upon, they refused our offer expressionlessly. They had done what they could, that's all. And in their "that's all" was deep, unspoken understanding—perhaps recognition, perhaps the same dreams.

Ladies and gentlemen, I never found in books any formula for writing poetry; and I, in turn, do not intend to leave in print a word of advice, a method, or a style that will allow young poets to receive from me some drop of supposed wisdom. If in this address I have recounted certain events from the past, if I have relived a never-forgotten adventure on this occasion and in this place so remote from that experience, it is to illustrate that in the course of my life I have always found the necessary affirmation, a formula, awaiting me, not to become enshrined in my words, but to lead me to an understanding of myself.

I found in that long journey the prescription for writing poetry. I was blessed by gifts from the earth and from the soul. I believe that poetry is a solemn and transient act to which solitude and unity, emotion and action, one's private world, man's private world, and the secret revelations of nature contribute in equal measure. I am similarly convinced that all this—man and his past, man and his commitment, man and his poetry—is preserved in an always expanding community, in an activity that will someday integrate reality and dreams, for this is how they are united. And I tell you that even after so many years I do not know whether the lessons I learned as I crossed a dizzying river, as I danced around the skull of a steer, as I lay in the purifying waters that flowed from the highest mountains—I tell you I do not know whether that experience originated in me, to be communicated later to other human beings, or whether it was a message sent me by other men as a demand and a summons. I don't know whether I lived it or I wrote it, I don't know whether the poems I experienced in that moment, the experiences I later sang, were truth or poetry, ephemera or eternity.

From such things, my friends, comes the kind of enlightenment the poet must learn from his fellow men. There is no unassailable solitude. All roads lead to the same point: to the communication of who we are. And we must travel across lonely and rugged terrain, through isolation and silence, to reach the magic zone where we can dance an awkward dance or sing a melancholy song; but in the dance and the song are consummated the most ancient rituals of awareness—the awareness of being men, and of believing in a common destiny.

The fact is that if some, or many, have thought that I was a sectarian, unable to break bread at the table of friendship and shared responsibility, I will make no attempt to justify myself. I do not believe that there is room for accusation or justification among the duties of the poet. After all, no one poet has administered poetry, and if one paused to accuse his fellows, or if another chose to waste his life defending himself against reasonable or absurd recriminations, I am convinced that only vanity leads us to such extremes. I say that the enemies of poetry are not to be found among its practitioners or patrons but in a lack of harmony within the poet. Thus it follows that no poet has a more fundamental enemy than his own inability to communicate with the most ignorant and exploited of his contemporaries; and this applies to all times and all nations.

The poet is not a "little god." No, he is not a "little god." He is not chosen for some cabalistic destiny superior to that of persons who perform different duties and offices. I have often said that the best poet is the man who delivers our daily bread: the local baker, who does not think he is a god. He fulfills his majestic yet humble task of kneading, placing in the oven, browning, and delivering our daily bread, with a true sense of community. And if a poet could be moved in the same way by such a simple conscience, that simple conscience would allow him to become part of an enormous work of art—the simple, or complicated, construction that is the building of a society, the transformation of man's condition, the simple delivery of his wares: bread, truth, wine, dreams. If the poet becomes part of the eternal struggle, if each of us places in the hands of the other his ration of commitment, his dedication and his tenderness toward the labor shared every day by all men, then the poet will be part of the sweat, the bread, the wine, the dream of all humanity. Only on this not-to-be-denied road of accepting our role as ordinary men will we succeed in restoring to poetry the amplitude chiseled away from it in every age, chiseled away by poets themselves.

The errors that have led me to relative truth, and the truths that have often led me to error, never permitted me—not that I ever attempted it—to define, to influence, or to teach what is called the creative process, the peaks and abysses of literature. But I have learned one thing: that it is we ourselves who create the phantoms of our own mythification. From the very mortar with which we create, or hope to create, are formed the obstacles to our own evolution. We may find ourselves irrevocably drawn toward reality and realism—that is, toward an unselective acceptance of reality and the roads to change—and then realize, when it seems too late, that we have raised such severe limitations that we have killed life instead of guiding it to growth and fruition. We have imposed on ourselves a realism heavier than our building bricks, without ever having constructed the building we thought was our first responsibility. And at the opposite extreme, if we succeed in making a fetish of the incomprehensible (or comprehensible to only a few), a fetish of the exceptional and the recondite, if we suppress reality and its inevitable deterioration, we will suddenly find ourselves in an untenable position, sinking in a quicksand of leaves, clay, and clouds, drowning in an oppressive inability to communicate.

As for the particular case of writers from the vast expanses of America, we hear unceasingly the call to fill that enormous space with creatures of flesh and blood. We are aware of our obligation to populate this space, and at the same time we realize our fundamental, our critical obligation to communicate in an uninhabited world which is no less filled with injustice, punishment, and pain because it is uninhabited. We also feel the obligation to revive the ancient dreams slumbering in our stone statues, in our ancient, ruined monuments, in the vast silences of our pampas, in our dense jungles, in our rivers that sing like thunder. We are called upon to fill with words the confines of a mute continent, and we become drunk with the task of telling and naming. Perhaps that has been the decisive factor in my own humble career; and in that case my excesses, or my abundance, or my rhetoric, will turn out to be nothing more than the simplest acts of routine American responsibility. Each of my verses strove to be palpable; each of my poems sought to be a useful tool; each of my songs aspired to be a sign in space to mark a gathering at the crossroads, or to be a fragment of stone or wood on which someone, others, those to come, could inscribe new signs.

Carrying the duties of the poet to their logical consequences, I decided, whether correctly or in error, that my commitment in society and in life should be that of a humble partisan. I decided this even as I witnessed glorious failures, solitary victories, stunning defeats. I understood, finding myself an actor in the struggles of America, that my human mission was none other than to add my talents to the swelling force of unified peoples, to join them in blood and spirit, with passion and hope, because only from that swelling torrent can be born the progress necessary for writers and for peoples. And though my position raised, or may raise, bitter or amiable objections, the fact is that I can accept no other road for a writer in our vast and harsh landscape if we want the darkness to flower, if we are to hope that millions of men who still have not learned to read us—or even to read—who still cannot write—or write to us—will live in a climate of dignity without which it is impossible to be a whole man.

We inherited the misery of peoples who have been marked by misfortune for centuries—the most Edenic, the purest peoples, peoples who built miraculous towers from stone and metal, jewels of dazzling splendor: peoples who suddenly found their lives dashed and silenced in a terrible era of colonialism that persists to this day.

Our original guiding stars are struggle and hope. But there is no such thing as solitary hope or struggle. In every man are joined all past ages, and the inertia, the errors, the passions, the urgencies of our time, the swift course of history. But what kind of man would I be if I had, for example, contributed in any way to the continuing feudalism of our great American continent? How could I hold my head high, graced by the great honor bestowed on me by Sweden, if I did not feel proud of having played a small part in the present changes in my country? We must look at the map of America, recognize its great diversity, the cosmic reaches of the space in which we live, to understand that many writers refuse to share in the curse of opprobrium and pillaging cast upon American peoples by dark gods.

I chose the difficult road of shared responsibility, and rather than reiterate my worship of the individual as the central sun of the system, I preferred to devote my humble services to the sizable army that may from time to time take the wrong turning but which advances relentlessly, marching forward day by day in the face of stubborn reactionaries, the impatient, and the uninformed. Because I believe that my duties as a poet embraced brotherhood not only with the rose and symmetry, with exalted love and infinite nostalgia, but with the thorny human responsibilities I have incorporated into my poetry.

Exactly a hundred years ago, a poor but splendid poet, the most tortured of the damned, prophesied: *"A l'aurore, armés d'une ardente patience, nous entrerons aux splendides Villes."*

I believe in that prophecy of the seer Rimbaud. I come from a dark province, from a country separated from others by a severe geography. I was the most abandoned of poets, and my poetry was regional, sorrowful, steeped in rain. But I always had confidence in man. I never lost hope. That may be why I am here with my poetry, and with my flag.

In conclusion, I say to all men of good will, to workers, to poets, that the future of man is expressed in Rimbaud's phrase: only with fiery patience will we conquer the splendid city that will shed light, justice, and dignity on all men.

Thus, poetry shall not have sung in vain.

TRANSLATED BY MARGARET SAYERS PEDEN

Arturo Uslar Pietri

Venezuela
(b. 1906)

———◆•◆◆◆———

Venezuelan Arturo Uslar Pietri made his first major impression on the literary world with his novel *Las lanzas coloradas* (1931). The novel can be categorized as one of the "novels of the land," produced in Latin America during the 1920s and 1930s. Like Mexican novelist Mariano Azuela and fellow Venezuelan Rómulo Gallegos, Uslar Pietri tried to portray the essential character of the nation through literature. His wide range of political roles, including minister of public education, secretary to the president, minister of the treasury, and head of the Venezuelan Democratic Party, pushed him away from fiction and toward a more journalistic style. Uslar Pietri has taught at the Universidad Central in Caracas and at Columbia University in New York. While working for his country's diplomatic corps in Paris, he shared an apartment with fellow writers Alejo Carpentier and Miguel Angel Asturias. Most of his literary activity reflects his deeply rooted interest in Venezuela's history and culture. His essays have been collected in *Veinticinco ensayos* (1969), *Vista desde un punto* (1971), *La otra América* (1974), *El globo de colores* (1975), and *Fantasmas de dos mundos* (1979), but Uslar Pietri may have made his greatest contribution in *Letras y hombres de Venezuela* (1946), in which he coined the term *magical realism*. Uslar Pietri devoted most of the 1980s to writing short pieces for Venezuelan newspapers discussing the nation's politics and cultural issues. "The Other America," written in Caracas, appeared in the August 1974 issue of Ortega y Gasset's prestigious *Revista de Occidente*.

The Other America

What many people call "Latin America" is, in a very meaningful way, the world from which the name has been taken away. There has always been a metaphor, a misnomer, or an understandable dissatisfaction about its name. The New World, the Indies, America, were all names dependent on chance and even ignorance. When in 1507 Martin Waldseemuller wrote the auspicious name on his map, he wrote it on the border of the southern continental mass. The northern part of the hemisphere did not come to be called America until much later.

From the moment in 1776 when the old English colonies of the north declared their independence and for lack of a name opted for the simple political definition "United States of America," which summarily described their form of government and their geographical situation, there arose the problem of what to call the South. When the new country's expansion and power became evident, the name "Americans" increasingly came to be ascribed to them. For the eighteenth-century French and English, Benjamin Franklin was "The American" while a man like Francisco de Miranda, who had better title to embodying the reality of the New World, was a *"criollo,"* an inhabitant of Terra Firma, or an exotic native.

That the name does not correspond to the thing exactly is not what matters. No name corresponds exactly to the thing it stands for. The origins of the names Asia, Africa, and Europe, not to mention Italy or Spain, were equally arbitrary. The problem has been the lack of a sufficient and secure identity.

It has gone on for four centuries; it has been long, arduous, unending, this search for the identity of the sons of the other America, which is still called by such objectionable, almost provisional names as Spanish America, Latin America, Iberoamerica, and even Indoamerica. The presence of this changeable modifier reveals the necessity of a not clearly determined but specific difference from the genus nearby.

Little importance would be given to the old or new, the ingenious or unaffected name, if behind its origin there were not hidden unsolved problems of definition and situation.

The peculiar attitude of the Latin American towards time and place has had much to do with all this. From the very beginning, his has been a situation that had to be changed. There, more than in any other place in history, one has thought in terms of future and distance. Tomorrow has always mattered more than today, the invisible more than the visible, the far more than the near. The search for El Dorado is a perfect, if extreme, example of this mentality. What did their solitary, meager cluster of huts matter in the face of the fact that they were on the road to El Dorado? They always found themselves facing a vastness to be conquered, compared with which what was known and possessed was disproportionately small. There was a Beyond in space and time where all would be good and plentiful.

From the arrival of the Conquistadores, the future was more looked to than the present. They came to make "inroads," to explore new lands, to look for treasure, to build for tomorrow, with a project in their imagination.

The fact that America was man's first great encounter with a geographical area that was completely unknown and in great part uninhabited had much to do with this phenomenon. More important than what there was, was what could be done. The name itself, the New World, reveals this visionary conception. They did not come to conquer cities and countries, but rather to found what did not already exist, without much taking into account what already did exist. Kingdoms, territories, and provinces were created the way an architect outlines a building project on paper. More than the present, what could be done in the future was stressed. They were going to make a New Spain, a New Castile, or a New Toledo; they were going to found the Order of the Knights of the Golden Spur, or, purely and simply, the Utopia of Sir Thomas More.

Latin America was conceived as a project. Everything the oldest official documents say refers to what can be done here. This runs from the letters of Columbus to the speeches of Bolívar, from the futuristic, astonished vision of the Jesuit Acosta in the sixteenth century to the description of the future's possibilities that fill Humboldt's prophetic work at the end of the Colonial period.

Independence itself has more to do with a future project than with an actual present. This is its chief characteristic. For tomorrow, we must create the most perfect republic that humankind has ever seen. The limitations and obstacles of the present do not matter. When in 1811 the Venezuelan congress declared the first Spanish American Constitution, it did not appear to take into consideration the real situation of the country, or its actual institutions, or its social organization, or its economy; rather it rushed, exempt and free from all ties to surrounding reality, to call for a political order which would require the complete transformation of existing reality to be able to function.

They turned to the remotest past, or they rushed toward the most utopic future. Anything but the present. In any case, the remote past, updated or resuscitated, of a golden legend has been a traditional mode of revolutionary thought. Revolution is fundamentally a kind of nostalgia, an attempt to return to the forgotten and lost Golden Age.

In the papers of the creators of the Spanish American revolution, this disdain for the immediate stands out. Miranda's papers abound with the evidence of this attitude. Miranda observed and studied the basis of the most advanced political institutions of the Europe of his time, from the armies and hospitals to the gardens and parliaments, in order to transport them at some opportunity to the New World; but when it came to giving a title to the leader of this immense new State which was to extend from Mexico to Argentina, he could find none better than "Inca." An "Inca" was to preside over the vast Mirandian republic, built upon the most modern political forms tested by England and Revolutionary France.

The first to take note of the hazards inherent in this position was Bolívar, whose Cartagena Manifesto and, above all, whose Angostura Speech of 1819 point out the repeated error of not taking into consideration the social reality created by history. This call to order went unheard. The continual battling of the nineteenth century is expressed in utopian proclamations that had little to do with surrounding reality. An abstract political perfection was being sought after, and it was needed for the morrow. All of this has never ceased being seen in caricature, has an undeniable tragic grandeur. So many years of struggle and destructive confrontation among the Spanish American nations could be looked upon with prideful disdain by the United States of the time and by the great powers of Europe as a proof of inferiority or incapacity for civilized life. At the same time, the Positivists arrived with their pessimistic diagnosis of the invincible factors of climate, race, and history that condemned us to barbarism or incapacity for civilized life. But a people who for so long and with so much passion have struggled in search of promises of justice, liberty, and equality reveal an extraordinary moral fiber. Certainly it would have been more useful and productive to resign themselves to the possible, to work within the given, and to give up looking for the superior forms of human dignity, but, stubbornly and almost unanimously, the hazardous and difficult path of the absolute was chosen.

In this connection, people have spoken of the Spanish American "nominalism"; to believe that the name is the thing itself, that to proclaim the republic is the republic, that to decree equality is equality. There is something of this, but this is not all. If this had been all, the countries would have remained quiet or hypnotized beside the renewed altars on which there had been set up the new idols of the great liberal principles. But this did not happen. Every time the promise or the hope did not become tangible reality, the struggle began anew. What caused the long wars that tore apart almost the entire Spanish American world in the past century and whose high points are such vast collective conflicts as the Mexican War of Reform, the Argentine crusade against Rosas, or the Venezuelan Federal war, was not only the proclamation of some political dogma, but a thirst for justice which, in vastly differing and sometimes very naive forms, reached all levels of society.

A world that has been able to struggle so much and for so long for the highest human ideals does not deserve such disdain and mocking commiseration.

Nonetheless, from the time of Queen Victoria and the French Third Republic, there has been an America worthy of admiration for its wealth, its virtues and its growing power, which was the one made up of the United States and perhaps also Canada; and another America, the hot countries, picturesque, primitive, at most good for colonization and exploitation. The land of parrots, vicuñas, feathered Indians, cowboys, and ignorant chieftains. The land of exotic colonial products: cocoa, coffee, rum, molasses, tobacco, and hides; and strange and impure poets.

It was not easy—it never has been—to identify Latin America, which presents so many and such contradictory faces, inside and out. What appears to be contradictory is nothing but a form of its irreconcilable jumble. It is full of the conflict of relics and novelties. Half a century after an amazed Humboldt listened to a discussion about the world's most recent major political events on the rocky old path from La Guaira to Caracas, Sarmiento was describing the stagnant life of seventeenth-century Mendoza. And when Bolívar reached Cuzco in 1825, he must have experienced the sensation of watching a deep, open cross-section through history. There, side by side, superimposed and barely fused, were the people, garments, and stones of the Incas and the Spanish churches, the missionary and doctrinaire priests, the doctors of Utraquism and an army that brought, along with its coarse gun-powder, Rousseau's and Montesquieu's ideas. He could hold Pizarro's standard in one hand and in the other, at the same time, a project for a democratic Constitution. They greeted him with the old ceremonial words proper for an Inca or Viceroy, while he spoke of "citizens" and "republic."

An Arrested Era

There was a Spanish era that remained arrested and backward on American soil. This is attested by the language, which evolved more slowly, by the archaism not only of idiomatic expressions but of customs that persisted in the life of *criollos* of the upper class. The Bourbons' arrival on the Spanish throne was only felt slowly and superficially in America. In essentials, it was the world and values of the House of Hapsburg that survived.

That old Castilian Christian who was the heir of a long history of the encounter of Christians, Moors, and Jews on the Peninsula, and who arrived, as Américo Castro put it, full of indestructible Castilian breeding, found himself not only in a different geographical and social milieu, but in the presence of other races as well as other cultures. We still do not know much about the vast and profound process of cultural fusion which took place so dramatically, painfully, and richly in the new lands. From city planning to temple architecture, from language to working conditions, from worship to cuisine, from agricultural methods to family and societal relations, the presence of the Indian and the Black made itself felt through a great variety of contributions. What happened in Spanish America during those three centuries resembles nothing that occurred on other continents in the encounters between Europeans and natives. It did not happen in North America, or Africa or Asia in the spheres of English or French control.

There is no equivalent to the Inca Garcilaso in Anglo-Saxon America. An Asian or an African baroque did not come into being as a legacy of the European encounter. No new social or artistic forms rose up; instead, the

European was imposed upon the indigenous, the contact zone was narrow and lifeless, the Presbyterian church stood next to the Hindu temple, the European minority was isolated from the autochthonous majority. It was impossible to produce an African Sarmiento or an American Caspicara or Aleijadinho. Impossible because the basic fact out of which arose those men and creations, a cultural and racial fusion, did not take place in any meaningful way in North America, or Africa, or Asia. Culturally there was, *avant la lettre*, apartheid.

If the United States was able to appropriate to itself the name "America" in the eyes of the world, obliging the other three-quarters of the hemisphere to look for a surname or other name, it was not the result of a clever move or a successful advertising campaign. Fundamentally, it was the effect of the immense disparity of development and power between it and the rest of America. Immense consequences of all sorts the world around have come out of the spectacular fact that in less than two centuries, England's thirteen fringe colonies on the American North Atlantic coast became the greatest economic, technological, and military power on the planet.

With surprising speed and efficiency, they managed to take possession of the immense continental mass that stretched from ocean to ocean and to establish an economic system of the highest productivity that man has ever known and a system of simple and effective public freedoms.

Many have been the causes and explanations given for such a great difference in growth, from climate and soil quality to the Protestant ethic and economic freedom.

In American territory, in cutting and dramatic form, the division of destiny and mentality occasioned by the Protestant Reformation in Europe has reappeared, between the North, which invented capitalism, rationalism, and parliamentarian government, and the South, which remained faithful to the medieval heritage of absolutism, the master-and-slave economy, the dominance of religious dogma.

The other America did not decide its own path, but rather in great part it was the consequence of decisions that almost coincided with its birth. As a result of the battle of Villahar it did not have representative government; owing to the Diet of Worms and seventeenth-century Hapsburg politics, it did not take part in the birth of capitalism, the development of scientific investigation, or the formulation of Rationalist thought.

In great part the difficulties in its history have derived from having to swim against the current, against the pull of those decisive factors that they inherited, in a desperate search for a possibility of incorporating themselves with another history and another era.

The antinomy between the inherited soul and the vital need to keep up with the world of progress explains many of its contradictions.

While Carlos II was staging an anachronistic *auto-da-fe* in Madrid's Plaza

Mayor to celebrate his marriage to the past, in the Hague the *Discours de la Méthode* was being written, in London the Royal Society and the Bank of England were being founded, and Newton was formulating his law of physics.

From that time on, the gap has not narrowed, and the leap which the countries of Hispanic heritage must attempt is of anxiety-provoking size. The times will change, or we ourselves must change.

The attempt to leap over the hereditary mentality has been the ferment of revolutionary disquiet in the Spanish American world, at least since the eighteenth century. The *criollos* soon discovered Rationalism, scientific progress, and the glitter of Enlightenment. Through the example of English America, through journeys and the books that arrived along with other contraband from the heretic islands, a new urge arose to modernize and repudiate the past. New voices, new ideas, new Utopias to replace the already forgotten ones began to appear. It was precisely the sons and heirs of the Conquest's privileges who were most active in throwing themselves into the revolution. José Domingo Díaz, a Venezuelan monarchist contemporary with the War of Independence, was moved by astonishment to write in his book, *Recollections of the Caracas Rebellion*: "There for the first time was seen a revolution plotted and executed by the people who stood to lose the most by it."

Now, with its equivocal name, its unsolved contradictions, its anxiety of the future and the absolute, its burden of defiant irrationality, the other America has entered the most unexpected and trying age the planet has known.

In the midst of the largest and swiftest transformation of all the relationships of value and change, in a confused panorama of new and growing possibilities of Utopia and risk, the old land of Utopia and risk must rethink its destiny and prepare itself for a future that can eventually be reconcilable with its visions.

New Forms of Power

New and large centers of power are forming of a size and consequence that the past never knew. It is no longer a question of the battleships and battalions of the old colonial powers. We are living in the nuclear bipolarity, in the Cold War, in the new forms of power represented by technological monopoly and complex transitional enterprises. We now see the possibility of new concentrations of power rise up. Now it is not the United States and the Soviet Union alone with their respective spheres of influence, but we can clearly see the resurgence of the total power of a unified Europe. Japan appears as the major center of technological and industrial power in Asia. And the possibility should not be discarded that there will be an alliance of nations of Anglo-Saxon culture, which could comprise the United States, Canada, South Africa, Australia, and New Zealand, and to which Great Britain would have to belong in some way.

Someday, Black Africa will find a way to unite, and the destiny of China and India will take shape facing that of Japan. In the world that will come out of the growing concentration and disparate advance of technological and economic power, what role will Latin America play?

To contemplate this possibility, it should be considered in conjunction with an immense sum of geographical space, natural resources of all kinds, climates and forests and waters and human beings: one of the largest land masses of the planet, an extraordinarily homogeneous cultural unity, which could constitute one of the most unified of human concentrations in the world to come.

Today, Spanish is the mother tongue of more than two hundred million persons. Numerically, it is the third largest language after Chinese and English. If we add up the countries speaking Spanish and Portuguese, whose linguistic border is very tenuous, they would represent more than three hundred million, the second largest linguistic community in the present world.

The possibility of a large total potential of power in the Hispanic world certainly exists. The organic complementing of its human and its natural resources, facilitated by its cultural and linguistic community, could create the bases for one of the important centers of world power in tomorrow's world.

The Hispanic world has experienced great moments of enlightenment in which it seems to have sensed some dark and powerful call of destiny.

The formation of the New World was one of those moments. We still have not justly evaluated everything meant by the quantitative extension of the political, economic, and cultural space, nor even less the qualitative changes introduced by this extension into its values and conceptions.

Another was the War of Independence; the Spanish Independence as well as the Latin American, two manifestations of a single phenomenon. The last vestige of the patrimonial myth of the Spanish Crown was broken, the lifeless flow of tradition was halted, and the countries had to face new circumstances. Throughout, there is a spiritual relationship and a coincidence of meaning in attitude and a contemporary correspondence of purpose which successively inspired Aranda, Miranda, Jovellanos, Bolívar, and Riego. One moment in the history of the West demanded an appropriate, swift answer from the Hispanic world.

Another of these moments was the vast, multiple phenomenon which, at the end of the nineteenth century, provoked a wholly anguished and profound reevaluation of the past as well as a search for the future in the thought and literature of the Spanish language. This is represented by men separated in space, but not in intent or sentiment, such as Martí, Ganivet, Unamuno, Darío, and Rodó. What in Spain is called the Generation of 1898 and in America is recognized as the Modernist movement, constitutes two spontaneous and analogous reactions to a common situation.

We still do not know how much all of Spanish America participated morally and in spiritual anguish in the Spanish Civil War. It was felt as a new tragic episode in the old heritage and the old common calling.

Today, we are living in a similar period. Great concentrations of world power are forming. Scientific and technological power, which is at the same time the basis today of economic, military, and political dominance, with all its implications, continues to concentrate itself in the Anglo-Saxon countries, the Soviet Union and its family of satellites, and Japan.

What is the Hispanic world going to do? Revolve in a passive, sterile orbit around an alien power? Or gather its resources and its forces into an effective whole to enter a dialogue in the drama of the creation of man's future?

Should we say, as in Unamuno's tragic *boutade*, "Let *them* invent," or should we ourselves begin to invent?

This is the time neither for optimisms nor for pessimisms, but rather for a cold, calculated realism that will take inventory of resources and define practical possibilities.

The other America, which is "other" not only because it is different from the Anglo-Saxon one, but because it needs to renew and redefine its present and find its future, and the other Spain, which must emerge, have no greater possibility than consciously to unite for the future what up till now has been nothing less than a tacit postponement, an unclaimed inheritance of the common past. The times are calling us.

TRANSLATED BY ANDRÉE CONRAD

José Bianco

Argentina

(1908–1986)

———◆•••◆———

Known for his deep human vision, Buenos Aires native José Bianco had already published two books of short stories and begun to write for several magazines by the age of eighteen. He published a collection of short stories, *La pequeña Gyaros* (1932), when he was twenty-four, and he went on to direct the Argentine magazine *Sur*, from 1938 to 1967, as well as the University Press in Buenos Aires. A man of letters whose editorial pen scratched the surfaces of major works by Jorge Luis Borges, Alfonso Reyes, Ezequiel Martínez Estrada, and Pedro Henríquez Ureña, among others, Bianco was a prolific *conversateur*, a superb translator of French and English works, but the author of only a handful of fiction titles. His essays, on the other hand, are abundant, both in terms of quality and of quantity. He wrote insightfully about Marcel Proust, Ambrose Bierce, Jorge Luis Borges, Julien Brenda, Albert Camus, José Ortega y Gasset, and Domingo Faustino Sarmiento. He received a Guggenheim grant in 1975 and was awarded the *Odre des Palmes Academiques* by the French government. Two novellas, *Shadow Play* (1941) and *The Rats* (1943), were critically acclaimed, as was his collection of essays, *Ficción y realidad* (1988), which includes the following insightful literary study of Tolstoy's classic, *Anna Karenina*. Bianco's essay was originally published in 1978.

Anna Karenina

"Why Karenina instead of Karenín? In the Russian language, the feminine endings of surnames correspond to the genitive *de* in Spanish that is used by married women in some Hispanic American countries (i.e., María Pérez *de* González), and there is no reason why one should apply the grammatical rules of one language when speaking or writing in another. Outside of Russia, surnames started to take on feminine endings at the turn of the century in order to identify certain famous dancers such as Pavlova and Karsavina; but Anna wasn't a dancer or an actor; she was a woman of the world."

That's what a Russian friend told me, and she's right; nevertheless, I will continue calling her "Anna Karenina" because many years ago I first read Tolstoy's novel in Spanish, and it was a bad translation at that. Anna

Karenina embodies the typical *femme fatale* that later became part and parcel of the film world (Greta Garbo, Marlene Dietrich) until it lost favor; today, the *femme fatale* is out of fashion, all of which has contributed to putting Anna Karenina above what's considered fashionable. First, it was her beauty, which was beyond her control and whose splendor is attenuated or exalted in the course of the novel; and there's her intelligence, her refinement, the simplicity of her behavior, and her vivaciousness. Over and over, Tolstoy refers to Anna Karenina's vivacity as if it were an abundance of repressed energy easily detected in her face. When, after much hesitation, she abandons her husband and child in order to join her lover (but rejects divorce, which was possible at the time), she submits to her instincts, which are not devoid of moral grandeur and religious foundation, but in direct opposition to the corruption and conventions of her society. Thomas Mann wrote that *Anna Karenina*, perhaps the most important social novel of all time, is a novel that works *against* society. In his Rousseau-like behavior, Levin, who is a male character of major consequence, is foreshadowed in the biblical quotation in the epigraph: "Vengeance is mine: I will repay, saith the Lord." Clearly, Tolstoy accuses the cold cruelty of the social laws of his era. Are the characters not taking on roles that do not correspond to them? Does society have the right to seek revenge against Anna Karenina by ostracizing her instead of having God punish her? In the hands of God, nevertheless, these same laws, whose cruelty is manifested in the novel, are the instrument of justice. The ill fortune that determines Anna Karenina's destiny and brings her to a tragic end stems from the moral precepts of her era; but Thomas Mann has indicated that God would not have been able to punish her if society had not acted the way it did. Although there is an apparent contradiction in the epigraph of the novel, it also explains the severe lucidity with which Tolstoy judges his heroine, despite his fondness for her.

From the beginning, he presents her as a woman who fights obstinately against her powers of seduction, of which she is fully conscious. When she compliments her future lover in front of the young woman who aspires to marry him, the incident at the train station is never mentioned—that is, when Vronski gave 200 rubles to the woman whose husband was killed by a train—because something tells her that the enthusiasm that she, Anna, has awakened in Vronski is not contrary to his generosity. That same night when she sees him at her brother's house, she admits that they have similar feelings about each other. Halfway through the second part of the novel, when Vronski achieves "his only goal in life," we see how feelings of love begin to grow ever so delicately, but also unequivocally, in Anna Karenina's heart. Pages before the impassioned scene where Anna gives herself over to Vronski, Tolstoy repeats the words of the epigraph, putting them in the mouth of the conventional Karenin, who at times also deserves our pity: "Your feelings appertain to your conscience, but because of you, myself, and God, I have the obligation to remind you of your responsibilities." Our lives are not united by men but by God; only crime can break this bond of union, and each crime has its "punishment." The crime is eventually consummated and the biblical maxim of the novel is carried out. But Tolstoy, who still hasn't fully revealed himself, is too much of an artist not to respect Anna Karenina's sense of humanity. Despite the opposition he creates between her adulterous love affair with Vronski and the chaste love of Levin and Kitty, the circumstances that vex Anna give the impression that they are inevitable and, from the point of view of the reader, the same ones that explain and justify her guilt.

This, from the point of view of the reader and, intermittently, from Tolstoy's own point of view. The mystery of destiny and the laws of morality seem to him more enigmatic than the mystery of religious faith. "It is not surprising," he writes in his *Diary*, "that God proclaims a piece of bread to be the body of his Son, but what is surprising, totally surprising, is to live without knowing why we live for and love Goodness, even though it is not written down anywhere that this is good or that is bad." Within the strict code of convention, Anna Karenina does not deny that her love for Vronski is immoral; however, when she becomes aware of that new love, a transformation takes place in her soul that allows her not only to discern what is bad about it ("I'm not strange, I'm immoral," she says to her sister-in-law before returning to St. Petersburg, a day after the dance), but also to comprehend that from then on it will be difficult, if not impossible, to endure married life. In sum, Tolstoy creates what has been called, as it is today, *a passion of sin*; and Anna Karenina, who is the first one to feel the weight of her own guilt, never gives in until she receives her fateful punishment. Tolstoy records the tenuous deviations of her conscience, from the lies that even surprise herself and disconcert her husband, Karenin, to the pleasure she receives as she controls the fascination men have over her, especially Levin's, the novel's intellectual hero who suspects that her lover will eventually abandon her. That suspicion intensifies the animadversion he feels toward Vronski. As time passes, Anna blames him for her forsaken life, for her probable eternal separation from her son, for her husband's continual vacillation at conceding a divorce, but who now seems to oppose it, and for Vronski's procrastination in taking up with her in the country in order to consecrate her role as his lover. And, to top it off, she is consumed with passion. "Then death occurred to her as the only way to avenge herself, to reconquer her love, to triumph over the malignant spirit engulfing her that she attributed to him. What did it matter to go to the country or not, or to obtain the divorce? Essential was the punishment." Caught up in a whirlwind of futile thoughts as she visits her sister-in-law, and upon reaching the train station on her way home, the idea of suicide crosses her mind. It should be pointed out that here, Tolstoy, long before Joyce, utilizes *stream of consciousness* with maximum competence, a technique whose invention was later disputed by English and French writers.

The image of the train—dark and ominous—is persistent throughout the novel, including the hissing steam, the huffing and puffing, the deafening noise, the smoke, and the shrill whistle, even the small man with the bushy beard who appears in Anna's dreams banging on metal and talking incoherently. Anna and Vronski first meet at a train station on the day that a drunken employee, or one who is too bundled up to hear the engine shunting along, falls under the wheels; Vronski, who is following Anna on her return to St. Petersburg, declares his love to her when she gets off the train somewhere along the way to take in some fresh air. Levin and Karenin first meet each other while traveling on the same train, a scene not described in the novel, and when the novel ends, that is, two months after Anna has committed suicide by throwing herself in front of a moving train, we are still privy to the vicious commentaries that provoked her death: a group of people have gathered at the station to send off a trainload of Russian volunteers who have joined the Serbian army in its war against Turkey. One of the volunteers is Vronski, and his mother is accompanying him; during a stop at a provincial city along the way, she asks Levin's brother to try to talk to her son, so they talk while they stroll up and down the platform. Vronski has joined the army because his life has become meaningless: "As a man, I'm nothing," he tells Levin's brother; he's grown old, numbed by grief and, because of another kind of pain, like a piercing toothache, one of those painful states that Tolstoy himself suffered, Vronski is unable to express himself. He remains silent, defeated by the toothache that leaves his mouth full of saliva, unable to take his eyes off the wheels of the train that approaches slowly down the tracks. The sight of the train wheels and his conversation with a man whom he has not seen since the mishap evoke in his memory a heartbreaking scene not described in the novel that suddenly blocks out his physical pain; that is, Vronski's confrontation with Anna's body:

"Her body was bloody, but still seemed to be alive; and her head was intact, thrown back, with heavy braids and slight curls of hair covering her temples. There was a strange and mournful expression on that beautiful face with eyes full of horror and parted lips that seemed to repeat the terrible words she had told him in their last and fatal discussion: 'You will regret this.' He tried to remember what she was like when he first met her at the train station, mysterious, enchanting, eager to love and to be loved; but now he could only remember her as threatening and triumphant, making him suffer his destiny: regret. He forgot about his toothache and began sobbing."

Anna Karenina's revenge brings its own destruction, allowing the words of Scripture to ring true. Tolstoy feels tenderness and loving kindness toward Anna; however, as a novelist, he is no less inexorable than God.

TRANSLATED BY DICK GERDES

Enrique Anderson Imbert

Argentina
(b. 1910)

While still in college at the University of Buenos Aires, Enrique Anderson Imbert began his journalistic career at the socialist daily *La Vanguardia*. Later, he taught at the University of Tucumán, but in 1947, under the regime of Juan Perón, he was forced into exile. He ended up settling in the United States, where he joined the faculties of such prestigious institutions as the University of Michigan and Harvard. Although a writer of ghost stories and what Borges called *lo fantástico*—most of which are anthologized in *El leve Pedro* (1976)—Anderson Imbert is best known as a literary critic. His widely read books include *Los grandes libros de Occidente y otros ensayos* (1957), *Crítica interna* (1961), *Historia de la literatura hispanoamericana* (1954–77), *La originalidad de Rubén Darío* (1967), *Genio y figura de Sarmiento* (1967), *Métodos de crítica literaria* (1969), *El realismo mágico y otros ensayos* (1976), *Estudios sobre letras hispánicas* (1977), *Los primeros cuentos del mundo* (1977), *Las comedias de George Bernard Shaw* (1978), and *Teoría y técnica del cuento* (1979). "In Defense of the Essay" dates back to 1945 and was included in *Los domingos del profesor* (1972). In it Anderson Imbert reflects on the value of the essay as a literary genre, compares it to the philosophical treatise, introduces a valuable definition, and, in passing, ponders thinkers of the caliber of David Hume and Benedetto Croce—all of this done with elegance and substance and without a hint of academic pomposity. Therein lies his contribution to this literary tradition: He brings ample scholarly wisdom to the form, but always keeps the lay reader, not a self-contained elite of the initiated few, as his target audience.

In Defense of the Essay

When I collected the essays of my youth in *La flecha en el aire* ten years ago, some good friends praised the modesty with which I confessed not having hit the bull's-eye. "Don't despair," they told me. "Sometimes you nailed it, and you will continue to nail it if you just refine your aim."

But the truth is that I was not being modest in that title. To the contrary. In the games with which Aeneas honored the tomb of his father, Anchises, a group of warriors pointed their bows at a pole upon which a dove was tied. The first put his arrow in the wood, the second cut the rope, the third hit the dove in mid-flight, but Acestes was the winner: he shot his arrow into the sky, and it burned in the clouds like a shooting star.

I am not saying that my arrows are that prodigious, but that what I value in myself are my imaginative shots: the arrow in the sky, burning and ephemeral, not the final possession of a pierced target!

However, circumstances do not allow me such a luxury. Since it is impossible to live by the pen in Argentina, and, furthermore, there is no literary journalism, I had to change careers and become a professor, upon which my intellectual strength immediately changed direction. Instead of "I," "we"; instead of the pleasure of *doxa*, the simulation of *episteme*; instead of joyful conversation, writing subject to a discipline that falsely promises an impossible objectivity. I am happy as a professor, in part because even in class I let the journalist inside me speak out, but I know that I will become sterilized if I keep fulfilling the rites of a conception of culture in which I do not believe. Above all, I do not believe that a systematic treatise, constructed with methods and bibliographies, like those that arouse professors, is worth more, necessarily, than a personal essay, spontaneous and audacious, on the same theme. Everything depends on the author and his fruit.

It is clear that the fanatics of philosophy will say that a philosophical system—above all if it is German—has more rigor, dignity, and hierarchy than an essay—above all if it is English. But, people, let us not talk about philosophy, first as if it monopolizes all offices of intelligence; and second as if it truly exists! I lament emphasizing philosophy, but I have no other choice: philosophy professors are those I have seen—with their very high eyebrows—disdaining essayists. Professionals of the concept, it would not be at all strange if they were to think that written genres have greater objectivity than writers.

The belief that concepts can become independent of the psychological process that elaborates them, substantiate themselves like the spiritualists' ectoplasm, convert themselves into "objective spirit," and resent the men who gave them life has always seemed a manifestation of madness to me. It was in a rage of sensibility that Aristotle elaborated his concept of poetic genres; but it was in a prolonged span of madness—from the Renaissance to Romanticism—that those genres were hypostatized into rhetorical realities and began to exercise an insulting power upon poets themselves. I respect the theoretical investigations of many sincere and original men whose work I envision as the concept of philosophy; but if they tell me, with the defiant air of a Quixote, that philosophy (from Toboso or wherever) demands something greater than respect, since it is the unparalleled queen of all intellectual disciplines, and I should obey it or die, then I rebel and swear I do not know that lady named Philosophy.

I am not absolute enough in my idealism to suppose that everything, even the elephant, is an illusion of my conscience. No. I believe in the heavy elephant. At least I believe that outside my being there is something that, upon entering my conscience, is represented to me as an image I call "elephant." But I refuse to believe that there is something called Philosophy, and much less that this Philosophy obliges me to be ashamed of my essays or to comply with academic methods. I do not know what an elephant is in itself, but it is enough for me to know that if that piece of noumenon puts a foot on me (or what I imagine is a foot) the noumenal foot will crush me. On the other hand, in the dominion of my conscience I am free, and there is nothing spiritual from the outside that can crush me. There are two elephants: the illusory and the other, which crushes me; but there is only one Philosophy, the illusory one, which cannot harm me.

I am skeptical, therefore, of the prejudice that an essay is less worthy than a philosophical treatise. The pellet is as round as the moon.

What happens is that many suppose that an essay is a rehearsal in something that one does not know well. A certain university professor (Argentine, of course) was upset because a colleague had published an essay. It seemed a trifling thing. "Why not rehearse at home," he exclaimed, "instead of rehearsing in public?" It seemed to him that to express oneself in informal, quick, and pleasant pages was to squander the theme and probably the brain!

But essays are not mumblings in an unlearned language; they are not the first steps on a path that others—the authors of treatises, theses, dissertations, and discourses—have already traveled to its end. Neither mumblings nor first steps were the pages by Montaigne, "the father of the essay." The history of the essay does not show us a limbo of indecisive people or apprentices, but of an emphatic assembly of spirits who felt confident, ingenious, and aware.

The essay's discredit in Argentina is due to snobs who have suddenly begun to make usurious calculations: if instead of being generous with periodicals—they say—they were to commit themselves to writing more extensive and systematic works, the country would grow in cultural import. Why? English literature is among the finest in the world thanks, in part, to the essay: Bacon, Cowley, Steele, Addison, Swift, Johnson, Goldsmith, Lamb, Hazlitt, Coleridge, Ruskin, Pater, Stevenson, Shaw, Chesterton, Woolf, Huxley, etc., are presences entirely on the face of a great literature, not loose threads hanging off the back of the tapestry. The essay is not always more humble than other literary genres. Who doubts that an essay by Addison is worth more than a tragedy by Addison? The essay is not always more ephemeral than a treatise. Great *Summae* have disappeared in the abyss and—as Paul Valéry says of the ancient empires—they have left us only their beautiful names. The word *Thomism*, for example; doesn't it sound beautifully phantom like the word *Babylonia*?

As I do not believe in genres, I do not believe in definitions either. A scholarly approximation would be this: the essay is a composition in prose, discursive but artistic through its richness in anecdotes and descriptions, brief enough that we can read it in one sitting, with an unlimited register of themes interpreted in all tones and with total liberty from a very personal point of view. If one considers this more or less current definition, one will see that the essay's very noble function consists of poeticizing the plain exercise of the writer's intelligence and fantasy, in prose. The essay is a conceptually constructed work of art; it is a logical structure, but one where logic begins to sing. I know that Croce would reject these opinions: he, who in one of his theoretical abuses arrived at denying poetic worth even to Dante's allegories, would not admit that there could be lyricism in an essay. "Where there is concept there is no poetry!" But conferring unity to something is already a poeticizing act. Any construction is animated with a touch of poetry when its interior unity has become visible, easy, and pleasant. There are philosophical systems, mathematical theories, scientific hypotheses, and historical characterizations that are converted into poems by the work and grace of a unifying spirit. And the essay is, above all else, a minimal unity, delicate and vivacious, wherein concepts may shine like metaphors.

TRANSLATED BY JESSE H. LYTLE

Eduardo Caballero Calderón

Colombia

(1910–1993)

Fiction was Eduardo Caballero Calderón's first pursuit as a writer, and he set his novels in his native Colombia, which he also depicts in his autobiography, *Memorias infantiles* (1964). Heavily influenced by Proust, his works often attempt to reconstruct his early life in Colombia. He worked as a journalist for *El Tiempo* and *El Espectador* and held diplomatic posts in Madrid and at UNESCO. Caballero Calderón settled in Madrid after leaving the diplomat corps and founded a publishing house, Editorial Guadarrama. He then branched into more intellectual essays, which can be found in *Suramérica: Tierra del hombre* (1942), *Latinoamérica: Un mundo por hacer*, and *Historia privada de los colombianos* (1960). Time in Spain and France led to *Americanos y europeos* and *Ancha es Castilla*. Later came *El nuevo príncipe: Ensayo sobre las malas pasiones* (1969), a philosophical work refuting Machiavelli, and *El Cristo de espaldas* (1958), an analysis of Colombia's struggle between liberals and conservatives. "Hermit Crabs," about writers as inhabitants of an ivory tower, is part of volume 2 of Caballero Calderón's *Obras completas* (1963). In its second part, his discussion of the role of the writer in Colombia is designed as an invitation to a type of democratic criticism where the observer is also observed and where no one— not the intelligentsia, not the political establishment—lives *sub specie aeternitatis*.

Hermit Crabs

We writers are like the fish that, living underwater, learn less about their own appearance than the fisherman casting his hook out from shore to catch them. We writers do not know our country as well as those who may have a wider perspective from which to pass judgment. They look at it from afar and above, with rods in one hand and pails for the fish within reach of the other. Hence, we can usually see better what lies beyond or afar, remote in history and distant in space, than what is proximal and recent, right before our eyes. And thus it is easier to write a book of memories than a diary. The latter is a landscape without perspective; whoever records it is like one who inspects individual cinematic frames, discovers many curious details that may escape a viewer in a movie theater, but does not understand anything of the film's sense as a whole.

225

The contemporary history of a country, even one covering a period of two or three generations that the writer has come to know, is a diary, a succession of film fragments seen too slowly and closely to be completely comprehended. We understand the history of the Greek people better than our own, the one in which we now swim and breathe, and of which we are but humble spectators. Better the history of the Greek people, I mean, than that of the contemporary French or Germans. But we see the Germans and the French as if projected in the distance, upon the screen of another continent, with the vast ocean in between; we can judge them with greater clarity than we can our own compatriots moving in our circles, among whom we are one of so many, one among all. Hence, this may appear absurd, or flippant and brash, yet it is still rigorously true: contemporary writers scrutinize the reality of Pericles's Greece in their darkest heart, while that of Hitler's Germany still eludes them. They can understand certain aspects of that nation's history, however, with greater perspicacity than aspects of their own, that of their very homeland, where they float without peeking their heads out, like fish in a pond.

It seemed appropriate to clarify these things before attempting to write an essay on Colombian reality, to determine its key points and follow the vectors of its historical coordinates. The difficulty of such an undertaking is great, for the reasons I just expressed by means of a handful of images. But along with this abstract and profound difficulty for writers of all countries and eras, Colombians and Hispanic Americans generally also bear the burden of native pride, which impedes us from accepting a universal hierarchy of values, within which ours occupy but a modest place. We have a certain propensity to take the recent to be important and what is in fashion to be the truly authentic.

It now may be worthwhile to digress slightly about the pernicious influence of current affairs upon the writer. He approaches his work with great fervor, and for a while lives in a strange world, absorbed in the contemplation of the characters he is building up, sleepless while obsessed by the reflections that suggest to him the historical facts demanding his attention. In this mood he picks up the morning paper, and he sees that a rocket launched by the clever Russians has just planted itself in the moon's corpse; or that there was another horrifying peasant slaughter in an interior village; or that the chief of state delivered a sensational speech on hot themes of foreign policy. All of a sudden the writer feels, with tremendous discouragement, that his writing does not have the slightest importance in the face of these pressing issues that claim the entire world's attention. It seems to him that his work is too personal within the universal tide of events, which crash with journalistic spray upon the shores of history. If he lets himself be defeated by such feelings of inferiority when faced with current reality, by those feelings of inadequacy when faced with universality, his book will remain in limbo and he will forever lack the will to finish it. The writer, then, must make a heroic effort to overcome himself, an effort not unlike that of the mystic. He must turn his back on the reality surrounding him—newspaper, radio, television, cinema, theater, the street—and submerge himself in the bottomless sea of his solitude. In contrast to the journalist, the writer is not a contemporary man: he is an extemporaneous man who lives before or after, above or below the surface upon which the others navigate toward nearby objectives, rising like islands on the horizon.

• • •

There is another concrete element that affects the Colombian writer. We like to judge ourselves according to foreign intellectual standards, and thus counterfeit and deform our own history to accommodate it to a certain succession of archetypes: Renaissance Spain, Revolutionary France, Manchester England, turn-of-the-century United States, Stalinist Russia; that is to say, a Catholic and colonial conception of society, later individualistic and romantic, then utilitarian and mercantilist, on to capitalist and pragmatic, and finally Marxist and revolutionary. However, that which is specifically Colombian, as I will explore in the course of this essay, relates only at a theoretical or intellectual level to ideas *induced* from foreign realities, which thus leaves only an interpreted view of our own.

Since the birth of logic and experimental sciences, ideas have been induced from reality, rising from the concrete to the abstract, and by compressing reproducible, phenomenal events into laws. Inclusively, when ancient peoples thought metaphysically, *deducing* reality from ideas and facts from a preestablished law, the former and latter were almost physical entities for those who blindly believed in the gods of Olympus, or later in the supremacy of theodicy upon all human experiences. Today, scientific thought, by induction and not deduction, is a common and current mode in those countries whose ideas we imitate; but we continue to be metaphysicists. With the ingenuousness of a medieval serf, we want our reality and history to be deduced from ideas that were never induced from our secular experiences. We are one of the most ignorant peoples on Earth: our illiteracy is desolating, our scientific and academic endeavors are making out dimly but go mostly unnoticed. To judge or interpret ourselves, we get lost while running in circles within the most *Byzantine* and sterile of intellectualisms. Dating back to pre-Independence, we have been in search of ideas and ideal systems that can accommodate us and find us an authorized explanation. For us, everything that is foreign and not ours carries authority. Hence, I say, we bear a striking resemblance to a certain astute variety of crustaceans, the hermit crabs of the San Andrés island, one of the prettiest in Colombia and perhaps the most irreducible to Colombian reality. Hidden in the beach sand, the crabs of San Andrés wait for other crustaceans to abandon their shells and then take them for themselves, like someone who suddenly moves into his neighbor's house. We put ourselves, I say, into the armor of exotic ideas and systems that belong to another species of crustaceans capable of constructing them through their own means.

Before attempting an interpretation of Colombian reality, we hermit writers must make a heroic effort to abandon our foreign shells and venture into the sun and open air: an effort to denude ourselves of foreign ideas, of common places, proper roles of national prejudices and petty feelings. We must expose our weakness and nakedness to the air and sun, with the patriotic aspiration of becoming real crustaceans someday, although then we will no longer be able to boast the strength and splendor of beautiful, stolen shells like the hermit crabs of San Andrés Island.

TRANSLATED BY JESSE H. LYTLE AND ILAN STAVANS

Ernesto Sábato

Argentina
(b. 1911)

———◦•••◦———

Upon leaving Argentina in 1934, Ernesto Sábato became disillusioned with the leftist beliefs he had acquired as a student, and he ended up studying physics in Paris, where he was introduced to surrealism and existentialism, whose influences are visible in his work. He later returned to Argentina and became a professor of physics at the University of La Plata. World War II shattered his belief in progress through science, and thus Sábato turned to a more humanistic and philosophical approach to the world. This approach can be seen clearly in *Uno y el universo* (1945), *Hombres y engranajes* (1951), and *Heterodoxias* (1953). From this point on, his essays branch out thematically: In *The Writer in the Catastrophe of Our Time* (1963), he discusses the novel; in *Tango, discusión y clave* (1953) and *La cultura en la encrucijada nacional* (1976) he muses about his native Argentina; with *Sartre contra Sartre* (1968), Sábato returns to more Europeanized themes, incorporating polemical critiques of Albert Camus, Jean-Paul Sartre, Simone de Beauvoir, and other French thinkers. His novels include *The Tunnel* (1952), *On Heroes and Tombs* (1961), and *Angel of Darkness* (1978). Sábato's fiction has been primarily devoted to the exploration and transformation of the psychological novel. His characters are incredibly alienated from the world and are often led to irrational acts by a compulsive dependence on rationality. The following discussion of the novel as a modern artifact is part of *The Writer in the Catastrophe of Our Time*. The novel's birth, Sábato believes, is the result of a deep crisis of identity and a direct response to the emergence of science and capitalism after the Middle Ages. In his eyes, novels like *Don Quixote* are designed to ponder existential questions once restricted to philosophers.

The Great Arc of the Novel

The rise of the novel in the West has to do with the deep spiritual crisis that unfolded after the Middle Ages. It was religious in that values were clear-cut and solid and then moved on into a profane era in which everything was to be put on trial and anguish and loneliness were to become more and more the attributes of alienated man. If we are to specify when this took place, I believe we can set it in the thirteenth century when the disintegration of the Holy Roman Empire began and when the Papacy, like the Empire, began crumbling in its universality. Between the two cynical and mighty powers in decline the Italian communes launched the new era of profane man, and the entire Old World was to begin collapsing. Soon man was to be ready for the rise of the novel; there was no solid faith, mockery and unbelief had replaced religion, man was again out in the metaphysical cold. And so, that curious genre was to be born that would bring the human condition under scrutiny in a world where God is absent, does not exist, or is doubted. From Cervantes to Kafka, this was to be the great theme of the novel, and hence a strictly modern and European creation since the conjunction of three great events was called for which had never taken place before anywhere in the world: Christianity, science, and capitalism with its industrial revolution. The *Quixote* is not only the first example but the most typical one, inasmuch as the chivalric values of the Middle Ages are held up to ridicule in it, from which stems not only the sensation of satire but the painful tragicomic feeling, the terribly sad rending that, evidently, its creator felt and which he transmits to his readers through his grotesque mask. Here, precisely, we have the proof that our novel is something more than a simple series of adventures. It is the tragic testimony of an artist for whom the secure values of a sacred community have collapsed. And the entry of a society into a crisis of ideals is like the ending of adolescence for a child; the absolute has broken to pieces and the soul remains facing despair or nihilism. Perhaps for that very reason the end of a civilization is felt more keenly by the young who do not wish to resign themselves ever to the collapse of the absolute and by the artists who are the only ones among adults who resemble adolescents. And so, this collapse of a civilization is attested to by the suffering youths who travel the roads of the West and the artists who in their works describe, investigate, and bear poetic witness to the chaos. The novel, in this way, could be situated between the beginning of Modern Times and their present decline, running parallel to this growing profanation (how significant this word turns out to be!) of the human creature, to this frightful process of demythification of the world. The Western novel originates, develops, and reaches its peak between these two great crises. And that is why it is useless and a waste of time to study it without reference to this formidable period which, since there is no choice, must be called "Modern Times." Without the Christianity that preceded them, restless and problematical consciousness would not have existed; without the technology that typifies them there would have been neither demythification, cosmic insecurity, alienation, nor urban loneliness. In this manner, Europe injected into the old legendary tale or simple epic adventure that social and metaphysical urgency to produce a literary genre that was to describe infinitely more phantastic territory than that of the countries of legend: man's consciousness. And it will be made to sink further each day that the end of the era draws closer into the dark and enigmatic universe that has so much to do with the reality of dreams.

Jaspers maintains that the great dramatists of ancient times poured tragic awareness into their plays that not only moved their audiences but transformed them. In that way, they were *educators of their people*, prophets of their *ethos*. But, then—he says—that tragic awareness was transmuted into an esthetic phenomenon and the audience as well as the poet abandoned their deep, primitive seriousness to provide images without blood. It is possible that in writing these words, the great German thinker had in mind a certain kind of convoluted literature that appears in the West, as it did in all periods of intellectual refinement, because how admit that Kafka's work is not as metaphysically weighty as Sophocles's? In man's confrontation of this total crisis of the race, the most complex and profound that he has faced in his entire history, tragic awareness has recaptured the ancient and violent need through the great novelists of our age. And even when it is a matter, superficially, of wars or revolutions, in the final analysis, those catastrophes serve to set the human creature at the frontiers of his condition through torture and death, loneliness or madness. Extremes of man's misery and grandeur which manifest themselves only in great cataclysms, permitting the artists who record them to reveal the ultimate secrets of the human condition.

It is man's body that situates him within the animal kingdom, but he is not body alone; nor is he only spirit, which is rather our divine aspiration. What has to be saved amidst this hecatomb is the specifically human, the soul, sundered and ambiguous ambiance, site of the perpetual struggle between carnality and purity, between the nocturnal and the luminous. Through pure spirit, through metaphysics and philosophy, man sought to explore the Platonic universe, invulnerable to the powers of Time; and perhaps he may have done it, if Plato is to be believed, through the memory he retains of his primordial confraternity with the gods. But his true homeland is only this intermediate and terrestrial region, this dual and mangled region from whence the phantoms of the novel arise. Men write fiction because they are incarnate, because they are imperfect. A God does not write novels.

TRANSLATED BY ASA ZATZ

Jorge Amado

Brazil

(b. 1912)

———◆•✦•◆———

One of Brazil's most prolific and popular writers, Jorge Amado has authored more than twenty novels. His works reveal the communist inclinations that led the government to confiscate his *Cacao* (1933) immediately after it was published. That would only mark the beginning of Amado's legal troubles with the Brazilian regime. He was arrested in 1937 for his involvement in an attempt to overthrow the dictatorial government of Gertúlio Vargas. His legal troubles forced him to flee to Argentina and then to Uruguay. An ill-conceived return to Brazil in 1941 resulted again in his arrest and he was ordered to remain in the city of Salvador. After the downfall of the Vargas regime, Amado was elected to the Brazilian Congress as a candidate for the Communist Party. When two years later the party was declared illegal, he fled to Paris and would not return to his homeland until 1952. Ironically, his literary style grew less dogmatic as the government intensified its campaign of political persecution. After 1955, he began to incorporate a lower-class vocabulary, folk songs, and religious ceremonies into his narratives. After returning to Brazil during the 1950s, his political stance also underwent a significant change as he urged the Communist Party to reevaluate the value of socialist realism and the legitimacy of Soviet policy in Eastern Europe. Although he never left the party as many of his political allies did, his later works continued to demonstrate a growing distance from communist orthodoxy. *Land of Carnival* (1932), the Bahian native's first novel, was published when he was just nineteen. Other novels are *Gabriela, Clove and Cinnamon* (1958), *Doña Flor and Her Two Husbands* (1962), *Showdown* (1984), *The Golden Harvest* (1992), and *The War of the Saints* (1993). When compared to his prolific novelistic career, his essays are small in size and number. In them he often uses magical realism to call attention to the dreamlike aspects of Brazilian daily life. And he also uses the form to reflect on contemporary events and to recount autobiographical incidents, as he does in *Navegação de cabotagem* (1992), in which the following segment is included. Written in Paris between July 1991 and June 1992, these vignettes find Amado in Moscow in 1952. They then switch to New York in 1986, return to Paris in 1949, and finally leap forward to 1991.

Notes for Memoirs I'll Never Write

I.
Moscow 1952: The Forgetful

Ilya Erenburg and I return in silence from a conversation with important figures in high circles about our friend, the Czech writer Jan Drda. It was about a request he'd made of me in Prague, where I'd been before coming to Moscow to receive the International Stalin Peace Prize. Winning the prize had given me some prestige.

It's January 1952, 20 below zero, an icy wind sweeps the streets of Moscow. As we drain our glasses of vodka in Ilya's apartment on Gorky Street, he says: "Jorge, we are two writers who will never be able to write our memoirs. We know too much." Still seriously disturbed by the conversation we've just had, I nod my head in agreement.

That did not keep Ilya from publishing—years later, during the Khrushchev period when Soviet obscurantism "opened," and a small light glowed in the darkness—seven volumes of memoirs. That's right, seven. In the seventh, my wife, Zélia, and I appear as rather charming characters. And that's not all. Ilya's daughter Irina told me in 1988 that she was organizing her father's papers so she could publish several other volumes he couldn't print even during the Khrushchev "opening." Ilya did know too much.

Over the course of my career as writer and citizen, I came to know facts, causes, and effects I promised to keep secret. I knew those things because I was a militant in a political party whose goal was to change the nature of society. I acted clandestinely, even carrying out subversive actions. Even though it's been years since I ceased to be a militant in the Communist party, even today when the Marxist-Leninist ideology that shaped the activities of the party is fading and dying, when the universe of real socialism is coming to its sad end, even today I do not feel released from the vows I made not to disclose information to which I had access because I was a militant Communist. While such disclosures no longer have the slightest importance, I do not feel I have the right to tell things revealed to me in confidence. From time to time I remember things about which I wrote no notes, but they will die with me.

II.
Moscow 1953: Valentina's Breasts

Ilya Erenburg uses a meeting of the Committee of the World Peace Council as an opportunity to gather Soviet and foreign friends—about a dozen people—around the figure of Kuo-Mo-Jo. Kuo-Mo-Jo is a world-famous Chinese savant, a legend in Asia. He's the only linguist who knows 50,000 ideograms: to read a newspaper you only have to know 3,000; a university professor knows 7,000; the truly erudite may know 10,000. Twice a minister under Chiang Kai-Shek, representing the Communists in their alliances with the nationalist leader, member of the Politburo of the Communist party, which four years earlier, in 1949, had assumed power and proclaimed the People's Republic of China, of which he is vice president. He is also vice president of the World Peace Council and of the selection jury for the International Stalin Prize. Those are just some of the many titles Kuo-Mo-Jo boasts of, or rather doesn't boast of: he's a simple man devoid of arrogance, amiable, and extremely sympathetic. One of the most notable figures in the socialist world, one of the most respected leaders in the international Communist movement, he's in his sixties but doesn't look it. The Chinese don't show age.

In the living room: a low table weighed down by food and drink, smoked fish, salmon, caviar, fruit, vodka, cognac, wines from Georgia and Moldavia. Seated around the table: Konstantine Fedin, Konstantine Simonov (writers), Pudovkin (filmmaker), Pierre Cot (French politician), Vercors (French writer), the Rumanian writer Mihail Sadoveanu, and the Italian politician Pietro Nenni. And yours truly with Zélia.

Simonov brought his wife, a famous stage actress, an extremely elegant woman whose Slavic beauty has been sung in prose and verse. Her prodigious breasts, milk white, leap over her décolleté a fatal vision. Her name is Valentina Ferova, and Simonov wrote for her a book of sensual, almost erotic, love poems which drew a reproof from Stalin himself: "Why do our publishers waste money bringing out a book of this kind?" That put the kibosh on all the love poetry in the Soviet Union, beginning with Mayakovsky's. A famous woman, then, this sublime Valentina: When she died, after having been separated from Simonov for a long time, he appeared at the wake; later he placed a thousand red carnations on her grave, one thousand, not one less.

Sitting opposite this beauty, disconnected from the conversation taking place in French—he doesn't speak any Western language although he speaks 18 Asian languages—and having sent his interpreter, Liu, to wait outside, Kuo-Mo-Jo dedicates himself to staring at the décolleté of Valentina's evening dress, his eyes captured by her solid, dazzling, abundant breasts. Blind to everything else, he politely empties the glass of vodka set before him. He drinks it down in one gulp to get rid of it, and Ilya's wife, Lluba, the perfect hostess, refills it. He empties it just as quickly.

In China, it's worth noting, women's breasts are the supreme erogenous zone. They are the most sacred objects, always hidden, and, from early on, restrained and bound close to keep them from growing—the small breasts

of Chinese women, hidden away, an absolute taboo. Valentina's monumental breasts, practically on full display, the eyes of the illustrious leader,
of the eminent statesman, locked, fixed on those voluptuous breasts.

Oblivious to the drama, we're heatedly arguing about literature, art,
movies, and only become aware of the catastrophe—is that the right
word?—when the absurd takes place: Kuo-Mo-Jo, apparently sober despite all the vodka he consumed, his face impassive, never raising his eyes
from those Russian, theatrical, superabundant bosoms, stands up, walks
around to the other side of the table, stops opposite Mrs. Simonov, extends
both hands and takes hold of her breasts. He holds on so hard it looks as
if he will be there forever.

Right before our horrified eyes, Kuo-Mo-Jo, vice president many times
over, historical Communist, the greatest savant in Asia, an eminence, with
both hands down Valentina Ferova Simonov's décolleté. One hand on the
right breast, the other on the left, holding fast, supreme happiness imprinted
on his frozen face. We too are completely frozen, paralyzed, speechless, a
silence like that hadn't been seen since the beginning of the world and will
never be seen again. We gape, mute, turned to stone.

Liu, who never takes his eye off his boss, comes in from the other room,
takes Kuo-Mo-Jo gently but firmly by the elbows, separates him from
Valentina, and leads him to the elevator. Ilya and Lluba, restored to life,
rush to say good-bye. In the living room the arguments about literature,
art, and movies, take up where they left off, all interest in the affair vanishes,
and it is as if nothing had ever happened. Ever since that night of horror,
I've had an even higher opinion of Kuo-Mo-Jo.

III.
Moscow 1957–Paris 1990: Poetry

Perhaps because of the plague of declamation, an epidemic in the Brazil of
the thirties, poetry for me was limited to readings that consisted, at the
most, of recitations by two people: reading love poetry with your sweet-
heart in a low voice is an exceptional pleasure. It's wonderful in Moscow,
in Gorky Park, to see young married couples enjoying Pushkin and Yesenin, their heads together, their fingers entwined over the pages of a book.
I fled from women who recited poetry as from yellow fever, but I must
also confess that more than once I was moved by listening to poetry.

Not long ago, at the Sorbonne, Zélia and I, together with the French
translator Alice Raillard, listened to Maria de Jesus Barroso, actress and
wife of President Mário Soares of Portugal, recite poetry by the great Por-
tugese poets: Camilo Peçanha, Mário Sá-Carneiro, José Régio, Fernando
Pessoa. With absolutely no grandiloquence, the actress lives each stanza,
envelopes us in limpid poetry born out of emotion. The Portuguese lan-

guage, as Maria de Jesus spoke it, has the accent of eternity, the poetry invades me, penetrates me, runs in my blood, strikes my bones.

The other time was in Moscow, a bit further off. It was during the Khrushchev thaw, and in the Satirical Theater they were putting on a play about Mayakovsky, the poet's life told through his poems. The script consisted exclusively of lines by Mayakovsky and accusations leveled against his poetry by critics and ideologues—the critics and ideologues defecated insults and denunciations from two latrines located above the stage, latrine criticism, disgusting. On the stage itself, four actors lived four different Mayakovskys: the revolutionary, the lover, the Surrealist, and the—what was the fourth? Or were there only three?

I neither speak nor understand Russian, but the profound power of the poetry got into my guts and almost moved me to tears. I will never forget the moment when the suicidal Mayakovsky stepped onto the stage to kill himself: He entered reciting the poem in which he castigated Yesenin for having committed suicide. I listened with my hair standing on end.

IV.
Moscow 1954: Le Crapaud

We arrive for lunch at the house of Lluba and Ilya. Lida, their cook, is one of my readers and pulls out all the stops when she knows I'll be there. And at the Erenburg's you only eat and drink the very best. Ilya's in conference with a bigshot from *Pravda* who's come to give the party's instructions for a series of articles on foreign policy, a subject in which Ilya is a kind of spokesman for the Soviet government. And while we wait, we drink wine from the cellars of Joseph Goebbels.

The president of the Academy of Sciences, a man with access to secrets, telephones Ilya with sensational, first-hand news, the kind available to only a privileged few. He can't contain himself. Ilya asks, "Was Beria sentenced to death?" The call, after all, came through just when sentence was being passed on the former head of the secret police. "Who cares about Beria?" asks the now out-of-control academic. "I'm calling about something of the greatest importance, and you start in with the Beria business, which doesn't matter a whit. I know for a fact that tomorrow morning the wines from Goebbels's cellars will be put on sale in the specialty shops in the center of Moscow. My advice to you is get up early and send all your people out so you can buy the largest number of bottles."

Among the valuables, the entire industries, the machines, the gold, and the silver commandeered by the Red Army when Berlin fell, was Goebbels's cellar, the largest in Europe, the richest in fine wines, all confiscated from the reserves, the best-stocked *caves* in the wine-producing nations occupied by Nazi troops, especially France. Stored for almost ten years, decanted into anonymous bottles, all with the same label, "wine," with no other indications, they were put on sale for prices lower than those paid for wines from Moldavia or Georgia. Up at dawn, Ilya and Lluba call in Lida, Lida's mother, their driver, their two secretaries, the parents of the secretaries, their daughter Irina, their son-in-law, and I just don't know who else: a battalion. All together they manage to get almost eight hundred bottles, or a few more. Then the lines grew, the Soviet citizens bought and paid without asking about what they were buying because things put on sale would quickly run out. That was the situation.

Opening each bottle is a game of Russian roulette: What will our prize be this time? No matter where it came from, what *cru*, what year, what *cuvée*, it was always the best wine, always the nectar of the gods, the wines from Goebbels's cellar, the sale of which was the most important event to take place between the death of Stalin and the opening of the XXth Congress, when Khrushchev made his famous denunciation of Stalin. Compared with that sale, Beria's being condemned to death was nothing more than a matter for the crime page, a minor event. While we waited, we tasted (beside the wines): caviar, smoked salmon, sprats—and if you've never had sprats, run out and get some so you can find out what something really good is.

Ilya comes out of his office, introduces me to the big shot from *Pravda*, and offers him a glass of Goebbels's wine. But the thug prefers vodka, which he downs in one gulp, and then leaves. Ilya has a glass of red, classifies it as a Bordeau, and savors it slowly, trying to guess the year and the chateau. After all, his knowledge of wines is part of his legend. While Lida serves lunch, placing steaming dishes before us, Ilya relates the details of the meeting with the party man.

The walls of Ilya's office were covered with etchings and drawings by French masters, a collection worth millions. Opposite the writing desk, there is an etching by Picasso, *Le Crapaud*, an artist's proof dedicated to Ilya. As soon as he lays eyes on the picture—a deformed, disintegrated toad—the man from *Pravda*, a theoretician of socialist realism, begins to tremble and averts his eyes from such ignominy: so this is what the capitalists call art, he exclaims, on the verge of apoplexy. How is it possible that Comrade Erenburg has such excrescences, this rot of the bourgeoisie hanging from the walls of his apartment. And this Picasso calls himself a Communist, that really beats all!

Ilya interrupts this fulmination:

"Comrade, do you know the title of this etching, what it represents?"

"No, I don't know . . . What I do know is . . ."

"It represents Yankee imperialism."

The ideologue relaxes, takes another look at the picture, and nods his head; now free of the threat of a heart attack, he practices autocriticism:

"Yankee imperialism? Now I understand; Picasso is a member of the French Communist party, isn't that so? A loyal comrade: what a talent!"

V.
Moscow 1954: Conspiracy

Anna Seghers calls me from the National Hotel, which is just opposite Red Square. Zélia and I are in the Metropol, opposite the Bolshoi, along with Pablo Neruda and Nicolás Guillén. "I've just arrived," she says nervously, "and must talk with you right away, a matter of the utmost importance." Anna came to Moscow as I and so many other artists from the five continents did, invited to the Second Congress of Soviet Writers, an event of the highest importance in the universe of the intellectual left.

Anna hadn't come only for the Congress; she was also a member of the jury for the International Stalin Prize. I'd already won the prize, the greatest honor I'd ever received until then. In the USSR, I have diplomatic status, the importance of a party official. It's about the Stalin Prize that Anna wants to speak with me. I don't know why, but some people around the world believe in me, attribute to me powers I do not have, the ability to resolve any problem. Anna Seghers is one of those irresponsible people. The problem bothering her and which she explains so I can give her advice seems to me of undeniable gravity—it has to do with Bertolt Brecht. I had dinner with Brecht in Anna's house: she and Brecht live in the same four-story building in East Germany, Anna on the second and he on the fourth floor, if I'm not mistaken. I'm also a friend of his wife, Helena Weil, from the time we were together on the jury of the International Peace Prize for the World Council. I only came to have greater contact with Brecht during the filming of the play *Mr. Puntila and His Servant Matti* by Wien Film. I think I attended so the theater man and the cineast could come to some understanding; at the beginning they simply didn't get along.

It happened that Brecht fell under the suspicion of the German Communist party, a party whose sectarianism went far beyond the unimaginable. Without taking into account the fact that his entire life had been dedicated to socialism, his extraordinary production was accused of being formalist, not squaring with the norms of socialist realism laid down by Zhdanov. To begin the adjustment, the party decided, Anna whispered to me, to deprive Brecht of the use of the theater the Soviets had left him when they withdrew from Berlin, the theater where Brecht and his Berliner Ensemble company had set themselves up and were accomplishing things that had worldwide repercussions.

As Anna departs, the conspiracy against Brecht grows. She's worried sick: "They'll make Bertolt's life impossible, you know how things are, I don't have to tell you. But there is one way, one single way, to stop all this and guarantee him security, tranquility, and the peace he needs for his work." And what would that be? "Getting the Stalin Prize for him; if he had that, no one would dare touch him or his theater. I want you to help me. The jury meets four days from now."

Then came a lot of scurrying around. First the chat with Erenburg in his apartment on Gorky Street, where Anna counts the votes solidly for Brecht on her fingers: Ilya, Neruda, her own . . . Who could tell about Aragon? Then Ilya, "the old man," interrupts her brusquely: "Don't waste time with that. The important thing is Sacha's support." Sacha is Alexandr Fadayev who represents the U.S. Communist party on the jury. He is a member of their Central Committee, and if he thinks it's a good idea, no one will dispute the point. There is only one thing to do: talk to him.

He picks up the telephone to dial the number, and as he dials, he recommends to Anna, "Take Jorge, Sacha likes him." It was true. Fadayev thought a lot of me and considered me a good comrade on whom he could depend. So off we went, Anna and I, to talk with the secretary general of the Union of Soviet Writers.

It was easier than we'd thought. Once Anna explained the problem, Fadayev never hesitated even for an instant. He gave his complete support to Anna's suggestion. He would place Bertholt Brecht's name on the list of candidates, replaced whoever it was who would have the final word—according to him, it was the Party Political Bureau. Could that be true? I don't know; it wasn't easy to know which was the truth and which a play of interests. In any case, Brecht won the prize, the German C.P. changed course and stopped annoying him. *Annoying*: A weak verb; it doesn't remotely give an idea of the miseries to which they would have subjected him, the pit of infamies in which they would have sunk him.

VI.
Moscow 1951: A Letter

With extreme care, Fedor Keliin opens the leather briefcase, removes the cardboard folder, separating it from the leaves of writing paper that protect it, opens it, and takes out the yellowed manuscript. A priceless treasure, a relic: a letter written by Maksim Gorky.

Literature in Spanish and Portuguese owes a great deal to Fedor Keliin. A historian of Hispanic culture, he translated and popularized authors from the Iberian peninsula and Latin America in the USSR. There were those who criticized him for using meter and rhyme when he translated Neruda's free verse—"In Russian, I'm a disciple of Pushkin," Neruda jokes—but the fact is that good old Keliin fought for our literature with publishers and literary magazines. During the thirties, he'd fought in vain to have the Portuguese novelist Eça de Queiroz published, but the publishers slammed their doors in Eça's face.

He shows me the letter, I see Gorky's writing in the Cyrillic alphabet; the author is one of my favorites, because through him I learned how to love vagabonds. I devoured his stories, novels, and plays. During my first trip to the Soviet Union, I ran to see *The Lower Depths* spoken in the language of Communist gringos. I almost wept. Keliin tells me about the contents of the letter, which won him a victory over the sectarianism of the publishers.

Eça had been translated at the start of the century, just one book which had not reappeared in bookstores since the October Revolution. With the manuscript of the translation of *The Crime of Father Amaro* under his arm, Keliin went from publisher to publisher. He was in despair when Gorky returned from Italy and became the leader of literary life. Keliin wrote to Gorky, asking him to intervene with the publishers. He expected no answer, hoped the intervention might take place, and thought that taking a risk doesn't cost anything. He did receive an answer, the letter he proudly showed me in my room at the Hotel Metropol.

He points out one line to me, and translates what Gorky says about Eça: "Eça de Queiroz is one of the high points in the world novel." Is it necessary to add that it wasn't long before the translation of *The Crime of Father Amaro* came out? Eça's *Relic* soon followed, Keliin not content to rest on his laurels.

Fedor Keliin puts the manuscript back in among the sheets of writing paper, puts it in the cardboard envelope, which he then puts into the leather briefcase. He'd brought it back with him from Spain, where he'd fought on the Madrid front during the war.

VII.
Moscow 1954: Monsieur le Prix

Pravda publishes a list of the candidates for the International Stalin Prize; it's prominently placed on the front page. I'm shaking with joy because among those worthy of this supreme honor I read the names of Bertholt Brecht and Nicolás Guillén. I got involved on Brecht's behalf with Sacha Fadayev, but Zélia and I try to keep Nicolás's spirits up during the agony of the waiting period.

Rosa stayed behind in Havana, so Nicolás invited Zélia to hand him the medal and the diploma, which he would receive in a plenary session of the Congress of Soviet Writers. It was for the Congress that we came to Moscow; we're on the same floor in the same hotel. Under any and all pretexts, he sends us notes, which he signs "Monsieur le Prix." He's as happy as a child, and so are we. His name is in the papers, his poems read on the radio and on television, and, a peculiar Soviet plague, recited by women. The poet invites us in and sits us down to listen to one of them recite: She's fat and hoarse, a dinosaur. Nicolás savors the poems in Russian with delight, identifies them, and praises the virago. We applaud too: Why should we ruin our friend's happiness?

I compose a telegram for Nicolás, which I ask Marina Kontrizin, our interpreter, to translate for me. Then I send it from the post office set up at the congress to Nicolás at the Metropol. It's a message filled with ardent passion, a declaration of love, an invitation to a tryst: I sign it with only the first name of this imaginary admirer, Natacha. It's all hyperbole: "My genial poet, my tropical bard, I was overwhelmed when I heard your poems on television. I've been set ablaze by the fire of your poetry. I want to meet you as soon as possible. . . ." It went on like that, from flame to flame. I do remember the ending: "I love you, I love you, I love you. Call me, call me. Natacha."

Telegram in hand and accompanied by the interpreter, Nicolás bursts into our room: "Comrades, there's a woman in Moscow madly in love with me. She's sent me a telegram, but she must be a bit thick. She wants me to call, but doesn't include her telephone number. . . ."

VIII.
Moscow 1953: Tears

I leave the plane that's brought Zélia and me from Vienna. It's five o'clock in the afternoon, the dead of night in Moscow: January and the harsh winter of 1953. It's our first visit to the Soviet Union since going back to Brazil. A few friends greet us at the airport, among them the Hispanist and member of the Academy of Sciences Vera Kuteichkova, enthusiasm personified. She will be our interpreter during our stay.

We had already become friends through correspondence when we met face to face in 1948. In charge of literature in Spanish and Portuguese at the Gorky Institute of Universal Literature, Vera wrote an essay on my work which appeared in a series of pamphlets published by *Pravda*. For Zélia and me, Vera and her husband, Lev, another renowned Hispanist with books on Lorca, Neruda, and Diego Rivera, are our Soviet family—we don't have to talk to understand each other.

Vera came to have breakfast with us at the hotel. I hand my copy of *Pravda* to her and ask her to translate the headline because it looks like something important. Vera had read the paper before leaving the house, but even so, before giving additional information, she takes the newspaper and translates. The article announces the discovery of a "heinous Yankee plot" to assassinate Stalin. The filthy, monstrous agents of the conspiracy are doctors, the most eminent doctors in the USSR, those whose responsibility it is to look after the health of the potentates in the Kremlin—"all of them Jews," *Pravda* adds.

My mouth hangs open, I don't know what to say or think. I look at Vera opposite me. Motionless, she closes her fists, bites her lips, tears flow from her eyes: We don't have to talk to understand.

IX.
Moscow 1948: The True Believer

Francisco Ferreira, Portuguese, works at Radio Moscow along with Satva Brandão on Portuguese-language broadcasts. He supplies ideology and encouraging news to the comrades in Brazil, Portugal, and the Portuguese colonies in Africa. A Young Communist, he fought in the International Brigades during the Spanish Civil War and was evacuated to the Soviet Union after the defeat of the Republic. He married a Spanish woman and is a competent radio announcer, a nice person, cordial and expansive, capable of human solidarity, clear proof of which he gave in his devotion to the sister and daughter of the Brazilian Communist leader Luis Carlos Prestes when they were exiled to Moscow. An exemplary member of the Portuguese party, his sectarianism knows no limits: It is absolute.

Since it's my first visit to the USSR, I try to find out about its life, its customs, its pluses and minuses.

"Thieves?" our good Ferreira is visibly disturbed. "In the fatherland of socialism, there is no theft. Thieves are things of the past, from the days of the Czars."

That afternoon, at the GUM department store, thieves twice tried to grab Zélia's purse. Vera Kuteichkova warned us: "You can't be too careful; there are thieves all over the place." I try to unmask our informer: Don't lie to us, Ferreira. But he simply will not admit a thing.

"Thieves exist, of course. I'm not going to hide that. They're left over from the war. But they're the cleverest thieves on the face of the earth. Last week, I was on a bus at lunch time; it was crowded. Only when I got home did I realize they'd stolen everything I had: They cut through my overcoat with a razor blade and did such a good job I didn't feel a thing. You won't find thieves like that anywhere else." Soviet pride with a Portuguese accent.

We comment about the differences in sexual habits in the capitalist West and the socialist East. Our Ferreira is peremptory:

"That degeneracy doesn't exist in the Soviet Union (he was referring to adultery). Soviet women are faithful to their husbands; proletarian morality is rigid, you know. An adventure, a false step, conjugal infidelity—

these are very rare things; you can count the instances on the fingers of one hand."

The information I already have from writers and workers—I make friends wherever I go—contradicts Chico Ferreira's unconditional statements. More than once I gently debunk his statements, because I see no other intention in his falsehoods than a desire to conserve the image of the USSR, which for him is sacred. For him and for me, for millions and millions of people around the world.

"Don't be a cynic, Chico. Women around here are available even without your having to ask, as you well know, since you work in that radio world so favorable to whoring around. Should I quote examples?"

He did want examples, because the puritanism of the regime did not reduce the interest of the comrades in the lives of others, especially when the comrades happened to be important figures in intellectual life. So I repeat some widely known gossip. Ferreira listens, makes me repeat things, asks for more details: a man of delicacy. When I'm finished, he confesses:

"They lie, yes they do, and a lot. But I'm going to tell you something, comrade. In the whole world, there are no women you can compare to Soviet women in bed. At least not in Spain or Portugal. I don't know about the rest."

Francisco Ferreira is clumsy. Everything in the USSR is the best in the world. To deny obvious truths is to play into the hands of Yankee imperialism. Soviet women are the best in the world, my dear Ferreira? Better than gypsy girls from Seville? Better than the country girls from the Minho district of Portugal? Poor Soviet women, victims of prejudice and ignorance: They know nothing of the *Kama Sutra*, tied to their families, they only find variety in adultery, which they practice with consistent assiduity. They change partners at the banquet table, but the menu is always the same: the same old potato boiled in the same old salt water, she on the bottom, he on top.

Translated by Alfred MacAdam

José Lezama Lima

Cuba

(1912–1976)

———•◦•◦•———

Perhaps best known for his novel *Paradiso* (1966), which was translated into English by Gregory Rabassa, José Lezama Lima is considered one of Cuba's most outstanding contemporary essayists and fiction writers. He was born in the Columbia Military Installation, in the Marianao section of Havana, and the city, the true center of his intellectual and social activities, became an essential personal and philosophical influence. In fact, he left Havana only twice—in 1949 to visit Mexico, and in 1950 for a trip to Jamaica—and died there. His main theme is the quest for unity and harmony. *Muerte de Narciso* (1937), his first poetry collection, is about Narcissus's search for his own essence. Other poetic works followed a similar theme: *Aventuras sigilosas* (1945), *La fijeza* (1949), and *Dador* (1960). An early supporter of Fidel Castro's revolution, Lezama Lima was named director of the Literature and Publications Department of the National Council of Culture and vice president of the National Union of Cuban Writers and Artists. However, he was later scapegoated by the regime during the revolution's cultural struggles. He was coeditor of the magazine *Orígenes* from 1945 to 1956. His oeuvre includes *Los grandes todos* (1968), *Poesías completas* (1970), and *La cantidad hechizada* (1970), as well as the posthumously published *Fragmentos a su imán* (1977) and *Oppiano Licario* (1977); but many consider his *Paradiso*—a labyrinthine work of incredible sophistication and maturity, recognized in Cuba only after it had enjoyed success abroad—one of the greatest, still underappreciated, Latin American novels of the twentieth century. In his essays, particularly in *La expresión americana* (1957) and *Tratados de La Habana* (1958), Lezama Lima attempted a baroque reading of his milieu. The influential essay "Summa Critica of American Culture," which resulted from five lectures he delivered from 16 January to 26 January at the Centro de Altos Estudios of Havana's Instituto Nacional de Cultura, and is part of *La expresión americana*, displays a wide range of references—from Picasso and Stravinsky to Whitman and Melville, from José Martí to the Argentine classic *Martín Fierro*—in its search for unity, originality, and authenticity in modern Latin American art and culture.

Summa Critica of American Culture

In the 1920s, with the eruption of cries from the so-called reservists of French literature, the concept of originality was bursting forth and proliferating like the crowing of a rooster at dawn. It judged itself favorably for being "something different," like flattery inciting gazes rallied together by sympathy. *Faire autre chose, faire le contraire* was the slogan impressed upon the new, emerging generations, born with a royal sign over the left nipple like the ancient kings of Georgia. A Picasso, a Stravinsky, a Joyce were judged in the context of the *sprit nouveau* [*sic*] according to their originality. Their rupture was so superior to their generational debt that their historical backbone dissolved into an amorphous and protocellular state. Cézanne and Picasso were two kings declaring their oaths while walking toward different trees, their backs to each other. They wished to forget that in their search for frenzied originality their feet were driven by fatigue like those lazy people who, with the arrival of a new season, suddenly throw open their windows, thrash their arms about, and beat the winter blanket with long sticks like a muleteer beating a pack of mules standing still at a crossroads.

Picasso was "something different" from the search for sensation; Stravinsky was "something different" from the fervent search for orchestral color. A writer like Joyce was "something different" from the moral satire of a Bernard Shaw. Thus, the *sprit nouveau* [*sic*] tenuously indicated the uneasiness with its isolation from its very beginning and forgot that its motto was a label made fashionable by Baudelaire during Paris of the Franco-Prussian War, a salute to the brass of Wagner, the diabolic infantilism of Louis of Bavaria, and the enigmatic performances of Jeanne Samary.

But after ten years had rolled by, scenography would refuse to produce "something different" to rejoin the strand of continuity that united the generations. We were engaged in demonstrating that it was "the same thing," under various names and restrained mutations, that coursed through the trajectory of expression. Behind the values that, a decade earlier, were appreciated as original, what now was admired as a compendium of logic, with the sensibility of concentrated criticism, was the shrewdness to prune those regions of the past where greenhouses of innovation had been established and remained unexpressed in their totality and which now were being presented as an additive fragment. They wished to remove Picasso from the French tradition of his first works of this century, from the era of experimentation and mutations, to link him, according to the discerning taste of the day, with the Spanish tradition, a tradition that took fewer risks, advanced more slowly, and thus provided a hardier stock for the exigencies of the temporal plane. (This perverse tradition had forgotten that El Greco as well as Goya owed much to historical synthesis and to products of *indigenismo*.) But this substitution aside, in Picasso's work, from the bulls of Spain to French Formalism, emphasis was placed with relish on his pastiches of El Greco and Lautrec, his Doric period, his travels to the dihedral rocks of the blessed Orta, his adaptations of Catalan Illuminists—in short, his elegant mastery of the panoply of stylistic historicism. Picasso was no longer being asked to be innovative and original, restless and quick, but rather to brace his work within the great tradition of Spanish painting, in solid and gravitating values, in structures, in carboniferous bones and petroglyphs, in the swelling of the tides.

With Stravinsky, whose fortune was more secure given that he was deeper inside an easy truth, a popular foundation, the sure advances in his handling of the orchestral mass in relation to that of Rimsky, assimilating and expanding upon the latter's discovery of [Giovanni] Pergolesi, the ragtime and tap, the jazz era—in short, all the bees of history were bearing him a cloak covered with the emblems of every epoch. In the case of Joyce, it was no longer his philological workshop, his verbal ferociousness but rather fathers Suárez and Sánchez, his Scholastic teachers chosen by the Jesuits, the trash cans of the working-class neighborhoods of Dublin, the instruments of specialized gynecology transformed by the giantology of Rabelais, the Odyssean design. So it was that in less than ten years our critics swung from side to side, corrected themselves, placed themselves staunchly in opposition: what had been considered original was the product of style; what had seemed a rupture was a secret continuum. That rendered the idea of generations, taken from the German university seminar, obsolete and anachronistic, for the generations must emerge from their creation, not from a headstrong *anti-*, from a battle against, in the dawn's projected divination of the future. The generations are not created out of the willful desire for difference, which is mere appearance, but in the core of creation, the attending entity of that which is truly novel. With the passage of a decade, that which is frantic and discordant, as we see in the greatest creators, turns out to be in essence a product of elaboration and measure. And having lost their compass, those who in their day played the *rôle* of the very youngest did not know whether they were faced with artistic actions or reactions, did not know whether, disguised as old men, they were combatting that which was new or if they were reacting to a doddering formalism with a realism that exhaled the noxious fumes of a grave, the rotten fever of twilight.

In truth, what was occurring with a new and genuine depth was more difficult to love and to signal. For above all it was a new position, forsaken by historicism altogether, undetermined by all prior reference. In my opinion, this was due to the emergence of a new manifestation of man in his struggle with form, a kind of creator able to complete his initial training nourished by the entire contribution of ancient culture, which, far from exhausting him, incited his creative faculties, rendering them remarkably surprising. A critical wisdom that was at the same time, and perhaps for that reason, very creative; an intuitive knowledge that hypostatized itself in the historical by means of a swift penetration of the regions of creation in the habitual confusion of the historical. Here it may be objected, and the objection is merely superficial, that Leonardo and Goethe produced this kind of culture, forged from great living syntheses, out of their rich ability to discover, through form, the contents of creation. But a single distinction between the two modes of synthesis appears sufficient for our purposes. The great figures of contemporary art have discovered regions that seemed to be submerged, forms of expression or knowledge that, though once misread, continued to be creative. Joyce's knowledge of neo-Thomism, even as a dilettante, was not a late echo of Scholasticism but rather that of a medieval world that, in making contact with him, became oddly creative. Stravinsky's arrival at Pergolesi was not an astute act of neoclassical cunning but rather the need to find a thread in the tradition that had come so close to reaching the secret of music, the canon of creation, stasis in metamorphosis, the rhythm of return. The great exception of a man like Leonardo or Goethe became in our time the signal expression that demanded a quick and intuitive knowledge of previous styles, the faces of that which has remained creative even after so many failures and an adequate placement in the polemics of the day, the balance point between that which withdraws into the shadows and the jet that leaps from the waters.

If Picasso leaped from the Doric to the Eritrean, from Chardin to Provençal, it seemed to us a most favorable sign of the times, but if an American studied and assimilated Picasso, *horresco referens*. At once, in a false and facile understanding that wishes to have done with all, people would speak of organic influences, of essential Pauline sustenance, and of vegetative influence, passive and useless. But before arriving at the solution to this problem, it might be pertinent here to repeat the words of that philosopher who, when faced with the Eleatic aporias, said: "I see the solution. What I don't see is the problem." Perhaps the problem lies here: Picasso has been more of a solution than a problem. But in these initial approaches, let us content ourselves with following this problem, providing it exists, back to its origin, where it is worthwhile remembering these lines by Tirso de Molina:

> You rob honey not your own,
> while I am the bear
> that bears the honey comb.

The most elegant elements of Minervine prudence lead us to choose Mexican painting, which is worth highlighting and then being toned down, for these parallelisms. In Guerrero Galván, the figure of a woman at the edge of the sea, the same motif as in Picasso, head of hair, hands and feet treated exactly alike. In Tamayo, a composition with melons and mandolins; in Picasso the reappearance of the very same choice of fruit and the same preference in musical instruments. Horses in Agustín Lazo that seem branded with the initials of Chirico. (Incidentally, we might recall the years 10 to 15 of our own century when Pablo of Málaga followed Chirico the Roman very closely.) It's not a question of making a hierarchy of influences in which certain ones turn out to be ephemeral and inefficient and others insightful and magical: nor is it one of mimetic regalia—hasn't Mann pointed out how the dimensions of great art are reduced in Goethe to Eros and parody?—for in our time, to signal the first in the mimetic chain, it would be necessary to combine the specters of Scotland Yard with the college of translators of Toledo working in cooperation with the syndic of Egyptian scribes.

Those objections made by Mexicans against Mexican painters generated a terror within us and a complex that led them to accusations, and so, when in 1944 our [Cuban] painters exhibited in Mexico, Diego Rivera, Siqueiros, and Rodríguez Lozano joined forces to accuse our painters of displaying the influence . . . of Picasso.

All those objections, engendered by multiple confusions and precipitation, dissipated as soon as we were able to locate a center of thematic references. That thematic reference had to arise from a new proposition: that Picasso, in the history of culture, had delivered and made visible certain very important secrets such as visual elements, cunning compositional tricks, and the discovery in all its plenitude of the authentically creative tradition in the fine arts. What was in the case of Cézanne a painful search with very few disciples, in Picasso became a perpetual encounter with good fortune, with timely opportunities. The new art that had been a painful adventure in the case of Cézanne, favoring the development of great personalities, had become with Picasso a shared secret. With the formulae he had found, resembling what in the eighteenth century was called *per canon* music—and every day there appear more unknown musicians from that century of great, craftsmanlike quality, innumerable armies of fine artists—they played at a variety of stylistic games with differing and various results. And this art, which at the end of the last century had still been favorable to the development of great personalities—a Cézanne, a Van Gogh, a Degas—was falling into stylism, into the combining of formulae and into colorist decoration. The fact that Picasso may have been the painter who has had the most influence on the world—far more than someone like El Greco, Piero della Francesca or Raphael—is more a sign of the hypertrophy of the culture of fine arts in our time than a qualitative measure. In our era, the man from Málaga has been the major influence, the one to provoke a newly accepted virtue in all the rest. Signs very much of our day played a part here as well. His eye was quick to catch what is creative in his immediate surroundings and to develop it, with a very Mediterranean instinct, into form and subsequent visibility. According to the well-known anecdote that every day seems more of a lie, he would visit young people's studios with excessive diligence in order to catch in the act what was in them larval and in its initial stages and then bring it to its maximum realization, always leaving on it his indelible and unquestionable mark of paternity. He was the son in his surprising assimilation and astonishing, nourishing deployment while at the same time maintaining his paternity in his finished form and his mastery of the offering. A living summary transformed into organic influence, he yielded a secret that, for he who received it, remained mysterious and placental. No painter has taught so many hidden things, revived so many styles, projected onto dead eras so many possible reencounters and beginnings. Like those peasants who, by slip of memory, began their daily conversation— without surprise—in classical Greek, he was made to discover in custom, in habitual styles, prodigious signs of lasting life, and it wouldn't surprise us if, before dying, he painted the resurrection of the flesh, indicating with grinning solemnity the splendor he will assume, as if that had been the topic of conversation he had sustained throughout his life with the angel of the worn-out name.

Thus, the young American painter, pricked by Picasso's fertilizing barb, was not acting out of an ungainly mimetic spirit nor with bewildered, watered-down blood, but rather, like the young Ukrainian, Puerto Rican, or Portuguese welcoming this St. Hieronymous of the fine arts who, in his own way, had also brought together the oral traditions of the Orient— the secret of surprising the narrator at his climax—with the Roman canon, the ecumenical sphere, Raphael's academy of philosophy, and the Theban Legion of El Greco.

Picasso and his happy android—the fount of influence—were without a doubt a unique manifestation offered by our time, yet there were great historical antecedents bolstering our confidence in the face of those ancestral riches, in the face of their critical recognition, which at times may fall like an avalanche on a historical era, on a city, or on a person. An avalanche so powerful that grace had always to come to his assistance, for greats are always the ones at the highest risk of greater dangers. And on the last horizon of the expanse, the fig tree never fails to appear on its reckless visits.

No more dangerous *carrefour* or crossroads exists than the heroic times of Greece. Between the Egyptian theocentrism and what we might call, without belaboring it to an excessively paradoxical point, the refined Persian hordes, that situation, far from diminishing them, from turning them to cowards, leads them instead, entwined in the cheerful dances of their confidence in a harmonious fate, to awaken into the expanse delimited by the light. In the struggle for superiority between the Egyptian and Greek gods, Herodotus, with concealed complacency, insists on demonstrating

that the Egyptian Hercules preceded the Greek Hercules by five generations. To do so, he reaches back to Tyre of Phoenicia, where a temple
dedicated to that deity once stood. Upon proving this, he is apparently
flooded with joy. "I saw it then, richly adorned with gifts aplenty and
amidst these gifts, two attractive columns, one of gold pure from the cupel
oven, the other of emeralds that sparkled magnificently at night." The
temple, Herodotus assures us, had been built at the time of the city of Tyre
of the Phoenicians, its ancient life spanning 2,300 years. It is appropriate,
Herodotus seems to conclude, that this god of strength should come to us
from the distant darkness and that we Greeks send it into battle against
hydras and serpents, forests and miserable cunning, that exhausted sexuality
and a sluggish generative drive might threaten us once again. . . .

But that confident Greek stance with regard to the Egyptian changes
when they get a glimpse of the Persians. With the prodigious illustration
of their senses, with their way of living as innate as the act of breathing,
they find that they can take unfinished forms from the Egyptians, gods that
can be transplanted to their own sacred mountains, but on the other hand,
they watch the Persian with suspicion, he who has come to despoil, the
sluggish monster, that flaccid organism no longer able to assimilate. The
Lydian voice advises Croesus not to fight the Persians: "Their dress is made
entirely of animal skins," he says, "their lands are harsh, they know not
wine nor the pleasure of the fig nor the delicacy of savory dishes. If you
vanquish them, what shall you take from them who have no possessions?
However if you are vanquished, reflect on all you have to lose." Here,
perhaps, is the most dangerous position the history of culture could offer;
between the Egyptian and the Persian worlds, the Greek happily intuited
from whence the wisest sails would come and whence the most sterile
curse. He partook of the Egyptian offerings with delight and prepared to
resist the formless dragon, vast and capricious.

The Europeans had taught us a previous lesson: to reduce the landscape
down to the scale of man, be it by means of the window as with certain
primitives of the medieval era or that of feudal opulence as we see in
Simone Martini, whom we quote, who abandoned the confining battlements of his castle. In America, however, the attempt is made to reduce
Nature to the size of man by dispensing with landscape. But what in fact
is landscape in the history of culture? So it is that when man takes a look
at that line that separates his self from the outside world, he already has a
square lodged within him, a definition of nature. Does landscape then
consist of a fence, a pleasantly polygonal reduction by which an expanse
of Nature is defined? Let's see; let's see if we can place that cactus on the
tablecloth of a still life and there take a silent, dialectic shot at it.

Above all, landscape leads us to the acquisition of points of view, of
fields of sight and of surroundings. If a mysterious, small arrow should be

fired at us, should our gaze let loose its warriors to defend its territory and the surroundings raise up its battlements before indifferent regions or hordes remind us of Genghis Khan. Landscape is one form of man's domination, like a Roman aqueduct, a sentence by Lycurgus, or the Apollonian triumph of the flute. Landscape is always dialogue, the reduction of nature placed on the level with man. When we speak of nature, the *panta rei* gobbles up man like a Leviathan in all its length and breadth. Landscape is nature befriended by man. If we accept the statement by Schelling, "Nature is visible spirit and spirit is invisible nature," we will find it easy to reach the conclusion that what this visible spirit most likes is to converse with man and that this dialogue between the spirit that reveals nature and man is landscape. First, nature must win over spirit, then man will go to meet it. The combination of that revelation and its conjunction with man is the evidence of landscape's sovereignty.

In America, wherever the possibility of landscape emerges, there must exist the possibility of culture. The most frenetic possession of the mimesis of all that is European is liquefied when the landscape that accompanies it has its own spirit and offers it, and we converse with it, albeit in dreams. The Valley of Mexico, the coordinates that coincide in the Bay of Havana, the Andean region upon which the baroque acted, in other words, the culture of Cuzco—are the pampas landscape or nature?—the constitution of the image in landscape, the line that leads from the dungeon of Francisco de Miranda to the death of José Martí, are all forms of landscape, that is to say, in the struggle between nature and man: it constituted itself as the landscape of culture, the triumph of man in the time of history. The dream of Sor Juana is nighttime in the Valley of Mexico: while she sleeps, it seems as if her wandering self were conversing with the valley and what appeared as terms from Scholastic dialectics become, transformed by her dream, the recognized signals of the secrets of that landscape. The simple artists of the Cuzco School filter a reverent sky onto their canvasses, a sky so distant from the clouds that pass from Botticelli to Murillo, more as an indecipherable omen than as tender company. And when we propose to discuss whether the pampas are nature or landscape, we hear, in the first invocations of *Martín Fierro* and *The Return of Martín Fierro* how the language has been revived with fresh pride, confidence, and courage by a nature that lowers itself to the ground in order to offer us its stirrup, transformed into landscape by the new language traveling over it. Hear the guitar of Martín Fierro accompanied by the human voice that tames it and elicits its warmest companionship:

> I sit down on these plains
> To sing out this tale
> —As if the wind were blowing

> I make the grass shiver—
> My mind plays around
> With gold, hearts, and clubs.
>
> In my own rodeo I'm but a bull,
> A raging bull in another's;
> I've always thought I was good,
> If you want to put me to the test
> Let others come out and sing
> And we'll see who's the lesser man.

And in *The Return of Martín Fierro*, this voice rests like a mass of stone next to placid rivers:

> Anyone who wants to set me straight
> Has to know quite a bit
> —He who is able to listen to me
> Has an awful lot to learn—
> He has much to ponder
> The man who wishes to understand me.

Following Mr. Baroque, firmly established at the center of his pleasure, landscape regains a more powerful and demonical magnetization. Man, displaced from his center, returns to his landscape though it proves to be irreconcilable, now and forever remote. Francisco de Miranda was unable to find a new center of a new landscape either in the French Revolution or in the charms of an Eros in the Enlightenment, in the court of Catherine of Russia or in the meticulous and coldly creative England of Pitt. He moves over all of Europe but it is not until he finds his center once again in a dungeon where he reconstructs his country in its absence that he feels himself again to be a Venezuelan at heart. His landscape is already sufficiently strong that wherever it unfolds, and it embraced one of the greatest scenarios of its time, it would envelop him; he would reclaim it again and place it at the center of his dungeon.

Every American landscape has always been accompanied by a special sowing time and its own abundant foliage. Civilization before Cortés was based on "the blond ear of corn," on maize, even the culture of the Mayas. It is the culture of corn, of the winnower that extends throughout the seasons. It engenders such notable leisure as that enjoyed by the Greeks or the *otium cum dignitate* of the Romans; the baroque *soconusco* chocolate bowl shows this lord in command of his voluptuousness. He feels weary again, a weariness that then extends into his slaves' quarters, into his great ballroom. By the nineteenth century, Romanticism had abandoned itself to the drought of the plain, to the wandering life that leaves no trail behind it. The umbra tree, the one that walks at night on the pampas, according to a great Argentinean, Ezequiel Martínez Estrada, offers its vegetal mansion along the dangerous distance to be crossed. If not the umbra, then the generative ceiba stands in its place with vindictive permanence. It soothes the fertile womb and shelters the sojourner with unity of place. And the frills, the fine countenance of the American-born European, cast in the smoke of tobacco leaves between the lazy pronunciation of syllables and the endings of phrases that contend to place a sharp note in the harmonious closure of their vowels. Ornate trees, venerable leaves, which in the American landscape take on the value of writing where a judgment is recorded regarding our destiny.

When Van Elst made a distinction between the Flemish primitives of the fifteenth century and the North American primitives of the eighteenth and nineteenth centuries, it was based on how the primitive Flemish painters did not have a "primitive spirit" but rather a refined technique. "It was the artifice in their technique," he tells us, "that warranted this categorization appropriate to the coarse and uncultured North American painters who would travel from state to state and who paid for their lodging and earned their living painting portraits of their hosts or political placards or works with explicit messages, which, if not artistic, were at least intensely patriotic." If we compare the Virgin painted by St. Lucas, attributed to Van der Weyden, and the York family in their home, a work by a North American primitive in the Museum of Modern Art in New York, we discover that it is not the difference in technique that distinguishes those two paintings—Van Elst believes this to be altogether obvious and conspicuous—but rather the landscape, framed in the first canvas by a window and in the other, situated on a painting hanging on the wall against which one finds the two figures. If we set up a parallel, a fair judge, between Van Eyck and General Washington studying Fort Cumberland, in the Osland Gallery of New York, there is a contrast not only between the two heads but in the landscape that in this Van Eyck appears to be facing the severe judge, thus in perspective, whereas in the background of the painting of George Washington, the rigorous placement of the troops with their blue and white uniforms is played out in a landscape of enormous white masses, in the succession of hills and a sky overcast in a fundamental chiaroscuro. But to follow this further, if we were to innocently place the portrait of Arnolfini and his fiancée next to them, we notice a window letting in enough light to reveal their faces while scarcely allowing us to distinguish the landscape sliced like a loaf by that window, whereas in *Conversation*, from the collection of Thomas Halliday, the typical landscape does not appear, but rather the anticipation of its unfolding with great profusion in the flowers held by the figure paying its respects and, on the ground, the gradation corresponding to a gamut of providential colors in the foreground of the composition.

But if the American landscape has us filled with joy and praise, let us return in expectable antithesis to the gloomy pessimism of Hegelian Protestantism. We already saw how, in the case of the Indian Kondori, the zoomorphic and photomorphic elements were integrated in such a way that required a baroque form. But now Hegel is once again bringing us the pessimism of food. But if I return to him, it is in part to mock him, indicating to his displeasure a time when the idea did not correspond to reality, for in that sovereign spirit it appears as though domesticated facts and empiricism were following their prior ideogram, the irritated demands of his conceptual world. "They assure us," says Hegel, "that the consumable animals in the New World are not as nutritious as those in the Old World. In America there are enormous herds of cattle but European beef is considered there to be an exquisite morsel." The hundred years that have since passed render those Hegelian declarations irrefutable and indeed ridiculous. They remain in their grotesque state without any further commentary or gloss. And the British epicures, readers of Hegel nearly every one of them, smile as they sink their teeth into an Argentinean steak. We find that in the first Gaucho poems the English are called *bisquetes* because of their voracious devotion to fillets, salted meat, or jerked beef from Uruguay. This amusing problem remains for the numerous London Hegelians from the Whitehead school who should concede us the new absolute in the problematics of ingestion.

For Hegel, *logos* acts in history in a theocentric form, that is to say, God is *logos*, meaning, having been unable to find with the ease required by the absolute nature of his apriorism, he grows mistrustful and bestows his disdain on us. He seeks the objective spirit in America and what he finds, as in Genesis, is the breath of God rippling the waters, like a small stone skipped edgewise over the placid liquid sheet. What still astonishes us is the unrestrained interest on the part of Ortega y Gasset regarding those seven or eight pages in which Hegel passes judgment on America, in his *Lectures on the Philosophy of World History*. He considers the *criollo*, the native-born white European, to be the sole cause of independence in America, after paradoxically emphasizing that the Negro's strength had dislodged the passivity of the Indian. His pages concerning Negro cultures demonstrate a scandalous lack of comprehension. He limits himself to signaling their state of innocence. As if it were possible that in a tribal state the idea of innocence, in the Catholic sense of paradise with which he uses it, could arise. Consider that the character of the Black Continent is its indomitable nature, in the sense that it is immune to development and education, he says. All it would take to refute this is that epic culmination of the baroque in Aleijadinho, who symbolizes the artistic rebellion of the Negro in his synthesis of the Negro and Hispanic worlds. Prompted by these Hegelian limitations, we find it imperative to repeat here the words of Alfred Weber, which seem to us a quite perceptive and precise appreciation of Hegelian values taken as a whole: "The first great opposition," he says, "in which German Idealism is made to face the ideological content of modern culture originating in the Western countries."

In the cases of Melville or Whitman, the question of their nutrition was safe from danger: theology or the body, like subtle essences, moved within the totality of their substance. Both Melville and Whitman maintain a relationship of course and recourse, action and reaction, one source of strength in failure and another source of liberation in praise of the body. While Melville moves in the gloomy world of Calvinist theology, sin, and the Fall, the symbols of evil, the dark labyrinths that make redemption impossible, taking up again the ancient moral tradition and binding himself to it—though it be in the form of a circular hell that yields to the absolute nature of grace—Whitman abstains from contemplating the gloomy messengers of good and evil and strides toward that world where Socrates is forced to define wisdom, haunted by the memory of Charmides' tunic. But within that man battling evil there is evil as well, such that in the battle he wages all his aesthetic possibilities are shattered. He knows that in that struggle against evil he cannot save anything in its totality and responding to his frantic shouting from the bridge of his ship are the voices of the monsters that surround him, a sort of negative hallelujah, for as the battle commenced its only justification was the size of the very greatness of the fall. When he rises it is only to contemplate the monster coiled in the darkness. His battle against evil enflames him in such a way that his fate, like that of a Greek hero, can only find its completion in death. At the end of his book we observe that evil doesn't seek him but, rather, on the contrary, is his complement; he needs the infernal action in order to bring his movement to a close. By the end he has understood his destiny, that his greatness at its height lies in the inner strength of its thanatos and that he has been walking toward his own destruction. He puts words to the apocalyptic descent into hell. In combatting the spirit of evil with the identical sign of rebellion, he finds death to be the only possible solution. He has confronted evil with equal strength and in that cold epic of the terror that destroys him, the two rebellions are evenly matched. Whitman seems to fill out Ahab's mutilated body anew and put the murky world of no redemption behind him.

There is no sense of frenzy in him but, rather, he is accompanied by a sense of the radiant body. It is not the line that divides good from evil that concerns him so much as energy, but an energy of such a different sign from William Blake's demonic energy. He is interested in that energy insofar as it impedes the integration of the spirit of evil. Whereas Ahab feels himself cut off from the world, and in that separation lies the destruction he craves, Whitman joins body with grass, grass with the star-filled sky, all the while living in the redemption of that which is essential, which for the world is the presence of his body. Melville and Whitman establish at the height of the nineteenth century the era of men at the origin of things. They have freed themselves from historicism, and to the absolute outrage of Hegel, their sustenance and essences have been as favorable as can be. The harpoon hurlings of Ahab as he pursues the monster of predestination reappear in our day as Kafka's fury to break a shell that no longer bears any relation to its embryo, but rather to its cold armor. And when the influences Kafka absorbed have all been indexed, and Whitman's is right next to that of Schelemaicher, that of Melville, we understand that the Protestant theology of the first of these men looked to Melville to rekindle its tradition. In search of a body in which he might insert himself, Whitman's exaltations reappear as well in the powerful scales of Paul Claudel's processional, only in Whitman the relationship is forged with an archaic, primitive world, and in Claudel the hierarchies are established in a theocratic world of exchange of the gifts of grace and the order of charity. But that relationship is not the only one established by the Americans of high style, pertaining to the Pindaric Greek tradition and the world of the Fall. In Gershwin, for example, the inverse is posed with equal greatness. He had absorbed mediated Western influences—the pianism of Liszt, the diluted symphonism of Tchaikovsky, the experimental composers of the First World War, early Honneger of the locomotive—but the fact that his early training was permeated by the popular culture of his country was sufficient for *Porgy and Bess*, or certain of his magnificent songs like "Blue Monday," to fully express his macrocosm. The stunning beauty of his rhapsody forms part of the experimental composers' laboratory of acoustical physics, but the popularly rooted syncopations of the jazz era, the nostalgia of the spirituals, were sufficient for its fullness to be organized above its negative influences. Its modernity is legitimate for, by initiating its exploration at the source of its tradition, an act which proclaims other fallen or impure traditions to be adventitious, serving as a prop or test, an erroneous tradition will expel it just as a healthy body rejects any fragmentary or damaged material that might be ingested.

This voraciousness, this incorporative protoplasm of the American had ancestral roots. It is these roots that have legitimized our newly acquired power whose essence is American. The French influence, from the auroral revolution and Romanticism, has been a creative force inasmuch as that same French influence had contributed to Hispanic culture: since the epoch of Alfonso VI, at the very height of the Middle Ages, the Burgundian influence, the Gallic ritual in the principal Episcopal cathedrals, had embedded itself in the structure of the highest ascent in the Hispanic world. Juan of Cologne, who worked for the House of Burgundy, finishes off the spires of the cathedral of Burgos[;] fifteen years after their bases were laid, according to the work of Mayer, [he and his assistants] head for Toledo with Annequin Egas of Brussels, sculptors from Belgium and France. And the statues from the thirteenth century within the same cathedral are all imbued with the potent spirit of the primitive French Gothic. One need only contemplate the towers of the cathedral of Burgos to see at once that their base is Hispanic, still engaged in a battle against the invasions of this French Gothic. "One can see clearly," Mayer says, "how, in general, it still preserves the continuity of the form as a whole, but this movement springs from a freedom unknown until then." Foundation and freedom at the root of the Hispanic Gothic. Foundation and freedom, the sign of all of Spanish history throughout the centuries. In Goya, a genius of Altamirano Spain, we find his influences to include the German rococo of Mengs and the French rococo of Watteau. Which is to say, with a history that obliges him to do so, the Spaniard has a temperament for incorporating influences. The warmest reception of Italian prose ever since the *trescento* of Bocaccio is the *andantino* of Cervantes's prose. Marini's *polifemaida* bows down before the magnificent Polyphemus of Cordoba.

The mimetic conception of American culture as a consequence of its cold and lazy nature dissolves away in the incorporative nucleus we receive from our Hispanic ancestry. Where was the center of gravity located in this amalgamation of influences? The center of Hispanic resistance is the rocky earth of Castile whose effect has been that, in Spain, influences cannot be capricious or haphazard, but rather essential and bearing ample historical justification. When they refract off the stony Castilian ground, what remains embedded must be equally strong and necessary as with an immense, primitive organism: the particles of nutrients must reach the center of its mass, the blind center wherein lies the indistinction of its functions. This is why the hard center of Spanish resistance receives influences with ethical reverence, with ascetic zeal. The predominant element of the American influence is what I might dare call the open, Gnostic space in which the insertion of the invading spirit is verified by the immediate comprehension by the gaze. The frozen forms of the European baroque— and all proliferation is the expression of an injured body—vanish in America on account of this Gnostic space, whose knowledge comes from the variety of its landscape, from the excesses of its gifts. The *simpathos* of this gnostic space is due to its legitimate ancestral world; it is a primitive with knowledge, one who inherits sins and curses, who inserts itself within the forms of dying knowledge, needing to justify itself paradoxically with a spirit in its initial stages. Why was the Western spirit unable to extend itself into Asia and Africa yet able to do so throughout America? Because that Gnostic space was waiting for a kind of vegetal fertilization where we find its delicacy allied with its expanse, was waiting for grace to raise it to an adequate temperature for the reception of the generative corpuscles.

We find proof of the vegetal demand of this Gnostic space in the tiny number of colonizers who inhabited—not in number but suitable to the space—an expanse that would otherwise have remained sterile. The delicacy is that porous sensation of a certain temperature, the absence of scorn for any possible agent of fertilization. In Europe of the Renaissance, which produces the *imago* propitious to the Discovery, the reception of the chaotic decomposition of the theological world, the revived concern with the Arcadian world, the good Indian was bent over once again like a straggling creation from the agricultural period. But this delicacy has nothing whatsoever to do with the Renaissance concept of the goodness of primitive man. Nature may also be refined and exceedingly demanding, reaching extremes never conceived of by man, and it is precisely primitive man who is most sensitive to that refinement and those demands. When the Inca Garcilaso sat down, surrounded by the nobility of his Inca ancestry, his accounts mingled with tears of nostalgia. Far from provoking bitterness in him, that lamentation, located in his ancestral roots, leads him to join the Italian Renaissance with the forms of the first great maturity of Hispanic culture, forms with which he plumbs the essence of Inca culture.

After the Middle Ages, the Counter-Reformation as well as the Loyalist spirit were forms of bitterness, of defensiveness from a cosmos that was collapsing and which was being shored up with the most rigid tension will could impose. Only at that moment does America establish an affirmation of and an escape from the European chaos. But only the American landscape could offer a new space that establishes a Renaissance in its past and then offer it again to its contemporaries. Pachacámac is an Inca god whose signification, according to Garcilaso, is "he who does with the universe what the soul does with its body." The relationship of soul, body, nature is in complete opposition to the chaos of values, to the *physis* leading up to the Renaissance. When man bleeds in his inability to make an enduring symbol, he creates the symbol of the weary stone that bleeds, a mirror that guarantees the endurance of his pain. No culture of battlements took the handling of large stones to the perfection of the Incas; without adequate locks, without advanced and refined methods, they achieved a perfection that our astonishment can only compare with the Babylonian walls. This handling of immense stones, which the conquistadors considered feats of wizardry, could only be realized by the Gnostic space, which interprets, through a very close relationship with man, nature as a form of refinement, of a delicacy. Pachacámac is an invisible god who acquires his visibility through nature and man. In no culture does mythology acquire such a degree of reality as it does with the Incas. The battle of the Chancas, in which approximately one hundred thousand warriors fought, was counseled by ghosts; the stones turned into warriors and then afterward, back into stones; the Inca Viracocha receives the reinforcements of which the ghost of his uncle had told him. The priests of the House of the Sun addressed their divinity, the Sun, as if it were a man their size, quenching its thirst in a huge golden jar, shortening all the days. Later, Viracocha builds a temple in memory of the ghost who counseled him in war. The relationship between man before Cortés and the Gnostic space means that his intermediate and somewhat oblique form of knowledge can scarcely be distinguished. Certain expressions from the last euphuism, "arcs which to their flaming flight,/were the interwoven eyelids of the flowers," appear to be occasioned by the return of American culture to the Hispanic South. The centuries that have passed since the Discovery have offered services, have been filled; we have offered unconscious solutions to the superconscious European problematic. In a densely populated setting such as Europe, in the years of the Counter-Reformation, we offered with the Conquest and colonization an escape from the chaos of a Europe that was beginning to bleed profusely. While the European baroque became an inert play of forms, here Mr. Baroque dominates his landscape and offers another solution when the Western scenography was tending to wearily prop itself within its plaster cast. When someone in European Romanticism exclaimed "I write, if not with blood, then with red ink in the inkwell," we offer the fact of a new integration that emerges from the *imago* of absence. And when language fails, we offer the Dionysian guitar of Aniceto el Gallo and the feast of the zenith in the rich idiomatic style of José Martí. And finally, when faced with the pale green chill of Minervan couplings or the anger of aged Pan anchored in the precise moment of his frenzy, we offer in our jungles the sudden downpour of the spirit, which once again ripples the waters and tranquilly distributes itself over the Gnostic space, over a nature that interprets and recognizes, prefigures and grieves.

TRANSLATED BY MARK SCHAFER

Leopoldo Zea

Mexico
(b. 1912)

————•◦•◦•————

Leopoldo Zea's philosophical training evidences itself unmistakably in his essays on Mexican identity. He was a disciple of Mexican philosopher José Gaos and a friend of Alfonso Reyes, whose essay "Notes on the American Mind" had a strong influence on Zea. Both his master's thesis, *Positivism in México* (1943), and his doctoral thesis, "Apogeo y decadencia del positivismo en México," were well received by Mexico's intellectual community. As a professor of philosophy at the Universidad Nacional Autónoma de México, Zea edited a collection of essays from his renowned Hyperion group entitled *México y lo mexicano*. His contribution as an essayist lies not in his style but in the persuasiveness and concentration of his arguments. He has worked in Mexico's Ministry of Foreign Relations, and also chaired the Department of Philosophy and Letters and been in charge of cultural affairs at the Universidad Nacional Autónoma de México. His personal works include *Dos etapas del pensamiento en hispanoamérica: romanticismo al positivismo* (1949), *La filosofía como compromiso* (1952), *Role of the Americas in History* (1955), and *Regreso de las carabelas* (1993). In "Concerning an American Philosophy," originally published in *Ensayos sobre una filosofía de la historia* (1948), Zea begins by discussing the contribution of Samuel Ramos and Alfonso Reyes to the study of Mexican thought, and he then moves to a study of what is European in America. His essay navigates the same territory as Oswald de Andrade's "Anthropophagite Manifesto" and José Lezama Lima's "Summa Critica of American Culture," but comes to a very different conclusion.

Concerning an American Philosophy

I

A few years ago a young Mexican writer, Samuel Ramos, published a book which aroused expectations. In this book, called *The Profile of Man and Culture in Mexico*, a first attempt was made to interpret the culture of Mexico, taking it as a theme for a philosophical interpretation. Philosophy descended from the world of ideal entities to a world of concrete entities like Mexico, a symbol of men who live and die in its cities and fields. This rashness was scornfully called "literature." Philosophy could be nothing but an ingenious game of words taken from a foreign culture, words which of course lacked a meaning, the meaning they had for that original culture.

Years later another writer, this time an Argentinian, Francisco Romero, emphasized that Spanish America had to begin to concern itself about themes proper to itself, about the need to turn to the history of its culture and draw from it themes for a new philosophic interest. But this time the exhortation was supported by a series of cultural phenomena indicated in an article entitled "On Philosophy in Spanish America" ("Sobre la filosofía en Iberoamérica"). In this article he shows us how interest in philosophic themes has been growing in Spanish America day by day. The outside world follows and eagerly asks for works of a philosophic type or character, out of which numerous publications have arisen: books, reviews, newspaper articles, etc., as well as the formation of institutes and centres of philosophic studies in which this activity is carried on. This interest in philosophy appears in contrast to other periods when this activity was the work of a few misunderstood men, something that did not pass beyond the esoteric circle or the university chair. Now a point has been reached which Romero calls "a stage of philosophical normality," that is, a stage where philosophical exercise is regarded as an ordinary function of culture, the same as other activities of a cultural nature. The philosopher ceases to be a queer fellow whom no one is interested in understanding, and becomes a member of the cultural élite of his country. There is established a kind of "philosophical climate," that is, a public opinion which pronounces judgement upon philosophical creation, obliging it to concern itself with themes that agitate those who form so-called "public opinion."

Well then, there is a question that concerns not merely a few men on our continent, but the man of America in general. This question is that of the possibility or impossibility of an American culture, and as a partial aspect of this question, that of the possibility or impossibility of an American philosophy. But to pose and attempt to resolve such a question, independently of whether the answer is in the affirmative or the negative, is already engaging in American philosophy, since it means trying to answer an American question affirmatively or negatively. Therefore works like those of Ramos, Romero, and others on such a theme, whatever their conclusions, are already American philosophy.

The question of the possibility of an American culture is one imposed by our times, by the historical circumstances in which we find ourselves. In the past the name of America had not become the topic of such a debate because no one cared about it. An American culture, a culture proper to the man of America, was a theme without interest; America was living comfortably in the shadow of European culture. Nevertheless, this culture is astir in our times, and seems to have disappeared from the entire European continent. The man of America who had lived so trustingly finds the culture upon which he relied failing him, facing an empty future, and the ideas in which he had placed his faith turning into useless, senseless contrivances, without value to their originators. He who had lived so confidently in the shade of a tree he had not planted finds himself unprotected when the planter cuts it down and casts it into the fire as worthless. He now has to plant his own cultural tree, and make his own ideas. But a culture does not rise up miraculously. The seed of such a culture must be procured somewhere, and must belong to someone. Well (and this is the matter that preoccupies the man of America), where can he procure this seed? That is, what ideas is he going to develop? In what ideas is he going to put his faith? Will he continue to trust and develop ideas inherited from Europe? Or are there ideas and topics to be developed that belong to the American setting? Or will it be necessary to invent those ideas? In a word, there is posed the problem of whether there are or are not ideas proper to America, as well as that of whether or not to accept the ideas of European culture now in crisis. More concretely, it is the problem of relations between America and European culture, and that of the possibility of an exclusively American ideology.

II

By the preceding we see that one of the first themes for an American philosophy is that of relations between America and European culture. Well, the first thing to ask is what kind of relationship exists between America and that culture. Some have compared this relationship to that which exists between Asia and the same European culture. It is assumed that America, like Asia, has assimilated only European technology. But if this were so, what would American culture have of its own? For the Asiatic, what has been adopted of European culture is considered to be something superposed, which it has had to adopt due to change of circumstance when the European intervened. But what he has adopted of European culture is not precisely the culture itself—that is, a way of life, a concept of the world—but only its instruments, its techniques. The Asiatic knows himself to be heir to a very old culture which has been passed down from father to son, and thus he knows himself to be in possession of a culture of his own. His concept of the world is practically the opposite to that of the European. From the European he has taken only his techniques, and this has been forced upon him by the European himself, by intervening with his techniques in what was a purely Asiatic circumstance. Our day is showing what an Asiatic can do with a concept of the world that is his own by utilizing European techniques. Such a man is totally indifferent to the fu-

ture of European culture, and will certainly try to destroy it if it interposes itself or continues to intervene in what he considers as his own culture.

Well then, can we of America take the same view with respect to European culture? Such a view means to regard ourselves as possessors of a culture which is our own and which perhaps has not attained expression because Europe has stood in our way. Then it would indeed be fitting to take this as the opportune moment to liberate ourselves culturally. In that case the crisis in European culture would be a matter of indifference to us. Instead of such a crisis presenting itself as a problem, it would present itself as a solution. But this is not the case: the crisis in European culture concerns us deeply, and we feel it as a crisis of our own.

And this is because the kind of relationship which as people of America we have with European culture is different from that possessed by the Asiatic. We do not feel ourselves, as the Asiatic does, heirs to a culture of our own continent, that is, autochthonous. An indigenous culture did indeed exist—Aztec, Mayan, Incan, etc.—but to us it does not represent, to us who live in America today, what the ancient Oriental culture represents to present-day Asiatics. While the Asiatic continues to view the world as it was viewed by his forefathers, we of America do not view the world as it was viewed by an Aztec or a Mayan. If we did, we should feel for the divinities and temples of pre-Columbian culture the same devotion that the Oriental feels for his very ancient gods and temples. A Mayan temple is just as alien and meaningless to us as a Hindu temple.

What is our own, proper to America, is not found in pre-Columbian culture. Is it something European? Well, with respect to European culture we are in a strange position—we use it but we do not consider it ours; we feel ourselves to be "imitators" of it. Our way of thinking, our concept of the world, is similar to that of the European. European culture has for us meaning that pre-Columbian culture lacks. And yet, we do not feel it is ours. We feel like bastards using property to which they have no right. We feel like one putting on a suit that is not his, and we feel it is too big for us. We adapt their ideas but we cannot adapt ourselves to them. We feel we should realize the ideals of European culture, but feel ourselves incapable of achieving them; we content ourselves with admiring them, thinking they are not made for us. In this lies the core of our problem: we do not feel ourselves heirs of an autochthonous culture, since this culture lacks meaning for us; and the culture which, like the European, has a meaning for us, we do not feel is ours. There is something inclining us towards European culture, but at the same time fighting against being part of that culture. Our concept of the world is European, but the achievements of this culture we feel are alien to us, and when we try to emulate them in America, we feel we are imitators.

What inclines us towards Europe and at the same time resists being

European is something peculiarly ours, the spirit of America. America feels inclined towards Europe like a son towards his father, but at the same time he resists being his own father. This resistance can be seen in the fact that despite its inclination towards European culture, when it achieves what that culture achieves, America feels itself to be an imitator, and does not feel that it is achieving something of its own, but something that only Europe can achieve. This explains our feeling of being inhibited, inferior to the European. The trouble is that we feel American things, our own possessions, to be something inferior. The resistance of the American against being European is felt as incapacity. We think like Europeans, but this is not sufficient for us; we also want to have the same achievements as Europe. The trouble is that we want to adapt American circumstance to a concept of the world which we inherited from Europe, and not adapt this concept of the world to American circumstance. This accounts for ideas and reality remaining unadapted. We need the ideas of European culture, but when we bring them into our setting we feel they are too big and do not dare to cut them down; we prefer to be ridiculous, like one who puts on a suit which does not fit him. This is explained by the fact that until a very short time ago the man of America wanted to forget he was of America in order to feel himself just another European. This is the same thing as a son forgetting he is a son and trying to be his own father; the result would have to be a poor imitation. And this is what the man of America feels who has tried to imitate instead of to realize his personal potential.

Alfonso Reyes very wittily portrays for us this resistance of the man of America to being American. The American felt, "on top of the misfortunes of being human and being modern, the very specific misfortune of being American; that is, born and rooted in a soil that was not the present focus of civilization, but a branch office of the world."* Until yesterday to be of America had been a great misfortune, because it did not allow us to be European. Now it is completely the reverse: not having been able to be European, in spite of our great determination, allows us now to have a personality. It allows us in this moment of crisis in European culture to discover that there is something peculiar to ourselves, and which therefore can serve to sustain us. What this something is, is one of the questions which American philosophy must consider.

III

America is a daughter of European culture, and is rising up in one of the latter's great crises. The discovery is not simply a matter of chance, but the

---

*Alfonso Reyes, "Notes on the American Mind," *Sur*, Buenos Aires, Sept. 1936, No. 24. See pp. 88–95.

result of a need. Europe needed America; in the mind of every European was the Idea of America, the idea of a Promised Land, a land to which the European could direct his aspirations, when once he could not keep on directing them to the air above him. He could no longer look to heaven. Thanks to the new physics, the heavens ceased to be the abode of ideals, to become transformed into something unlimited, into a mechanical infinity which was for that reason dead. The idea of an ideal world came down from the heavens and was set in America. For that reason the European went out in search of the ideal land and found it.

The European needed to rid himself of a concept of life with which he felt himself sated; he needed to free himself from his past and begin a new life. He needed to make a new history, well planned and calculated, in which there would be neither scarcity nor surfeit. What the European did not dare to propose openly in his own land, this new land called America took for granted. America was the pretext for criticism of Europe. What they wished Europe to be was in their imagination realized in America. In these lands were imagined fantastic cities and governments which corresponded to the ideal of the modern man. America was presented as the idea of what Europe should be. America was the European Utopia, the ideal world in conformity with which the old Occidental world was to be remade. In a word: America was the ideal creation of Europe.

America comes into history as a land of projects, a land of the future, but projects which are not its own, and a future not its own either. These projects and this future belong to Europe. The European who set foot in America—becoming involved in the American scene, bringing into being the man of America—was not able to see the genuine America, for he had eyes only for what Europe wanted it to be. Not finding what European fancy had put on the American continent, he felt disappointed, which gives rise to the uprooting of the man of America with respect to his environment. The man of America feels himself to be European in origin, but inferior to the European on account of his dwelling-place. He becomes an unadapted person, considers himself superior to his environment and inferior to the culture which formed him. He feels scorn for anything American and resentment towards anything European.

The man of America, instead of trying to realize possibilities that were America's own, strove to realize a European Utopia, naturally coming into conflict with American reality which resists becoming anything but what it is, namely, America. This is the cause of the sense of inferiority of which we have already spoken. The surrounding reality is considered by the man of America to be inferior to what he believes to be his destiny. This feeling has shown itself in Anglo-Saxon America as an eagerness to achieve on a large scale the same thing that Europe achieved to satisfy needs peculiar to itself. North America has striven to be a second Europe, a copy magnified.

Creation of one's own is of no importance; the important thing is to copy the European models on a large scale and with maximum perfection. Everything is reduced to numbers: so many dollars or so many metres. At heart all they are trying to do in this is to conceal a sense of inferiority. The American of the United States tries to show that he is just as capable as the European, and his way of showing it is to do on a large scale, and with the greatest technical perfection, the same thing that the European has done. But in this he has not demonstrated cultural capability, but simply technical ability; for cultural capability is shown in the solution given to problems which pose themselves to man as he lives, and not in the mechanical imitation of solutions which other men have arrived at in solving their own problems.

As for the Spanish American, he has resigned himself to feeling inferior not only to the European, but also to the American of the United States. Not only does he not try to conceal his sense of inferiority, but he displays it by depreciating himself. The only thing he has tried to do up to the present has been to live as comfortably as possible in the shadow of ideas he knows are not his own. The important thing is not ideas, but the way one lives by them. Therefore our political organization has been turned into a bureaucracy. Politics ceases to be an end and is turned into an instrument for obtaining a certain bureaucratic post. Banners and ideals are of no importance; what matters is that these banners or ideals should open the way to a certain position. This explains those miraculous and rapid changes of banner and ideals; it also explains those everlasting projects and that constant planning, without ever achieving definitive results. Projects and plans are continually inspired by ever shifting ideologies. There is no plan to be carried through by the nation as a whole, because there is no sense of nationhood. And there is no sense of nationhood for the same reason that there is no feeling for things American. Anyone feeling inferior as a man of America also feels inferior as a national, as a member of one of the nations of the American continent. And do not think that the rabid nationalist has a sense of nationhood, the one who talks about making a culture that is Mexican, Argentinian, Chilean, or of any other country of America, excluding everything with a foreign smell. No, basically he will try only to eliminate everything before which he feels inferior. Such is the case with all those who think this the opportune moment to eliminate everything European from our culture.

This would be a false position; whether we like it or not, we are children of European culture. From Europe we have our cultural body, what we may call the framework: language, religion, customs; in a word, our view of the world and of life is European. To break away from it would be to break away from the kernel of our personality. We cannot renounce that culture, just as we cannot renounce our parents. But as without renouncing our parents we have a personality which prevents anyone from confusing us with them, so also we shall have a cultural personality without renouncing the culture from which we sprang. Consciousness of our true relationship to European culture eliminates every sense of inferiority, giving rise to a "sense of responsibility." This sense is what animates the man of America in our day. He regards himself as having attained his "majority," and like any man who has reached that age, he recognizes that he has a past and does not renounce it, in the same way that none of us is ashamed of having had a childhood. The man of America knows himself to be heir to Western culture and claims his place in it. The place he claims for himself is that of contributor. A son of such culture does not wish to continue to live by it, but he wants to work for it. In the name of this America with a sense of responsibility, a man of America, Alfonso Reyes, claimed from Europe "the right to the universal citizenship which we have won," considering that now "we have attained our majority."* America stands at the historic point where it must carry out its cultural mission. What this mission is to be is another theme, to be developed by what we have called American philosophy.

IV

Having recognized our cultural relations with Europe, another of the tasks of this possible American philosophy would be to continue the development of philosophic themes which belong to that culture, but especially the themes which European philosophy considers as universal themes; that is, themes whose abstractness makes them valid for any time or place. Such themes are those of being, knowledge, space, time, God, life, death, etc. An American philosophy would contribute to Occidental culture by trying to solve the problems which such themes would pose and which had not been solved by European philosophy, or whose solution was not satisfactory. Well then, those interested in formulating a philosophy with an American stamp might think that this is of no concern in a philosophy preoccupied with the strictly American. Nevertheless this would be untrue, because both the questions we have called universal and the questions peculiar to American circumstance are intimately bound together. When we deal with certain questions we must also deal with others. Abstract questions will have to be viewed from circumstances applicable to the man of America. Every man will see in these questions what has the closest connection with his circumstance, and will focus them from the point of view of his interest, which is determined both by his mode of life and by his capacity or incapacity—in a word, by his circumstance. In the case of

---

*A. Reyes, "Notes on the American Mind."

America, its contribution to the philosophy of these themes will be coloured by the American circumstance. Hence, when we approach abstract questions we shall focus them as questions of our own. Being, God, etc., while questions valid for any man, will be questions to which solutions would be given from an American point of view. Concerning these questions we should not be able to say what they are for every man, but what they are for us as men of America. Being, God, death, etc., would be what such abstractions represent for us. Do not forget that all European philosophy has worked on the same questions in an endeavour to offer solutions of a universal character. Nevertheless, the result has been a number of philosophies differing from one another. In spite of all their striving for universality, there have come out a Greek philosophy, a Christian philosophy, a French philosophy, an English philosophy, and a German philosophy. In the same way, independently of our trying to create a philosophy of America, and in spite of our endeavour to give solutions of a universal character, our solutions would bear the stamp of our circumstance.

Another kind of question that could be treated by our philosophy would be any that is related to our own circumstance; that is, this future philosophy of ours must try to solve problems which our circumstance poses. This point of view is as legitimate as the preceding, and valid as a philosophic theme. As men of America we have a number of problems that arise only in our circumstance, and which therefore only we can solve. The posing of these problems does not diminish the philosophic character of our philosophy, because this philosophy attempts to solve problems which are set before man in his existence. Hence the problems set before the man of America will have to be peculiar to the circumstance in which he exists.

Among these themes is that of our history. History is part of man's circumstance: it gives him his figure and profile, making him capable of performing certain tasks and incapable of performing others. This is why we must consider our history, for in it we shall find the basis of our capacities and incapacities. We cannot continue to be ignorant of our past, refusing to consider our experience, for without this knowledge we cannot consider ourselves mature. Maturity, attaining our majority, means experience. Anyone ignorant of his national history lacks experience, and anyone who lacks experience cannot be a mature, responsible man.

Concerning the history of our philosophy, it will be thought that we cannot find in it anything but bad copies of the European philosophic systems. In fact, this will be what is found by anyone seeking in it philosophic systems, peculiar to our America, that are as important as the European systems. But this would be a wrong point of view; we must go to the history of our philosophy with a different perspective. This must be that of our negations, of our incapacity to do anything but make bad copies of our European models. We must ask ourselves why we do not have a philosophy of our own, and the answer may just be that philosophy itself, since we should be discovering in ourselves a way of thinking that is our own, which perhaps has not acquired expression in the forms used by European philosophy.

We must further ask ourselves why our philosophy is a "bad copy" of European philosophy, because possibly in this fact of being a bad copy there may also be the thing that is essential to an American philosophy; for being a bad copy does not imply that it must be bad, but that it is simply different. Perhaps our sense of inferiority has caused us to think of anything of our own as bad, merely because it does not match or come up to its model. To acknowledge that we cannot produce the same systems that European philosophy has produced does not mean that we confess our inferiority to the makers of that philosophy; it is simply to acknowledge that we are different. Starting from this angle, we shall not see in what our philosophers have done a mass of bad copies of European philosophy, but interpretations of this philosophy made by men of America. The American element will be present in spite of our philosophers' endeavour to be objective. The American element will be present regardless of attempts to depersonalize.

V

Philosophy in its universal character has been preoccupied by one of the problems which have most agitated man in all times, that of man's relations with society. This theme has been posed as a political matter, the organization of our living together. These relations are the responsibility of the State, and for this reason philosophy has inquired by whom it ought to be formed, and who ought to govern. The State must see that the balance is not disturbed between the individual and society; it must see that it does not fall into either anarchy or totalitarianism. Well, to achieve this balance a moral justification is required. Philosophy tries to offer this justification, whereby any metaphysical abstraction culminates in an ethic and a political scheme. Any metaphysical idea serves as a basis for a concrete fact, as a justification for a type of political organization that is almost always proposed.

We have a great many philosophical examples in which metaphysical abstraction serves as a basis for a political construction. One example we have in Platonic philosophy, of which the theory of Ideas serves as a basis and justification for the *Republic*. In St. Augustine's *City of God* we have another example; the Christian community, the Church, is supported by a metaphysical entity which in this case is God. The Utopias of the Renaissance are other examples in which rationalism justifies forms of government out of which has arisen our present-day democracy. Some thinker has said that the French Revolution finds its justification in Descarte's *Discourse on Method*. Hegel's dialectics inverted by Marxism have given rise to forms of government like Communism. The same totalitarianism has tried to justify itself metaphysically by seeking that justification in the ideas of Nietzsche, Sorel, or Pareto. Many further examples may be found in the history of philosophy, in which metaphysical abstraction serves as a base for social or political practice.

By this we see how theory and practice must go together. Man's material acts must be justified by ideas, because this is what differentiates him from the animals. Now, our age has been marked by the rupture between ideas and reality. European culture finds itself in a crisis on account of this rupture. Man finds himself lacking a moral theory to justify his acts, and so he has not been able to solve the problem of his living in society, and the only thing he has achieved is going to extremes, to anarchy or totalitarianism.

The different crises in Western culture have been crises caused by lack of ideas to justify human acts, and the existence of man. When certain ideas have ceased to justify that existence, it has been necessary for man to seek another set of ideas. The history of Western culture is the history of the crisis which man has suffered by the rupture of the co-ordination which existed between ideas and reality. Western culture has gone from crisis to crisis, sometimes saving itself with ideas, sometimes with God, at other times with reason, until our own day, when it has been left without ideas, God, or reason. Culture is crying out for new bases on which to support itself. Well, the answer to this cry, from our point of view, appears practically impossible to obtain. And yet, this point of view is that of men in crisis, and it could not be otherwise, because if it seemed to us that such a problem was easy to solve, we should not be men in a crisis. But the fact that we are in a crisis, and that we do not possess the solution longed for, does not mean that no solution exists. Men in other ages who have found themselves, like us, in a crisis, have suffered from the same pessimism; nevertheless, the solution has been found. We do not know what values can replace those we see lost, but one thing certain is that they will appear, and it is up to us as men of America to make our contribution to this work.

By the above we can be led to another kind of task for a possible philosophy of America. The Western culture of which we are sons and heirs requires new values for its support. Well, these values will have to be extracted from new human experiences, from experiences which come when man finds himself in new circumstances like those which are now arising. America, given its particular position, can bring to culture the novelty of its still unexploited experiences. Hence it is necessary that it proclaim to the world its truth, but a truth without pretensions, a truth that is sincere.

The fewer pretensions it has, the more sincere and authentic that truth will be. America must not have aspirations to set itself up as a director of Western culture; its aspiration must be, purely and simply, to produce culture. And this can be done by trying to solve the problems that come up from its own, the American, point of view.

After this crisis America and Europe will find themselves in similar situations. Both will have to solve the same problem: that which concerns the form of life they will adopt in the new circumstances that confront them. Both will have to continue the work of universal culture which has been interrupted, but with the difference that this time America will not be able to continue to linger in the shadow of what Europe is achieving, because now there is no shadow, and no place to find support. On the contrary, it is America that finds itself in a privileged situation which may be of short duration, but which must be utilized to take on the appointed task of one that has become an adult member of Western culture.

An American philosophy will have to initiate this work, which consists in seeking the values that will serve as a basis for a future type of culture. And this work will have as its aim the safeguarding of the human essence, that by which man is man. Now, man in his essence is both an individual and a social being, and thus it is necessary to preserve the balance between these two components of his essence. This balance is what has been disturbed by carrying man towards his extremes: individualism to the point of anarchy and a sociability so complete that he has become one with the mass. It is therefore necessary to find values which make sociability possible without detriment to individuality.

This universal type of work, and not one that is simply American, will have to be the supreme goal of this possible philosophy of ours, which must not be limited to problems strictly American, to those of American circumstance, but must include those of that broader circumstance, in which we also have our place as the men we are, the circumstance called humanity.

It is not enough to try to discover an American truth, we must also try to discover a truth valid for all men, even though we may not in fact succeed. We must not consider things American as ends in themselves, but as frontiers of a more extensive purpose. That is why any attempt to form an American philosophy, with the sole aim that it be American, will be doomed to failure. One must endeavour to form a philosophy, purely and simply, and the American part will be added unto it. For the philosophy to be American, it will suffice that those who philosophize are American people, in spite of the attempt to depersonalize them. If the opposite way is taken, what will suffer will be philosophy.

In attempting to solve man's problems, whatever his situation in space or time, we shall have to start from ourselves as the men we are; we shall have to start from our circumstances, our limitations, from the fact of being of America, just as the Greek started from a circumstance called Greece. But like him, we cannot limit ourselves to remaining inside that circumstance. If we do remain there, it will be in spite of ourselves. Thus we shall form American philosophy just as the Greek developed Greek philosophy in spite of himself.

Only by starting from these bases can we fulfil our mission in the context of universal culture, contributing to it in the consciousness of our capabilities and our incapabilities, conscious of our reach as members of that cultural community called humanity, and of our limitations as the product of a circumstance, which is peculiar to us and to which we owe our personality, a circumstance called America.

TRANSLATED BY H. W. HILBORN

Adolfo Bioy Casares

Argentina
(b. 1914)

Adolfo Bioy Casares dismissed the first five books he published and claimed that *The Invention of Morel* (1940) represented the inception of his career. A sophisticated fantasy modeled after *The Island of Dr. Moreau* by H. G. Wells, *The Invention of Morel*, to which Bioy Casares's close friend and Argentine compatriot Jorge Luis Borges wrote a famous prologue, offers a sample of Bioy Casares's psychological, scientific, and philosophical bents. It inspired an important French experimental film, *Last Year at Marienbad*, directed by Alain Resnais in 1961. Bioy Casares and Borges collaborated on numerous projects, most importantly on several volumes of detective parody, including *Six Problems for Don Isidro Parodi* (1941), as well as in the *Antología de literatura fantástica* (1940), for which Bioy Casares's wife, Silvina Ocampo, Victoria Ocampo's sister and a novelist in her own right, also served as coeditor. He has a vast corpus of literary publications, including *Plan of Escape* (1945), *La trama celeste* (1948), *Dream of Heroes* (1954), *Historia prodigiosa* (1956), *Guirnalda con amores* (1959), *El lado de la sombra* (1962), *El gran serafín* (1967), and, with Silvina Ocampo, *Los que aman, odian* (1946). "Books and Friendship" is a reminiscence Bioy Casares wrote in 1987. It was later incorporated into the anthology *La invención y la trama* (1988) and appeared in the first volume of his autobiography, *Memorias* (1994). In it he recounts his early collaborative efforts with Borges and the impact the friendship had on him personally and on Argentine culture in general.

Books and Friendship

I think that my friendship with Borges began with our first conversation in 1931 or 1932, traveling between San Isidro and Buenos Aires; at the time, Borges was the most promising of our young writers and I was even younger, having published one book secretly and another using a pseudonym. When he asked me about my favorite authors, I spurned my shyness and, responding in broken sentences, I applauded the gaunt prose of a minor writer who was in charge of the literary section of a local daily newspaper. Striving to be more suggestive perhaps, he restated the question:

273

"Sure," he conceded, "but besides him, who else do you admire in this century or any other time?"

"Gabriel Miró, Azorín, James Joyce," I answered.

What could anyone say about an answer like that? In my case, I was in no position to explain why I admired Miró's ample narrative fresco paintings of biblical and Scholastic content, Azorín's provincial scenes, or, hardly understanding why, Joyce's garrulous narrative cascade that, like a rainbow-hued vapor, condensed into the prestige of what was considered hermetic, strange, and modern. Borges said something to the effect that young writers find it sufficient to read literature written by those who are enchanted by words; then, referring to his admiration for Joyce, he added:

"Of course. It's the intention, an act of faith, a promise. The promise that they [referring to young people] will like him when they read him."

Today, I have only vague memories of that era when we would walk around the neighborhoods of Buenos Aires or among the country houses in Androgué and talk endlessly and passionately about books and their themes; however, I remember one afternoon: we were on the outskirts of the Recoleta and I told him about the idea I had for *"Perjurio de la nieve,"* a story which I wrote several years later; on another occasion, as we were making our way down Austria Street, I met Manuel Peyrou, who was playing *La Mauvaise Priere*, sung by Damia, on his record player, which we listened to out of courtesy.

In 1935 or 1936, we spent a week on a ranch in Pardo in order to coedit a commercial advertisement, which seemed scientific, about the merits of a semi-Bulgarian food product. It was cold outside, the house was in near ruins, and we took refuge in the dining room, where we kept a fire going with eucalyptus branches in the chimney.

That pamphlet signified an important learning experience for me; after we had finished editing it, I was a different writer, much more experienced and at ease with my craft. Each collaborative project with Borges was equivalent to many years of work.

We also worked on a sonnet based on enumeration, but I can't remember how we accounted for the tercets by using windmills, angels, and L's; then we thought about producing a detective story—the ideas always came from Borges—that would deal with a certain Dr. Praetorius, a large, easygoing German school principal who, by using annoying means (obligatory games, never-ending music), would torture and kill young children. That story, which was never written, is the starting point for the writings by Bustos Domecq and Suárez Lynch.

Among all the forgotten conversations we had, I remotely remember one from that week in the country. I was convinced that absolute liberty was indispensable for artistic and literary creation; based on *idiocy*, it was a liberty that one of my writers had been demanding, which revolved around the repetition of two words—*brand new*; hence, I began to reflect on the importance of dreams, irrationality, and absurdity. But I received a big surprise: Borges advocated cogitative art and sided with Horace and the academics, against my heroes—the dazzling Vanguard poets and painters. We live in our own little worlds and we know little about our fellow-creatures; and we definitely look like that book dealer, one of Borges's friends, who for thirty years has been offering in timely fashion all the new biographies of the insignificant princes of the English royal family or the most complete manual on trout fishing. Borges let me have the last say in that conversation, which I attributed to the significance of my opinions; the next day, however, or maybe even that same night, I changed my mind: I had begun to discover that many writers' works were not as great as they had been described in the book review section of the newspapers. After that I strove to be more judicious in creating and writing my stories.

Despite our differences as writers, there was always room for friendship because we both shared the same passion for books. During many afternoons and evenings, we discussed Johnson, De Quincey, Stevenson, fantastic literature, detective-story plots, *L'Illusion comique*, literary theory, Toulet's *contrerimes*, problems of translation, Cervantes, Lugones, Góngora, Quevedo, the sonnet, free verse, Chinese literature, Macedonio Fernández, Dunne, time, relativity, Idealism, Schopenhauer's *Metaphysical Fantasy*, Xul Solar's neocriol, and Mauthner's criticism of language.*

How can I re-create what I felt during those conversations? Thanks to Borges and his observations, I could see things in a new light: poetry, critical thought, and narratives that I had already read; and what I had not read became a world of adventure, like an amazing dream that for a few moments seems real.

In 1936, we founded the journal *Destiempo*; the title referred to our desire to break away from the conventions of our era. In particular, we objected to the tendency of some critics who avoided the intrinsic value of literature by focusing only on folkloric or telluric aspects, or solely on literary history or sociological trends. We believed we would be better off forgetting about not only the cherished dictates of literary schools, but also the probable (or inevitable) trilogies dedicated to the gaucho or the fashion-monger of the middle class, etcetera.

On that September morning when we left the printer's shop on Hortiguera Street in Colombo with the first issue of the journal in hand, Borges proposed—half jesting, half serious—that we have a picture taken together

---

*At the end of the Spanish original, Bioy Casares includes a long list of subjects he discussed with Borges. *Editor's Note*

for posterity; and so we did in a small studio nearby. The picture disappeared so fast that I can't even remember what it looked like. The pages of *Destiempo* included illustrious writers and we produced three issues.

I have collaborated with Borges on diverse projects, such as writing detective and fantastic stories, scripts for movies (with little remuneration), and producing editions of classical works. Among my fondest memories are the nights we spent editing Sir Thomas Brown's *Urn Burial, Christian Morals,* and *Religio Medici,* and Gracián's *Agudeza y arte del in genio.* During the previous winter, other writers we chose for our *Book of Fantasy* included Swedenborg, Poe, Villiers de L'Ille Adam, Kipling, Wells, and Veerbohm. Borges excels in any literary undertaking because he has an alert mind, for he avoids convention, ritual, laziness, and snobbery; he has an extensive memory and an acute ability to discover hidden but significant and authentic relationships; he has a fertile imagination and his creative energy is boundless; and he distinguishes, with much clarity, of course, between marginal activities and his true mission. Once, at the very beginning of our friendship, he cautioned me: "If you want to write, don't edit books or journals. Read and write."

Years later, I commented on that advice: "That's why when one writes a lot, most of it's bad; you should see the books I published back then."

"The sooner one can determine his shortcomings, the better," he responded. "There was a time when I wrote using archaic Spanish, then the Buenos Aires street slang *lunfardo,* and even Vanguard expressions from the Ultraísmo movement. When I run across similar writing, I remind myself that I'm free, because I already made those errors."

Every one of the books I wrote in the 1930s must have prompted him to think that the person with whom he had become friends—so pedestrian but somewhat prudent when he talked—was really an inferior writer who was embarrassingly prolific. Borges was generous in his comments about those books, praising whatever was worth praising, but he was always trying to inspire me, too.

One afternoon in 1939, Borges, Silvina Ocampo, and I were in San Isidro discussing a possible story (another one of those stories that never got written). It was to take place in France, and the protagonist was a young writer from the provinces who had brought fame—celebrated by literary circles that he himself had invented—to a writer who had died some years before. The protagonist worked laboriously, searching everywhere, in order to collect the famous writer's works: a lecture, published as a pamphlet, consisting of a series of banalities written in good style and correct grammar, praising the mighty sword of academia; a short monograph, dedicated to [Désiré] Nisard, focusing on the *Tratado de la lengua latina,* by Varrón; and some poems, *Corona de sonetos,* unemotional both in form and content. The young admirer located the castle where the writer had been living and managed to gain access to his papers. He discovered impressive manuscripts, all helplessly abandoned. Following herewith, lastly, he discovered a list of prohibitions that we later jotted down on the withered cover and blank pages of a copy of *An Experiment with Time.*

In literature, one should avoid:

—Psychological curiosities and paradoxes; homicides from benevolence, suicides from happiness. Psychologically, who would deny that everything is possible? Misogyny in Don Juan, etc.

—Peculiarities, complexities, hidden talents in secondary or minor characters. The philosophy of Maritornes. Do not forget that a literary character consists of the words that describe him or her (Stevenson).

—Pairs of characters that are crudely dissimilar: Quixote and Sancho, Sherlock Holmes and Watson.

—Novels with pairs of heroes: references that switch back and forth between the two are bothersome. In addition, these novels create difficulties: if the author provides an observation about one character, he will necessarily invent a symmetrical one for the other, without trying to abuse contrasts or create feeble coincidences, a situation that is practically impossible: *Bouvard et Pécuchet.*

—Eccentrics in order to create differences among characters, i.e., Dickens.

—Acquiring virtue through novelty or surprise: trick stories. To seek what has not yet been said seems to be a task unbecoming of a writer from an educated society; civilized readers will not be pleased with the discourtesy caused by surprise.

—Playing vainly with time and space when developing plots, i.e., Faulkner, Priestly, Borges, Bioy, etc.

—The discovery that in a certain work the real protagonist is the pampa, the virgin jungle, the sea, the rain, or the beyond; the writing or reading of works about which one could make this statement.

—Poems, situations, or characters with which the reader can identify.

—Phrases of general application or ones that risk becoming proverbs or well-known expressions (they are incompatible with *un discours cohérent*).

—Characters that could become myths.

—Characters, scenes, or phrases from an intentional place. Local color.

—Fascination with the words themselves, as objects. Sex and death appeal, angels, statues, bric-a-brac.

—Chaotic enumeration.

—Lavish vocabulary. Any word that could be used as a synonym. Inversely, *le mot juste*. Eagerness to be precise.

—Exuberant descriptions. Emphasis on the material world. Cf. Faulkner.

—Backgrounds, environments, climate. Tropical heat, drinking binges, the radio, repeated phrases like the refrain of a song.

—Meteorological genesis and cessation. Meteorological or psychic coincidences. *Le vent se leve!* . . . *Il faut tenter de vivre!*

—Metaphors in general. In particular, visual ones; more specifically, agricultural, naval, financial types. See Proust.

—Any type of anthropomorphism.

—Novels that contain some kind of parallelism with another book. Joyce's *Ulysses*.

—Books that simulate menus, albums, itineraries, concerts.

—Anything that illustrations might suggest. The same with films.

—Censoring or praising literary criticism (according to Ménard's rules).* It is enough to include simply the literary effects. There is nothing more ingenuous than those "dealers in the obvious" who proclaim the ineptness of Homer, Cervantes, Milton, or Moliere.

—In criticism, any historical or biographical reference. The author's personality. Psychoanalysis.

—Family scenes or eroticism in murder mysteries. Dramatic scenes in philosophical dialogue.

—Expectation. The pathetic and the erotic in romance novels; enigmas and death in murder mysteries; ghosts and phantoms in fantasy novels.

—Vanity, modesty, pedantry, the lack of pederasty, suicide.

The few friends to whom we read this catalogue were outright disgusted; perhaps they thought we were usurping the role of guardians of the learned professions. Who knows if they suspected that sooner or later we would impose the prohibition of writing freely; maybe they didn't understand what we were actually proposing. On that point, they were partially right, because the criteria of our list are not clear; it includes sensible methods and remonstrative practices. I imagine that if we had written the document, any reader would be able to determine the significance of

---

*We were unaware of how literally this is applied; in North America, professors and university thesis directors; in Europe, and here, quick imitators.

the prohibitions, that is, the writer without a text, which would explain the impossibility of writing comprehensibly.

Menard, the one whose "rule" is mentioned above, is the hero of "Pierre Menard, Author of the *Quixote*."* The invention of both stories, the published version and the unwritten one, correspond to the same year and almost to the same day; if I'm not mistaken, that afternoon when we wrote down the prohibitions, Borges mentioned "Pierre Menard" to us.

Borges directly confronts his tasks with prodigious intensity of intention: I have seen him become delirious over Chesterton, Stevenson, Dante, a series of women (all of them singularly unique), etymology, Anglo-Saxonism, and, as always, literature. This latter passion bothers a lot of people, who quickly draw swords over the habitual conflict between books and life. Beyond that, Borges has said himself that his first stories "are not, nor do they pretend to be, psychological." Over time, though, critics have discovered that Borges seems to be more interested in plot than in his characters, and one can speculate that circumstance does reveal his intimate preference for plot over characterization. Wouldn't the same remark apply to the anonymous authors of *A Thousand and One Nights*? I believe Borges falls into the tradition of the great novelists and short-story writers, that is, the tradition of the storytellers.

The image of Borges isolated from the world—as some would have him—seems unacceptable. I won't confirm here his stubborn attitude toward tyranny, nor his concern for ethics, but simply make a literary reference: when we meet to work on short stories, Borges usually declares that he has some news about one character or another; as if he had just seen them, or had been living with them; he tells me what Frogman or Montenegro had been doing the day before, or what Bonavena or Mrs. Ruiz Villalba had said. He's attracted not only to the characters but also to the comedy intertwining them. An acute observer of idiosyncracy, he's a veritable but sensitive caricaturist.

I wonder if a part of today's Buenos Aires that is destined to become a part of posterity doesn't really consist of situations and characters from a novel invented by Borges. That's probably what has happened, because I have determined that Borges's words make his characters more real than life itself.

TRANSLATED BY DICK GERDES

---

*See pp. 153–61.

Julio Cortázar

Argentina

(1914–1984)

One of the master storytellers of all of Latin America, Julio Cortázar was born and raised in Argentina, but he moved to France with his wife in 1951. His most famous book, *Hopscotch* (1963), was written to be read in multiple sequences of chapters. His stories also display this creativity, intermingling fantasy and reality and blending in his own poetry, photos, and sketches. A voracious reader with a remarkable curiosity, Cortázar's works demonstrate his interest in romantic poetry, jazz, Oriental philosophy, the supernatural, and puzzles. Although his career as an essayist has brought him less attention, it nevertheless earned him high critical praise. In general, his literary style is promiscuous and, as with Borges, it is often difficult to know where a story ends and an essay begins. Thus, some critics consider *Cronopios and Famas* (1969) a hybrid collage—part fiction and part anecdote. Similarly, *A Certain Lucas* (1984), reminiscent of Italo Calvino's *Mister Palomar*, is written using an essayistic tone. But Cortázar also wrote more clearly defined essays, all of which manage to be both inventive and irreverent. Their value lies in their untraditional approach to their subject: They amuse, unsettle, even annoy the reader, but hardly ever try to prove a point by means of persuasive argumentation. Also, Cortázar's intellectual agenda can be more clearly seen in his essays than in his fiction—particularly those written toward the end of his life, such as *Nicaraguan Sketches* (1978), in which his inventiveness frequently falls victim to a dogmatic approach to socialism. Other volumes of essays are *Around the Day in Eighty Worlds* (1967), *Buenos Aires, Buenos Aires* (1968), *Ultimo Round* (1969), *Viaje alrededor de una mesa* (1970), *Literatura en la revolución y revolución en la literatura* (1970), *Prosa del observatorio* (1972), and *Territorios* (1978). "To Dress a Shadow," vintage Cortázar, is part of *Around the Day in Eighty Worlds*.

To Dress a Shadow

The hardest thing is to surround it, to fix its limit where it fades into the penumbra along its edge. To choose it from among the others, to separate it from the light that all shadows secretly, dangerously, breathe. To begin to dress it casually, not moving too much, not frightening or dissolving it: this is the initial operation where nothingness lies in every move. The inner garments, the transparent corset, the stockings that compose a silky ascent up the thighs. To all these it will consent in momentary ignorance, as if imagining it is playing with another shadow, but suddenly it will become troubled, when the skirt girds its waist and it feels the fingers that button the blouse between its breasts, brushing the neck that rises to disappear in dark flowing water. It will repulse the gesture that seeks to crown it with a long blonde wig (that trembling halo around a nonexistent face!) and you must work quickly to draw its mouth with cigarette embers, slip on the rings and bracelets that will define its hands, as it indecisively resists, its newborn lips murmuring the immemorial lament of one awakening to the world. It will need eyes, which must be made from tears, the shadow completing itself to better resist and negate itself. Hopeless excitement when the same impulse that dressed it, the same thirst that saw it take shape from confused space, to envelop it in a thicket of caresses, begins to undress it, to discover for the first time the shape it vainly strives to conceal with hands and supplications, slowly yielding, to fall with a flash of rings that fills the night with glittering fireflies.

TRANSLATED BY THOMAS CHRISTENSEN

Octavio Paz

Mexico
(b. 1914)

———◆◆◆◆———

Considered an essayist and poet unmatched in production and versatility by any other Latin American writer, Octavio Paz's poetic talent clearly shines through in his prose. Studying in the United States, Paz gained remarkable insight into his native Mexico and its relationship to other nations and societies, laying the foundation for his great analysis of Mexican culture, *The Labyrinth of Solitude* (1950). Diplomatic duties in France, Japan, and India led to his interest in surrealism and to his collection of essays *La búsqueda del comienzo*, while *Conjunctions and Disjunctions* (1969) explores eroticism in Eastern and Western cultures. Paz also served as Mexico's ambassador to India, which led to his writing of *The Monkey Grammarian* (1974). His essays reveal a Renaissance mind with an insatiable curiosity, but their underlying message seems a product of a cross between structuralism and Hegelian dialectical idealism. Despite being a contemporary of Alejo Carpentier, Miguel Angel Asturias, and Gabriel García Márquez, he seems to have developed an aversion to magical realism—his objective is not to call attention to the surreal in Latin America, but to explain why foreigners are so captivated by these stereotypical views, and he does so by contrasting civilizations and comparing cultural viewpoints. Other important works include *The Arch and the Lyre* (1956), *Las peras del olmo* (1957), *Puertas al campo* (1966), *Claude Lévi-Strauss o El nuevo festín de Esopo* (1967), *Alternating Current* (1967), *Los signos de rotación y otros ensayos* (1971), *Traducción: Literatura y literalidad* (1971), *Las cosas en su sitio* (1971), *Apariencia desnuda* (1973), *El signo y el garabato* (1973), *Children of Mire* (1974), *Xavier Villaurrutia* (1978), *The Philanthropic Ogre* (1979), *The Other Voice* (1991), and *The Double Female: Love and Eroticism* (1993). He is also responsible for an outstanding biography, *Sor Juana: The Traps of Faith* (1982), which not only follows closely the intellectual odyssey of Sor Juana Inés de la Cruz, the remarkable seventeenth-century Mexican poet and nun, but also explores political, social, religious, and cultural life in colonial Mexico. Paz's critical talents are immense and have produced extraordinary works, and the editor attempting to select a representative essay of his faces a considerable challenge, since no single piece will satisfy every reader. The following is a book review of *Mexican Churches*, a pictorial volume by American photographers Eliot Porter and Ellen Auerbach, published in the *New York Times* on 20 December 1987. By intertwining the personal and the historical, it evidences Paz's magisterial scope and vision.

Mexican Churches

It is difficult to describe the gamut of feelings I've experienced looking over the photographs of Mexican churches taken by Eliot Porter and Ellen Auerbach in the winter of 1955–1956: delight in identifying forgotten churches and altars that have been recovered through the eyes of these two artists of photography, as well as in discovering others unknown to me or now seen in an unexpected angle, bathed in a light that transfigures them. Also sadness and anger, since some of the churches and altars photographed by Mr. Porter and Ms. Auerbach have either disappeared or have been disfigured by negligence and "progress."

And finally melancholy: Those pictures made me think back to my youthful field trips to convents, temples, pyramids and ruins. Like most Mexicans, during my childhood I frequently went to church and took part in the rites and mysteries of the Roman Catholic faith. In the village I lived in, there was a Dominican convent from the sixteenth century and many churches and chapels, including two from the seventeenth century. One of them was my neighborhood church. I didn't consider it a monument but saw it as it was and is—both an intimate and public place where one went to talk to God, to the other believers and to oneself. The church offered solitude and communion—and something more profane; every Sunday the procession of girls on their way to Mass gave my friends and me a chance to meet them and invite them to the movies or some other entertainment. In Latin countries, the dim lights inside churches have always been favorable to courtship. Even Don Juan is buried in the atrium of a church in Seville.

It was later, when I entered high school, that I discovered the religious art of Mexico. High schools had just been newly formed, established around 1926 to take the place of the former lycée system. The Government had made a number of reforms modeled after the North American system—faint echoes of John Dewey's ideas about education. I came from a Catholic grammar school and the new methods bewildered me. The principal of my school was a kind, simple soul. As a worshiper of science, it occurred to him to give each section the name of a scientist. I passed from the Congregation of the Saints and Virgins to the Academy of the Immortals. The first year, I found myself in the section named after Archimedes, and during my second and third years, in the Newton and Lavoisier sections.

Our principal loved nature and organized field trips every other week. He made attendance mandatory at least once a month. During the stops on our walks, before eating and resting, we would gather around him. Leaning back on a rock or on a tree stump, he would pull out a sheet of paper and read us a poem. He was a poet and the themes that inspired him were scientific—the mysteries of the triangle and the sphere, the wonders hidden in the periodic table. He never suspected that those field trips led me to discover yet another wonder, the richness of religious art in Mexico. I have forgotten the ode to the parallelepiped and the sonnet to electrons and valence, but not the shapeliness of a white bell tower, a blue dome or the rose tinge of a convent.

The journey that Eliot Porter and Ellen Auerbach made to Mexico was, in a certain sense, a distant and indirect consequence of D. H. Lawrence's experiences in Mexico. In 1946, Mr. Porter settled in Santa Fe, N.M., where, through Georgia O'Keeffe, he met Spud Johnson, a poet living in Taos who had accompanied Lawrence on his trips from Taos south into Mexico. Fascinated by Johnson's accounts, Mr. Porter made his first journey in February 1951, accompanied by his wife and O'Keeffe. What he saw in the Mexican villages inspired him to return several years later to take photographs of the churches, especially their interiors and altars.

Mr. Porter, his wife and Ms. Auerbach left for Mexico early in December 1955, and their journey lasted five months. Traveling in a Chevrolet van—as well as by bus, plane and train—they covered the territory from northern Nogales to the southernmost states of Chiapas and Yucatán. A few years earlier, during World War II, an accelerated, and if not always fortunate, process of modernization had begun in Mexico, one that would only come to a standstill sometime after 1970. But the Mexico that Mr. Porter and Ms. Auerbach saw still retained some of its most characteristic features. They took more than 3,000 photographs, almost all of them in color—not that many if one stops to think of the incredible amount of churches, chapels and icons in Mexico. Ellen Auerbach confessed that they "were frustrated by the feeling of not having even scratched the surface."

*Mexican Churches** offers only 88 of those 3,000 photographs. This rigor is rewarding; almost all are excellent, some are magnificent and a few are masterpieces. Among these is the photograph on the cover of the book. It shows the ochre stains and burnt orange of a cracked wall on which hangs a paper garland of red, yellow and purple roses. Below, on the changing shades of the ground—the color of a Franciscan's habit—a black bottle and a glass in which a poppy is drowning. This is a composition in which the animation of colors and the richness of tones dramatically contrast with the poverty of the materials—paper, glass, plaster, cement, stains of moisture—tools with which time makes and destroys appearances. The paper garland, a sumptuous rag, seems to be a crown for a destitute king, Christ. It is remarkable how the eye of the artist isolates this humble reality and

---

*University of New Mexico Press, 1987.

transforms it into living art. It has been years since that garland was thrown into the garbage can and the wall, if it still stands, has been painted over several times. But the image in Mr. Porter's photograph lives. Photography redeems.

Another picture which surprised me is by Ms. Auerbach, depicting a sculpture of the crucified Christ in a niche painted with flowers and geometric motifs. Mexican religious art uses and abuses Expressionism but, within this tradition, this blood-stained Christ is not terrible; it is liberating. The figure, animated by the spiritual impulse to levitate, with arms extended like a human bird, seems to detach itself from the cross and fly. One has the impression that the dome is going to open up to let out the prodigious bird.

A clear and lucid essay by Donna Pierce, the curator of Spanish Colonial collections at the Museum of International Folk Art in Santa Fe, accompanies the photographs. It is a complete synthesis of the evolution of religious art in Mexico and a discussion of Catholicism's central influence over Mexican sensibility, imagination and life. Ms. Pierce underlines the syncretism of Mexican Catholicism, which has adopted pre-Hispanic divinities purged of their most horrible aspects, among them (and most important) the ancient goddesses of fertility. A comparison with Anglo-Saxon Protestantism is significant. In Mexico, Indian gods were converted, as it were, to Christianity, while in the United States they vanished. The spiritual richness of Mexican Catholicism is astonishing. I'm not just thinking of the examples of love and charity that have ennobled the interior life of the people, or the images like the Virgin of Guadalupe or the Christ of Chalma which have enriched their sensibility, I'm also thinking of the masterworks in architecture, painting, sculpture, music and poetry. There is nothing like this in North American culture.

Perhaps it isn't very fair to compare the United States with Mexico with respect to religious art and images. Mexico is still, in many respects, a traditional society (which is where its strengths and weaknesses lie), while the United States is the first truly modern society in history. As to the absence of female images in the religious life of North America, the Protestant God is male and abstract and there is no Virgin Mary to reign at His side. Capitalist culture, based on work, savings and competitiveness, is also distinctly masculine. Maybe a comparison of Mexico with India, another traditional society, is more enlightening. In Mexico, Catholic monotheism blends with native polytheism through saints, virgins, martyrs and demons. In India there is a strict and sometimes fratricidal separation between Hindu polytheism and Moslem monotheism. Not only was there never a fusion or cultural exchange, but the two religions engendered two clearly distinct cultures and two adversary political causes.

Mexican syncretism has been, and is, a creation of its people. It isn't the result of the theories of a handful of theologians; it is the spontaneous expression of a people who, in order to face their misfortunes, *had* to believe. For centuries religion has not been the opium but the balm of the Mexicans. With the same freedom and confidence in the supernatural with which they converted the ancient gods into saints and Christian demons, the Mexicans have adopted and transformed Western artistic forms. Art in Mexico has always been an art of crossbreeding and a conjunction of opposites. It's not only an Indian characteristic, but a Spanish one. The first churches and convents built by the Spaniards were hybrids, a mixture of styles—Gothic, Mudejar (Moorish-Christian) and Renaissance. The presence of Indian sensibility is visible from the beginning of the Spanish presence in the Americas. It is a presence that has never vanished, not in the splendor of the Baroque period (which in Mexico has its own characteristics) nor in the heyday of neo-classicism.

Two architectural trends have always coexisted in Mexico, formal and popular. The Chapel del Rosario in Puebla is an example of the first, the apex of the Baroque and full of classical reminiscences, much in the way a poem by the seventeenth-century Mexican writer Sor Juana is studded with Greco-Roman allusions. The Church of Santa Maria Tonanzintla, whose dancing virgins and Indian angels seem possessed by a kind of pagan and sacred inebriation, is an example of the second. Mr. Porter and Ms. Auerbach didn't photograph the most important places from a historical point of view but with an eye to what is most characteristic and spontaneous, those things which, as Ms. Pierce nicely says, are true "portraits of faith." They don't offer us a manual but a book of living images.

The technical expertise of Mr. Porter and Ms. Auerbach is no less extraordinary. Most of their photographs are of church interiors, a number of them photographed for the first time, and many, no doubt, for the last. Indeed, not only have many of these churches been renovated—not always skillfully—but the use of electricity has radically changed the traditional look of those interiors with their play of shadow and light. Mr. Porter and Ms. Auerbach refused to use electrical lighting or any other form of interior illumination; they photographed the altars, niches and sculptures in the half light. We see those images just the way the parishioners saw them. All this required long exposures but the results more than compensate for the hours of waiting; the photographs re-create with intense accuracy the emotional atmosphere of the interiors, the shadows crossed by the faltering lights of candles and the reflections of the colored glass.

Human figures don't appear in any of the photographs. I find this omission to be one of the best achievements of the artists; we imagine the believers praying, surrounded by dancing lights and shadows. Many times Mr. Porter and Ms. Auerbach had to overcome the resistance of the parishioners who considered, with good reason, both church and icons to be theirs. Between each sacred image and its devotee there is an intimate, filial relationship; the believer sees the saint as a supernatural protector but also as a confidant. This relationship isn't stated but implicit in "Mexican Churches." In the invisible but real presence of the worshipers lies the secret fascination that many of these photographs radiate. There are two families of artists—those, like Picasso, who use their models to serve them, and those who, like Velázquez, serve their models. Mr. Porter and Ms. Auerbach belong to this second category.

TRANSLATED BY ROBERT PEGADA

Augusto Roa Bastos

Paraguay
(b. 1917)

Augusto Roa Bastos was born in Paraguay, a country that has never enjoyed great literary acclaim. He worked as a journalist before he was pressured to immigrate to Argentina during the civil war of 1947. Poetry was his initial medium, but he eventually moved on to prose, which he found to be a better vehicle for his voice. He produced a collection of short stories in 1953 entitled *El trueno entre las hojas*, but his greatest accomplishment came with *Son of Man* (1960), a historical novel about politics and the human condition in Paraguay. *El naranjal ardiente* (1960) was his final volume of poetry, and was followed by the anthologies *El baldío* (1966) and *Moriencia* (1969), and by the magisterial novel *I, the Supreme* (1974), an encyclopedic, polyphonic account of the solitary life of José Gaspar Rodríguez de Francia, known as "El Supremo," a tyrant who ruled Paraguay from 1814 to 1840. Roa Bastos's work also includes *Vigilia del almirante* (1992), *El fiscal* (1993), and *Contravida* (1995). Much like the prose of Carlos Fuentes and Gabriel García Márquez, he has been particularly concerned with the quest for origins. Roa Bastos's complex readings of Paraguayan society often force the reader to dismiss the distinction between history and fiction. Roa Bastos returned to Paraguay in the 1970s only to be exiled again in 1982, two years after publishing his *Antología personal*. "Writing: A Metaphor for Exile" first appeared in Spain's daily *El País* on 8 July 1985. It offers a personal account of the displacement and nostalgia most Paraguayans experienced as a result of the repressive regime of General Alfredo Stroessner, in power from 1954 to 1991. Stroessner's dictatorship is only one of several since "El Supremo" ruled the nation.

Writing: A Metaphor for Exile

The political, social, and cultural picture presented by Paraguay under the dictatorship of longest standing on the Latin American continent dramatically reveals the devastating effect that the latter has had on the creative sources of society in their various manifestations. In this backward society endlessly playing out, as a sort of punishment, the "ongoing hallucination of its history"—the culmination of a century of intermittent, endemic dictatorships resembling tropical fevers—the phenomenon of exile, through this perversion of history, forms part of its nature and its destiny.

Exile, first of all, of the country itself within its landlocked prison, marked by territorial segregations, by migrations and emigrations, by mass exoduses: among them, that of its native peoples, the first at the time of the expulsion of the Jesuits (1767), which in turn represented the first banishment of foreigners in colonial Paraguay. This nonetheless did not prevent the country, once it had become independent, from attaining the status of the most advanced nation, materially and culturally, in Hispanic America. Under the rule of the famous Dr. Francia, founder of the Republic and builder of the nation-state in accordance with the principles of the Enlightenment and the French Revolution, there took place in Paraguay the first successful experiment in autonomous government and independence in the history of Latin America: something that the liberators of the continent themselves were not able to achieve after the battles for emancipation. The economic interests—the penetration and domination of the British Empire in that part of the world—could not permit the utopia of self-determination to prosper in this little isolated, landlocked country and thus set a dangerous example. At the instigation of the British and with their aid, the financial centers of the Brazilian Empire and the oligarchies of the Río de la Plata, who were dependent on England, contrived to bring about the so-called War of the Triple Alliance. Lasting for five years (1865–1870), this war devastated Paraguay, exterminated two-thirds of its population, and stripped it of more than half its territory. Paraguay was thus reduced to ruins. All that was left of this unfortunate nation was a "great catastrophe of memories" and in its midst a raving mad reality blowing tremendous gusts of their history into the faces of the survivors, in the words of the Spaniard Rafael Barret, writing at the beginning of this century.

The emptiness of the past, its isolation, its lack of communication, its harassment by neocolonialist interest kept even the echoes of cultural currents that were transforming the ideas, the arts, the literatures of Latin America from reaching this enclave, withdrawn into itself and brooding upon its national calamities. To all of this there must be added the double barrier of its bilingual culture: Paraguay is the only totally bilingual country in Latin America; the native oral language, Guaraní, is the real national language of the people. This is the space of mestizo culture, where more than four centuries of purely oral expression has turned writing into an absent text: the root metaphor of exile.

This cultural and linguistic exile hence aggravates, from within, all the other forms of alienation that inner exile implies, since it means the destruction of the last freedom by fear: fear installed as public conscience in a country crushed by the system of totalitarian repression that holds that country in contempt.

The fragmentation of Paraguayan culture, the imbalance of the forces of production, the overwhelming fear that has taken over the functions of a conscience at once public and secret, individual and collective, have profoundly affected the creative powers of a society that lives, as a sort of ironic punishment, on the shores of one of the most beautiful rivers in the world, that river that gave its mythic name to the country: *Paragua'y: plumed-water or river-of-crowns.*

Brutality and terror have dammed those sources that nourish the works of writers and artists and project the originality of a people. It is evident that this expressive process can take place only when such works fuse the social energy of the collectivity and the essence of its life, its reality, its history, its cultural, social, and national myths that fecundate the creative subjectivity of poets, novelists, artists. The greatest alienation of that collectivity is to live torn between reality as it ought to be and reality as it is: between the plenitude of life that has been stolen from it and the monstrosity of the vegetative life that causes foreign to its historical and social nature have imposed upon it.

The writer cannot comport himself like an ethnologist. Passivity, keeping his distance, are not his forte. Paraguayan writers, authors of fiction, poets belong to a culture whose internal structure continues to be oral, stubbornly resistant to the signs of *cultivated* writing, which stands for artificiality and domination. Imagination thus remains a prisoner of this twofold alienation: that of language, in expressing a reality that overwhelms it; and that of a reality that is polyphonic sound, a reality that manifests itself only through orality, the inflections and modulations of verbal expression. And as we are well aware, it is not good intentions that make a literary work; it is, rather, the meanings of its internal structure, the instinctive force that emanates from it, the mediation of "an art that is undoubtedly conscious, yet in search of a form not conscious of itself," an art that is not ideological yet cannot escape ideology.

In the inventory of the forms of exile of the Paraguayan writer (outward exile and inner, dispossession of life not lived, deprivation of work not yet done, segregation from his reality, lack of communication with his national public among those scattered in the diaspora, lack of communication with those suffering from inner exile), linguistic exile is their paradigm, the true metaphor of reality transformed into unreality.

The problem of the Castilian–Guaraní polarity may be the key sign of this sort of linguistic schizophrenia. In which of the two languages is the Paraguayan writer to write? If literature is fundamentally a matter of language, and hence of communication, the choice should be or would seem to be inevitable: Castilian Spanish. But on writing in Castilian, the writer, and the author of fiction in particular, feels that he is suffering his most intimate alienation, that of linguistic exile. To what desperate straits might he be driven if he thus keeps at a distance that portion of reality and collective life that is expressed in Guaraní, of Paraguayan culture bearing the indelible mark of its oral nature, of original mythic thought? As he sits writing in Castilian he feels he is engaged in making only a partial translation of a linguistic context that is split in two. And as he does so, he splits himself in two. He will always have something left that has not been expressed. This brings the Paraguayan writer face-to-face with the need to *make* a literature that as yet has no place in literature; to speak against the word, to write against writing, to invent stories that are the transgression of official history, to undermine, with subversive, demystifying writing, the language loaded with the ideology of domination. In this sense, the new generations of fiction writers and poets find themselves committed to the task of advancing this *literature without a past* that comes from a past without literature, of expressing it in their own language.

The Guaraní cosmogony conceived of human language as the foundation of the cosmos and the original nature of man. The nucleus of this myth of origin is the esoteric and untranslatable *ayvú rapytá* or *ñe'eng mbyte râ* as the very essence of the soul-word: the *ayvú* of the beginning of time. Noise or sound impregnated with the wisdom of nature and of the cosmos engendering itself through the austere and melodious Father of the beginning and the end; originator of the word that founds. A secret word that is never uttered in the presence of strangers, and the one that forms, along with *tataendy* (flame-of-the-sacred-fire) and *tatachiná* (mist-of-the-creative-power), the trinity of prime elements in the cosmogony of the ancient Guaranís. Their primordial divinities did not fulminate punitive laws against one who aspired to wisdom. They brought about the communion between knowing and doing, between unity and plurality, between life and death. Every man was God on the way to purification, and God—or the many gods of that theogony—was both the first man and the last. They did not impose exile, but the pilgrimage of the *multitude-person* to the *land-without-evil* that each one bore within and amid all.

In present-day Paraguayan society, thrown out of balance by oppressive power, the ancestral voice—that last language in which a threatened and persecuted people takes refuge—has also been confiscated. A language without writing that in another time contained within itself the very essence of the soul-word—seed of the human and the sacred—it is today trying to find its space as a word, the irradiation of reality through the unreality of signs.

Contemporary Paraguayan writers are aware that they find themselves at an extreme point of a historic succession. This makes them abnormally conscious not only of the problems of their society but also of their artistic task. For those writers subjected to internal exile, as for those forced to scatter in the diaspora, the work of literature once again means the imperative need to embody a destiny, to find their place once more in the vital reality of a collectivity, their own, in order to nourish themselves in its profoundest essences and aspirations, and from there go on to embrace the universality of humankind.

These narrators understand that achievements of this sort, by their very nature, can be realized only on the aesthetic plane, on the plane of the word and of writing, through the very conception of the art of narration, which is not only, as is commonly thought, the art of describing reality in words but also the art of making the word itself real.

This commitment tends to penetrate beneath the skin of human destiny as deeply as possible; to bring into being, in short, the most complete image possible of the individual and of society, the most intimate image possible of the vital and spiritual experience of the human person of our time. It is in this way that, allying personal subjectivity with historical and social conscience, creative imagination with moral passion, Paraguayan writers can overcome their dramatic lack of communication and isolation of today and become an integral part of the whole of the literature whose language is Hispanic.

TRANSLATED BY HELEN LANE

Augusto Monterroso

Guatemala
(b. 1921)

———•◦•••◦•———

Honduran by birth, Augusto Monterroso spent his childhood and adolescence in Guatemala, and the majority of his career in Chile and Mexico. Forced both to educate and support himself during his adolescence, he devoted his free time to the reading of classics at the National Library of Guatemala. Before his departure in 1944, he collaborated with the political movements opposed to the dictatorship of General Jorge Ubico. However, despite his activism, Monterroso never displayed any interest in using literature as a tool for his political agenda. Monterroso began writing after his arrival in Mexico in 1944. His flexible, ironic voice is evident in his first anthology, *Complete Works and Other Stories* (1959). He has served as a diplomat, translator, and professor at the Universidad Nacionol Autónoma de México over the last forty years. Monterroso, who like Borges and Cortázar cultivated the art of the literary essay, is known for the brevity and meticulousness with which he composes his works. His reluctance to "repeat himself" has led him to experiment with diverse art forms: He has published a book of fables titled *The Black Sheep and Other Fables* (1969); an autobiographical essay, *La letra e.: Fragmento de un diario* (1987); and a brief memoir, *Los buscadores de oro* (1993). His other works include *Perpetual Movement* (1972), *La vida y la obra de Eduardo Torres* (1978), and *La palabra mágica* (1983). Internationally celebrated, Monterroso holds the record for the shortest short story (heralded by Italo Calvino in his *Six Memos for the Next Millennium* as an incomparable accomplishment); also, he is known as the author of the shortest of literary essays, entitled "Fecundity," which is part of *Perpetual Movement* and is reproduced here. Ironically, the essay is introduced by a much longer epigraph by Jean Jaures.

Fecundity

> *Between the provocation of hunger and the passion of hatred, Humanity cannot think about the infinite. Humanity is like a great tree full of flies buzzing angrily beneath a stormy sky, and in that buzz of hate, the deep, divine voice of the universe cannot be heard.*
>
> —Jean Jaures, "Regarding God"

Today I feel well, like a Balzac; I am finishing this line.

Translated by Edith Grossman

Emir Rodríguez Monegal

Uruguay
(1921–1985)

———◆•••◆———

Born in Melo, Uruguay, Emir Rodríguez Monegal did his undergraduate studies at the Lycée Français in Montevideo and in Rio de Janeiro, and his postgraduate work at Cambridge University. In his early career he edited such Uruguayan magazines as *Marcha* and *Número*, from which he drew material for later studies, such as *Narradores de esta América* (1962). He was also a teacher and prolific critic, publishing major biographies on Horacio Quiroga, Pablo Neruda, Jorge Luis Borges, and Andrés Bello. Rodríguez Monegal stepped into the international spotlight when he moved to Paris in 1966 to direct *Mundo Nuevo*, a magazine rumored to be sponsored by the CIA, which focused on contemporary Latin American prose and poetry, and helped launch the Boom generation of the 1960s. Teaching stints at Harvard, the University of Liverpool, and Yale followed. In addition to his biographical studies, he wrote *El juicio de las parricidas* (1956), *El arte de narrar* (1968), *Vínculo de sangre* (1968), and *El boom de la novela latinoamericana* (1972). Rodríguez Monegal's 1978 biography of Borges, filled with bibliographic and anecdotal details but somehow lacking a coherent style, appeared in different versions in Spanish and English. His most lasting contribution is the ambitious two-volume *Borzoi Anthology of Latin American Literature* (1977), in which he was assisted by Thomas Colchie. "Horacio Quiroga in the Mirror" served as the introduction to his biography of Quiroga, published in Argentina in 1968. It illustrates his approach to the essayistic genre: Rodríguez Monegal uses the first person to penetrate his subject's mind. He also employs the third person to perceive Quiroga from a distance. He places words in Quiroga's mouth and turns him into a kind of existential hero.

Horacio Quiroga in the Mirror

I'm alone like a cat . . . like a dot in the immensity of the rainy landscape.

It's Saturday. Two o'clock in the afternoon and it's been raining nonstop since dawn. From the windows of his stone house, the man (small, thin, and bearded) sees the curtain of rain take form against the tall palm trees of the mesa. At the bottom, impossible to distinguish but vivid in the observer's repeated experience, the immense river is gliding along. He's pondered the smooth silver ribbon thousands of times from the same large window. Through his efforts he's tamed the currents of the powerfully savage crest of the Paraná River thousands of times as well. But today (June 27, 1936) the rain has worn away the landscape. It's wet, sad, and dark. Also dark is the 57-year-old man who ponders the rain. It's been exactly five months since the woman and his daughter left, downstream, for Buenos Aires. And for exactly five months, the man who looks at the landscape is sick and alone, so sick that not even he (despite old medical claims) is capable of realizing the seriousness of his *maladie*, as he likes to write. Sick without knowing it, consciously alone, he meditates.

There's a sheet of paper in front of him. This man, who has scribbled on and used up entire reams of paper during an intense life dedicated (among other things) to the difficult art of writing, now sets down a few lines on the paper. It's not one of those stories that made him famous everywhere Spanish is read. It's been five long years since he's written stories. Nor is it one of those chronicles about animals, which lately, with the use of direct and almost autobiographical notes, has substituted the old inventing. What he is now writing, alone and numb from the cold, in front of the curtain of rain, is a letter. The sheet of paper is like a mirror, his mirror.

In that letter—which, like the woman he lost, should also go downstream along the wide river to Buenos Aires—the man writes about his days, details the trivialities of his solitude, the anguish, the broken heart. He writes: "Two o'clock. It warms my heart to see it raining since dawn. From my large windows I see the wet, sad, and dark landscape. I'm alone like a cat. This morning my maid, her little daughter, and her husband went to Santa Ana in a truck; they'll return late tonight, or in the morning. I heated the soup that I prepared last night, and here I am in the living room, like a dot in the immensity of the rainy landscape." The hand keeps writing on the paper, the letter continues flowing like the river and the rain, filled with memories, of books read and experienced, of invocations to the absent friend (the younger brother, he calls him), of things too difficult to endure alone. When he finishes, the postal service should be responsible for delivering it into the hands of Ezequiel Martínez Estrada. The letter will be opened. The quiet, distant voice of Horacio Quiroga will flow from the letter and the monologue will start again.

But now, while Quiroga writes pondering the rain, the letter is a mirror. "I'm alone like a cat." Upon reading this "absurd" (the label also pertains to him) letter again, he has experienced the final days, the final months, the final years of that life. This man is (today, June 27, 1936) one of the greatest narrators of Hispanic America, one of its most long-lasting storytellers. He has known early success in his native city (Salto, located above another wide river, the Uruguay); has achieved the attention and envy of the Plate Basin capitals (Montevideo and Buenos Aires); and has been edited, translated, and reviewed in Madrid, New York, and Paris. His work was acclaimed by Leopoldo Lugones, Rodó, Sanín Cano, Roberto J. Payró, Waldo Frank, José Eustasio Rivera, and Alberto Zum Felde. Still, for the man who now appears in front of the mirror of that letter, all that success is meaningless. Solitude has invaded him to the very core. He has lost the eagerness to create with words; he's gotten to the point where the burden he's acquired in 57 years of an intense and ravenous life finally breaks one's back. Facing the whiteness of the paper, Quiroga is pondering his annihilation; he feels "like a dot in the immensity of the rainy landscape."

The failure of a second marriage (after intervals of various crises, María Elena left five months ago), the disinterestedness of the new generations toward his work, an inexplicable discouragement that reflects the dark labor of the sickness over his most cherished tissues, including an unconscious preparation for the final encounter, have all been undermining his will to live and have forced him, in the end, to face his solitude as a purifying experience. Thin, small, and bearded, Quiroga is facing himself in the mirror of that letter for the first time, with his total being. What the sheet of paper, which is being covered with his slanted, nervous, and almost illegible handwriting, reflects is the man's final disguise. Although it might be invisible to him, this is the face of an exiled man.

Born 57 years ago on the border of another big American river, Quiroga needed to pull himself violently away from his indifferent homeland to fulfill his ambition; he wanted to transplant his roots to Paris, with the absurd intent of conquering it; he found a winter residence in the modern sections of Montevideo and Buenos Aires until a master stroke of luck (which is also called destiny) allowed him to discover his habitat, that land with which he was mysteriously satisfied, in the forest of Misiones. As if in a dream, Quiroga discovered St. Ignatius and guessed (before his intelligence could register it) that he should put down roots there. Without knowing it, Quiroga chose a destiny of exile in order to look for and find his true homeland. He had once said, "Weeds don't exist; they're plants that aren't in their place." Outside Misiones, Quiroga felt like a weed; in Misiones he turned himself into a profound tropical plant.

From the damp region of San Ignacio, from the mesa he created with his hands and his imagination, from the stone house, the man in exile looks at the heavy rain and measures the extent of his solitude. He doesn't yet know (today, June 27, 1936) that the die is already cast. He is still unaware that at last the roots have found the final land. He touches his solitude with a trembling hand, timidly sinks his fingers into that painful heart, delicately advances to the tissues already devoured by the unknown cancer, and finds only solitude.

He's at the edge of the final experience. Fifty-seven years of life, successes and grief, rage, happiness and tragedy, remain behind. The journey from the idle glory of Salto in the summer of 1878 to that rainy Misiones winter of 1936 has truly been long. Only now can the man ponder his real face in the paper mirror. Only now does he understand that throughout the course of an intense life he has worn out many disguises. Only now is he capable of returning ("a victim of memory") and discovering his true face. One after the other, the successive images have been dropping away: the stupid and ill-bred boy; the young village musketeer; the insufferable degenerate of a multitude of barbiturates and shoes riddled with holes; the punished conqueror of Paris wearing down his hunger in the Luxembourg Gardens; the hysterical poet who scandalizes his still provincial surroundings of Montevideo; the dyspeptic photographer who travels to the Jesuitical Misiones and catches a glimpse of the promised land; the oppressive Chaco cotton farmer; the literature professor who is always on the lookout for the puberty of his female students; the literary settler of that Misiones, which gave him a world and took away a wife; the gentle and tyrannical father that exposes his children to the dangers of the jungle in order to make them true inhabitants of a frontier land; the *homme de lettres*, the aging citizen who stirs up the enthusiasm of the young people and the women around him; the storyteller who Hispanic America finally hails as our Kipling after having been discovered as our Poe; the master ignored by new generations, who ends up taking refuge in his land in order to find, in the failure of a second marriage, in the rain and solitude, in the cancer, his final image.

The sheet of paper is a mirror. As it traces his peculiar calligraphy, Quiroga unveils his true image. Fifty-seven years have ripened him to this nakedness, this stripping, this "simple bitter almond." Quiroga looks back and ponders the rapid succession of days and beings. He looks at the bottom and discovers a small river city, elevated on top of powerful hills overlooking a river that causes an uproar as it flows into waterfalls very close to the port, a city eternalized in the siestas of infancy, heavy with sleep and discoveries. Perhaps he sees the first image.

TRANSLATED BY HARRY MORALES

Alvaro Mutis

Colombia
(b. 1923)

————◆◆◆◆————

Accustomed to radical changes of setting even at a young age, Alvaro Mutis spent his early life in Brussels. Although his family would later settle in their native land permanently, his earliest contact with Colombia came through the family's vacations. During the late 1940s and 1950s, he decided to break with Colombia's poetic tradition. He joined other Colombian poets in a group named *Mito*, which began to explore the limits of their art form through technical innovations. He moved to Mexico in 1956, and both his productivity and the recognition he received increased dramatically. Mutis's life as a Colombian exile in Mexico made a powerful impact on his craft. A master of the novella form, he is responsible for the ongoing saga of Maqroll, an elusive sailor whose love for literature and adventure takes him to the most remote and exciting corners of the world. In a career in which his writing has maintained a distance from political ideology, Mutis has created a style that is both Colombian in character and international in its appeal. His books include *Diario de Lecumberri* (1960), *Summa de Maqroll el Gavillero* (1982), and *La última escala del tramp steamer* (1988). In English, the novellas with Maqroll as protagonist have been collected in two volumes: *Maqroll* (1992) and *The Adventures of Maqroll* (1995). The following brief essay, "Interlude in the South Atlantic," from the anthology *La muerte del estratega* (1988), is an enchanting tribute to the Polish-born British novelist Joseph Conrad, a figure whose influence south of the Rio Grande is considerable and whose essential affinity with Mutis is obvious: marine adventure. We see here the way in which Mutis explores the identity of the author of *Heart of Darkness* by pondering the various names he went by in his life, from Konrad Korzeniowski to Joseph Conrad.

Interlude in the South Atlantic

For Santiago Mutis D.

In the small though comfortable cabin of the second mate of the *Torrens*, a sleek, three-masted 1,234-ton sailing vessel, two men spoke amid the vast silence of a night strewn with stars, the likes of which one sees only in the Southern Hemisphere. The ship, one of the last to carry both cargo and passengers between Australia and London, advances in silence, the wind in its sails, bound for the capital of the Empire.

The second mate, who holds the rank of captain, has found himself obliged to take this job, which pays a salary of 8 pounds a month, owing to the scarcity of positions available to command a ship. He is a man of small stature, with nervous and aristocratic gestures, black hair and eyes of the same color, which do not for a moment stop their searching movement, a strange combination of nearly feminine gestures, proper to a court in the central empires, a steely virility that emanates from his eyes, ready to assume command, and the sharp, well-timbred voice of a man accustomed to making decisions. He speaks an impeccably correct English, though with a heavy Slavic accent that often renders him incomprehensible. The conversation partner of this salty dog with the manners of a count is an agreeable young man whose tie shines with the colors of Cambridge and who, without intending to do so, reveals a solid classical education as he speaks and a pleasant familiarity with the big names in literature of the day. He has entered the second mate's cabin to return several manuscripts the latter had lent him so as to hear, later on, the opinion of a person versed in such matters. The mariner's fine, small hands hold the pages written in a tiny script, practically illegible and of uneven, feverish strokes. After a long silence, the second mate stares at the other man and asks: "What do you think? Did you like it? Do you think it is worth pursuing?" The other man answers with the economical conviction typical of a well-educated Englishman: "Quite." A bell rings signaling the changing of the guard. The second mate of the *Torrens* stands up and, putting on a short jacket of thick nautical flannel, opens the door to let his guest and passenger out ahead of him. He doesn't speak another word except for a curt and cordial "good evening."

After going on watch, the second mate leans back against the railing of the foredeck and looks at the dark and mild disarray of the water. "So," he thinks, "it's worth pursuing." This story of Almaayer, the Dutch businessman devoured by the climate of the archipelago, subjected to the infantile and capricious tyranny of his Malayan wife, his slow fall, and his sordid adventures with the rajah, in whose lands lies the factory entrusted to him by Lingard, will become, one day, the subject of a novel read by innumerable and anonymous readers. A curious fate. Over twenty years at sea and now, all of a sudden, he considers beginning a career as a writer. It isn't the first time that chance led him to such a crossroad. How many others does the uncertain future hold in store for him? By the time his watch is over he has made a decision. Upon arrival in London, he will finish his novel and will send it to an editor. Which one? It doesn't matter. Any editor will do.

He slowly removes his clothing as the cabin's oil lamp sways, causing the ring in the ceiling from which it hangs to squeak. Absorbed, the seaman thinks about what name he should use in his new life: Konrad Korzeniowski? Joseph K. Korzeniowski? The K has something coarse and irritating about it. Better Conrad. Yes. Joseph Conrad.

And that night, under the illuminated dome of the Atlantic Ocean at rest, one of the greatest, most disturbing, and most original storytellers of his and of all times is born.

TRANSLATED BY MARK SCHAFER

Claribel Alegría

Nicaragua
(b. 1924)

———◆◆◆◆◆———

The daughter of a militant anti-interventionist, Claribel Alegría left her native country at an early age and spent most of her life in exile—primarily in El Salvador, Mexico, Chile, and Uruguay. She did not return to Nicaragua until 1979, when the Frente Sandinista de Liberación Nacional (FSLN) overthrew the Somoza dictatorship. In 1943 she moved to the United States, and earned a bachelor's degree from George Washington University. In 1947 she married Darwin J. Flakoll, an American journalist who died in 1992 and with whom she collaborated on numerous projects, mostly reportage, exposés, and anthologies with a left-wing bent, including *New Voices of Hispanic America* (1962), *Nicaragua: La revolución sandinista* (1982), and *Death of Somoza* (1996). Most are collective volumes, assembled in the form of a collage. The technique Alegría and Flakoll employed involves interviewing a wide range of people on a specific subject; they then assemble the material in an engaging fashion, carefully avoiding any editorial intrusion. Her novels include *Ashes of Izalco* (1966), *Sobrevivo* (1978), *Family Album* (1982), and *Luisa in Realityland* (1987). Along with the Mexican Elena Poniatowska, Alegría has perfected the essay as testimonial, which she calls *letras de emergencia*. She puts literature at the service of her strong commitment against injustice and in favor of women's rights. An earlier version of "The Writer's Commitment," whose title announces its overall content, appeared in 1984 in *Fiction International*.

The Writer's Commitment

Political commitment, in my view, is seldom a calculated intellectual strategy. It seems to me more like a contagious disease—athlete's foot, let's say, or typhoid fever—and if you happen to live in a plague area, the chances are excellent that you will come down with it. Commitment is a visceral reaction to the corner of the world we live in and what it has done to us and to the people we know. Albert Camus penned a phrase in "The Myth of Sisyphus" that impressed me profoundly. "If a man believes something to be true yet does not live in accordance with that truth," he said, "that man is a hypocrite."

Each of us writers, I have found, is obsessed with the personal equation

301

and, however successfully he or she camouflages it, is surreptitiously pushing a world view.

"What am I doing here? Where am I going?"

These are the eternal existential—and profoundly political—questions, and the creative writer dedicates his life to communicating the answers he has stumbled across while negotiating the booby traps and barbed wire barricades of this twentieth-century obstacle course.

Let me be unashamedly personal, then. I spent the greater part of my life writing poetry, without the slightest notion that I had an obligation to commit myself literarily or politically to what was happening in my country—El Salvador—or my region—Central America.

There were political antecedents that marked me, of course. Thirty thousand peasants were slaughtered in El Salvador when I was seven years old. I remember with hard-edged clarity when groups of them, their crossed thumbs tied behind their backs, were herded into the National Guard fortress just across the street from my house, and I remember the *coup de grace* shots startling me awake at night. Two years later, I remember just as clearly my father, a Nicaraguan exile, telling me how Anastasio Somoza, with the benediction of the Yankee minister, had assassinated Sandino the night before.

I left El Salvador to attend a U.S. university; I married, had children, and wrote poetry, convinced that Central American dictators—Martínez, Ubico, Carías, Somoza—were as inevitable and irremediable as the earthquakes and electrical storms that scourge my homeland.

The Cuban revolution demonstrated that social and political change was possible in Latin America, but surely the Yankees with their helicopter gunships and Green Berets would never permit such a thing to happen again. Nevertheless Fidel and Che sensitized me to the currents of militant unrest just below the surface of the American *mare nostrum* in the Caribbean. We watched the eddies and whirlpools from Paris and later from Mallorca while I nourished my growing burden of middle-class guilt. What was I doing sitting on the sidelines while my people silently suffered the implacable repression of the Somoza dynasty in Nicaragua and the rotating colonel-presidents in El Salvador? Some of my poems took on an edge of protest, and my husband and I wrote a novel about my childhood nightmare: the 1932 peasant massacre.

I caught the political sickness from the Sandinista revolution. Shortly after Somoza's overthrow in 1979, my husband and I went to Nicaragua for six months to research a book about the historical epic of Sandino and his successors of the FSLN. We were in Paris, on our way home to Mallorca, when we heard of the assassination of Archbishop Oscar Arnulfo Romero, the only Salvadoran figure of international prestige who had served as the voice of the millions of voiceless in my country. In response to that brutal and tragic event, all but two or three of El Salvador's artists and intellectuals made the quiet decision, without so much as consulting each other, to do what we could to try to fill the enormous vacuum left by his death.

Since then, I have found myself writing more and more poems and prose texts that reflect the misery, the injustice, and the repression that reign in my country. I am fully aware of the pitfalls of attempting to defend a transient political cause in what presumes to be a literary work, and I have tried to resolve that dilemma in a roughshod way by dividing my writing into two compartments: the "literary-poetic," if you will, and what I have come to think of as my "crisis journalism."

Political concerns do have a way of creeping into my poetry, however— simply because the Central American political situation is my major obsession, and I have always written poetry under obsession's spur. When I think back, though, I can truly say that my "commitment" to literature has always been, and remains, a simple attempt to make my next poem less imperfect than the last.

But there is something further: in Central America today, crude reality inundates and submerges the ivory tower of "art for art's sake." What avant-garde novelist would dare write a work of imagination in which the Salvadoran people, in supposedly free elections, could only choose between Robert D'Aubuisson, the intellectual author of Monseigneur Romero's assassination and the recognized mentor of the infamous "Squadrons of Death" and José Napoleón Duarte, who, as the nation's highest authority for the greater part of the last four years, has systematically failed to bring the known perpetrators and executors of that sacrilegious deed to justice?

What Hollywood writer four short years ago could have envisioned a script in which all the horrors of Vietnam are being reenacted on the Central American isthmus?

> America, America, God shed his grace on thee,
> and crowned thy good with brotherhood,
> from sea to shining sea.

Can this be the America that sends Huey helicopter gunships, A-37 Dragonflies, and "Puff, the magic dragon" to rain napalm and high explosives on the women, children, and old people in El Salvador's liberated zones, to convert the village of Tenancingo among others into a second Guernica? Is this the nation that christens Somoza's former assassins of the National Guard as "freedom fighters" and "the moral equivalent of the Founding Fathers" and sends them across the Nicaraguan border night after night to spread their message of democracy by slaughtering peasants, raping their women, and mowing down defenseless children while blowing up the cooperatives and health clinics and schools the Nicaraguans have so painfully constructed over the past six years?

How has America become entrapped in this morass of blood and death? An American President, John F. Kennedy, made a prophetic statement twenty-five years ago. His words were: "Those who make peaceful evolution impossible, make violent revolution inevitable."

Anastasio Somoza, Jr., made peaceful evolution impossible in Nicaragua, so the Nicaraguan people had no choice but to overthrow him. Again today, as it has so often in the past, the U.S. government has allied itself with the forces in El Salvador who make peaceful evolution impossible: the forces that have put an abrupt end to the limping agrarian reform program, have encouraged a recrudescence of the Squadrons of Death— and have forced a suspension of peace negotiations with the FMLN-FDR.

The burning question for all of us today is: how will America find its way out of this bloody swamp?

Central American reality is incandescent, and if there be no place there for "pure art" and "pure literature" today, then I say so much the worse for pure art and pure literature. I do not know a single Central American writer who is so careful of his literary image that he sidesteps political commitment at this crucial moment in our history, and were I to meet one, I would refuse to shake his hand.

It matters little whether our efforts are admitted into the sacrosanct precincts of literature. Call them newspapering, call them pamphleteering, call them a shrill cry of defiance. My people, sixty percent of whom earn less than eleven dollars per month, know that only through their efforts today will it be possible for their children and grandchildren to eventually have equal opportunity to learn the alphabet and thus gain access to the great literature of the world: a basic human right that has been denied most of their elders.

TRANSLATED BY THE AUTHOR

José Donoso

Chile

(1924–1996)

One of his country's most oustanding writers, José Donoso is known as a master of both the novel and the short story. The Princeton graduate's first stories were published in 1950 in his alma mater's literary magazine, *MSS*, and, five years later in Santiago, Chile, he produced the well-received *Veraneo y otros cuentos*. *Coronation* (1957), a book about social disarray that received the 1962 Faulkner Foundation prize for the best Latin American novel, competes for status as Donoso's masterpiece with *The Obscene Bird of Night* (1970), a baroque, nightmarish narrative reminiscent of the paintings of Goya and Hieronymous Bosch, about a deceiving deaf-mute protagonist seeking refuge in an asylum for old women. Donoso later moved to Spain, but he returned to Santiago in the 1980s, at the end of General Augusto Pinochet's reign. Among his other acclaimed works are *El Charleston* (1960), *This Sunday* (1966), *Hell Has No Limits* (1966), *Sacred Families* (1973), *A House in the Country* (1978), *Curfew* (1986), and the groundbreaking *TriQuarterly Anthology of Latin American Literature* (1969). As an essayist he devoted his energy to political commentaries and to literary memoirs, like *The Boom in Spanish-American Literature: A Personal History* (1978). The following essay, "Ithaca: The Impossible Return," in which Donoso again evaluates the relevance of the literary Boom and, in particular, his own role in it, was written in English and published in 1982 in the *City College Papers* in New York.

Ithaca: The Impossible Return

To be here at all, facing an audience that is sure to expect a learned argumentation in favor of or against solid intellectual convictions and theories, makes me feel slightly uneasy. I possess little or no academic learning beyond the kind that a gentleman of my years with a college education naturally has: I'm a writer who has "small Latin and less Greek." Mine is a scrappy, unorganized mind, wholly subjective, completely arbitrary, a kind of warehouse that happily stores all sorts of apparently useless odds and ends, and rejects what it shouldn't reject. Ideologies and cosmogonies are alien to me: they can be amusing, even challenging, but their life is too short and they are too soon proved wrong, their place immediately taken by another explanation of the world. I read a lot, mostly novels, memoirs, literary biographies, but I don't know how to crack a book open with those formidable instruments that are the works of critics. I know their names, of course, Lacan and Chomsky, Barthes and Dérrida, and a little of what they have to say, but I prefer to leave their use in the hands of scholars who can surely do this sort of thing with much more flair than I could ever hope to achieve. I'm more interested in the *how* than in the *why*, that tyrannical demand for explanations which reduces phenomena to the rational. Like Nietzsche, I believe that the question *why* is the seed of all conflict and nihilism, and that Socrates, who gave that question the currency in the spell of which we still abide, was really the first decadent. No real, unequivocal history exists. What we believe to be history is no more than an accumulation of conflicting interpretations; the power of the rational lies in its nonrational sources. I'd rather read Klee and the letters of Gauguin on art, or Flaubert and Virginia Woolf on the *how* of the literary endeavor: the thing itself, and the how of the thing—not the consequences or the meaning of the thing—are, to me, what is really exciting, rather than all-encompassing explanations. Thus, my convictions, political, aesthetic, and philosophical, never achieve the status of convictions since they waver so, and tend to be contradictory.

Yet I do possess one kind of knowledge which scholars can come by only secondhand: the knowledge that springs from the experience of writing books. I'm a novelist, only tenuously an intellectual, though I couldn't be farther from the coy anti-intellectualism of the guts and muscle, and slice-of-life literary persuasion, still so prestigious in Spanish and Latin American writing. I can claim that, as an inventor of fiction, I live primarily within the world of metaphor, a world which is never wholly transparent though it can be so radiant that it causes blisters. I think of the world of literature as the open world of the tentative, of hesitation, rarely one of assertion, and believe that the universe of literature is not one of meaning but of being. I thus cringe from formulating general ideas in connection with literature—let me be specific and say *novels*, which is what I know most about—because novels to me are, if anything, the art of the particular: if they are literature at all they will never unveil the secret of themselves as metaphor, no matter how much you tease them with theory. For metaphor exists first and foremost in and of itself, an object whose essence is placed outside the world of meaning, not a sign to be substituted for another kind of notation. (Such as it appears in fiction, metaphor is like a palimpsest of meanings. Isn't it?)

Yet it seems useless to pretend there are no wires electrically connecting these metaphors among themselves and to other phenomena, thus tempting us to place them in some kind of order. Things literary perversely happen with a symmetry, or a regularity, facing which one has to look at least twice. Certain intervals appear which are difficult to ignore. For at least a while, certain forms in certain places share tone, diction, theme, scope: schools sprout. Then they wither. And periods of drought set in, inviting hypotheses to explain them. Metaphor, then, no matter how irritated one can become by theory overpowering the created object, is not an isolated occurrence, but a shared experience glittering with many, often contradictory, facets.

Exile—and I shall use this word, perhaps inappropriately, meaning both political and voluntary absence from one's own country—exile, then, is one of those knots of live-wires, a shared, a collective experience, from which I think the greater part of Latin American contemporary fiction derives its strength. It is sure to become the great theme of the novel of the eighties, once all this pain and rage is hopefully remembered in tranquility: but not yet. We're too busy surviving, being confused and beset by doubts, to undertake that task just yet and metabolize it into metaphor. But living isolated, as an expatriate in Spain in the sixties and seventies, remote from the shattering experiences of those who stayed behind in my country—or in my continent, for that matter—is the strongest collective experience I have undergone, no matter how paradoxical this may seem. I have lived away from Chile for seventeen years now, and gone back only twice, for a month each time—I must hasten to add, lest I'm taken for a hero, that I could have returned any day I wished to, since neither persons nor ideologies banned me—with the result that the greater part of my work has been written in Spain, a country I feel few cultural bonds with. What really surprises me once I come to think of it, is that I'm far from being an exception. Looking around me at the major Latin American novelists of my generation, I find that every single one of them has written the most important part of his *oeuvre* away from his country. Cortázar wrote *Hopscotch, Los premios* and his best short stories in Paris. García Márquez wrote *One Hundred Years of Solitude* not in his native Columbia, but in Mexico. Vargas Llosa wrote *The Time of the Hero* in Paris, *Captain Pantoja and the Special Service* in Barcelona, *The Green House* in England, large chunks of *Conversation in the Cathedral* in Barcelona and elsewhere, and I hear he's recently been writing in Brazil. Roa Bastos wrote practically everything in political exile in Buenos Aires. Carlos Fuentes has lived abroad for so long and in so many different places that it is impossible to chart the itinerary of his books. Cabrera Infante has written everything either in Brussels or in London: he's also a political exile. As regards Manuel Puig, he wrote his first three novels in Buenos Aires, but after that I believe all his other novels were written abroad. Speaking for myself, I wrote my first two collections of short stories and my first novel in Chile. My next two novels were written in Mexico, and all the rest of my books in Spain.

Are we, then, a generation of cosmopolites, of expatriates, rooted into new soil? I think the contrary is true. On the one hand, we are evidently wanderers: I belong to a floating community of Latin American rootless novelists, all of them ailing of this infirmity which is our strange relationship with our own countries: our inability to live or write there. This certitude provided the only feeling of community I have experienced for a long while. The advent of Salvador Allende, first, and then the irruption of General Pinochet on the scene, reversed things in my mind, and made me realize there was still another level to the idea of community. I found that the old bond, which I had thought dead, was still alive. On the other hand, although we have lived abroad for such extended periods, the Latin American novelists of my generation all obsessively write about our own countries, or of countries of the imagination closely resembling those we grew up in. If the Latin American living abroad becomes an expatriate, his literature never does. As Gertrude Stein said of another distinguished generation of writers living abroad: "It all happened in Paris, but it was an American experience." Latin American literature, especially the novel now in its maturity, no matter how cosmopolitan the writer, always stays pretty close to the motherland. In many ways it's an Oedipal literature, guilty, dependent, an ambivalent literature of love and of accusation, yearning and damning at the same time. It is in fact probable that in most cases this very acceptance of ambivalence has given the contemporary Latin American novel its stature. The novelists who stayed home did not recognize the guilt of incest and accepted it without questioning the nature and consequences of this love. Plato talks of the artist who is only able to render the "sensory appearances of the material world," as contrasted to those who go beyond that: we made the voyage and went beyond sensory appearances. Those who stayed behind mostly reported only the given truth.

How have we gone beyond it, these contemporary wanderers of the Latin American novel? We refuse to live at home. We reject the idea of writing about the contingent problems of our countries in the present day. We are critical. Sometimes unkind. We accept foreign influences. We become involved in things not national. We do not write about the countries we now live in, or about the circumstances of our exile.

Yet something quite strange happens to the writing of these wanderers: we obsessively write about our homelands. It is as if we were substituting imaginary maps of our countries, within which we *can* live without guilt, for our actual countries, where we can't live. The details of the past, transformed into an imaginary present, flood the mind and cover pages. In my opinion, this establishes what I want, for the time being, to call the novel of *absence*, which I would like to propose as one of the defining elements of the Latin American novel of my generation.

Sometimes, it is true, Latin American novelists don't go back to their countries for political reasons. But one must accept the fact that the political radicalism—now, in any case, notoriously in abeyance—which is supposed to keep most Latin American novelists away, is a position taken after, not before, they become expatriates by choice. Cabrera Infante and Roa Bastos are two exceptions. Some left their native Ithacas, like Odysseus, with the purpose of fighting in the great ideological wars of the world and thus transcend the meagre experiences they found within their own boundaries. Most of us left because our little island offered paltry intellectual stimulation. All of us, in any case, left in order to do, in one way or another, what Cavafy advises his traveler to do:

> Stop at Phoenician markets,
> and purchase fine merchandise,
> mother of pearl and corals, amber and ebony,
> and pleasurable perfumes of all kinds.
> Buy as many voluptuous perfumes as you can;
> visit hosts of Egyptian cities,
> to learn and learn from those who have knowledge.

Yet it turns out that no matter how long we stay away from our countries—ten, twenty years—the only "voluptuous good" we acquire during absences which become no longer voluntary, but which habit makes compulsive, is the *guilt of absence*. Our roots do not sink deep into foreign soil. What we learn from Egyptian sages is mostly academic, worldly, never "voluptuous," that is to say, never related to pleasure and pain and love, which would shoot these experiences into the mainstream of our lives and thus find their way into our books. We write as if from a no man's land, rejecting the obligations of home, rejecting the voluptuousness of abroad, rooted more than anything in an absence that is not nostalgic. Unlike Odysseus in Calypso's island, we do not *"weep by the shore where so oft, consumed with tears, sighs and pains he fixed his gaze upon the sterile sea, weeping bitterly."*

What is it, then, that we do if we don't weep by the shore? One must acknowledge that the attitude of Odysseus was not an enlightened one. He wanted to go back to his Ithaca, barren and un-beautiful, and to his no longer young wife, while nymphs and princesses vied for his favors. T. E. Lawrence, in his Translator's note to his *Odyssey*, after saying of it: *"Crafty, exquisite, homogeneous . . . whatever great art may be, these are not its attributes,"* concedes that *"it is the oldest book worth reading for its story and the first novel of Europe."* He calls Odysseus *"that cold-blooded egotist"* and adds that *"it is sorrowful to believe that these were really Homer's heroes and exemplars."* I would add that there was a side to Odysseus which was very much "the common man with commonplace aspirations": a wily man of action, not a reflective man for whom the experience of the voyage, the first and still the definitive voyage of our literature, would have been fine material and the best solace.

Yet, far from our countries, not wanting to go back, or to relinquish the experience of a voyage which, although it has become a habit, we do not allude to it in our books, we never write under the spell of feeling of loss, sighing to be in England now that April's there, so to speak. Nor do we bewail the more general loss of Keats:

> The day is gone and all its sweets are gone
> sweet voice, sweet lips, soft hand and softer breast.
> Warm breath, light whisper, tender semi-tone . . .

You will never find this note of nostalgia in our writing. For the point is that we are aware that we have lost our capacity to return home, no matter how much we write about our countries. We know it is advisable to stay away; our Ithacas are stifling and provincial. We know that within their bounds literary vanity and/or jealousy can kill. Above all we realize that the demand for public action is such that it can imperil and destroy our identities by making us "public" and our writing "useful."

Little of our international experience, however, occupies any space in our work. We have not recorded exile in any of its forms. No one, like Henry James in England, has given up his national identity as a writer, although I hear that Cortázar has become a French citizen and Cabrera Infante a British subject. However French, however English the Latin American writer, we all, without exception, in our major work, obsessively write about our own Ithacas using the detritus of our different vernaculars still floating in our memories: in order to keep our Ithacas at a safe distance we recycle them into metaphors. There is no foreign locale, no use of a foreign language or of a different vernacular, no creation of the international literary Latin American Spanish . . . nothing to be equated with the importance of French in Beckett, say, or of places like Spain in Hemingway, or Paris in Gertrude Stein. Cavafy warned us, "*Always keep Ithaca fixed in your mind.*"

We do, obsessively, and I'd say, guiltily. Our literature is not "committed" to the struggles of our countries. It was the past generation of Latin American novelists, those who never became expatriates, that wrote the useful novels, the didactic novels, immersed in struggle.

How is it that we don't? All interviewers ask the same question. Why do we not take part in the social and political struggles of our countries? In the Argentine, the police ferrets out writers and persecutes and imprisons those who refuse to play up the military. In Uruguay, a whole generation of writers was wiped out. In Chile, when Pinochet came along, a huge exodus of *literati* took place: the terror of those first years was not only the terror of being killed, it was also the problem of being intolerant of an intolerable situation. Things have changed, they say, in Chile. Writers, even some known to have been communists, are now returning with permission from the Junta, as the cases of Alfonso Alcalde and Gonzalo Rojas have recently proved. But if Cavafy tells his traveler to *". . . pray that the road is long . . . ,"* he also reminds him that *"to arrive there is your ultimate goal."* How can this be done? How to keep away from collective action in Chile? How can a writer continue writing within his own limitations, those which define him, when tyrannized by the immediate need for action on any front, with any weapons? Better to keep away for the time being. Not a heroic attitude, although most of us share it to some extent. But who said that writers were supposed to be exemplary human beings?

What we have tried to avoid by not going back is not action itself, but writing as action. This may be difficult for a contemporary American to grasp as an "obligation" since it is not an American tradition. There's evidently no "public" side in the writing of Cheever, or Updike, or Truman Capote, and no guilt because there isn't. But there is an exceedingly long tradition in Latin America of the writer considered "serious" only if there is a public, useful, didactic, civic side to his writing, and if he leads an exemplary life of action. Our tradition of the President-poet, of the diplomat-man-of-letters, of the politician-novelist is a much respected one even today.

There is yet another tradition, the one of exile: Andrés Bello, the Venezuelan man of letters living in exile in Chile and in London, wrote his *Ode to the Agriculture of the Torrid Zone* to delve into the prosaic realities of the New America. The Argentinian José Mármol, living in political exile in Montevideo, wrote his novel *Amalia* as a tract against his enemy, the dictator Rosas. The Chilean Blest-Gana wrote *Martín Rivas* as a diplomat in Paris, where he eventually died, as a study of the rising middle class of his country. Miguel Angel Asturias wrote his diatribe against dictators while in exile in Paris.

I feel that our dependence for our source-material and our diction derives so compulsively from our own countries due more than anything to an overriding feeling of guilt for not being connected with action. This is a romantic tradition. Lord Byron wrote to Lady Melbourne: "I prefer the talents of action—of war, of the senate, even of science—to all the speculations of our mere dreams . . ." The exile of the English Romantic poets stood for many things: their stance flaunted conventionality and stood for the liberal ideas of the times. There was even something exemplary about them all dying abroad: Keats in Rome, Byron in Missolonghi, Shelley in the Gulf of La Spezia—when he put out to sea in a storm aboard his yacht the *Ariel*, and Trelawney went out to look for his body in Byron's yacht called, in an uncanny way which seems to tie all these themes together, the *Bolivar*.

I'd venture to say that it was in order to escape that tyrannical superego demanding exemplary lives linked to action through literature, to write useful books pointing to exemplary public lives, to be concerned with the immediate and put it down on paper, that most of us took abode in countries abroad, from where we could manage our perspectives and be as private as we chose. I think it is this lack of the immediacy of the pressing public reality, this perspective, the time and the void for the imagination to grow in and to preen and prattle and prance, to be free and subjective, that has given the novel of my generation, written in un-useful and un-heroic style, its character and its stature.

In the previous generation it was the poets who fled and made Latin American poetry internationally renowned, not being respected at home until they came back with their heads wreathed in foreign laurels. When I went to teach in Iowa in the mid-sixties and suggested a seminar on contemporary Latin American fiction in translation, they made the counterproposal that I give one on Latin American poetry: it was so much more distinguished. Rubén Darío, Gabriela Mistral, Octavio Paz, Pablo Neruda, César Vallejo, Vicente Huidobro, were all invoked. It was, indeed, a most brilliant galaxy of writers.

All of them lived abroad for extended periods of their lives and were defined by that fact. Rubén Darío fled Nicaragua and became as European as Henry James became English. In Chile, the tradition of the expatriate poets is a legend. Vicente Huidobro not only lived in France, but wrote in French, publishing in such *avant-garde* magazines as *Nord-Sud*, side by side with Apollinaire and Tristan Tzara. Gabriela Mistral led as wandering an existence abroad as Rilke's. Their language was their only homeland.

The case of Neruda is slightly different. No writer ever professed to be more attached to his Ithaca than he. His first books were grey in tone, subjective and personal, in a way defined by the circumstances and size of Chile in the early twenties. Then he left for Ceylon, Burma, Indonesia, where his perspective shifted abruptly and he wrote *Residence on Earth*: in this shift, we can at once perceive the meaning of "the voyage," because it was then that Neruda gained an altitude and a speed of flight which he thereafter never lost. This wise traveler returned to Ithaca laden with beautiful objects. He stayed home only six months. Then he left again, this time for Buenos Aires, thence to the Spain of the Civil War, thence to the Mexico of the great muralists. I believe, however, that it was after his return to Chile, many years later, when for political reasons he had to live incognito, an exile in his own country until he was forced to escape for another five years, that he came to full fruition: in political exile, this time, all his previous absences seem to have *set*, so to speak, once and for all, into the monumental metaphor of the *Canto general*. It is an impassioned reconstruction in *absence*, of Ithaca. In *absence*, he does not weep by the shore, like Odysseus: out of the void in time and space grows that huge metaphor that he substitutes for the lost world and fills his absence with it.

If I compare the semantic field of the word *absence*, in English, to that of the word *ausencia*, in Spanish, which is what I mean, I discover that both semantic fields do not coincide. Absence, in English, carries, I think, little or no connotation of sorrow or loss: I'd say it is an emotionally inert word. In Spanish, however, its equivalent, *ausencia*, carries with it an almost elegiac semantic field. It is an emotionally charged word, rich with connotations of dreaminess, of guilt and punishment, of sleep, of recall, even of madness. I must hasten to correct myself, then, and explain that I'm speaking of the contemporary Latin American novel as a novel of *ausencia*, not of absence. I also detect in the Spanish word a sort of *will to stay away*, a determination taken, pulling the word out of shape, then to one side. But it also suggests a sorrow for staying away, pulling it out of shape to the other side: it establishes a conflict, and contains an implicit desire to return, and an implicit acknowledgment that it is impossible to return. This tension pulls the word apart in such a way as to leave a sort of void in the middle of it, filled with our guilt for not returning to be diplomat-poets, politician-novelists, senator-men-of-letters, President-translators of Dante, engaged in useful and admirable struggles, thrust into prison, tortured, persecuted, impoverished. Therefore, in that void, we reconstruct countries of the imagination where in *ausencia* we can live as we are, without guilt. It is from this unresolved ambivalence of guilt that the best novels of my generation spring.

What language should we use to write the novel of *ausencia?* None of us has turned into a Nabokov or a Beckett. To illustrate this all-important point of language let me talk a little about Guillermo Cabrera Infante's recent *Infante's Inferno*. This novel of *ausencia* does not possess the literary glory of *One Hundred Years of Solitude*, or of *Hopscotch*, or even Cabrera's earlier *Three Trapped Tigers*, where the vernacular of each country—recalled and re-created abroad—undergoes the mystical transmutation of becoming the metaphor itself. In these novels the vernacular simply *is*, it cannot and need not be explained in order to be the flesh of the metaphor: its semantic field either reaches you or it doesn't. *Infante's Inferno* is a long monotonous narrative dealing with the amours of the young author with a seemingly endless parade of Cuban females who barely achieve identity. The spontaneous Cuban vernacular of *Three Trapped Tigers* is very far in the past. If language is a form of action, the writer must continuously limber up for it, if he doesn't want to lose his power to handle it. Cabrera seems no longer fit in that sense. The vernacular is no longer the star, the novel itself. But he obsessively reconstructs an autobiographical Havana detained in the past, packed with minutiae. A void of time is placed between the period of the narrative and the late seventies, *when* he is writing. That void in time becomes equated with the void in space separating Havana and London, *where* he is writing. He can't go back to Ithaca because the angry, bearded Poseidon banished him from his island. This space-time void is filled with a strange silence. It is the sad silence of the lost vernacular, the absence of a valid Cuban Spanish which made *Tres tristes tigres* what it is. This Cuban Spanish of a certain class and a certain age was the marrow and the nerve itself of the novel, the code which it was written. In *Infante's Inferno* something quite different happens: it is written mostly in flat, colorless Spanish, punctured by Cabrera's usual puns. When he does use the vernacular, it is either in dialogue, or more interestingly, seen *from the outside*: Cabrera has to account for it and explain it, using it as in between inverted commas. These inverted commas define the territory of Cabrera's *ausencia*. As an example, he carefully explains what the Cuban idiom *amor trompero* means: "Amor trompero, cuantas veo, cuantas quiero. Hace tiempo que no lo oigo pero no he olvidado lo que quiere decir." The whole of *Infante's Inferno* is the anecdote of "amor trompero," but not the metaphor for it, since the vernacular is lacking, and it and everything becomes explained from the outside. The homeland of a writer is not really a place, but a language. Not even a language, but a certain section, a fraction of that language with which one identifies. The return voyage to Ithaca is an effort to regain one's vernacular, which the intervening silence of years and space has rendered powerless, and plug into it again, even when one lives abroad.

It seems to me that much of the power of the Latin American novel of my generation, written in *ausencia*, comes from the monumental effort of reconstructing and regaining one's vernacular, or inventing a vernacular that will take its place and possess a charged semantic field. Words *are* time and space if they are to be timeless. When used in *ausencia*, that time and that space placed in an order or perspective provided by distance become alive, and they form that structure which we call fiction.

The case of Manuel Puig may clarify things further. His is an artificial form of the vernacular. He claims to have always been an exile from reality, living in the fantasy world of films. Puig's Argentinian Spanish is not an Argentinian of *his* personal reality. It grows out of the subculture of the old films, out of fashion magazines, out of soap operas. Puig, as an individual, does not share this language. He stands at a distance from its mindlessness. He has lived away from his country for a long time. Yet he cannot use anything but what I'd call an artificial vernacular—not a "natural" one as in the case of Cabrera, or a "cultural" one as in the case of Cortázar's *Hopscotch*—with artifical origins: this language is Puig's metaphor. Without its avowed artificiality, a certain world of the mind—and of an Argentinian reality of a space and time now vanished—could not be conveyed. I'd venture to say that even when he is not being Argentinian, this world of the mind is conveyed by means of the artificial Argentinian vernacular that he has invented, which defines a space and time. In Puig's *ausencia*, Ithaca is reached by means of an ironic code that is not the writer's own language, not one that embodies his own values: it is what I'd call a language of *disguise*. I'd venture to say that all of Puig's fiction is created by means of disguise. He pretends that it is all true, that it is the only language possible, but we know this is not true for him, and furthermore, the whole point is that we must be aware that it is not. Heidegger said when he was writing about Nietzsche: "The greatness of a thinker is measured in terms of what he did not know he was putting into his work." I wonder if Puig knows how much compassion he puts into his novels by means of using this disguise of an artificial vernacular. And compassion is important since it is a rare commodity in the pyrotechnical display of Latin American fiction: in Puig, the time–space void can be equated with the vernacular that is pure disguise, and disguise is a metaphor for indefinite *ausencia*. Puig can go on writing novels indefinitely by means of the false vernacular he has invented. He is, however, not the only one: Mario Vargas Llosa, in *Captain Pantoja and the Special Service* and in *Aunt Julia and the Scriptwriter* wrote two novels of disguise with a somewhat different result. These two authors seem to me oddly symmetrical in their literary endeavors.

To wind up, let me talk a little about my own experience during these long seventeen years of *ausencia*. To quote Cavafy again:

> Ithaca has given you a beautiful voyage.
> Without her you would have never taken the road.
> But she has nothing more to give you,
>
> And if you find her poor, Ithaca has not cheated
>   you.
> With the great wisdom you have gained, with so
>   much experience,
> You must surely by then have understood what
>   Ithaca means.

The stanzas are moving. The reasoning excellent, as always in Cavafy. As always, he points to intellectual pleasure, besides sensual pleasure—he tends to equate the two—as the greatest of gains. The voyage has made it possible—and that is the reason why it is not important if Ithaca is found to be poor—for us to understand not only our own Ithaca but, more important, the meaning of all Ithacas, which is what the traveler ostensibly in quest of voluptuous goods was really after.

The most important thing about the voyage, then—in other words about *ausencia*—is acquiring not a limited experience, but an experience that can be expanded into knowledge by means of a return to Ithaca, which will make the meaning of all Ithacas accessible. I myself, as a Latin American writer who stays away although he could go back, have to accept that one's essential knowledge is to be limited to the singular case of our own Ithaca, in contrast to the universal Ithaca of the completed return. I must begin by accepting the ambivalence: the return is stifling—I will find it poor— but it will give me full knowledge of all Ithacas. The acceptance of return, of the particular *experience* of my own historical circumstances, is also the recuperation of a vernacular.

Return would be easy in my case if I felt a moral, social, or political obligation. But not feeling those urges is a limitation of my personality which I cannot ignore. I can do nothing more effective for my community than writing, and writing about my own limited universe. Now that seventeen years have gone by in *ausencia*, I find that I'm asking myself whether I can keep away from my country any longer, and yearning, in other words, for my lost vernacular. My first two volumes of stories and my first novel were written in Chile in a "natural" realistic language that never questioned its validity. Then, for years, I became entangled with a huge novel, a *summa* of my Chilean experience, getting right to the bottom of my language: but no matter how much I worked I couldn't place things in perspective and the novel was throttling me. I thus spent years in Chile accomplishing nothing at all. Then I left Chile. The year following my flight, in Mexico, I wrote two novels, *Hell Has No Limits* and *This Sunday*: Chilean locale, Chilean characters, Chilean language: none of it questioned, but the sudden, and much needed experience of *ausencia* enabled me to write. In a way, though, both novels fall into the tradition of serious, useful realistic fiction: they are true, they stuck to the examination of class distinctions, there was an easy code to crack. But the years were going by and I was still obsessively at work at my labyrinthine *The Obscene Bird of Night*. I did not finish it until 1969, six years after leaving Chile. I think that novel both embodied all of my Chilean experience, and exhausted it. It is my contribution to the novel of *ausencia*.

After *The Obscene Bird of Night*, something quite odd began to happen. I began to become unable to use the unquestioned, "natural" Chilean-Spanish vernacular which, no matter how literary it became, I had used without qualms up until then. Chilean diction, tone, vocabulary, syntax, words, and turns of phrases that expressed experiences alien to me, especially those which were being formed during the Unidad Popular, seemed so odd that I, indeed, felt *ausente*. Even the use of the old vernacular I had grown up with, and perhaps even helped to create, seemed, now that so much time had gone by, unmanageable on the written page. I was living in Spain. But academic Spanish, or even the Spanish of the streets and everyday life—the Spanish that my very young daughter spoke to me, in fact—was just as foreign, just as unmanageable for me as was Chilean Spanish. I was living, then, within the silent limbo of *ausencia*. So I wrote *The Boom in Spanish American Literature: A Personal History* which, being a memoir, did not require anything more committed than a clear style.

There was, then, no language for me to write in. What I did was to try the language of disguise: I wrote *Sacred Families: Three Novellas*, in pseudo-Catalan Spanish, about Catalan people similar to the people I knew all over the world.

What to do next? *The Obscene Bird of Night* was inscribed in the group of large *summas* written by novelists from all over Latin America, who, each using his own vernacular, in *ausencia*, created whole countries of the imagination: its size, moreover, pointed to a certain period in time, now completely over. What I had to do was to get out of the linguistic limbo I was trapped in. I applied to the Guggenheim Foundation for a grant to return to Allende's Chile for a year in order to verify how bad my relations with Chilean Spanish were, and what I could do about them. I wanted to write a musical comedy about the Bavarian Romantic painter Rugendas who painted and lived in Chile at the beginning of the nineteenth century, and recorded all the popular *types* of the recently born nation. After that, and as part of my project, I meant to write a novel about what it was like to produce a musical comedy about Rugendas in Chile during Allende's time. It was an ambitious and interesting project, and I was given the grant. But then along came Pinochet, so I naturally gave up my trip to Chile and stayed in Spain. It was during this most horrifying period of *ausencia*, in the anguish of those first years, that *A House in the Country* began to grow out of what was by now a huge time–space void resulting in a sort of linguistic schizophrenia. The new novel could not, of course, be written *about* experience that not only I had not undergone, but that I was separated from for so many years. But at least on some levels the new novel could touch upon ideas and emotions that I had a right to feel and think, even though I had been neither a victim nor a witness of the terror. I could not use Chilean characters because I no longer knew what they were like. Or Chilean locales, which I'd lost the *bouquet* of. Or Chilean vernacular, which, by now, had become foreign to me without my acquiring a new one. From the desperate void of my *ausencia* sprang the whole travesty of *disguise* in *A House in the Country*. Diction in disguise, locale in disguise, characters in disguise, problems in disguise. It became the only way to solve the problem of writing a novel about my feeling for what had happened during my *ausencia*. This is what I think I did. But there is much in that novel—and some say they are the best parts—which, as Heidegger said, I did not know I was putting in. The imagination was let loose by means of its many fancy dresses, and the metaphor was created.

Fancy dress or not, on one level it would be a return to Ithaca: a useful, committed novel, a novel to teach and discuss, a novel with a "public face" within the old Latin American tradition. Yet not only that. I blush to confess that I hoped to make the problem of a tragic Chile in fancy dress a metaphor for all our Ithacas, and thus, for the first time in my life, I consciously chose to be an exemplary writer. A little bit absurd to my mind, but I realized it underwrote the guilt of my long years abroad, and gave my *ausencia* some sort of meaning. Besides, it did something else for me: it helped me to avoid the existential problem of what to do with my life-language, with my language-life, which was solved in that book.

Now I am again in a linguistic limbo. *A House in the Country* was published during the last month of 1978. This is early 1980. What have I been up to in the meantime? Could I wait it out in Madrid, with its penetrating idiomatic Spanish eroding the credibility of the remnants of my Chilean Spanish? I did use my Chilean vernacular, with a vengeance, in my spoken Spanish. But on paper it was impossible: it was blank, bereft of connotations, a semantic field lying, by now, in waste.

I am now on my way to Chile to see how things look there. I want to verify which of the conflicting tales are true. But also, and for me a much more important thing, to find out whether I can feel that the Chilean language is not a kind of *fancy dress*, as unfortunately I feel now. I feel it as totally alien as I feel Academic Spanish, another disguise, as *madrileño* street-Spanish is a disguise. I don't want to spend the rest of my life caught in linguistic travesty.

Meanwhile, in this quandary, having for the present soothed my conscience with the knowledge that, whatever *A House in the Country* is, and I hope it may be many things, at least it grew out of an emotion that was fully committed to an experience. I began to cast about for what to do next, since I'm of the persuasion that one doesn't write a book in order to say something, but to find out what one has to say. I have assumed, for the moment, disguise as a necessity while I solve other matters. I am writing a series of novellas which, collected, are to be called *Four Traditional Experiments*. They are four short, unrelated novels, written each in a different form that I've never tried before and for which I feel no particular concern or preference: an erotic novel, a political novel, a thriller, and a science fiction novella.

I tried my hand, first of all, with the erotic novella. Immediately, without even being conscious of what I was doing, all the disguises urged themselves upon me. I remembered an old collection of Spanish magazines which I had spent all one summer reading, while my wife looked down on me because she was absorbed in Marcuse. But the far away memory of those magazines suddenly sprang to my rescue: the new novella was to take place in Madrid, in the 1920s; it was not to be straight erotica but tongue-in-cheek, following a tradition of popular *madrileño* fiction, now completely forgotten, but which is nevertheless interesting and atmospheric; Felipe Trigo, Caballero Audaz, Pedro Mata, Alberto Insúa. In about two months I wrote *La misteriosa desaparición de la marquesita de Loria*, which will be published when I return to Spain in April, with all the news from Ithaca. The next novella will be about how Lenin, in 1908 in Paris, got money to publish one of his many clandestine papers and will also be comic. I can't predict what the result will be. I know, from writing *La misteriosa desaparición de la marquesita de Loria*, that comedy is necessary because it is another protective layer of disguise. *Taratuta*, this Lenin novel, will require a lot of historical research, but the idea is enticing because I'll write about a historical reality different from my own, thus using another layer of fancy dress which at this point I find necessary to be able to write. But what shall I do for the actual language of *Taratuta?* I don't really know. I don't want to live for the rest of my life in *fancy dress*. I'd like to feel under my feet the secure soil of a vernacular in which to write. Even if I do go back to live in Chile, will I be able to assume the language I left in a completely different stage of its evolution, so many years ago? I don't know. I do know that the novel of *ausencia*, written in voluntary or political exile, which was the experience of my generation, has evolved into something else that I can't yet figure out. I know that it was at least as enthralling as the poetry of *ausencia*, a generation before. There are hordes of Argentinians in exile in Europe, lawyers washing dishes, professors of philosophy from Uruguay tending bars, long queues to get working permits, marriages broken up, Chileans like me who have lost or are in danger of losing their identity, architects making *empanadas* to sell, or little, unattractive bead necklaces no longer in fashion, *batik*, toys, pictures, anything. I know the political uncertainty, the terror that suddenly strikes when news of more killing suddenly arrives, and the ambivalent guilt of the few who have been able to make a go of it at their own thing, the lack of security, of faith in everything but especially in words, the frustration of being considered fifth-class citizens in France, of hating Swedish weather notwithstanding the security offered, the gradual loss of everything . . . yes, I've known this sorry crowd in Eastern and Western Europe alike.

I've begun to wonder, though I'm no political exile and can go back to Chile whenever I choose, whether this rootless community is not the only community I really belong to now . . . whether it is not my new Ithaca. But the language, the swear-words, the love-words that carry pictures and memories with them, which one didn't put there on purpose, what is its language, besides that of rage and frustration? I don't know.

But eventually I will perhaps find out. Just as it was necessary, at one point, to leave Chile, and introduce a distance, an *ausencia*, a linguistic silence so I could write—an experience shared with so many novelists of my generation—I may have to go back to the first Ithaca I came from in order to write about the uprooted and lonely people, younger than I, to

whose breed, with its debilitated national identity and lost national vernacular, I now seem to belong. Yes, absent from the experience itself of
being adrift, tucked away in Ithaca, I may be able to find the language to
write out their, our story, and write about my long voyage without the
need of disguise.

Sebastián Salazar Bondy

Peru

(1924–1965)

Although Sebastián Salazar Bondy made his living from journalism, his expertise lay in the arts. He was not only an art critic but also an anthropologist, poet, novelist, playwright, and essayist. Despite spending 1947 to 1951 in Buenos Aires, he produced the majority of his work upon returning to his native Peru, where he was a college professor, editor of *El Comercio,* and director of the Institute of Contemporary Art. Many of Bondy's pieces focus on pre-Hispanic Peru and various facets of art, such as his *Arte milenario de Perú* (1958), *Del hueso tallado al arte abstracto* (1960), *Cerámica peruana prehispánica* (1964), and *Lima: Su moneda y su cerámica* (1964). He also compiled *Poesía quechua* (1964) and adapted the Incan *Ollantay* to the modern stage. Toward the end of his life, Salazar Bondy traveled widely—to China, Russia, Japan, Cuba, Mexico, Italy, and Yugoslavia—and his journalistic pieces serve as evidence of his globetrotting adventures. His most important book, *Lima la horrible* (1964), which includes the essay "Aberrant Nostalgia," is a social and cultural critique of Peru's capital and of the neocolonialist mentality of the nation's aristocracy, written with a baroque flair. When first published, it scandalized a vast segment of its audience. Salazar Bondy died at the age of forty-one.

Aberrant Nostalgia

> *I have learned nothing about Peru in Lima: there, it is not a matter of anything pertaining to the public happiness of the empire. . . . [C]old-hearted vanity tyrannizes everyone, and he who does not suffer from it himself does nothing to protect anyone else from it.*
>
> —*Baron Humboldt,* Correspondence

As if the future and even the present did not exist, Lima and its inhabitants are permeated with the past. This reality has been imposed on us by those who believed they could unravel the enigma of our being, about which we are always inquiring with some perplexity in an effort to determine our destiny. They have determined that our city is impregnated with "something like an aberrant nostalgia" (Raúl Porras Barrenechea), but this is true more in reference to our deviant feelings than the feelings

321

themselves, because, historically speaking, we need only ask in which way we really do look. We see a hardly idyllic mirage of an era whose attributes were imposed by a rigid caste system and the economic privileges and well-being of a select few at the expense of a less-fortunate majority.

The Colonial period—an idealized Arcadia—has yet to be properly evaluated by scrupulous critics. Through articles, stories, and essays, we are given the image of a period of abundance and serenity that excludes the unimaginable tension between masters and slaves, between foreigners and natives, between potentates and their unfortunate subjects—a tension that must have shaken the very underpinnings of the entire society; but no one knows for sure the extent of that ostensible conflict among opposing social strata, and those of us who suspect the presence of social fissures in that historical terrain rarely have had the possibility of acknowledging it. The thankless task of challenging the image of Colonial Arcadia will always be painful because the majority of us have unsuspiciously assimilated more than a century of innumerable pages written by erudite experts working under delusion. Despite his liberal affiliation, Ricardo Palma, who was caught up in his own charisma, became the most propitious creator of that literary wonder; his formula, as he himself explained, consisted of "mixing tragedy and comedy, history and fiction."

We will not commit here the sacrilegious act of judging his works with the usual verbose conclusiveness to which they are accustomed. Owing to his wit, patience, and good humor, Palma created a myth out of the ancient archives, but his characters are only occasional heroes, because they never function as rebels or liberators (Riva-Agüero, to his credit, made the same observation); only a gallery of respectful and respectable courtesans were born from the pen of the great writer, and neither they nor their behavior put anyone into danger, certainly not his fabulous embellishment of the regal representatives, their coquettish but chaste wives, or the clergy that was less licentious than concupiscent and all of whom were highly unscrupulous in their profane ways, but never in matters involving dogma or theology.

It is true that the author of *Tradiciones peruanas* produced nothing less than a fragile, agrarian *comédie humaine*, but failed to include anyone who was unhappy and free, or who might have wanted to question conformity or confront the patronizing social institutions; similarly, his version of the grandees of Independence was tempered by the soporiferous aroma of vice-regal salons and bedrooms. The Colonial invention, which was a total success, had realized its initial satirical proposal but also became its own saboteur. It is undeniable that "Palma's stories undermined history" (Luis A. Sánchez) and instead of imparting true viceregal history, he bequeathed a digressive theory of his own world—Lima—from a narrow, provincial perspective that even today cannot be refuted by a general, scientific perspective; so strong is our intellectual laziness that we find ourselves comfortably immersed in the quicksand of delusion. Whoever refuses to accept the legend as one's past and the phantoms that make it come alive as if they were a part of our venerated ancestors is, by consensus, transformed like larva into an alien bird, indeed, a dangerous and rapacious bird.

Porras Barrenechea, in writing that "our past is still alive in Lima, and it allures with undeniable persistence," was not mistaken. It has nothing to do with the survival of monuments that have suffered deterioration over time yet still serve as tangible examples, but rather refers to that contrivance already known for its regressive nature called "Colonialism" (José Carlos Mariátegui) and "Perricholismo" (Luis A. Sánchez) that, when reduced to a few words, is the cult of noble ostentation to which everyone aspired (such as Villegas who sought to bed Amat) no matter what their social station might have been. Because of politics, there are those who make it to the venerated Court. Perricholismo, which is passionless and verbose, like the syrupy vengeance of Mexican "malinchismo," is the driving force behind Lima and its inhabitants. Today, if the country's President lives in Pizarro's Palace, like he did 140 years ago, it does not mean that whoever is camping out there considers himself a Spanish Viceroy or, in political contrast, a descendant of an Incan king. A person who hails from Lima typically begins his career in a government position, as a political delegate, or through elected office, and triumphantly winds up in power or receiving the official favors of whoever irrigates the 400-year-old fig tree in the patio of the founder. The literary or intellectual "Perricholismo" to which Sánchez refers is less obstinate than its corresponding social manifestation; more hypochondriacal in its reminiscences—although Palma is the talented exception—Perricholismo, sooner or later, founders in the shallows of one's local reputation, which constitutes, on the contrary, an existential form of success that is dependent upon sacrificing ideas, principles, everything.

Our attraction for the past is something less than what happens in reality; indeed, we are alienated from it not only because it is the source of our popular culture, but also because it is our national kitsch that provides a code of social behavior for every poor soul who aspires to become Mr. Somebody, because contemporary times reproduce a caricature of earlier times; and because, in essence, there is no way to escape from looking backwards when one is hypnotized by the mysteries of the past and blind to the future. The past is everywhere—in our homes and schools, politics and the news media, folklore and literature, religion and everyday life; our elders, for example, echo outmoded Colonial wisdom, our schools propagate Arcadian lies, the government's golden carriages fill our streets, and our newspapers are continually paying festive homage to a lost paradise. We sing and dance Creole waltzes that stubbornly evoke traditional colonial neighborhoods, and we continue to print books of anecdotes and memories about that which José Gálvez coined as "the Lima that's disappearing." Amid the smoke of the food being cooked on the street corner, old and new processions make their way down the street, while the gregarious devotee is rejuvenated by other similar odors. And we attend— what option do we have?—idle rituals like weddings and funerals, all of which are based on hypocritical conventions. Every street is filled with the potholes of Colonial Arcadia, and it is not easy to avoid them.

On an entirely different matter, it should be noted that Lima is not Peru, although it strives to be; while there is no question that a certain splendor irradiates out from the capital to the rest of the country, it does little to enlighten it. Despite the opposition to the invasion of modernity that has, nevertheless, given those trapped by nostalgia their cars, transistor radios, penicillin, nylon, etc., Lima has ceased being a tranquil city based on religious customs, once so revered by its inhabitants that the Frenchman Radiguet became filled with emotion when he saw it; instead, it has become an urban hub where, in order to survive, two million people bump into each other in the midst of honking horns, blaring radios, stifling human congestion, and other stupidity: two million people jostled about "abriendo paso," or "elbowing one's way through" (a colloquial phrase that Francisco Monclova has noted for its egotistical demeanor), among wild beasts that have formed a human conglomeration of underdevelopment. Thanks to capitalism, civil chaos, which has been stimulated by the cancerous velocity of a ravenous urban hodgepodge, has become the ideal: blinded, the entire populace desires to be consumed by it, letting its proximity stoke a spiritual holocaust. It's all due to improvisation and malice: the traffic jams downtown and along the avenues, the noise of the street vendors and vagabonds, the fatiguing lines of people waiting for a bus, the housing crisis, the overflowing sewers, and the terrible telephone service, all of which spawns neurosis. Like the eyes of a serpent, haphazardness and malevolence beguile us while, at the same time, provincial candor bites its own tail with infected and tangling absurdity. The monastic solitude that nineteenth- and even early twentieth-century travelers to Lima had grown to associate with the powers of meditation was swept away amid a demographic explosion. However, the mutation was only quantitative and superficial; the sudden incursion of urban growth has only veiled, but not suppressed, the melancholic vocation of the "limeño," because today Colonial Arcadia has become an archetypal model of longing.

At bottom, only a fleeting image convinces the tourist that any surviving remnants of the Colonial period have been transcended; but we should not rely on a traveler's mistaken impressions. The alienated past is buried not only in the hearts of those families who have lived in Lima for generations, but also in those people who, hailing from the provinces and overseas, have moved to Lima; they arrive in the capital overflowing with expectations for the future and, for no apparent reason, after many years find themselves undermined by the very hopes that had motivated them to go to Lima. Their original aspirations are replaced with the feeling of satisfaction brought about by knowing that they have been integrated into the Colonial society of Lima, which means they have begun to construct their own personal Viceroyalty and, thanks to that process, through matrimony, by association, or through complicity, they begin to participate in the power exercised by the masters and the landlords that has been retained by the Great Families. Their dream of achieving aristocracy (whose titles are determined by those belonging to the elite circles of power) disseminates from the metropolitan empire out to the rest of the nation where, in every city, town, and village, the specter of opulence is re-created like a trial run before making its appearance in the capital.

Here, then, we must confront the Great Families. It is impossible to deny that they are the ones who have disseminated the perfidious notion that "there's nothing like the past," while, on the one hand, totally ignoring the precedent set by Jorge Manrique's poetic sway and, on the other, adding to this fiction the idea that of all prior periods in history, the one possessing a paternalistic heritage and dependence on foreigners was the happiest time of all. Those Great Families know full well that socially and economically those times are long gone; hence, they increase their opulence and seek to prosper according to the reality of the present moment. Afraid, however, as they have always lived, of any potential outbreak of unhappiness or violence, they continue to perpetuate—thanks to the little or nonexistent knowledge that our schools teach about the subject— the idyllic metaphor of the Colonial period and its psychological and moral influence. Their religious paintings of the Cuzco School, their neo-colonial-style houses with baroque furnishings, their inbred marriages— only accidentally interrupted by a transfusion of foreign blood—their legitimate or false family heralds, the prurience of the well-served gentleman, their Hispanism based solely on bull fighting and flamenco music, and, finally, their nobility—stamped into genealogical histories and driven by the desire for economic success—give refined proof of the reigning confusion that has become a sign of their indisputable destiny.

It is not a matter of a platonic love for history, nor a lack of perspective regarding the progress of man, nor some crazy anachronism; indeed, none of that, but rather the preservation of a sickly fetish, that is, the continuing dependence of the land and those who work it on its owner, the Señor; as a result, the entire system becomes a sham, propped up by tradition, literature, and nostalgia, that is, false tradition, poor literature, and aberrant nostalgia; nevertheless, it cannot be denied that the story of Colonial Arcadia has been a success and, in fact, those of us who have been liberated, if not held captive in its web, at least forming a group of admirers, find it difficult to emancipate ourselves from the attractive nature of those alluring elements of fiction: viceroys, royal dignity, Colonial auditors, veiled women, saintly types, which are all strategically positioned in the old, winding neighborhoods, in the fickle but catchy words of a contemporary song, in the proverbial bar, in the commotion of typical urban life. . . .

As it became popularized and formed a part of our national pride, this aberrant nostalgia has crystallized into what is called "criollismo," a kind of national folklore. In the end, it is hardly anything born out of fantasy or past history that allows "criollismo" to justify the continuity of Colonial Arcadia; but it is highly dangerous because it has no identity, be it in terms of style, customs, obsessions or distortions. Paradise lost, yes, but according to the recipe, it can be rescued and brought to life through parody and sluggish innovation.

TRANSLATED BY DICK GERDES

Rosario Castellanos

Mexico
(1925–1974)

————————

Born in Mexico's Federal District, Rosario Castellanos is known as one of Mexico's most prolific female voices. Raised in an aristocratic landholding family, Castellanos and her family moved to Mexico City after their land was confiscated in accordance with President Lázaro Cárdenas's "Land Reform" program. While studying at the National University of Mexico, she joined a group of Mexican and Central American writers who grew to be known as the "Generation of 1950." In 1951, after postgraduate work in Madrid, she worked as the director of the cultural program in Chiapas. She pursued an academic career from 1951 to 1971, when she was appointed Mexico's ambassador to Israel. There she died tragically, three years later. A master of demolishing any myths that pervade accounts of women's experiences, Castellanos devoted much of her literary career to the exploration of gender in Mexican culture. Her work spanned many genres in novels like *Balún-Canán* (1957) and *Oficio de tinieblas* (1962); short story collections such as *City of Kings* (1960), *Los convidados de agosto* (1964), and *Album de familia* (1971); poetry like *Meditation on the Threshold* (1985); essays, like those included in *Juicios sumarios* (1966) and *El mar y sus pescaditos* (1975); and plays, such as *El eterno femenino* (1975). She worked as the press and information director for the National University of Mexico and was a visiting professor at the Universities of Wisconsin, Colorado, and Indiana. Her essays often mix her analysis with biographical data and anecdotes, and many analyze the lives of women in Mexico through pseudomythical figures such as the Malinche and the Virgin of Guadalupe. "Once Again, Sor Juana" is a discussion of the relevance of Sor Juana Inés de la Cruz. Not until the early twentieth century was Sor Juana rediscovered, and writers like Castellanos, Amado Nervo, Xavier Villaurrutia, and especially Octavio Paz have helped establish her as a classic to be read and reread. The piece, written on 26 October 1963 and collected in *Juicios sumarios*, is an enlightening view on the role of women in society, religion, and literature south of the Rio Grande.

Once Again, Sor Juana

There are three figures in Mexican history that embody the most extreme and diverse possibilities of femininity. Each one of them represents a symbol, exercises a vast and profound influence on very wide sectors of the nation, and arouses passionate reactions. These figures are the Virgin of Guadalupe, Malinche, and Sor Juana.

Only positive elements seem to converge in the Virgin of Guadalupe. In spite of her apparent fragility, she is the sustainer of life, the one who protects us against danger, the one who comforts our sorrows, presides over the most pompous events, legitimizes our joys, in short, the one who saves our body from sickness and our soul from the devil's stealth. How can we but help loving her, revering her, converting her into the dearest, most beloved core of our emotional life? That is precisely what Mexicans do—even to the point of separating their religious beliefs from the personality of the Virgin of Guadalupe in order to safeguard her, in the event these beliefs conflict with each other, undergo crisis, or must go into hiding due to circumstantial pressures. A classic example is the case of our atheists, who suffer no pangs of conscience when they make their annual pilgrimage to her shrine at La Villa.

Malinche incarnates sexuality in its most irrational aspect, the one least reducible to moral laws, most indifferent to cultural values. Because sexuality is a dynamic force that is projected outward and is manifested by deeds, Malinche has become one of the key figures of our history. Some call her a traitor, others consider her the foundress of our nationality, according to whatever perspectives they choose to judge her from. Because she is not dead, she still wails in the night, crying for her lost children throughout the most hidden corners of our land, just as she still makes her annual appearance disguised as a giant at Indian festivals and she continues to exercise her fascination as a woman, a female, and a seductress of men. Before Malinche, consciousness remains alert, vigilant, and forced to qualify her and understand her in order not to succumb to her power, which like Antheus' is always renewed whenever she comes into contact with the earth again.

The attitudes toward the Virgin of Guadalupe or Malinche are clear ones because their figures are also very clear-cut: the former, a woman who sublimates her condition in motherhood, the latter, a woman of our roots, uninterested in the process of its development, indifferent to the results. But Sor Juana? The initial enigma she poses for us is not her genius (sufficient to worry many doctors) but her femininity. She speaks of it in different passages of her writing, not in terms of a consummated and assumed fact but rather as a hypothesis that perhaps cannot be proven. She states, for example, in a ballad:

> I don't understand these things,
> I only know that I came here.

So that if I be woman
No one can truly say.

Such explicit confession and evident purpose constitute the stumbling block for scandal among Sor Juana's admirers. Either they look through her, or they prefer to ignore evidence that in the long run has the value of being first hand and prefer to continue to construct her according to their own tastes: frivolous damsel of the viceregal court, a bird that allows herself to be caught in the snare of an impossible love from which her only escape is to beg asylum behind the consecrated walls of a convent. There she finds the solace of solitude and drowns her sorrows in sonnets and other minor matters. Like all the chosen of the gods, Sor Juana dies young and fee fi foe fum our story is done.

There's a paragraph written by Sor Juana in her *Letter in Reply to Sor Philotea* that is a type of autobiography, in which she spoke of the many doubts that assailed her before she took the veil. She knew her own character very well, her preference for solitude, how difficult it would be for her to submit to the discipline of a community life. In the end she chose the convent because the only other alternative was marriage, for which she felt an unconquerable aversion.

That paragraph has not prevented many persons from praising her monastic vocation, finding her obedience to the orders of the several superiors that she endured to be irreproachable, her zeal in the fulfillment of her vows excessive, and her final sacrifice and her charity toward her suffering sisters nothing less than saintly. For all of these reasons there has been no lack of those who, carrying their admiration to the utmost, have begged the pertinent authorities to canonize her. Naturally, the cause has not advanced. The Church straddles the Rock of Ages and resorts to very painstaking procedures before elevating anyone to its altars.

However, the attitudes that we have just described are, in the final instance, naïve and thus inoffensive. There is another attitude that takes on all the trappings of science, placing the curious specimen under the microscope in order to classify it.

Why so curious? Not because she chose the convent, a very commonplace deed in the New Spain of her time. Not because she wrote somewhat charming verse, because it was already a saying that in this newly founded metropolis there were more poets than fertilizer (and fertilizer was very abundant). No, it was because it was a woman who wrote those poems. Because she was a woman who had an intellectual vocation. Because, in spite of all the resistance and barriers of her environment, she exercised that vocation and transformed it into literary work. It was a body of work that provoked the astonishment and admiration of her contemporaries, not for its intrinsic qualities but because it sprang from a hand whose natural employment should have been cooking or sewing. A body of work greeted by silence, beset by the scorn of centuries, now comes to light once again, thanks to the research of scholars, among whom first place goes to Father Alfonso Méndez Plancarte.

Thus, Sor Juana returns to the present, not only as an author but as a person. We see her dissected by the instruments of psychoanalysis, thanks to the Germanic curiosity (and being Germanic it is thorough and solemn) of Ludwig Pfandl.

His diagnosis does not do her any favors. Moreover, it is a catalog of all the complexes, traumas, and frustrations that can victimize a human being. Naturally, in her relationship with her family there are all those ambiguities that are explained, thanks to the dummy card of Oedipus. Naturally, due to her beauty and her talent, she was a narcissist. Did she confess an eagerness to know more? She's a neurotic. Does she use symbols? Was she effusive to someone? Careful! That's either mistaken affection or an unconscious urge to kill.

A book conceived in this fashion is insulting, not for its partiality but because criteria like these have been superseded by other broader ones. Wouldn't it be fairer to think that Sor Juana, like any other human being, possessed a backbone, that it was her own vocation, and that she chose among all the different kinds available to her, the one she was most able to count on achieving?

TRANSLATED BY MAUREEN AHERN

Clarice Lispector

Brazil

(1925–1977)

Perhaps the greatest female figure in Brazilian literature, Clarice Lispector and her work are well-known in Europe and Latin America. Born in the Ukraine and a descendant of Eastern European Jews, she grew up in the Brazilian state of Recife. Following the death of her mother, Lispector's family moved to Rio de Janeiro in 1937. She obtained a law degree in 1944 and left Brazil with her husband, a fellow lawyer who worked for Brazil's diplomatic corps. Most of her life was lived abroad. Lispector's prose had an immediate impact on Brazil's literary circles. Although some criticized her style and the voice of her narrators, her introspective characters gained her immediate praise. Not concerned with social or political problems, Lispector wrote unconventionally and in an innovative fashion. She was primarily concerned with the exploration of the individual's psyche and its reactions to the outside world. Her works often take the reader through the deepest and most confusing aspects of the human mind and its search for a universal truth or supreme being. Her versatile voice allowed her to produce a variety of essays, novels, short stories, and children's literature. In many of her pages the influence of Virginia Woolf, Lispector's idol, is evident, in their poetic awareness and in their ruminations on human existence. Among her more celebrated works are *The Passion According to G. H.* (1964), *Family Ties* (1960), *An Apprenticeship or The Book of Delights* (1969), *The Apple in the Dark* (1961), and *The Hour of the Star* (1977). The following newspaper piece, written by Lispector on 20 June 1970 and collected in her posthumously published volume *Discovering the World*, is a reflection on the beauty and the ugliness of modern urban architecture, and on the frightening coldness of Brasilia, the most artificial and utopian of Latin America's modern cities.

Creating Brasília

Brasília is built on the line of the horizon. —Brasília is artificial. As artificial as the world must have been when it was created. When the world was created, it was necessary to create a human being especially for that world. We are all deformed through adapting to God's freedom. We cannot say how we might have turned out if we had been created first, and the world deformed afterwards to meet our needs. Brasília has no

331

inhabitants as yet who are typical of Brasília. —If I were to say that Brasília is pleasant, you would realize immediately that I like the city. But if I were to say that Brasília is the image of my insomnia, you would see this as a criticism: but my insomnia is neither pleasant nor awful—my insomnia is me, it is lived, it is my terror. The two architects who planned Brasília were not interested in creating something beautiful. That would be too simple; they created their own terror, and left that terror unexplained. Creation is not an understanding, it is a new mystery. —When I died, I opened my eyes one day and there was Brasília. I found myself alone in the world. There was a taxi standing there. No sign of the driver—Lúcio Costa and Oscar Niemeyer are two solitary men. —I look at Brasília the way I look at Rome: Brasília began with the starkest of ruins. The ivy had not yet grown. —Besides the wind there is another thing that blows. It can only be recognized in the supernatural rippling of the lake. —Wherever you stand, you have the impression of being on the edge of a dangerous precipice. Brasília stands on the margin. —Were I to live here, I should let my hair grow down to my feet. —Brasília belongs to a glorious past which no longer exists. That type of civilization disappeared thousands of years ago. In the fourth century BC, Brasília was inhabited by men and women who were fair and very tall, who were neither American nor Scandinavian, and who shone brightly in the sun. They were all blind. That explains why there is nothing to collide with in Brasília. The inhabitants of Brasília used to dress in white gold. The race became extinct because few children were born. The more beautiful the natives of Brasília, the blinder, purer, and more radiant they became, and the fewer children they produced. The natives of Brasília lived for nearly three hundred years. There was no one in whose name they could die. Thousands of years later, the location was discovered by a band of fugitives who would not be accepted in any other place; they had nothing to lose. There they lit a bonfire, set up their tents, and gradually began excavating the sands which buried the city. Those men and women were short and dark-skinned, with shifty, restless eyes, and because they were fugitives and desperate, they had something to live and die for. They occupied the houses, which were in ruins, and multiplied, thus forming a human race which was much given to contemplation. —I waited for night, like someone waiting for shadows in order to steal away unobserved. When night came, I perceived with horror that it was hopeless: wherever I went, I would be seen. The thought terrified me: seen by whom?—The city was built without any escape route for rats. A whole part of myself, the worst part, and precisely that part of me which has a horror of rats, has not been provided for in Brasília. Its founders tried to ignore the importance of human beings. The dimensions of the city's buildings were calculated for the heavens. Hell has a better understanding of me. But the rats, all of them enormous, are invading the city. That is a newspaper headline. —This place frightens me. —The construction of Brasília: that of a totalitarian state. This great visual silence which I adore. Even my insomnia might have created this peace of never-never-land. Like those two hermits, Costa and Niemeyer, I would also meditate in the desert where there are no opportunities for temptation. But I see black vultures flying high overhead. What is perishing, dear God? —I did not shed a single tear in Brasília. —There was no place for tears. —It is a shore without any sea. In Brasília there is no place where one may enter, no place where one may leave. —Mummy, it's nice to see you standing there with your white cape fluttering in the breeze. (The truth is that I have perished, my son.) —A prison in the open air. In any case, there would be nowhere to escape to. For anyone escaping would probably find himself heading for Brasília. They captured me in freedom. But freedom is simply what one achieves. When they beat me, they are ordering me to be free. —The human indifference which lurks in my nature is something I discover here in Brasília, and it flowers cold and potent, the frozen strength of Nature. Here is the place where my crimes (not the worst of them, but those I would not understand), where my crimes would not be crimes of love. I am off to commit those other crimes which God and I understand. But I know that I shall return. I am drawn here by all that is terrifying in my nature. —I have never seen anything like it in the world. But I recognize this city in the depths of my dream. In those depths there is lucidity. —For as I was saying, Flash Gordon . . . —If they were to photograph me standing in Brasília, when they came to develop the film only the landscape would appear. —Where are the giraffes of Brasília? —A certain twitching on my part, certain moments of silence, cause my son to exclaim: 'Really, grown-ups are the limit!'—It is urgent. Were Brasília not populated, or rather, over-populated, it would be inhabited in some other way. And should that happen, it would be much too late: there would be no place for people. They would sense they were being quietly expelled. —Here the soul casts no shadow on the ground. —During the first two days I had no appetite. Everything had the appearance of the food they serve on board aeroplanes. —At night, I confronted silence. I know that there is a secret hour when manna falls and moistens the lands of Brasília. —However close one may be, everything here is seen from afar. I could find no way of touching. But at least there is one thing in my favour: before arriving here, I already knew how to touch things from afar. I never became too desperate: from afar, I was able to touch things. I possessed a great deal, and not even what I have touched knows of this. A rich woman is like this. It is pure Brasília. —The city of Brasília is situated outside the city. — *'Boys, boys come here, will you. Look who's coming on the street, all dressed up in modernistic style. It ain't nobody but . . . '* (Aunt Hagar's Blues, played by Ted Lewis and his Band, with Jimmy Dorsey on the clarinet.)—Such astonishing beauty, this city traced out in mid-air. —Meantime, no samba is likely to be born in Brasília. —Brasília does not permit me to feel weary. It almost hounds me. I feel fine. I feel fine. I feel fine. I feel just fine. Besides, I have always cultivated my weariness as my most precious passiveness. —All this is but today. Only God knows what will happen to Brasília. Here the fortuitous takes one by surprise—Brasília is haunted. It is the motionless outline of something. —Unable to sleep, I look out of my hotel window at three o'clock in the morning. Brasília is a landscape of insomnia. It never sleeps. —Here the organic being does not deteriorate. It becomes petrified. —I should like to see five hundred eagles of the blackest onyx scattered throughout Brasília. —Brasília is asexual. —The first instant you set eyes on the city you feel inebriated: your feet do not touch the ground.

How deeply one breathes in Brasília. As you breathe here you begin to experience desire. And that is out of the question. Desire does not exist here. Will it ever exist? I cannot see how. —It would not surprise me to encounter Arabs on the street. Arabs of another age and long since dead. —Here my passion dies. And I gain a lucidity which makes me feel grandiose for no good reason. I am wonderful and futile, I am of the purest gold. And almost endowed with the spiritualistic powers of a medium. —If there is some crime which humanity has still to commit, that new crime will be initiated here. It is so very open, so well suited to the plateau, that no one will ever know. —This is the place where space most closely resembles time. —I am certain that this is the right place for me. But I have become much too corrupted on earth. I have acquired all of life's bad habits. —Erosion will strip Brasília to the bone. —The religious atmosphere which I sensed from the outset, and denied. This city was achieved through prayer. Two men beatified by solitude created me here, on foot, restless, exposed to the wind. How I should love to set white horses free here in Brasília. At night, they would become green under the light of the moon—I know what those two men wanted: that slowness and silence which are also my idea of eternity. Those two men created the image of an eternal city. —There is something here which frightens me. When I discover what it is, I shall also discover what I like about this place. Fear has always guided me to the things I love; and because I love, I become afraid. It was often fear which took me by the hand and led me. Fear leads me to danger. And everything I love has an element of risk. —In Brasília you find the craters of the Moon. —And the beauty of Brasília is to be found in those invisible statues.

TRANSLATED BY GIOVANNI PONTIERO

Angel Rama

Uruguay

(1926–1983)

———•••••———

Angel Rama and Emir Rodríguez Monegal, both Uruguayans born in the same decade, are the two indisputable titans of twentieth-century Latin American literary criticism. Their approaches are complementary: Rama used Marxism to study literature as a social phenomenon; Rodríguez Monegal chose psychoanalysis to approach writers as self-centered individualists. A critic, editor, and scholar of continental importance, Rama died in a plane crash together with his wife, art critic Marta Traba, and novelist Jorge Ibargüengoitia. Rama's promotion of Latin American literature came as a result of his association with Biblioteca Ayacucho in Venezuela, an extensive publishing project devoted to rescuing and standardizing works written in Spanish and Portuguese since the time of the Conquest. Rama's books were numerous. They include *Los dictadores latinoamericanos* (1976), *Rubén Darío y el Modernismo* (1979), *Transculturación narrativa en América Latina* (1982), and *The Lettered City* (1984). He was a regular columnist for *El Nacional* and other Venezuelan newspapers and journals. The following essay, "Literature and Exile," was first published in the American journal *Review*. By Rama's own account, he wanted at first to tackle the inexhaustible theme of exile in Latin America from a continental perspective, which could easily have resulted in a book-length monograph. But he changed his mind. "The history of exile [in the region] is so extensive," Rama once said, "the countries involved are so numerous and the political and cultural problems it entailed so complex, that to try to deal with the entire subject in a few pages would be futile." So he decided, instead, to limit his scope to his native area, broadly defined as the "Southern Cone," which he knew so well—Argentina, Chile, Paraguay, and Uruguay.

Literature and Exile

The turbulent political history of Latin America, including the constant confrontation between the civilian-minded intellectual sector and the military forces or political bosses and warlords which began immediately following the wars of independence, has continued up to the present moment, complicated by new factors, such as the economic migrations occurring in this century. It would be casuistry to separate these related factors from a discussion of political exile.

1. The People of the Diaspora

The millions of Mexicans who have migrated to California or Texas, the equally numerous Paraguayans who have made Buenos Aires the major Paraguayan city, the Dominicans or Colombians who have settled in Venezuela, as well as the Chileans, Argentines, and Uruguayans who have recently scattered throughout the world are part of a migratory phenomenon that cannot be exclusively attributed to seemingly impartial economic reasons unlinked to politics. In many cases one will find that the root cause is a political oppression that, by maintaining a rigid and unjust social structure, limits the possibilities of people and impels them toward an emigration similar to the one that took place in Europe during the second half of the 19th century.

At best, such migrations testify to the inability of governments to provide citizens with basic necessities, in this sense underscoring the bond between economics and politics. From 1930 on, massive displacements have increased in Latin America: on the one hand, the internal migration that results in uncontrolled urban growth and whose immediate cause is the impoverishment of rural areas stemming from the new distribution of labor occurring throughout the world; on the other hand, exacerbating the process, the external migrations toward such poles of attraction within Latin America as Buenos Aires, São Paulo, Mexico, and more recently Caracas and outside of Latin America toward various North American cities, ranging from Miami to Los Angeles.

The somewhat elitist distinction between the exile and the emigrant should be corrected, particularly in view of the subtle semantic shift that has replaced such nineteenth century words as "banishment" and the legal term "ostracism" with the new term of foreign origin: exile. The exile is no longer the citizen expelled from his homeland—a somewhat chivalric measure that repressive regimes have stopped practicing—but rather one who voluntarily abandons his land to avoid persecution, prison or death, or, more frequently, in order to continue his work in a country which provides more appropriate conditions; this work often includes the struggle against the exile's own government. Although among exiles, members of the intellectual sector—politicians, professionals, and writers—are more notorious, laborers, white collar workers, students, and even businessmen are much more numerous. If we consider the deep roots of contemporary mass migrations together with the modern realities of exile we can see how the rigid boundaries between exile and migration disappear.

Only by looking at the process as a whole can one understand the problems of exiled writers: as they cease to be isolated centers of attention, they become distinguished members of a wide stratum of educated persons displaced along with entire populations. All make up the Latin American people of the diaspora, in search of countries and cities where a higher degree of civil liberties and greater possibilities of employment, education, and social mobility amount to a fuller expression of human rights. Writers as well as emigrants, by being faithful to such ideals, are unfaithful to their native countries in which such principles are denied, and they are constantly reproached for this with the emotionalism that accompanies national sentiment. The answer to such reproaches is the work that these exiles are accomplishing abroad and their intent to return to their homelands when they are finally able to make their ideals and national realities coincide.

When José Martí appealed to the fishermen and laborers of Tampa for their indispensable support for the cause of Cuban independence, he set up a model of the cooperative effort linking intellectuals and emigrants devoted to a common cultural and political cause which has benefited from the survival of the national culture abroad as well as from the experience of a non-colonial way of life that is more democratic than that of the homeland. Thus, a process of subtle transculturation has been characteristic not only of the diaspora in general but of the experience of the individual intellectual, subjected to the same unsettling social experiences and abrupt changes as the Mexican day laborer living on the outskirts of Los Angeles, the Colombian peasant settled in Maracaibo or Caracas and the Paraguayan in Buenos Aires. The shock of modernization experienced in the United States may be more drastic but it is not essentially different from that experienced by peasants from areas of traditionally strong Indian influence when they settle in teeming Latin American cities modernized according to European or North American norms.

Although better educated, with greater ability to adapt and more universal perspectives, the intellectual sector is also affected by transculturation in both the sense of culture shock (as noted above) and in the discovery of the cultural diversity traditionally obscured by the belief that the continent is a homogeneous unit. Not only must one stress the flagrant cultural differences that distinguish the Andean region from the River Plate area or the Antilles from the zone of cultural influence of the Mexican plateau; one must also recognize that in spite of all the speeches, international agreements and ceremonious artistic exchanges, there is much less communication among different regions in Latin America than in Europe. For example, there is no cultural bridge between Argentina and Mexico: the highly developed intellectual sectors of both countries are notoriously ingrown and find common ground only when looking abroad, particularly toward France or the United States. Writers such as Jorge Luis Borges or Octavio Paz have had rewarding intellectual careers which have not involved an awareness of the rest of Latin America: their axis has been national culture in relation to Europe. This is why Argentine exiles who have recently settled in regions with which they had practically no previous contact—the America of mestizos and mulattoes—are discovering exotic realities similar to those encountered in the Orient by Europeans during the last century.

Brazilian intellectuals, scattered throughout the Latin American countries when the Goulart regime fell to the military (1964), have had a similar experience, which promises to have beneficial results, now that they are returning to their country. These intellectuals "discovered" Spanish America, not only in its political pecularities, but also in its cultural modes: Mario Pedroza in Chile, Ferreira Gullar in Buenos Aires, Darcy Ribeiro in Montevideo, and Francisco Juliao in Mexico, all went on to become ambassadors for their own unknown culture and analysts of the familiar and yet remote countries of others. An imaginative and intelligent work such as Darcy Ribeiro's *The Americas and Civilization* would have been impossible without those long years of exile. If one adds to this the large professional sector from the Southern Cone which has settled in Brazil in the last decade, we can state that, for the first time in almost two centuries, the traditional lack of communication between the two large hemispheres of Latin American culture is being remedied. This seems to me to be an event of major importance.

2. A Macrostructual Vision of Latin America

The above tends to confirm a paradoxical truth I have already suggested with respect to intellectual exile: it is actually the dictators whom we must thank for the acceleration of cultural exchange and unification in Latin America—ideals so often espoused on paper and so rarely practiced. Interregional contacts have been established to a degree improbable under normal circumstances, a situation that has facilitated not only the exchange of knowledge but also a cultural confrontation which could have rich and unforeseen consequences. Such links have helped shape an overall vision that is better informed and better structured; they have also led to joint ventures based on global interpretations. The process was already evident in the vigorous development of the social sciences in Latin America, but it has now involved other intellectual groups, strengthening the development of a general critical discourse about the region.

Moreover, unlike the generalizing vision of previous decades, rooted in Paris, London or New York and often dangerously schematic, the new discourse, practiced mainly by Latin Americans, has begun to function from within Latin America (Mexico, above all, but Caracas and Havana as well), with curious results, because its predictable political and social belligerence and all-encompassing scope do not exclude the rigorous methodology and solid documentation that were frequently lacking before.

National or regional compartmentalization has been replaced by a better articulated comprehensive vision. Obviously this is due not only to the clusters of exiled writers in some cities, but also to the advances in the disciplines they practice, advances which in turn have benefited from the macrostructural and universal perspectives now characteristic of the most varied studies in fields ranging from economics to linguistics.

This change in focus has had repercussions for literature, in both creative works and critical studies. Writers and critics alike have attempted to coordinate the vastness of time in Latin America with the vastness of its space: an ambitious enterprise in which the obsession with current events that dominated the earlier literature has given way to the broader purpose of not only recapturing the past along the straightforward lines established by the Romantic historians but structuring past and present in a single signifying discourse. The past has reappeared in our literature—the colonial period, even the earlier, autochthonous cultures, and, of course, our vibrant nineteenth century in works that focus less on the exoticism of phenomena than upon the complex relationships that weave them into patterns: *I, the Supreme* by Augusto Roa Bastos, *Terra Nostra* by Carlos Fuentes, *El estrecho dudoso* by Ernesto Cardenal, or *One Hundred Years of Solitude* by Gabriel García Márquez are landmarks of this tendency. For other writers, dealing with the vastness of time is not sufficient and so they also attempt to articulate the equally vast Latin American space. Sociological literary essays such as *The Open Veins of Latin America* by Eduardo Galeano have shown the way. The title of a recent novel is revealing: *Homérica Latina*. More than the search for similarities and differences, which from Alfonso Reyes to Ezequiel Martínez Estrada motivated a generation of essayists, what we are seeing now is a search for the macrostructure that might be able to explain to us the functioning of a continent and project a valid future for it. Pedro Orgambide, Abel Posse, and Luis Britto García have proposed differing models of this structure.

3. The Writer and His Public

The central problem lies in the relationship between the writer and his public. When exile occurs, a writer is often surprised to discover that that relationship had not been functioning in a single direction, from author to reader, but that the sender and receiver had been nourishing each other, sharing in the same cultural effort, within the same frame of reference and in constant communication.

Now the situation has changed. The exiled writer functions in relation to three potential publics: that of the country or culture in which he has temporarily settled; that of his native country, with which he tries to maintain communication in spite of dictatorial restraints; and the public of his compatriots, who make up the people of the diaspora, as part of which he will probably now function as in a cultural ghetto. Although it is possible to choose a single public, it is more common to try to reach all of these diverse publics: another example of the trend toward macrostructure that we have just examined in the context of themes and which now becomes more intrinsic to the writer's work because it affects its very conception. If one keeps in mind the high degree of cultural, semantic, and linguistic complicity within which literary works are generated, one will easily see that the writer is at a crossroads of conflicting intentions and even contradictions. Paradoxically, this situation can be more intense when he has moved to a country where his own language is spoken than if he had settled in a linguistically foreign locale, since in the latter case the difference is so drastic that he can either abandon his language or fall back completely on his cultural origins, which is the more common of the two choices. He can be Conrad or he can be Kavafis. The long, self-imposed exile of Julio Cortázar in Paris led him to such total concentration on the language of Buenos Aires (even more than that of Argentina) that all his characters, regardless of origin, are linguistically homogeneous in their use of the *porteño* speech.

This is a difficult situation for the poet, who works so deeply inside his language. It is not a matter of replacing "auto" with "car," but rather of the emotional charge words carry, the rich semantic plurality a culture gives them as live beings—multifaceted, ambiguous, mysterious, sometimes deceptive, capable of suddenly startling us. "Aduana lingüística," the custom house of language, is the title of an essay by Alfonso Reyes, in which he compares the use of erotic and obscene language in various American regions. What speaker of Spanish is unaware of the strength of those secret words in which insult, love, and the entire body burn? And of how those words, in another linguistic community, melt like rubber watches that no longer mark time? And of how the distinctive patterns of that other linguistic community are powerless to express our feelings? This is what happens to words, and it is with words that the writer constructs his work. This linguistic phenomenon is part of a larger one which can only be called cultural, since each Spanish American region responds to specific cultural norms that are inevitably reflected in its language.

These are not insurmountable barriers, but they are hurdles that impede communication. They put the exiled writer in the position of temporary guest of a culture. He is given more of a right to associate with his native community than with the one that he has circumstantially adopted. I will not speak here of jealousy and xenophobia, two scourges more widespread than courtesy and caution would let us admit. There remains the dialogue with the writer's two other publics: that of his homeland, which is in captivity and barely hears his words, and that of the diaspora, which is his most fertile public and the one most interested in his message. This public lives in the same circumstances as the writer: expatriation, homesickness, the hope of return, and worry over the children who, as is normal, begin to sever their links with the past as they become part of the new society in which they are living. In relation to both these publics, the writer assumes a role familiar to all of us from past experience: that of guardian and upholder of his cultural heritage and interpreter of the political solutions that might enable that heritage to survive and prosper.

4. Custodians of the Cultural Legacy

One of the most pernicious traits of dictatorships has been anti-intellectualism. Writers have been viewed by the military as responsible for the social unrest which tries to change the political structures of a country. Although the blame has been exaggerated, there is some truth in the charge. The democratic exchange of ideas among intellectuals capable of analyzing fundamental problems initiated the questioning of archaic structures within the various countries of Latin America by calling for a modernizing, and at times revolutionary, transformation. The military saw in the universities and intellectual journals a danger greater than that coming from the ranks of the workers. They responded by dismantling the universities, destroying the publishing houses, persecuting intellectuals, and by prohibiting any activity, however harmless, that could lead to the restoration of cultural life. From Guatemala to Uruguay the intellectuals who have stayed in their own countries have been silenced and nothing which might contribute to a cultural dialogue has been allowed in from abroad.

The military order established a rhetorical and official rule in schools and academies. Cultural life was totally suspended: a situation worsened by economic impoverishment. The military imposed a rigid set of values diametrically opposed to those of intellectual freedom. Therefore the writer in external exile, who enjoys freedoms denied the writer in internal exile, has had to become the custodian and defender of his endangered culture. In fact, an overwhelming majority of writers in exile have worked within national cultural traditions (a healthy sign of a new kind of nationalism), striving for the restoration of the creative values of their native culture, and at the same time taking up its causes, its protests, and even its grudges.

This tendency has been most acute in literature, with its peculiar ability to explore and express the causes of the great upheavals experienced by a community, when those upheavals cease, either temporarily or definitively. At that moment literature appears responding to the demands of the public, in this case the people of the diaspora. Time and time again, Latin America has seen these literary explosions after great social upheavals: the literature that grew out of the Mexican Revolution; the literature of violence in Colombia, which started with the "pax" of Rojas Pinilla; the literature of testimony in Venezuela since 1968. The period in which action leaves room only for slogans is followed by another in which reflection, explanation, reminiscence and the testimony of suffering are translated into literature. It is true that the spectre of Edmond Dantès hovers above these works, which at times are heart-rending cries. Nevertheless, in them a community is coming to terms with itself.

It is a literature of the defeated. Someone once observed that our defeats have inspired more eloquent works than have our victories, perhaps because, requiring a more tenacious effort, such works lead to the very limits of literature. A literature of the defeated is not necessarily a sign of resignation but rather a time out for thought. The writer's perspective stands to gain from this brief but necessary respite which allows past events to be seen and interpreted as a coherent whole. Artistically and intellectually, such a period of reflection can be even more profitable than the militancy of an earlier period. *The Poem of the Cid*, the work upon which Spanish literary language is founded, opens with the banished turning back for a last look at their abandoned homes, "tears streaming from their eyes." The *Cid* is the poem of exile and also of the hope of return. And Latin American writers in exile are also writing this long and painful poem. But in sharing their obsession with a national past, they are also founding the Latin American literary community of the future.

TRANSLATED BY PAMELA PYE

Carlos Fuentes

Mexico
(b. 1928)

———◆•◆◆◆◆———

Carlos Fuentes has lived, studied, and lectured in Europe, the United States, and Latin America. A native of Mexico City, Fuentes sets many of his works in the Federal District, as is, most notably, his breakthrough novel, *Where the Air Is Clear* (1958). As one of the original Boom writers, Fuentes helped renovate the literary language of Spanish America. His prose is fluid, but his writing is complex, filled with word games and experimentation with temporal, spatial, and narrative perspectives. In addition, Fuentes, more so than other writers of the Boom, defined the theoretical origins and boundaries of the movement through several of his essays. Fuentes's essays and prose works often dismiss the validity of traditional historical analysis and have sparked a general interest in the boundaries dividing history and fiction. His works are primarily concerned with the search for a Mexican identity, or rather, the search for the culture's undefined origins. After the follow-up *Las buenas conciencias* (1959), he published the fantastic *Aura* (1962) and *The Death of Artemio Cruz* (1962). *A Change of Skin* won him the Premio Biblioteca Breve in 1967, and was followed by *Christopher Unborn* (1987), and *The Orange Tree* (1994). Fuentes has also produced a number of plays, short stories, and essay collections, in which one can sense the influence of fellow countryman Octavio Paz. His distinguished diplomatic career has allowed him to travel widely and to broaden his international appeal. When compared with his earlier work, his writing from the late 1980s and 1990s— from his novel *Diana* (1994), about his romance with actress Jean Seberg, to his essays in *New Mexican Time* (1994)—has a more autobiographical bent. Belonging to this latter period and originally written in English, "How I Began to Write" first appeared in the British magazine *Granta*. It was later incorporated into *Myself with Others* (1988). This selection illustrates Fuentes's peculiar dual identity: the mode of the essay is Jamesian in its descriptiveness, but the tone is Hispanic in its ornate flair.

How I Started to Write

I

I was born on November 11, 1928, under the sign I would have chosen, Scorpio, and on a date shared with Dostoevsky, Crommelynck, and

Vonnegut. My mother was rushed from a steaming-hot movie house in those days before Colonel Buendía took his son to discover ice in the tropics. She was seeing King Vidor's version of *La Bohéme* with John Gilbert and Lillian Gish. Perhaps the pangs of my birth were provoked by this anomaly: a silent screen version of Puccini's opera. Since then, the operatic and the cinematographic have had a tug-of-war with my words, as if expecting the Scorpio of fiction to rise from silent music and blind images.

All this, let me add to clear up my biography, took place in the sweltering heat of Panama City, where my father was beginning his diplomatic career as an attaché to the Mexican legation. (In those days, embassies were established only in the most important capitals—no place where the mean average year-round temperature was perpetually in the nineties.) Since my father was a convinced Mexican nationalist, the problem of where I was to be born had to be resolved under the sign, not of Scorpio, but of the Eagle and the Serpent. The Mexican legation, however, though it had extraterritorial rights, did not have even a territorial midwife; and the Minister, a fastidious bachelor from Sinaloa by the name of Ignacio Norris, who resembled the poet Quevedo as one pince-nez resembles another, would have none of me suddenly appearing on the legation parquet, even if the Angel Gabriel had announced me as a future Mexican writer of some, albeit debatable, merit.

So if I could not be born in a fictitious, extraterritorial Mexico, neither would I be born in that even more fictitious extension of the United States of America, the Canal Zone, where, naturally, the best hospitals were. So, between two territorial fictions—the Mexican legation, the Canal Zone—and a mercifully silent close-up of John Gilbert, I arrived in the nick of time at the Gorgas Hospital in Panama City at eleven that evening.

The problem of my baptism then arose. As if the waters of the two neighboring oceans touching each other with the iron fingertips of the canal were not enough, I had to undergo a double ceremony: my religious baptism took place in Panama, because my mother, a devout Roman Catholic, demanded it with as much urgency as Tristram Shandy's parents, although through less original means. My national baptism took place a few months later in Mexico City, where my father, an incorrigible Jacobin and priest-eater to the end, insisted that I be registered in the civil rolls established by Benito Juárez. Thus, I appear as a native of Mexico City for all legal purposes, and this anomaly further illustrates a central fact of my life and my writing: I am Mexican by will and by imagination.

All this came to a head in the 1930s. By then, my father was counselor of the Mexican Embassy in Washington, D.C., and I grew up in the vibrant world of the American thirties, more or less between the inauguration of Citizen Roosevelt and the interdiction of Citizen Kane. When I arrived here, Dick Tracy had just met Tess Trueheart. As I left, Clark Kent was meeting Lois Lane. You are what you eat. You are also the comics you peruse as a child.

At home, my father made me read Mexican history, study Mexican geography, and understand the names, the dreams and defeats of Mexico: a nonexistent country, I then thought, invented by my father to nourish my infant imagination with yet another marvelous fiction: a land of Oz with a green cactus road, a landscape and a soul so different from those of the United States that they seemed a fantasy.

A cruel fantasy: the history of Mexico was a history of crushing defeats, whereas I lived in a world, that of my D.C. public school, which celebrated victories, one victory after another, from Yorktown to New Orleans to Chapultepec to Appomattox to San Juan Hill to Belleau Wood: had this nation never known defeat? Sometimes the names of United States victories were the same as the names of Mexico's defeats and humiliations: Monterrey. Veracruz. Chapultepec. Indeed: from the Halls of Montezuma to the shores of Tripoli. In the map of my imagination, as the United States expanded westward, Mexico contracted southward. Miguel Hidalgo, the father of Mexican independence, ended up with his head on exhibit on a lance at the city gates of Chihuahua. Imagine George and Martha beheaded at Mount Vernon.

To the south, sad songs, sweet nostalgia, impossible desires. To the north, self-confidence, faith in progress, boundless optimism. Mexico, the imaginary country, dreamed of a painful past; the United States, the real country, dreamed of a happy future.

The French equate intelligence with rational discourse, the Russians with intense soul-searching. For a Mexican, intelligence is inseparable from maliciousness—in this, as in many other things, we are quite Italian: *furberia*, roguish slyness, and the cult of appearances, *la bella figura*, are Italianate traits present everywhere in Latin America: Rome, more than Madrid, is our spiritual capital in this sense.

For me, as a child, the United States seemed a world where intelligence was equated with energy, zest, enthusiasm. The North American world blinds us with its energy; we cannot see ourselves, we must see *you*. The United States is a world full of cheerleaders, prize-giving, singin' in the rain: the baton twirler, the Oscar awards, the musical comedies cannot be repeated elsewhere; in Mexico, the Hollywood statuette would come dipped in poisoned paint; in France, Gene Kelly would constantly stop in his steps to reflect: *Je danse, donc je suis.*

Many things impressed themselves on me during those years. The United States—would you believe it?—was a country where things worked, where nothing ever broke down: trains, plumbing, roads, punctuality, personal security seemed to function perfectly, at least at the eye level of a young Mexican diplomat's son living in a residential hotel on

Washington's Sixteenth Street, facing Meridian Hill Park, where nobody was then mugged and where our superb furnished seven-room apartment cost us 110 pre-inflation dollars a month. Yes, in spite of all the problems, the livin' seemed easy during those long Tidewater summers when I became perhaps the first and only Mexican to prefer grits to guacamole. I also became the original Mexican Calvinist: an invisible taskmaster called Puritanical Duty shadows my every footstep: I shall not deserve anything unless I work relentlessly for it, with iron discipline, day after day. Sloth is sin, and if I do not sit at my typewriter every day at 8 A.M. for a working day of seven to eight hours, I will surely go to hell. No *siestas* for me, alas and alack and *hélas* and *ay-ay-ay*: how I came to envy my Latin brethren, unburdened by the Protestant work ethic, and why must I, to this very day, read the complete works of Hermann Broch and scribble in my black notebook on a sunny Mexican beach, instead of lolling the day away and waiting for the coconuts to fall?

But the United States in the thirties went far beyond my personal experience. The nation that Tocqueville had destined to share dominance over half the world realized that, in effect, only a continental state could be a modern state; in the thirties, the U.S.A. had to decide *what to do* with its new worldwide power, and Franklin Roosevelt taught us to believe that the first thing was for the United States to show that it was capable of living up to its ideals. I learned then—my first political lesson—that this is your true greatness, not, as was to be the norm in my lifetime, material wealth, not arrogant power misused against weaker peoples, not ignorant ethnocentrism burning itself out in contempt for others.

As a young Mexican growing up in the U.S., I had a primary impression of a nation of boundless energy, imagination, and the will to confront and solve the great social issues of the times without blinking or looking for scapegoats. It was the impression of a country identified with its own highest principles: political democracy, economic well-being, and faith in its human resources, especially in that most precious of all capital, the renewable wealth of education and research.

Franklin Roosevelt, then, restored America's self-respect in this essential way, not by macho posturing. I saw the United States in the thirties lift itself by its bootstraps from the dead dust of Oklahoma and the gray lines of the unemployed in Detroit, and this image of health was reflected in my daily life, in my reading of Mark Twain, in the images of movies and newspapers, in the North American capacity for mixing fluffy illusion and hard-bitten truth, self-celebration and self-criticism: the madcap heiresses played by Carole Lombard coexisted with the Walker Evans photographs of hungry, old-at-thirty migrant mothers, and the nimble tread of the feet of Fred Astaire did not silence the heavy stomp of the boots of Tom Joad.

My school—a public school, nonconfessional and coeducational—reflected these realities and their basically egalitarian thrust. I believed in the democratic simplicity of my teachers and chums, and above all I believed I was, naturally, in a totally unselfconscious way, a part of that world. It is important, at all ages and in all occupations, to be "popular" in the United States; I have known no other society where the values of "regularity" are so highly prized. I was popular, I was "regular." Until a day in March—March 18, 1938. On that day, a man from another world, the imaginary country of my childhood, the President of Mexico, Lázaro Cárdenas, nationalized the holdings of foreign oil companies. The headlines in the North American press denounced the "communist" government of Mexico and its "red" president; they demanded the invasion of Mexico in the sacred name of private property, and Mexicans, under international boycott, were invited to drink their oil.

Instantly, surprisingly, I became a pariah in my school. Cold shoulders, aggressive stares, epithets, and sometimes blows. Children know how to be cruel, and the cruelty of their elders is the surest residue of the malaise the young feel toward things strange, things other, things that reveal our own ignorance or insufficiency. This was not reserved for me or for Mexico: at about the same time, an extremely brilliant boy of eleven arrived from Germany. He was a Jew and his family had fled from the Nazis. I shall always remember his face, dark and trembling, his aquiline nose and deep-set, bright eyes with their great sadness; the sensitivity of his hands and the strangeness of it all to his American companions. This young man, Hans Berliner, had a brilliant mathematical mind and he walked and saluted like a Central European; he wore short pants and high woven stockings, Tyrolean jackets and an air of displaced courtesy that infuriated the popular, regular, feisty, knickered, provincial, Depression-era little sons of bitches at Henry Cooke Public School on Thirteenth Street N.W.

The shock of alienation and the shock of recognition are sometimes one and the same. What was different made others afraid, less of what was different than of themselves, of their own incapacity to recognize themselves in the alien.

I discovered that my father's country was real. And that I belonged to it. Mexico was my identity yet I lacked an identity; Hans Berliner suffered more than I—headlines from Mexico are soon forgotten; another great issue becomes all-important for a wonderful ten days' media feast—yet he had an identity as a Central European Jew. I do not know what became of him. Over the years, I have always expected to see him receive a Nobel Prize in one of the sciences. Surely, if he lived, he integrated himself into North American society. I had to look at the photographs of President Cárdenas: he was a man of another lineage; he did not appear in the repertory of glossy, seductive images of the salable North American world. He was a mestizo, Spanish and Indian, with a faraway, green, and liquid look in his eyes, as if he were trying to remember a mute and ancient past. Was that past mine as well? Could I dream the dreams of the country suddenly revealed in a political act as something more than a demarcation of frontiers on a map or a hillock of statistics in a yearbook? I believe I then had the intuition that I would not rest until I came to grips myself with that common destiny which depended upon still another community: the community of time. The United States had made me believe that we live only for the future; Mexico, Cárdenas, the events of 1938, made me understand that only in an act of the present can we make present the past as well as the future: to be a Mexican was to identify a hunger for being, a desire for dignity rooted in many forgotten centuries and in many centuries yet to come, but rooted here, now, in the instant, in the vigilant time of Mexico I later learned to understand in the stone serpents of Teotihuacán and in the polychrome angels of Oaxaca.

Of course, as happens in childhood, all these deep musings had no proof of existence outside an act that was, more than a prank, a kind of affirmation. In 1939, my father took me to see a film at the old RKO–Keith in Washington. It was called *Man of Conquest* and it starred Richard Dix as Sam Houston. When Dix/Houston proclaimed the secession of the Republic of Texas from Mexico, I jumped on the theater seat and proclaimed on my own and from the full height of my nationalist ten years, "Viva México! Death to the gringos!" My embarrassed father hauled me out of the theater, but his pride in me could not resist leaking my first rebellious act to the *Washington Star*. So I appeared for the first time in a newspaper and became a child celebrity for the acknowledged ten-day span. I read Andy Warhol *avant l'air-brush*: Everyone shall be famous for at least five minutes.

In the wake of my father's diplomatic career, I traveled to Chile and entered fully the universe of the Spanish language, of Latin American politics and its adversities. President Roosevelt had resisted enormous pressures to apply sanctions and even invade Mexico to punish my country for recovering its own wealth. Likewise, he did not try to destabilize the Chilean radicals, communists, and socialists democratically elected to power in Chile under the banners of the Popular Front. In the early forties, the vigor of Chile's political life was contagious: active unions, active parties, electoral campaigns all spoke of the political health of this, the most democratic of Latin American nations. Chile was a politically verbalized country. It was no coincidence that it was also the country of the great Spanish-American poets Gabriela Mistral, Vicente Huidobro, Pablo Neruda.

I only came to know Neruda and became his friend many years later. This King Midas of poetry would write, in his literary testament rescued from a gutted house and a nameless tomb, a beautiful song to the Spanish language. The Conquistadors, he said, took our gold, but they left us their gold: they left us our words. Neruda's gold, I learned in Chile, was the property of all. One afternoon on the beach at Lota in southern Chile, I saw the miners as they came out, mole-like, from their hard work many feet under the sea, extracting the coal of the Pacific Ocean. They sat around a bonfire and sang, to guitar music, a poem from Neruda's *Canto General*. I told them that the author would be thrilled to know that his poem had been set to music.

What author? they asked me in surprise. For them, Neruda's poetry had no author, it came from afar, it had always been sung, like Homer's. It was the poetry, as Croce said of the *Iliad*, "d'un popolo intero poetante," of an entire poetizing people. It was the document of the original identity of poetry and history.

I learned in Chile that Spanish could be the language of free men. I was also to learn in my lifetime, in Chile in 1973, the fragility of both our language and our freedom when Richard Nixon, unable to destroy American democracy, merrily helped to destroy Chilean democracy, the same thing Leonid Brezhnev had done in Czechoslovakia.

An anonymous language, a language that belongs to us all, as Neruda's poem belonged to those miners on the beach, yet a language that can be kidnapped, impoverished, sometimes jailed, sometimes murdered. Let me summarize this paradox: Chile offered me and the other writers of my generation in Santiago both the essential fragility of a cornered language, Spanish, and the protection of the Latin of our times, the lingua franca of the modern world, the English language. At the Grange School, under the awesome beauty of the Andes, José Donoso and Jorge Edwards, Roberto Torretti, the late Luis Alberto Heyremans, and myself, by then all budding amateurs, wrote our first exercises in literature within this mini-Britannia. We all ran strenuous cross-country races, got caned from time to time, and recuperated while reading Swinburne; and we were subjected to huge doses of rugby, Ruskin, porridge for breakfast, and a stiff upper lip in military defeats. But when Montgomery broke through at El Alamein, the assembled school tossed caps in the air and hip-hip-hoorayed to death. In South America, clubs were named after George Canning and football teams after Lord Cochrane; no matter that English help in winning independence led to English economic imperialism, from oil in Mexico to railways in Argentina. There was a secret thrill in our hearts: our Spanish conquerors had been beaten by the English; the defeat of Philip II's invincible Armada compensated for the crimes of Cortés, Pizarro, and Valdivia. If Britain was an empire, at least she was a democratic one.

In Washington, I had begun writing a personal magazine in English, with my own drawings, book reviews, and epochal bits of news. It consisted of a single copy, penciled and crayonned, and its circulation was limited to our apartment building. Then, at age fourteen, in Chile, I embarked on a more ambitious project, along with my schoolmate Roberto Torretti: a vast Caribbean saga that was to culminate in Haiti on a hilltop palace (Sans Souci?) where a black tyrant kept a mad French mistress in a garret. All this was set in the early nineteenth century and in the final scene (Shades of Jane Eyre! Reflections on Rebecca! Fans of Joan Fontaine!) the palace was to burn down, along with the world of slavery.

But where to begin? Torretti and I were, along with our literary fraternity at The Grange, avid readers of Dumas *père*. A self-respecting novel, in our view, had to start in Marseilles, in full view of the Chateau d'If and the martyrdom of Edmond Dantès. But we were writing in Spanish, not in French, and our characters had to speak Spanish. But, what Spanish? My Mexican Spanish, or Roberto's Chilean Spanish? We came to a sort of compromise: the characters would speak like Andalusians. This was probably a tacit homage to the land from which Columbus sailed.

The Mexican painter David Alfaro Siqueiros was then in Chile, painting the heroic murals of a school in the town of Chillán, which had been devastated by one of Chile's periodic earthquakes. He had been implicated in a Stalinist attempt on Trotsky's life in Mexico City and his commission to paint a mural in the Southern Cone was a kind of honorary exile. My father, as chargé d'affaires in Santiago, where his mission was to press the proudly independent Chileans to break relations with the Berlin–Rome Axis, rose above politics in the name of art and received Siqueiros regularly for lunch at the Mexican Embassy, which was a delirious mansion, worthy of William Beckford's follies, built by an enriched Italian tailor called Fallabella, on Santiago's broad Pedro de Valdivia Avenue.

This Gothic grotesque contained a Chinese room with nodding Buddhas, an office in what was known as Westminster Parliamentary style, Napoleonic lobbies, Louis XV dining rooms, Art Deco bedrooms, a Florentine loggia, many busts of Dante, and, finally, a vast Chilean vineyard in the back.

It was here, under the bulging Austral grapes, that I forced Siqueiros to sit after lunch and listen to me read our by then 400-page-long opus. As he drowsed off in the shade, I gained and lost my first reader. The novel, too, was lost; Torretti, who now teaches philosophy of science at the University of Puerto Rico, has no copy; Siqueiros is dead, and, besides, he slept right through my reading. I myself feel about it like Marlowe's Barabbas about fornication: that was in another country, and, besides, the wench was dead. Yet the experience of writing this highly imitative melodrama was not lost on me; its international setting, its self-conscious search for language (or languages, rather) were part of a constant attempt at a breakthrough in my life. My upbringing taught me that cultures are not isolated, and perish when deprived of contact with what is different and challenging. Reading, writing, teaching, learning, are all activities aimed at introducing civilizations to each other. No culture, I believed unconsciously ever since then, and quite consciously today, retains its identity in isolation; identity is attained in contact, in contrast, in breakthrough.

Rhetoric, said William Butler Yeats, is the language of our fight with others; poetry is the name of our fight with ourselves. My passage from English to Spanish determined the concrete expression of what, before, in Washington, had been the revelation of an identity. I wanted to write and I wanted to write in order to show myself that my identity and my country were real: now, in Chile, as I started to scribble my first stories, even publishing them in school magazines, I learned that I must in fact write in Spanish.

The English language, after all, did not need another writer. The English language has always been alive and kicking, and if it ever becomes drowsy, there will always be an Irishman. . . .

In Chile I came to know the possibilities of our language for giving wing to freedom and poetry. The impression was enduring; it links me forever to that sad and wonderful land. It lives within me, and it transformed me into a man who knows how to dream, love, insult, and write only in Spanish. It also left me wide open to an incessant interrogation: What happened to this universal language, Spanish, which after the seventeenth century ceased to be a language of life, creation, dissatisfaction, and personal power and became far too often a language of mourning, sterility, rhetorical applause, and abstract power? Where were the threads of my tradition, where could I, writing in mid-twentieth century in Latin America, find the direct link to the great living presences I was then starting to read, my lost Cervantes, my old Quevedo, dead because he could not tolerate one more winter, my Góngora, abandoned in a gulf of loneliness?

At sixteen I finally went to live permanently in Mexico and there I found the answers to my quest for identity and language, in the thin air of a plateau of stone and dust that is the negative Indian image of another highland, that of central Spain. But, between Santiago and Mexico City, I spent six wonderful months in Argentina. They were, in spite of their brevity, so important in this reading and writing of myself that I must give them their full worth. Buenos Aires was then, as always, the most beautiful, sophisticated, and civilized city in Latin America, but in the summer of 1944, as street pavements melted in the heat and the city smelled of cheap wartime gasoline, rawhide from the port, and chocolate éclairs from the *confiterías*, Argentina had experienced a succession of military coups: General Rawson had overthrown President Castillo of the cattle oligarchy, but General Ramírez had then overthrown Rawson, and now General Farrell had overthrown Ramírez. A young colonel called Juan Domingo Perón was General Farrell's up-and-coming Minister of Labor, and I heard an actress by the name of Eva Duarte play the "great women of history" on Radio Belgrano. A stultifying hack novelist who went by the pen name Hugo Wast was assigned to the Ministry of Education under his real name, Martínez Zuviría, and brought all his anti-Semitic, undemocratic, pro-fascist phobias to the Buenos Aires high-school system, which I had suddenly been plunked into. Coming from the America of the New Deal, the ideals of revolutionary Mexico, and the politics of the Popular Front in Chile, I could not stomach this, rebelled, and was granted a full summer of wandering around Buenos Aires, free for the first time in my life, following my preferred tango orchestras—Canaro, D'Arienzo, and Anibal Troilo, alias Pichuco—as they played all summer long in the Renoir-like shade and light of the rivers and pavilions of El Tigre and Maldonado. Now the comics were in Spanish: Mutt and Jeff were Benitín y Eneas. But Argentina had its own comic-book imperialism: through the magazines *Billiken* and *Patoruzú*, all the children of Latin America knew from the crib that "las Malvinas son Argentinas."

Two very important things happened. First, I lost my virginity. We lived in an apartment building on the leafy corner of Callao and Quintana, and after 10 A.M. nobody was there except myself, an old and deaf Polish doorkeeper, and a beautiful Czech woman, aged thirty, whose husband was a film producer. I went up to ask her for her *Sintonía*, which was the radio guide of the forties, because I wanted to know when Evita was doing Joan of Arc. She said that had passed, but the next program was Madame Du Barry. I wondered if Madame Du Barry's life was as interesting as Joan of Arc's. She said it was certainly less saintly, and, besides, it could be emulated. How? I said innocently. And thereby my beautiful apprenticeship. We made each other very happy. And also very sad: this was not the liberty of love, but rather its libertine variety: we loved in hiding. I was too young to be a real sadist. So it had to end.

The other important thing was that I started reading Argentine literature, from the gaucho poems to Sarmiento's *Recuerdos de provincia* to Cané's *Juvenilia* to Güiraldes's *Don Segundo Sombra* to . . . to . . . to—and this was as good as discovering that Joan of Arc was also sexy—to Borges. I have never wanted to meet Borges personally because he belongs to that summer in B.A. He belongs to my personal discovery of Latin American literature.

II

Latin American extremes: if Cuba is the Andalusia of the New World, the Mexican plateau is its Castile. Parched and brown, inhabited by suspicious cats burnt too many times by foreign invasions, Mexico is the sacred zone of a secret hope: the gods shall return.

Mexican space is closed, jealous, and self-contained. In contrast, Argentine space is open and dependent on the foreign: migrations, exports, imports, words. Mexican space was vertically sacralized thousands of years ago. Argentine space patiently awaits its horizontal profanation.

I arrived on the Mexican highland from the Argentine pampa when I was sixteen years old. As I said, it was better to study in a country where the Minister of Education was Jaime Torres Bodet than in a country where he was Hugo Wast. This was not the only contrast, or the most important one. A land isolated by its very nature—desert, mountain, chasm, sea, jungle, fire, ice, fugitive mists, and a sun that never blinks—Mexico is a multi-level temple that rises abruptly, blind to horizons, an arrow that wounds the sky but refuses the dangerous frontiers of the land, the canyons, the sierras without a human footprint, whereas the pampa is nothing if not an eternal frontier, the very portrait of the horizon, the sprawling flatland of a latent expansion awaiting, like a passive lover, the vast and rich overflow from that concentration of the transitory represented by the commercial metropolis of Buenos Aires, what Ezequiel Martínez Estrada called Goliath's head on David's body.

A well-read teenager, I had tasted the literary culture of Buenos Aires, then dominated by *Sur* magazine and Victoria Ocampo's enlightened mixture of the cattle oligarchy of the Pampas and the cultural clerisy of Paris, a sort of Argentinian cosmopolitanism. It then became important to appreciate the verbal differences between the Mexican culture, which, long before Paul Valéry, knew itself to be mortal, and the Argentine culture, founded on the optimism of powerful migratory currents from Europe, innocent of sacred stones or aboriginal promises. Mexico, closed to immigration by the TTT—the Tremendous Texas Trauma that in 1836 cured us once and for all of the temptation to receive Caucasian colonists because they had airport names like Houston and Austin and Dallas—devoted its population to breeding like rabbits. Blessed by the Pope, Coatlicue, and Jorge Negrete, we are, all eighty million of us, Catholics in the Virgin Mary, misogynists in the stone goddesses, and *machistas* in the singing, pistol-packing *charro*.

The pampa goes on waiting: twenty-five million Argentinians today; scarcely five million more than in 1945, half of them in Buenos Aires.

Language in Mexico is ancient, old as the oldest dead. The eagles of the Indian empire fell, and it suffices to read the poems of the defeated to understand the vein of sadness that runs through Mexican literature, the feeling that words are identical to a farewell: "Where shall we go to now, O my friends?" asks the Aztec poet of the Fall of Tenochtitlán: "The smoke lifts; the fog extends. Cry, my friends. Cry, oh cry." And the contemporary poet Xavier Villaurrutia, four centuries later, sings from the bed of the same lake, now dried up, from its dry stones:

> In the midst of a silence deserted as a street before
> the crime
> Without even breathing so that nothing may disturb
> my death
> In this wall-less solitude
> When the angels fled
> In the grave of my bed I leave my bloodless statue.

A sad, underground language, forever being lost and recovered. I soon learned that Spanish as spoken in Mexico answered to six unwritten rules:

- Never use the familiar *tu*—thou—if you can use the formal you—*usted*.
- Never use the first-person possessive pronoun, but rather the second-person, as in "This is *your* home."
- Always use the first-person singular to refer to your own troubles, as in "Me fue del carajo, mano." But use the first-person plural when referring to your successes, as in "During our term, we distributed three million acres."
- Never use one diminutive if you can use five in a row.
- Never use the imperative when you can use the subjunctive.
- And only then, when you have exhausted these ceremonies of communication, bring out your verbal knife and plunge it deep into the other's heart: "Chinga a tu madre, cabrón."

The language of Mexicans springs from abysmal extremes of power and impotence, domination and resentment. It is the mirror of an overabundance of history, a history that devours itself before extinguishing and then regenerating itself, phoenix-like, once again. Argentina, on the contrary, is a tabula rasa, and it demands a passionate verbalization. I do not know another country that so fervently—with the fervor of Buenos Aires, Borges would say—opposes the silence of its infinite space, its physical and mental pampa, demanding: Please, *verbalize* me! Martin Fierro, Carlos Gardel, Jorge Luis Borges: reality must be captured, desperately, in the verbal web of the gaucho poem, the sentimental tango, the metaphysical tale: the pampa of the gaucho becomes the garden of the tango becomes the forked paths of literature.

What is forked? What is said.

What is said? What is forked.

Everything: Space. Time. Language. History. Our history. The history of Spanish America.

I read *Ficciones* as I flew north on a pontoon plane, courtesy of Pan

American Airways. It was wartime, we had to have priority; all cameras were banned, and glazed plastic screens were put on our windows several minutes before we landed. Since I was not an Axis spy, I read Borges as we splashed into Santos, saying that the best proof that the Koran is an Arab book is that not a single camel is mentioned in its pages. I started thinking that the best proof that Borges is an Argentinian is in everything he has to evoke because it isn't there, as we glided into an invisible Rio de Janeiro. And as we flew out of Bahia, I thought that Borges invents a world because he needs it. I need, therefore I imagine.

By the time we landed in Trinidad, "Funes the Memorious" and "Pierre Ménard, Author of Don Quixote" had introduced me, without my being aware, to the genealogy of the serene madmen, the children of Erasmus. I did not know then that this was the most illustrious family of modern fiction, since it went, backwards, from Pierre Menard to Don Quixote himself. During two short lulls in Santo Domingo (then, horrifyingly, called Ciudad Trujillo) and Port-au-Prince, I had been prepared by Borges to encounter my wonderful friends Toby Shandy, who reconstructs in his miniature cabbage patch the battlefields of Flanders he was not able to experience historically; Jane Austen's Catherine Moreland and Gustave Flaubert's Madame Bovary, who like Don Quixote believe in what they read; Dickens's Mr. Micawber, who takes his hopes to be realities; Dostoevsky's Myshkin, an idiot because he gives the benefit of the doubt to the good possibility of mankind; Pérez Galdós's Nazarín, who is mad because he believes that each human being can daily be Christ, and who is truly St. Paul's madman: "Let him who seems wise among you become mad, so that he might truly become wise."

As we landed at Miami airport, the glazed windows disappeared once and for all and I knew that, like Pierre Menard, a writer must always face the mysterious duty of literally reconstructing a spontaneous work. And so I met my tradition: *Don Quixote* was a book waiting to be written. The history of Latin America was a history waiting to be lived.

III

When I finally arrived in Mexico, I discovered that my father's imaginary country was real, but more fantastic than any imaginary land. It was as real as its physical and spiritual borders: Mexico, the only frontier between the industrialized and the developing worlds; the frontier between my country and the United States, but also between all of Latin America and the United States, and between the Catholic Mediterranean and the Protestant Anglo-Saxon strains in the New World.

It was with this experience and these questions that I approached the gold and mud of Mexico, the imaginary, imagined country, finally real but only real if I saw it from a distance that would assure me, because of the very fact of separation, that my desire for reunion with it would be forever urgent, and only real if I wrote it. Having attained some sort of perspective, I was finally able to write a few novels where I could speak of the scars of revolution, the nightmares of progress, and the perseverance of dreams.

I wrote with urgency because my absence became a destiny, yet a shared destiny: that of my own body as a young man, that of the old body of my country, and that of the problematic and insomniac body of my language. I could, perhaps, identify the former without too much trouble: Mexico and myself. But the language belonged to us all, to the vast community that writes and talks and thinks in Spanish. And without this language I could give no reality to either myself or my land. Language thus became the center of my personal being and of the possibility of forming my own destiny and that of my country into a shared destiny.

But nothing is shared in the abstract. Like bread and love, language and ideas are shared with human beings. My first contact with literature was sitting on the knees of Alfonso Reyes when the Mexican writer was am-bassador to Brazil in the earlier thirties. Reyes had brought the Spanish classics back to life for us; he had written the most superb books on Greece; he was the most lucid of literary theoreticians; in fact, he had translated all of Western culture into Latin American terms. In the late forties, he was living in a little house the color of the *mamey* fruit, in Cuernavaca. He would invite me to spend weekends with him, and since I was eighteen and a night prowler, I kept him company from eleven in the morning, when Don Alfonso would sit in a café and toss verbal bouquets at the girls strolling around the plaza that was then a garden of laurels and not, as it has become, of cement. I do not know if the square, ruddy man seated at the next table was a British consul crushed by the nearness of the volcano; but if Reyes, enjoying the spectacle of the world, quoted Lope de Vega and Garcilaso, our neighbor the *mescal* drinker would answer, without looking at us, with the more somber *stanze* of Marlowe and John Donne. Then we would go to the movies in order, Reyes said, to bathe in con-temporary epic, and it was only at night that he would start scolding me: You have not read Stendhal yet? The world didn't start five minutes ago, you know.

He could irritate me. I read, against his classical tastes, the most modern, the most strident books, without understanding that I was learning his lesson: there is no creation without tradition; the "new" is an inflection on a preceding form; novelty is always a variation on the past. Borges said that Reyes wrote the best Spanish prose of our times. He taught me that culture had a smile, that the intellectual tradition of the whole world was ours by birthright, and that Mexican literature was important because it was literature, not because it was Mexican.

One day I got up very early (or maybe I came in very late from a binge) and saw him seated at five in the morning, working at his table, amid the aroma of the jacaranda and the bougainvillea. He was a diminutive Buddha, bald and pink, almost one of those elves who cobble shoes at night while the family sleeps. He liked to quote Goethe: Write at dawn, skim the cream of the day, then you can study crystals, intrigue at court, and make love to your kitchen maid. Writing in silence, Reyes did not smile. His world, in a way, ended on a funeral day in February 1913 when his insurrectionist father, General Bernardo Reyes, fell riddled by machine-gun bullets in the Zócalo in Mexico City, and with him fell what was left of Mexico's Belle Epoque, the long and cruel peace of Porfirio Díaz.

The smile of Alfonso Reyes had ashes on its lips. He had written, as a response to history, the great poem of exile and distance from Mexico: the poem of a cruel Iphigenia, the Mexican Iphigenia of the valley of Anáhuac:

> I was another, being myself;
> I was he who wanted to leave.
> To return is to cry. I do not repent of this wide
>   world.
> It is not I who return,
> But my shackled feet.

My father had remained in Buenos Aires as Mexican chargé d'affaires, with instructions to frown on Argentina's sympathies toward the Axis. My mother profited from his absence to enroll me in a Catholic school in Mexico City. The brothers who ruled this institution were preoccupied with something that had never entered my head: sin. At the start of the school year, one of the brothers would come before the class with a white lily in his hand and say: "This is a Catholic youth before kissing a girl." Then he would throw the flower on the floor, dance a little jig on it, pick up the bedraggled object, and confirm our worst suspicions: "This is a Catholic boy after . . ."

Well, all this made life very tempting. Retrospectively, I would agree with Luis Buñuel that sex without sin is like an egg without salt. The priests at the Colegio Francés made sex irresistible for us; they also made leftists of us by their constant denunciation of Mexican liberalism and especially of Benito Juárez. The sexual and political temptations became very great in a city where provincial mores and sharp social distinctions made it very difficult to have normal sexual relationships with young or even older women.

All this led, as I say, to a posture of rebellion that for me crystallized in the decision to be a writer. My father, by then back from Argentina, sternly said, Okay, go out and be a writer, but not at my expense. I became a very young journalist at the weekly *Siempre*, but my family pressured me to enter law school, or, in the desert of Mexican literature, I would literally die of hunger and thirst. I was sent to visit Alfonso Reyes in his enormous library-house, where he seemed more diminutive than ever, ensconced in a tiny corner he saved for his bed among the Piranesi-like perspective of volume piled upon volume. He said to me: "Mexico is a very formalistic country. If you don't have a title, you are nobody: *nadie, ninguno.* A title is like the handle on a cup; without it, no one will pick you up. You must become a *licenciado,* a lawyer; then you can do whatever you please, as I did."

So I entered the School of Law at the National University, where, as I feared, learning tended to be by rote. The budding explosion in the student population was compounded by cynical teachers who would spend the whole hour of class taking attendance on the two hundred students of civil law, from Aguilar to Zapata. But there were great exceptions of true teachers who understood that the law is inseparable from culture, from morality, and from justice. Foremost among these were the exiles from defeated Republican Spain, who enormously enriched Mexican universities, publishing houses, the arts, and the sciences. Don Manuel Pedroso, former dean of the University of Seville, made the study of law compatible with my literary inclinations. When I would bitterly complain about the dryness and boredom of learning the penal or mercantile codes by heart, he would counter: "Forget the codes. Read Dostoevsky, read Balzac. There's all you have to know about criminal or commercial law." He also made me see that Stendhal was right that the best model for a well-structured novel is the Napoleonic Code of Civil Law. Anyway, I found that culture consists of connections, not of separations: to specialize is to isolate.

Sex was another story, but Mexico City was then a manageable town of one million people, beautiful in its extremes of colonial and nineteenth-century elegance and the garishness of its exuberant and dangerous nightlife. My friends and I spent the last years of our adolescence and the first of our manhood in a succession of cantinas, brothels, strip joints, and silver-varnished nightclubs where the bolero was sung and the mambo danced; whores, mariachis, magicians were our companions as we struggled through our first readings of D. H. Lawrence and Aldous Huxley, James Joyce and André Gide, T. S. Eliot and Thomas Mann. Salvador Elizondo and I were the two would-be writers of the group, and if the realistic grain of *Where the Air Is Clear* was sown in this, our rather somnambulistic immersion in the spectral nightlife of Mexico City, it is also true that the cruel imagination of an instant in Elizondo's *Farabeuf* had the same background experience. We would go to a whorehouse oddly called El Buen Tono, choose a poor Mexican girl who usually said her name was Gladys and she came from Guadalajara, and go to our respective rooms. One time, a horrible scream was heard and Gladys from Guadalajara rushed out, crying and streaming blood. Elizondo, in the climax of love, had slashed her armpit with a razor.

Another perspective, another distance for approximation, another possibility of sharing a language. In 1950 I went to Europe to do graduate work in international law at the University of Geneva. Octavio Paz had just published two books that had changed the face of Mexican literature, *Libertad Bajo Palabra* and *The Labyrinth of Solitude*. My friends and I had read those books aloud in Mexico, dazzled by a poetics that managed simultaneously to renew our language from within and to connect it to the language of the world.

At age thirty-six, Octavio Paz was not very different from what he is today. Writers born in 1914, like Paz and Julio Cortázar, surely signed a Faustian pact at the very mouth of hell's trenches; so many poets died in that war that someone had to take their place. I remember Paz in the so-called existentialist nightclubs of the time in Paris, in discussion with the very animated and handsome Albert Camus, who alternated philosophy and the boogie-woogie in La Rose Rouge. I remember Paz in front of the large windows of a gallery on the Place Vendôme, reflecting Max Ernst's great postwar painting "Europe after the Rain," and the painter's profile as an ancient eagle; and I tell myself that the poetics of Paz is an art of civilizations, a movement of encounters. Paz the poet meets Paz the thinker, because his poetry is a form of thought and his thought is a form of poetry; and as a result of this meeting, an encounter of civilizations takes place. Paz introduces civilizations to one another, makes them presentable before it is too late, because behind the wonderful smile of Camus, fixed forever in the absurdity of death, behind the bright erosion of painting by Max Ernst and the crystals of the Place Vendôme, Octavio and I, when we met, could hear the voice of *el poeta Libra*, Ezra, lamenting the death of the best, "for an old bitch gone in the teeth, for a botched civilization."

Octavio Paz has offered civilizations the mirror of their mortality, as Paul Valéry did, but also the reflection of their survival in an epidemic of meetings and erotic risks. In the generous friendship of Octavio Paz, I learned that there were no privileged centers of culture, race, or politics; that nothing should be left out of literature, because our time is a time of deadly reduction. The essential orphanhood of our time is seen in the poetry and thought of Paz as a challenge to be met through the renewed flux of human knowledge, of *all* human knowledge. We have not finished thinking, imagining, acting. It is still possible to know the world; we are unfinished men and women.

I am not at the crossroads;
                    to choose
        is to go wrong.

For my generation in Mexico, the problem did not consist in discovering our modernity but in discovering our tradition. The latter was brutally denied by the comatose, petrified teaching of the classics in Mexican secondary schools: one had to bring Cervantes back to life in spite of a school system fatally oriented toward the ideal of universities as sausage factories; in spite of the more grotesque forms of Mexican nationalism of the time. A Marxist teacher once told me it was un-Mexican to read Kafka; a fascist critic said the same thing (this has been Kafka's Kafkian destiny everywhere), and a rather sterile Mexican author gave a pompous lecture at the Bellas Artes warning that readers who read Proust would proustitute themselves.

To be a writer in Mexico in the fifties, you had to be with Alfonso Reyes and with Octavio Paz in the assertion that Mexico was not an isolated, virginal province but very much part of the human race and its cultural tradition; we were all, for good or evil, contemporary with all men and women.

In Geneva, I regained my perspective. I rented a garret overlooking the beautiful old square of the Bourg-du-Four, established by Julius Caesar as the Forum Boarium two millennia ago. The square was filled with coffee-houses and old bookstores. The girls came from all over the world; they were beautiful, and they were independent. When they were kissed, one did not become a sullied lily. We had salt on our lips. We loved each other, and I also loved going to the little island where the lake meets the river, to spend long hours reading. Since it was called Jean-Jacques Rousseau Island, I took along my volume of the *Confessions*. Many things came together then. A novel was the transformation of experience into history. The modern epic had been the epic of the first-person singular, of the I, from St. Augustine to Abélard to Dante to Rousseau to Stendhal to Proust. Joyce de-Joyced fiction: Here comes everybody! But H. C. E. did not collectively save the degraded Ego from exhaustion, self-doubt, and, finally, self-forgetfulness. When Odysseus says that he is nonexistent, we know and he knows that he is disguised; when Beckett's characters proclaim their nonbeing, we know that "the fact is notorious": they are no longer disguised. Kafka's man has been forgotten; no one can remember K the land surveyor; finally, as Milan Kundera tells us, nobody can remember Prague, Czechoslovakia, history.

I did not yet know this as I spent many reading hours on the little island of Rousseau at the intersection of Lake Geneva and the Rhône River back in 1951. But I vaguely felt that there was something beyond the exploration of the self that actually made the idea of human personality possible if the paths beyond it were explored. Cervantes taught us that a book is a book is a book: Don Quixote does not invite us into "reality" but into an act of the imagination where all things are real: the characters are active psychological entities, but also the archetypes they herald and always the figures from whence they come, which were unimaginable, unthinkable, like Don Quixote, before they became characters first and archetypes later.

Could I, a Mexican who had not yet written his first book, sitting on a bench on an early spring day as the *bise* from the Jura Mountains quieted down, have the courage to explore for myself, with my language, with my tradition, with my friends and influences, that region where the literary figure bids us consider it in the uncertainty of its gestation? Cervantes did it in a precise cultural situation: he brought into existence the modern world by having Don Quixote leave his secure village (a village whose name has been, let us remember, forgotten) and take to the open roads, the roads of the unsheltered, the unknown, and the different, there to lose what he read and to gain what we, the readers, read in him.

The novel is forever traveling Don Quixote's road, from the security of the analogous to the adventure of the different and even the unknown. In my way, this is the road I wanted to travel. I read Rousseau, or the adventures of the I; Joyce and Faulkner, or the adventures of the We; Cervantes, or the adventures of the You he calls the Idle, the Amiable Reader: you. And I read, in a shower of fire and in the lightning of enthusiasm, Rimbaud. His mother asked him what a particular poem was about. And he answered: "I have wanted to say what it says there, literally and in all other senses." This statement of Rimbaud's has been an inflexible rule for me and for what we are all writing today; and the present-day vigor of the literature of the Hispanic world, to which I belong, is not alien to this Rimbaudian approach to writing: Say what you mean, literally and in all other senses.

I think I imagined in Switzerland what I would try to write someday, but first I would have to do my apprenticeship. Only after many years would I be able to write what I then imagined; only years later, when I not only knew that I had the tools with which to do it, but also, and equally important, when I knew that if I did not write, death would not do it for me. You start by writing to live. You end by writing so as not to die. Love is the marriage of this desire and this fear. The women I have loved I have desired for themselves, but also because I feared myself.

IV

My first European experience came to a climax in the summer of 1950. It was a hot, calm evening on Lake Zurich, and some wealthy Mexican friends had invited me to dinner at the elegant Baur-au-Lac Hotel. The summer restaurant was a floating terrace on the lake. You reached it by a gangplank, and it was lighted by paper lanterns and flickering candles. As I unfolded my stiff white napkin amid the soothing tinkle of silver and glass, I raised my eyes and saw the group dining at the next table.

Three ladies sat there with a man in his seventies. This man was stiff and elegant, dressed in double-breasted white serge and immaculate shirt and tie. His long, delicate fingers sliced a cold pheasant, almost with daintiness. Yet even in eating he seemed to me unbending, with a ramrod-back, military bearing. His aged face showed "a growing fatigue," but the pride with which his lips and jaws were set sought desperately to hide the fact, while the eyes twinkled with "the fiery play of fancy."

As the carnival lights of that summer's night in Zurich played with a fire of their own on the features I now recognized, Thomas Mann's face was a theater of implicit, quiet emotions. He ate and let the ladies do the talking; he was, in my fascinated eyes, a meeting place where solitude gives birth to beauty unfamiliar and perilous, but also to the perverse and the illicit. Thomas Mann had managed, out of this solitude, to find the affinity "between the personal destiny of [the] author and that of his contemporaries in general." Through him, I had imagined that the products of this solitude and of this affinity were named art (created by one) and civilization (created by all). He spoke so surely, in *Death in Venice*, of the "tasks imposed upon him by his own ego and the European soul" that as I, paralyzed with admiration, saw him there that night I dared not conceive of such an affinity in our own Latin American culture, where the extreme demands of a ravaged, voiceless continent often killed the voice of the self and made a hollow political monster of the voice of the society, or killed it, giving birth to a pitiful, sentimental dwarf.

Yet, as I recalled my passionate reading of everything he wrote, from *Blood of the Walsungs* to *Dr. Faustus*, I could not help but feel that, in spite of the vast differences between his culture and ours, in both of them literature in the end asserted itself through a relationship between the visible and the invisible worlds of narration. A novel should "gather up the threads of many human destinies in the warp of a single idea"; the I, the You, and the We were only separate and dried up because of a lack of imagination. Unbeknownst to him, I left Thomas Mann sipping his demitasse as midnight approached and the floating restaurant bobbed slightly and the Chinese lanterns quietly flickered out. I shall always thank him for silently teaching me that, in literature, you know only what you imagine.

The Mexico of the forties and fifties I wrote about in *Where the Air Is Clear* was an imagined Mexico, just as the Mexico of the eighties and nineties I am writing about in *Christopher Unborn* is totally imagined. I fear that we would know nothing of Balzac's Paris and Dickens's London if they, too, had not invented them. When in the spring of 1951 I took a Dutch steamer back to the New World, I had with me the ten Bible-paper tomes of the Pléiade edition of Balzac. This phrase of his has been a central creed of mine: "Wrest words from silence and ideas from obscurity." The reading of Balzac—one of the most thorough and metamorphosing experiences of my life as a novelist—taught me that one must exhaust reality, transcend it, in order to reach, to try to reach, that absolute which is made of the atoms of the relative: in Balzac, the marvelous worlds of *Séraphita* or *Louis Lambert* rest on the commonplace worlds of *Père Goriot* and *César Birotteau*. Likewise, the Mexican reality of *Where the Air Is Clear* and *The Death of Artemio Cruz* existed only to clash with my imagination, my negation, and my perversion of the facts, because, remember, I had learned to imagine Mexico before I ever knew Mexico.

This was, finally, a way of ceasing to tell what I understood and trying to tell, behind all the things I knew, the really important things: what I did not know. *Aura* illustrates this stance much too clearly, I suppose. I prefer to find it in a scene set in a cantina in *A Change of Skin*, or in a taxi drive in *The Hydra Head*. I never wanted to resolve an enigma, but to point out that there *was* an enigma.

I always tried to tell my critics: Don't classify me, read me. I'm a writer, not a genre. Do not look for the purity of the novel according to some nostalgic canon, do not ask for generic affiliation but rather for a dialogue, if not for the outright abolition, of genre; not for one language but for many languages at odds with one another; not, as Bakhtin would put it, for unity of style but for *heteroglossia*, not for monologic but for dialogic imagination. I'm afraid that, by and large, in Mexico at least, I failed in this enterprise. Yet I am not disturbed by this fact, because of what I have just said: language is a shared and sharing part of culture that cares little about formal classifications and much about vitality and connection, for culture itself perishes in purity or isolation, which is the deadly wages of perfection. Like bread and love, language is shared with others. And human beings share a tradition. There is no creation without tradition. No one creates from nothing.

I went back to Mexico, but knew that I would forever be a wanderer in search of perspective: this was my real baptism, not the religious or civil ceremonies I have mentioned. But no matter where I went, Spanish would be the language of my writing and Latin America the culture of my language.

Neruda, Reyes, Paz; Washington, Santiago de Chile, Buenos Aires, Mexico City, Paris, Geneva; Cervantes, Balzac, Rimbaud, Thomas Mann: only with all the shared languages, those of my places and friends and masters, was I able to approach the fire of literature and ask it for a few sparks.

Gabriel García Márquez

Colombia
(b. 1928)

————————

Perhaps the greatest ambassador of Latin American letters to the international literary scene, Gabriel García Márquez authored what is considered one of the greatest books written in the Spanish language: *One Hundred Years of Solitude* (1967). This masterpiece inherited many of its themes and characters from earlier works, such as *Leaf Storm* (1955), *La mala hora* (1962), *No One Writes to the Colonel* (1962), and *The Funerals of Mama Grande* (1962). His exquisite manipulation of magical realism and brilliant insight into Latin American society have made him both a favorite of scholars and a best-selling author. In his works, he has been primarily concerned with the modern exploration of Greek myths, literary experimentation with both time and space, and psychoanalytic applications of dreams. García Márquez is perhaps the most renowned of Latin America's Boom writers. Vastly credited for bringing global recognition to the continent's literary offerings, he was awarded the Nobel Prize for literature in 1982, the fourth Latin American writer to be honored by this prize. His subsequent international successes include *Chronicle of a Death Foretold* (1982), the masterpiece *Love in the Time of Cholera* (1985), the story collection *Strange Pilgrims* (1993), and the short novel *Of Love and Other Demons* (1994). García Márquez has also devoted much of his lifelong intellectual energy to journalism and screenwriting. Intertwining fiction with nonfiction, his essayistic work appears in the form of semiobjective reportage and is featured in *The Story of a Shipwrecked Sailor* (1955), *Obra periodística* (4 vols., 1981–83), *The Adventures of Miguel Littín: Clandestine in Chile* (1987), and *Noticia de un secuestro* (1996). Since the early 1960s he has remained close to the Communist regime of Fidel Castro, and has often served as liaison between the Havana government and major amnesty organizations. "Uses and Abuses of the Umbrella" is reminiscent of the minimalist essayistic style of Julio Cortázar. Published in June 1955, in Columbia's *El Espectator*, it belongs to García Márquez's early career as a journalist. Thus, the piece could not actually have been influenced by his Argentine friend, Cortázar, whom he met in Paris a decade or so later. Astute, precise, and humorous, the piece is both a critique of social mannerisms and an entertaining literary game.

Uses and Abuses of the Umbrella

If one were to produce a careful statistical tabulation of the men who use umbrellas, one would determine that when the rains begin the umbrellas disappear. It's only natural: the umbrella is too fine, too delicate and lovely an article for water to be allowed to ruin it.

The umbrella, though we are led to believe otherwise, was not made for the rain. It was made to be carried on the arm like an enormous ornamental bat and to allow one the opportunity to put on British airs as the atmospheric conditions demanded. If one were to research the history of the umbrella, one would discover that it was created with a purpose far different from that which formal umbrellists wish to attribute to it—those gentlemen who mistakenly take their umbrellas to the street when it looks like rain, unaware that they are exposing their precious devices to a washing that never figured into their plan.

Cork hats and newspapers of more than eight pages were invented for the rain. Furthermore, before the cork hat and the newspaper of more than eight pages, rain had been invented for just this purpose: to fall on the happy pedestrian who has no reason in the world not to enjoy a shower of pure water from the heavens, still the best prevention against baldness ever invented.

The reduction in umbrellas during the rainy season demonstrates that there are still a goodly number of gentlemen who know what that black, molded tree with metal branches is for, a device invented by someone who grew desperate in the face of the compelling concept of being unable to fold up a bush and take it for a stroll, dangling from his arm. An intelligent woman once said: "The umbrella is an article proper to the desk." And so it is, and it is well that it is so, for it presumes that next to every desk there ought to be a coat rack and, hanging on the coat rack, an umbrella. A dry one, however. For a wet umbrella is an accident, a barbarism, a spelling mistake that must be spread open in a corner until it is fully corrected and has become a true umbrella once again. An item to be carried in the street, to be used to startle friends and—in the worst of cases—to fend off one's creditors.

TRANSLATED BY MARK SCHAFER

Jorge Ibargüengoitia

Mexico
(1928–1983)

———•••———

Jorge Ibargüengoitia spent his youth in Mexico City and pursued his studies as an engineer. However, he did not complete his training; instead, he began studying dramatic art at the National University. Theater lured him back into academia, and under the tutelage of Rodolfo Usigli, he wrote the play *El atentado* (1964). Unappealing historical research for that play and an unfavorable letter from Usigli encouraged him gradually to turn away from theater. Ibargüengoitia then moved to writing novels, beginning with *The Lightning of August* (1964). His main thematic concerns are the negative impacts of urban and industrial growth and the grotesque structures populating modern cities. He worked extensively as a theater critic and columnist, and proceeded to write a handful of novels, including *Maten al león* (1969), *The Dead Girls* (1977), *Estas ruinas que ves* (1979), *Two Crimes* (1979), and *Los pasos de López* (1982), and volumes of stories. Early in his career he also took part in a couple of prestigious literary forums, the *Revista Mexicana de Literatura* and the *Revista de la Universidad*. This exposure in Mexico's printed media continued as he moved to the daily *Excélsior* and then to Octavio Paz's monthly, *Vuelta*. Having already spent time in Europe, the United States, and Cuba, he was awarded a Rockefeller Fellowship to study theater in New York and a two-year fellowship from the Centro Mexicano de Escritores. Ibargüengoitia died tragically in an airplane crash at Barajas, Madrid, in 1983. Ironically, he often wrote about his fear of flying in his columns. "Solve This Case for Me" was written as an obituary for Agatha Christie and denotes his interest in mysteries and popular culture. It first appeared in *Excélsior* and was reprinted in Ibargüengoitia's posthumously published collection of newspaper notes, *Autopsias rápidas* (1988). In English it was part of a special issue of the *Literary Review* in 1994, devoted to detective and science fiction from Latin America.

Solve This Case for Me

In the last few weeks three different people have asked why didn't I write an article about Agatha Christie under the pretext of her death. I told all three the same thing: that to me the lady's books seem unreadable, because the ones I have read or tried to read have caused me one of two experiences: I have found out on page 40 who the murderer was because of my own intuition, for which she isn't to blame (for instance, I think that if a gentleman's only characteristic is that he winds all the clocks in the house every day, he must be the criminal), or, on the contrary, I finish the novel not knowing which way is up and I can't understand the explanation Poirot gives at the end.

But this mundane and contemptuous attitude is, on second thought, false. I think what actually happens to me with Agatha Christie and with any detective story is that I'm hopeless at solving mysteries.

When I examine my past, the opposite of what happens to Hercule Poirot happens to me: I see in the shadow of the past a forest of unanswered cases.

Not that I have found cadavers when entering the dining room, nor shoes by the swimming pool, nor received a letter signed with little drops of blood. The cases that I have tried to solve are of another nature. If I may, they are small mysteries but no less needling. Above all, no easier to solve.

One of the most unsolvable: Who took the nutcrackers?

In my house there were two identical nutcrackers that had been in my family's possession for at least seventy years. They were old but not so very old (my mother would classify them as old rubbish), not well designed (their form resembled instruments of torture from the Middle Ages), nor were they of precious metal (they were heavy with a peeling silver coating).

This is the *corpus delicti*. The suspects are the ten of us who ate at the house one Sunday in August 1967. Among the fruits there were figs and nuts, and since that day, in my house, there is only one nutcracker. I have gone over that scene many times in my mind, and I always get wrapped up in its complexity. Of the ten of us who were sitting there, no one has a criminal record, nor has gotten money illegally, nor do we know of anyone who blacks out before a metallic shine. All, I'm sure, have nutcrackers in their respective homes. And I'm also sure that a nutcracker identical to the one I now hold would have seemed endowed with irresistible beauty to anyone. Nevertheless, there is but one nutcracker.

Another disquieting possibility is that the nutcracker was thrown into the trash, with the nut shells and the fig peel. Who would dare discard this alternative?

Another unsolvable mystery that haunts me is represented by a fork with a different design from the rest that are to be found in my house. It appeared in the silverware drawer in 1950. If I am not mistaken this fork was the property of the Herrasti family. I am the guilty party in that crime. This is clear. The mystery is the circumstance that led me to commit it.

There is another mystery that I think is solved. I'm going to explain it because I believe its solution represents a triumph, not of logic but of parabolic deduction.

I'll start at the end. A few months ago we had a fairly large group of people over for dinner. When the guests left, my wife discovered a very long platinum blonde hair tangled in the bristles of her brush. Later on she noticed that the pot we mix the mustard in had disappeared. In one instant we solved the mystery: at the party there was only one woman with platinum blonde hair. We imagined her using the brush and then putting the mustard pot in her handbag.

But this deduction led me to an even more important conclusion: that woman had been present on another occasion many years before, the night that half a chicken pie disappeared. The triple crime was solved.

TRANSLATED BY FERNANDA SOICHER

Guillermo Cabrera Infante

Cuba

(b. 1929)

───•⟩•⟨•───

Guillermo Cabrera Infante grew up in Cuba and witnessed firsthand the rise of Fidel Castro. He founded and directed *Lunes de Revolución*, the first and only major Cuban literary periodical, which disappeared as the place of the artist in the revolution was questioned. He began his literary career as a film critic, publishing under the pseudonym of G. Caín. After writing his first book of stories, *Así en la paz como en la guerra* (1960), he was sent to Belgium and Luxembourg in a diplomatic role. He subsequently published a volume of film criticism entitled *Un oficio del siglo veinte* (1963). In 1965 Cabrera Infante denounced the Cuban revolution and moved to London. While in exile, he produced a superlative novel, *Three Trapped Tigers* (1967), a playful baroque account of pre-Castro Havana that earned him international fame. In the tradition of *Tristram Shandy*, the novel captures the Spanish language spoken in the Havana of the 1950s and the characters who inhabit the decadent nightlife of that epoch. The book is loosely structured, without standard plot, and subverts our traditional view of the novel by assembling anecdotes, vignettes, translations, parodies, letters, psychiatric sessions, dreams, and more without much interest in a progressive narrative. Cabrera Infante is also responsible for the autobiographical novel *Infante's Inferno* (1979) and for a book-long essay on cigars in Western culture, *Holy Smoke* (1988). Since then he has written for several British and European newspapers in both English and Spanish. Although his fiction has earned him great recognition, critics are in awe of his career as an essayist, particularly since he is able to write superbly in the two languages. The following piece, written in February 1992, was included in Cabrera Infante's *Mea Cuba* (1992), a collection of lectures, correspondence, and journalistic pieces. Its central question is speculative: What if Christopher Columbus had not discovered America? The answer is humorous and not without a political undertone.

Scenes of a World without Columbus

A hypothesis is hype with the consistency of a dream—or of a nightmare—and it has almost as much reality. But *really*—can you imagine a world without Christopher Columbus? Or maybe that Columbus had never come to the New World? That nobody, *nobody*, had discovered America? As an aid more to imagination than to navigation, I make lists.

Let us imagine, the reader and I, that the mutiny attempt on board the *Santa María* on 3 October 1492, spirited out of his ship's log later by the Grand Admiral himself, had really taken effect the night of the sixth—only *six* days before the Discovery. Instead of backing his admiral, Martín Alonso Pinzón comes to the flagship to add himself to the so-called 'rising of the Biscayans'. Columbus, in the midst of the confusing betrayal, upbraids the mutineers and confronts them with their outrageous villainy: they are not respecting their oath of loyalty made when they left the port of Palos. Now Columbus invokes the Capitulations of Santa Fe and the confidence placed in him by Their Catholic Majesties. Besides the grace of his sovereigns to which he alludes, the Grand Admiral of the Ocean Sea addresses sailors and officers and cabin boys: the whole crew and stowaways. Then he makes a last plea that they desist: 'If you don't do it for the King—do it for the Queen.'

Fatum O'Nihil, the only Irish sailor on board, inquires: 'Isabella? What about Queen Isabella?' But Columbus cannot answer him. Not because he doesn't know English but because at that moment he is carried on the crew's shoulders, like bullfighters in triumph, barely bearing his bearing. Columbus is thrown, without the ceremony that would accompany a dead body entrusted to the depths, headfirst into the sea. (Which just at that moment has ceased to be an ocean: no more Atlantic, quasi Caribbean.) He does not last long among the waves: he is not the floating Admiral. Columbus, ladies and gentlemen, didn't know how to swim! (As will be seen right away.) What is still visible of his body—flapping arms, a face of *horror vacui* (or rather *aquae*), fair hair that the black night makes dark— sinks in 'the frozen waters of egoist calculations' (see *Communist Manifesto*), as another Jew said on another occasion. Moments after sinking a third time, which is the last, Christovoro Colombo, born in Genoa, Italy, of doubtful age and discoverer by profession, disappears for ever from the face of the earth.

The captain's flagship, now without a captain, after this drowning that recalls the fall of Icarus according to Brueghel, changes its heading and followed always by the *Pinta* and the *Niña*, heads the helm back to the Canary Islands and finally to Spain.

Centuries later a recorded *guaracha* records the extreme wantonness of the act:

> About the Discoverer:
> All the Pinzón brothers
> were fags & mothers.
> Friends of the Lady Bobadilla

they liked to eat tortilla.
That's all we uncovered.

Since Columbus did not discover America, there would be no America. That Italian usurper Amerigo Vespucci, who has as much of Marco Polo as of Machiavelli, would never come to America and would not write what an obscure German geographer would not call his *Quattuor Americi Navigationes*—or insist that the Southern hemisphere be called *'ab Amerigo'*. Vespucci himself would not write his letters from America because there would not be a Casa de Contratación de Indias to hire him nor would he defect, because he would have no motive or rancour, to Portugal—to not discover Rio de Janeiro. The whole immense Brazil would not end up in Portuguese hands.

Meanwhile Father Bartolomé de Las Casas (whom a writer, who would never be called Borges, would not have injured with the epithet of 'a curious variation of the philanthropist') would not have copied Columbus's *Diary*, which one Pinzón (or the other) would have destroyed because it was evidence of the mutiny and of the murder. So the good Father would not have described the forests of Cuba, 'on top of them and from branch to branch a squirrel could traverse the island from one extreme to the other'—among other things because in Cuba there were no squirrels. Besides the island itself would not exist by not being on the maps.

The Aztecs would persist in their splendour of Metshiko, feeding themselves, literally, on other tribes. From time to time they would celebrate their rites, in which the *pièce de résistance* would be to take the beating heart out of Toltec virgins with a stone knife. The Mayas, already in their dour decline, would have left behind (uselessly) their magnificent pyramids that Japanese tourists would never be able to photograph. But the equivalent of the Greek goddess of victory, Niké, would be called Nikon. Even though the invention of the hand camera would still be delayed because there never was an inventor named Edison to not invent film nor did another man named Eastman create the Kodak camera.

Since the Viking sailors did not write ships' logs North America would not take place. Without the USA the German defeat in the First World War (that did happen) would be converted into a victory, to which England would have to make adjustments and France would be saved the humiliation of the Occupation and the opportune collaborators of later on. Hitler of course would have had to continue his career as a house-painter (from house to house) and Mussolini would perhaps have debuted in La Scala—as a *partichino*. Neither would there be *partigiani* to fight his wrong notes with imported Bronx cheers and rotten tomatoes.

Lenin would not have travelled (in the historic first-class coach of a sealed German train) to the Finland Station because the Germans, having no reason to do so, would not have offered him a ticket to ride. Kerensky, conveniently embalmed, would occupy today Lenin's place in the St Petersburg mausoleum, because, among so many things that would not happen, Moscow would not become capital of Russia again. Marx, on the other hand, would exist, but as an amateur economist whose capital work, *Das Kapital*, would be his revenge for too many boils. Nobody would read this book, or translate it into any other languages. So it would never become the Bible of state capitalism. Karl yes, damn it, but no Groucho, alas.

If Martín Alonso Pinzón had carried out what he intended once (or twice) and the rabble on board, who wanted to get back home in time for their gazpacho more than to reach America, had mutinied and murdered the obstinate mad mariner or had forced him to take a nautical U-turn, there would have been neither Communism in Russia nor its consequences, Nazism and Fascism. Franco, of course, would have retired with the pension of a general who never won a battle. His lieutenant, Manuel Fraga, would not now put on the airs of a flying statesman, nor have had to inaugurate a museum in his parent's house in Cuba, because there would have been no Galician emigration to a land that never existed.

In Stockholm they would not have ignored the great Darío, who as a pure Indian and not a *mestizo* would not have written a single line of verse in Spanish. (They still would have given the prize to Juan Ramón Jiménez, who would not have been a follower of Darío but perhaps an original poet.) As with Borges, they would have given the Nobel neither to Neruda nor to Miss Mistral, because they would not have existed. But perhaps Asturias would have received a consolation prize for being Indian. Although the Indians, without a Columbus to come to the Indies to name them, would not be Indians either.

In Spain no one could go partying (such sweet sorrow) to a *guateque* or smoke *puros* (but *porros* yes) or cigarettes made of tobacco and they wouldn't call their politicians *caciques*. A third of the *Dictionary of the Royal Academy*, which would continue to be royal, would remain blank from an absence of Americanisms. In the non–*guateques* nobody would dance rumbas or *sones* (which would never be called salsa) or mambos, although the chachacha, because of what it has of a Madrid schottische, would perhaps have been created by a Jorrín de Jérez. But, think about it, there would be no Antonio Machín to sing boleros. Worse still, there would be no Olga Guillot or Celia Cruz or Beny Moré—or Pérez Prado to put the pain of Spain in the mambo. Nor would there be *habanera* competitions in Tarraza nor would anyone dance tangos like Valentino in *Apocalypse* then. Nor would there be jazz or blues or rock or rap because there wouldn't be blacks in an America that never existed. As there was no slavery, the whole continent would end up as an infinite Indian boredom and the only entertainment, to the sound of fifes and flutes, would be the *tamborito* in the south—while in the north there would be the tribal wars to perform, in which the Cheyennes would try to exterminate the Sioux, and the redskins would finish off the darker Apaches without even using the horse or the repeating rifle. But worse than no horses, no Westerns or John Ford—and, what is worse still, there would be no Westerns by John Ford.

Nobody, of course, would eat potatoes, neither French fried nor as Spanish straw. But there would not be the great famine in Ireland in the last century because of the failure of the potato harvest and no Irishman would have emigrated to some United States that never existed. (Perhaps thus the world would have been freed of the Kennedy blight for ever.) There would have been bananas but Africa grown and there would be neither avocado nor tomato to make a mixed salad. There would be coffee but there would be no chocolate and the Godiva lady would end up being naked for ever. There would be no Panama and so, no Panama hats. And though there would be opium and morphine and heroin, there would be no cocaine, that stimulant so dear to the movie world.

But there would be no movies because the Lumière Brothers only adopted and adapted an invention by Edison, who as we have already seen was an inventor who never invented. There would be no Hollywood therefore and though sooner or later the Germans would have invented the *Kino*, nobody would call Berlin the Mecca of the Kino. There would be photography thanks to Daguerre and to Niepce but never *le cinéma* in France. There would be no Marilyn Monroe alive or dead. Nor would there be Ginger Rogers's gorgeous bare back or Kim Novak's true sacred cow beauty or Cyd Charisse's legs too. And though there would have been a Rita Hayworth, called Margarita Cansino in Seville, she wouldn't be the same—believe me. Greta Garbo would have stayed in Sweden, still named Gustafson. There would be no Fred Astaire, although there would be a gypsy dancer in Cádiz named Alfredo del Aire. And, think about it, there would never have been a round world to go around.

If Columbus had not invoked the Catholic Kings, Christ and God himself, who had created the pole star to guide the flagship. If Martín Alonso Pinzón had not rowed from his caravel to the *Santa María* and backed up the Grand Admiral in his vision of an Asia for the Europeans. If Columbus had not praised himself as a saint before King and Queen on his return (yes, from America) declaring that he was guided more by Isaiah's prophecy than by the celestial bodies, which governed only his compass and his astrolabe but not his luck. If the hallucinating Admiral, God's secret agent, had not seen the American dawn, none of the aforementioned would exist—not even as a negation. And I have left out more, much more. (Or rather, less, much less.)

Without Columbus there would have been no America, but no Latin America either and the natives of the centre and of the south, pure Indians all, would not be called Latins, a tag they do not understand in a language they do not speak and would be Aztecs or Mayas or Chibchas or Incas or Araucanians or Quechuas or Guaranís who bear a Latinity as the baptism of a lay religion. Or a mockery.

If Christopher Columbus had not discovered America, I would never have written this vertiginous list that you will read perhaps with equal vertigo. But neither would Fidel Castro have existed nor the totalitarian horror that he implanted.

If the price of leaving nothingness for a moment only to enter nothingness again, which is being, were not being, I would pay with content the other nothingness. So with the pleasure of knowledge I would see the mutineers of the 9 October 1492 converted into exterminating angels of history—to throwing the hated Genoese once and for all into the sea.

TRANSLATED BY KENNETH HALL

Roberto Fernández Retamar

Cuba
(b. 1930)

––––––•◦•◦•––––––

One of the most important and influential voices of the Cuban Revolution, Roberto Fernández Retamar has taught at Yale and the University of Havana, is a well-known critic, and has edited the magazine *Casa de las Américas*. Before the armed struggle led by Fidel Castro at the end of 1958, Fernández Retamar was known as an academic, but it was the triumph of the *guerrilleros* that pushed him toward a clear political commitment. His poetry is light and colloquial and can be found in a number of volumes, including *Poesía reunida: 1948–65* (1966). His essays analyze subjects involving cultural, intellectual, and ideological conditions and the radical transformation necessary for Communism to prevail in a Latin American society. He is also known for exploring the relationship between his generation of writers and Castro's regime in critical works such as *Papelería* (1962) and *Ensayo de otro mundo* (1967). Other important works include *Buena suerte viviendo* (1967), *Qué veremos arder* (1970), *A quien pueda interesar* (1970), and *Cuaderno paralelo* (1973). Fernández Retamar is best known for his long essay *Caliban: Notes toward a Discussion of Culture in Our America*, in which the following essay serves as an introduction. Originally published in Havana in *Casa de las Américas*, in the September/October 1971 issue, and translated into English three years later in the *Massachusetts Review*, the essay is a Marxist discussion of authenticity dwelling on the dichotomies of civilization and barbarism and of the characters Ariel and Caliban in Shakespeare's *The Tempest*. The discussion returns to a topic popularized by the Modernista critic José Enrique Rodó in his classic *Ariel*.

Caliban: A Question

A European journalist, and moreover a leftist, asked me a few days ago, "Does a Latin American culture exist?" We were discussing, naturally enough, the recent polemic regarding Cuba which ended by confronting, on the one hand, certain bourgeois European intellectuals (or aspirants to that state) with a visible colonialist nostalgia; and on the other, that body of Latin American writers and artists who reject open or veiled forms of cultural and political colonialism. The question seemed to me to reveal one of the roots of the polemic, and could also be expressed another way:

"Do you exist?" For to question our culture is to question our very existence, our human reality itself, and thus to be willing to take a stand in favor of our irremediable colonial condition, since it suggests that we would be but a distorted echo of what occurs elsewhere. This elsewhere is of course the metropolis, the colonizing centers, whose "right wings" have exploited us and whose supposed "left wings" have pretended and continue to pretend to guide us with pious solicitude; in both cases, with the assistance of local intermediaries of varying persuasions.

While this fate is to some extent suffered by all countries emerging from colonialism—those countries of ours which enterprising metropolitan intellectuals have ineptly and successively termed *barbarians, peoples of colour, underdeveloped countries, third world*—I think the phenomenon achieves a singular crudeness with respect to what Martí called "our *mestizo* America." Although the unquestionable thesis that every man and even every culture is *mestizo* could easily be defended, and although this seems especially valid in the case of colonies, it is nevertheless apparent that in both the ethnic as well as the cultural aspects, capitalist countries long ago achieved a relative homogeneity. Almost before our eyes certain readjustments have been made. The white population of the United States (diverse, but of common European origin) exterminated the aboriginal population and thrust the black population aside, thereby affording itself homogeneity in spite of diversity, and offering a coherent model which its Nazi disciples attempted to apply even to other European conglomerates—an unforgiveable sin that led some members of the bourgeoisie to stigmatize in Hitler what they applauded as a healthy Sunday diversion in Westerns and Tarzan films. Those movies proposed to the world—and even to those of us who are kin to the communities under attack and who rejoiced in the evocation of our own extermination—the monstrous racial criteria which has accompanied the United States from its beginnings to the genocide in Indochina. Less apparent (and in some cases perhaps less cruel) is the process by which other capitalist countries have also achieved relative racial and cultural homogeneity at the expense of *internal* diversity.

Nor can any necessary relationship be established between *mestizaje* [racial intermingling; racial mixture—ed. note] and the colonial world. The latter is highly complex* despite basic structural affinities. It has included countries with well-defined millennial cultures, some of which (India, Vietnam) have suffered (or are presently suffering) direct occupation, and others, such as China, which have suffered indirect occupation. It also comprehends countries with rich cultures, but less political homogeneity, which have been subjected to extremely diverse forms of colonialism (the Arab world). There are other countries, finally, whose fundamental struc-

*Cf. Yves Lacoste. *Les pays sous-developpés* (Paris, 1959), pp. 82–4.

tures were savagely dislocated by the dire activity of the European (the peoples of black Africa), despite which they continue to preserve a certain ethnic and cultural homogeneity. (Indeed, the latter occurred despite the colonialists' criminal and unsuccessful attempts to prohibit it.) In these countries, *mestizaje* naturally exists to a greater or lesser degree, but it is always accidental and always on the fringe of its central line of development.

But within the colonial world, there exists a case unique to *the entire planet*: a vast zone for which *mestizaje* is not an accident, but rather the essence, the central line: ourselves, "our *mestizo* America." Martí, with his excellent knowledge of the language, employed this specific adjective as the distinctive sign of our culture—a culture of descendants, both ethnically and culturally speaking, of aborigines, Africans, and Europeans. In his "Letter from Jamaica" (1815), the Liberator Simón Bolívar had proclaimed: "We are a small human species: we possess a world encircled by vast seas, new in almost all its arts and sciences." In his message to the Congress of Angostura (1819), he added:

> Let us bear in mind that our people is neither European nor North American, but a composite of Africa and America, rather than an emanation of Europe; for even Spain fails as a European people because of her African blood, her institutions and her character. It is impossible to assign us with any exactitude to a specific human family. The greater part of the native peoples have been annihilated; the European has mingled with the American and with the African, and the latter has mingled with the Indian and with the European. Born from the womb of a common mother, our fathers, different in origin and blood, are foreigners; all differ visibly in the epidermis, and this dissimilarity leaves marks of the greatest transcendence.

Even in this century, in a book as confused as the author himself but full of intuitions (*La raza cósmica*, 1925), the Mexican José Vasconcelos pointed out that in Latin America a new race was being forged, "made with the treasure of all previous ones, the final race, the cosmic race."*

---

*A Swedish summary of what is known on this subject can be found in Magnus Mörner's study, *La mexcla de razas en la historia de América Latina*, translation, reviewed by the author, by Jorge Piatigorsky, Buenos Aires, 1969. Here it is recognized that "no part of the world has witnessed such a gigantic mixing of races as the one that has been taking place in Latin America and the Caribbean [Why this division?] since 1492," p. 15. Of course, what interests me in these notes is not the irrelevant biological fact of the "races" but the historical fact of the "cultures": *vid.* Claude Lévi-Strauss: *Race et histoire* (1952), (Paris, 1968), *passim.*

This singular fact lies at the root of countless misunderstandings. Chinese, Vietnamese, Korean, Arab or African cultures may leave the Euro-North American enthusiastic, indifferent, or even depressed. But it would never occur to him to confuse a Chinese with a Norwegian, or a Bantu with an Italian; nor would it occur to him to ask whether they exist. Yet, on the other hand, some Latin Americans are taken at times for apprentices, for rough drafts or dull copies of Europeans, including among these latter whites who constitute what Martí called "European America." In the same way our entire culture is taken as an apprenticeship, a rough draft or a copy of European bourgeois culture ("an emanation of Europe," as Bolívar said). This last error is more frequent than the first, since confusion of a Cuban with an Englishman or a Guatemalan with a German tends to be impeded by a certain ethnic tenacity. Here the *rioplatenses* appear to be less ethnically, although not culturally, differentiated. The confusion lies in the root itself, because as descendants of numerous Indian, African, and European communities, we have only a few languages with which to understand one another: those of the colonizers. While other colonials or ex-colonials, in metropolitan centers, speak among themselves in their own language, we Latin Americans continue to use the languages of our colonizers. These are the *linguas fancas* capable of going beyond the frontiers which neither the aboriginal nor creole languages succeed in crossing. Right now as we are discussing, as I am discussing with those colonizers, how else can I do it except in one of their languages, which is now also *our* language, and with so many of their conceptual tools which are now also *our* conceptual tools? This is precisely the extraordinary outcry which we read in a work by perhaps the most extraordinary writer of fiction who ever existed. In *The Tempest*, William Shakespeare's last play, the deformed Caliban—enslaved, robbed of his island, and taught the language by Prospero—rebukes him thus: "You taught me language, and my profit on't/ Is, I know how to curse. The red plague rid you/ For learning me your language!" (*The Tempest*; Act 1, Scene ii.)

TRANSLATED BY LYNN GARAFOLA, DAVID ARTHUR McMURRAY,
AND ROBERT MÁRQUEZ

Antonio Benítez Rojo

Cuba
(b. 1931)

———◆•••◆———

avana, Antonio Benítez Rojo received degrees in economics, finance, and accounting from the University of Havana in 1955 and the American University in Washington, D.C. His early childhood was spent traveling with his family throughout Latin America, and he grew up to become an important Cuban cultural figure of the 1960s. He worked in succession as a statistician for the Cuban Ministry of Labor, the Cuban Telephone Company, and the Council of Urban Development. Then, in 1965, he turned to journalism, finding his true calling: literature. At that point Benítez Rojo established an association with the Casa de las Américas Foundation, where he edited numerous anthologies and was involved in the judging of several prestigious literary awards granted by the Cuban government to Latin American writers. In 1980 he defected while serving on a Cuban delegation in Paris and eventually settled in the United States. While still in Cuba he published *Tute de Reyes* (1967), which was awarded a Casa de las Américas prize, *El escudo de hojas secas* (1969), *El mar de las lentejas* (1979), and *El enigma de los esterlines* (1980), among other works. Once in the United States, Benítez Rojo produced *The Repeating Island: The Caribbean and the Postmodern Perspective* (1989), a voluminous critical work reevaluating Caribbean identity from Fray Bartolomé de las Casas to the writers Alejo Carpentier, Wilson Harris, and Edgardo Rodríguez Juliá; he also published the English translation of *Sea of Lentils* (1990), a book banned in Cuba after its 1979 publication. He has taught at the Universities of Pittsburgh, California-Irvine, Brown, and at Amherst College. The essay "Apocalypse and Chaos," became the introduction to *The Repeating Island*. In it Benítez Rojo examines the particular nature of Caribbean identity.

Apocalypse and Chaos

I can isolate with frightening exactitude—like the hero of Sartre's novel—the moment at which I reached the age of reason. It was a stunning October afternoon, years ago, when the atomization of the meta-archipelago under the dread umbrella of nuclear catastrophe seemed imminent. The children of Havana, at least in my neighborhood, had been evacuated; a grave silence fell over the streets and the sea. While the state bureaucracy searched for news off the shortwave or hid behind official speeches and communiqués, two old black women passed "in a certain kind of way" beneath my balcony. I cannot describe this "certain kind of way"; I will say only that there was a kind of ancient and golden power between their gnarled legs, a scent of basil and mint in their dress, a symbolic, ritual wisdom in their gesture and their gay chatter. I knew then at once that there would be no apocalypse. The swords and the archangels and the beasts and the trumpets and the breaking of the last seal were not going to come, for the simple reason that the Caribbean is not an apocalyptic world; it is not a phallic world in pursuit of the vertical desires of ejaculation and castration. The notion of the apocalypse is not important within the culture of the Caribbean. The choices of all or nothing, for or against, honor or blood have little to do with the culture of the Caribbean. These are ideological propositions articulated in Europe which the Caribbean shares only in declamatory terms, or, better, in terms of a first reading. In Chicago a beaten soul says: "I can't take it any more," and gives himself up to drugs or to the most desperate violence. In Havana, he would say: "The thing to do is not die," or perhaps: "Here I am, fucked but happy."

The so-called October crisis or missile crisis was not won by J.F.K. or by N. K. or much less by F. C. (statesmen always wind up abbreviated in these great events that they themselves created); it was won by the culture of the Caribbean, together with the loss that any win implies. If this had happened, let's say, in Berlin, children there would now be discovering hand tools and learning to make fire with sticks. The plantation of atomic projectiles sown in Cuba was a Russian machine, a machine of the steppes, historically terrestrial. It was a machine that carried the culture of the horse and of yogurt, the cossack and the mouzhik, the birch and the rye, the ancient caravans and the Siberian railroad; a culture where the land is everything and the sea a forgotten memory. But the culture of the Caribbean, at least in its most distinctive aspect, is not terrestrial but aquatic, a sinuous culture where time unfolds irregularly and resists being captured by the cycles of clock and calendar. The Caribbean is the natural and indispensable realm of marine currents, of waves, of folds and double-folds, of fluidity and sinuosity. It is, in the final analysis, a culture of the meta-archipelago: a chaos that returns, a detour without a purpose, a continual flow of paradoxes; it is a feedback machine with asymmetrical workings, like the sea, the wind, the clouds, the uncanny novel, the food chain, the music of Malaya, Gödel's theorem and fractal mathematics. It will be said that in that case Hellas does not meet our canon for meta-archipelagoes. But yes, it meets it. What's happened is that Western thought has kept on thinking of itself as the diachronic repetition on an ancient polemic. I am referring to the repressive and fallacious machine made up of the binary opposition

Aristotle *versus* Plato. Greek thought has been subjected to such sleight of hand that Plato's version of Socrates has been accepted as the limit of the tolerable, while the glowing constellation of ideas that made up the Greek heaven by way of the Pre-Socratics, the Sophists, and the Gnostics has been ignored or distorted. This magnificent firmament has been reduced almost as if we were to erase every star in the sky but Castor and Pollux. Certainly, Greek thought was much more than this philosophical duel between Plato and Aristotle. It's just that certain not entirely symmetrical ideas scandalized the faith of the Middle Ages, modern rationalism, and the functionalist positivism of our time, and it's not necessary to pursue this matter, because we're speaking here of the Caribbean. Let's say good-bye to Hellas, applauding the idea of a forgotten sage, Thales of Miletus: water is the beginning of all things.

Then how can we describe the culture of the Caribbean in any way other than by calling it a feedback machine? Nobody has to rack his brains to come up with an answer; it's in the public domain. If I were to have to put it in one word I would say: performance. But performance not only in terms of scenic interpretation but also in terms of the execution of a ritual, that is, that "certain way" in which the two Negro women who conjured away the apocalypse were walking. In this "certain kind of way" there is expressed the mystic or magical (if you like) loam of the civilizations that contributed to the formation of Caribbean culture. Of course there have been some things written about this too, although I think that there's a lot of cloth left to be cut. For example, when we speak of the genesis of Caribbean culture we are given two alternatives: either we are told that the complex syncretism of Caribbean cultural expressions—what I shall call here *supersyncretism* to distinguish it from similar forms—arose out of the collision of European, African, and Asian components within the Plantation, or that this syncretism flows along working with ethnological machines that are quite distant in space and remote in time, that is, machines "of a certain kind" that one would have to look for in the subsoils of all of the continents. But, I ask, why not take both alternatives as valid, and not just those but others as well? Why pursue a Euclidian coherence that the world—and the Caribbean above all—is very far from having?

Certainly, in order to reread the Caribbean we have to visit the sources from which the widely various elements that contributed to the formation of its culture flowed. This unforeseen journey tempts us because as soon as we succeed in establishing and identifying as separate any of the signifiers that make up the supersyncretic manifestation that we're studying, there comes a moment of erratic displacement of its signifiers toward other spatio-temporal points, be they in Europe, Africa, Asia, or America, or in all these continents at once. When these points of departure are nonetheless reached, a new chaotic flight of signifiers will occur, and so on ad infinitum.

Let's take as an example a syncretic object that has been well studied, let's say, the cult of the Virgen de la Caridad del Cobre (still followed by many Cubans). If we were to analyze this cult—presuming that it hasn't been done before—we would necessarily come upon a date (1605) and a place (el Cobre, near Santiago de Cuba); that is, within the spatio-temporal frame where the cult was first articulated upon three sources of meaning: one of aboriginal origin (the Taino deity Atabey or Atabex), another native to Europe (the Virgin of *Illescas*), and finally, another from Africa (the Yoruba *orisha* Oshun). For many anthropologists the history of this cult would begin or end here, and of course they would give reasons to explain this arbitrary break in the chain of signifiers. They would say, perhaps, that the people who today inhabit the Antilles are "new," and therefore their earlier situation, their tradition of being "a certain kind of way," should not count; they would say that with the disappearance of the Antillean aborigine during the first century of colonization these islands were left unconnected to the Indoamerican mechanisms, thus providing a "new" space for "new" men to create a "new" society and, with it, a "new" culture that can no longer be taken as an extension of those that brought the "new" inhabitants. Thus the Virgen de la Caridad del Cobre would turn out to be exclusively Cuban, and as the patron saint of Cuba she would appear in a kind of panoply along with the flag, the coat of arms, the statues of the founders, the map of the island, the royal palms, and the national anthem; she would be, in short, an attribute of Cuba's civic religion and nothing more.

Fine; I share this systemic focus, although only within the perspective offered by a first reading in which—as we know—the reader reads himself. But it happens to be the case that after several close readings of the Virgen and her cult it is possible for a Cuban reader to be seduced by the materials that he has been reading, and he should feel a reduced dose of the nationalism that he has projected on to the Virgen. This will happen only if his ego abandons for an instant his desire to feel Cuban only, a feeling that has offered him the mirage of a safe place under the cover of a nationality that connects him to the land and to the fathers of the country. If this momentary wavering should occur, the reader would cease to inscribe himself within the space of the Cuban and would set out venturing along the roads of limitless chaos that any advanced rereading offers. This being so, he would have to leap outside of the statist, statistical Cuba after searching for the wandering signifiers that inform the cult of the Virgen de la Caridad del Cobre. For a moment, just for a moment, the Virgen and the reader will cease to be Cuban.

The first surprise or perplexity that the triptych Atabey-Nuestra Señora-Oshun presents us is that it is not "original" but rather "originating." In fact, Atabey, the Taino deity, is a syncretic object in itself, one whose signifiers deliver to us another signifier that is somewhat unforeseen: Orehu, mother of waters to the Arawaks of the Guianas. This voyage of signification is a heady one for more than one reason. In the first place it involves the grand epic of the Arawaks; the departure from the Amazon basin, the ascension of the Orinoco, the arrival at the Caribbean coast, the meticulous settlement of each island until arriving at Cuba, the still obscure encounter with the Mayans of Yucatan, the ritual game of the ball of resin, the "other" connection between both subcontinental masses (such was the forgotten feat of these people). In the second place, it involves also the no less grand epic of the Caribs: the Arawak islands as objects of Carib desire; construction of large canoes, preparations for war, raids on the coastal islands, Trinidad, Tobago, Margarita, ravishing the women, victory feasts. Then the invasion stage, Grenada, St. Vincent, St. Lucia, Martinique, Dominica, Guadeloupe, the killing of the Arawaks, the glorious cannibalism of men and of words, *carib, calib, cannibal,* and *Caliban;* finally, the Sea of the Caribs, from Guyana to the Virgin Islands, the sea that isolated the Arawaks (*Tainos*) from the Greater Antilles, that cut the connection with the South American coast but not the continuity of cultural flow: Atabey-Orehu, the flux of signifiers that crossed the spatio-temporal barrier of the Caribbean to continue linking Cuba with the Orinoco and Amazon basins; Atabey-Orehu, progenitor of the supreme being of the Tainos, mother of the Taino lakes and rivers, protector of feminine ebbs and flows, of the great mysteries of the blood that women experience, and there, at the other end of the Antillean arc, the Great Mother of Waters, the immediacy of the matriarchy, the beginning of the cultivation of the yucca, the ritual orgy, incest, the sacrifice of the virgin male, blood and earth.

There is something enormously old and powerful in this, I know; a contradictory vertigo which there is no reason to interrupt, and so we reach the point at which the image of Our Lady venerated in el Cobre is, also, a syncretic object, produced by two quite distinct images of the Virgin Mary, which were to wind up in the hands of the chiefs of Cueiba and Macaca, and which were adored simultaneously as Atabey and as Nuestra Señora (this last in the form of an amulet). Imagine for a moment these chiefs' perplexity when they saw, for the first time, what no Taino had seen before: the image, in color, of the Mother of the Supreme Being, the lone progenitor of Yucahu Bagua Maorocoti, who now turned out to be, in addition, the mother of the god of those bearded, yucca-colored men; she who, according to them, protected them from death and injury in war. *Ave María*, these Indians would learn to say as they worshiped their Atabey, who at one time had been Orehu, and before that the Great Arawak Mother. *Ave María*, Francisco Sánchez de Moya, a sixteenth-century Spanish captain, would surely say when he received the commission and the order to make the crossing to Cuba to start copper foundries in the mines of El Prado. *Ave María*, he would say once again when he wrapped the image of Nuestra Señora de Illescas, of whom he was a devotee, among his shirts to protect him from the dangerous storms and shipwrecks of the hazardous passage to the Indies. *Ave María*, he would repeat on the day he placed it upon the humble altar in the solitary hermitage of Santiago del Prado, the merest hut for the poor Indians and Negroes who worked the copper mines.

But the image, that of Nuestra Señora de Illescas, brought to Cuba by the good captain, had a long history behind it. It is itself another syncretic object. The chain of signifiers now takes us across the Renaissance to the Middle Ages. It leads us to Byzantium, the unique, the magnificent, where among all kinds of heresies and pagan practices the cult of the Virgin Mary was born (a cult unforeseen by the Doctors of the Church). There in Byzantium, among the splendors of its icons and mosaics, a likeness of the Virgin Mary and her Child may have been plundered by some crusading and voracious knight, or acquired by a seller of relics, or copied on the retina of some pious pilgrim. At any rate the suspicious cult of the Virgin Mary filtered surreptitiously into Europe. Surely it would not have gone very far on its own, but this happened at the beginning of the twelfth century, the legendary epoch of the troubadours and of *fin amour*, when Woman ceased to be Eve, the dirty and damned seducer of Adam and ally of the Serpent. She was washed, perfumed, and sumptuously dressed to suit the scope of her new image: the Lady. Then, the cult of Our Lady spread like fire through gunpowder, and one fine day it arrived at Illescas, a few miles away from Toledo.

Ave María, the slaves at the El Prado mines repeated aloud, and quickly, in an undertone that the priest could not hear, they added: *Oshun Yeye*. For that miraculous altar image was for them one of the most conspicuous *orishas* of the Yoruba pantheon: Oshun Yeye Moro, the perfumed whore; Oshun Kayode, the gay dancer; Oshun Aña, the lover of the drum; Oshun Akuara, she who mixes love potions; Oshun Ede, the *grande dame*; Oshun Fumike, she who gives children to sterile women; Oshun Funke, the wise one; Oshun Kole-Kole, the wicked sorcerers.

Oshun, as a syncretic object, is as dizzying as her honeyed dance and yellow bandanas. She is traditionally the Lady of the Rivers, but some of her avatars relate her to the bays and the seashores. Her most prized objects are amber, coral, and yellow metals; her favorite foods are honey, squash, and sweets that contain eggs. Sometimes she shows herself to be gentle and ministering, above all in women's matters and those of love; at other times she shows herself to be insensitive, capricious, and voluble, and she can even become nasty and treacherous; in these darker apparitions we also see her as an old carrion-eating witch and as the *orisha* of death.

This multiple aspect of Oshun makes us think at once of the contradictions of Aphrodite. Both goddesses, one as much as the other, are at once "luminous" and "dark"; they reign over a place where men find both pleasure and death, love and hate, voluptuousity and betrayal. Both goddesses came from the sea and inhabit the marine, fluvial, and vaginal tides; both seduce gods and men, and both protect cosmetics and prostitution.

The correspondences between the Greek and Yoruba pantheons have been noted, but they have not been explained. How to explain, to give another example, the unusual parallel of Hermes and Elegua? Both are "the travelers," the "messengers of the gods," the "keepers of the gates," "lords of the thresholds"; both were adored in the form of phallic stone figures, both protect crossroads, highways, and commerce, and both can show themselves in the figure of a man with a cane who rests his body's weight on one foot alone. Both sponsor the start of any activity, make transactions smooth, and are the only ones to pass through the terrible spaces that mediate the Supreme Being and the gods, the gods and the dead, the living and the dead. Both, finally, appear as naughty, mendacious children, or as tricky and lascivious old men; both are the "givers of discourse" and they preside over the word, over mysteries, transformations, processes, and changes; they are the alpha and omega of things. For this reason, certain Yoruba ceremonies begin and end with Elegua's dance.

In the same way, Africa and Aphrodite have more in common than the Greek root that unites their names; there is a flow of marine foam that connects two civilizations "in another way," from within the turbulence of chaos, two civilizations doubly separated by geography and history. The cult of the Virgen de la Caridad del Cobre can be read as a Cuban cult, but it can also be reread—one reading does not negate the other—as a meta-archipelagic text, a meeting or confluence of marine flowings that connects the Niger with the Mississippi, the China Sea with the Orinoco, the Parthenon with a fried food stand in an alley in Paramaribo.

The peoples of the sea, or better, the Peoples of the Sea proliferate incessantly while differentiating themselves from one another, traveling together toward the infinite. Certain dynamics of their culture also repeat and sail through the seas of time without reaching anywhere. If I were to put this in two words, they would be: performance and rhythm. And nonetheless, I would have to add something more: the notion that we have called "in a certain kind of way," something remote that reproduces itself and that carries the desire to sublimate apocalypse and violence; something obscure that comes from the performance and that one makes his own in a very special way; concretely, it takes away the space that separates the onlooker from the participant.

TRANSLATED BY JAMES MARANISS

Alejandro Rossi

Venezuela
(b. 1931)

———◆•◆◆•◆———

Although Alejandro Rossi was born in Florence, Italy, became a Venezuelan early on, and has lived in Mexico most of his life, he has traveled to and resided in various other Latin American countries. This globe-trotting life helped make him one of the most outstanding examples of Hispanic intellectual cosmopolitanism. His essays are always far-ranging in scope and meticulously Borgesian in style. They deal with philosophical issues—again, often from a Borgesian perspective—and they discuss major nineteenth- and twentieth-century authors, such as Samuel Johnson, Stendhal, and Alexander Solzhenitsyn. Rossi studied philosophy in Mexico, England, and Germany. He founded the magazine *Crítica* and is responsible for such essayistic works as *Lenguaje y significado* (1976), *Sueños de Occam* (1979), *El cielo de Sotero* (1982), and *La fábula de las regiones* (1988). For many years he remained devoted to Octavio Paz's monthly *Vuelta*, publishing in its pages a wide range of pieces. His fame is closely tied to *Manual del distraído* (1978), a much-reprinted collection of essays. "The Perfect Page," a homage to Borges, is part of that collection.

The Perfect Page

To write about Jorge Luis Borges's work is to resign oneself to being the echo of some Scandinavian commentator or a persevering, erudite, eager North American professor; it is to resign oneself, perhaps, to writing once more page 124 of a doctoral dissertation, which is most likely being defended by its author at this very moment. In the bibliography compiled by Horacio Jorge Becco—covering the years 1923 to 1973—the section "Criticism and Biography" lists 1,010 works. They cover the spectrum: books, monographs, reviews, oceanic essays and minuscule exegeses, recollections, portraits, amends, speeches, titles that aspire to elegance—*Jorge Luis Borges ou la mort au bout du Labyrinthe, Masques, miroirs, mensonges et labyrinthe*—others that dream of an academic career—*Eine Betrachtung seiner Lyrik im Rahmen des Gesamtwerkes*—those that try for the brief paradox— *The Subject Doesn't Object*—and those that achieve an utter lack of taste: *A Blind Writer with Insight.* (Anyone in search of the horrific shall find it: *Borges, Poor Babbling Blind Man.*) Not to forget, of course, the unavoidable *J.L.B.: The Genius and the Man.* To write about Borges is to compete with an author who never ceased to think about himself, in all his works and before the innumerable tape recorders that have surrounded him. Indeed, the aforementioned bibliography collects book-length interviews; conversations that go on for 144 pages; less laborious, perhaps informal chats—five, seven, ten pages long; and even a brief encounter whose title deserves transcription: *My Unhappy Note (Five Minutes, Forty Seconds with Jorge Luis Borges)*. I myself have no filing cabinets—only a mediocre memory, his books, the habit of reading them, and the tendency to imitate them. I renounce erudition and venture into plagiarism. Like he who is fulfilling a desire, I am becoming one more citation in the next edition of Horacio J. Becco's bibliography.

I imagine that Borges is not particularly interested in literary immortality. I don't think he stays awake imagining how many pages will be dedicated to him in future literary histories or the figure of his potential statue. Regarding that other immortality, the personal one, he has for a long time now maintained that "perhaps we all know deep down that we are immortal" ("Funes the Memorious"). Very recently, on July 21 [1976] (*La Nación*, Buenos Aires), he confessed that he viewed this protraction as a threat. I also recall having read that he found the idea of overcoming death inconceivable. I don't presume to put these beliefs in order—beliefs susceptible to alteration from one moment to the next, given an unanticipated experience, a fear, hope, or abandonment. I don't wish to digress concerning an intimacy that is his alone. My intention is to speak of another form of overcoming death, no less mysterious, and which has been a constant preoccupation of Borges. I am thinking of something one might call the fate of the literary work.

In an essay from 1930—"The Superstitious Ethic of the Reader"— Borges describes the perfect page: "[The] page on which no word may be altered without causing damage is the most precarious of all. Shifts in language wipe away lateral meanings and nuances. The 'perfect' page is the one composed of those delicate values and which is eroded with the slightest effort. Inversely, the page with a vocation for immortality is capable of withstanding errata, of approximate versions, inattentive readers, and misunderstandings without ever risking its soul." A technical observation and a conviction cohabit this paragraph. The former tells us that the history and evolution of language do away with certain connotations, certain resonances, allusions, and their dependent meanings. The text is thus transformed into a trifle, a stupidity, or else an incomprehensible object. Here, Borges is characterizing the perfect page as that which sustains itself entirely through the values of language. I don't know whether he also thinks that these values always work to the exclusion of others. In any case, he is suggesting that the perfect page is, in a certain sense, the empty page, a purely linguistic artifact. It can't withstand the passage of time because it is nothing but language: it is destroyed by the inattention of a linotypist, by the variance of usage, by change—in short, by life itself. The conviction that enlivens these lines of Borges is that this project is essentially a trivial one, or alternately, an erroneous calculation. In a previous work on Quevedo, we read that this author "is not inferior to anyone, but he has not found a symbol capable of seizing people's imagination. Homer has Priam, who kisses the homicidal hands of Achilles; Sophocles has a king who solves riddles and the Fates who must decipher the horror of his destiny; Lucretius has the infinite starry abyss and the dissonance of the atoms; Dante, the nine circles of hell and the Rose of paradise; Shakespeare, his spheres of violence and music; Cervantes, the happy oscillation of Sancho and Quixote." The work that manages to invent or discover such a symbol will last; that which doesn't find it or fails to seek it shall disappear or retreat into the literary obscurity of a particular country. The condition has changed and is more determined, but the emphasis remains the same: that which transcends language is that which survives. To discourage that project, Borges relies on yet another sort of reasoning. The search for the new metaphor, for example, is by necessity a futile, pointless task given that true metaphors, those that formulate intimate connections between one image and another, have always existed. The metaphors we can still invent are false ones, metaphors that are not worth inventing (*Other Inquisitions*). In a story from *Doctor Brodie's Report*, he restates the idea that "commonplace metaphors are the best because they are the only true ones." Writers, he adds, are barely slivers of a trunk, the passing interpreters of a linguistic tradition that imposes specific limits. His conclusion is practically an act of surrender: "Individual experiments are truly insignificant except when the innovator resigns himself to constructing a museum piece, a diversion destined to be discussed by literary historians or simply to cause a commotion, like *Finnegan's Wake* or *Soledades*" (prologue, *Selected Poems*). I believe that Borges is revealing here not so much a literary precept as the fears and skepticism that his own work provokes in him. It is a tension, a mistrust that he has never put behind him: as if he suspected the splendor of his verbal gifts, his love of words, his enjoyment of games, of surprises, of parodies, his fear of mannerism or of the vacuous baroque, of what he saw in Quevedo—the production of an enormous amount of prose to say nothing. His mistrust of his own powers and inventions, his fear that time would reduce them to specious stylings, to marginal eccentricities, the danger that someone, tomorrow, would describe them as "Labyrinths, puns, emblems/ Frozen and tedious trifles" ("Baltasar Gracián," *Selected Poems*). These qualms—excessive in a writer as lucid, as measured and economical as Borges—are perhaps what encourages that gospel of simplicity as recommended in ironic, pointed, joking prologues, wholly resembling what they presume to repudiate. The pages of Borges are damaged by errata, but they are not empty. They are frequently perfect and never foolish. I don't know whether or not Bustos Domecq and Suárez Lynch hit upon a universal symbol, but the language they employ certainly places them in a specific geography. Nevertheless, these two have created extraordinary verbal parodies. I don't understand why they are diminished by the impossibility of translating them into Czech. We can, we must, defend ourselves against the theoretical asceticism Borges shows toward his own work.

The fate of a work of literature implies, on the other hand, the question of its identity, one aspect of which, for Borges, is the (fascinating) lack of proportion between results and intentions. Chesterton wished to write as an orthodox apologist, the polemicist who defends a clear, pure doctrine. Nevertheless, in one form or another, he was always dark, umbrageous, satanic, and full of despair. "Something in the very substance of his self inclined toward nightmares, something secret, blind, and essential" (*Other Inquisitions*). Swift set about writing a sort of accusation against the human race and ended up producing a book for children (*Discussion*). Borges tends to offer us two explanations. The first suggests that the doctrines pronounced by an author are not necessarily the motivating force and sinew of his work. The second, more a corollary to the first, regards his insistence that "the practice of literature is mysterious" (prologue, *Doctor Brodie's Report*). Writing is an intentional dream, he tells us: artistic creation is the act of opening oneself to uncontrolled and unconscious forces and influences. The author may be his worst interpreter and be unaware of the quality of his work. Should it last, it may differ from what the author imagined. What is his own—Swift's lament for the human race—disappears; what is not, lasts—the entertaining adventures of Gulliver. But beyond this, a book, a poem, any text whatsoever allows for an infinite number of readings, depending on period, preference, conventions, or superstitions. "The words *amica silentia lunae* now mean the intimate moon, silent and bright, and in the *Aeneid* meant the interlude, the darkness that allowed the Greeks to enter the citadel of Troy" (*Other Inquisitions*). That interference—the reader—produces multiple identities. A work of literature lasts when someone reads it, but that reading transforms it. "Pierre Menard, Author of the *Quixote*" is the extreme and perfect elaboration of that idea. "[Cervantes] indulges in a rather coarse opposition between tales of knighthood and the meager provincial reality of his country. [Menard] chooses as 'reality' the land of Carmen during the century of Lepanto and Lope." Menard's Quixote—an exact reproduction of the original—is nevertheless different: in one passage, Cervantes offers a rhetorical eulogy to history; Menard, in the same words, evokes pragmatist doctrines. Cervantes's style is of his time; Menard, on the other hand, prefers an archaic style. Who, now, is the author of *Don Quixote*? The concept of identity, with regard to literary work, turns elastic and precarious. Borges, in writing about Kafka, advances the thesis that every writer *creates* his precursors: from the time of Kafka onward, we are able to detect "Kafkaesque characteristics." Beforehand, it was impossible to discover them for they simply didn't exist. As if the writer were saying: Perhaps I am writing the pages that will illustrate—dimly—the traits of some future writer. From this moment on, I am the follower of a master who does not yet exist; I am the representative of a school whose manifesto I have never seen. He who *will* define me does not yet exist. I am not a precursor, but rather the irresolute material that will acquire form and meaning through another. To hazard a hypothesis regarding the future of a poem or story implies then knowing that which is impossible to know *now*: the identity of the poem and the story.

I don't know what Borges's future readers will think of him. Perhaps he will seem somewhat obvious, for his epithets, his syntax, his habit of using verbs as qualifiers; his innovations will all have been incorporated into common usage and, thus, what for us was astonishing for them will be standard, a somewhat more articulated conversation. His prose shall be more sedate, more modest; it will flow calmly and effortlessly. I am sure that Borges would not be displeased with this outcome. My wish, however, is different: that they won't find him so natural but neither will they need the assistance of philologists, a potentially eternal species. I hope those readers shall approach him as we did: with the certainty that we were in the presence of an exception. That his work might be magical and meticulous for them too. Perhaps they shall discover a Borges even greater than our own.

TRANSLATED BY MARK SCHAFER

Salvador Elizondo

Mexico
(b. 1932)

Salvador Elizondo was born and raised in Mexico, but he has traveled extensively throughout the Americas and Europe. He has penned numerous poems, short stories, and translations, many of which have seen publication in an array of literary reviews and periodicals. The style of Elizondo's writing and its reflection of his interest in photography, metafiction, modernist literature, and Eastern philosophy are reminiscent of the American critic Susan Sontag's work: Both writers are not only highly intelligent and widely read, but they both have a highly controlled style and an experimental approach to criticism. Elizondo founded the magazine S. Nob in 1962 and three years later directed the film *Apocalipsis 1900*. In the fashion of the French *nouveau roman*, his literature is unconventional and intense. Novels such as *Farabeuf* (1965) and *Narda o el verano* (1966) are more collages than linear narratives. Among his other principal works are *El hipogeo secreto* (1968), *Cuaderno de escritura* (1969), and *El grafógrafo* (1972). Elizondo's essays are frequently self-reflective and bookish, and they abound in references to ancient and Oriental philosophical systems. Like Alejandro Rossi, Elizondo has been much influenced by Borges. "My Debt to Flaubert," originally published in January 1980, is part of Elizondo's collection *Camera lúcida* (1983).

My Debt to Flaubert

I read Flaubert at a time in my life when I wasn't worried about studying technique or incurring literary debts; I read for the sheer pleasure of reading. So I am all the more surprised to find myself twenty years later paying a literary debt I contracted without even realizing it. Two years ago I reread *Un coeur simple*, which I still consider the best of the works I remember reading. The first book I read, in Spanish, at the age of thirteen, was *La légende de Saint Julien L'Hospitalier*; to this day I retain the painful and persistent memory of many of the atrocious images of this book: hunting with bow and arrow, the mother's death, the cruel expiation. In the interval between these polar readings, my state of mind and passing moods have taken me to the pages of Flaubert with varying consequences. When I tried to read *L'Education sentimentale* (the second version), I was still under the splendorous spell of *Le rouge et le noir*. Perhaps that's why I waded through that wealth of minute detail with the sense that Flaubert's fastidious dissection of emotional conflicts, observed from the blurred perspective of an alien era and society, added up to little more than a lesson on literature or rhetoric aimed at trying to beat Stendhal at the game of psychological introspection and careful writing, and why, on balance, it struck me as tedious and tiresome. Despite that uncomfortable sensation, in the course of my arduous reading I almost unconsciously became aware of certain qualities that would later help me understand several interesting aspects of the evolution of contemporary literature—and of my own literary sensibility as well—an effect Flaubert has had, I believe, on a number of writers of my time.

The first quality of Flaubert's writing that attracted my attention was the tone. Much later I discovered the precise key to that tone, which through the medium of writing allowed one to feel dangerously close to the author: the tone was achieved through the careful transmutation of real feelings into forms capable of being transposed into the written word. Flaubert never ventures—as Céline does, for example—beyond the limits of a possible writing, that is to say, a writing sufficiently profound or perfect as to be capable of transmitting undecipherable sensations that lack a fixed or comprehensible point of reference. It seems to me that he obtains his most rarefied effects through the process of tonal elaboration of his prose in *Salammbô* and in *La Tentation de Saint Antoine*. Both books are constructed in the same way, through the accumulation of documentary detail, recorded so minutely that each one of the details considered separately has more importance than the whole they form a part of. It is well known that his uncompromising will to perfection often led Flaubert to rewrite a phrase thirty times. The second *Education* is a version perfected over a span of twenty years.

Flaubert's attitude clearly reveals the eminently *artistic* status that the genre of the novel enjoys in his work. The novel never ceases to be a reflection of life, but it becomes a reflection of the author's inner life and subjectivity. This is why Flaubert is the first modern novelist and the first to direct the current of pure art into the river of narrative. I believe that all writers openly acknowledge this debt to him. I would enter my balance in the opposite column. Flaubert is the inventor of the "author-character"; he would insert an identity between the terms that have been the springboard of the modern novel: *Madame Bovary c'est moi!*—he cries in order to justify himself before his judges. There would not be space in this brief settling of accounts with Flaubert to specify the formidable consequences and unsuspected developments which the application of this succinct and enigmatic formula has produced to date. It is sufficient to mention that every work that intimates or actualizes the technique of *interior monologue*—

despite what Jung says to the contrary—has its literary origin in the identity that famous affirmation establishes between author and character. Flaubert introduces a measure of rational rigor in the apparently chaotic discourse of the emotions and the imagination; he reduces this dimension of the poetic spirit to the implacable rules of an imperceptible but omnipresent rhetoric and makes us experience that identity, perhaps almost too insistently.

I have thought a great deal about Emma Bovary—especially since I found out that she was Gustave Flaubert. I have never been very good at clearly discerning the differences between the souls of men and women; aside from physicial differences, I perceive no other distinctions between them. Emma's soul manifests itself too urgently as an archetype for my taste. Her hollow head is full of foolish notions, stirred by all kinds of banalities that Flaubert knew how to sublimate by means of a writing style whose unsurpassed perfection stirs many contemporary novelists to secretly attempt to emulate it. In general terms, I believe that seldom has such mastery been placed at the service of such inanity.

I would remain with a balance in my favor if I did not recognize the magnitude of a literary effort the mere concept of which would make my head reel even without its having been realized in a particular book— unfinished and flawed—one of the most monotonous and at the same time most interesting of all Flaubert's works. In *Bouvard and Pécuchet*, published posthumously in 1881, we have the only concrete example of what on various occasions throughout his vast correspondence Flaubert proclaimed to be his maximum literary aspiration—an aspiration that caused his name to be inextricably linked to that of Mallarmé: to write a book about nothing.

The concern for nothing runs parallel to the concern for pure writing. It is not possible to conceive of the latter except as text uncontaminated by sense or form, reduced to its essential condition of object of the senses; a writing that has its origin in nothing and that fulfills itself in itself. If *Bouvard and Pécuchet* is an attempt at the magnum epic of nothing, *Un coeur simple* is its perfect realization on a small scale. Its sense of emptiness and absence is more profound and terrifying, its desolation more intense, its loneliness more cruel; the silence that dominates that flat but sharp-edged writing, terse with the force of pent-up emotion, suppresses dialogue and "talk," which Flaubert relegates to the domain of the parrot.

On balance, I think the true substance of Flaubert's legacy lies in his having placed the novel at the level of pure writing. His concern is of an aesthetic rather than a critical order, although the latter was essential to his constant pursuit of the aesthetic absolute—an aspiration that informs some of the most significant works of modern literature, *Ulysses* and *Finnegan's*

Wake, to mention only two. Contemplated from the perspective of the hundred years that have passed since his death, Flaubert's work is radiant with that quality Ezra Pound attributes to him in a famous verse of his anti-autobiographical poem *Mauberly: His true Penelope was Flaubert* . . . , reminding us that the love of art for art's sake and the search for rarefied aestheticism are the origin and destiny of great works.

TRANSLATED BY JO ANNE ENGELBERT

Manuel Puig

Argentina
(1932–1990)

———◆•◦•◦•———

Although he began his career unsuccessfully as a filmmaker, Argentine Manuel Puig achieved both critical and popular fame with his novels. *Betrayed by Rita Hayworth* (1967) preceded his first major success, *Heartbreak Tango* (1969). The latter deals with provincial life and sexuality, two of Puig's favorite themes, and was later made into a motion picture. *The Buenos Aires Affair* (1973) delves even deeper into the human psyche. Puig's greatest triumph remains *Kiss of the Spider Woman* (1976), a novel-turned-movie-turned-Broadway-musical of tremendous critical acclaim and popularity. The story takes place in a small prison cell, in an unnamed South American country. The two protagonists are a Marxist militant and a confessed homosexual. As in the tales of Sheherazade in *A Thousand and One Nights*, the homosexual man keeps his companion awake by recounting, and often reshaping, old Hollywood movies of the 1940s. In the end, a kiss between them—which scandalized Puig's audience—takes place. The novel was followed by other works, including a volume with the screenplays *La cara del villano* (1985) and *Recuerdo de Tijuana* (1985), in which the essay "Cinema and the Novel" appears as a prologue, and his last novel, *Tropical Night Descending* (1989). As his career matured, Puig sharpened a novelistic style very much of his own. Most of his books are explorations of kitsch and camp art (in Spanish, *lo cursi*). They examine the interrelationship between life and popular culture. Perhaps as a result of his obsession with theater and cinema, Puig's preferred narrative approach is dialogue. He often builds his plots by presenting his protagonists in the first person and eliminating all traces of a third-person narrator. Puig's contribution to the essay form was comparatively small, but the essays he did write include powerful memoirs, as if he understood this literary genre as an exercise in autobiography. His obsession with Hollywood and his adolescent dream of becoming a film director are both apparent in the evocative essay that follows, in which he claims that "reading movies" is an artistic experience unlike any other.

Cinema and the Novel

To be living in a small town in the Argentine pampas is far from ideal for someone who feels ill at ease with the reality around him. Any other reference points were far off: it took fourteen hours by train to reach

Buenos Aires, a whole day's journey to the sea, nearly two to the mountains of Córdoba or Mendoza. My survival instinct led me to create another point of reference much closer to home: that of the town's cinema screen, where a parallel reality was projected. A reality? So I believed, for many years. A reality which, I was convinced, existed somewhere beyond my town, and in all three dimensions. The first evidence to the contrary came to me from Buenos Aires, where I went to study for my end of school exams in 1946. There I encountered only variations of the same despotic *machismo* that prevailed in the *pampa*. Prestige always came from wielding authority, whether that of money or of the fists.

So the reality of pleasure, my desired reality of the cinema screen, did not exist in Buenos Aires either. Perhaps outside Argentina then? It was difficult for me to leave my country: I was twenty-three by the time I had saved enough to pay for the three-week boat trip which in those days separated Buenos Aires from Europe. I very soon discovered that my longed-for reality did not exist in Rome either. Above all, it had no place in the official film school, the *Centro Sperimentale di Cinema*, built in the heart of Cinecittà itself. The pantheon of gods I worshipped when I arrived there was highly inappropriate: Von Sternberg, Frank Borzage, the great stars: Greta, Marlene, Michèle Morgan; the poet Prévert. We were in 1956, and the reigning ideology was neo-realism. The school was dominated by two seemingly opposed kinds of oppression, which were basically akin to each other. This was a state-run school, and the Christian Democrats were in government. Consequently, the director and the administration were ultra-Catholic, of the kind still common in the 1950s, puritanical to an extent that would be laughable today. For example, they would object to actresses' necklines, they insisted on "decorum," and any hint of sexual activity was considered an offense. This was the asceticism of a convent. Right-wing oppression by the administrators was in theory countered by the neo-realism of the teaching staff, who were all followers of this movement, begun shortly after the war with *auteur* films such as Rossellini's *Rome, Open City*, De Sica's *Shoe-shine boy*, and Visconti's *Terra Trema*. Unfortunately in Italy a number of critics and theorists of the cinema had tried to construct dogma from these films, a series of principles which they used as a bludgeon against any sort of cinema which differed from that espoused by Zavattini and his followers. They were seeking, above all, and quite rightly, to get away from Hollywood formulas, to experiment with a more enquiring cinema. They wanted an intelligent, thought-provoking cinema of social protest. But this determination led them into a grave mistake: one of Hollywood's chief concerns had always been to construct a solid plot, but since, according to the neo-realists, all Hollywood was synonymous with reactionary cinema, the ability to tell a story also became a reactionary characteristic. Any attempt to give a film a dramatic structure was dismissed as cheap melodrama or *pièces-à-ficelles*. I can recall an example of 'pure cinema' dreamt up by Zavattini: a working woman leaves her house to go shopping: she looks in shop windows, compares prices, buys shoes for her children; and all this in the real time such actions would take, so that the typical ninety minutes of screening time would easily be filled. And, of course, the director's own vision was to be kept strictly out of it: it was a mortal sin if the director were to be suspected of guiding things subjectively. The cold, impersonal, but revealing camera was their answer to everything. Exactly what did the camera reveal? In all probability, only a photographic, superficial reality. Obviously, not only was the art of narration reactionary, but the director's art as well. A movement which had grown out of the work of *auteurs* such as Rossellini and De Sica ended by establishing an *anti-auteur* theory.

I should add that 1956 was a year of deepest crisis for the neo-realist critics. The cinema public was shrinking and this, instead of making the critics stop and think, merely reinforced the rigidity of their concepts. 1956 saw the launch of De Sica's *Il Tetto*, filmed under Zavattini's reign of terror, which failed both with audiences and at the international film festivals. The only people who defended it were the neo-realist critics, because it had been made in strict accordance with their house style: which almost succeeded in stifling even De Sica's creative spirit. What was the final outcome of all this? The producers refused to back any serious efforts, and that was the end of what had started, ten years earlier, as a brilliant crusade led by directors rather than critics. Why did the producers withdraw? Because the public was voting with its feet: this cinema of political protest had become so purist, so rarefied, that only an elite could follow it. The mass audience, the lower or working classes who in Italy have a real passion for the cinema, could not understand this kind of film, though it was supposedly aimed at them. It may well be that all aesthetic theories tend to the extreme and at some point become oppressive; in this particular case, the neo-realist dogma went so far as to deny validity to anything that did not fit its own canons.

Even after so many years, it is this desire to exclude which I find the most alarming of critical phenomena. At the time I was immensely shocked to find this act of castration being carried out in the name of the Left. I was from a country where repression invariably came from the Right. Furthermore, these critics were highly refined, and met in the most expensive cafés. They were nothing like my hybrid pampa-MGM view of what Bohemia should be.

Emotionally, I was split. On the one hand, a popular cinema of protest appealed to me; but on the other, I also liked cinema with a story, and this apparently classed me as a diehard reactionary. In the midst of all this, I was struggling with my first screenplays, which were little more than imitations of old Hollywood films. I got enthusiastic while writing them, but this feeling vanished once I had finished them. I was fascinated by the possibility of re-creating moments of being a child cocooned in his cinema seat, but awakening from that brought no pleasure. The dream itself did, but not the waking. I finally thought it might be more interesting to explore the anecdotal possibilities of my own reality, so I set about writing a film script which inevitably turned into a novel. Why *inevitably?* I did not consciously decide to switch from a film to a novel. I was roughing out a scene in the script in which the off-screen voice of an aunt of mine was introducing the action in the laundry room of a typical Argentine house. Though her voice was supposed to take up at most three lines of dialogue, she went on without stopping for thirty pages or more. There was no way I could shut her up. Everything she said was banal, but it seemed to me that the accumulation of these banalities lent a special meaning to what she was saying.

It was one day in March 1962 that this accident of thirty pages of banalities happened. I think it was my desire for more narrative space which led me to change my medium of expression. Once I had managed to face reality, after so many years escaping from it into films, I was keen to explore and scrutinize it as deeply as possible in order to try to understand it. The traditional ninety minutes offered by films was simply not enough. The cinema requires synthesis, whereas my themes needed the opposite: they called for analysis, the accumulation of details.

After that first novel, I went on to write two more, convinced that I had said goodbye to the cinema. However, in 1973 the Argentine director Leopoldo Torre Nilsson wanted to buy the film rights to *Heartbreak Tango*, which, after much hesitation, I accepted, also agreeing to adapt the book myself. As producer and director, Torre Nilsson gave me complete creative freedom, but this work of adaptation didn't feel right! I had to follow the opposite process to the one which had helped free me. I had to compress and cut the novel, to find ways of making a synthesis of all that had originally been set out analytically. Once the script was finished, I returned with a sigh of relief to writing novels, and began *Kiss of the Spider Woman*.

Four years later, I had another call from the world of cinema. From Mexico, the director Arturo Ripstein asked me to adapt José Donoso's novella *Hell Has No Limits*. At first I said no, but Ripstein insisted, so I read the book again. It was more of a long short story than a novel, so in this case the problem was to add material to round out the script. I enjoyed this far more, and my good working relationship with Ripstein led to another project, which I myself suggested: the adaptation of a story by the Argentine writer Silvina Ocampo, *El impostor*, which meant a return to the cinema for the producer Barbachano Ponce. What did *Hell Has No Limits* and *El impostor* have in common? On the surface, only their length: they were both short novels, or long short stories. But, once I had finished this third adaptation, I could see another obvious common denominator. Both stories were allegories, poetic in tone, without any claims to realism, even though basically they dealt with well-defined human problems.

My novels, on the other hand, always aim for a direct reconstruction of reality; this led to their—for me, essential—analytic nature. Synthesis is best expressed in allegory or dreams. What better example of synthesis is there than our dreams every night? Cinema needs this spirit of synthesis, and so it is ideally suited to allegories and dreams. Which leads me to another hypothesis: can this be why the cinema of the 1930s and 1940s has lasted so well? They really were dreams displayed in images. To take two examples, both drawn from Hollywood: an unpretentious B-movie like *Seven Sinners*, directed by Tay Garnett, and *The Best Years of Our Lives*, directed by William Wyler, a 'serious' spectacular which won a clutch of Oscars and was seen as an honour for the cinema.

Forty years on, what has happened to these two films? *Seven Sinners* laid no claim to reflect real life. It was an unbiased look at power and established values, a very light-weight allegory on this theme. *The Best Years of Our Lives*, by contrast, was intended as a realistic portrait of US soldiers returning from the Second World War. And as such, it was successful. But, after all these years, all that can be said of this film is that it is a valid period piece, whereas *Seven Sinners* can be seen as a work of art. When I look at what survives of the history of cinema, I find increasing evidence of what little can be salvaged from all the attempts at realism, where the camera appears to slide across the surface, unable to discover the missing third dimension beyond two-dimensional photographic realism. This superficiality seems, strangely enough, to coincide with the absence of an *auteur* behind the camera. That is to say, of a director with a personal viewpoint.

Having outlined the differences I think I can discern between cinema and literature, I should like to turn to a question that is often asked nowadays: do the cinema and television mean the end of literature, or more specifically of narrative? I'm inclined to say no, that this is impossible, because the two involve different kinds of reading. In films, one's attention is attracted by so many different points of interest that it is very difficult, if not impossible, to concentrate on a complicated conceptual discourse. In the cinema, one's attention is split between the image, the dialogue, and the background music. Also, the demands made by the moving image are especially important. This is not the same as the demands made by looking at a painting, in which the image remains static. Because of the greater attention that can be focused on the written page, the narrator there has the possibility for another kind of discourse, which can be more complex conceptually. Moreover, a book can wait, its reader can stop to think; this does not apply to images in a film.

To conclude: some kinds of stories can only be dealt with in literature, because of the limits of the reader's attention. It is the human capacity for attention which decides the matter in the end. There are definite limits: one can focus on so much material, and no more. Beyond that, one grows tired: so, one can take in more from the written page than one finds possible on the screen. I myself had a curious experience in this respect. About three years ago, I saw an Italian film: *Il sospetto*, by Maselli. It has a very complicated political plot, and is very well made. Half way through the screening I began to grow alarmed: I simply could not follow the story. The characters were raising questions whose importance I could not grasp. I guessed that if they had been written down, those same chunks of dialogue would have been more comprehensible. Or would they? What was going on? Was it all nonsense, or was it merely that the spectator's attention could not grasp all that was being presented? I was intrigued, and through my publisher in Rome I got hold of the original film script. I read it through, and understood everything perfectly. There were one or two somewhat obscure passages, but they became clear on a second reading. This of course had been impossible in the cinema. There is no way of turning back the projector.

This all goes to explain why I think that the 'reading' a cinema spectator makes is different from that performed by the reader of a novel, and that the former, while it does relate to a literary reading, is also closely akin to looking at a painting. This would mean that it involves a third kind of reading which, while encompassing some of the characteristics of 'reading' literature and works of art, is distinct from both of them.

TRANSLATED BY NICK CAISTOR

Elena Poniatowska

Mexico
(b. 1933)

————◆•※•◆————

Although she was born and lived in Poland until she was eight, Elena Poniatowska is known as one of Mexico's outstanding female voices. Her most acclaimed work may still be *Massacre in Mexico* (1971), a dramatic account of the 1968 student massacre by the national army. The incident helped shape modern Mexico, and Poniatowska's book is directly linked to it in Mexico's consciousness. Composed of interviews, newspaper clippings, and firsthand accounts of the tragedy in Tlatelolco Square, the book attracted great publicity because of President Gustavo Díaz Ordaz's government's vocal anger at its publication. Since then, it has been reprinted numerous times and has acquired the status of a canonical text. Poniatowska's early works include the masterpiece *Hasta no verte, Jesus mío* (1962), a fascinating hybrid—part anthropology, part fictional autobiography—chronicling the life of a resilient peasant woman in Mexico, spanning the better part of the twentieth century, and *Los cuentos de Lilus Kikus* (1967), followed later by *Dear Diego* (1978), *Gaby Brimmer* (1979), *De noche vienes* (1979), *Flor de lis* (1988), *Tinísima* (1992), and *Luz y luna, las lunitas* (1994). Poniatowska's writing mixes journalism, creative fiction, and the chronicle to produce poignant yet flowing prose in which Mexican culture comes alive. Together with Carlos Monsiváis, she belongs to a generation of intellectuals enchanted with the American style of New Journalism of Tom Wolfe. Her topics range from the photography of Graciela Iturbide to Subcomandante Marcos, from middle-class women in the nation's capital to Frida Kahlo. Poniatowska has lectured extensively in the United States and is also known as the translator into Spanish of *The House on Mango Street*, by Chicana Sandra Cisneros. "And Here's to You, Jesusa," published in Octavio Paz's monthly *Vuelta* in 1978, is an invaluable window to Poniatowska's mind. The essay explains the relationship between the writer and Jesusa Palancares, the subject of *Hasta no verte, Jesus mío*, and it ponders the degrees of separation between fiction and reality.

And Here's to You, Jesusa

Out there where Mexico grows scrubbier every day, where the streets meander off and peter out and lie in greater disrepair every day, out there is where Jesusa lives. Along those streets the squad car winds its way, cruising slowly all through the day, the policemen drowsy with the heat; and it parks at the corner for hours on end. The general store is called "El Apenitas," The Just Barely. The cops get out for something to drink, but by now the ice in the *Victoria* and *Superior* coolers is only a pool of water where beers and sodas float. Women's hair sticks to the napes of their necks, plastered down with sweat. The heat buzzes, just as the flies buzz. How greasy and wringing wet the air coming from that direction! People out there live in the same skillets in which they fry their tortillas and their potato and squash-blossom quesadillas, that daily bread the women pile up on rickety tables along the street. Some squashes are being dried on the flat roofs.

Jesusa is dried out too. She keeps time with the century. She's seventy-eight now, and the years have shrunk her the way they've shrunk the houses, curving her spine. They say old people shrink so as to take up as little space as possible on this earth. Little red veins show in her weary eyes. Around the pupil, the iris is earthen, grey, and the coffee pigment is slowly fading away. Her eyes no longer water, and the tear ducts are blood red. There is no moisture under her skin either, and that is why Jesusa is constantly repeating: "I'm shriveling away." Still, the skin remains taut over her protruding cheekbones. "Every time I move, I shed some scales." First, a front tooth fell out and she decided: "When another one on the side falls out, I'll get myself a piece of gum, chew it real good, and stick it back." She has lost her beautiful hair, that hair that made the soldier boys call her "Queen Xochitl." What bothers her most are her two stringy braids, and now when she goes to town for bread or milk, she covers her head with a shawl. She walks along stooped, hugging the wall, bent over herself; nonetheless, I like her two graying, thin braids, the whisps of white hair curling at her temples over her wrinkled, cloth-covered brow. She also has those big spots on her hands. She says they come from her liver, but I think they come from time. With age, men and women become covered with mountain ranges and furrows, hills and deserts. Each day Jesusa looks more and more like the earth; she is a walking clod of soil, a little mountain of clay packed down by time and now dried out by the sun. "I've got four stumps left," and she raises her fingers, deformed by arthritis, to point to the gaps in her mouth.

Over the years, Jesusa has also tamed down. When I first knew her, she was gruff, remiss, not even saying "Come on in." Now, if you visit her, she offers you a seat.

"What brings you? What brings you here?"

"I'd like to chat with you."

"With me? Look, I work. If I don't work, I don't eat. I can't sit around gabbing."

Grudgingly, Jesusa agreed to my seeing her on the only day of the week she had free: Wednesday, from four to six. I began to live a little from Wednesday to Wednesday. Jesusa, on the other hand, did not give up her hostile attitude. When her neighbors let her know from the doorway that she should come tie up the dog so I could go in, she would mutter peevishly: "Oh, it's you." Tied to a very short chain, the black dog guarded the whole building. He was big and strong: a vicious dog. He blocked the way, narrow as it was, to all strangers. When I slipped past with a huge tape recorder, I was aware of his hot breath and his barking as surly as Jesusa's hostility. The building had a central corridor and was cut up into rented rooms on either side. The two "sanitary facilities," with no running water and always filled to the top, were at the back. Nobody kept an eye on them; there was a toilet to sit on but the dirty paper accumulated on the floor. The sun scarcely entered Jesusa's room, and oil fumes from the stove made your eyes water. The walls were decaying with saltpeter, and despite the corridor's being very narrow, half a dozen shoeless boys were playing there and peering in at the various neighbors. Jesusa asked them: "Want a taco, even if it's just with beans? No? Well, don't go begging from door to door then." Rats would peer in too.

In those years, Jesusa did not spend much time at home, because she left early for a printshop that still employed her. She'd leave her room locked up tight, her animals suffocating inside, along with her potted plants. At the printer's she cleaned, swept, picked up, mopped, washed the metal plates, and she brought home the overalls and, often, the workers' own clothes. The first time I asked her to tell me about her life (because I had overheard her talking at a laundry, and her language struck me as fearsome, especially the degree of her indignation), she responded: "I don't have time." She pointed to her work: the pile of overalls, the five chickens she had to take out in the sun, the dog and the cat to feed, the two caged birds that looked like sparrows, prisoners in a cage that grew smaller day by day. "See? Or are you going to give me a hand?" I said I would. "OK, then put the overalls in the gasoline." That's when I found out what overalls really are. I took hold of a hard object, shriveled with age, stiffened with grime, covered with large greasy stains, and I soaked it in a washtub. It was so stiff the water couldn't cover it; it was an island in the middle of the water, a rock. Jesusa ordered me: "While it's soaking, put the chickens out in the sun on the sidewalk."

So I did, but the chickens started cackling and scattering across the street. I got frightened and flew back inside. "A car's going to run them over."

"You mean you don't know how to sun chickens?" she asked me angrily. "Don't you see the cord? You have to tie them by the feet." In a second she had gotten the chickens back in, and she started scolding me again. "Who would think of putting chickens out like that?"

Remorsefully, I asked her: "How *can* I help you?"

"Well, put the chickens out in the sun on the roof, even if it's only for a little while."

Full of fear, I did it. The building was so low that from down on the ground I could see the hens flutter, fluff themselves, and happily peck out fleas. That pleased me, and I thought: "Well, I'm doing something right." Jesusa yelled at me again: "All right, and what about the overalls?"

When I asked: "Where's the washing machine?" she pointed to a ribbed board scarcely ten or twelve inches wide and twenty long, saying "No washing machine, not even a pot to piss in! Scrub it yourself, on that!" She took a basin out from under the bed. She looked at me sarcastically: I wasn't able to scrub anything. The uniform was so stiff, it was difficult even to get hold of it. Then Jesusa exclaimed: "Just look what a waste you are! One of those stuck-up women too good to get their hands dirty." And she made me stand aside. Later she acknowledged that the overalls had to soak overnight in gasoline, and, shoving the full tub back under the bed, she commanded: "Now we have to go get food for the animals." I offered her my VW. "No, it's just down the corner."

She walked rapidly, change purse in hand, never looking at me. In contrast to the silence she had maintained with me on the way, she joked in the shop with the butcher, softsoaped him, and bought a miserable heap of scraps wrapped in tissue paper that immediately became soaked with blood. Back home, she flung the offal on the floor, and the cats, with their tails on end, electrified, pounced on it. The dogs were slower. The birds didn't even chirp.

I tried to plug in my tape recorder, nearly the size of a navy-blue coffin and with a speaker big enough for a dance hall, and Jesusa protested: "You're going to pay for my electricity, right? Don't you see you're stealing my current?" Later, she gave in. "Where are you going to put your beast? I'll have to move all this filth." And besides, the recorder was borrowed: "How come you go around with other people's things? Aren't you scared to?"

The following Wednesday I asked her the same questions again.

"Wait, didn't I tell you all that last week?"

"Yes, but it didn't record."

"Then that monster of yours doesn't work?"

"Sometimes I'm not aware whether it's recording or not."

"Then don't bring it anymore."

"It's just that I can't write quickly, and we'll waste a lot of time."

"That's just it. Better let's stop here, since neither of us is getting much out of this."

After that I started writing in a notebook, and Jesusa sneered at my handwriting: "So many years of study to come up with such a scrawl."

That method helped me, though, because when I returned home at night I could reconstruct what she had told me. I was always afraid that on the least expected day she would "hang up" on our conversations. She didn't like the neighbors seeing me nor my greeting them. One day, when I asked after the smiling girls in the doorway, Jesusa, from inside her room, explained: "Don't call them girls, call them whores. Yes, little whores. That's what they are."

One Wednesday I found Jesusa lying on her bed, wrapped in a gaudy sarape—red, yellow, parakeet green, with big, loud stripes. She got up only to let me in, and went back to stretch out under the sarape, entirely covered from head to foot. I had always found her seated in the darkness in front of the radio, like a little bundle of age and loneliness, but listening, attentive, alert and critical. "They're telling complete lies in that box! They only say what suits them! When I hear them mention Carranza on the radio, I shout 'Damn Crook!' Every government boasts about what suits it. Now they call him the Baron of Four Marshes, and I think it's because his soul was all smeared with mud." Or: "So now they're going to put Villa's name up in gold letters on a church! How can they if he was a filthy killer, a cattle thief, a rapist? To me, those revolutionaries are like a kick in the . . . , well, that is, if I had balls. Nothing but thieves, highway robbers, protected by the law!" I looked at the unfamiliar sarape and sat down on a small chair at the foot of the bed to wait. Jesusa didn't utter a single word. Even the radio that was always playing while we talked was turned off. I waited for about half an hour in the darkness.

From time to time, I would ask: "Jesusa, are you feeling ill?"

She did not answer me.

"Jesusa, don't you feel like talking?"

She did not budge.

"Are you angry?"

Total silence. I chose to wait. Jesusa was often in a bad mood when our interviews began. After a while, she would compose herself but not lose her cranky, contemptuous attitude.

"Have you been sick? Haven't you gone to work?"

"No."

"Why not?"

"I haven't gone in more than two weeks."

Once again we fell into absolute silence. You couldn't even hear the chirping of her birds, who always made their presence known with a lament, a gentle, humble notice of here I am, under the rags covering the cage. Discouraged, I waited a long while and then launched another attack:

"Aren't you going to talk to me?"

She did not answer.

"Want me to go?"

Then she lowered her sarape down to her eyes, then to her mouth and spat out:

"Look. You've been coming here for two years and bugging me and bugging me and you don't understand a thing. So it's better if we put a stop to it right here and now."

I left hugging my notebook against my breast like a shield. In the car I thought to myself: "My God, what an old woman! She doesn't have anyone in her life. I'm the only person who visits her, and she's capable of telling me to go to hell." (On one occasion she had already said: "Go straight to hell!")

On the following Wednesday I was late (it was an unconscious slip), and I found her outside on the sidewalk. She grumbled: "Well, what happened to you? Don't you see I don't have the time? After you leave, I have to go to the barn for my milk, go for my bread. You annoy me when you leave me here waiting."

Then I went with her to the dairy, because in the poor districts the countryside comes right up to the city limits—or the other way around—even though nothing may smell like country and everything smacks of dust, garbage, swarms of people, and rot. "When we poor people drink milk, we drink it straight from the cow, not that junk in bottles and cartons you people drink." In the bakery Jesusa bought four rolls. "No pastry. That stuff doesn't fill you up, and costs more."

I came into contact with poverty, real poverty—the poverty of water drawn in pails and carried carefully so as not to spill a drop, of laundry done on the metal scrubbing board because there is no washing machine, of electricity stolen by rascals, of hens that lay eggs without shells ("just clear membrane") because the lack of sunlight never lets them harden. Jesusa belongs to the millions of men and women who do not live, who merely survive. Just getting through the day and making it to nighttime costs them so much effort that all their hours and energy are expended that way. How hard it is to stay afloat, to take one peaceful breath, even if only for a moment at dusk, when the chickens are no longer cackling behind their wire-mesh fence, and the cat is stretching out on the trampled ground.

Nevertheless, on Wednesday afternoons at sundown, in that little room almost always in shadow, in the midst of children's shrieks from the other rented rooms, the slamming of doors, the shouting, and the radio at full blast, another sort of life emerged, Jesusa's life, both her past and what she was reliving now in retelling it. Jesusa informed me that this was the third time she had come to earth and that if she suffered and was poor now that was because in her last incarnation she had been a queen. "I'm here on earth paying my debt, but my life is elsewhere. In reality, anybody alive on earth is here on loan. He's only passing through, and when his soul is freed from the sack of skin and bones we're all wrapped in, when he leaves his misery below ground, that's when he begins to live. We are the dead ones, turned inside out so we can see. We think we're alive, but we're not. We only came to earth in seeming flesh to fulfill one mission. We make our way encountering obstacles, and when He calls us to our final reckoning we die materially. The flesh dies and they bury it, but the soul returns to the place where it was released. We are reincarnated every thirty-three years after we die." Thus, between one death and another, between one coming to earth and another, Jesusa had invented a previous, interior life that made her present misery tolerable. "Now you see me in this dung-hill, but I had my glorious garment, and Pierrot and Columbina carried my train because I was their sovereign, they my subjects."

Through Jesusa Palancares I learned of a doctrine that is widespread in Mexico: *spiritualism*. At the Government Ministry they informed me that in the Federal District alone there were more than 176 spiritualist churches, and I was able to visit various gathering places, meet mediums in Portales, Tepito, Luna Street, in the poor neighborhoods. The Catholic Church condemns spiritism and spiritualism equally, and yet this doctrine has much of Catholicism in it. Obviously it is a sect, and the faithful adopt it because they receive—just as in the banks—"more personalized attention." They refer to themselves as "Marist Trinitarians," alluding to the Virgin Mary and the Trinity, and they never completely break with the Roman Catholic Church although they stop attending it because they prefer the Spiritualist Opus.

The Spiritual Opus always seemed rather hazy to me, incomprehensible sometimes, and Jesusa got annoyed when I made her repeat some idea: "But didn't I already talk with you about that? How many times am I going to have to tell you?" She spoke of Allan Kardec, of her priest and protector Manuel Antonio Mesmer, and thus I discovered Franz Anton Mesmer, the founder of mesmerism and the famous *baquet magnetique*. Visiting a spiritist temple under the Nonoalco Bridge, the Midday Temple on Luna Street, I was introduced to a brotherhood and listened to a holy lecture on revelation and radiance that the priests and the "Guide" delivered to a reverent congregation who kept their eyes closed.

The United States anthropologist Isabel Kelly and the poet Sergio Mondragón point out that there is a difference between spiritism and spiritualism. The people interested in spiritism are educated and economically well off; many of them are politicians (Madero, for example, was a spiritist), and their interest focuses on appearances, ectoplasms, the effects of light and sound, levitation, and spiritual writing. They meet in private homes or in a rented space (in Gante, on the top floor of a building from the days of Porfirio Díaz, a select and elegant group of spiritists used to meet and was sometimes visited by Gutierre Tibón). They conduct their sessions in the dark. Joining hands in a circle that must not be broken, the power of their spirits vibrates out to the beyond, and the response is not long in coming: the dead descend to earth and make themselves known, the table moves, the curtain rises, the supernatural breaks through, communication begins.

On the other hand, poverty dominates spiritualism, and many inhabitants of the poorer neighborhoods search out spiritualist temples to receive treatment and cures, since the spiritual doctors usually charge between three and five pesos, and sometimes the operations are more effective than those in hospitals and, of course, have a much more uplifting effect: a shot of Coramine is hardly the same as a cleansing with a spray of seven herbs: hypericum, lavender, rue, sweet scabious, pepper tree, fennel, and clove. Twenty-two days of cleansings: seven cleansings with the bunch of herbs, seven of fire, and seven of vapors; a vigorous rubdown with Siete Machos lotion, and a massage that ends in ecstasy.

Men and women of all ages experience a sort of transport when they are spiritually possessed by their protectors: Mesmer, Adrian Carriel or Alan Cardel (possibly Allan Kardec), Light of the East, and many Mexican spirits, such as Pedrito Jaramillo, Rogelio Piel Roja, and others who obey Roque Rojas, that is, Father Elías. Roque Rojas is the founder of spiritualism, and in 1886 he was transformed into Father Elías. His photograph looks as though it had been taken from some volume of the Larousse. His eyes attempt to be penetrating. Alongside him and his prodigious miracles, Jesus Christ pales. Moreover, Roque possesses, he penetrates, his flock. When he enters them, after a violent trembling, women and men start speaking out loud in a trance, their eyes closed and their bodies agitated by spasms, and they unburden themselves: the conflicts, the frustrations, the husband's impotence, the fear of old age, the hatred for the woman next door all tumble out in a torrent. Afterward, the faithful return to their homes feeling very much relieved. And they return in a week and suddenly rise up and emerge from the gathering: rigid, with their eyes shut and their mouths covered with saliva, in expectation of divine possession, they sway back and forth because their protector rocks them as he massages them. And then! It happens: the floodgates open and the torrent of their misery pours out.

Most of these people are mestizos with very low wages. They are part of this monstrous city, part of its rootless, floating population composed of immigrants from the countryside and provinces who have traded their traditional culture for television and radio. For them, Catholicism is far less satisfactory than spiritualism, with its more powerful emotions that give them a sense of individuality. For example, at one time the Spiritual Opus was the only thing that gave meaning to the life of Jesusa Palancares, and she even went so far as to have herself baptized in it at a ceremony at "El

Pocito," on the road to Pachuca, a ceremony that caused her to cry a great deal. Her protectress, the priestess Trinita Pérez de Soto, pressed a triangle of light on Jesusa, first on her forehead, then on her skull, ears, mouth, brain, feet, and on her hands with their palms turned up. This divine triangle prevents storms, winds, floods, whirlpools, and it also "calms the storms within one, the spiritual ravages, because it is a defense against all evils on earth." That day Jesusa saw a spiritual hand make a sign of the cross on the water of El Pocito, and she saw a "vision" that consoled her— three roses on the water: one white, one yellow, and one pink. From that moment on she spoke with her dead relatives, her parents and her brothers, whom she had rescued from darkness and who, thanks to her, no longer wandered lost in infinity, flying about with no one to remember what sort of life they had lead on earth. But Jesusa broke with the Spiritual Opus because other priestesses in white nylon gowns and with large, tightly woven sprays of amaranth scorned her, refused to yield her proper place to her, and demanded that she move away. As she herself relates it: "At the time when I was entering into ecstasy, and all of us were seated so the beings could take possession of us, they gave me an elbow: 'Sister, move someplace else, a little farther back.' " Until one day Jesusa became angry and shouted at them: "All right, there are your chairs, and you can go squash your rumps on them."

Listening to Jesusa, I imagined her young, swift, independent, rugged and I experienced along with her all her rages and pains, her legs that went numb with the snow from up north, her reddened feet. Seeing her act in her own story, capable of making her own decisions, my own lack of character made itself plain to me. I especially liked to imagine her in the ocean, facing out to sea, the wind on her face tugging her hair back, her naked feet on the sand, lapped by the water, her hands cupped to taste the sea, to discover its saltiness, its tang. "You know, there's a lot of ocean." I also saw her running, petticoats between her legs and glued to her firm body, her pretty head sometimes in a shawl, sometimes covered with a straw hat.

Imagining her haggle at the market with a stallkeeper was a thrill for me; imagining her traveling on the roof of a train was the best of movies. While she was talking, images sprang to mind, and they all filled me with joy. I felt strengthened by everything I have not experienced. I would arrive home and tell them: "You know, something is being born inside me, something new that didn't exist before." But they did not respond at all. I wanted to tell them: "I feel stronger and stronger. I'm growing. Now, for sure, I'm going to be a woman." What was growing—or maybe what had been lying dormant there for years—was my Mexican self, the forging of me as a Mexican, the feeling that Mexico, identical to Jesusa's Mexico, lay within me, and that by the merest cracking of my shell it would emerge.

I was no longer the eight-year-old girl who had arrived on *The Marquis of Comillas*, a boat carrying refugees. I was no longer the daughter of eternally absent parents, of transatlantic travelers, the daughter of ships and trains. Instead, Mexico was inside me; it was a beast (as Jesusa called my tape recorder) inside, a powerful, vigorous animal that grew larger until it filled the whole space. Discovering it was like suddenly holding a truth in your hands, a brightly lit lantern that casts its circle of light on the floor. I had only seen lamps float in the dark and then disappear: the kerosene lantern of the station chief or the switchman's, which sways to the rhythms of his steps only to vanish finally; but this solid, steady lamp gave me the security of a home. My grandparents and my great-grandparents used to use a pat phrase: "I don't belong." One night, before falling asleep and after identifying myself for a long time with Jesusa, reviewing all my images of her one by one, I was able to tell myself in a whisper: "I *do* belong."

For months, I would fall asleep thinking about Jesusa. Just one of her phrases, barely sensed, was enough to humiliate me and dash my hopes. I heard her within me just as when I was a child lying in bed, I had heard myself growing in the night. "I know I'm growing because I can hear my bones rumble ever so quietly." My mother had laughed. Jesusa laughed inside me, sometimes scornfully, and sometimes she hurt me. Always, always she made me feel more alive.

Bit by bit, a cautious, timid love developed between Jesusa and me. I used to arrive with my spoiled pet's burden of woe, and she would take me to task: "Woman, what's getting into you? Everybody, not just you, has his burden to bear here."

It was a healthy blow to my self-esteem and a way of minimizing the oldest problem in the world: either being in or out of love, heads or tails of the same coin. There we were, the two of us, afraid of hurting one another. That same afternoon she brewed a bitter tea for my biliousness and handed me her fifth hen: "Here, take it home to your mama so she can make broth for you." But I already had another image of hens; and when I saw the plucked, yellow chicken on the table at home, I was thinking about the five hens squabbling at her house in Cerro del Peñón and how they were already my friends. One Wednesday I got there and fell asleep on her bed, and she sacrificed her soap operas to let me sleep. And Jesusa *lives* for the radio! It's her means of communication with the outside, her only link to the world. She never turns it off, she never left it even to tell me the most intimate episodes of her life. Little by little the confidence between us was growing, the "fondness" as she says but which we never mentioned out loud nor even named. I think that Jesusa is the human being I most respect after Mane. . . . And she is going to die on me, just the way she wants to. That's why every Wednesday my heart skips a beat at the thought she might not be there. "Someday when you come,

you're not going to find me anymore. You'll only bump into thin air."
And, after her showing two legs dangling in coarse-ribbed cotton stockings
and my hearing her soap opera, she lets me in. Grumbling and muttering,
she greets me with her little hands knobby from so much washing, the
yellow and brown spots on her face, her stringy braids, her sweaters fastened
with a pin. And I beg God to let me take care of her right to the grave.

When I traveled to France, I wrote to her, especially postcards. The first
replies, by return mail, were hers. She went to public letter writers in Santo
Domingo Square, dictated her letters, and deposited them in the main post
office. She related what she thought would interest me: the arrival in Mexico of the President of Czechoslovakia, the external debt, highway accidents; but in Mexico she and I never spoke about current events or
newspapers. Jesusa always was unpredictable. One afternoon I found her
seated, glued to the radio, a notebook on her lap, a pencil between her
fingers. She wrote the letter "u" upside down and "n" with three descending strokes, and she did it with infinite slowness. She was taking a radio
course in writing. Foolishly, I asked her: "And why do you want to learn
that now?" And she answered me: "Because I want to die knowing how
to read and write."

On different occasions I tried to get her to go out: "Jesusa, let's go to
the movies."

"No, because I can't see good anymore . . . in the old days I used to
enjoy the serials, movies with Lon Chaney."

"Then," I would propose, "let's go out for a walk."

"And what about the chores? It's easy to see you don't have any chores."

I suggested a trip to Tehuantepec Isthmus to see her home province
again, something I thought would please her, until it dawned on me that
the hope of something better upsets her, makes her aggressive. Jesusa is so
used to her condition, so warped by her solitude and her poverty, that the
possibility of a change seems like an affront to her:

"Get out of here. You-know-it-all. Get out, I tell you. Leave me in
peace."

Then I realized that there comes a time when one has suffered so much
that one can no longer cease to suffer. The only respite that Jesusa allowed
herself was that single "Farito" she smoked slowly around six in the afternoon, with her radio always turned on even while she was speaking to me
out loud. She unwrapped and rewrapped gifts very carefully. "So they're
not mistreated." That was how I learned about her box of dolls, all new
and untouched. "There're four. I bought them for myself. As a girl, I never
had any."

Jesusa might have every justification for dying, but she does the impossible to stay alive. And to sleep. Sleeping is an adventure for her. Each
night she awaits the sleep that will put her, once again, in contact with the

beyond. She has revelations that reach the point of scenting the air as though the resin known as copal were being burnt. Sometimes her humble palace smells of citrus blossoms, at others of verbena, fruit, or musk, and the room is showered in a pale violet light.

Moreover, Jesusa is a woman who fends off men, not like some saint (because she herself admits to being a big drinker, a big dancer: "Lots of men fell in love with me, hear? A bunch of real men chased my skirts.") but as a whole person who respects herself. I see her as a temple, a temple in the sense we conceived of it as children when they told us that there is a sacred place inside us that we must never desecrate. I have always had that image of purity when thinking of Jesusa.

In writing *Hasta no verte, Jesús mío [Here's Looking at You, Jesus]*, I faced a problem: the problem of nasty language. In an early version, Jesusa never talked that way, and it pleased me to think about her discretion, her reserve. The possibility of writing a story without bad words made me happy, but as the trust developed between us, and especially when I came back from almost a year in France, Jesusa let herself go. She opened up her world to me, no longer watching what she said; and she herself admonished me: "Don't be an ass. You're the only one who believes in people. You're the only one who thinks people are good." I had to look some of her words up in the dictionary of Mexicanisms, to trace others—like *hurgamaderas, bellaco*—back to the most archaic Spanish. She threw my absence in my face: "You and your self-centered interest! You'll keep coming to see me so long as you can get something out of me that benefits you, and afterwards not a trace, not even your taillights. That's how it always is: everybody's trying to milk the other person dry."

Like all old people, she recounted a long series of ailments and complaints: her weak ribs, the aching backs of her knees, how badly they drive trucks, the awful quality of food supplies, rent you can't afford any longer, neighbors who are lazy drunks. Tiresome, she returned time after time to the same subject, seated on her bed, her legs dangling over the edge since the bed was raised up on bricks on account of the water that came into the rooms, flooding them, especially during the rainy season when Doña Casimira, the owner, didn't bother to have the drain in the corridor opened.

Over a period of ten years, I saw her change houses three times, and each time she had to move farther away, because the city drives its poor people out, pushing them to the city limits, forcing them away, as it expands. Jesusa first lived close to Lecumberri, to the north, in Iguarán; later she moved to Cerro del Peñón. Now she has landed on the highway to Pachuca, near a few settlements named Aurora, Tablas de San Agustín, San Agustín Gardens, which use blue arrows pointed in the four cardinal directions to announce *drainage* (spelled with a "j"), *water* (with an "h"), and *electricity* (with an "s"). There is no *drainaje*, no *whater*, no *electrisity*. Nor is there a single tree on those untilled flatlands, nor a blade of grass, not even a bush, except for those carted in by the settlers in their Mobil Oil cans. The dust storms look like the Hiroshima mushroom itself, and they are no less deadly since they carry all the world's debris and swallow up even the people's souls.

Jesusa now lives in two small 12' × 12' rooms built for her by her adopted son Perico, and she observes: "Here everybody's from Oaxaca, so that's why we help each other out." The settlers huddle together according to state and, recognizing each other by their native region, they help each other or, at least, do not harm each other. Jesusa expresses it well: "When all's said and done, I don't have a country. I'm like the Hungarians—from nowhere. I don't feel like a Mexican, and I don't acknowledge Mexicans. The only thing here is pure convenience and self-interest. If I had money and possessions, I'd be Mexican; but since I'm less than trash, I'm nothing. I'm garbage the dogs pisses on and then trots away. The wind comes up and carries it off, and that's the end of everything."

If previously when I went to see her I had had to cross streets, when I visited her in her new home I drove across open tract after open tract, with nothing but the car's tires raising clouds of yellow dust. There was no highway, nothing, only the desert. Suddenly, far away, in the middle of an open stretch, I saw a little black dot, and, as I approached, this dot turned into a man squatting in the baking sun. I thought to myself: "What will happen to this poor man? He must be sick." I drove up close and asked him from the car window: "Don't you want . . . ?" I stopped dead. The squatting man was defecating. Annoyed, he looked at me. Starting up the car, I thought about the oddity of this man's walking who knows how far to defecate in the middle of the land, so to speak, on the cusp of the world. I told Jesusa about it, and, irritated, she spat out: "You're always making a jackass out of yourself."

To write the book about Jesusa I used a journalistic device: the interview. Two years earlier I had worked for a month and a half with the U.S. anthropologist Oscar Lewis, author of *The Children of Sánchez* and other books. Lewis asked if I would help him edit *Pedro Martínez, The Life of a Tepoztlán Peasant*. Lewis worked with a team that inquired into the facts and did a sort of topographical survey of poverty. His informants came to see him at his apartment in Gutenberg Street, where he turned on his tape recorder and asked questions. It was my job to revise and prune those stories, that is, to eliminate repetitions and useless digressions. Undoubtedly this experience left its mark on me in writing *Here's Looking at You, Jesus*; nevertheless, since I am not an anthropologist, my work may be viewed as a testimonial novel and not an anthropological or sociological document. I made use of the anecdotes, the ideas, and many of Jesusa Palancares's expressions, but I would never be able to assert that the narrative is a direct transcription of her life because she herself would reject that. I killed off the characters who got in my way, I eliminated as many spiritualist sessions as I could, I elaborated wherever it seemed necessary to me, I cut, I stitched together, I patched, I invented. After finishing, I had some feeling of having stayed on the surface; I had not brought the essential, the depths of Jesusa's character, to light. With time, however, I have come to think that if I did not do that it was because I was treading on what was most vital without really being conscious of it: I limited myself to *divining* Jesusa.

I collected incidents, I always got ahead of her, I did not know how to portray those moments when the two of us remained silent, alone, almost not thinking, waiting for the miracle. We were always a little feverish; we always yearned for the hallucination.

Since I could turn to the tape recorder only when she let me use it, I would reconstruct what she said each Wednesday in the evening. In her voice I heard the voice of the nanny who taught me Spanish, the voice of all the maids who passed through our house like drafts, with their expressions, their way of looking at life, if they looked at it at all, because they only lived in the cold light of day and had no reason to dream. These and other women's voices added their choir to the main one: Jesusa Palancares's voice; and that is why I think my book contains words, expressions, proverbs—many proverbs—not only from Oaxaca, Jesusa's home state, but from all over the Republic, from Jalisco, Guerrero, the Puebla mountains, the Federal District.

On some Wednesdays, Jesusa spoke only about her obsessions of the moment: the sealed drain in the corridor, for example; but in the marasmus of routine and the difficulties of living, there were moments when we cried together, very gently, because she had suffered and continues suffering quietly to this day; moments when happiness burst in from who knows where, and we took the hens out from behind their chicken wire and settled them comfortably on the bed as if they were our children; when we met at a corner, and from far away, with my heart beating fast, I saw her raised arm hailing me down, because she, who saw nothing, had been warned by Mesmer that I was going to come.

On Wednesday afternoons I went to see Jesusa, and in the evenings I accompanied my mother to some cocktail party at one embassy or another. I always tried to maintain a balance between the extreme poverty I shared in the afternoon and the glitter of the receptions. My socialism was two-faced. Climbing into my really hot bath, I recalled Jesusa's washtub, under her bed, in which she soaked the overalls and bathed herself on Saturdays. All I could think was: "I hope she never comes to know my house, never learns how I live!" When she did come to know it, she told me: "I'm never coming back. They're not going to think I'm a beggar." And yet our friendship persisted: the link had been forged, and Jesusa and I loved each other. She never stopped criticizing me, but she never offended me: "I've known for a long time that you put on airs." When I was in the hospital, she wanted to stay and sleep there: "I'll just stretch out, even if it's under your bed." I have never gotten so much from anyone; I have never felt more to blame. All I did was move over a little in the bed: "Come, Jesusa, there's room for both of us." But she did not want to. She said goodbye at 5 A.M., and I still said to her: "Oh, come on, since there's room!" And she answered: "The only bed with room enough for the two of us is mine, because it's a poor woman's bed."

When I had retyped the first version of her life, I brought it to her in a sky-blue binder. She said: "What do I want this for? Get this crap out of here! Don't you see I can't have anything else in the way?" I had thought she would like it for its bulk and because Ricardo Pozas had once told me that Juan Pérez Jolote had been disappointed with the second edition of his life story as published by the Fondo de Cultura Económica and yearned for the yellow binding of the Instituto Nacional Indigenista's edition: "That edition was two inches thick!" On the other hand, even if Jesusa did reject the typed version, I chose the image of the Infant of Atocha, who presided over the darkness of her room, for the cover of the printed book; and, as a matter of fact, when she saw it, she asked me for twenty copies, which she gave to the boys in the shop so they would know what her life had been like, the many rocky roads she had had to travel.

Her reactions always unsettled me. Right in front of me she ripped into a thousand pieces some photos that Hector García had taken of us one afternoon: "This shows a lack of respect! This is filth! What I wanted was one like this!" She did not like to see herself with an apron, standing in the middle of the entrance to her building. "I thought it was going to come out like this!" And she pointed to her large sepia portrait hanging in a wooden frame. "That's a Marcel wave, with three or five waves, according to the size." (The size of what? Her head?)

In 1968 she made her hatred of the students clear. "They're a bunch of troublemakers. Why aren't they studying instead of rioting? I despise them." She also hated unions. "Union dues and more union dues, and I ask you: what for? So the leaders can get rich, get fat on our money? I used to march on the first of May with the barbers' union and the wood-workers', until I saw Cárdenas up close, smothered in streamers; but when I realized it was a matter of out and out robbery, I shouted at them: 'Take your harp, I'm not playing your tune anymore.' " She also censured and rejected teachers, nuns, and priests: "Those nuns, I've watched them, and that's why I tell them right out: 'Hypocritical little daughters of Eve, stop playing the fool and let yourselves go, out in the open.' Besides, how ugly priests and nuns are, always chasing after each others' skirts." Oddly enough, she always accepted homosexuality: "Women are such pigs these days, a young man doesn't know who to lay anymore. . . ." Then she observes: "Don Lucho was a good sort, because queens are better than machos." And that is how she also justifies her friend Manuel the Cradle-snatcher: "Maybe women disgusted him because he got the clap or they cheated on him, and so he was better off devoting himself to boys. He had lots of fun with them and used to say that men are less expensive than women and much more amusing." And yet she always kept her own man under the wraps of great modesty. This is her only reference to her love life: "When Pedro went on military duty, then he used me. I never took off my trousers, just dropped them when he used me, and that was that. We had to keep our trousers on so that when they sounded the trumpet: 'Fall in, everybody up!' we could go wherever. My husband wasn't a man for much petting, not at all. He was a very serious man. Nowadays I see kids over there necking and hugging in the doorways. It seems odd to me because my husband never went around making such foolish faces. He had what it took and he did it and that was it."

Jesusa is no more explicit about her puberty: "These days everybody blabs everything: they wave the flag of their filthiness and worse. Back in those days, if you bled, well, you bled, and that was that. If you had your period, then you did, and if not, not. They never told me anything about using rags or anything. I bathed two or three times a day and did so all my life. I never went around with such filthiness there, stinking like a dead dog. And I didn't get my clothes dirty. There was no reason to get dirty. I'd go, wash myself, change my clothes, hang them up to dry, and put them on again perfectly clean. But I never suffered, or thought about it; I never hurt or said anything to anyone."

As for Mexican politics, her reaction was one of anger and disillusion-ment, and it aroused totally Buñuelian images in my mind: "So many banquets! So many banquets! And why doesn't the president invite the hordes of beggars walking the streets? Come on, why not? A real revolu-tionary s.o.b. With each passing day we are trampled on more and more, and everything that comes along gnaws away at us, leaves us toothless, crippled, maimed, and they build their mansions out of our bits and pieces." Nor do other people console her: "This not dying on time is really tough. When I'm sick, I don't open my door all day long; I spend entire days locked inside. I just boil tea or corn-meal mush or something I make for myself. But I don't go outside to quarrel with anybody, and nobody stops at my door. The day I'm stuck here dying like an animal, my door will be bolted. . . . Otherwise, the neighbors poke their heads in to see that you're dying, that you're grimacing, since most people come to laugh at a person in their death throes. That's life. You die so others can laugh. They mock your visions. You're left with your legs spread, bent in two, twisted, with your lips swollen, mouth open, and your eyes popping out. Tell me if this life's not hard, to die in such a way. That's why I bolt my door. They'll drag me out of here, stinking, but come here to look at me and say this or that—no, nobody, . . . nobody . . . only God and me."

Ultimately, I would have liked to place Jesusa Palancares within Mexican literature, to speak of her role as a follower of the troops during the Revolution, of her ancestors, to say that she is a heroine in the cast of those spontaneous fighters, the women who went on strike, who did not "give in," either in her life or her work, but I felt that it was out of place, pedantic. I tried to emphasize Jesusa's personal qualities, to stress what distinguishes her from the traditional figure of the Mexican woman: her rebelliousness, her independence: "In the end, the more you give the more they drive you into the ground. I think that right in Hell there must be a place for all the women who gave in. Well, let 'em get shafted!" Her combativeness: "Before they land one on me, it'll be because I landed two on them." I came to the conclusion that it was not up to me to analyze her character historically. To what end? What I can indeed assure you, however, is that Jesusa continues to live in me, in other women, in my daughter, in other girls who will come along, in the daughters of Guayaba. She is not a militant member of any party, she is not political, she does not attend any demonstrations—nor does she invade countries. I cannot set her to standing guard beneath any red/black flag or to march in the ranks of the unions. She's seen it all. While I am on my way there, she's already come back.

"You can pull the wool over my eyes once; twice, never." If I were to transform her into a neighborhood Zapata, I would betray all those hours we had together. I seem to see Jesusa in the sky, on the earth, and everywhere in Mexico—like that, as God once was, Him, the masculine one.

TRANSLATED BY GREGORY KOLOVAKOS AND RONALD CHRIST

Luis Rafael Sánchez

Puerto Rico
(b. 1936)

Although he is esteemed chiefly as a playwright, Luis Rafael Sánchez is also known in his native Puerto Rico and around the world as a dramatist, actor, poet, and short story writer. Influenced by the works of such figures as Tennessee Williams and Federico García Lorca, Sánchez's plays are known both for their artistic merit and for their sociopolitical acuity. His career has been devoted to the exploration of the language and internal codes of the Caribbean, particularly of Puerto Rico. His writings often integrate elements from mass media television campaigns, soap operas, and popular music. Works such as *La espera* (1959) and *La pasión según Antígona Pérez* (1968) highlight his dramatic career, a career that also produced *Sol 13* (1961), *El cuerpo de camisa* (1966), and *Farsa del amor compradito, o casi el alma* (1966). "Espuelas," "Memoria de un eclipse," and "La parentela" are among his better-known short stories. But his talents as a novelist have brought him even greater acclaim. His novels include *Macho Camacho's Beat* (1976), which was translated into English by Gregory Rabassa, and *La importancia de llamarse Daniel Santos* (1989). Sánchez, who divides his time between Puerto Rico and New York, is a tenured professor at the University of Puerto Rico and the City University of New York, where he is Distinguished Professor of Romance Languages. The following essay, published in the New York magazine *Review* in 1994, is a voyage through Caribbean identity as it manifests itself in musical sounds. An unparalleled *joie de vivre* infuses his prose, and his passion for popular black culture in the archipelago makes the reader understand the region anew.

Caribbeanness

The Cuban Alejo Carpentier writes "The Caribbean sounds, the Caribbean resounds." His affirmation flows out with the rhythm of poetry. But it isn't really poetry. It's Carpentier's prose explanation of the cultural fabric some call the Caribbean and others call the Sea of the Antilles. His explanation is convincing because it's beautiful and because it's right.

Caribbean nature has more pleasing sounds than any guitar. The ineluctable sea sends its sound through the islands—the fickle ocean sound that either rocks you to sleep or scares you out of your wits, that relaxes

418

you or gives you insomnia. And the breeze of morning soothes the skin the way the cooing of the birds soothes the ear. It is no surprise, then, that one's first impression of the Antilles is of a paradise without a serpent.

After the sounds of nature, come the human sounds that punctuate Caribbean nights and days, the ones that make love last longer, turn labor strikes fanatical, and embellish the solitude of death. Has anyone ever seen lovers without a song? Could anyone convince a picket line to give up bongos and tambourines? Does the noble music played during funerals commit some sacrilege against the peace of the grave? Perhaps on another corner or in some other house in the world. Not on the Caribbean islands.

This enslaving fondness for music is characteristic of Caribbean men and women. Every self-respecting government office can boast at least one radio continually playing dance music. The act of renewing a driver's license, for example, becomes a musical one when set to a *bachata* by the stupendous Juan Luis Guerra or a ballad crooned by the tremendous Lucecita Benítez. The tail-end of a song escapes from the radio hidden in the medicine chest of more than one emergency room. The downward flow of intravenous serum becomes music in a *guaguancó* by the eternal Celia Cruz or in a super-bolero by the divine Danny Rivera. In the Caribbean, if people aren't hearing, life is difficult. In the Caribbean, if there is no music, even death is spoiled.

Insipid advertising refers to Caribbean men and women as "children of the sun." "Children of sound" would be better. Fondness for sound in all its manifestations. Even the sound that emanates from bodies in motion.

A famous *merengue* describes the pernicious effect of carnal sounds: "You've got a way of walking that's got me all messed up." A famous *guaracha* describes another kind of walk that seems to swing back and forth between sensuality and indecency: "That little blond Ophelia. Walks down the street. And she walks like this, walks like this. Walking like this." Even a flat imagination can visualize both walks after hearing the sound of the *guaracha* and the *merengue*.

But let's take up a carnal sound that has a full name.

The memory of anyone who ever heard Lucy Fabery automatically records the magnetic strangeness of her voice. And then the diffuse spasms of her body; spasms that strip spectators of their serene detachment. Listening to the wonderful sound of Lucy Fabery, seeing the singer Lucy Fabery elevate physical movement to the level of a concert by a full orchestra, we see the truth expressed by Carpentier when he writes, "The Caribbean sounds, resounds."

At the same time, the Puerto Rican poet Luis Palés Matos sees the mulatto or black element as the common denominator of the islands set in the sea some call the Caribbean and others the Sea of Columbus. The streets of the Antilles, lit up by *cocolos* [mulattoes] with black faces are, again and again, the stage for Palés Matos's best poetry.

The sonorous word, the stanza that demands an actor's voice, and all the implications of gestural grace together transform Palés Matos's black poetry into a banquet for declaimers of verse. It's only natural that such recitation would make his poetry popular and that it be quoted constantly, that a series of incisive and unforgettable lines, disconnected from the poem in which they appear, should become something like a homage to the poet's powers of invention.

But the repercussions of Palés Matos's ideas transcend mere sonority, poses, and charm. Palés Matos's black poetry doesn't waste time with impertinent demagoguery or weak rhetoric. It spends its time wisely in an enumeration of Black contributions to the culture of the Antilles. How Palés Matos transforms his vision of the double lifestyle of the Blacks into a careful meditation is wonderful to see, as wonderful as how he frames that double lifestyle in rhythmic onomatopoeia: the hiss of the maracas and the delicious percussion of the drums. The Caribbean sounds and resounds because the Caribbean is black, black.

Language and history change from Jamaica to Haiti, from Aruba to the Spanish Caribbean, but blackness links the Antillean archipelago. The ineluctable Black presence authorizes the racial preeminence in the Caribbean Luis Palés Matos confers upon it.

The commonsensical eye of the people also recognizes it. The old saying "if you're not Dinga then you must be Mandinga" makes a joke of the white fervor of the absurd aristocracies of the Antilles. Fortunato Vizcarrondo, whose poetry is still waiting for an imaginative critic to reveal its brilliance and originality, composes defiant verses:

> Yesterday you called me black,
> so today I'm going to answer back.
> My Grandma receives people in the hall,
> I'm not sure you've got one at all.

Which is to say: neither a denial of grandparents nor the concealment of frizzy hair under an obliging turban—all denounced in Francisco Arriví's extremely important play *Vejigantes* [Masks]—can manage to deny that mixed blood and blackness constitute the destiny of the Antilles.

The Dominican poet Pedro Mir goes in a different direction in his search for an Antillean common denominator. In one of his greatest poems, "Countersong to Walt Whitman," Mir inserts a short autobiographical aside:

> a son of the Caribbean,
> quite precisely from the Antilles.

Primitive product of a naïve
Borinquen girl
and a Cuban worker,
justly and poorly born
on the soil of Quisqueya.

Constant changes of address and racial mixture constitute the binding element in the Caribbean according to Pedro Mir's poetry, the indelible sign of a great people scattered over a poor archipelago. Pedro Mir's verses, so rich despite their calculatedly laconic character, synthesize a perfect portrait in words of the hybrid Caribbean. A moving simplicity energizes these verses by the Dominican master: the same simplicity that links the three Hispanic nations of the Caribbean. Political oppression, dictatorships as a matter of course, the scourge of misery, and the growing greed of the privileged classes make Puerto Rico today, the Dominican Republic yesterday, and Cuba the day before take turns as the capital of interbreeding in the Hispanic Caribbean.

The labors of pilgrimage and the compromises of exile lead to this mixing because so many people from the Antilles have survived over the centuries as pilgrims and exiles. From the illustrious to the tarnished. From those who travel by airbus to those who risk being eaten alive by sharks. From those legitimized by passports to those whose only identification is their age-old hunger. From those the Great Society takes in and protects to those the Great Society stigmatizes and rejects.

Pilgrimage and exile have also produced clans that carry two compromising loyalties. Sometimes conciliating, sometimes problematic, these new clans have adventures worthy of being heard. The adventures of the Cuban–Puerto Ricans and the Cuban-Dominicans. Adventures of the Puerto Rican–Cubans and the Dominican-Cubans.

Music, blackness, and wandering define the Caribbean according to three of the Caribbean's essential writers: Alejo Carpentier, Luis Palés Matos, and Pedro Mir. A language both useful and artistic crystallizes in the definitions they offer. The literature considered central establishes a pact between language considered useful and language that satisfies as art.

But music, blackness, and wandering do not merely define, characterize, or indicate the Caribbean. They are the flag of the entire Caribbean. A protective, historical, authorized flag with three stripes. One intimate, one unifying, the third bitter.

TRANSLATED BY ALFRED MACADAM

Mario Vargas Llosa

Peru
(b. 1936)

———◆◆◆◆◆———

Peruvian-born and educated in Bolivia, Mario Vargas Llosa burst onto the literary scene with his second work, *The Time of the Hero* (1963). He is considered one of the greatest living writers in the Spanish language, his prose demonstrates his vast learning and the meticulousness with which he constructs his works. He followed his initial success with other notable novels: *The Green House* (1966), *The Cubs* (1968), and *Conversation in the Cathedral* (1969). Included in his extensive catalog are also *Captain Pantoja and the Special Service* (1973), *Aunt Julia and the Scriptwriter* (1977), *The War of the End of the World* (1981), *Mayta* (1984), and *In Praise of the Stepmother* (1988). He has, in addition, written theatrical pieces, excellent critical works, especially on Gabriel García Márquez, and numerous essays that have been collected in various volumes, among them *La orgía perpetua* (1976), *Contra viento y marea* (2 vols., 1982–86), and his autobiographical *A Fish in the Water* (1994), about his ill-fated candidacy for Peru's presidency in 1990. Vargas Llosa was inducted into the Spanish Royal Academy and was made an honorary citizen of Spain in 1995. He has lectured at Harvard, Princeton, and Georgetown Universities, among other institutions in the United States. His essays are incisive in tone, yet conventional in structure. "Novels Disguised as History," delivered as a lecture in Edinburgh, Scotland, when he was the 1986 Neil Gunn International Fellow, was repeated at Syracuse University in 1988 and published, in shorter form, in the *Times Literary Supplement* and *Harper's* magazine. In this essay Vargas Llosa revisits a lifelong obsession of his—the theme of literature as "a convenient lie." He investigates what he calls the "questions of conquest" by exploring the imagination of the first Spanish chroniclers of Peru and inviting us to a "literary reading" of history. The piece eventually became the first chapter of *A Writer's Reality*, edited by Myron I. Lichtblau.

Novels Disguised as History

The historian who mastered the subject of the discovery and conquest of Peru by the Spaniards better than anyone else had a tragic story. He died without having written the book for which he had prepared himself his whole life and whose theme he knew so well that he almost gave the impression of being omniscient. His name was Raúl Porras Barrenechea.

422

ied man with a large forehead and a pair of blue
nated with malice every time he mocked some-
illiant teacher I have ever had. Marcel Bataillon,
had a chance to listen to at the Collège de France
Peruvian chronicle, seemed to be able to match
uence and evocative power as well as his aca-
.....ven the learned and elegant Bataillon could cap-
tivate an audience with the enchantment of Porras Barrenechea. In the big
old house of San Marcos, the first university founded by the Spaniards in
the New World, a place which had already begun to fall into an irreparable
process of decay when I passed through it in the 1950s, the lectures on
historical sources attracted such a vast number of listeners that it was necessary to arrive well in advance so as not to be left outside the classroom
listening together with dozens of students literally hanging from the doors
and windows.

Whenever Porras Barrenechea spoke, history became anecdote, gesture,
adventure, color, psychology. He depicted history as a series of mirrors
which had the magnificence of a Renaissance painting and in which the
determining factor of events was never the impersonal forces, the geographical imperative, the economic relations of divine providence, but a
cast of certain outstanding individuals whose audacity, genius, charisma, or
contagious insanity had imposed on each era and society a certain orientation and shape. As well as this concept of history, which the scientific
historians had already named as romantic in an effort to discredit it, Porras
Barrenechea demanded knowledge and documentary precision, which
none of his colleagues and critics at San Marcos had at that time been able
to equal. Those historians who dismissed Porras Barrenechea because he
was interested in simple, narrated history instead of a social or economic
interpretation had been less effective than he was in explaining to us that
crucial event in the destiny of Europe and America—the destruction of
the Inca Empire and the linking of its vast territories and peoples to the
Western world. This was because for Porras Barrenechea, although history
had to have a dramatic quality, architectonic beauty, suspense, richness,
and a wide range of human types and excellence in the style of a great
fiction, everything in it also had to be scrupulously true, proven time after
time.

In order to be able to narrate the discovery and conquest of Peru in this
way, Porras Barrenechea first had to evaluate very carefully all the witnesses
and documents so as to establish the degree of credibility of each one of
them. And in the numerous cases of deceitful testimonies, Porras Barrenechea had to find out the reasons that led the authors to conceal, misrep-
resent, or overclaim the facts, so that knowing the peculiar limitations,
those sources had a double meaning—what they revealed and what they

distorted. For forty years Porras Barrenechea dedicated all h
intellectual energy to this heroic hermeneutic. All the works he ʝ
while he was alive constitute the preliminary work for what shoulﬞ
been his magnum opus. When he was perfectly ready to embark upoɪ
pressing on with assurance through the labyrinthine jungle of chroniclﬞ
letters, testaments, rhymes, and ballads of the discovery and conquest thaʋ
he had read, cleansed, confronted, and almost memorized, sudden death
put an end to his encyclopedic information. As a result, all those interested
in that era and in the men who lived in it have had to keep on reading the
old but so far unsurpassed history of the conquest written by an American
who never set foot in the country but who sketched it with extraordinary
skill—William Prescott.

Dazzled by Porras Barrenechea's lectures, at one time I seriously considered the possibility of putting literature aside so as to dedicate myself to
history. Porras Barrenechea had asked me to work with him as an assistant
in an ambitious project on the general history of Peru under the auspices
of the bookseller and publisher Juan Mejía Baca. It was Porras Barrenechea's task to write the volumes devoted to the conquest and emancipation.
For four years I spent three hours a day, five days a week, in that dusty
house on Colina Street where the books, the card indexes, and the notebooks had slowly invaded and devoured everything except Porras Barrenechea's bed and the dining table. My job was to read and take notes on
the chronicles' various themes, but principally the myths and legends that
preceded and followed the discovery and conquest of Peru. That experience has become an unforgettable memory for me. Whoever is familiar
with the chronicles of the conquest and discovery of America will understand why. They represent for us Latin Americans what the novels of chivalry represent for Europe, the beginning of literary fiction as we understand
it today.

Permit me here a long parenthesis. As you probably know, the novel
was forbidden in the Spanish colonies by the Inquisition. The Inquisitors
considered this literary genre, the novel, to be as dangerous for the spiritual
faith of the Indians as for the moral and political behavior of society, and,
of course, they were absolutely right. We novelists must be grateful to the
Spanish Inquisition for having discovered before any critic did the inevitable subversive nature of fiction. The prohibition included reading and
publishing novels in the colonies. There was no way naturally to avoid a
great number of novels being smuggled into our countries; and we know,
for example, that the first copies of Don Quixote entered America hidden
in barrels of wine. We can only dream with envy about what kind of
experience it was in those times in Spanish America to read a novel—a
sinful adventure in which in order to abandon yourself to an imaginary
world you had to be prepared to face prison and humiliation.

Novels were not published in Spanish America until after the wars of independence. The first, *The Itching Parrot*, appeared in Mexico in 1816. Although for three centuries novels were abolished, the goal of the Inquisitors—a society free from the influence of fiction—was not achieved. They did not realize that the realm of fiction was larger and deeper than that of the novel. Nor could they imagine that the appetite for lies, that is, for escaping objective reality through illusions, was so powerful and so deeply rooted in the human spirit that, once the novel could not be used to satisfy it, all other disciplines and genres in which ideas could freely flow would be used as a substitute—history, religion, poetry, science, art, speeches, journalism, and the daily habits of the people. Thus by repressing and censuring the literary genre specifically invented to give the necessity of lying a place in the city, the Inquisitors achieved the exact opposite of their intentions.

We are still victims in Latin America of what we could call the revenge of the novel. We still have great difficulty in our countries in differentiating between fiction and reality. We are traditionally accustomed to mixing them in such a way that this is probably one of the reasons why we are so impractical and inept in political matters, for instance. But some good also came from this novelization of our whole life. Books like *One Hundred Years of Solitude*, Cortázar's short stories, and Roa Bastos's novels would not have been possible otherwise. The tradition from which this kind of literature sprang, in which we are exposed to a world totally reconstructed and subverted by fantasy, started without doubt in those chronicles of the conquest and discovery that I read and annotated under the guidance of Porras Barrenechea. I now close the parenthesis and return to my subject.

History and literature, truth and falsehood, reality and fiction mingle in these texts in a way that is often inextricable. The thin demarcation line that separates one from the other frequently fades away so that both worlds are entwined in a completeness which the more ambiguous it is the more seductive it becomes because the likely and the unlikely in it seem to be part of the same substance. Right in the middle of the most cruel battle, the Virgin appears, who, taking the believer's side, charges against the unlucky pagans. The shipwrecked conquistador, Pedro Serrano, on a tiny island in the Caribbean, actually lives out the story of Robinson Crusoe that a novelist invented centuries later. The Amazons of Greek mythology became materialized by the banks of the river baptized with their name as they wounded Francisco de Orellana's followers with their arrows, one arrow landing in Fray Gaspar de Carvajal's buttocks, the man who meticulously narrated this event. Is that episode more fabulous than another, probably historically correct, in which the poor soldier, Manso de Leguízamo, loses in one night of dice playing the solid-gold wall of the Temple of the Sun in Cuzco that was given to him in the spoils of war? Or more fabulous perhaps than the unutterable outrages always committed with a smile by the rebel Francisco de Carvajal that octogenarian devil of the Andes who merrily began to sing "Oh mother, my poor little curly hairs the wind is taking them away one by one, one by one," as he was being taken to the gallows, where he was to be quartered, beheaded, and burned?

The chronicle, a hermaphrodite genre, is distilling fiction into life all the time as in Borges's tale "Tlon, Uqbar, Orbis Tertius." Does this mean that its testimony must be challenged from a historical point of view and accepted only as literature? Not at all. Its exaggerations and fantasies often reveal more about the reality of the era than its truths. Astonishing miracles from time to time enliven the tedious pages of the *Crónica moralizada*, the exemplary chronicle of Father Calancha: sulphurous outrages come from the male and female demons, fastidiously catechized in the Indian villages by the extirpators of idolaters like Father Arriaga to justify the devastations of idols, amulets, ornaments, handicrafts, and tombs. This teaches more about the innocence, fanaticism, and stupidity of the time than the wisest of treatises.

As long as one knows how to read them, everything is contained in these pages written sometimes by men who hardly knew how to write and who were impelled by the unusual nature of contemporary events to try to communicate and register them for posterity, thanks to an intuition of the privilege they enjoyed, that of being the witnesses and actors of events that were changing the history of the world. Because they narrated these events under the passion of recently lived experience, they often related things that to us seem like naïve or cynical fantasies. For the people of the time, this was not so; they were phantoms that credulity, surprise, fear, and hatred had endowed with a solidity and vitality often more powerful than beings made of flesh and blood.

The conquest of the Tahuantinsuyo [the name given to the Inca Empire in its totality], by a handful of Spaniards, is a fact of history that even now, after having digested and ruminated over all the explanations, we find hard to unravel. The first wave of conquistadores, Pizarro and his companions, were fewer than two hundred, not counting the black slaves and the collaborating Indians. When the reinforcements started to arrive, this first wave had already dealt a mortal blow and taken over an empire that had ruled over at least twenty million people. This was not a primitive society made up of barbaric tribes like the ones the Spaniards had found in the Caribbean or in Darién, but a civilization that had reached a high level of social, military, agricultural, and handicraft development which in many ways Spain itself had not reached.

The most remarkable aspects of this civilization, however, were not the paths that crossed the four *suyos*, or regions, of the vast territory, the temples and fortresses, the irrigation systems, or the complex administrative organization, but something in which all the testimonies of these chronicles coincide. This civilization managed to eradicate hunger in that immense region. It was able to distribute all that was produced in such a way that all its subjects had enough to eat. Only a very small number of empires throughout the whole world have succeeded in achieving this feat. Are the conquistadores' firearms, horses, and armor enough to explain the immediate collapse of this Inca civilization at the first clash with the Spaniards? It is true the gun powder, bullets, and the charging of beasts that were unknown to them paralyzed the Indians with a religious terror and provoked in them the feeling that they were fighting, not against men, but against gods who were invulnerable to the arrows and slings with which they fought. Even so, the numerical difference was such that the Quechua ocean would have had to shake in order to drown the invader.

What prevented this from happening? What is the profound explanation for that defeat from which the Inca population never recovered? The answer may perhaps lie hidden in the moving account that appears in the chronicles of what happened in the Cajamarca Square the day Pizarro captured the Inca Atahualpa. We must above all read the accounts of those who were there, those who lived through the event or had direct testimony of it like Pedro Pizarro. At the precise moment the emperor is captured, before the battle begins, his armies give up the fight as if manacled by a magic force. The slaughter is indescribable, but only from one of the two sides. The Spaniards discharged their harquebuses, thrusted their pikes and swords, and charged their horses against a bewildered mass, which, having witnessed the capture of their god and master, seemed unable to defend itself or even to run away. In the space of a few minutes, the army, which had defeated Prince Huáscar and which dominated all the northern provinces of the empire, disintegrated like ice in warm water.

The vertical and totalitarian structure of the Tahuantinsuyo was without doubt more harmful to its survival than all the conquistadores' firearms and iron weapons. As soon as the Inca, that figure who was the vortex toward which all the wills converged searching for inspiration and vitality, the axis around which the entire society was organized and upon which depended the life and death of every person, from the richest to the poorest, was captured, no one knew how to act. And so they did the only thing they could do with heroism, we must admit, but without breaking the thousand and one taboos and precepts that regulated their existence. They let themselves get killed. And that was the fate of dozens and perhaps hundreds of Indians stultified by the confusion and the loss of leadership they suffered when the Inca emperor, the life force of their universe, was captured right before their eyes. Those Indians who let themselves be knifed or blown up into pieces that somber afternoon in Cajamarca Square lacked the ability to make their own decisions either with the sanction of authority or indeed against it and were incapable of taking individual initiative, of acting with a certain degree of independence according to the changing circumstances.

Those one hundred and eighty Spaniards who had placed the Indians in ambush and were now slaughtering them did possess this ability. It was this difference, more than the numerical one or the weapons, that created an immense inequality between those civilizations. The individual had no importance and virtually no existence in that pyramidal and theocratic society whose achievements had always been collective and anonymous—carrying the gigantic stones of the Macchu Picchu citadel or of the Ollantay fortress up the steepest of peaks, directing water to all the slopes of the cordillera hills by building terraces that even today enable irrigation to take place in the most desolate places, and making paths to unite regions separated by infernal geographies.

A state religion that took away the individual's free will and crowned the authority's decision with the aura of a divine mandate turned the Tahuantinsuyo into a beehive—laborious, efficient, stoic. But its immense power was in fact very fragile. It rested completely on the sovereign god's shoulders, the man whom the Indian had to serve and to whom he owed a total and selfless obedience. It was religion rather than force that preserved the people's metaphysical docility toward the Inca. The social and political function of his religion is an aspect of the Tahuantinsuyo that has not been studied enough. The creed and the rite as well as the prohibitions and the feasts, the values, and devices all served to strengthen carefully the emperor's absolute power and to propitiate the expansionist and colonizing designs of the Cuzco sovereigns. It was an essentially political religion, which on the one hand turned the Indians into diligent servants and on the other was capable of receiving into its bosom as minor gods all the deities of the peoples that had been conquered, whose idols were moved to Cuzco and enthroned by the Inca himself. The Inca religion was less cruel than the Aztec one, for it performed human sacrifices with a certain degree of moderation, if this can be said, making use only of the necessary cruelty to ensure hypnosis and fear of the subjects toward the divine power incarnated in the temporary power of the Inca.

We cannot call into question the organizing genius of the Inca. The speed with which the empire in the short period of a century grew from its nucleus in Cuzco to become a civilization that embraced three quarters of South America is incredible. And this was the result not only of the Quechua's military efficiency but also of the Inca's ability to persuade the neighboring peoples and cultures to join the Tahuantinsuyo. Once this became part of the empire, the bureaucratic mechanism was immediately set in motion enrolling the new servants in that system that dissolves individual life into a series of tasks and gregarious duties carefully programmed and supervised by the gigantic network of administrators whom the Inca sent to the furthest borders. Either to prevent or to extinguish rebelliousness, there was a system called *mitimaes*, by which villages and people were removed en masse to faraway places where, feeling misplaced and lost, these exiles naturally assumed an attitude of passivity and absolute respect, which of course represented the Inca system's ideal citizen.

Such a civilization was capable of fighting against the natural elements and defeating them. It was capable of consuming rationally what it produced, heaping together reserves for future times of poverty or disaster. And it was also able to evolve slowly and with care in the field of knowledge, inventing only that which could support it and deterring all that which in some way or another could undermine its foundation—as, for example, writing, or any other form of expression likely to develop individual pride or a rebellious imagination.

It was not capable, however, of facing the unexpected, that absolute novelty presented by the balance of armored men on horseback who assaulted the Incas with weapons transgressing all the war-and-peace patterns known to them. When, after the initial confusion, attempts to resist started breaking out here and there, it was too late. The complicated machinery regulating the empire had entered a process of decomposition. Leaderless with the murder of Inca Huayna Capac's two sons, Huáscar and Atahualpa, the Inca system seems to fall into a monumental state of confusion and cosmic deviation, similar to the chaos that, according to the Cuzcan sages, the Amautas, had prevailed in the world before the Tahuantinsuyo was founded by the mythical Manco Capac and Mama Ocllo.

While on the one hand caravans of Indians loaded with gold and silver continued to offer treasures to the conquistadores to pay for the Inca's rescue, on the other hand a group of Quechua generals, attempting to organize the resistance, fired at the wrong target, for they were venting their fury on the Indian cultures that had begun to collaborate with the Spaniards because of all their grudges against their ancient masters.

Spain had already won the game, although the rebellious outbreaks, which were always localized and counterchecked by the servile obedience that great sectors of the Inca system transferred automatically from the Incas to the new masters, had multiplied in the following years up to Manco Inca's insurrection. But not even this uprising, notwithstanding its importance, represented a real danger to the Spanish rule. Those who destroyed the Inca Empire and created that country which is called Peru, a country that four and a half centuries later has not yet managed to heal the bleeding wounds of its birth, were men whom we can hardly admire. They were, it is true, uncommonly courageous, but contrary to what the edifying stories teach us, most of them lacked any idealism or higher purpose. They possessed only greed, hunger, and in the best of cases a certain vocation for adventure. The cruelty in which the Spaniards took pride and which the chronicles depict to the point of making us shiver was inscribed in the ferocious customs of the times and was without doubt equivalent to that of the people they subdued and almost extinguished.

Three centuries later, the Inca population had been reduced from twenty million to only six. But these semiliterate, implacable, and greedy swordsmen who even before having completely conquered the Inca Empire were already savagely fighting among themselves or fighting the pacifiers sent against them by the faraway monarch to whom they had given a continent, represented a culture in which, we will never know if for the benefit or disgrace of mankind, something new and exotic had germinated in the history of man. In this culture, although injustice and abuse often favored by religion had proliferated, by the alliance of multiple factors—among them chance—a social space of human activities had evolved that was neither legislated nor controlled by those in power. On the one hand this evolution would produce the most extraordinary economic, scientific, and technical development human civilization has ever known since the times of the cavemen with their clubs. On the other this new society would give way to the creation of the individual as the sovereign source of values by which society would be judged.

Those who, rightly so, are shocked by the abuses and crimes of the conquest, must bear in mind that the first men to condemn them and ask that they be brought to an end, were men like Father Bartolomé de Las Casas, who came to America with the conquistadores and abandoned the ranks in order to collaborate with the vanquished, whose suffering they divulged with an indignation and virulence that still move us today.

Father Las Casas was the most active, although not the only one of those nonconformists who rebelled against the abuses inflicted upon the Indians. They fought against their fellow men and against the policies of their own country in the name of a moral principle that to them was higher than any principle of nation or state. This self-determination could not have been possible among the Inca or any of the other pre-Hispanic cultures. In these cultures, as in the other great civilizations of history foreign to the West, the individual could not morally question the social organism of which he was a part because he only existed as an integral atom of that organism and because for him the dictates of the state could not be separated from morality. The first culture to interrogate and question itself, the first to break up the masses into individual beings who with time gradually gained the right to think and act for themselves, was to become, thanks to that unknown exercise, freedom, the most powerful civilization in our world.

It is useless to ask oneself whether it was good that it happened in this manner, or whether it would have been better for humanity if the individual had never been born and the tradition of the antlike societies had continued forever. The pages of the chronicles of the conquest and discovery depict that crucial, bloody moment, full of phantasmagoria, when, disguised as a handful of invading treasure hunters, killing and destroying, the Judeo-Christian tradition, the Spanish language, Greece, Rome, and the Renaissance, the notion of individual sovereignty, and the chance of living in freedom all reached the shores of the Empire of the Sun. So it was that we as Peruvians were born. And of course the Bolivians, Chileans, Ecuadoreans, Colombians, and others.

Almost five centuries later, this notion of individual sovereignty is still an unfinished business. We have not yet, properly speaking, seen the light. We do not yet constitute real nations. Our contemporary reality is still impregnated with the violence and marvels that those first texts of our literature, those novels disguised as history or historical books corrupted by fiction, told us about.

At least one basic problem is the same. Two cultures, one Western and modern, the other aboriginal and archaic, hardly coexist, separated from one another because of the exploitation and discrimination that the former exercises over the latter. Our country, our countries, are in a deep sense more a fiction than a reality. In the eighteenth century, in France, the name of Peru rang with a golden echo. And an expression was then born: *Ce n'est pas le Pérou*, which is used when something is not as rich and extraordinary as its legendary name suggests. Well, *Le Pérou ce n'est pas le Pérou*. It never was, at least for the majority of its inhabitants, that fabulous country of legends and fictions, but rather an artificial gathering of men from different languages, customs, and traditions whose only common denominator was having been condemned by history to live together without knowing or loving each other.

Immense opportunities brought by the civilization that discovered and conquered America have been beneficial only to a minority, sometimes a very small one; whereas the great majority managed to have only the negative share of the conquest, that is contributing to their serfdom and sacrifice, to their misery and neglect, and to the prosperity and refinement of the westernized elites. One of our worst defects, our best fictions, is to believe that our miseries have been imposed on us from abroad, that others, for example, the conquistadores, have always been responsible for our problems. There are countries in Latin America, Mexico is the best example, in which the Spaniards are even now severely indicted for what they did to the Indians. Did they really do it? *We* did it; we are the conquistadores.

They were our parents and grandparents who came to our shores and gave us the names we have and the language we speak. They also gave us the habit of passing to the devil the responsibility for any evil we do. Instead of making amends for what they did, by improving and correcting our relations with our indigenous compatriots, mixing with them and amalgamating ourselves to form a new culture that would have been a kind of synthesis of the best of both, we, the westernized Latin Americans, have persevered in the worst habits of our forebears, behaving toward the Indians during the nineteenth and twentieth centuries as the Spaniards behaved toward the Aztecs and the Incas, and sometimes even worse. We must remember that in countries like Chile and Argentina, it was during the Republic (in the nineteenth century), not during the colony, that the native cultures were systematically exterminated.

It is a fact that in many of our countries, as in Peru, we share, in spite of the pious and hypocritical indigenous rhetoric of our men of letters and politicians, the mentality of the conquistadores. Only in countries where the native population was small or nonexistent, or where the aboriginals were practically liquidated, can we talk of integrated societies. In the others, discreet, sometimes unconscious, but very effective apartheid prevails. Important as integration is, the problem to achieving it lies in the huge economic gap between the two communities. Indian peasants live in such a primitive way that communication is practically impossible. It is only when they move to the cities that they have the opportunity to mingle with the other Peru. The price they must pay for integration is high—renunciation of their culture, their language, their beliefs, their traditions and customs, and the adoption of the culture of their ancient masters. After one generation they become *mestizos*. They are no longer Indians.

Perhaps there is no realistic way to integrate our societies other than by asking the Indians to pay that price. Perhaps the ideal, that is, the preservation of the primitive cultures of America, is a utopia incompatible with this other and more urgent goal—the establishment of societies in which social and economic inequalities among citizens be reduced to human, reasonable limits and where everybody can enjoy at least a decent and free life. In any case, we have been unable to reach any of those ideals and are still, as when we had just entered Western history, trying to find out what we are and what our future will be.

If forced to choose between the preservation of Indian cultures and their complete assimilation, with great sadness I would choose modernization of the Indian population because there are priorities; and the first priority is, of course, to fight hunger and misery. My novel *The Storyteller* is about a very small tribe in the Amazon called the Machiguengas. Their culture is alive in spite of the fact that it has been repressed and persecuted since Inca times. It should be respected. The Machiguengas are still resisting change; but their world is now so fragile that they cannot resist much longer. They have been reduced to practically nothing. It is tragic to destroy what is still living, still a driving cultural possibility, even if it is archaic; but I am afraid we shall have to make a choice. For I know of no case in which it has been possible to have both things at the same time, except in those countries in which two different cultures have evolved more or less simultaneously. But where there is such an economic and social gap, modernization is possible only with the sacrifice of the Indian cultures.

One of the saddest aspects of the Latin American culture is that, in countries like Argentina, there were men of great intelligence, real idealists, who gave the moral and philosophical reasons to continue the destruction of Indian cultures that began with the conquistadores. The case of Domingo F. Sarmiento is particularly sad to me, for I admire him very much. He was a great writer and also a great idealist. He was totally convinced that the only way in which Argentina could become modern was through westernization; that is, through the elimination of everything that was non-Western. He considered the Indian tradition, which was still present in the countryside of Argentina, a major obstacle for the progress and modernization of the country. He gave the moral and intellectual arguments in favor of what proved to be the decimation of the native population. That tragic mistake still looms in the Argentine psyche. In Argentine literature there is an emptiness that Argentine writers have been trying to fill by importing everything. The Argentines are the most curious and cosmopolitan people in Latin America, but they are still trying to fill the void caused by the destruction of their past.

This is why it is useful for us Latin Americans to review the literature that gives testimony to the discovery and the conquest. In the chronicles we not only dream about the time in which our fantasy and our realities seem to be incestuously confused. In them there is an extraordinary mixture of reality and fantasy, of reality and fiction in a united work. It is a literature that is totalizing, in the sense that it is a literature that embraces not only objective reality but also subjective reality in a new synthesis. The difference, of course, is that the chronicles accomplished that synthesis out of ignorance and naïveté and that modern writers have accomplished it through sophistication. But a link can be established. There are chronicles that are especially imaginative and even fantastic in the deed they describe. For instance, the description of the first journey to the Amazon in the chronicle of Gaspar de Carvajal. It is exceptional, like a fantastic novel. And, of course, García Márquez has used themes from the chronicles in his fiction.

In the chronicles we also learn about the roots of our problems and challenges that are still there unanswered. And in these half-literary, half-historical pages we also perceive—formless, mysterious, fascinating—the promise of something new and formidable, something that if it ever turned into reality would enrich the world and improve civilization. Of this promise we have only had until now sporadic manifestations, in our literature and in our art, for example. But it is not only in our fiction that we must strive to achieve. We must not stop until our promise passes from our dreams and words into our daily lives and becomes objective reality. We must not permit our countries to disappear, as did my dear teacher, the historian Porras Barrenechea, without writing in real life the definite masterwork we have been preparing ourselves to accomplish since the three caravels stumbled onto our coast.

TRANSLATED BY MYRON I. LICHTBLAU

Severo Sarduy

Cuba

(1937–1993)

———•:•:•———

Born in Cuba, Severo Sarduy was one of the few writers who, like Guillermo Cabrera Infante, openly opposed and defied the dictatorship of Fulgencio Batista. His complex cultural origins (Spanish, African, and Chinese) had a profound impact on his works, as he often tried to superimpose his three cultural identities within an experimental but fluid narrative. A former medical student who excelled as a poet, literary critic, novelist, and even a painter, Sarduy began publishing his work in *Ciclón, Carteles,* and *Lunes de Revolución,* the official newspaper of Fidel Castro's guerrilla forces. He left for Paris in December 1960 on a government scholarship to study art criticism and decided to stay in France permanently, as the Cuban revolutionaries were shifting toward totalitarianism. Sarduy, who ended up spending the rest of his life in Paris, was immediately successful in his new setting. He soon joined one of Paris's premier intellectual circles as a member of the magazine *Tel quel* and was able to enjoy some of the financial success of the Boom period of Latin American literature. Although his works did not sell as well as those by Vargas Llosa, García Márquez, Fuentes, or Cortázar, they had a profound impact on Spanish American letters and were subsequently translated into several languages. He was closely tied to both literary production and critique in France, which is reflected in many of his own writings, especially *Gestos* (1963). Sarduy's essays, particularly those in *Escrito sobre un cuerpo* (1969), reveal both his command of modern literary criticism and his knowledge of art history. They are experimental in structure and baroque in style, which makes them demanding to read. His novels, such as *From Cuba with a Song* (1967) and *Cobra* (1972), also rely on the superpositions of various realities and cultures, contexts not unlike his native Cuba. "Writing and Transvestism," written as a commentary on José Donoso's novel *Hell Has No Limits* (1978), about a drag queen named Manuela, shows Sarduy at his best. By deconstructing the act of transvestism, he delivers a powerful thesis: All literature is a form of performace and, as such, an act of sexual transgression.

Writing/Transvestism

Although it is perforce restrained, a hint of ridicule is apparent in Goya's reverent and polished portraits. The absurd, the compulsive force of the ridiculous, as if it were tearing the canvas to shreds, eats away at those ladies of the Spanish court until they are transformed into placid monstrosities.

If we see, simultaneously, respect and derision, piety and mockery, in those figures it is because there is something in the royal entourage which suggests that it is all *false*. I am thinking of Queen María Luisa in *The Family of Carlos IV*, jewel-encrusted and plump, with a diamond arrow piercing her coiffure, and, above all, of the Marquesa de la Solana, crowned with a huge flower made of pink felt.

The subliminally false in these examples—*without having to alter a single element of their basic form*—changes the jewels into paste, the gowns into disguises, the smiles into grimaces.

I make these references to Goya because they all seem related to, and ultimately explained by, the character Manuela in José Donoso's *Hell Has No Limits*. In Manuela, queen and scarecrow, we see falsity, we see the abomination of the *postiche*. The portrait becomes a blot and the outline a blur because we are dealing here with a transvestite, with someone who has carried inversion to its limits.

The goyesque in Manuela appears when, on the level of gestures and sentences cast in the feminine gender, we suddenly realize that they all refer—*without having to alter a single element of their basic form* (grammatical form)—to Manuel González Astica, the dancer who came to town one day to brighten up a party at La Japonesa's bordello. He was "as skinny as a broom stick, with long hair and with his eyes as heavily made-up as those of the Farías sisters [obese harpists]" and the execution of a *tableau vivant* along with the madame made him a father.

The central inversion, Manuel's, provokes a chain reaction of inversions, and these make up the novel's basic structure. In this sense, *Hell Has No Limits* continues the mythical tradition of "the world turned upside down" so assiduously cultivated by the Surrealists. The novel's meaning—more than simple transvestism (the outward expression of sexual inversion)—is inversion itself. The progress of the narrative is dominated by a metonymic chain of "upsets," of displaced *dénouements*.

Manuela, who novelistically (grammatically) is defined as a woman—initial inversion—*functions* as a man, since it is as a man that he attracts La Japonesa. It is this attraction which induces the curious madame to execute the *tableau vivant*; her ambition (the village bourgeois promises her a house if she can excite the apocryphal dancer) is nothing more than a pretext, one in which money justifies all transgressions.

Inside this inversion there arises another: in the sexual act, Manuela's role—he having been termed masculine by the narrative—is passive. Not that it is feminine—we are dealing with an inversion within an inversion and not with a simple return to the initial transvestism—but rather that it is of a passive man, one who engenders *malgré lui*. La Japonesa possesses him by having herself possessed by him. She is the active element in the *act* (also to be taken in its theatrical sense: a single glance is enough to create the space of the show, to crystalize the Other, the scene). The succession of adaptations, the metaphor of the Russian doll, could be diagrammed.

Inversions:

1st. A man dresses up as a woman
2nd. who attracts because of whatever there is in her which is masculine
3rd. which is *passive* in the sexual act.

This formal chain, which gives shape to narrative space as it marks out its coordinates, is "reflected" thematically on the level of emotional attraction: Pancho Vega, the official *macho* of the hamlet, besieges Manuela, fascinated, in spite (or because) of scandal, of the mask or of the goyesque imposture. The final sadistic act, which Pancho and his follower Octavio perpetrate, is a substitute for an act of possession. The *macho*—that reverse form of transvestism—incapable of confronting his own desire, of assuming the image of himself which his desire wills he assume, becomes an inquisitor, an executioner.

Donoso skillfully disguises his sentence; he masks it in order to locate it symbolically at Manuela's emotional level. He does this to delegate the "responsibility" of the tale to her (the third-person narrator seems to be just another means of hiding the facts), to an ego which is lurking, dissimulated, the real subject of the sentence: the entire *he/she* structure is a cover-up; a latent "I" threatens it, undermines it, cracks it. As in that other place without limits, dreams, everything here says "I."

Verbs with an aggressive meaning (*kick, punch*) are often "dubbed" with others which have sexual connotations (*pant*), with metaphors of desire (*men are hungry*), of penetration (*their drooling and hard bodies wounding his*), of pleasure (*their hot bodies twisting around*). One sentence, finally, as if the subterranean discourse relaxed for a second, makes the sadistic joy explicit: "delighted to the depth of their painful confusion."

Another inversion may be seen on the level of social functions: the present madam of the bordello (La Japonesita) is a virgin, and as if to underline the fact that in this inverted world the only possible attraction is that which is governed by disguise, no one desires her.

This game of "upsets" which I have outlined may be extended to the entire narrative: Donoso substitutes for the tale-within-a-tale an inversion-within-an-inversion. If this system of twists, one within another, never straightens out into an image analogous to that of the "right-side-up world," but goes on spinning further and further, it is because the thing inverted in each case is not the totality of the surface—economics, politics, class tensions, none of these is changed in the upsets, and they always correspond to "reality"—but only its constantly changing erotic signifiers, certain verbal levels, the topology which certain words delineate.

Appearances Deceive

We are deceived by those things which constitute the supposed "exterior" of literature: the page, the blank spaces, all that comes out of those spaces to appear between the lines, the horizontality of writing, the writing itself, etc. This appearance, this display of visual signifiers—and through them (the visual aspects) those which are phonetic—and the relationships which are created in that privileged place in the association that is the *plane* of the page, the *volume* of the book. These are the things that a persistent prejudice has considered the exterior face, the obverse of something which must be what that face *expresses*: content, ideas, messages, even a "fiction," an imaginary world, etc.

That prejudice, manifest or not, sweetened with various vocabularies, taken up in various dialectics, is that of realism. Everything in it, in its vast grammar, backed up by culture, the guarantee of its ideology, supposes a reality outside the text, outside the "literalness" of writing. That reality, which the author should limit himself to expressing, to translating, should direct the movements of the page, its body, its languages, the material quality of writing. The most ingenuous people suppose that it is the reality of the "world around us," the reality of events; the wisest displace that fallacy in order to present us with an imaginary entity, something fictitious, a "fantastic world." But it's all the same: pure realists—socialist or not— and magic realists promulgate and have recourse to the same myth. It is a myth rooted in aristotelian, logocentric knowledge, knowledge about a "source," about something primitive and *true* which the author brings to the blank page. And it is to this kind of thinking that we may relate the *fetishization* of this new singer, this demiurge recovered by Romanticism.

The progress of certain theoretical studies, the complete turnabout those studies have brought about in literary criticism, have made us reevaluate all of what had been considered as an outside, an appearance:

(1) the unconscious considered as a language subject to its own rhetorical laws, its own codes and transgressions; the attention given to signifiers, which create an *effect* which is the sense, the attention given to the manifest substance of dream. (Lacan)
(2) the "content" of a work considered as an absence, metaphor as a sign without content and it is "that distance from meaning which the symbolic process designates." (Barthes)

The apparent exteriority of the text, the surface, that "mask" which fools us, "since if there is a mask there is nothing behind it; a surface which doesn't hide anything but itself; a surface which, because it makes us suppose that there is something behind it, stops us from thinking it a surface. The mask makes us believe that there is a depth, but what the mask covers is itself: the mask feigns dissimulation to dissimulate that it is nothing more than a simulation."

Transvestism, as Donoso's novel practices it, is probably the best metaphor for what writing really is: what Manuela makes us see is not a woman *under whose outward appearance* a man must be hiding, a cosmetic mask which, when it falls will reveal a beard, a rough, hard face, but rather *the very fact of transvestism itself.* No one cannot know, and it would be impossible not to know it, given the obvious falsity of the disguise, that Manuela is a tired-out dancer, a dissimulated man, a goyesque *capricho.* What Manuela reveals is the coexistence, in a single body, of masculine and feminine signifiers: the tension, the repulsion, the antagonism which is created between them.

By means of a symbolic language this character comes to signify a painting-over, a concealment, a hiding of something. Painted eyebrows and beard: that mask would enmask its being a mask. That is the "reality" (limitless, since everything is contaminated by it) which Donoso's hero enunciates.

Those planes of intersexuality are analogous to the planes of intertextuality which make up the literary object. They are planes which communicate on the same exterior, which answer each other and complete each other and define each other. That interaction of linguistic textures, of discourses, that dance, that parody, is writing.

TRANSLATED BY ALFRED MACADAM

Rosario Ferré

Puerto Rico
(b. 1938)

One of the more versatile contemporary Latin American authors, Puerto Rican–born and Manhattan College-educated Rosario Ferré is the daughter of Luis Ferré, a powerful Puerto Rican entrepreneur whose assets include the daily *El Nuevo Día*. Ferré now divides her time between Maryland and San Juan. She has written poetry, short stories, a novella, and criticism, and is responsible for translating her own oeuvre into English. This work ranges from children's stories to fantasies to social and cultural commentaries. A fascination with the human imagination pervades her work, from the story collection *The Youngest Doll* (1976) to the short fiction *Sweet Diamond Dust* (1986). Some of her works denounce Puerto Rico's class structure and the place of women in society. Her female characters are often the silent victims of a culture that forces them to internalize their feelings of inferiority. However, some of Ferré's writings are devoid of the political. Such is the case with her children's stories, which often portray life optimistically and celebrate Puerto Rico's popular culture. Ferré has also written an essay collection, *Sitio a Eros* (1980), and a volume of poetry entitled *Fábulas de la garza desangrada* (1982). Her stories have been featured in numerous anthologies and magazines, including *Zona de carga y descarga*, which she edited during the mid-1970s. Her novel *The House on the Lagoon* (1995), written in English, was nominated for a National Book Award. The following essay, part of her volume *The Youngest Doll*, is an insightful examination of the bilingual writer's double life and of the uses and abuses of bilingualism and self-translation.

On Destiny, Language, and Translation; or, Ophelia Adrift in the C. & O. Canal

> *Language is the most salient model*
> *of Heraclitean flux . . .*
> *So far as we experience and realize*
> *them in linear progression,*
> *time and language are intimately*
> *related; they move and*
> *the arrow is never in the same place.*
> —George Steiner, After Babel

What is translation? On a platter
A poet's pale and glaring head,
A parrot's screech, a monkey's chatter,
And profanation of the dead.
—Nabokov, *"On Translating Eugene Onegin"*

A few weeks ago, when I was in Puerto Rico, I had an unusual dream. I had decided, after agonizing over the decision for several months, to return to the island for good, ending my five-year stay in Washington, D.C. My return was not only to be proof that Thomas Wolfe had been wrong all along and that one *could* go home again; it was also an anguishedly mulled over decision, which had taken me at least a year to arrive at. I wanted to come in contact with my roots once again; to nurture those hidden springs of consciousness from which literary inspiration flows, and which undoubtedly are related to the world we see and dream of as infants, before we can formulate it into words.

In my dream I was still in Washington, but was about to leave it for good. I was traveling on the C. & O. Canal, where horse-towed barges full of tourists still journey picturesquely today, led by farmers dressed up in costumes of Colonial times. I had crossed the canal many times before, entering the placid green water which came up to my waist without any trouble, and coming out on the other side, where the bright green, African-daisy-covered turf suspiciously resembled the Puerto Rican countryside. This time, however, the canal crossing was to be definitive. I didn't want my five professionally productive years in Washington to become a false paradise, a panacea where life was a pleasant limbo, far removed from the social and political problems of the island. I felt that this situation could not continue, and that in order to write competently about my world's conflicts, as war correspondents have experienced, one has to be able to live in the trenches and not on the pleasant hillocks that overlook the battlefield.

As I began to cross the canal, however, and waded into the middle of the trough, I heard a voice say loudly that all the precautions of language had to be taken, as the locks were soon to be opened and the water level was going to rise. Immediately after this someone opened the heavy wooden gates of the trough at my back and a swell of water began to travel down the canal, lifting me off my feet and sweeping me down current, so that it became impossible to reach either of the two shores. At first I struggled this way and that, as panic welled up in me and I tried unsuccessfully to grab onto the vegetation which grew on the banks, but I soon realized the current was much too powerful and I had no alternative but to let it take hold of me. After a while, as I floated face up like Ophelia over the green surface of the water, I began to feel strangely at ease and tranquil. I looked at the world as it slid by, carried by the slowly moving swell of cool water, and wondered at the double exposure on both shores, the shore of Washington on my right and the shore of San Juan on my left, perfectly fitted to each other and reflected on the canal's surface like on a traveling mirror on which I was magically being sustained.

The water of the canal reminded me then of the mirror on the door of my wardrobe when I was a child, whose beveled surface entranced me when I crawled up to it because, when one looked closely into its edge, left and right fell apart and at the same time melted into one. The canal had the same effect on me; in it blue sky and green water, north and south, earth and vegetation ceased to be objects or places and became passing states, images in motion. The water of words, the water in the C. & O. Canal where "all the precautions of language had to be taken," was my true habitat as a writer; neither Washington nor San Juan, neither past nor present, but the crevice in between. Being a writer, the dream was telling me, one has to learn to live by letting go, by renouncing the reaching of this or that shore, but to let oneself become the meeting place of both.

In a way all writing is a translation, a struggle to interpret the meaning of life, and in this sense the translator can be said to be a shaman, a person dedicated to deciphering conflicting human texts, searching for the final unity of meaning in speech. Translators of literary texts act like a writer's telescopic lens; they are dedicated to the pursuit of communication, of that universal understanding of original meaning which may one day perhaps make possible the harmony of the world. They struggle to bring together different cultures, striding over the barriers of those prejudices and mis- understandings which are the result of diverse ways of thinking and of cultural mores. They wrestle between two swinging axes, which have, since the beginning of mankind, caused wars to break out and civilizations to fail to understand each other: the utterance and the interpretation of meaning; the verbal sign (or form) and the essence (or spirit) of the word.

I believe that being both a Puerto Rican and a woman writer has given me the opportunity to experience translation (as well as writing itself) in a special way. Only a writer who has experienced the historical fabric, the inventory of felt moral and cultural existence embedded in a given lan- guage, can be said to be a bilingual writer, and being a Puerto Rican has enabled me to acquire a knowledge both of Spanish and English, of the Latin American and of the North American way of life. Translation is not only a literary but also a historical task; it includes an interpretation of internal history, of the changing proceedings of consciousness in a civili- zation. A poem by Góngora, written in the seventeenth century, can be translated literally, but it cannot be read without taking into account the complex cultural connotations that the Renaissance had in Spain. Lan- guage, in the words of George Steiner, is like a living membrane; it provides a constantly changing model of reality. Every civilization is imprisoned in a linguistic contour, which it must match and regenerate according to the changing landscape of facts and of time.

When I write in English I feel that the landscape of experience, the fields of idiomatic, symbolic, communal reference are not lost to me, but are relatively well within my reach, in spite of the fact that Spanish is still the language of my dreams. Writing in English, however, remains for me a cultural translation, as I believe it must be for such writers as Vladimir Nabokov and Vassily Aksyonov, who come from a country whose cultural matrix is also very different from that of the United States. Translating a literary work (even one's own) from one language to another curiously implies the same type of historical interpretation that is necessary in translating a poem of the seventeenth century, for example, as contemporary cultures often enclaved in different epochs of time coexist with each other. This is precisely what happens today with North American and Latin American literatures, where the description of technological, pragmatic, democratic modern states coexists with that of feudal, agrarian, and still basically totalitarian states. Translating literature from Spanish into English (and vice versa) in the twentieth century cannot but take into account very different views of the world, which are evident when one compares, for example, the type of novel produced today by Latin American writers such as Carlos Fuentes, Gabriel García Márquez, and Isabel Allende, who are all preoccupied by the processes of transformation and strife within totalitarian agrarian societies, and the novels of such North American writers as Saul Bellow, Philip Roth, and E. L. Doctorow, who are engrossed in the complicated unraveling of the human psyche within the dehumanized modern city-state.

Translating has taught me that it is ultimately impossible to transcribe one cultural identity into another. As I write in English I am inevitably translating a Latin American identity, still rooted in preindustrial traditions and mores, with very definite philosophical convictions and beliefs, into a North American context. As Richard Morse has so accurately pointed out in his book "*Prospero's Mirror, a Study in the Dialectics of the New World,*" Latin American society is still rooted in Thomistic, Aristotelian beliefs, which attempt to reconcile Christian thought with the truths of the natural universe and of faith. Spain (and Latin America) have never really undergone a scientific or an industrial revolution, and they have never produced the equivalent of a Hobbes or a Locke, so that theories such as that of pragmatism, individual liberty, and the social contract have been very difficult to implement.

Carlos Fuentes's novel *Terra Nostra*, for example, tries to point out this situation, as it analyzes the failure of the Latin American totalitarian state (the PRI in Mexico), founded both on the Spanish tradition of absolute power established by Philip the II during the seventeenth century and on the blood-soaked Aztec Empire. Fuentes's case, however, as well as that of Alejo Carpentier, can be said to be exceptions to the rule in the Latin American literary landscape, as both writers make an effort in their novels to escape arbitrary descriptions of their worlds, and often integrate into their novels rationalistic analyses which delve into Latin American traditions from diverging points of view.

Translating my own work, I came directly in contact with this type of problem. In the first place, I discovered that the Spanish (and Latin American) literary tradition permits a much greater leeway for what may be called "play on words," which generally sound frivolous and innocuous in English. In Puerto Rico, as in Latin America, we are brought up as children on a constant juggling of words, which often has as its purpose the humorous defiance of apparent social meanings and established structures of power. In undermining the meaning of words, the Latin American child (as the Latin American writer) calls into question the social order which he is obliged to accept without sharing in its processes. This defiance through humor has to do with a heroic stance ("el relajo," "la bachata," "la joda") often of anarchic origin which is a part of the Latin personality, but it also has to do with faith, with a Thomistic belief in supernatural values. It is faith in the possibility of Utopia, of the values asserted by a society ruled by Christian, absolute values rather than by pragmatic ends, which leads the Puerto Rican child to revel in puns such as "Tenemos mucho oro, del que cagó el loro" (We have a lot of gold, of the kind the parrot pukes) or "Tenemos mucha plata, de la que cagó la gata" (We have a lot of silver, of the kind the cat shits), which permit him to face, and at the same time defy, his island's poverty; or in popular Puerto Rican sayings of the blackest humor and unforgiving social judgment such as, "el día que la mierda valga algo, los pobres nacerán sin culo" (the day shit is worth any money, the poor will be born without assholes).

But faith in the magical power of the image, in the power to transform the world into a better place through what Lezama Lima calls the "súbito," is only one of the traditions that enable Latin American writers to revel in puns and wordplay; there is also a historical, geographic tradition which I believe helps to explain the elaboration of extremely intricate forms of expression. It is not casually or by expediency that the literary structures in Alejo Carpentier's *The Lost Steps*, Guimarães Rosa's *The Devil to Pay in the Backlands*, or Nélida Piñón's *Tebas de mi corazón* often remind us of the baroque altarpieces of the churches of Brazil, Mexico, and Peru, where baroque art reached its maximum expression. When the Spanish conquerors reached the New World in the fifteenth and sixteenth centuries they brought the Spanish language and tradition with them, but that language and tradition, confronted by and superimposed on the complex realities of Indian cultures, as well as the convoluted forms of an equally diverse and till then unknown flora and fauna, began to change radically. In this sense Spanish literature in itself had received, by the time the seventeenth century had come around, considerable cultural influence from the Latin American continent. Don Luis de Góngora y Argote, for example, who never visited the Spanish colonies, would probably never have written the *Soledades* (a poem considered the apex of baroque literary expression) in which a shipwrecked traveler reaches the shores of a Utopian New World, if Spanish had not been the language in which Mexico and Peru were discovered and colonized. None has put it more clearly than José Lezama Lima, the Cuban poet, in an essay entitled "La curiosidad barroca." Lezama points out there how the baroque literary art of Góngora, as well as that of his nephew, the Mexican Don Carlos de Sigüenza y Góngora and of the Mexican nun Sor Juana Inés de la Cruz, evolves parallel to the carved altarpieces of Kondori, an Indian stonecarver from Peru, which represent "in an obscure and hieratic fashion the synthesis of Spanish and Indian, of Spanish theocracy with the solemn petrified order of the Inca Empire." Lezama's own novel, *Paradiso*, whose linguistic structure is as convoluted as the labyrinths of the Amazon jungle, remains today the most impressive testimony to the importance of baroque aesthetics in the contemporary Latin American novel.

A third characteristic that helps define Latin American tradition vis-à-vis North American tradition in literature today has often to do with magical occurrences and the world of the marvelously real ("lo real maravilloso"), which imply a given faith in the supernatural world which is very difficult to acquire when one is born in a country where technological knowledge and the pragmatics of reason reign supreme. We are here once again in the realm of how diverging cultural matrices determine to a certain extent the themes that preoccupy literature. In technologically developed countries such as the United States and England, for example, the marvelous often finds its most adequate expression in the novels of writers like Ray Bradbury and Lord Dunsany, who prefer to place their fiction in extraterrestrial worlds where faith in magic can still operate and the skepticism inherent in inductive reasoning has not yet become dominant.

As I began to translate my novel, *Maldito amor*, the issues I have just mentioned came to my attention. The first serious obstacle I encountered was the title. "Maldito amor" in Spanish is an idiomatic expression which is impossible to render accurately in English. It is a love that is halfway between doomed and damned, and thus participates in both without being either. The fact that the adjective "maldito," furthermore, is placed before the noun "amor," gives it an exclamative nature which is very present to Spanish speakers, in spite of the fact that the exclamation point is missing.

"Maldito amor" is something very different from "Amor maldito," which would clearly have the connotation of "devilish love." The title of the novel in Spanish is, in this sense, almost a benign form of swearing, or of complaining about the treacherous nature of love. In addition to all this, the title is also the title of a very famous danza written by Juan Morell Campos, Puerto Rico's most gifted composer in the nineteenth century, which describes in its verses the paradisiacal existence of the island's bourgeoisie at the time. As this complicated wordplay would have been totally lost in English, as well as the cultural reference to a musical composition which is only well known on the island, I decided to change the title altogether in my translation of the novel, substituting the much more specific "Sweet Diamond Dust." The new title refers to the sugar produced by the De Lavalle family, but it also touches on the dangers of a sugar which, like diamond dust, poisons those who sweeten their lives with it.

The inability to reproduce Spanish wordplay as anything but an inane juggling of words not only made me change the title; it also soon made me begin to prune my own sentences mercilessly like overgrown vines, because, I found, the sap was not running through them as it should. How did I know this? What made me arrive at this conclusion? As I faced sentence after sentence of what I had written in Spanish hardly two years before (when I was writing the novel), I realized that, in translating it into English, I had acquired a different instinct in my approach to a theme. I felt almost like a hunting dog which is forced to smell out the same prey, but one which has drastically changed its spoor. My faith in the power of the image, for example, was now untenable, and facts had become much more important. The dance of language had now to have a direction, a specific line of action. The possibility of Utopia, and the description of a world in which the marvelously real sustained the very fabric of existence, was still my goal, but it had to be reached by a different road. The language of technology and capitalism, I said to myself, must above all assure a dividend, and this dividend cannot be limited to philosophic contemplations, or to a feast of the senses and of the ear. Thus, I delved into a series of books on the history and sociology of the sugarcane industry in Puerto Rico, which gave me the opportunity to widen the scope of the novel, adding information and situating its events in a much more precise environment.

Is translation of a literary text possible, given the enormous differences in cultural tradition in which language is embedded? I asked myself this, seeing that as I translated I was forced to substitute, cancel, and rewrite constantly, now pruning, now widening the original text. In the philosophy of language and in reference to translation in general (not necessarily of a literary text) two radically opposed points of view can be and have been asserted. One declares that the underlying structure of language is universal and common to everyone. "To translate," in the words of George Steiner, "is to descend beneath the exterior disparities of two languages in order to bring into vital play their analogous and . . . common principles of being." The other one holds that "universal deep structures are either fathomless to logical and psychological investigation or of an order so abstract, so generalized as to be well-nigh trivial." This extreme, monadistic position asserts that real translation is impossible, as Steiner says, and that what passes for translation is a convention of approximate analogies, "a rough-cast similitude, just tolerable when the two relevant languages or cultures are cognate. . . ."

I lean rather more naturally to the second than to the first of these premises. Translating literature is a very different matter from translating everyday language, and I believe it could be evaluated on a changing spectrum. Poetry, where meaning can never be wholly separated from expressive form, is a mystery which can never be translated. It can only be transcribed, reproduced in a shape that will always be a sorry shadow of itself. That is why Robert Frost pronounced his famous dictum that "poetry is what gets lost in translation" and Ortega y Gasset evolved his theory on the melancholy of translation, in his *Miseria y esplendor de la traducción*. To one side of poetry one could place prose and poetic fiction, where symbolic expression may alternate with the language of analysis and communication. Here one could situate novels and prose poems which employ varying degrees of symbolic language and which are directed toward both an intuitive *and* an explanatory exposition of meaning. On the far side of the spectrum one could place literary texts of a historical, sociological, and political nature, such as the essays of Euclides Da Cunha in Brazil, for example, and the work of Fernando Ortíz in Cuba or of Tomás Blanco in Puerto Rico. These texts, as well as those of literary critics who have been able to found their analytic theories on a powerfully poetic expression (such as Roland Barthes), are perhaps less difficult to translate, but even so the *lacunae* which arise from the missing cultural connotations in these essays are usually of the greatest magnitude.

Translating one's own literary work is, in short, a complex, disturbing occupation. It can be diabolic and obsessive: it is one of the few instances when one can be dishonest and feel good about it, rather like having a second chance at redressing one's fatal mistakes in life and living a different way. The writer becomes her own critical conscience; her superego leads her (perhaps treacherously) to believe that she can not only better but surpass herself, or at least surpass the writer she has been in the past. Popular lore has long equated translation with betrayal: "Traduttore-traditore" goes the popular Italian saying. "La traduction est comme la femme, plus qu'elle est belle, elle n'est pas fidèle; plus qu'elle est fidèle, elle n'est pas belle" goes the chauvinst French saying. But in translating one's own work it is only by betraying that one can better the original. There is, thus, a feeling of elation, of submerging oneself in sin, without having to pay the consequences. Instinct becomes the sole beacon. "The loyal translator will write what is correct," the devil whispers exultantly in one's ear, "but not necessarily what is right."

And yet translation, in spite of its considerable difficulties, is a necessary reality for me as a writer. As a Puerto Rican I have undergone exile as a way of life, and also as a style of life. Coming and going from south to north, from Spanish to English, without losing a sense of self can constitute an anguishing experience. It implies a constant re-creation of divergent worlds, which often tend to appear greener on the other side. Many Puerto Ricans undergo this ordeal, although with different intensity, according to their economic situation in life. Those who come from a privileged class, who form a part of the more recent "brain drain" of engineers, architects, and doctors who emigrate today to the States in search of a higher standard of living, can afford to keep memory clean and well tended, visiting the site of the "Lares" with relative assiduity. Those who come fleeing from poverty and hunger, such as the taxi drivers, elevator operators, or seasonal grape and lettuce pickers who began to emigrate to these shores by the thousands in the forties, are often forced to be merciless with memory, as they struggle to integrate with and become indistinguishable from the mainstream. It is for these people that translation becomes of fundamental importance. Obliged to adapt in order to survive, the children of these Puerto Rican parents often refuse to learn to speak Spanish, and they grow up having lost the ability to read the literature and the history of their island. This cultural suicide constitutes an immense loss, as they become unable to learn about their roots, having lost the language which is the main road to their culture. I believe it is the duty of the Puerto Rican writer, who has been privileged enough to learn both languages, to try to alleviate this situation, making an effort either to translate some of her own work or to contribute to the translation of the work of other Puerto Rican writers. The melancholy of the Puerto Rican soul may perhaps this way one day be assuaged, and its perpetual hunger for a lost paradise be appeased. Memory, which so often erases the ache of the penury and destitution suffered on the island, after years of battling for survival in the drug-seared ghettos of Harlem and the Bronx, can, through translation, perhaps be reinstated to its true abode.

I would like now to talk a bit about the experience of being a woman writer from Latin America, and how I suspect being one has helped me to translate literary works. As a Latin American woman writer I feel a great responsibility in forming a part of, and perpetuating, a literary tradition which has only recently begun to flourish among us. I feel we must become aware that we belong to a community of countries that cannot afford to live at odds with each other; a community whose future, in fact, depends today on its ability to support and nurture itself, helping to solve each other's problems. A sense of belonging to a continental community, based on an identity which was first envisioned by Simón Bolívar, must rise above nationalistic passions and prejudices. In this respect, Brazilian women writers have always been at the forefront, for they were the first to write not solely for the women of Brazil, but for all those Latin American women who, like the feminine protagonists of Clarisse Lispector and Nélida Piñón in stories like "Una gallina" and "Torta de Chocolate," have suffered a stifling social repression.

As a woman writer who has lived both in Anglo America and Latin America I have had, like Ophelia drifting down the canal or the child that looks in the beveled mirror of her wardrobe, to be able to see left become right and right become left without feeling panic or losing my sense of direction. In other words, I have had to be able to let go of all shores, be both left-handed and right-handed, masculine and feminine, because my destiny was to live by the word. In fact, a woman writer (like a man writer), must live traveling constantly between two very different cultures (much more so than English and Spanish), two very different worlds which are often at each other's throats: the world of women and the world of men. In this respect, I have often asked myself whether translation of feminine into masculine is possible, or vice versa (here the perennial question of whether there is a feminine or a masculine writing crops up again). Is it possible to enter the mind of a man, to think, feel, dream like a man, being a woman writer? The idea seems preposterous at first, because deep down we feel that we cannot know anything but what we are, what we have experienced in our own flesh and bones. And yet the mind, and its exterior, audible expression, language or human speech, is mimetic by nature. Language, in Leibnitz's opinion, for example, was not only the vehicle of thought but its determining medium. Being matterless, language (thought) can enter and leave its object at will, can actually become that object, creating it and destroying it as it deems necessary. In this sense the cabalistic tradition speaks of a logos, or a word which makes speech meaningful and is like a hidden spring which underlies all human communication and makes it possible. This concept of the word as having a divine origin confers upon it a creative power which may perhaps justify the writer's attempt to enter into modes of being (masculine, Chinese, extraterrestrial?) in which she has not participated in the course of her own human existence.

I like to believe that in my work I have confronted language not as a revelation of a divine meaning or of an unalterable scheme of things, but as a form of creation, or re-creation of my world. If writing made it possible for me to authorize (become the author of) my own life, why may it not also permit me to enter into and thus "create" (translate?) the lives of other characters, men, women and children? These are questions I ask myself often, which I may never be able to answer, but I believe it is important to try to do so.

TRANSLATED BY THE AUTHOR

Carlos Monsiváis

Mexico
(b. 1938)

———◆•◆•◆———

Carlos Monsiváis, born and educated as a Protestant in Mexico City, quickly aban-doned his study of economics in favor of following the emerging art and political worlds of the 1960s. An essayist, critic, journalist, and translator, he has contributed a vast quantity of work to Mexican literary journals and periodicals, among them the weekly *La cultura en México*. An active leftist, he was especially known for his chron-icles on Mexican art and society. In fact, Monsiváis, who has lectured at Harvard and the University of California–Santa Cruz and who in 1962 received a one-year fellow-ship from the Centro Mexicano de Escritores, is considered the almost single-handed revitalizer of the chronicle (in Spanish, *la crónica*) as an essayistic form. His approach is unique, now often imitated: Using middle- and lower-class popular jargon, he explores all dimensions of everyday culture as if his readers were from the lower and middle class, when in fact they belong to an educated elite capable of proc-essing his sarcasm. His analyses of life in Mexico often incorporate history, mythol-ogy, legend, and street language. He has published an autobiography, *Carlos Monsiváis* (1966), and a portrait of his generation, in *Días de guardar* (1970). But his most acclaimed books are *Amor perdido* (1970), which includes the following ques-tionnaire first drafted in 1969, *A ustedes les consta: Antología de la crónica en México* (1980), *Nuevo catecismo para indios remisos* (1982), *Entrada libre: Crónicas de la sociedad que se organiza* (1987), and *Los rituales del caos* (1995). "Guess Your Decade" is Monsiváis at his shrewdest. It forces the reader to understand his or her role in history by fetishizing popular items and lampooning European, Amer-ican, and Mexican cultures.

Guess Your Decade: A Questionnaire

Faithful to one's era: a euphemism meaning something like "historically numbed." And nevertheless, according to fashion—that ridiculous, de-plorable, transient ghost which makes us live on our knees—one has always felt the need to demand affiliations, to be chronologically classified. The thesis is simple: everyone is from his own moment and moments are usually defined by decade. Precision has become necessary: which is your decade? with whom do you fit? with the twenties, the thirties, the forties, the sixties, the seventies, the nineteenth century, or the Middle Ages? How

451

do I know if my neighbor is stuck in the forties or that I have been unable to abandon the fifties? Faced with the eternally nightmarish urgency to place one's self and everyone else, an exploratory, symptomatic questionnaire is proposed. An interpretive key is provided following the questions for each decade.

The Neurotic Twenties

Are you absolutely convinced that Paris is the center of the world, and that beyond Paris lies the kingdom of the philistines?

Do you believe that alcoholism is the supreme vice?

Do you find yourself drastically sure that going to the Chiapas missions is the only way to save your soul?

When you hear "Yes sir, that's my baby," do you feel the absolute joy of living?

At gatherings, do you heatedly defend the absolute equality of men and women?

In conversation, do you usually adopt the violent, arch-synthetic tone of Hemingway's characters?

Do you declare yourself partisan to intense emotions like Scott Fitzgerald?

Do you believe in the necessity of socialism, as long as it does not inhibit spiritual elevation?

Do you insist Technology is the great enemy of Humanity?

Do you believe the defeat of José Vasconcelos scared knowledge away from power?

Do you find yourself firmly convinced the United States has Technology but Latin America possesses Culture?

Key
Five affirmative answers: you are definitely from the twenties; six to eight answers: for you, nothing beats the Charleston; nine questions: at night,

you should dress like a flapper or Al Capone; ten questions: you are all that remains of Rudolph Valentino.

The Militant Thirties

Do you trust only those political causes accompanied by three demonstrations per week?

Can nobody or nothing dissuade you from believing that "There is nothing else like Mexico"?

Are you indignant when you remember Chamberlain's treachery and Leon Blum's sinister doubts?

Are you gloriously convinced that muralism is the best painting in the world?

Do you think that Rancho Grande is the image of our Paradise Lost and that the struggle between the province and the capital is the duel between virtue and vice?

Can you conceive the world without your social security number?

Are you moved by the novels of John Steinbeck and Erskine Caldwell?

Do you agree that Proust, living in the ivory tower, separated himself from popular struggle, or does the word "Trotsky" make you indignant?

Do you associate the XEW Radio, Voz de la América Latina from Mexico, with all your sentimental memories?

Do you agree that there is no sound more beautiful than a union rally?

Do you solidly believe "that we must admit the Indian is right, even if he is not"?

Key
Five affirmative answers: convicted and confessed, you will eternally live in the Decade of Compromise; six to eight answers: the most important thing to you is the defense of the Popular Front; nine answers: the meeting will be tonight at Teatro Iris; ten answers: are you sure you are not Vicente Lombardo Toledano, reincarnated?

The Traumatic Forties

Do you wake up in the morning humming "My beloved Mexico, how beautiful is your flag, should anyone blemish it, I would split his heart"?*

Do you enthusiastically dance to Glenn Miller's music?

Do you frequently use the terms "chicho" and "gacho"?†

Do you distrust the "fast lane" and prefer, as a catharsis, to spend the night awake, drinking and talking with friends?

Do you feel that living in the margins of society is no different from the severe and dramatic accusation "Traitor to the Country"?

Have you read Curzio Malaparte's *La pelle* [*The Skin*] twice?

Do you believe there will be no more wars?

Would you like to know why there are people who enjoy Juan Orol's films?

Do you have erotic dreams involving Veronica Lake or Ann Sheridan? Or José Cibrián and Luis Aldás?

Do you know which celebrated poem features these verses: "I am a poor bum/with no home and no fortune/and I know no/earthly joys"?‡

Key
Five affirmative answers: consider yourself a perpetual militant from the forties; six to eight answers: we share the pain of not having participated in the battle of Iwo Jima; nine answers: we are sorry not to have an autographed photo of Winston Churchill; ten answers: but of course we recognize you, Mr. Traitor.

---

*The original verse reads "Mi México querido, qué linda es tu bandera, si alguno la mancilla, le parto el corazón." *Translator's Note*
†These two terms lack English analogs from the 1940s. "Chicho" is related to "egotist" or "big man on campus," while "gacho" is a sort of "bully" or "tough guy." *Translator's Note*
‡The original verses are "Soy un pobre vagabundo/sin hogar y sin fortuna/y no conozco ninguna/ de las dichas de este mundo." *Translator's Note*

The Schizophrenic Fifties

Did you see a genuine symbol of rebellion in Elvis Presley?

If it were not for your analyst, would you have already committed suicide?

Are you sure that the continuance of the human figure in plastic arts is like, as the old metaphor goes, a bull in a china shop?

Do you detest injustice, but prefer to remain silent?

Do you believe that the definitively contemporary image is someone on a motorcycle, with blue jeans and leather jacket with a skull on the back?

Are you partisan to the Third Position?

Can you spend an entire day listening to old recordings of King Oliver and Leadbelly and Louis Armstrong?

Do you feel the end of Hollywood is imminent?

Do you accept your sympathy for James Dean's misunderstood image?

Do you identify with Holden Caulfield, Salinger's hero?

Do you attend Marxist seminars, not because you consider yourself a revolutionary, but because you like to know everything?

Key
Five affirmative answers: you may declare yourself an undistinguished citizen of the silent decade; six to eight answers: of course we have nothing against high society; nine answers: we are sure you have at least six Bill Haley LPs at home; ten answers: don't say anything compromising: Senator McCarthy could accuse you of social dissolution.

The Unforgettable Sixties
[drop formalities; use "tú" in all cases]

Do you call everyone born before 1945 "la momiza"?*

---

*"La momiza" is slang derived from "momia," or "mummy," whose closest analogs may be "the old guard" or "the system." *Translator's Note*

Are you so concerned about being solemn that you haven't looked up "archaic" in the dictionary?

Do you associate the phrase "riot police" with the idea of "hospital"?

Does the banal and frivolous game of "in" and "out" bother you so much that when they practice it all around you, you feel "out"?

Are you certain that Dostoyevsky is psycho-camp?

Does jazz bore you as much as the Beatles excite you?

What do you think of King Kong? Is he a symbol superior to the capacities of our Establishment?

Did you participate in (at least) ten demonstrations, thirty brigade marches, two hundred assemblies, and one detention?

When they say "There is nothing else like Mexico," do you usually add, "fortunately"?

Do you associate fashionable themes like "El papel de la juventud en nuestro tiempo" ["The role of youth in our time"] and "La duda del hombre frente al cosmos" ["Man's doubt facing the cosmos"] with the traumas of infancy?

If somebody admits an inferiority complex to you, do you thank them for the chance to hear an archaism again?

When they ask you to describe the Battle of Padierna or the Taking of Zacatecas, do you apologize and say you've never seen any Argentine movies?

Do you dislike being friendly with people who bear a solemn attitude?

Key

Five affirmative answers: for starters, consider yourself "in"; six to eight positive responses: you have surpassed the limitations of being "in"— you've already discovered the System; nine answers: do not trust the immediate nor the long-term economic future; ten answers: better run, here come the tanks; thirteen answers: we're with you, comrade. And we hope you get out really soon.

TRANSLATED BY JESSE H. LYTLE

Luisa Valenzuela

Argentina
(b. 1938)

———•◆••◆•———

Daughter of author Luisa Mercedes Levinson, Luisa Valenzuela is perhaps the greatest female literary innovator to come out of Argentina, if not all of Latin America. She was assistant editor for the Sunday literary supplement of the legendary Buenos Aires daily *La Nación* but was forced into exile by the Argentine military rulers, spending considerable time in the United States. She was at the Iowa Writers' Workshop, became a writer-in-residence at Columbia University, and taught for years at New York University, only rarely returning to her homeland. Finally, with the triumph of Raul Alfonsín in 1984 and the establishment of a civilian government, Valenzuela returned to Argentina to settle down. Her works often deal with the darker and more sobering aspects of Latin American life. Her lively, unpredictable style has made works such as *Clara: Thirteen Short Stories and a Novel* (1976), *Strange Things Happen Here* (1979), *Other Weapons* (1982), *The Lizard's Tail* (1983), and *Open Door* (1988) into great successes. Other novels include *Hay que sonreír* (1966), *El gato eficáz* (1972), *Como en la guerra* (1977), *Black Novel with Argentines* (1990), and *Bedside Manners* (1990). This last title is a semiautobiographical examination of Argentina's fragile democracy from the viewpoint of a mature female writer returning to Buenos Aires after decades of absence. Valenzuela has not been prolific as an essayist. Nevertheless, in a handful of instances she has explored the limits of this literary genre, always with a political overtone in mind, and the results are intriguing. "Little Manifesto," part of the Fall 1986 issue of the *Review of Contemporary Fiction*, explains Valenzuela's view of the duty of writers. In her eyes they ought not be judges of an epoch but witnesses. This role forces them to be utterly responsible and alert to terror, and to approach society without preconceived ideas.

Little Manifesto

We tend to forget that behind every writer there is a dormant human being, ready to jump at the smallest provocation of the world around him and/or at the slightest tickle of the quill. If for Borges man (meaning the human being) is a literary animal, one can also say that the human being is a political animal. And it's not a question of a clear or easy option, but rather of a conflictive duality with which we must learn to

457

coexist. The literary animal in each writer requires inner tranquillity and some inclination or ability to withdraw from external preoccupations. The political animal doesn't allow him to do that, every so often awakening him from his daydream with a treasonous clawing. The world continues and we are part of the world, and if they invade Grenada or if the Radical Party in Argentina wins the elections, we know that, for better or worse, matters will no longer be the same and neither will we be the same.

Should we write for or against these topics? Perhaps in some newspaper article, a territory where opinions have a direct value. Because literature is something else, literature is the site of the crosswaters—the murky and the clear waters—where nothing is exactly in its place because there is no precise place. We have to invent it each time.

If we believe we have an answer to the world's problems, it befits us to be politicians and attempt to solve them with the power politics provides. Literature doesn't pretend to solve anything. It disturbs and stirs ideas, keeping them from becoming stale.

But it is precisely at these crosswaters that it becomes necessary to have a lucid ideology as a base from which problems may be focused on, new options explored.

I don't believe we writers are or should be judges; neither should we pretend to be the blind, beautiful Justice. We are simply witnesses with our antennae alert, witnesses to our external and internal realities, intertwined as they always are. Forget about crude social realism or diffuse metaphysical surrealism. The literary act is a mixture of both. For me, it centers neither on the marionette nor on the hand which moves it, but tries to capture the elusive threads which go from one to the other. And trying to see these threads forces us to squint. The clarity of our vision will be greater the less we try to impose a preconceived image and the more we alert ourselves to terror.

We write in order to discover, to disclose, and also to point out that which we would much rather forget.

It's a game of constant questioning and it is a dangerous one, not because we might be fighting against some kind of censorship but rather because we can never permit ourselves the comfortable solid ground of absolute security, where dwell those who have killed the political animal or the literary animal inherent in themselves and so are called, respectively, literati or politicians.

TRANSLATED BY LORI CARLSON

Eduardo Galeano

Uruguay
(b. 1940)

———◆◆◆◆◆———

A native of Montevideo, Eduardo Galeano began his career in journalism, an influence that pervades his fiction and essays. *The Open Veins of Latin America* (1971),
widely read, and *Guatemala, país ocupado* (1967) both originated from his work as
a reporter and are examples of "combative literature," a type of essay with clear
left-wing convictions invoking a metaphor of Latin America as a battlefield of merciless foreign investors and repressed native voices. Although his insights earned
early critical acclaim, his prose took time to refine, to become sharp and precise.
From the rough *Los días siguientes* (1963) to later successes like *Los fantasmas del
día de león* (1967), *Siete imágenes de Bolivia* (1971), *Days and Nights of Love and
War* (1983), *The Book of Embraces* (1991), and *We Say No: Chronicles: 1963–1991*
(1992), one can see a marked stylistic maturation. Closely linked to the Buenos Aires
literary monthly *Crisis*, Galeano owes his international reputation to his trilogy *Memories of Fire* (1985–88), an anecdotal history of Latin America as told by the people
themselves. The volumes are made up of numerous vignettes, newspaper clippings,
short tales, and curious data in which luminaries and working people recount their
own existential odysseys. The following piece, part of volume 2 of *Faces and Masks*,
is a miniature essay about the European search for El Dorado, a mythical paradise of
gold that attracted explorers to the Americas from 1492 to the late nineteenth century. Its precise style, historical background, and engaging images are representative
of Galeano's extraordinary trilogy.

Temptation of America

In his study in Paris, a learned geographer scratches his head. Guillaume
Delisle draws exact maps of the earth and the heavens. Should he include
El Dorado on the map of America? Should he paint in the mysterious lake,
as has become the custom, somewhere in the upper Orinoco? Delisle asks
himself whether the golden waters, described by Walter Raleigh as the size
of the Caspian Sea, really exist. And those princes who plunge in and swim
by the light of torches, undulating golden fish: are they or were they ever
flesh and bone?

The lake, sometimes named El Dorado, sometimes Paríma, figures on

459

all maps drawn up to now. But what Delisle has heard and read makes him doubt. Seeking El Dorado, many soldiers of fortune have penetrated the remote new world, over there where the four winds meet and all colors and pains mingle, and have found nothing. Spaniards, Portuguese, Englishmen, Frenchmen, and Germans have spanned abysses that the American gods dug with nails and teeth; have violated forests warmed by tobacco smoke puffed by the gods; have navigated rivers born of giant trees the gods tore out by the roots; have tortured and killed Indians the gods created out of saliva, breath, or dream. But that fugitive gold has vanished and always vanishes into the air, the lake disappearing before anyone can reach it. El Dorado seems to be the name of a grave without coffin or shroud.

In the two centuries that have passed since the world grew and became round, pursuers of hallucinations have continued heading for the lands of America from every wharf. Protected by a god of navigation and conquest, squeezed into their ships, they cross the immense ocean. Along with shepherds and farmhands whom Europe has not killed by war, plague, or hunger, go captains and merchants and rogues and mystics and adventurers. All seek the miracle. Beyond the ocean, magical ocean that cleanses blood and transfigures destinies, the great promise of all the ages lies open. There, beggars will be avenged. There, nobodies will turn into marquises, scoundrels into saints, gibbet-fodder into founders, and vendors of love will become dowried débutantes.

TRANSLATED BY CEDRIC BELFRAGE

Isabel Allende

Chile
(b. 1942)

———◆•◦•◦•◦———

A relation of Chile's socialist president Salvador Allende, Isabel Allende left her native country as a result of the military coup by General Augusto Pinochet. She lived in Venezuela for many years with her husband and children, wrote for women's magazines and feminist periodicals, and had a popular radio show. She began writing her international best-seller, *The House of the Spirits* (1982), at night, after her children had gone to bed. Strongly influenced by Gabriel García Márquez's *One Hundred Years of Solitude*, the novel underwent many versions and revisions before it reached the public. Allende sent the finished manuscript to several Venezuelan publishing houses; upon their rejections she mailed it to the prestigious Spanish agent Carmen Balcells, who sold it within six months. Partly as a result of her success, Allende divorced and moved to San Francisco. She is also the author of *Of Love and Shadow* (1984), *Stories of Eva Luna* (1989), *The Infinite Plan* (1992), and a memoir of the tragic death of her daughter, *Paula* (1994). Allende has not fully cultivated the essay. Still, her forays into its tradition are engaging, as is the case with "The Spirits Were Willing," originally delivered as a lecture at Montclair State College and published in *Discurso Literario* in 1984. In this essay she discusses how her debut novel was written, the link between literature, politics, and history, and the magic that makes a work of art come to life.

The Spirits Were Willing

Someone has said that books have a guardian angel. The angel doesn't always do its job, but sometimes it does it so well that the book avoids every obstacle in its travels through the world. Born under a lucky star, *The House of the Spirits* has had this good fortune. It was published a few months ago in Spain, and one day I saw it for the first time on a bookstore counter. It was hiding in a corner, timid and frightened. I was afraid for my novel; I knew that it no longer belonged to me, that now there would be nothing I could do to help it. There it was, exposed to the gaze of persons who might judge it without mercy. But as time passed I began to relax, and I now believe that there really is a spirit that watches over it.

They say that every first novel is autobiographical, especially those writ-

461

ten by women. That's not exactly true in my case, because I'm not in the book. I am not any of the characters, but I don't deny that I have known many of them and that their passions and suffering have touched me very deeply. Some of the anecdotes in its pages are things I heard from the lips of my mother or grandfather or read in my grandmother's notebooks of daily life. I could say that all together these stories comprise a kind of family tradition.

People often ask me why I chose to write something as vast and complex as a family saga. The answer is that you don't choose a theme, the theme chooses you. Somehow this story began to grow inside me. I carried it in my heart for many years and fed it tirelessly. For this reason, in order to talk about the history of this book I'm going to have to talk about the history of my family and of my country.

My father disappeared from my life when I was very young, leaving so few traces that even if I ransack my memory I cannot even remember his face. My mother went back to her parents' home to live, along with her children, an event that had a critical impact on my childhood. I think that this explains why the book gives such importance to the big house full of spirits where the Truebas live out their lives. Our house was neither so large nor so luxurious as theirs; it didn't have a garden with singing fountains and Olympian statues nor an army of servants like the house built by the protagonist of my novel. But to me it seemed enormous, shadowy and drafty, and I was sure it was haunted by ghosts who rattled the wardrobes and slipped in and out of mirrors. There I grew up, absorbed in solitary games and excursions to the basement, a mysterious treasure trove of useless junk. That place was my Pandora's box. It contained the past, captured in old love letters, travel diaries, and portraits of bishops, maidens, and explorers with one foot on a Bengal tiger. My fantasy was fed by all that and also by my books. My legacy from my father was a great stack of books: novels by Jack London, Jules Verne, Emilio Salgari; the Tesoro de Juventud collection; classic works of all times. Two eccentric bachelor uncles lived with us, one of whom had more books than you could even count. No one guided or censored my reading, so at ten I wept over the tragedies of Shakespeare, tried to decipher Freud, and became thoroughly confused reading the Marquis de Sade. I envied people who could write and I filled countless notebooks with my impossible tales. Thirty years later, when I could not postpone any longer the decision to write a novel, I took some dreams, experiences, and fears from that era of my life and concocted a group of characters who go up in a balloon, invent fabulous machines, travel to India in search of the 999 names of God, get lost in the jungle looking for treasure, or die in a tenement disguised as the Queen of Austria.

My grandfather was a patriarch, a strong, intolerant man shaken by uncontrollable passions who died when he was nearly a hundred in full possession of his faculties, frail and lame, but without a wrinkle, with a lion's mane of hair and the piercing blue eyes of a boy of twenty. He was a marvelous character for a book.

I had a magnificent grandmother who died too young but whose spirit still accompanies me. She was a luminous, transparent being whom I named Clara in my book. There was little to invent; I took her from reality, although I did exaggerate a bit. Perhaps it was true that my grandmother could move a three-legged table with the power of her thought, that she helped the poor, sheltered poets, and floated above human frailties with an eternal smile and the most limpid eyes in the world.

I grew up in my grandparents' house and lived there until my mother married a diplomat, and we set out on a trip that took us to several countries. Later I was separated from her for long periods. I am bound to my mother by a profound, happy, and absolute affection. We developed the habit of writing letters to each other every day, which trained me to be an alert observer of the world, to be aware of people's emotions, to decipher symbols and discover keys, perceiving the hidden side of reality. It also gave me the discipline of writing, something I am grateful for every time I sit down before a blank sheet of paper.

I have no vocation for the nomadic life. All the years I spent wandering about the world I kept yearning to recover the stability of my childhood. That's why when I finally returned to Chile, I took a very deep breath of the air of my country, looked up at its snow-covered peaks and set about putting down roots. "This is where I'm staying; I will live here and be buried here one day under a bough of jasmine," I said.

How can I put into words what I felt then or what I feel even now every time I pronounce the name of Chile? Pablo Neruda described the country as a long petal. . . . He wrote poems to its forests, lakes, and volcanoes and to the *cordillera* that accompanies it from north to south, crumbling into a dust of islands before it disappears in the ice of the Antarctic. It is a region of balmy valleys where grapes grow, of lunar deserts, copper mountains, and steep cliffs battered by the waves of the Pacific Ocean. A mad geography inhabited by a hospitable people steeped in poverty and suffering. The Chileans are accustomed to calamity; they live on the crest of catastrophe, waiting for the next earthquake, flood, drought, or political upheaval. It is a land to love with passion and serve with joy, a land to tell about in books.

When I wrote *The House of the Spirits*, my ambition was to paint in broad strokes a fresco of all Latin America. I am aware of the many differences that exist among our countries, but I think that the similarities and affinities are even more striking. I am convinced that a single inexorable and prodigious destiny unites us all and that one day there will be a single country stretching from the Rio Grande to the frozen reaches of the South Pole. In honor of that Utopia I did not place the Trueba family in a particular country. The Truebas could exist anywhere on the continent, and their turbulent passions, their collective, shared suffering, their victories, and their defeats would be identical. This is so much the case that I receive letters from all over South America from readers who tell me that they have identified with the characters and their story, which is similar to their own.

I returned to Chile when I was fifteen years old, beginning to sense my womanhood and to dream about love. I wrote some dreadful poetry, belligerent prose, and the inevitable letters to my mother. I think I already knew then that I wanted to be a writer. Agatha Christie was my ideal because she produced many novels and still had free time for afternoon tea and rose gardening in the English countryside. I had no idea how arduous writing was.

One night at a party a boy asked me to dance. It was the chance I had been waiting for, and after arguing with him for four years, I succeeded in convincing him that we should get married. We have been together ever since. I knew love, had children, and a very full era of my life began. It was the age of the twist, the miniskirt, hippies and marijuana, women's liberation, and the political and social struggles of my country. I worked as a journalist, which is a kind of oblique way of approaching literature. An older colleague gave me my first lessons. He gave me a bit of advice I still heed because it never fails: "Tell the truth. Only the truth can touch your reader's heart."

My life was passionate and active. I was always at the forefront of whatever was going on; nevertheless, a part of me was always looking toward the past.

And so, loving and working and storing up history, I went on living my life. Until one fateful Tuesday—September 11, 1973—when I woke up to a new reality. That day a military coup overthrew the constitutional government of Chile, putting an end to a history of democratic rule that distinguished my country on a continent plagued by dictatorships. What happened in Chile has special characteristics, but it is not very different from what happens in other tyrannies. Outside the country one merely has to read the international press to get information. Inside the dictatorship, on the other hand, information is censored, because control of public opinion is critical to the regime. Thanks to my job as a journalist I knew exactly what was happening in my country; I experienced it firsthand, and those cadavers, torture victims, widows, and orphans left an indelible impression in my memory. The last chapters of *The House of the Spirits* recount those events. I based that account on what I saw with my own eyes and on the direct testimony of people who lived through the brutal experience of the repression.

For those who know and love liberty, it is impossible to adapt to a dictatorship. Many people around us were imprisoned, killed, or forced underground. The time came for me to leave, despite the promise I had made myself to live and die in that country. My husband spread out a map of the world, and we looked for a place to go. That's how we arrived in Venezuela, a hot, green country that took us in together with many other refugees and emigrants. We arrived with our children, with very little luggage, and with sorrow in our hearts.

The enchanted trunks of my uncles were left behind along with the books in the basement, the family portraits, the letters and travel diaries, my grandmother's three-legged table, and her crown of orange blossoms. My grandfather stayed behind also, sitting in a rocking chair, infinitely desolate and lonely, with a hundred years of memories and no one to share them with.

Far away from my country, I felt like a tree whose roots have been cut off and which is doomed to shrivel and die. Nostalgia, rage, and sadness kept me paralyzed for a long time. Nevertheless, little by little, my emotions were purified, I acquired a larger perspective of reality, and the new country won my heart. Then I felt the necessity of recovering the benevolent spirits of the past, the landscape of my country, the people I knew, the streets of my city, the winter rains, and the peaches of summer. In January of 1981 I woke up one morning with an extravagant idea. I had the thought that if I set down in writing what I wanted to rescue from oblivion, I could reconstruct that lost world, revive the dead, unite the dispersed, capture the memories forever, and make them mine. Then no one could ever take them away from me. I bought paper and sat down to write a story.

When I put the first piece of paper in the typewriter, I didn't know how to accomplish any of this, but I knew I should write. I remembered the words of my old reporter friend: tell the truth. I wanted to talk about the suffering of my people and of other people of that tormented continent so that the truth would touch the hearts of my readers.

It's true that I wrote for the pleasure of writing and because I had waited almost forty years for that moment. But I also did it because of an unavoidable obligation.

Latin America is living a tragic moment of its history. In our lands fifty percent of the population is illiterate and yet writers are listened to and respected. They are the voice of those who suffer in silence. All of us who write and who are fortunate enough to be published should assume the commitment of serving the cause of freedom and justice. We have a mission to accomplish at the front lines. We must combat the obscurantism that oppresses several countries of our continent through the force of our words, with reason, and with hope. We must put letters at the service of mankind. The worst enemy of barbarism is ideas.

I wanted what I wrote to be part of the effort to make our reality known. I wrote the story of a family like mine and like many others, of a country like mine and like any other in Latin America. The story spans almost a century; I started at the beginning, with the things most remote in time, things that had been told to me—transformed, of course, by magic, emotion, and the vagaries of memory. Once I had begun, I kept recounting things in order and without pause straight to the end.

I did not know that this book would change my life. I lacked experience in literature, and I did not imagine the impact that the written word could have.

While the ink was still fresh I had the opportunity to prove that there were spirits that protected my book: its acceptance in Spain was immediate and very warm. That surprised me, since I had thought that Europe was very far from Latin America. Later I learned that this is not so and that human beings are alike all over the world. All that is needed is a little effort for us to understand and accept one another.

Because of the strict censorship in Chile in 1982, I thought that *The House of the Spirits* would not be read in my country. I resigned myself to the idea that my compatriots would never read that story, one that speaks of injustice, fear, and suffering, but also of solidarity, courage, and love as they exist in a country like ours.

I never could have imagined what happened.

The book entered Chile like a pirate, hidden in the suitcases of brave travelers or sent by mail without covers and cut into two or three pieces so that it could not be identified. The few copies that entered the country this way multiplied by magic art. People who had a copy made photocopies that passed from hand to hand. There were lists of people who wanted to read it, and I am told that there were even a few people who rented out copies of it.

Months later the government decided that it was necessary to lift the censorship of books in order to improve its image, although there is still a suffocating muzzle over the mouths of those using the mass media. Along with other books that had been banned for the previous ten years, *The House of the Spirits* entered Chile legally and has headed sales lists since last August.

It moves me to think that the book is being translated into so many languages and that the spirits that live in its pages will be in contact with readers in remote places, offering them a breath of this fabulous continent where I was born. It's hard for me to imagine the Truebas speaking English, German, or Norwegian, but I trust they will get along just fine.

I wrote out of urgent need, as I said in the first line of the book: "to reclaim the past and overcome my terrors." I did not suspect that the benevolent spirit of my grandmother would protect those pages, watching over them in their travels through the world. I like to think about this, to imagine, for example, that Clara, clear, clairvoyant Clara, is here at my side at this moment, wearing her white gown and her woolen gloves, with her false teeth hanging on a chain around her neck.

Yes . . . It's a beautiful idea that books have their own guardian spirit.

TRANSLATED BY JO ANNE ENGELBERT

Ariel Dorfman

Chile
(b. 1942)

———◦•◦•◦———

Ariel Dorfman is perhaps best known for his poignant commentary on cultural imperialism, *How to Read Donald Duck* (1971), but the Argentine-born Chilean citizen has also authored a number of other works. Dorfman's *Death and the Maiden* (1992) met critical and popular success on Broadway and was adapted into a film directed by Roman Polanski. One of the few writers who have consciously switched from one language to another during their literary careers, Dorfman currently writes in both English and Spanish. He is primarily concerned with the theme of silent suffering (such as is experienced by the silent victims of totalitarian regimes) and the impact of totalitarianism upon the collective memory. Many of his pieces are vivid portrayals of the society of Chile, a country from which he was exiled after the 1973 coup. *The Empire's Old Clothes* (1983) is a nonfiction piece, while *The Last Song of Manuel Sendero* (1982), *Widows* (1981), and *My House Is on Fire* (1988) are fiction; Dorfman has also written a poetry collection entitled *Last Waltz and Other Poems of Exile* (1988). He is Research Professor of Literature and Latin American Studies at Duke University. Dorfman's essays are of two types: strictly academic, like those included in *Some Write to the Future* (1991), and the more journalistic, like "Adiós, General," included here. Originally written for *Harper's* magazine, it is a farewell to General Augusto Pinochet, whom Dorfman met briefly in 1973 while the ill-fated socialist president Salvador Allende was still in power in Chile. This essay highlights both Dorfman's role as an intellectual antagonist to military dictatorship in Latin America and his use of literature to combat it relentlessly.

Adiós, General

It was an afternoon in late August of 1973 when I held my first, and only, conversation with General Augusto Pinochet. At the time, of course, I had no way of knowing that he would all too soon become the master of my life and my country.

Those were the tense, waning days of Chile's experiment in creating socialism through peaceful means, and our democratically elected president, Salvador Allende, was fighting a losing battle against the forces that would soon overthrow him. As an unofficial adviser to Fernando Flores,

Allende's chief of staff, I spent a lot of time at La Moneda, the colonial building in the capital of Santiago that houses the offices of the executive branch. That afternoon I was trying to work out with Flores a way to involve some singers and writers in a government media campaign in support of Allende. The phone rang. Flores had stepped away from his desk for a few minutes, so I picked up the receiver. When a gruff voice demanded the chief of staff, I asked who it was. The answer was impatient and abrupt: "El General Augusto Pinochet Ugarte." I was duly impressed and buzzed Flores immediately. Pinochet had just been named commander in chief of the army. He was thought to be one of the few generals still committed to civilian rule, still willing to oppose what seemed to be an imminent coup.

When there was a coup, less than two weeks later, it was led, as the world now knows, by the man whose voice I had fleetingly heard over the phone. I have had many years to brood over the other phone calls he must have made in the days that followed: the call ordering fierce Hawker Hunters to bomb the presidential palace, where Allende died; the call ordering the Chilean Congress disbanded; the call to arrest Orlando Letelier and the call to execute Freddy Taberna and the call to disappear Fernando Ortiz and the call to cut the throat of José Manuel Parada.

From afar—from the distance of my exile, which began in December 1973 when I fled the crackdown of a military that had publicly burned my books—that voice started to take on for me satanic dimensions. When I read in a human-rights report that in the first year of the dictatorship 180,000 people had been summarily detained, and that an estimated 90 percent of them were reported to have been tortured; when I greeted in France my friend Oscar Castro, expelled from Chile after a two-year term in a prison camp for having staged an antimilitary play, and tried to console him about his mother's disappearance at the hands of the secret police; when I would read in one paper or another that 27 percent of Chile's population was receiving 3.3 percent of the country's total income and would try to conjure from these dry statistics the desperate hunger of the poor—always it was Pinochet and Pinochet and Pinochet who was responsible.

And yet, even while the general was the one person I blamed (aware as I was that many men were behind him) for Chile's suffering and despair—and for my not being able to return to my land or live a normal life while away—he remained for me, at the same time, strangely ethereal, almost unreal. I had photos of him clipped from the Chilean papers I combed for news and even had some of his speeches on tape, but all of this had the curious effect of making him seem even more disembodied, distant. He was for me corporeal only in the utter naked intensity of those three brief innocent seconds when I had heard his voice over the phone.

He was everything, and nothing.

I was permitted to return to Chile for the first time in September 1983. I had always imagined that this first trip back would coincide with the return of democracy—even, perhaps, with a Pinochet trial, the general exposed to public scrutiny and scorn for crimes against humanity. In September 1983, however, the general was still very much in control.

Yet strangely, it turned out that even in Santiago, Pinochet was everything and nothing. Few of my friends had ever caught a glimpse of him. He lived behind an imposing wall of security. He lived, as I did, at a distance from Chile—or do I mean to say he kept the Chile I had known at a distance from its people? I was returning to a land of exiles, men and women who inhabited a place that bore scant resemblance to the country in which they had been born.

It was one evening during that trip, as I was returning to uptown Santiago from one of the city's miserable shantytowns, that I finally saw General Pinochet for the first time—or saw at least part of him. I had spent most of the afternoon with a group of poor youngsters. They told me of brutal police raids, of the lack of jobs (for in that zone of Santiago the unemployment rate was estimated to be 70 percent). Some spoke of their addiction to benzene fumes, the cheapest, quickest escape.

My brother-in-law had driven me to that slum, and on our way back, at the exact intersection of the streets Antonio Varas and Eleodoro Yáñez, our car was brought to a halt by a screeching siren and a hive of braking motorcycles. "It's Pinochet, it's Pinochet," my brother-in-law murmured urgently. A caravan of black cars raced by, and just as they passed us, a white-gloved hand darted out of one of the windows and waved, in the typical gesture of dignitaries acknowledging a cheering crowd. It was absurd, because there was nobody there except us.

And then he was gone. An apparition.

Pinochet, of course, had no idea that I was watching him. And yet I felt that Pinochet was mocking me—that his ghostly hand in the dusk was gesturing defiantly: I am here to stay, this is as near as you and your kind will ever get to me, this is the only farewell you will ever see from me.

Five years later, on October 5, 1988—as the world also knows—the people of Chile found a way of telling Pinochet that perhaps, after all, he was not to be a permanent part of their lives. They used a plebiscite, one the general himself had confidently scheduled years before, to vote No—no to military rule, no to Pinochet. The following day, hundreds of thousands of those voters (I was among them) streamed into the streets of Santiago, and some of us marched to the presidential palace waving handkerchiefs as white as his glove—mocking him, bidding him adieu. *Adiós, General*, we shouted to the man we still could not see. *Adiós, General. No vuelva nunca más*—never come back again. It was a magical moment, as if the man who was inside those walls would indeed fade instantly and forever from our lives.

That very same night, however, the general made a regal appearance. On television, dressed in full uniform, he conceded that the opposition had won this round—but not the war. He did not intend to resign. On March 11, 1990, he would hand over the presidency to the winner of a new, open election, to be held in December 1989. Meanwhile, he was informing us: I will be around.

He has been around. Weakened, unable to stop the presidential election, which Patricio Aylwin, the candidate of a coalition of opposition parties, Concertación de Partidos por la Democracia (CPD), is expected to win comfortably, the general has spent his last long months in office making sure that his ghostly presence will continue. That hand I saw waving at me in the crepuscular Santiago light has been carefully binding the country up, leaving it *bien atado*, well tied. He has been carefully fastening a series of knots that will obstruct and entangle Aylwin's efforts to truly democratize the country.

Economic knots: the change in status of the Central Bank that will allow it to dictate monetary policy independently of the new government, and some of whose directors cannot be dismissed for ten years.

Political knots: His electoral laws allow him to name 9 of 38 senators and all but 16 of the land's 325 mayors, and to gerrymander legislative districts so that ultraconservatives can be elected with a third of the votes that an opposition candidate needs. He has also offered exceptionally munificent retirement benefits to several members of the country's Supreme Court, which can declare laws unconstitutional. This has allowed him to name younger judges for life, all of them fervid Pinochet supporters.

Terror knots: Death squads—linked to Pinochet in the past—have again sprung into action. A prominent left-wing politician was murdered recently.

Military knots: Pinochet has announced his intention of remaining commander in chief of the army for another eight years. From that post, he can threaten to intervene each time the new government tries to loosen his other knots and, more ominously, can threaten another coup if, say, as happened in Argentina, military men are put on trial for torturing and disappearing.

Aylwin has stated quite clearly that his first act as president will be to ask Pinochet to resign, and that he will seek to overturn each piece of antidemocratic legislation enacted after the October 1988 plebiscite. Even if many of Pinochet's knots can be painfully untied, it means that a great part of the democratic energies of Chile, instead of being directed to undoing the more terrible legacies of Pinochet—for instance, the "trickle down" effects on the poor of Chile's $16.7 billion foreign debt, the second largest per capita debt in Latin America—must still first be expended on simply trying to get the man responsible for these calamities out of the way.

Still, Pinochet's power *has* been receding, and as it has we have gotten a stark and satisfying view of the forces behind him, forces in no way as immaculate as his white glove. The secret police are feuding among themselves; former members thought to be willing to testify at trials for human-rights violations have been threatened or gunned down. The right-wing forces that backed Pinochet are in disarray, bitterly divided between those who want to distance themselves from his policies and those who are determined to continue them. (It is this division that has allowed major changes in the constitution to be arranged, in spite of Pinochet's desperate attempts to foil them.) And, although editors and producers still hear Pinochet's voice on the other end of intimidating phone calls—he recently saw to it that a noted television reporter was booted for having been "too soft" on Aylwin—he cannot stop the media from reporting the opposition's criticism of his dictatorship. For Chileans, many of whom for years shut their eyes to the general's mistakes and abuses, a more detailed profile of the man who has ruled them since 1973 is gradually coming into focus.

Above all, it is the psychological climate that has changed in Chile. This is particularly true for those who never shut their eyes. After such a long time quietly struggling to oust him, putting their lives on the line, almost incredulous at having survived his incessant repression, people are breathing serenely, trying to prepare for a world without Pinochet.

This is not as easy a task as it may seem.

Chile has been marked indelibly by Pinochet. I have visited my country a number of times in recent years, staying as long as six months. And on every visit I have observed the consequences of his misrule. A generation has grown up without knowing what democracy or freedom is, and a country has had to learn to bite its tongue and live with uncertainty, humiliation, terror. Unbridled pollution, countless slums where extended families share two-room shacks, hospitals without bandages or penicillin, thousands of beggars exploring garbage dumps in search of food, delinquency rising each year, eyes that avoid looking directly at you, bowed shoulders: over and over, signs of a ravaged land. Pinochet will haunt every effort at redressing this situation.

The consequences of extraordinary evil, such as child abuse, tend to live on, often for generations. Who has not seen the flocks of psychologists descending upon the victims of a hostage-taking, or upon schoolchildren terrorized by a gunman, or upon the survivors of a maniac who opened fire in a fast-food restaurant? Who has not heard it said that some of those who have experienced this trauma may be scarred for life? Pinochet has held my country hostage for more than sixteen years. His shadow was cast on every activity, every thought. This was most obviously true for those he could damage at the snap of his fingers because they remained "inside." But it was true as well for those of us who spent the years abroad, in relative safety, far from immediate retaliation. Even for exiles, Pinochet, by taking possession of our landscape and the people we loved, became the owner of our future—unless, that is, we were prepared to turn our backs on the suffering of our country and become indifferent.

A dictatorship has a perverse effect on a nation used to democracy. Normality is taken away from everybody—from those who, out of fear, weariness, or self-interest, blind themselves to what is happening and become apathetic, hopeless, guilty accomplices of a sort; from those who decide to dedicate their lives to getting rid of the dictator and fill their existence with his presence, leaving space for hardly anything more; and from all the rest, the majority who fluctuate between ignorance and resistance. In all cases, the general weighs at the center of one's life, a dark anchor narrowing the range of every choice. Thus, it will be difficult to grow accustomed to his absence. He is burned into our memory, into our customs, into the way we speak, into our dreams. How are we to exorcise him?

This dictator is our creature. We Chileans created the conditions that allowed him to take power. We continue to grapple with him and his legacy.

He will be exorcised. Enough people in Chile believed that Pinochet was not here to stay and were ready to risk their lives for that belief. There has not been one moment of his awful reign when part of Chile has not been resisting him, creating inner zones as well as more visible spaces he could not command. There has not been one moment when he was not defied by thousands of Chileans who, if they could not organize their lives as if he did not exist, were able to act as if he had already been defeated.

Although I cannot shake from my head and heart the feeling that the general, like the worst nightmares, may well be with us forever, I also trust that perhaps my fractured visions of him—the disembodied voice, those faded newspaper clippings, the white, white glove—were, after all, prescient, prophetic. Could it not be that the voice on the phone and the gloved hand waving are the exact metaphors? Is it not true that, in the final analysis, he is departing because he was never wholly among us?

Perhaps it is *we* who have been waving good-bye to *him* all these years. *Adiós, General.*

Edgardo Rodríguez Juliá

Puerto Rico

(b. 1946)

Born in Rio Piedras, Puerto Rico, Edgardo Rodríguez Juliá is one of the most important figures of contemporary Puerto Rican literature. As part of a group of writers who emerged during the 1970s, he addresses the island's concern for its cultural and political identity in a style that is less solemn than that of his predecessors. An offspring of Puerto Rico's industrial development, Rodríguez Juliá presents readings of modern Puerto Rico that are multidisciplinary, his essays often including references to sports, literature, music, art, and soap operas. While he explores the origins of Puerto Rico's national consciousness in the eighteenth century in works such as *La noche oscura del Niño Avilés* (1984), in others like *Una noche con Iris Chacón* (1986) he chronicles the complex reality of contemporary Puerto Rico. Other titles by Rodríguez Juliá are *La renuncia del héroe Baltasar* (1974), *Las tribulaciones de Jonás* (1981), *El entierro de Cortijo* (1983), *Campeche, o los diablejos de la melancolía* (1989), and *El cruce de la bahía de Guánica* (1989). He was awarded a Guggenheim Fellowship in 1986 and is a professor at the University of Puerto Rico. In the tradition of the Latin American chronicle practiced by Carlos Monsiváis, "Melancholy at the Hotel Empress," written on 6 November 1986 and included in *El cruce de la bahía de Guánica*, illustrates Rodríguez Juliá's irreverent experimental style and his satirical approach to popular culture. The piece is not without its offensive elements.

Melancholy at the Hotel Empress

I am writing a novel about adultery. It will be entitled *Cartagena*. I am baring my every wound to the sun at the seaside bar of the Hotel Empress. The line of the horizon and the curve of the El Alambique beach calm my cluttered mind: The sentimental conflicts that have filled so many pages of my writing are summed up by the words to that always timely *bolero* playing on the bar tape player: "*I am master and slave of love, a child and an old man, one woman loves and spoils me, the other just plays around.*" Eddie, the bartender, turns out to be a nice guy while at the same time respectful of that solitude the melancholy drinker seeks. This open-air bar, thatched with palm leaves and spreading onto a spacious terrace that practically seems to touch that big island known in days past as Isla Verde, must be, without a doubt, one of the great bars in this country.

• • •

There is something painfully kitschy about this place: It evokes that vision of the languid tropics an Italian from Brooklyn or Atlantic City might have. The boardwalk, or the boarded section that doubles as a terrace, seems a response to an infantile fantasy dreamed up next to the surging waters of some northern sea. We then move from fantasy to a kind of kitsch surrealism: Rising from the Jacuzzi next to the pool is a Venus de Milo watched over by the American and Puerto Rican flags. The taste is JC Penney according to the Constitution of the Commonwealth. I drink with my back to the monstrosity. But the terrace has also been decorated with enormous clay pots overflowing with tropical vegetation. Over the entrance to the hotel, once again, Venus de Milo. . . .

• • •

I prefer this bar to the one in the Hotel La Playita. The latter is the lower-middle-class version of hot-to-trot mistresses in the hippest por-to-ri-can *yuppie* restaurant, the infamous Amadeus. Whereas conversations here tend toward *the cruise I took around the Greek Isles*, the latest flick at the Cine Arte, and the omnipresent Bay, in La Playita the women would always ask me if I'm a psychologist, that is to say, if I was a priest.

• • •

There is a particular sexual anxiety that pervades the bar at La Playita. It is nothing short of intolerable. The anxiety of Amadeus is success and happiness according to BMW. In La Playita, it is the loathsome fuckfest. It is the women, above all, who generate that particular anxiety. They always come in pairs; it is the institution of the chaperones brought up to date.

This always results in a great inconvenience for the loner. (Puerto Rican society is relentlessly gregarious.) Let us imagine him for a moment: If the lady accompanying my pickup is seduced by the owner of a gas station or a coke freak, a hellish night of gibberish, of *y'know* and *I mean*, awaits me. There is something about me—a stranger at heart—that brings out the worst in people from this and other classes: that desire, that effort to speak to me byoo-tee-full-ee! Such are the professional grievances of a writer and professor.

The rooms in La Playita cost thirty dollars. In the Hotel Empress they cost sixty with a color television, cable, and nice decoration . . . according to Eddie. It is clear that the Italian owners of the Empress do not wish to turn their little tropical hotel into a fuck palace. Perhaps that is why they installed that smoked glass elevator with the panoramic view. It would be altogether impossible given the *al fresco* timidity of the Puerto Rican to ride the elevator up to his room with a woman. (We should recall the failure of sidewalk cafés in Puerto Rico.) Eddie says to me: *"Think if your neighbor saw you . . . he's got your number. . . . The other day a couple was there. They were talking for something like eight hours and then, you guessed it. . . . They took a room but they didn't ride the elevator, kiddo. . . . Not on your life. They bolted up the stairs."*

* * *

The bar in the Empress is diametrically opposed to the bar at Los Chavales: The latter is an enclosed capsule, *a camera obscura* where one gets drunk without knowing when the sun set. The door to this bar has a peephole. When the peephole is completely dark, we know that we have been busy drinking for several hours: the submarine syndrome, the space capsule syndrome, as David calls it. It is the ideal place for the euphoric drinker.

Here in the Hotel Empress, the bar is open to the breeze and the stifling heat at the end of the afternoon. Every shift of light at dusk is reflected in the sea. It is the ideal place for melancholy drinking. The person who goes to Los Chavales feeling the slightest bit sad is asking for depression guaranteed. In the bar at the Hotel Empress, melancholy languishes, is soothed by the sinuous passage of time, measured by each special effect of light over the murmur of the waves.

Los Chavales is the perfect gentleman's bar. Conquests there are tallied, not dramatized. The bartenders, Tollinchi and Freddie, preside over the bar with the severity of Jesuits on a Lenten retreat: Mistresses are frowned upon, are allowed but not encouraged.

In the bar at the Hotel Empress, I always drink the colonial *al fresco* cocktail *par excellence: Gin and tonic—Beefeater or Tanqueray, por favor!* At Los Chavales, I'm incapable of drinking anything but that damned martini.

* * *

The bar at the Hotel Empress is not fashionable. It opened in November of last year; it still has no traditions of any kind, no tribe or crowd has gelled there yet.

At five o'clock, the time of day when I walk along the beach to the Hotel Empress, the place looks somewhat deserted. Later, there is merengue every night—which I hear the way Cavafis's Marco Antonio heard the murmuring of life as it receded from him—from the window of my apartment on the tenth floor of Marbella East. Happy hour starts at five, lasts till seven. There may be, as in La Playita, Ladies' Night, Gentlemen's Night. . . . On Sundays I think they play calypso. . . . My prevailing misanthropy frightens me: When the throng of men and women from the party scene arrive, I leave, like a venerable professor thought up by one of the Mann brothers.

• • •

But the party scene pursues me. Another drinker arrives, twenty-something years old. He knows how to drink though he's not a drunk, which is to say, his eyes don't turn red with the second drink; also, he smokes. . . . No one smokes in the bar at Los Chavales. Those damn signs of anxiety. . . .

• • •

A young macho on the make comes in with the girl he just picked up at La Playita. He's about thirty, she's twenty-five. He can't speak English, she's a Nuyorican. The easy lay is a whirlwind of anxiety; he has the good nature of a business student. He endures her like someone putting up with a cold or a rash; he's ready to screw her, that's all. . . . My grim misanthropy focuses its peephole on those anxious Nuyoricans: They almost always produce in me a visceral repulsion; the most integrated and cosmopolitan ones are vulgarly sophisticated, monstrously denatured, like those fried plantains filled with caviar they serve at the Amadeus.

The management student seems all right to me. . . . Suave and laid back with one of those little mustaches Puerto Rican men display along with chubby cheeks, like emblems of their virility. He's a bona fide macho waiting for the women to stew in their own anxiety.

She is dressed the part of the *femme fatale*: A black jersey miniskirt, black glasses, violent suntan, her hair tousled and slightly dried from the sun and salt, a body built like a brick house—she hasn't even given birth in her imagination—the slightest hair, red, strapless, high-heeled shoes, flat feet but a fine ass and fine tits, truly exquisite if she just didn't breathe fire from her mouth.

He asks for a gin and tonic. She asks for a *margarita frozen*. Eddie, a true gentleman in his forties, wearing blue jeans and with the arms of a long-shoreman, prepares the drink for her in a plastic cup; it looks delicious, *muy, muy* frozen, coooooooold, perfect for this time of day. . . . But no, the easy lay protests in English: *Is that a frozen margarita?* The bartender stops short, smiles at her insipidly, but he's met too many like her. That fucked-up thing women have with complicated drinks, with concoctions! Why don't they order perfectly standard drinks like a Cuba Libre, a martini, or a scotch and soda? . . . *(Do you know how to make a Red Russian? . . . Kahlúa with milk and grenadine. . . .)* Eddie turns up his insipidity and responds in Spanish with a certain edge to his voice: *Yes, it's a frozen margarita.* She says cuttingly: *It doesn't look like one. . . .* When she gets mad she feels an obligation to speak in English. She comments to the potential owner, a bit under her breath: *It just doesn't look like one, too mushy. . . .* Enough to strangle her. The bartender backs down: He knows her type well.

She seems smothered, goes to the phone again, asks Eddie how he prepares a frozen margarita, forgets her sunglasses at the phone, goes to get them. The business student smiles at the bartender, establishes a complicity between him, me, and himself, the scholar of managerial mysteries. The other drinker—not a drunk, it's like the difference between a *pitcher* and a *thrower*—remains aloof, smoking, with a certain air about him—his khaki pants and military belt, his unbleached linen aviator's shirt—characteristic of a funky yuppizoid from the Amadeus gone somewhat astray. I'm already starting not to like him. He's so fucking good-looking, so sharply dressed, far from the suave style of the management student who *will probably go on to study law.*

In a moment of exasperation, the Nuyorican asks her companion in Spanish: *Why don't the people here speak English?* And he says, brandishing the sucusumucu (sly, take socks off while leaving shoes, not malicious) wood knife of a born and bred *boricua: I find it very hard. . . .*

The Nuyorican asks the bartender for another drink, *anything but a margarita. . . .* Eddie makes her a Sea Breeze: a squeeze of lemon, cranberry juice and vodka . . . *refreshing* he says. . . . She tastes it. Doesn't look convinced. When Eddie asks her if she likes it she responds *all right,* which is not the same thing as *so-so.*

Two girls walk in and sit next to me. I put the ugliest scowl on my face I can manage. Soon they are both smiling. They realize they are in the presence of an alien. They make conversation with me. Ask when the place opened. I emerge distractedly, partly from the alcoholic mists and partly from my premature deafness; I tell them that the place opened last November. I add sarcastically that there is Ladies' Night on Wednesday, Gentleman's Night on Thursdays, merengue, and on Sundays they play calypso. When I mention *Ladies'* Night on Wednesday, I do so with a jeering smile. . . . *Cynic!* they must be saying to themselves. What I fear the most: They don't appreciate my sense of humor *even in the slightest.* One of them, the oldest, the one displaying a bandanna *a la* Yvonne Goderich, *because someone told me I look like her,* like that TV actress, snaps back in indignation: *The men here, just because you're sitting in this kind of a bar, they think you're . . . What were you referring to when you said "ladies"? . . .* So, the so-and-so took offense. I think: *Now I'm screwed! . . .*

I don't respond very belligerently. I'm interested in the other one, in the friend. . . . She is an attractive young woman. The only ominous detail is that she wears an enormous punk braid in her hair. Kindred spirits, selective affinity: They both have rags around their head or over their forehead. They are both pro-statehood: One of them, Linda, is a Republican pro-statehooder; the other one belongs to Hernán's band.

Though we Puerto Ricans continue to employ ideology and party affiliation as calling cards, the times have indeed been a-changin'. Just as in the sixties it was somewhat chic to say you were an *independentista*, now these statehooders are acquiring that libertarian and stylish disposition for belonging to the perpetual opposition. Now being a government official and a Republican is considered *progressive*.

The drinker-smoker gets up and crudely approaches Miss Yvonne Goderich: *Don't I know you from somewhere?* . . .

I take on Linda. She invites me to sit next to her; I insist that she be the one to get up and sit over here. She agrees.

"How old are you?"

"Twenty-two. I was born in 1964. . . . But I've gone out with older men. I'm going out with Doctor . . ."

(What a condescending bitch, this easy lay: At the same time she's giving me the green light she's reminding me of my hardened middle-age appearance.)

Sensing a certain utopian nostalgia in me, she talks about and questions me on The Sixties. I tell her very seriously that that's all over now, that the Eddie Palmieri concert in 1972 at the university was, for me, the very melancholy twilight of those crazy and anarchic years. A bit surprised by my best halting whiskey voice, she reassures me: "I was born in 1964 but I greatly admire that era. It was a traumatic era, an era of changes. . . . I wrote a song about The Sixties. . . ."

Later on in the conversation her true nature rears its head: that of a Late Eighties girl. She tells me about Sra. Nivia Mclintock, a committeewoman in the Republican Party, and of Don Luis A. Ferré, whom she knows, and Poto Paniagua too, though he's a Democrat of course, *and I always sit in his box seat when the baseball season starts up, and it's not because I'm a social climber.* . . .

I don't have any money left. The perverse idea passes through my mind of bumming a drink off an attractive, twenty-two-year-old girl—I've already told her my oldest son is seventeen—affiliated with the Republican Statehood Party, the *P.E.R.*, of Garcías Méndez and Luis A. Ferré, *the man, the leader.* . . . I make my attack. She accepts. Eddie, who can't stand to see me sink so low, realizes the jam I'm in, serves me a *drink on the house*. It's Happy Hour!

I go on the offense, still pretending to be deafer than I am and with an astigmatism in my right eye. "I like you. . . . You have . . . How shall I put it? . . . Firm ideological convictions, you're clear, you are very intelligent. . . . And that's what I find most attractive . . . in anyone . . . you know. . . ."

"Thank you. . . . I like you too. . . ."

"Let's go have dinner. . . . I'll stop at my apartment for a second to change."

"The thing is, I'm with my friend. . . ."

"I'm not so sure. . . . She's already with someone. . . . Haven't you noticed? . . ."

"Yes, but the thing is we came here together and she'd get upset if I left. . . ."

Those damned chaperones! The Republican variation on the *dolce vita* according to Villa Carolina!

But the tender little thing is not altogether heartless. She writes down three telephone numbers on the Guest Check Eddie provides her with. . . . I listen to muddled instructions on how to call her.

"I didn't catch that . . ." (I press my ear forward. I come on a little tipsy and even more astigmatic. The quite perverse young woman has already told me again that she went out with a seventy-five-year-old lawyer. . . .)

"This is *Mami*'s phone number. . . . You can call me here and tell me where I can find you. . . . These other two numbers are Sylvette's; you can call me there on Fridays. . . . Or better yet, call *Mami* and leave a message. . . . I live with her although I'm going to school and work at the IRS. Though I'm alone. . . . But you understand, I live with her, I'm divorced and have a baby, a ten-month-old baby. . . ."

"Well, it's a pleasure to meet you. . . ."

I walk along the beach somewhat light of step. The gin and tonics have accentuated the euphoria of this nearly forty-year-old conquistador. I feel like a Cluniac monk about to turn into the sugar daddy of a succubus raised on the finest from the Avenida Campo Rico.

I fold up the piece of paper with the phone numbers and carefully hide it in my wallet, to lie there in the limbo between my Visa Citibank Preferred Gold Card and my *Auxilio Mutuo* membership card.

Linda Ortiz: 260-5243 (mami); 351-4512/462-7346 (Sylvette)—Fridays.

Thank you. Call again.

TRANSLATED BY MARK SCHAFER

Subcomandante Marcos

Mexico
(b. 1954)

————•◦••◦•————

A guerrilla freedom fighter, Subcomandante Marcos stomped into the world's consciousness on 1 January 1994. In a military operation by the ill-equipped Ejército Zapatista de Liberación Nacional (EZLN) in various small towns in the southern Mexican state of Chiapas, he used television, radio, and especially the printed media to get his revolutionary message across. The indigenous people of Chiapas, he argued, had been betrayed by the tyrannical ruling party of Mexico, the Partido Revolucionario Institucional. The goal of EZLN was to overthrow the regime of President Carlos Salinas de Gortari and establish a more equitable ruling system. Sarcastic, irreverent, his face always covered by a dark ski mask, Subcomandante Marcos quickly became known in Mexico and abroad as a prolific writer of letters and communiqués to the press through the Internet, messages fresh in style, postmodern in nature. By mid-1995, the Mexican government, tired of negotiating with EZLN, built a campaign to defame Subcomandante Marcos: It announced that his true identity was that of Rafael Sebastián Guillén Vicente, an ex-academic from Mexico City's left-wing Universidad Autónoma Metropolitana in Xochimilco. But despite this smear campaign, his reputation as the region's Robin Hood has only grown with time. Most of his written electronic messages are included in *Shadow of Tender Fury* (1995), to which the following letter serves as a prologue. While Subcomandante Marcos is obviously a distinguished member of the tradition of Latin American *guerrilleros* (Enriquillo, Ernesto "Ché" Guevara, Edén Pastora, and Abimael Guzmán are some others), he holds the unique position of having used the written word as his sharpest, most explosive weapon. The Mexican political establishment was able to neutralize the EZLN rebels, but it could not dismantle Subcomandante Marcos's intellectually unsettling persona. He remains one of the most imaginative revolutionaries of this century and an essayist of the first order, and his writing exemplifies a true crossroads where Latin American politics and literature meet.

Letter of 30 June 1994

June 30, 1994

To all the large, medium–sized, small, marginal, pirate,
buccaneer, and etcetera presses who are publishing the

communiqués and letters of the EZLN and have written asking for a prologue for your respective publications, or have requested an exclusive of some kind or other.

From Subcomandante Insurgente Marcos
EZLN General Headquarters
Mountains of the Mexican Southeast
Chiapas, Mexico

I received your request for a kind of prologue or introduction to the book that is being published by _____ (note: fill the empty space with the name of the large, medium-sized, small, marginal, pirate, buccaneer, etcetera publishing house which has asked for this exclusive introduction) containing the communiqués, letters, and other materials of the EZLN.

As far as I can see, my reputation for being a scatterbrain is not sufficient to dissuade you from sending me questions and problems about publications, prologues, and other equally absurd things. So I am going to answer, ad hoc, your questions about such transcendent problems. And there is nothing better for this purpose than to tell you a little story that happened to us many moons ago.

It was 1986. I left our base camp with a column of combatants on a short exploratory march. All my boys were novices; the majority of them had been with us for less than a month and they were still arguing about what was the worst part of trying to adapt: the diarrhea or the nostalgia. The two "veterans" in the group had been with us for two and three months, respectively. So there I was, sometimes dragging them, sometimes pushing them, through their political and military training. Our mission was to open a new route for our military maneuvers and to train the recruits in the tasks of exploration, marching, and setting up camp. The work was hard because there was not enough water and we had to ration what we had taken with us from the base camp. So survival practice was added to the training, as the lack of water made cooking difficult. The maneuvers were to last four days, with approximately one liter of water per person, per day, and only *pinole* with sugar to eat. An hour after we left the base we found that our route took us through some steep, difficult hills. The hours passed and we ascended and descended hills on paths that would frighten the most experienced mountain goats.

Finally, after seven or eight hours of non-stop up and down, we arrived at the top of a hill where I decided to set up camp, as the afternoon was beginning to give way to twilight shadows. The water ration was distributed, and most of the recruits, despite my warnings to save a little liquid for the *pinole*, "burned their ships" and immediately chugged down their whole ration, as they were very thirsty, and the psychological effect of knowing the water was rationed only made their anxiety worse. When the time came to eat, they saw the consequence of their foolishness: no matter how much they chewed, they were unable to swallow—without water they were not able to get the *pinole* with sugar to go down their throats. There were two hours of such silence that we could clearly hear the crunching between their teeth, and the sounds from their throats when they finally managed to swallow a piece of the sugared corn dust. The next day, having learned their lesson, they all saved a part of their water ration for their morning *pinole*. That day we left on the maneuver at 09:00 hours and returned at 16:00, so it was seven hours of walking and cutting paths, going up and down hills, without any water except what we sweat.

We spent three days like that; on the fourth, the weakness of the whole group was evident. During the meals (?), the sado-masochism that seems to characterize insurgents appeared: between bites of *pinole* and little sips of water, we began to talk about taquitos, tamales, cakes, steaks, soft drinks, and other things that could only make us laugh because our bodies didn't have enough water to cry. To top it off, the day we were going to return to our base, we found a nearby river, and that night the mountain mischievously honored us with a strong downpour which soaked us before we managed to get under cover. We did not lose our good humor and we swore endlessly at the roof, the rain, and the jungle, and all their respective kin. But really this was all part of the training and was not surprising. The work was completed, in general the people responded well, although one person nearly fainted carrying his load up a particularly difficult hill.

All of this is nothing but the "scenery" for the story I want to tell you. On one of these days of exploration, we returned to the camp, as always, completely wiped out. While the rations of *pinole* and water were being distributed, I turned on the short-wave radio to catch the evening news, but out of the radio came only the strident song of parrots and macaws. I then remembered a work by Cortazar (*Ultimo Round? El Libro de Manuel? Cronopios and Famas?*) that talks about what would happen if "things-were-out-of-place." But I didn't let such a small incident bother me, as I was accustomed to seeing in these mountains things as apparently absurd as a little deer with a red carnation in its mouth (probably in love, because if not, why a *red* carnation?), a tapir with violet ballet shoes, a herd of wild boar playing cards and, with their teeth and hooves, tapping out the rhythm of "we will break down the house to see Doña Blanca. . . ." As I say, I wasn't much surprised and I moved the dial looking for another station, but there wasn't anything but the songs of the parrots and macaws. I changed to the medium-wave mode, with the same results. Without losing hope, I took the apparatus apart to find the scientific reason for this toneless song.

When I opened the back of the radio, I found the logical and dialectical cause of this irregular transmission: a bunch of parrots and macaws flew out, screaming with joy at regaining their freedom. I managed to count 17 parrots, 8 female macaws and 3 males, as they all scrambled out. After a rather tardy self-criticism for not having cleaned the apparatus, I prepared to give it the maintenance it required. As I was taking out the feathers and droppings (and even the skeleton of a little parrot that the others had taken care to give a Christian burial, and above whose tomb shined a carefully made cross and a stone with the inscription in Latin? *Requiescat in Pace*), I found a little nest with a little gray egg, speckled with green and blue, and beside it was a little envelope, that—with barely concealed eagerness—I quickly opened. It was a letter, addressed "To whom it may concern." In a tiny script, the little parrot had written her sad and melancholy story.

She had fallen in love with a young and elegant macaw (so said the letter) and he loved her back (so said the letter). But the other parrots, concerned about the purity of their race, did not approve of such a scandalous romance and absolutely prohibited the parrot from seeing the handsome young macaw (so said the letter). And so the great love that united the couple (so said the letter) obliged them to see each other clandestinely, behind one of the transistors of the radio. As "a macaw is fire, and a parrot dry wood, along came the Devil and told them they should" (so said the letter) and soon one thing led to another and this little egg that I now had in my hands was the forbidden fruit of their illicit relation. The parrot requested (so said the letter) that whoever should find the egg should protect it and support it until the little one would be able to take care of itself (so said the letter), and finally there was a list of maternal recommendations for care, and a tearful lament for her cruel fate, etcetera (so said the letter).

Overwhelmed by the enormous responsibility of becoming an adopted father and cursing the impulse that led me to clean the radio, I tried to find moral and material support from one of my combatants, but all of them were already asleep, probably dreaming of mountain springs of coffee with milk and rivers of coca-cola and lemonade. Following the often cited maxim that "There is no problem so big that you can't walk away from it," I abandoned the egg, putting it by the side of my hammock, and got myself ready to enjoy a well-deserved rest. It was useless; my guilt feelings (deep down, very deep down, I actually have a good and noble soul) would not let me sleep and soon I picked up the little egg and found a comfortable spot for it on my belly. At midnight, a very unfortunate hour, it began to move. At first I thought it was my stomach protesting the lack of food, but no, it was the little egg that was moving and beginning to break. With an inexplicable maternal instinct I made myself ready to witness the sacred moment when I would become a mother . . . I mean . . . a father. And how great my surprise to see come out of the shell neither a macaw nor a parrot, not even a baby chicken or a little dove. No, what came out of the shell was . . . a little tapir! Seriously, it was a little tapir with green and blue feathers. A plumed tapir! In a moment of clarity (which now come to me less and less often) I understood the true meaning of this sordid little story: the crux-of-the-matter-as-I-don't-know-who-said. "Eureka!" I screamed, exactly-as-had-screamed-I-can't-remember-who-either.

What had happened was the parrot was "double dealing," that is, she had a liaison with a tapir, they sinned, and she was trying to frame the macaw. But everything had now fallen apart, given the radio problems and all the other etceteras. "They are all the same," I sighed. Having figured out the mystery, the only thing left was to decide what the hell I was going to do with the bastard tapir. . . . And I am still trying to decide. For the time being I carry her hidden in my knapsack and give her a little of my food. I don't deny that we like each other, and my maternal instinct (excuse me, paternal) has given way to an insane passion toward the tapir, who throws me ardent glances which don't have very much to do with polite gratefulness but rather with a badly controlled passion. My problem is severe: if I fall into temptation, I will not only commit a crime against nature, but also incest, because, after all, I am her adopted father. I have thought about abandoning her, but I can't, she is more powerful than I. In short, I don't know what the hell to do . . .

As you can see, I have too many problems here to be able to attend to yours. I hope that now you will understand my continued silence in regard to the questions that you insist on putting before me. Of course, the CCRI-CG of the EZLN approves your request, and gives you permission to publish the materials and to write some kind of prologue or introduction. You're welcome.

Vale, and as-you-can-find-out-who-said, "Books are friends that will never betray you." *Salud*, and please send me a veterinary manual for wild animals of the tropics.

From the mountains of the Mexican Southeast
Subcomandante Insurgente Marcos
Mexico, June 1994

A FORGETFUL P.S.: Yes, I seem to have forgotten the purpose of all this: an introduction or prologue to the book of communiqués called: "From the First to the Second Declaration of the Lacandon Jungle" or I don't know what you are going to call the damned book from _____ Press. (Note once again: Fill the space with all the appropriate names, publishing houses, etcetera, etc.)

And so it happens, I imagine, that something ought to be said to the readers of this book. Taking advantage of the fact that there is a respite between airplanes, tapirs, and communiqués, I write this letter disguised as a postscript:

To the readers of this book who are going to know what it is called
　From Supmarcos
　June 1994

This book contains the communiqués of the EZLN from the First Declaration of the Lacandon Jungle to the Second Declaration of the Lacandon Jungle, that is, from December 31, 1993, to June 10, 1994. It also brings together a series of letters that present and then reiterate some of the principal political and ideological positions of the Zapatista Army of National Liberation.

It is worthwhile to speak a little about the procedure used to produce the communiqués of the Revolutionary Indigenous Clandestine Committee-General Command of the EZLN. All the communiqués signed by the CCRI-CG of the EZLN were approved by the members of the committee, sometimes by all the members, sometimes by their representatives. The writing of the texts was one of my jobs, but the communiqués themselves are produced in two different ways:

One is that the members of the committee, or a collective of the committee, see the need to make a pronouncement about something, that is, "to say their word." First, the principal points of what is going to be said are proposed and debated, and then they order me to write it up, using the debate as my general orientation for what to say. Later I present the written communiqué, they revise it, take out some things, add some others, and, finally, approve it or reject it.

The other method is that, on the arrival of information from far off parts or confronted by a fact that I think merits it, and seeing the value of commenting on it, I propose to the committee that we send out a communiqué. I then write it and present it as a proposal. It is discussed and approved or rejected.

Did I say "rejected"? Yes, even though the current circumstances contribute to the appearance that Subcomandante I. Marcos is the "head" or "leader" of the rebellion, and that the CCRI is just the "scenery," the authority of the committee in the communities is indisputable. It is impossible to sustain a position there without the support of the leadership of this indigenous organization. I have made various proposals for communiqués that were rejected, some for being "too hard," others for being "too soft," and some others because "they confuse things, rather than clarifying them." Also, some communiqués were sent out despite my objections. It is not worth citing examples, but the correctness of the judgment of my compañeros on the committee has been demonstrated throughout these six months of war.

There are also texts that I often write to introduce the communiqués. I am more "loose" in these, but the committee keeps a close eye on them too. More than one of my "Letters of Introduction" has merited a reproof from members of the CCRI-CG.

It took a long time for the communiqués to arrive, and they arrived irregularly. The "untimely" nature of our pronouncements is something we have tried to remedy, with no success whatsoever. The speed with which some of the communiqués reached the press was due to lucky circumstances that, unhappily, were never a result of anything we planned.

Nevertheless, I believe that the lack of "speed" of the Zapatista answers are understandable to most of the readers who now are face to face with this book. What you probably cannot understand is the complex and anonymous heroism of the couriers who carried, from our lines to the cities, these white pages with black letters that spoke our thought. There are various anecdotes about these anonymous Zapatistas who risked all to cross enemy lines time and again, wearing out their mounts, with their feet destroyed by the cold and the rain in January and February, and by heat and thorns in the later months. These routes of misery and oblivion, the ancient tracks and steep trails, carried, from the mountains to the asphalt, the Zapatista words of dignity and rebellion. As of now these messengers have not faced cameras or tape recorders, have not received letters or been interviewed, there have been no testimonies as to the *"sex appeal"* of their anonymity, no recognition for their efforts to make *our word, their word,* reach other ears. This is a good place to recognize them for their silent—and effective—work.

I spoke in a letter that appears in this book about the reasons we delivered our word to some particular media for publication in their pages or for broadcast on their radio stations. I will not push it too hard, but a word should be said about the part these media played. The honest press made ways for Zapatista thought to appear in the pages of newspapers and magazines, and in some radio broadcasts. I believe that whatever the outcome of our collective desire for dignity, the honest press will feel, always, the satisfaction of having fulfilled their duty.

There is something else about this passionate moving of words, something that does not appear in any postscript or any communiqué. It is the anxiety, the uncertainty, the galloping questions that assault us every time one of the couriers leaves with one, or several, communiqués. Questions and more questions fill up our nights, accompany us on our rounds to check the guards, sit beside us on some broken tree trunk looking at the food on the plate, are carried in the hand that divides up the provisions, and move in the feet that walk back and forth. "Were these words the best ones to say what we wanted to say?" "Were they the right words at this time?" "Were they understandable?" We were never satisfied with any communiqué at the time it was sent.

In general, we make an effort to differentiate between the communiqués of the CCRI-CG and the introductory letters. While the first were written in capital letters and signed by the committee, the second are in capital and small letters, and signed by "Subcomandante Insurgente Marcos." We believe that both types did the job they needed to do. What their future will be in this book form is uncertain, but the word of those who speak the truth will always find its way.

There is something more to say about the Zapatista "editorial line." We follow the motto: "Now or maybe never." Given the conditions of war and isolation in which we find ourselves, we don't "measure" what we say and we try to throw it all out at once . . . because every communiqué could be the last one.

That is why from the first communiqués on, the position and ideas of the EZLN have been defined, and repeated, continually. This anxious word forever stumbling all over itself comes out of a situation which can only be understood by those who find themselves now, or have been, in the same circumstances.

On the one hand, we cannot give ourselves the luxury of lying. One becomes spontaneous when living on the thin edge of war, and we have discovered that lying requires at least a little bit of planning. On the other hand, we have not been able to "measure out" our word, and look for the "opportune moment" to say it, nor wait cunningly for conditions to be just right. The clearest examples of this Zapatista "editorial line" are the letters of the January 18, 1994 ("Who must ask for pardon and who can grant it," number 13) and January 20, 1994 ("The sup will take off his mask, if Mexico takes off its mask," number 14). The one of January 20 (the one which presents the result of the trial of Absalón Castellanos Domínguez) seen from a distance, and after everything that has happened, could appear exaggerated—and that is the way it seems to me now. But at that moment, face to face with the typewriter, anxiety moved my fingers, and it seemed to me that there was no other way to say what I had to say. This is not a question of pessimism or optimism, it is something more . . . more . . . more immediate, a spontaneous and unadorned judgment of the dramas that were happening to us, and those that might happen.

I am sorry if I am disillusioning someone with this "horrible" secret, but we never planned beforehand what we were going to say, nor the form in which we were going to say it. We had, and we have, a clear understanding of who we are and who we are not, what we can do and what we cannot, and what we ought to do and what we ought not. From this general standard, or from this foundation, the letters and communiqués were sent out, in the same way we walked in the mountains: one worries about the step one is taking, and does not plan the next step; it is enough to know that you are still walking, and later . . . later . . . there might never be a later.

There is also in these letters and communiqués the constant presence of death. I know that this has bothered more than one reader, but on this side of the war, in the same way that one says "book," "weapon," or "love," one says "death," and so it must be written. I remember as I was writing one letter, I told myself to stop insisting on this theme, but I remind you of what I explained above about the "Zapatista editorial line." Later, when I reread that letter in the newspaper, it turned out to be one of the most gloomy I had written. In short, since we don't write to please, but rather to explain, one is able to put aside these worries about writing what one believes respectable people would want one to write.

Vale. Health and a good appetite, reading is nourishment which, fortunately, never fills one up.

I don't know if all that I have pointed out here will help or hurt the rereading of the materials that are compiled in this book. I tried, as much as possible, to write a communiqué about the communiqués, a letter about the letters. I see, with pleasure, that once again the Zapatista "editorial line" has imposed itself on me, and that what I have written about these letters is only what has occurred to me right now. Therefore, on the improbable chance that another introduction will be needed later, and that bad luck marks me out to do it again, I will put the date, hour, and place on this prologue, so that the readers will know that I finished writing this one before dawn on the morning of June 28, 1994, that the watch on my left wrist read 02:30 hours, it was raining hard, and that a good while ago Tacho told me he was going to sleep. The place, for a change, is

From the mountains of the Mexican Southeast
Subcomandante Insurgente Marcos
Mexico, June 1994

P.S. about the P.S.'s: Of course a little digression about the postscripts should go in a postscript. It happens that one feels that something has remained between the fingers, that there are still some words that want to find their way into sentences, that one has not finished emptying the pockets of the soul. But it is useless, there will never be a postscript that can contain so many nightmares . . . and so many dreams . . .

TRANSLATED BY FRANK BARDACKE

Rigoberta Menchú

Guatemala
(b. 1958)

A Guatemalan peasant woman, Rigoberta Menchú entered public life after her family was killed by the Guatemalan army. She learned Spanish and became an activist, publicizing her plight, a plight typical of the terrible injustices suffered by the indigenous peoples of much of Latin America. *I, Rigoberta Menchú* (1983) is the vivid, moving account of her life and times, edited and introduced by the Latin American anthropologist Elisabeth Burgos-Debray, and the following passage chronicling her origins is illustrative of her style. The original Spanish title is somewhat longer and more ideologically charged: *Me llamo Rigoberta Menchú y así me nació la conciencia*—My Name Is Rigoberta Menchú, and Thus My Political Conscience was Born. Menchú was awarded the Nobel Peace Prize in 1992. While she often relies on help in her writing, her control of written Spanish and the structure of her exposition are outstanding. Of particular significance is her appropriation of the language of the conquerors to denounce their repression of the Indian population in southern Mexico and Central America. She is considered the most illustrious member of a solid tradition of aboriginal writers south of the Rio Grande (others are the Bolivian Domitila Barrios and the Mexicans Juan Pérez Jolote and Renata López), who use both the oral and the written word as invaluable political weapons. The following segment is the first chapter of *I, Rigoberta Menchú*. In reading one should keep in mind that Menchú was first interviewed by Burgos-Debray and that transcription and various rewritings took place before her story reached printed form. That is, while Menchú's fresh oral voice is still present, it has been adulterated and modified by a Westernized social scientist acting as translator.

I, Rigoberta Menchú

We have always lived here: we have the right to go on living where we are happy and where we want to die. Only here can we feel whole; nowhere else would we ever feel complete and our pain would be eternal.
—Popol Vuh

My name is Rigoberta Menchú. I am twenty-three years old. This is my testimony. I didn't learn it from a book and I didn't learn it alone.

I'd like to stress that it's not only *my* life, it's also the testimony of my people. It's hard for me to remember everything that's happened to me in my life since there have been many very bad times but, yes, moments of joy as well. The important thing is that what has happened to me has happened to many other people too: My story is the story of all poor Guatemalans. My personal experience is the reality of a whole people.

I must say before I start that I never went to school, and so I find speaking Spanish very difficult. I didn't have the chance to move outside my own world and only learned Spanish three years ago. It's difficult when you learn just by listening, without any books. And, well, yes, I find it a bit difficult. I'd like to start from when I was a little girl, or go back even further to when I was in my mother's womb, because my mother told me how I was born and our customs say that a child begins life on the first day of his mother's pregnancy.

There are twenty-two indigenous ethnic groups in Guatemala, twenty-three including the *mestizos*, or *ladinos*, as we call them. Twenty-three groups and twenty-three languages. I belong to one of them—the Quiché people—and I practise Quiché customs, but I also know most of the other groups very well through my work organising the people. I come from San Miguel Uspantán, in the northwest province of El Quiché. I live near Chajul in the north of El Quiché. The towns there all have long histories of struggle. I have to walk six leagues, or 24 kilometres, from my house to the town of Uspantán. The village is called Chimel, I was born there. Where I live is practically a paradise, the country is so beautiful. There are no big roads, and no cars. Only people can reach it. Everything is taken down the mountainside on horseback or else we carry it ourselves. So, you can see, I live right up in the mountains.

My parents moved there in 1960 and began cultivating the land. No one had lived up there before because it's so mountainous. But they settled there and were determined not to leave no matter how hard the life was. They'd first been up there collecting the *mimbre* that's found in those parts, and had liked it. They'd started clearing the land for a house, and had wanted to settle there a year later but they didn't have the means. Then they were thrown out of the small house they had in the town and had no alternative but to go up into the mountains. And they stayed there. Now it's a village with five or six *caballerías* of cultivated land.

They'd been forced to leave the town because some *ladino* families came to settle there. They weren't exactly evicted but the *ladinos* just gradually took over. My parents spent everything they earned and they incurred so many debts with these people that they had to leave the house to pay them. The rich are always like that. When people owe them money they take a bit of land or some of their belongings and slowly end up with everything. That's what happened to my parents.

My father was an orphan, and had a very hard life as a child. He was born in Santa Rosa Chucuyub, a village in El Quiché. His father died when he was a small boy, leaving the family with a small patch of maize. But when that was finished, my grandmother took her three sons to Uspantán. She got work as a servant to the town's only rich people. Her boys did jobs around the house like carrying wood and water and tending animals. But as they got bigger, her employer said she didn't work enough for him to go on feeding such big boys. She had to give away her eldest son, my father, to another man so he wouldn't go hungry. By then he could do heavy work like chopping wood or working in the fields but he wasn't paid anything because he'd been given away. He lived with these *ladinos* for nine years but learned no Spanish because he wasn't allowed in the house. He was just there to run errands and work, and was kept totally apart from the family. They found him repulsive because he had no clothes and was very dirty. When my father was fourteen he started looking around for some way out. His brothers were also growing up but they weren't earning anything either. My grandmother earned barely enough to feed them. So my father went off to find work on the *fincas* near the coast. He was already a man and started earning enough money to send to my grandmother and he got her away from that family as soon as he could. She'd sort of become her employer's mistress although he had a wife. She had to agree because she'd nowhere else to go. She did it out of necessity and anyway there were plenty more waiting to take her place. She left to join her eldest son in the coastal estates and the other boys started working there as well.

We grew up on those *fincas* too. They are on the south coast, part of Escuintla, Suchitepequez, Retalhuleu, Santa Rose, Jutiapa, where coffee, cotton, cardamom and sugar are grown. Cutting cane was usually men's work and the pay was a little higher. But at certain times of the year, both men and women were needed to cut cane. At the beginning things were very hard. They had only wild plants to eat, there wasn't even any maize. But gradually, by working very hard, they managed to get themselves a place up in the *Altiplano*. Nobody had worked the land there before. My father was eighteen by this time and was my grandmother's right arm. He had to work day and night to provide for my grandmother and his brothers. Unfortunately that was just when they were rounding young men up for military service and they took my father off, leaving my grandmother on her own again with her two sons. My father learnt a lot of bad things in the army, but he also learnt to be a man. He said they treated you like an object and taught you everything by brute force. But he did learn how to fight. He was in the army for a long hard year and when he got back home he found my grandmother was dying. She had a fever. This is very common among people who come from the coast where it's very hot straight to the *Altiplano* where it's very cold. The change is too abrupt for them. There was no money to buy medicine or to care for my grandmother and she died. My father and his brothers were left without parents or any other relatives to help them. My father told me that they had a little house made of straw, very humble, but with their mother dead, there was no point in staying there. So they split up and got work in different parts of the coast. My father found work in a monastery but he hardly earned anything there either. In those days a worker earned thirty to forty *centavos* a day, both in the *fincas* and elsewhere.

That's when my father met my mother and they got married. They went through very difficult times together. They met in the *Altiplano* since my mother was from a very poor family too. Her parents were very poor and used to travel around looking for work. They were hardly ever at home in the *Altiplano*.

That's how they came to settle up in the mountains. There was no town there. There was no-one. They founded a village up there. My village has a long history—a long and painful history. The land up there belonged to the government and you had to get permission to settle there. When you'd got permission, you had to pay a fee so that you could clear the land and then build your house. Through all my parents' efforts in the *fincas*, they managed to get enough money together to pay the fee, and they cleared the land. Of course, it's not very easy to make things grow on land that's just been cleared. You don't get a good yield for at least eight or nine years. So my parents cultivated the land and eight years later, it started to produce. We were growing up during this period. I had five older brothers and sisters. I saw my two eldest brothers die from lack of food when we were down in the *fincas*. Most Indian families suffer from malnutrition. Most of them don't even reach fifteen years old. When children are growing and don't get enough to eat, they're often ill, and this . . . well . . . it complicates the situation.

So my parents stayed there. My mother found the trees and our amazing mountains so beautiful. She said that they'd get lost sometimes because the mountains were so high and not a single ray of light fell through the plants. It's very dense. Well, that's where we grew up. We loved our land very, very much, even if we did have to walk for a long time to get to our nearest neighbour. But, little by little, my parents got more and more people to come up and cultivate the land so there would be more of us to ward off the animals that came down from the mountains to eat our maize when it was ripe, or, when the ears were still green. These animals would come and eat everything. My father said that one of them was what they call a racoon. Soon my mother started keeping hens and a few sheep because there was plenty of room but she didn't have the time to look after them properly so they'd wander off to find other food and not come back. The mountain animals ate some of them, or they just got lost. So they lived there, but unfortunately, it was many years before our land really produced anything and my parents still had to go down and work in the *fincas*. They told us what it was like when they first settled there, but when we children were growing up and could spend four or five months of the year there, we were very happy. There were big rivers rushing down the mountainside below our house. We didn't actually have much time for playing, but even working was fun—clearing the undergrowth while my father cut down trees. Well, you could hear so many different types of birds singing and there were lots of snakes to frighten us as well. We were happy even though it was very cold because of the mountains. And it's a damp sort of cold.

I was born there. My mother already had five children, I think. Yes, I had five brothers and sisters and I'm the sixth. My mother said that she was working down on a *finca* until a month before I was born. She had just twenty days to go when she went up to the mountains, and she gave birth to me all on her own. My father wasn't there because he had to work the month out on the *finca*.

Most of what I remember is after I was five. We spent four months in our little house in the *Altiplano* and the rest of the year we had to go down to the coast, either in the *Boca Costa* where there's coffee picking and also weeding out the coffee plants, or further down the South coast where there's cotton. That was the work we did mostly, and I went from when I was very little. A very few families owned the vast areas of land which produce these crops for sale abroad. These landowners are the lords of vast extensions of land, then. So we'd work in the *fincas* for eight months and in January we'd go back up to the *Altiplano* to sow our crops. Where we live in the mountains, that is, where the land isn't fertile, you can barely grow maize and beans. The land isn't fertile enough for anything else. But on the coast the land is rich and you can grow anything. After we'd sown our crops, we'd go down to the coast again until it was time to harvest them, and then we'd make the journey back again. But the maize would soon run out, and we'd be back down again to earn some money. From what my parents said, they lived this harsh life for many years and they were always poor.

TRANSLATED BY ANN WRIGHT

Ilan Stavans

Mexico
(b. 1961)

————•••••————

Born in Mexico to a Jewish family of Eastern European descent, Ilan Stavans immigrated to New York City at the age of twenty-five, studied at the Jewish Theological Seminary and at Columbia University, and joined the faculty of Amherst College in 1993. His first literary language was Yiddish, but most of his oeuvre is written in either Spanish or English. His essayistic work deals with translingualism, the clash between highbrow and popular culture, as well as issues of religious identity. Stavans's essays can be found in *La pluma y la máscara* (1993), *Bandido* (1995), *The Hispanic Condition* (1995), and *Art and Anger: Essays on Politics and the Imagination* (1996). He is also the author of two novellas and several short stories, published in *Talia y el cielo* (1989) and *La pianista manca* (1992); many of these have been published in English in *The One-Handed Pianist and Other Stories* (1996), which was awarded the Latino Literature Prize and the Gamma Prize. "The Verbal Quest" is included in *Art and Anger*. First published in the journal *Metamorphoses* in December 1994, it deals with the Tower of Babel and the challenges of polyglotism and translation in the modern world.

The Verbal Quest

> *"We will build our Temple here,"* said they, *simultaneously, and with an indescribable conviction that they had at last found the very spot.*
> —*Nathaniel Hawthorne,* Twice-Told Tales

For quite some time I have been interested in the link between language and religion—more specifically, in the search of a primal tongue that precedes all others, one whose virtue is not lessened by time. Can such a proto-language be at once divine and secular? Can its meaning and interpretation be standardized? My interest is also targeted toward translation: Would such a proto-language symbolize, once and for all, the abolition of the act of translation? Such miscellaneous questions rumbled in my mind not long ago, as I was reading two thought-provoking essays, one by the Mexican poet and essayist Octavio Paz: "Edith Piaf among the Pygmies"; the other: "The Ephemerality of Translation" by Ray Harris, an Oxford professor. While both share a common theme—the reaches and limitations of translation—their asymmetrical relationship is fascinating. Paz argues that the job of translating a text from one language to another is simply impossible. He offers as an example a television documentary he once saw about several Pygmies who heard Edith Piaf's voice magically reproduced by a phonograph an ethnologist had turned on for them to hear. Whereas the ethnologists could identify with the song by the French pop singer, a song about jealousy and violent love, the Pygmies immediately became quite frightened: they covered their ears and ran away. They fled because they were unable to recognize such passionate groans. What seemed to be an aesthetic experience for the scientists was horrifying to the Pygmies. Inspired by Claude Lévi-Strauss's book *Tristes Tropiques*, Paz explains that, had the ethnologists tried to translate the song, surely the Pygmies would have felt even more repulsed. The Petrarchian concepts of courtly and passionate love in Piaf's lyrics were totally alien to them: unrecognizable, unapproachable. One could argue, of course, that the Pygmies indeed understood Piaf's message; otherwise they would have made it clear, through a subtle gesture of annoyance, that they disapproved of her groans. Precisely because both the content of the lyrics and the musical form in which these were expressed were so aggressive, so passionate, there was a misunderstanding, a loss in the act of translation. They probably could not picture a woman screaming vehemently without knowledge of the context from which such suffering was born. Perhaps they could not understand why the fragile threads that make a relationship between a Western man and a woman become the source of such misery. In short, they simply could not understand. Paz concludes that translating moral, aesthetic, scientific, or magical concepts from one language to another, from one culture to another, is a hopeless task; it requires that the recipient in the translation process stop being himself—which means that each translation, by its very nature, creates an insurmountable abyss between civilizations, one impossible to bridge.

At first sight, Paz's argument might seem too emphatic, a statement against translation, but it isn't. Without translations our world would be even more chaotic than it already is. Translations result from dialogue, communication, encounters between disparate entities. Although much can be, and in fact is, lost in translations, they ultimately emerge as an attempt to unite, a desire to reach out. In other words, the translation act, in spite of cultural abysses, cannot so easily be discharged: it is a necessity the modern world cannot afford to live without; it provides an essential taste our intellectual life has become accustomed to, the seasoning that keeps our cosmopolitan spirit afloat. And yet, translation is framed by time and space. Before beginning the task, each translator knows, consciously or otherwise, who his reader will be. If *The Iliad*, in its original language, can overcome the passing of numerous generations of readers and still be accessible, with translations we tend to have little patience: when a translation loses vitality, when it becomes obscure, impenetrable, we replace it with a new one; that is, whereas the original text is treated as invaluable and of primary importance, translations are disposable.

This is where Harris's thesis becomes relevant. More and more new translations of literary classics are required, he claims, because mass culture, in love with disposable products, is always in need of new commodities, always involved in prefabricating past goods. From 1947 to 1972, at least eleven translations into German of Wilde's *Portrait of Dorian Gray* were made; and between 1949 and 1969, at least eight translations of Flaubert's *Madame Bovary* were cast into English. To make a new translation is to recycle an already appealing product, to commercialize it once again in order to make it accessible to a new readership. Publishers and the academy have found a logic to justify such a multiplication of items on library shelves: modern translations are needed because the language of the original becomes outdated with the passing of time. History wears language down and erases formal structures. It invents new meanings for old words, it introduces neologisms, it reshapes syntax. Since our present civilization is in the process of eternal renovation, retranslating a text is a form of renewal, a strategy for rediscovering who we are, for once again posing old questions in search of meaningful answers. For obvious reasons, marketing plays a crucial role here: each translation entering the literary market promises to be even more "perfect," even more faithful to the original—even more accurate. But accuracy is a tricky word: an accurate depiction is one in which a reader fully believes the portrait a writer delivers; that is, his social model is reflected in the literary model. History is made up of a never-ending drive to reinterpret old models, to reevaluate ancient epochs. The fall of the Aztec city of Tenochtitlán, for instance, had been understood quite differently in the seventeenth, nineteenth, and late twentieth centuries: The fall of Tenochtitlán is constant but the implications of the disaster vary. The same applies to translation. As consumers, we get trapped in the uncontrollable torpedoing of new translations, texts that reproduce old texts, texts that revise well-known texts—which, at the end, do nothing but annihilate the utopian dream of ultimate perfection.

Of course, no translation can ever be perfect: as a human endeavor, each attempt is doomed to fail before it was ever begun; it will be useful to a generation of readers and then, when language changes, a new translation will become necessary and available. Like everything else around us, new translations add up to the never-ending flow of life-and-death cycles generated by nature. Volumes pile up, shelves are constantly expanded, and our poor, disorganized, incoherent, and illegible Western culture remains imperfect despite our strivings for coherence.

Clearly, Paz's and Harris's arguments are two facets of one ample, ir-resolvable matter: Do translations serve a purpose? Are we only falsifying the original message? I use the verb "to falsify" with some uncertainty and awe; translators, not without reason, thoroughly dislike it. After all, no one proud of his career would want to perceive his livelihood as the treason the famous adage urges: *traduttore, traditore*.* An act of betrayal involves dishonesty and deception; a falsification implies fakery, infidelity, and even misrepresentation. The dedicated translator spends hours, days, perhaps months and years finding *le mot juste*, the perfect equivalent for a simple word, only to be accused later on of betraying the original—no doubt in a display of ingratitude by readers who were expected to respond positively. But translations do carry in themselves a measure of distance from the original text and although, at times, a writer might confess that his text in a certain translation reads better than in the original, the natural flavor has magically disappeared. Hence, by the verb "to falsify" I mean to distance, to pervert, to switch words and meanings so as to make a specific message accessible to a foreign culture. I want to be cautious enough and not to inject the translation with negative powers, however. Although translations are falsifications, we desperately need them to communicate, to find each other across borders.

In translations one frequently gets the feeling that while the taste of the translated text is legitimate and even acceptable, it carries in itself a form of removal, a distancing from the source. Cervantes thought that reading a translation was the same as seeing a Turkish tapestry from behind: as a silhouette, a shadow, not the real object. Robert Frost used to say that poetry is what gets lost in translation. And Isaac Leibush Peretz, a Yiddish master from the turn of the century, author of *Into the Marketplace* and the memorable short story "The Kabbalists," felt that approaching a translation is like kissing a bride through the wedding veil: the physical contact is indeed experienced but only through a degree of separation. Paz begins his article in an interesting way. He tells us that the search for a common language, one that could transcend all languages, is a way to resolve the opposition between unity and multiplicity which does not cease to intrigue the human spirit: he posits one language of languages *vis-à-vis* a multiplicity of idioms and dialects, the one and the many. I suggest that that original tongue could be approached in at least a couple of ways: as silence, the absence of language, which, of course, is also a form of language; and as music, which, according to Plotinus, is the natural rhythm of the celestial spheres. Music, dance, and pictorial art are enviable forms of creativity

---

*I first wrote about translation in "Octavio Paz and the Kabbalists," published in 1985. That essay, a rough draft for this English version, appeared under a different title in my book *Prontuario* (Mexico: Joaquín Mortiz, 1992), pp. 19–24.

because they are never in need of translation: the original message can never be lost. But music, what Hegel considered the true language of the soul, has an even more nearly unique quality: its ceaseless, ephemeral, innate, abstract nature makes it universal. Anywhere, at any time, music seems to contain a religious ingredient: it links the earthly and the heavenly terrain, it elevates nature to a supernatural level. Spoken language, on the other hand, precludes an education: it depends on context, and thus, it carries an equivocal message. As a result, the longing for a universal language reflects a need as ancient as humankind: to eliminate error, to make words indefinite, unconfined, open to everybody. Latin, Sanskrit, Hebrew are tongues injected with sacred universality: in spite of their imperfect metabolism, they are the closest we can get to the musicality of the original proto-language. Music and silence are what human languages long for.

Another way to resolve the conflict between unity and multiplicity, Paz says, is through translations. Before the erection of the Tower of Babel, the Old Testament myth claims that all nations on earth spoke the same sacred tongue, a human version of God's proto-language. Everyone understood each other. Words were less equivocal and thus less poetic. Meanings were standardized. As humans we will always long for that primal language. We will look for it in the dark corners of our creativity. Shelley once wrote, for instance, that all the poems of the past, present, and future are episodes or fragments of a single infinite poem, written by all the poets on earth—a proto-poem in a proto-language. Borges thought that "every man should be capable of all ideas." And in "Poetry and Imagination," Ralph Waldo Emerson wrote:

> Poetry is the perpetual endeavor to express the spirit of the thing, to pass the brute body and search the life and reason which cause it to exist—to see that the object is always flowing away, whilst the spirit or necessity which causes it subsists. Its essential mark is that it betrays in every word instant activity of mind, shows in new uses of every fact and image, in preternatural quickness or perception of relations. All its words are poems.

And we are attached to poetry, with its plurality of meanings, because, as George Steiner has claimed, after Babel human communication became a casualty: it was lost—irrevocably lost in the chaos of translation.

The interpretation given by rabbinical Judaism to the causes and echoes of Babel can be easily summarized: The desire to unravel the enigmas of the universe and the desire to understand (e.g., explain) God's mysteries made the Almighty angry. He exploded by creating a majestic idiomatic rupture in the universe: the resulting fragmentation was His revenge against man's daring to understand the impossible. Consequently, today everyone speaks a different language and no one understands anything at the same time. Unity has given way to multiplicity and interpretation has become a sort of religion: to interpret is to understand and vice versa. Our human temples are built on multiplicity. We inhabit a world where meaning is relative, equivocal, malleable. Which means that we are always in search of a completely meaningful language but will never be able to find it. Interpretations are hence often for sale. After the oceanic confusion at Babel, man's presumptions have been in the open, and human communication has been ruled by our lack of understanding. Since early on, the search for a universal language, a *lingua franca*, a tongue meaningful to all, was a dream dreamt by prophets, necromancers, and apocryphal messiahs: the abolition of interpretation, the unificational meaning, a return to the source. Classical Latin of the Middle Ages, unlike its vulgar counterpart, upheld this inspiration. In the modern era, two attempts can be noted: Esperanto, invented by the Polish linguist Ludovic Zamenhof in 1887; and the so-called International Auxiliary Language Association, which originated in 1951. Paz did not quite develop the theme of universal language; instead, he chose to develop the concept of the art of translation. Nevertheless, the drive for a language of languages has always led us to a dead end: while we long for unity, we will always be surrounded by multiplicity—our religiosity, our most profound philosophical questions emerge from such a fracture of the many from the ultimate one. But his logic also leads Paz to discredit the phenomenon of translation: Edith Piaf will never be understood by the Pygmies, who will always run away from her groans.

When talking about language, meaning, and communication, what Paz leaves out, and what Harris does not attempt to address, is a third aspect, as important as a universal language and translation, polyglotism. In a sense, polyglotism, the plurality of fluency in languages in a single speaker, unity *in* multiplicity, is the only possible human triumph of a universal tongue: a speaker capable of many tongues—a multifaceted entity; or better, a speaker, the source of many speeches. Polyglotism, it goes without saying, also carries within itself a high dose of imperfection: it is self-centered and solipsistic; but it is an option that manages to eliminate needless obstacles in the search of an entirely meaningful act of communication—and as such it is a metaphor of God's stream of consciousness—in which speaker and listener are one.

At this juncture, I need to center on the nature of the Hebrew language and to bring to my readers' attention the linguistic plight underscored in the theory and practice of Kabbalah, a system of thought which I studied under Moshe Idel (a successor of Gershom Scholem) at the Jewish Theological Seminary in New York City. Among Jewish mystics in medieval and Renaissance times, and above all in the esoteric texts *Ra'ya Mehemmá* and *Ticuné Zohar*, written between 1295 and 1305 by a certain disciple of

THE VERBAL QUEST \ 501

Moisés de León, the principle author of *Sefer ha-Zohar*, we see the idea that the Law that Moses received at Mount Sinai had been thought out and even written in its entirety in advance by the Almighty; that is, that Moses served only as a confidant, a vehicle through whom God dictated the past, present, and future history. Nothing resulting is random; everything has been predetermined. We are only actors in a multicast epic saga that began on the first day of Genesis, in the first chapter of the Hebrew Bible, and will end when God's text reaches its final line. Divine language, the Kabbalah suggests, is different from human language (*lashon adoni* and *ashon beni adam*). They are as incompatible as oil and water. Yet in order to make himself understood, the Almighty had to translate Himself, to make His message comprehensive, accessible to earthly creatures, almost mundane. Thus, He communicated with the people of Israel in a human tongue: that is to say, in Hebrew—the sacred language, the universal tongue, the language of the synagogue and holy scriptures and the vehicle that unites heaven and earth—which does not imply that God spoke Hebrew to Himself. The Almighty is most likely beyond words. He chose Hebrew, *lashon bnei adam*, to find a channel of communication with His chosen people. Consequently, to speak biblical Hebrew is to elevate oneself to the linguistic code of heaven, to sanctify oneself. Understandably, Jewish literati in the diaspora who spend their lives creating in pagan languages—the cases of Kafka, Scholem, Walter Benjamin, Cynthia Ozick, to name a few—often crave a return to the origin, an ascendance to paradise, a desire to master the Hebrew language.

Translation, then, is a synonym of transformation, of alteration and movement. It is not an aftermath of the Babel confusion: it actually precedes the event. It is not simply a human act, it is also a divine activity. But translation does not preclude interpretation; on the contrary, it incorporates the original in its womb: to understand a text, one has to uncover its secret truths, those truths God carefully hides from us: the mysteries and enigmas of the universe. To translate the Bible into Yiddish or into English does not imply simplifying God's word: it implies an interpretation. It serves to disseminate the divine teachings in a partial manner. Whoever would like to learn the original significance should read the Hebrew. Was the communication between God and Israel in Hebrew mutually understood? Probably not. Probably something was lost in translation . . . with a bit of conceit, says the *Sefer ha-Zohar* as well as Maimonides in his mysterious *Guide for the Perplexed*. The meaning behind God's words and actions is, and will always be, hidden, unclear, mysterious. The fabric of the Divine Mind, the secrets of nature, cannot be completely understood by humans—but it can be interpreted. Interpretation is a way to clarify, to adapt, to make accessible to human ears. It is also often the case that Hebrew is spoken only by a handful of sages. During the Diaspora, the 2,000-

year exile, Israel has come into contact with numerous nations and the need to learn new languages also has become an imperative: Russian, German, Ladino, Polish, Yiddish, Arabic, Czech, French, Latin, Greek, Italian, Spanish, English, Portuguese are secular, pagan tongues used to establish earthly communication. But through these languages the rabbis also want to explain the hidden meanings in the Bible. To speak many languages is to exist in different dimensions, to search in vain for the sole evasive meaning: it helps reduce the degree of misunderstanding although it does not solve the confusion that reigns in human affairs. Like translation, polyglotism is a desire to penetrate what is not ours; but it is a more authentic, less confusing attempt: after all, there is no third player in the game; the bridge, the intermediary between reader and author is the translator. In a multilingual existence, the translator and the receiver can be one and the same. Multilingualism, thus, is the journey to penetrate different cultures without accessories and without the necessity for change. What is written in Hebrew—the Bible above all—is original; everything else is vulgar reproduction. And yet, to attempt a translation, to make a life of interpreting texts, which is what rabbinical existence longs for, is an act worthy of the heavens.

While translation and interpretation are two very different activities, they are also part of the same linguistic process: to translate is to interpret; and simultaneously, to interpret is to translate. It is true that a diaphanous and integral translation of meanings between cultures is utterly impossible. It is an impossible feat stemming from our fallible and awkward human condition. To create a universal language, a tongue meaningful to all, is also impossible because it could imply the inversion of the Tower of Babel, a return from multiplicity back to unity, and such a fanciful return to the origin can happen only in mythology, not in the real world. The third solution is a polyglot existence necessary in our civilization: it is obviously the more difficult to accomplish simply because it requires an infinite amount of human energy. But it is the solution that transgresses the original meaning the least. Perhaps it is a solitary device, but the search for a perfectly meaningful language can be accomplished only when the one is inhabited by the many: when God and man are one.

Of course multilingualism has an extraordinary capacity to live in many words at once. Besides, scientists have shown that a polyglotic child must activate more brain cells and ultimately acquires a higher I.Q. than children exposed to a single tongue. Knowledge of many languages also allows one to understand the nuances that distinguish one culture from another. As for translation, I spend a good many hours of my day reading literature removed from its original source. I do so mechanically, to the point where I, like millions of other readers, forget it is a translation I am reading. That, precisely, is the nature of technological communication in our mass culture:

a reality where every encounter seems to contain a degree of separation. Encounters today come through sophisticated artifacts—phone, TV, radio, computers; direct human contact is becoming a casualty of modernity. Translations can thus be perceived as metaphors for our reluctant accessibility to dialogue: our original voice is often replaced by a secondary source. As for interpretation, we are children of Einstein's relativity and pupils of Rashomon, thriving in finding multiple perspectives, multiple truths. Such multiplicity pushes us to a bizarre form of idolatry: Truth, the Truth spelled with a capital *T*, becomes fragmented, departmentalized, broken into numerous pieces. Interpretation gives way to deception. But again, we cannot do without it: I interpret, thus I exist.

To return to my main interest, the bridge where language and religion intertwine, the more I reflect on the subject, the more I am persuaded to believe in a neo-Platonic structure linking the two: first comes the original language, a proto-language—be it silence or music—through which the Almighty communicates with Himself and, at the same time, narrates the history of the universe; second comes a sacred though imperfect tongue— Hebrew for the Jews—a bridge between heaven and earth; and third comes the plurality of languages we use daily to communicate with one another. Hence, the search for an original language can be understood as an impossible journey, an emanation process that craves a return to the Origin of origins through stops in many linguistic spheres. A proto-language, it seems to me, is a corpus in which every word is simultaneously reduced to one meaning and still keeps a dose of poetry; a vehicle of communication in which words contain within themselves the ancestral memory of everything that once was and will ever be;* a tongue in all places at once; a set of infinite words impossible to misunderstand—a linguistic temple that reverses, once and for all, the idiomatic fracture that came after the destruction of the Tower of Babel. It is an abstraction made of smoke rings, of course. The closer we want to get to it, the more we burn the energy that enables us to travel in search of the original tongue. We waste it without any revenue. Some would, of course, suggest that the pilgrimage in search of the primal tongue can also be approached as an end in itself; that the object of the search is always in the searcher. But this opinion leads us nowhere, for nothing can replace the original proto-language: like paradise, its true worth is beyond human reach. We therefore must find satisfaction in dissatisfaction, happiness in multiplicity. As Borges wrote in "The Analytical Language of John Wilkins": "The impossibility of penetrating the divine scheme of the universe cannot dissuade us from outlining human schemes, even though we are aware that they are provisional." Unity, as

---

*I have written about language and memory in my introduction to *Cuentistas judíos* (Mexico: Editorial Porrúa, 1994), pp. iii–xvi.

a result, is but a dream: we shall always aspire to reach it but will inevitably fail to attain it. The human language thrives in alternatives to the unifying dream in translation, in polyglotism, even in Esperanto; but these are all self-consuming forms of confusion. I am reminded of Stéphane Mallarmé's poem equating the soul to a cigar:

> Toute l'âme résumé
> Quand lente nous l'expirons
> Dans plusieurs ronds de fumée
> Abolis en autres ronds
>
> Atteste quelque cigare
> Brulant savamment pour peu
> Que le cendre se sépare
> De son clair blaiser de feu . . .

Acknowledgments

———◆—◆—

Alegría, Claribel: "The Writer's Commitment" by Claribel Alegría, translated by D. J. Flakoll, from *Lives on the Line*, edited by Doris Meyer (University of California Press, 1988). Reprinted by permission of the author.

Allende, Isabel: "The Spirits Were Willing" by Isabel Allende, translated by Jo Anne Engelbert, from *Lives on the Line*, edited by Doris Meyer (University of California Press, 1988). Copyright ©1984, 1988 by Isabel Allende. Reprinted by permission of Agencia Literaria Carmen Balcells, S.A.

Amado, Jorge: "Notes for Memoirs I'll Never Write" by Jorge Amado, translated by Alfred MacAdam, first appeared in *Review* 47 (Fall 1993), 32–38, as "Sailing the Shore: Notes for Memoirs I'll Never Write." Copyright © 1993 by the Americas Society, Inc. Copyright © 1992 by Jorge Amado. Reprinted by permission of the editors of *Review* and Agencia Literaria Carmen Balcells, S.A.

Anderson Imbert, Enrique: "In Defense of the Essay" by Enrique Anderson Imbert, translated for this anthology by Ilan Stavans, was published in Spanish as "Defense del ensayo" in *Los domingos del profesor* (Ediciones Gure, 1972). Translated by permission of the author.

Andrade, Mário de: "Of Hypocrisy" by Mário de Andrade, translated for this anthology by José Matosantos, was published in Spanish as "De la hipocresía" in *Obra escogida*, 1979. Translated by permission of the publisher Fundación Biblioteca Ayacucho.

Andrade, Oswald de: "Anthropophagite Manifesto" by Oswald de Andrade, translated by Chris Whitehouse, first appeared in *Art in Latin America*, edited by Dawn Ades. Text copyright © 1989 by the South Bank Centre and the authors. Published by Yale University Press and the South Bank Centre. Reprinted by the permission of the publishers, translator, and the author's estate c/o Luciana Freire Rangel.

Arciniegas, Germán: "Do They Know Us? Do We Know Them? Do We Know Each Other?" by Germán Arciniegas, translated for this anthology by Jesse H. Lytle, was published in Spanish as Nos conocen? ¿Los conocemos? ¿Nos conocemos?"in *América, ladina*, 1993. Translated by permission of the publisher Fondo de Cultura Económica, S.A.

Asturias, Miguel Angel: "Lake Titicaca" by Miguel Angel Asturias, translated for this anthology by Jesse H. Lytle, was published in Spanish as "El lago Titicaca" in *América, fábula de fábulas* (Monte Avila Editors, 1972). Translated by permission of Agencia Literaria Carmen Balcells, S.A.

Benítez Rojo, Antonio: "Apocalypse and Chaos" by Antonio Benítez Rojo, translated by James Maraniss, first appeared as "From Apocalypse to Chaos" in *The Repeating Island: The Caribbean and the Postmodern Perspective*, pp. 10–16. Copyright © 1992 by Duke University Press. Reprinted by permission of the publisher.

Bianco, José: "Anna Karenina" by José Bianco, translated for this anthology by Dick Gerdes, was published in Spanish as "Ana Karenina" in *Ficción y reflexión* (Fondo de Cultura Economica, S.A., 1988). Reprinted by permission of Ana María Torres.

Bioy Casares, Adolfo: "Books and Friendship" by Adolfo Bioy Casares, translated for this anthology by Dick Gerdes, was published in Spanish as "Libros y amistad" in *La invención y la trama* (Fondo de Cultura Economica, 1988). Copyright © 1988 by Adolfo Bioy Casares. Translated by permission of Agencia Literaria Carmen Balcells, S.A.

Borges, Jorge Luis: "Pierre Menard, Author of the *Quixote*," by Jorge Luis Borges, translated by Anthony Bonner, first appeared in *Ficciones* . Copyright ©1962 by Grove Press, Inc. Used by permission of Grove/Atlantic, Inc., and Weidenfeld & Nicolson.

Caballero Calderón, Eduardo: "Hermit Crabs" by Eduardo Caballero Calderón, translated for this anthology by Jesse H. Lytle, was published in Spanish as "Cangrejos ermitaños" in *Obras, vol. 2* (Editorial Bedout, 1963). Translated by permission of Beatriz Caballero.

Cabrera, Lydia: "El Socorro Lake" by Lydia Cabrera, translated by Alfred MacAdam, first appeared in *Review* 52 (Spring 1996), 6–7. Copyright©1996 by the Americas Society, Inc. Published in Spanish in *La Laguna Sagrada de San Joaquín* (Madrid: Ediciones R, 1973). Reprinted by permission of the editors of *Review* and Isabel Castellanos.

Cabrera Infante, Guillermo: "Scenes of a World without Columbus" by Guillermo Cabrera Infante, translated by Kenneth Hall and the author, first appeared in *Mea Cuba*. Translation copyright © 1994 by Farrar, Straus & Giroux, Inc. Reprinted by permission of the publishers Farrar, Straus & Giroux, Inc., and Faber & Faber, Ltd.

Cardoza y Aragón, Luis: "A Macaw at the Pole " by Luis Cardoza y Aragón, translated for this anthology by Jo Anne Englebert, was published in Spanish as "Un guacamayo en el polo" in *Guatemala: las líneas de su mano*, 1965. Reprinted by permission of the publisher Fondo de Cultura Económica, S.A.

Carpentier, Alejo: "Prologue: *The Kingdom of This World*" by Alejo Carpentier, translated by Alfred MacAdam, first appeared in Review 47 (Fall 1993), 28–31. Copyright ©1993 by the Americas Society, Inc. Reprinted by permission of the editors of *Review*.

Castellanos, Rosario: "Once Again, Sor Juana" by Rosario Castellanos, from *A Rosario Castellanos Reader*, edited by Maureen Ahern, translated by Maureen Ahern and others. Copyright © 1988. By permission of Maureen Ahern, Universidad Veracruzana, and the University of Texas Press.

Cortázar, Julio "To Dress a Shadow" by Julio Cortázar, translated by Thomas Christensen, first appeared in *Around the Day in Eighty Worlds* (North Point Press, 1986). Copyright © 1967 by Julio Cortázar and the heirs of Julio Cortázar.

The Literary Review, volume 38, no. 1, Fall 1994. Reprinted by permission of Joy Laville Ibargüengoitia and Fernanda Soicher.

Lezama Lima, José "Summa critica of American Culture" by José Lezama Lima, translated for this anthology by Mark Schafer, was published in Spanish as "Sumas críticas del americano" from *Obras completas*, vol. 2 (Ediotiral Aguilar, 1977). Copyright © the heirs of José Lezama Lima. Reprinted by permission of Agencia Literaria Latinoamericana.

Lispector, Clarice: "Creating Brasília" from *Discovering the World* by Clarice Lispector, translated by Giovanni Ponteiro. Published by Carcanet Press, Ltd., in 1992. Reprinted by permission of the publisher.

Mallea, Eduardo: "To Be Argentine" by Eduardo Mallea, translated for this anthology by Jesse H. Lytle, was published in Spanish as the preface to *Historia de una pasión argentina*, 1968. Translated by permission of the publisher Editorial Sudamericana, S.A.

Mañach Robato, Jorge: "America's Quixotic Character," translated for this anthology by Mark Schafer, was published in Spanish as "El quijotismo y América" in *Examen del quijotismo* (Editorial Sudamericana, 1950). Translated by permission of Nena Mañach Goodman.

Marcos, Subcomandante: "Letter of 30 June 1994" from *Shadow of Tender Fury* by Subcomandante Marcos, translated by Frank Bardacke et al. Copyright ©1995 by Monthly Review Press. Translation ©1995 by Frank Bardacke and Leslie López. Reprinted by permission of Monthly Review Foundation.

Mariátegui, José Carlos: "Art, Revolution, and Decadence" by José Carlos Mariátegui, translated by Ann Wright, first appeared in *Art in Latin America,* edited by Dawn Ades. Text copyright © 1989 by the South Bank Centre and the authors. Published by Yale University Press and the South Bank Centre. Reprinted by the permission of the publishers, translator, and the estate of the author c/o Comisión nacional del centenario de José Carlos Mariátegui.

Martínez Estrada, Ezequiel: "Thoreau" by Ezequiel Martínez Estrada, translated by Gregory Kolovakos, first appeared as "Taking Sides with Nature," in *Review* 17 (Spring 1976), 32–34. Copyright © 1976 by the Center for Inter-American Relations, Inc. Reprinted by permission of the editors of *Review*.

Meléndez, Concha: "A Visit to the Alphonsine Chapel," by Concha Meléndez, translated for this anthology by Harry Morales, was published in Spanish as "Visita a la Capilla Alfonsina y 'El fuego y su aire'" in *Literatura de ficción en Puerto Rico*, vol. 13, published by Editorial Cordillera, Inc., l971, pp. 185–95. Translated by permission of the publisher.

Menchú, Rigoberta: "I, Rigoberta Menchú" by Rigoberta Menchú, translated by Ann Wright, first appeared in *I, Rigoberta Menchú: An Indian Woman in Guatemala*, edited by Elisabeth Burgos-Debray in 1984. Reprinted by permission of the publisher, Verso.

Mistral, Gabriela: "My Homeland" by Gabriela Mistral, translated for this anthology by José Matosantos, was published in Spanish as "Chile" in *Lecturas para mujeres* (Editorial Porrua, S.A., 1973). Translated by permission of Doris Dana for the Estate of Gabriela Mistral.

Monsiváis, Carlos: "Guess Your Decade: A Questionnaire" by Carlos Monsiváis, translated for this anthology by Jesse H. Lytle, was published in Spanish as "Adivine su década" in *Amor perdido*, 1977. Copyright ©1977. Translated by permission of the publisher Ediciones Era, S.A.

Monterroso, Augusto: "Fecundity" from *Complete Stories and Other Works* by Augusto Monterroso, translated by Edith Grossman. Copyright © 1995. By permission of the University of Texas Press.

Mutis, Alvaro: "Interlude in the South Atlantic," by Alvaro Mutis, translated for this anthology by Mark Schafer, was published in Spanish as "Intermedio en el Atlántico Sur" in *La muerte del estratega: narraciones, prosas y ensayos*, 1988. Translated by permission of the publisher Fondo de Cultura Económica, S.A.

Neruda, Pablo: "Toward the Splendid City: Nobel Lecture" by Pablo Neruda, translated by Margaret Sayers Peden. Copyright © 1972 by The Nobel Foundation. Reprinted by permission of Farrar, Straus & Giroux, Inc.

Ocampo, Victoria: "Women in the Academy" by Victoria Ocampo, translated by Doris Meyer, from *Victoria Ocampo: Against the Wind and the Tide* by Doris Meyer. Copyright © 1979, 1990. By permission of the University of Texas Press.

Ortiz, Fernando: "Tobacco and Sugar" from *Cuban Counterpoint: Tobacco and Sugar* by Fernando Ortiz, translated by Harriet de Onís. Copyright 1947 by Alfred A. Knopf, Inc. Reprinted by permission of the publisher.

Paz, Octavio: "Mexican Churches" by Octavio Paz, translated by Robert Pegada, first appeared as "Here People Talk to God"in *The New York Times Book Review*, 20 December 1987. Copyright © 1987 by the New York Times Company. Reprinted by permission.

Poniatowska, Elena: "And Here's to You, Jesusa," by Elena Poniatowska, translated by Gregory Kolovakos and Ronald Christ, first appeared in *Lives on the Line*, edited by Doris Meyer (University of California Press, 1988). Copyright © by Elena Poniatowska. Translation copyright © 1988 by Gregory Kolovakos and Ronald Christ. Reprinted by permission of the author, Ronald Christ, and the estate of Gregory Kolovakos.

Puig, Manuel: "Cinema and the Novel" by Manuel Puig, translated by Nick Caistor, first appeared in *On Modern Latin American Fiction*, edited by John King. (Faber & Faber, 1987). Reprinted by permission of the Thomas Colchie Literary Agency and the translator.

Rama, Angel: "Literature and Exile" by Angel Rama, translated by Pamela Pye, first appeared in *Review* 30 (September–December 1981), 10–13 as "Founding the Latin American Literary Community." Copyright ©1982 by the Center for Inter-American Relations, Inc. Reprinted by permission of the editors of *Review*.

Ramos, Graciliano: "Jail: Prison Memoirs" by Graciliano Ramos, translated by Thomas Colchie, first appeared in *Review* 73, Winter 1972. Reprinted by permission of the Thomas Colchie Literary Agency.

Ramos, Samuel: "The Use of Thought" from *Profile of Man and Culture in Mexico* by Samuel Ramos, translated by Peter G. Earle. Copyright ©1962. Reprinted by permission of the University of Texas Press.

Reyes, Alfonso: "Notes on the American Mind," by Alfonso Reyes, translated by H. W. Hilborn, from *The Modern Mexican Essay*, (The University of Toronto Press, 1965). Published in Spanish in *El ensayo mexicano moderno*, edited by José

Luis Mart'nez, published by Fondo de Cultura Económica, 1958. This translation reprinted by permission of the publishers.

Roa Bastos, Augusto: "Writing: A Metaphor for Exile" by Augusto Roa Bastos, translated by Helen Lane, first appeared in *Lives on the Line*, edited by Doris Meyer (University of California Press, 1988). Translation copyright © 1988 by Helen Lane. Copyright © by Augusto Roa Bastos. Reprinted by permission of Agencia Literaria Carmen Balcells, S.A., and the translator.

Rodríguez Juliá, Edgardo: "Melancholy at the Hotel Empress," translated for this anthology by Mark Schafer, was published in Spanish as "Melancolia en el Hotel Empress" in *El cruce de la Bah a de Guánica* (Eitorial Cultural, 1989). Translated by permission of the author.

Rodríguez Monegal, Emir: "Horacio Quiroga in the Mirror" by Emir Rodríguez Monegal, translated for this anthology by Harry Morales, was published in Spanish as "El espejo de papel" in *El deterrado, vida, y obra de Horacio Quiroga* (Editorial Losada, S.A., 1968). Translated by permission of the Thomas Colchie Literary Agency.

Rossi, Alejandro: "The Perfect Page" by Alejandro Rossi, translated for this anthology by Mark Schafer, was published in Spanish as "La página perfecta" in *Manual del distraído*, 1987. Translated by permission of the publisher Fondo de Cultura Económica, S.A.

Sábato, Ernesto: "The Great Arc of the Novel" from *The Writer in the Catastrophe of Our Time* by Ernesto Sábato, translated by Asa Zatz. Copyright © 1990. Copyright © 1986 by Editions du Seuil. Reprinted by permission of Council Oaks Books.

Salazar Bondy, Sebastián: "Aberrant Nostalgia" by Sebastián Salazar Bondy, translated for this anthology by Dick Gerdes, was published in Spanish as "La extraviada nostalgia" in *Lima la horrible* (Ediciones Era, 1964). Translated by permission of Irma de Moncloa.

Sánchez, Luis Rafael: "Caribbeanness" by Luis Rafael Sánchez, translated by Alfred MacAdam, first appeared as "Voyage to Caribbean Identity," in *Review* 47 (Fall 1993), 20–22. Copyright © 1993 by the Americas Society, Inc. Reprinted by permission of the editors of *Review*.

Sanín Cano, Baldomero: "Theodore Roosevelt" by Baldomero Sanín Cano, translated for this anthology by Harry Morales, was published in Spanish as "El coronel Teodoro Roosevelt" pp. 172–75 of *El oficio de lector* de Baldomero Sanín Cano (1991). Translated by permission of the publisher Fundacion Biblioteca Ayacucho.

Sarduy, Severo: "Writing/Transvestism" by Severo Sarduy, translated by Alfred MacAdam, first appeared in *Review* 9 (Fall 1973), 31–33. Copyright © 1973 by the Center for Inter-American Relations, Inc. Reprinted by permission of the editors of *Review*.

Sarmiento, Domingo Faustino: "Niagara" by Domingo Faustino Sarmiento, translated by Andrée Conrad, first appeared in *Review* 17 (Spring 1976), 64–66. Copyright © 1976 by the Center for Inter-American Relations, Inc. Reprinted by permission of the editors of *Review*.

Stavans, Ilan: "The Verbal Quest" by Ilan Stavans first appeared as "The Original Language" in *Metamorphoses*, vol. 3, no. 1, 1994. Published in *Art and Anger:*

Essays (1986–1995) by Ilan Stavans (University of New Mexico Press, 1995). Reprinted with the permission of the publisher.

Uslar Pietri, Arturo: "The Other America" by Arturo Uslar Pietri, translated by Andrée Conrad, first appeared in *Review* 14 (Spring 1975), 42–47. Copyright ©1975 by the Center for Inter-American Relations, Inc. Reprinted by permission of the editors of *Review*.

Valenzuela, Luisa: "Little Manifesto" by Luisa Valenzuela, translated by Lori Carlson, first appeared in the *Review of Contemporary Fiction*, Fall 1986. Reprinted by permission of the editor.

Vargas Llosa, Mario: "Novels Disguised as History: The Chronicles of the Birth of Peru" from *A Writer's Reality* by Mario Vargas Llosa, translated by Myron I. Lichtblau. Reprinted by permission of Syracuse University Press.

Vasconcelos, José: "Books I Read Sitting and Books I Read Standing" by José Vasconcelos, translated by H. W. Hilborn, from *The Modern Mexican Essay* (The University of Toronto Press, Inc., 1965), was published in Spanish as "Libros que leo sentado y libros que leo de pie" in *El ensayo mexicano moderno*, edited by José Luis Martínez (Fondo de Cultura Económica, 1958). Reprinted by permission of the publishers.

Zea, Leopoldo: "Concerning an American Philosophy" by Leopoldo Zea from *The Modern Mexican Essay*, translated by H. W. Hilborn (The University of Toronto Press, 1965), was published in Spanish as "En torno a una filosfía americana" in *El ensayo mexicano moderno*, edited by José Luis Martínez (Fondo de Cultura Económica, 1958). Reprinted by permission of the publishers.

Topical Listing of Contents

Politics and Foreign Relations

Reading and Writing

Author Index